VICTORIA MARMOT

The Complete Collection

Virginia McClain

Cover design by Natasha Snow

ISBN 13: 978-1-9994612-9-4

Works by Virginia McClain

The Victoria Marmot series:
Victoria Marmot and the Meddling Goddess
Victoria Marmot and the Inconvenient Prophecy
Victoria Marmot and the Shadow of Death
Victoria Marmot and the Dragon's Rage
Victoria Marmot and the Road to Hell

The Chronicles of Gensokai series:
Blade's Edge
Traitor's Hope

Short Stories
Rain on a Summer's Afternoon

To Tom, for being a best friend and brother.
To Aurora, for being a best friend and a superhero disguised as an editor.

VIRGINIA McCLAIN

VICTORIA MARMOT
AND THE
MEDDLING GODDESS

VICTORIA MARMOT BOOK ONE

To Lee, for all the hours spent with the sapling.

VICTORIA MARMOT WAS unrolling her sleeping bag in a quiet mountain glade, the clearing surrounded by tall pines and a single oak with branches that gave it a shape rather like a hooded person carrying a scythe.

"Hello?"

She paused, as though unsure of where to find the best view of the star-filled night sky.

"Who is saying that?"

Her chestnut hair barely reflected the starlight, her mint-green eyes flashing with confusion as her caramel skin darkened to the color of milk chocolate with increasing ire.

"Who the fuck is hiding in the woods describing me like a damned dessert?"

She stared furiously into the woods, unable to ascertain the origin of the mysterious voice even as she reached for the knife on her belt.

"I will put a damned blade through the origin of the voice if it doesn't show itself RIGHT. FUCKING. NOW."

"Well, that seems uncalled for."

"Who said that?"

"I did," and, with a dramatic flourish few possess, a beautiful, milk-skinned redhead appeared in the forest before the young adventurer.

"Okay, crazy, naked nut job. Please stop narrating every damn thing that happens and go away."

"I can't. That's my job. I'm your narrator." With another flourish the graceful redhead produced a fabulous set of deerskin leathers and a flowing blouse to highlight her gorgeous figure.

"I don't need a narrator. Thank you for putting clothes on. And what the actual fuck is going on right now? Are you a hologram or something?"

"So tetchy! You do need a narrator. You're on an adventure."

"I'm on my weekly backpacking trip. I do this specifically to avoid people, especially people who refer to themselves in the third person, so please go back to whatever asylum you escaped from and leave me alone. I was about to enjoy some star gazing before falling into a blissfully exhausted sleep."

"You come out here every week to find a sense of normalcy after losing your parents in a freak boating accident six months ago, and don't pretend that you're ever exhausted enough to sleep properly since you lost your family."

Victoria's jaw hung open as she stared at the glorious redhead who seemed poised to turn all her carefully constructed escapism on its head.

"I know what my jaw is doing, you don't have to say it out loud! There's no one else to hear you. And how in seven hells do you know anything about me or my parents?"

"I told you, I'm your narrator. I'm supposed to be omniscient. I know everything about you, even things that you don't know about yourself."

"That doesn't make any sense. Why would I have a narrator? I'm not a character in a book. I'm a teenager *trying* to enjoy a nice little solo backpacking trip for the weekend. I do not need a psychotic hologram following me through the woods and analyzing me. I need to go to sleep. Preferably after catching the start of the meteor shower tonight."

"You *do* need a narrator because you are embarking on a great adventure."

"I'm backpacking on the side of freaking Mt. Humphreys. That is not a great adventure. It's a day hike that I'm drawing out as long as possible because I didn't have enough time to drive very far this weekend. Why on earth would this trip warrant a narrator, and seriously, even if you can answer that question, why the fuck would I believe that *you* are my narrator and not just some crazy woman who likes to wander the woods and freak out nature enthusiasts by popping up naked in front of them?"

Gwen carefully shaped her mouth into an attractive pout.

"I can see you doing it, I do NOT need you to tell me about it."

"I'm not saying it for you! I'm saying it for them."

"Who is THEM? There is no one else here, and if anyone were here, they would be able to see you too, so you don't need to narrate it. Unless you've brought a bunch of blind people here? Are there blind people hiding in this forest now too?"

Victoria threw a concerned glance at the woods that surrounded the small clearing where she'd unrolled her Therm-a-Rest and sleeping bag.

"Dude, seriously. Are you going to keep doing that? It is creeping me the fuck out!"

"Someone *has* to narrate this story. I can't just leave it unsaid, or they'll have no idea what's happening."

"They who— no, wait, you know what? Never mind. Fuck it. We're not getting anywhere that way. You said *someone* has to narrate this story. Does that someone have to be you?"

"I suppose not."

"Could that someone be me?"

"I suppose…. I *hate* first person narration. It seems like something only an angsty teen would do."

"Ok. Ms. Literati. Sorry to burst your critical bubble, but first person point of view is a perfectly valid form of narrative style, so you and your angsty teen comments can suck it."

"I'm only saying—"

"What were you going to do for the parts in my head?"

"What?"

"When it got to the parts where I think something important to the story, how were you going to narrate that?"

"Italics, I suppose. Why?"

"Just wondering if I could do the narration job with just my thoughts. You know, without saying everything I'm doing aloud, to avoid acting like an insane person."

"You keep throwing around those insane accusations. I'll have you know that's very offensive to sufferers of mental illness, who are often very productive members of society."

"Fine. You're right. I'm sorry. I know lots of people with mental health issues who are great, and decidedly not insane, but I don't know how else to describe someone who can't let go of an alternate reality that differs substantially from observable fact."

"*I* would call that a person stuck in a dimensional pocket, but that's neither here nor there."

"What? That's—never mind. Look, can I narrate in my head, or not?"

"Yes. I suppose that would work just fine."

"Fine. Then make me the narrator."

Gwen looked uncomfortable for a moment, as though that were a decision she didn't wish to make—

"Would you PLEASE stop—"

And then she did. Thank fuck. I no longer had to hear the delusional woman in front of me describe each of her own actions in detail.

"Thank you," I said. I wasn't sure if I was the one "narrating" now, but I didn't really care. I had just wanted her to cut that the fuck out. It was incredibly eerie to have someone describe your every move aloud, and it had been making it difficult to think.

"Ok…. So, can you go away now?" I asked, still unsure of whether or not I would even stay behind once this character left. I didn't know what a person with delusions like this was likely to do, and I didn't really feel like getting stabbed to death in my sleep. Despite what I'd acknowledged about lovely people with serious mental health problems—all true—I didn't know this woman at all, and a tiny percentage of people with mental health issues were truly unhinged and dangerous. The unhinged and dangerous ones likely just needed a better therapist and the right meds, but that wasn't going to make me any less dead if Gwen were one of them and found herself unable to resist the voices telling her to take my head as a trophy.

"Well, I'm afraid I haven't quite taken care of my role this evening," Gwen said, startling me out of my dark imaginings of her waving my bloody severed head in the wind. "I *was* your narrator, but I er… have another purpose too. Tonight, mainly, it's to get you started on your quest."

"My quest?"

"Yes, your quest." And with that statement, the leathers she was wearing somehow became a flowing gown that definitely brought forth Lady of the Lake style imagery, all flowing blue silks and shit. "The DM was supposed to show up for this, but he ran into a scheduling conflict, and since I was going to be here anyway, I offered to help out."

"The DM? Are you kidding me? Is this whole thing just an elaborate role playing game? I mean, honestly, that explains just about everything, including the sudden costume changes, but seriously, you need to let people know when they're going to be part of a LARPing event. Just showing up naked and calling yourself a narra—"

"No, no, The DM is just the name he goes by now, he's one of the original Fates, actually. Just likes to keep up with the times. Anyway, he can't make it tonight, so I suppose it doesn't really matter."

"The Fates? Seriously? You expect me to believe—" Gwen raised her voice and kept on going, as though I'd never interjected.

"And I'm SUPPOSED to tell you...."

She cleared her throat.

"Yes?"

"Are you finally listening?"

"Will it make you go away?"

"Yes."

"Then I'm listening."

"Your quest, Victoria Adelaide Marmot, is to find out what really happened to your parents."

And then, I shit you not, she literally disappeared. Yes. Literally. Not figuratively, and not as some asshats misuse literally to mean "very." She straight up evaporated into nothing. Where once she had stood was now empty space, and there was no trace of her in any direction. She hadn't even snapped her fingers.

So, thoroughly shitting my pants (figuratively of course), I packed up my overnight pack and booked it the hell back to my car. I was freaked out enough by her disappearing act to run away, but the thing that spooked me most was how much she had known about my weekend adventures and the real reason behind them.

She had been right on the money. I ran into the wilderness every weekend because it was the only place I could find a semblance of peace in a world that had snatched my parents away from me, over a year before I would graduate high school. And now, some lady who liked to stalk people in the woods and describe them like tasty snacks had shown up, known about my parents' deaths, and implied that they hadn't died the way I thought they did.

And that was more than I could fucking take, tonight.

CRAWLING INTO MY own bed, in the large, empty house my parents had willed to me, didn't made me feel any better. Part of me wished I hadn't allowed Gwen to scare me away from my campsite. Watching the meteor shower from the side of the mountain would have been spectacular, and probably worth the risk of getting stabbed to death by a delusional woman delivering quests, but I had been too agitated to think it through at the time. Returning to my newly acquired home had seemed the more reasonable option, even if it was depressingly devoid of other people. Pulling up to the darkened doorstep of my blue clapboard-covered home, in its quaint, gently-wooded Flagstaff neighborhood, hadn't made me feel any more secure than I had felt alone in the woods, and walking into the house was just one more reminder that I was alone in the world. Well, I suppose I had my great-uncle Algernon, but… that wasn't much comfort when he wasn't actually in town.

Getting ready for bed, my mind played the conversation I'd had with a total stranger in the woods on a endless loop. When my brain finally let me sleep, I was more agitated than I had been since my parents had failed to come home from their round-the-world journey.

I woke up so angry it was a physical sensation.

As I stared down my reflection, while brushing my teeth, I was practically vibrating with rage.

Who the fuck was this Gwen person anyway?

And I don't mean that in the figurative, "who does she think she is," type way, although, hey, that too while we're at it. But—who *was* she? She was the kind of nut job who went around claiming to be a narrator and a deliverer of quests, that's who she was. I should just ignore her and her ridiculous claims about my parents, but…

But she'd disappeared like she was straight out of Hogwarts. That could be some kind of special effect. It's not like I searched every inch of woods for her right after she ammscrayed from my line of sight, or like I could have searched well enough to eliminate the possibility that she'd used smoke, mirrors, and a hologram to fake her disappearance, even if I had tried to. She could totally be putting one over on me. It's not as though vanishing made the rest of what she said true. It was just that…

What she'd said about my parents…

Damn it!

I'd spent so much time trying to accept my parents' death. Every day since I'd gotten the call six months ago, it had been the main thing I'd been doing with myself. Gwen hadn't been wrong when she'd accused me of running into the wilderness to hide from people and…process things. It was what I was doing with every weekend backpacking trip, with every afternoon trail run I took into the mountains…

But I had researched my parents' death as fully as any seventeen year old could without retracing their every step. I had tracked down all of the records from their GPS, all of their emergency logs. Everything that their beacon broadcast the day that their boat was lost…. All of it.

It had taken me months to even accept that they were dead. That it wasn't all some ridiculous mistake. The possibility that they hadn't died that day…but was that even what the naked narrator lady was implying? That my parents were still alive? Or was she just suggesting that they hadn't died by drowning in the Indian Ocean?

I shook myself from where I'd gotten lost in the mirror and swore loudly when I checked the time on my phone.

Great. On top of everything else, I was going to be late for my first day at my new school.

<center>~~~</center>

I must have still been furious when I rushed into my first period physics class that morning. That's the only explanation I can come up with for why I decided to sass the teacher when she asked me why I was late. Well, that, or the fact that the bell had rung *while* I was walking through the door.

"Why are you tardy, Miss… Marmot? What a quaint name."

The teacher was a middle aged woman with lank black hair and what looked like a permanent sneer. I rushed past multiple rows of black-topped desks, each with pairs of stools supporting a variety of fellow teenagers, barely noticing any of the people around me, or the vaguely generic science paraphernalia around the room, and took a seat at the back. I replied while rummaging through my backpack for my notebook.

"Sorry. It's my first day. I got lost on the way here."

No. That wasn't the sassy part.

"And you believe that excuses your tardiness?"

I stared at her for a moment before replying.

"Well, it's kind of a one time excuse, so… yeah."

There we go! Sasstastic!

"Well, class, Ms. Marmot believes the rules don't apply to her. How does that make the rest of you feel?"

"We should punish her!" shouted an enthusiastic blonde kid from the front row.

Great. Next up, I expected someone to accuse me of turning them into a newt.

Before anyone could get my funeral pyre ready, though, the voice next to me spoke up.

"She smells amazing."

I turned, incredulous at the inanity of that statement, and found possibly the most handsome boy I'd ever seen staring at me with a disturbing look in his eye.

"What was that, Edik?" the teacher asked.

"Nothing, Ms. Rebuke. I said 'no hazing.' The school rules dictate that we shouldn't—"

I snickered and he stopped speaking. I hadn't meant to let the noise escape me, but… Rebuke?

"Do you find something funny, Ms. Marmot?"

Now the woman was suddenly standing right in front of my desk and I was too mesmerized by how quickly she'd moved to come up with a witty retort.

"No, Ms. Rebuke."

I barely managed not to chuckle saying her name. I felt bad though. Most people had no choice in their last names.

"If you are so intent on entertaining this class, Ms. Marmot, perhaps you can entertain us with today's lesson. The topic is dark matter. Please, why don't you enlighten us with your extensive knowledge on the subject."

Well, that was an odd punishment. I was a little surprised that dark matter was today's lesson, even though this was an AP physics class. It wasn't exactly an intro topic, but whatever, far be it from me to discourage interesting lesson plans. I shrugged.

"Ok. Do you want me at the front of the class? The chalkboard would be handy."

Ms. Rebuke said nothing, only glared at me.

I decided to stay in my seat.

"Dark matter is a popular theoretical explanation for all the excess mass in the universe," I began.

Did I mention that binge-watching Neil deGrasse Tyson's Cosmos remake was another way in which I dealt with my parents' death? Honestly binge-watching anything on Netflix should be considered an official stage of grief. Somewhere after denial and anger, but before acceptance.

"On its largest scale, the universe behaves in a way that suggests that there is far more mass in it than we can currently detect. The theory is that most of the universe's mass, therefore, is matter that we cannot see, sense, or detect with current instruments. Something like 99% of the universe is made up of this non-detectable mater, in fact—"

"That's enough Ms. Marmot! You may visit the principal's office at any time now. You certainly aren't needed here, as you've made it clear that you're already an expert on today's subject."

"Wait, are you kicking me out of—"

"Go!"

Ms. Rebuke sounded like she was ready to spit flames, so I didn't argue. I really hadn't meant to give her any grief to start with, but being marked tardy as I walked in while the bell was ringing, on my very first day at a new school, in a new town, when I had already woken up angry… I wasn't at my best. I had started to pack up my stuff when the stupidly handsome boy next to me spoke up again.

"I'll take her," he said, in the tone of someone who had been asked to help the less fortunate. "She won't know how to get there."

"Excellent, Edik. Please come right back."

I had a school map in my pocket, and the look in Edik's eyes still freaked me out a bit, so I headed for the door without looking to see if he was behind me.

UNFORTUNATELY, MR. DAZZLING Eyes was indeed with me as I walked out the door.

"You don't have to take me, really. I can find the office on my own."

As if I hadn't spoken, the dude wrapped his arm around my shoulder and started talking.

"Don't worry about Ms. Rebuke. She doesn't even teach physics, normally. She's the chemistry teacher. Just subbing, for some reason. Not sure where the real physics teacher is today, but have no fear, I won't allow her to harm you."

"Um…dude, can you take your arm off me, please?"

I like to ask before I force people to move in ways that are likely to hurt them.

"Oh, of course, my dear. How terribly forward of me! Wouldn't want to give anyone the wrong impression, would we? I'm awfully sorry. I simply… got caught up in you."

"That's weird, Eric."

"It's Edik, not Eric."

"Oh. Sorry."

I wasn't particularly sorry, because this guy was setting off my creep-o-meter something fierce, but I did like to get people's names right. I was in favor of people being addressed in whatever way they preferred to be addressed.

Edik though…. Not only was this guy's accent decidedly inappropriate for Arizona, but his manner of speaking was entirely wrong for this century.

However, talking oddly wasn't a reason to bestow violence on anyone, and as he had removed his arm from my shoulders I decided he didn't require a knee to the balls just yet. Still, he was doing himself no favors with his "let me save you" talk and his lack of personal boundaries.

I spent the rest of our brief stroll through the featureless hallways trying to surreptitiously walk farther away from my escort, but he refused to give me more than a handsbreadth of personal space. Thankfully, a few well-marked turns down blandly lit hallways delivered me to an office that was leaking small, disturbing wisps of smoke from the crack where door met frame. Just as I was trying to tactfully tell Edik to hit the road, he saved me the trouble.

"I hate to leave you, my darling, but I cannot abide the smell of this place. Fare thee well!"

And before I could even thank Too Creepy To Be Handsome Anymore dude for unnecessarily guiding me to the door quite clearly labeled "Principal," he was gone.

"That… was decidedly weird," I muttered, before cautiously knocking on the door.

I am not overly versed in recreational drugs, but even I could tell it reeked of pot in this hallway, so I wasn't sure what I was expecting to see when the door opened.

A bushy-browed, grey-haired, long-bearded man in a crushed velvet bathrobe was definitely not on the list of things that crossed my mind in the few seconds' between when I knocked and when the door opened.

The giant wave of pot smoke that billowed around him was also a bit of a surprise. At least, in the sense that it was pooling out of an office clearly labeled "Principal" in the middle of a school day. It wasn't surprising given that wisps of smoke and pot reek had been pouring out of the office before the door even opened.

"Umm… is now a bad time?" I asked, unsure how to proceed.

"Is he gone?" the man asked.

"Is who gone?"

"That vampire twat, Edik."

"Umm… Edik left, yes."

"He hasn't got to you, has he?"

"What does that mean?"

"You're not in love with him, are you?"

"What?!"

"It's a long story."

The old man, who was speaking with a decidedly British accent, peered suspiciously down the hallway in each direction and then gestured me into the office.

I hesitated, if only because I didn't particularly want the contact high I was fairly certain would result from walking into that room.

"Come, come. If he's left, then now is the perfect time to talk."

"Ok."

I was a bit baffled. I hadn't even had a chance to explain what I was doing here.

"Ms. Rebuke sent me," I began, planning to confess my sassy sins, but the grey-haired man shut the door behind me and cut me off.

"I know, I know. Not sure what's got her knickers in a bunch today. I suppose she's miserable about substituting for Physics again, but Ms. Squirrel is still unwell. Anyway, that hardly matters at this point. Come here, child, let me look at you."

Uh… weird. That was definitely a weird request. People I'd only just met asking to get a closer look at me was not something I was entirely comfortable with, but I wasn't getting any leering vibes from the old dude, so I let it slide. But then he was staring deeply into my eyes and tearing up, and that was a bit more than I could handle, creepy vibes or no. It was disturbing enough that I looked around the room. Anything to keep from locking eyes with the ones behind the half-moon spectacles in front of me.

The room was still smoky, but underneath the smoke it reminded me of an old cat lady's living room, minus the cats, plus a couple of very large lizards.

I was just about to ask about the origins of the six-foot-long iguana that lay along the back of a red velvet wingback chair, when my thoughts were completely derailed.

"You have your mother's eyes."

"What?!" I almost shouted, my eyes snapping back to the grey ones in front of me.

"Your mother, Tenzin, you have her eyes."

"You knew my mother?"

"Yes. Of course. Didn't you know?"

"Mister, I don't even know who you are!"

It was true. I assumed that this man was the principal of the school, but the pot smoke had made me doubt that a bit, and I certainly didn't know his name. I most assuredly had no inkling that he had known my mother.

"Didn't your parents tell you about me? Professor Bumblebee? I taught them both."

"What?"

I sat down in the red velvet wingback, despite the hissing of the iguana.

"Your parents both studied with me. Didn't they tell you? Surely you've wondered how they learned it all?"

"Learned what? My father was an English professor and my mother was a professional triathlete. I wasn't aware that they'd ever studied the same subjects."

My tone was probably bordering on insolence, but I couldn't help it. Between crazy ladies in the woods telling me that my parents hadn't died the way I thought they had and this guy revealing that he was an old family friend… I just didn't have enough energy left to stay polite.

"Well, let's see. Where to begin? What do you know exactly?"

"About what, Mr. Bumblebee?"

"Oh, call me Albert."

"Ok, Albert."

I would have asked why I was supposed to call my school principal by his first name, but a knock on the door stopped the words in my throat. I was so desperate to have a conversation that wasn't emotionally draining that I almost hoped it was Edik come to escort me to my next class.

It wasn't.

Albert opened his office door to reveal another student who looked about my age. He was slightly taller than me, and had long, black hair pulled into a ponytail to reveal high cheekbones, startling amber eyes, and skin the same shade as mine. For some reason, I couldn't take my eyes off of him.

"Mr. Topaz sent me to get the new student."

His voice was deep and quiet, and far more alluring than it should have been. I shook myself and turned to Mr. Bumblebee.

"Oh? Yes, yes. I suppose she should go to classes anyway." He turned his half-moon spectacles in my direction then. "Do come back, dear. We have much to discuss."

I nodded, numbly, and then stepped out the door and stood awkwardly next to the student who had come to retrieve me.

"Umm… hi," I muttered, lamely. What the hell. I was never tongue-tied in front of guys. "I'm Vic." I cleared my throat and proffered my hand.

"Seamus," he said, taking my hand and shaking it firmly before dropping it like it was hot.

If he had felt the same electric jolt up his arm that I had just felt up mine while shaking his hand, then I didn't blame him.

"Nice to meet you," I said, after an interminably long pause during which we said absolutely nothing but just stared at each other as if we'd never seen another human before.

"You smell good," he replied.

Right. Well, my day was officially stupid.

"I'M SORRY ABOUT that," Seamus mumbled.

"What?" I asked, no longer sure that we were both speaking English.

"Saying you smell good. That's creepy as hell. It's just… true."

I nodded. "Ok. As long as you acknowledge it's creepy and don't expect me to be flattered or anything…"

"Gods, no! I just… said it before I could think. I'm sorry. I've never said anything that weird before. I mean, not since I was like five."

"Right. Ok. You can stop apologizing now."

He nodded. I tried to take a deep, calming breath, and then realized that he smelled *amazing*. Like a pine forest and a mountain breeze and… gingerbread with chocolate sauce? What the hell!? I shook myself and looked pointedly towards the hallway that I thought we should be walking down instead of standing awkwardly in front of Mr. Bumblebee's door.

Seamus finally caught on and gestured towards the hallway with one hand, while standing well back from me.

"Shall we?" he asked.

"Sure."

I gave him the same wide berth he'd given me. The man smelled better than anyone I'd ever met, and sent sparks shooting up my arm when we touched…. Did not need more of that right now.

~~~

"So, where are you from?" Seamus asked, as we wandered yet another
~~~

bland institutional hallway lined with lockers. Honestly, this school was so drab it could have been any public high school in the US. How it managed to hide within its walls a cadre of teachers, seemingly all hailing from the UK, piloted by a oddball hot-boxing principal, was a mystery that would have fully enveloped my attention had I not been distracted by Seamus' attempts at conversation.

"What makes you think I'm not from here?" I asked, before I could stop my typical knee-jerk response to the question.

"Well, you're new here, but you're a senior… I just assumed you moved here from somewhere else."

I took a deep breath and tried to remember that not everyone who saw my skin tone and eye shape assumed I was from a different country. It was hard, because I got that a lot.

"Sorry. I'm not having the best day. Colorado, I suppose."

"You're not sure?"

"Well, before Colorado we moved once or twice, and I spent most of my summers on a boat until recently."

"Well, that sounds interesting. Wanna talk about it?"

I chuckled. Seamus set me at ease for some reason, despite the annoying electric buzz I'd gotten when we first shook hands, and the weird smell comment. He didn't seem… demanding.

"I'd love to, but I suppose we should wait until after class."

I nodded towards the closed door that was labeled with the number that corresponded to the folded-over schedule I had wrestled out of my pocket on the walk here.

"Oh, yeah. Probably. Though I wonder sometimes if he'd even notice if we all left the room…"

"Huh?"

"You'll see. Come on."

He pushed open the door and we shuffled in, just ahead of a handful of other students who had arrived from the opposite direction. I followed Seamus to a low table in the back of the room. The tables were set up in rows, with one aisle down the middle and three chairs per table. The room was drearily devoid of decoration save for a lone poster from the Dead Poets' Society.

It seemed as though our class wasn't full, as no one tried to sit with us and there was also plenty of room to spare at the other desks. I usually preferred to sit up front for my classes, but today apparently wasn't my day for it.

After class got started, I understood Seamus' seating choice perfectly.

The teacher, a balding man without a single memorable feature, started by reading some truly terrible poetry, and continued... by reading more of it. No one asked a single question and indeed, the man just paced the front of the room reading aloud from his book without even looking at a single student.

Despite my best efforts to pay attention, around the seventh poorly rhymed verse about a whale frolicking somewhere in Scotland I gave up.

Besides, Seamus' notes were too distracting. Mostly because they consisted of hilarious sketches about whatever oddity Topaz was describing in poem form.

A whale being harpooned, a royal carriage, a collapsed bridge… it was hard not to laugh aloud when he finally handed me a sketch of a blundering stick figure holding a goose.

This is truly terrible poetry, I wrote in reply. *Does he seriously do this every class?*

Seamus wrote back, *I think so. I mean, last year I only had him for a week as a sub, but this was all he did.*

I was amazed. Still, it wasn't long before we had abandoned the topic of Topaz's terrible poetry.

Is Vic short for Victoria? Seamus asked.

Yep. Not sure why my parents went full-on boring cat lady when they named me, but that's my legacy.

I watched Seamus smile while reading my reply, and swallowed hard. I was doing my best to think of him in purely friendly terms, but my body kept reacting to him in a really… emphatic way.

Not sure what my parents were thinking when they named me Seamus, TBH, he replied.

I raised an eyebrow at that.

I just assumed you were part Irish.

That was a lie. I hadn't assumed that at all. He didn't look even remotely Irish, but now that I thought about it seemed plausible enough.

Good guess. I am, actually. But I'm mostly Navajo, and I'm still bummed that I didn't get a much cooler name than Seamus.

Seamus sounds pretty cool to me.

Yeah, until you realize it's just Irish for James.

Huh. Do you have a nickname you prefer?

Nah. I just stick with Seamus. What about you? he asked.

At this point we weren't even pretending not to pass notes, we were just both hunkered over my notebook right in the middle of the table.

I already told you to call me Vic.

No, I mean heritage-wise. The Navajo is pretty obvious, but I just admitted to being part Irish. I was wondering what awesomeness produced those eyes…

I could feel blood rushing to my cheeks as I read the comment about my eyes. Part of me wanted to hurl at my own reaction. It was just a compliment, but, whatever, I was touchy about my eyes. Having someone appreciate them was… whatever. It made me blush.

Honestly, I don't know that my heritage does much to explain my eye-color, but since you "admitted" to being Irish… just Tibetan on my mom's side, and Dad's is more of a mystery. He never talked about his family much. If I had to guess, based on what he did say… Euro-Mutt and… African? Not the entire continent, obviously, but I seriously have no idea which country, or even which region, really.

Seamus had just started penning his reply when the door to the classroom flew open and slammed against the wall, loud enough to actually cause Mr. Topaz to pause in his reading.

Edik stood in the doorway, and I watched with growing dismay as his eyes scanned the tables until they reached the one where Seamus and I were sitting.

Before I could blink, Edik was standing in front of me and glaring at Seamus.

"What are you doing sitting next to *him?*"

"Um… listening to terrible poetry. What the seven hells are you doing here?"

I felt safe making the terrible poetry comment because as soon as Edik had left the doorway, Mr. Topaz had started up again without the slightest indication that he objected to Edik's batshit crazy entrance.

"Victoria, darling, you cannot possibly entertain this mongrel. He's absolutely beneath you."

"Edik. Seriously. What are you doing here? I'm in the middle of class."

"I came to tell you the truth. Your scent is so compelling that I cannot keep it to myself any longer."

I really didn't want to know where this was going. "Edik. You need to leave now. Keep whatever it is to yourself and just go, please."

"I cannot! I must tell you. It is a truth I cannot keep from you. We are meant to be. I am a creature of the night, and I love you."

I HAD NEVER been more relieved in my life to smell the earthy, cloying scent of marijuana than when Albert Bumblebee had wandered into Topaz's class for a "surprise audit."

Edik hadn't even said goodbye before glaring daggers at the principal and storming out.

As a bonus, Topaz had seemed reluctant to continue reading from what appeared to be a leather-bound journal of his own poetry after Bumblebee's arrival, and instead we had started a somewhat lively discussion of Twelfth Night, which had been part of the assigned summer reading.

Honestly, the rest of my day was pretty normal after that. At least until I got to swim practice.

Swimming was on the list of the few things in life that grounded me, much like backpacking, rock climbing, and trail running, so I had been looking forward to this first practice ever since I had woken up vibrating with anger.

My anticipation hadn't exactly diminished when I'd learned that Seamus was also on the swim team. Still, as I walked, dripping, from the showers in the locker room into the humid, chlorine-laden air of the pool, I was determined that even Seamus' mostly naked presence wouldn't distract me from getting into the zone.

That proved more difficult than expected.

He wasn't decidedly better looking than most guys who swim competitively, and I was *very* used to seeing guys who swim competitively wearing next to nothing. It was literally part of my everyday existence during swim season, and I had been swimming competitively since I was ten.

So, why, why, WHY could I feel Seamus' body in the lane next to me as if it were radiating flames?

Luckily, swimming isn't the kind of sport that allows you to stop and ogle the swimmers nearby while you're in the water. But it shouldn't have been such a damned challenge to keep myself from trying to do just that.

I'd had crushes on guys on my team before, had even dated a teammate for a little while at my old school, but, usually, once I hit the water, nothing else mattered.

At least, on a normal day.

Today was clearly not a normal day.

As evidenced by the completely naked creep swimming right underneath me.

"WHAT THE ACTUAL FUCK!?!?" I screamed, pulling myself from the pool as though the water were lava.

Everyone was staring at me as I stood on the pool side shaking with rage, I could tell, but my eyes were fixed on the water, where Edik—still butt naked—was blithely hanging out near the bottom of the pool, without coming up for air, and waving gaily at me as though this were all terribly amusing and wouldn't we laugh about it later.

Before I could even draw breath to ask if anyone else saw what was happening, a giant ball of fur shot past my left arm and flew into the water, going straight for the nudist.

Suddenly the water was a giant froth of wolf, blood, and naked crazy person.

Despite what my brain tried to tell me about the low likelihood of a wolf diving into a school pool during swim practice, my eyes were quite convinced by the evidence to the contrary. I was too familiar with wolves to mistake it for anything else. The coat, the size, the lankiness, the flash of amber eyes that I saw briefly at one point when it came up for air… all of it shouted wolf. Especially the giant canines that were visible just before they tore into Edik's arm again.

Once the initial shock wore off, I took a quick look around and saw that the same shock was nowhere close to wearing off for my fellow swimmers. Indeed, many of them had already run for the changing rooms. Even Seamus was nowhere in sight.

Right. So this was going to be on me, then. Fine.

I had a moment of wanting to just let the wolf ravage the batshit weirdo who had been swimming naked underneath me, because, honestly… just…

ew. But Edik probably didn't deserve to die for his crimes, and… well, I really didn't want the wolf to get killed. Although, since the wolf was attacking humans it was probably already sick, and there was no way it would be getting out of here alive if authorities of any type showed up. Besides, what the hell did I think I could do to stop a wolf from attacking someone, anyway? Other than lose an arm, that is.

Then a quiet voice spoke up beside me and I almost jumped out of my skin.

"Do you plan to just let them go on like that?" the voice asked.

I turned to see Mr. Topaz, of all people, standing there still wearing the three-piece suit he'd donned for our class that morning.

"Um… did you have any ideas for getting them to stop?" I asked.

He shrugged.

"No. And it wouldn't bother me, normally, but I like that Seamus bloke and I wouldn't want him to get hurt. Edik's a git, anyway."

"What does Seamus have to do with any of this?"

I was beginning to wonder if Topaz was actually as batty as his poetry suggested.

"The wolf," he said, nodding at the churn of water ahead of us, "is your friend Seamus."

It might have been a bit early to deem Seamus a friend, but he seemed like a nice enough kid. He did not, however, seem like 130 pounds of canine fury.

"I am fairly certain that Seamus is *not* a timber wolf."

"Really? Interesting. Is he a mexican red or something? But he's all black… I'm not very good with animals."

This conversation was getting away from me fast. Just then, I heard a small scream and turned to see none other than Seamus, locked in Edik's unyielding grip. The wolf was nowhere in sight.

I wanted to ask what had happened to the wolf, or how Seamus had shown up without my noticing, or why he was suddenly naked, but I didn't take the time. I had been somewhat absorbed in talking to Topaz, anyway, so Seamus must have come running from the changing rooms just as the wolf ran off, and it all must have happened while I was staring in disbelief at my English teacher, who was suggesting that Seamus was somehow also a wolf. Giving up on figuring out how it had gone down, I went to split up what had now become a simple fist fight—well within my purview, and unlikely to lose me any extremities.

Not bothering to walk around the edge of the pool, I dove straight for the two young men entangled in the water, and as soon as I broke the surface on my way up, I also broke Edik's hold on Seamus' neck with the simple expedient of a punch to the face. Fun fact: getting punched in the face will distract most people who aren't used to it—and very few people are used to it. As soon as Edik loosened his grip, I grabbed Seamus by the shoulder and swam him towards the side of the pool. By the time Edik recovered, I had already thrown Seamus into a beached whale position on the side of the pool. I spun back to Edik, ready to receive whatever attack he might throw at me, my legs treading water and my hands in a fighting stance. I wasn't used to fighting in water (I would have to ask my sensei about incorporating that into an upcoming class though, it would be fun) but I was willing to bet that Edik wasn't used to it either, and by this stage I was looking forward to kicking his ass.

I was disappointed, though. As soon as Seamus was out of the water, Edik stopped trying to attack.

"Are you alright, my darling?" he asked.

I propelled myself towards the deck as quickly as I could.

"Get away from me, creep!" I shouted, while pulling myself out of the water as quickly as possible. Seamus was gone. That was weird as hell, since he'd seemed almost unconscious when I'd pulled him from the water and I'd only turned my back on him for a handful of seconds to see if Edik was going to keep fighting.

While my eyes tried, and failed, to locate Seamus, I felt a hand touch my ankle and kicked backwards, connecting solidly with what felt like Edik's nose. It gave a satisfying crunch and he gasped in pain, but I didn't turn back to see what he was doing. I just made a beeline for the ladies' locker rooms and hoped to hell he wouldn't follow me in there.

I WAS STILL shaking a bit when I stepped into the warm afternoon that awaited me outside of the pool building. I closed my eyes, letting the mountain sun heat my face up a bit before I started my walk home. With my eyes closed and the fall-scented mountain breeze in my lungs, I could almost pretend I was back home in Colorado. Almost. Opening my eyes always brought a tinge of disappointment as I took in a view that lacked a full range of white-capped Rocky Mountains. At least the view had *a* mountain. It could have been worse. It could have been the flatlands.

I still wasn't sure why my parents had kept a home in Northern Arizona that I'd never known about, or why they had left it to me only on the condition that I occupy it. It had required leaving the high school I'd been attending for the past three years, and all the friends I'd made there, and starting over from scratch. When I'd first read the will I'd thought that had been particularly cruel. High school was hard enough without having to be the new kid in your senior year… but then I realized that my parents probably hadn't been planning on dying. I suppose they hadn't really expected any of this to come up just yet.

So the only odd thing, then, was that I hadn't known about the place at all. I mean, isn't it a little weird that they owned a whole house that I never knew about? Also odd that they'd made a provision in their will for me to occupy the house alone, even if I was underage still. Technically, my great-uncle Algernon was my legal guardian, but he was only required to check on me once a month. We didn't have to live together. My lawyers (yes, my inheritance had come with lawyers) told me that was rare. But whatever, at least I had a place to live, even if it was in a different state from everyone I'd known for most of my life.

Still, after all the awkward silences, pitying looks, and sympathy hugs I'd gotten after my parents had died, moving twelve hours away from my friends had seemed like a fine idea when the time came. Not to mention how impossibly lonely our Colorado home had seemed after the accident.

I hadn't even made it a block away from the nondescript concrete building that was Flagstaff High School when I felt a hand on my shoulder, and Seamus wound up eating dirt.

I realized who it was halfway through the throw and did what I could to help him land well, but he still hit the ground with the kind of gasp that lets everyone know that it's going to take a minute to start breathing again.

"Shit. Sorry, Seamus. Don't do that."

Seamus still didn't have air in his lungs, so I just tried to help him to a standing position while he worked on re-inflating his lungs.

"My bad," he muttered, when he finally had a enough air to speak. "I should have known you'd be on edge."

I shrugged.

"Not a good idea to grab me when I can't see you, anyway. Muscle memory takes over."

He raised an eyebrow at that.

"I've been studying mixed martial arts since I was ten."

"Right. Ok. Mental note. Do not touch Vic without her explicit permission."

I nodded.

"Not a bad rule for all humans, really."

Seamus thought about that. He nodded, but then frowned.

"I'm pretty cuddly with my friends, though. Male or female, doesn't matter. I like to hug, and wrap my arm around people's shoulders and stuff."

I smiled.

"I'm not saying you shouldn't touch people, Seamus, just make sure they're cool with it first. You don't need a written waiver every damned time, but, you know, pay attention to body language and facial expressions, and if you're ever in doubt, just ask."

He still looked upset, so I continued.

"I, for one, love hugs from my friends. I just need to be able to see them coming. And if I ever don't feel like being touched, I sure as hell will let you know."

"Preferably before you knock the wind out of me," Seamus said.

I shrugged again.

"Preferably, but I make no guarantees. Don't sneak up on me. I've been trained to hurt people who do."

"Fair enough," he said. Then he hunched his shoulders and stepped back a bit. "Well, this makes half of my mission seem obsolete."

"Oh? What was your mission?"

"To thank you for saving my butt in there," he began, "and to offer to walk you home in case Pervy McPerverson decides to show up again."

That made me smile.

"I appreciate the gesture, Seamus, but I think I can handle Mr. McNoPants if I need to. After all, he's made it extremely easy for me to kick him in the nuts."

Seamus chortled briefly before looking serious again.

"I don't like the idea of you going home alone now that he's set his sights on you."

I was no longer smiling.

"Dude. Keep your overprotective alpha male shit to yourself. I can defend myself, and you have no responsibility to protect me. I'll see you tomorrow."

With that, I turned on my heel. I liked Seamus. He had a good sense of humor and he seemed like good company, but I had zero tolerance for patriarchal bullshit.

"Vic, wait! I didn't mean…"

I did not wait. At least he was smart enough not to try to make me stop walking away.

About a block later I caught a strange, dark form out of the corner of my eye, but when I turned to look at it, I saw nothing. My house was basically a straight shot down the road from where I stood, but I decided to make a detour to see if whatever I'd glimpsed was following me.

Sure enough, after I turned right down a side street, I saw it again. This time I waited until I was sure the dark patch was in my peripheral vision and didn't break my stride, then suddenly flipped around and saw clearly what was following me.

A wolf.

And not just any wolf.

The same black wolf that had launched itself into the pool after Edik had shown up.

What. The. Fuck.

I stared at the wolf. It stared back. I considered my options.

It whined.

I ran.

RUNNING AWAY FROM a wolf is a stupid thing to do. It elicits a prey-chasing response in them and is not anywhere near the top of the list of things you should do if you *don't* want a wolf to chase you.

Which is why I was running towards the wolf.

It probably sounds stupid to you, but really, I was just trying to convince the wolf that I was the bigger, badder predator, and that it should run for the hills. Honestly, we were in the middle of Flagstaff ,which, aside from not generally harboring wolves to begin with, was full of other humans, so the wolf should have been wary to begin with. Me charging him should have thoroughly convinced him that his jaunt into Humanville was over and he should head back to wherever he might have friends waiting.

Should have.

But didn't.

I stopped when I was only a few feet away from the creature, which was staring at me like I'd lost my mind.

I lowered my arms and coughed, as though that covered up the insane yelling I'd been doing up until a few seconds ago.

"Go away. There are humans here who would hurt you, especially after you attacked that guy in the pool."

Look, it's not like I thought talking to the wolf was going to work. But old habits die hard, and after my stint volunteering with the Colorado Wolf and Wildlife center, I was in the habit of talking to wolves. I didn't expect him to listen to me. I'd spent a year's worth of weekends and vacations working with wolves who had always seemed like they were listening, but then went ahead and did whatever it was they had planned to do to begin with. Which, to be honest, I attribute to wolves just not giving a fuck, rather than wolves not understanding human speech, but however you slice it, wolves don't just take advice from humans and do what they say.

"Go on, bud. I know it's interesting here with all the weird smells and free food and stuff, but it's not safe and… and ok, you're really starting to creep me out with that."

That last part was in response to the wolf looking for all the world like he was chuckling when I said the words free food.

"Please go away," I tried again.

Then the wolf stretched a bit, nodded once, and walked away.

THAT NIGHT I was exhausted. Pants-shittingly eerie wolves aside, it had been a weird day, no matter how you cut it.

I had been ready to collapse into bed as soon as I got home, especially after the night I'd had previously, full of crazy narrators and bomb drops about my parents' deaths, but I decided to be a responsible not-quite-adult and microwave myself some leftover Chinese food before showering and collapsing into bed with a good book.

Luckily, none of my classes had assigned much in the way of homework, seemingly wanting to ease students into the transition from summer. I'd have to give an oral account of everything I'd done over summer vacation in Spanish tomorrow, but since I'd grown up speaking Spanish with my father anyway, I didn't feel the need to prepare.

I wasn't sure what time it was when I finally drifted off to sleep, several chapters into the latest Twenty-Sided Sorcerer book, but I was disconcerted to find the lights turned out when I woke up a few hours later. I didn't remember turning them off. Nor did I remember leaving the window open, but the breeze that caressed my face definitely brought with it the smell of pine needles and fresh earth, and those were not smells that originated inside my air conditioning unit.

I casually reached for my bedside lamp with one hand, all the while sliding my other hand under the pillow to grasp for the cell phone I vaguely recalled shoving under there after spending more time than I'd actually wanted to checking Facebook before starting to read.

At the same moment my left hand turned on the bedside light, my right hand connected with my cell phone.

The light blinded me briefly, even though I'd closed my eyes as it came on, but soon I was able to see a dark figure standing on the far side of the room.

"Step any closer, and I'll call the cops," I said, brandishing my cell phone. Of course, I'd already hit my speed dial for police dispatch, but whoever the fuck was standing inside of my room didn't need to know that just yet.

"I'm sorry, Victoria," said a vaguely familiar voice, as the figure stepped out of the shadows. "I didn't mean to startle you."

My jaw dropped as Edik stepped into the light of the lamp.

"What in the name of ten kinds of hell are you doing in MY BED-ROOM?!" I shouted.

The small, closed-mouth smile that had been gracing Edik's lips fell, and his eyebrows raised in confusion.

"I just came to watch you sleep," he said.

"What the fuck do you mean, you came to watch me sleep?! That's the creepiest godsdamned thing I've ever heard. GET OUT OF MY HOUSE, YOU FUCKING PERV!"

Edik looked as though I had slapped him, but I wasn't about to be deterred.

"Seriously, get out of my house before the cops get here," I said, as he took a step closer.

"You called the cops?" he asked, looking for all the world like a stricken puppy.

"Yes, I called the cops. THERE'S A STRANGE MAN IN MY BED-ROOM."

I have to admit I was partially yelling to make sure that whoever was listening over dispatch heard what I was saying. I had to hope that the GPS chip in the phone would give them my location.

"But it's just me. Surely you don't need them to come now?"

"Edik, did I say or do anything today that made you think I wanted you to visit me at all, let alone IN MY BEDROOM?"

"No, not exactly but… but can't you feel it, Victoria? Don't you feel the connection between us?"

"No, Edik. I do not. I feel no connection. All I know is that you're a very attractive, but probably sociopathic, classmate who has shown up uninvited not only to my HOUSE, but to my freaking BEDROOM, after, let's not forget, showing up to my swim practice butt naked and swimming underneath me like some kind of psychotic seal. Now, I'm going to ask you one more time to GET THE FUCK OUT OF MY HOUSE."

I was beginning to feel that Edik might be a little bit slow, as he persisted in not walking away from me, even though I could hear sirens in the distance already.

"But you're supposed to be the one who understands me, the one who is finally able to love me despite my being… being a… m-m-monster."

The way his lips pouted as he said that last part really made me want to hit him. So far he seemed like he WAS a fucking monster. After all, what the hell else do you call someone who breaks into your house at night to watch you sleep and then doesn't leave even after you call the cops?

"Get. Out. OF. MY. HOUSE!"

Instead of doing as I asked, the asshole insisted on stepping even closer to the bed, and I finally decided to stand up and back away, lest he try to pin me down.

This appeared to have been a mistake, as he covered the distance between us so fast that I couldn't even track it, and then pinned me to the wall. His body pressed against mine, and his arms pushed my shoulders back. At least I was standing upright.

"Do you have any idea how your smell drives me to distraction?" he asked, face buried in my hair, winning the award for creepiest shit ever said to me in my entire life.

"No, and you have one more second to back away from me before I will be forced to kick your ass," I said, with more confidence than I actually felt. Edik was a good six inches taller than I was, and had at least fifty pounds on me if I was any judge of muscle mass, but I was banking that he'd never been taught how to fight, especially after how quickly he'd backed down at the pool earlier.

"Victoria, I—"

His second was up. I'd really only given it to him to gather my own courage, not because he deserved any sort of second chance.

I stepped hard on his instep and buckled his arms at the elbow with simultaneous strikes from my forearms, then reached forward to grab the back of his head and pull his nose down to meet my forehead. Even as I did this, my knee came up and rammed into his crotch as hard as it could.

Edik collapsed into a pile on the floor just as I'd hoped, but I felt like I'd head-butted a tree, and slowly braced myself against the wall to hold the dizziness at bay.

Just as I sank to the floor with my back to the wall, I heard a rush of footfalls coming up the stairs. Without any announcement, the door burst open and a bunch of armed officers in uniform flowed through with their guns raised. I'd never been happier to see a cop, or seven.

I was just working on staggering back to my feet when one of the officers crouched down in front of me.

"Are you alright, miss?" she asked.

The voice caused a faint tremor of recognition to pass through me. I looked into the woman's face and tried to focus my blurring eyes for a moment. Focusing hurt, but through the pain I had a moment of full recognition, just before my vision started to darken.

"What are you doing here?" I asked the wild-haired redhead in uniform.

"Shh…" she said, holding a finger to my mouth, as blackness overtook me.

"Damn it, Gwen," I muttered, slumping to the floor as consciousness fled.

I'D WANTED TO ask Gwen a number of questions, but, of course, she was gone as soon as I came to.

It took a while for the rest of the cops and EMTs to leave, but luckily they were willing to take my statement in my own kitchen instead of making me go to the local precinct. I'd had a much harder time convincing the EMTs not to drag me to the hospital, but I downplayed the head-butt to Edik's brick-like skull and played up shock as the reason for my fainting. It wasn't that I wanted to ignore a concussion, it was just that I couldn't handle the thought of spending the night in a hospital alone.

The cops asked who they could call for me, but the only family I had nearby was my great-uncle Algernon, who was 85 and probably didn't need the hassle of being woken up by the cops at 2AM, so I said no one.

When everyone had filed out, I heaved a sigh of relief and turned to head up to my bedroom. I desperately needed to get some sleep. But just as I turned towards the staircase, I heard a scratching noise on my front door.

"What the…"

I wandered to the door and looked out the peephole. I couldn't see anything, but the scratching redoubled, coupled with a light whining sound.

I reached for the lock, then thought better of it. I turned around, went to the nearest closet, grabbed my field hockey stick, and THEN went to turn the lock on the door, field hockey stick brandished threateningly all the while.

My open door revealed none other than the wolf who had been following me home earlier.

"What are you doing here?"

It was a sign of how exhausted I was that I was talking to the wolf instead of panicking about having a large predator on my doorstep.

It whined again, and nudged its head towards the door, as though asking to come in.

"No. Dude. I need to sleep. Whatever wolfy business you think you have with me is gonna have to wait."

The whining increased, and the wolf stared at me resolutely.

"Seriously, I just need to get some slee—"

I didn't finish my thoughts on getting a full eight hours of rest, because at that moment both the wolf and I turned to look up the stairs, where we'd just heard a ridiculously ominous bump from my bedroom floor.

"YOU'VE GOT TO be fucking kidding me," I mumbled, even as the wolf let forth a low growl that made my skin crawl. I glanced at him, just to be sure that the growl wasn't directed at me, but sure enough, he was staring at the ceiling.

"Well, should we head upstairs and see what's making all that racket?" I asked, even as I moved towards the staircase.

I was experiencing a weird mixture of fear and anger. Honestly, if I hadn't been so pissed off at the idea of Edik breaking into my bedroom *again,* especially after he'd just been carted off by the cops, I think I would have been cowering in a corner. As it was, I was ready to tear someone's fucking head off. Or at least laugh maniacally while I watched the wolf do it.

I took a deep breath as I neared the top of the stairs. If I was too worked up, I might incite the wolf to violence before it was strictly necessary. Although, I was having a more and more difficult time believing that the response to Edik shouldn't just be an immediate grab for the jugular.

Maybe one more calming breath before I opened the door…

The wolf was right on my heels, his head pushed up against my hip, as he tried to wrangle positioning so that he would enter the room first.

"Hey, there, Fang," I whispered. "No need to go all overprotective male on me. I can handle this. You're just here in case I knock myself out head-butting this asshole a second time."

The wolf growled, but took a step back.

"Look, if the nut shot works as well as it did before, you can pee on him while he's down."

The snarl that followed looked like it was supposed to be an imitation of a smirk. I shook my head. *Wolves do not emulate human facial expressions,* I reminded myself.

One more deep breath, and…

I pulled the door open and then instantly bent down to grab the wolf by the neck as he attempted to lunge past me, a deep-throated growl on his lips.

"Hold up!" I shouted to the enraged wolf that I had no business trying to restrain. Luckily, he decided not to turn his ire on me and continued to growl at the figure that sat in the middle of my floor.

"That," I said, standing up, but keeping one hand nestled in the fur of the wolf's neck, "is not Creepy McStalkerpants."

"GWEN?" I ASKED, unsure where to start. "What the fuck are you doing here? And why didn't you stick around earlier, if you were just going to show up again?"

"If you don't want me around, I can leave." Gwen stood up as she spoke, wiping imaginary dust from her spotless leather leggings.

"I didn't say that. But you know… you could have come and knocked on the door or something, instead of appearing here in my bedroom. Or even… I don't know, called me, like a normal human being."

"Phones are a hassle, you were busy with the cops and I didn't want to disturb you, and… I dropped something up here earlier."

That sounded like a blatant lie.

"Right…" suddenly I was glad that the wolf was here with me, even though it should have scared the crap out of me. I kept my field hockey stick raised. Just in case.

"I was just looking for the light switch when I ran into the end of your massive bed."

"Oh?" I guess that explained why she'd been on the floor when we'd come in.

"Why do you have a king sized bed, anyway?"

"Because I like to spread out when I sleep. Why do you care?"

"Because I like to move stealthily and the damned thing knocked me on my ass."

"I don't see how that's the bed's fault."

"You wouldn't."

"Mind telling me why you're here?"

Gwen just leveled her emerald eyes at me and stared until I blinked.

"I have a message for you."

"Ok…"

She flipped her fiery hair over her shoulder and looked pointedly at the wolf.

"Just you."

"Seriously? He's a wolf. Who's he going to tell? And besides, I don't really trust you at the moment, so I'd rather he stayed, thanks."

It might be insane to trust a wild animal I'd just met more than another human, but I'd had a bad streak with humans lately, and I'd never had a wild animal do anything I wouldn't expect it to do. Well, ok, yes, except this guy following me and seeming like he was listening to me, but you get what I'm saying.

"Fine, he can stay, but I'm still casting a silencing spell on the room."

"A what?"

"A silencing spell."

"Am I supposed to know what that is?"

"I think the name is pretty self-explanatory."

"Yes, but the name implies… you know… magic."

"What tipped it off? The word spell?"

"Yeah, but… since magic isn't real, I assume you'll explain what you're *actually* going to do."

"Who said magic isn't real?"

"Um… everyone? For like the last 200 years or so?"

"Tsk, tsk, little girl, didn't your parents teach you *anything*?"

I didn't bother to reply, simply because I wasn't used to arguing with crazy people. If Gwen wanted to believe there was magic, how on earth was I going to argue with her? It's like when someone says that you can't prove to them that there aren't teeny, tiny, weightless, invisible unicorns who become insubstantial whenever you try to touch them dancing on your head right now. You can't disprove that kind of thing, you just know better.

Gwen gestured around the room for a bit, and then her eyes glowed a bright green for a few seconds. That weirded me out, but I wasn't sold on the idea that it was magic. You could buy all kinds of fancy contacts these days. I knew a girl who would put white contacts in her eyes and go sit in a park for hours at night, just to freak out the neighborhood kids. Folks need their hobbies.

"So, did you set up our cone of silence?"

"This is *not* an episode of Get Smart."

"You sure? It kinda feels like one."

Gwen just glared at me again. I felt that was an unfair number of malevolent eye gestures in my direction, when she was the one who had abandoned me after I'd been attacked AND the one who had broken into my house afterwards, making me think that my stalker was back.

I tried to return the glare, but wound up merely squinting. I probably looked like I had gas.

"Wanna tell me why you're here, now?" I said, when I'd given up on the staring contest.

"Are you sure you're ready? Would you like to sit down first?" she asked.

"Gwen, for fuck's sake, just tell me!"

"Tomorrow the triangle will be complete!"

I WOULD LOVE to tell you what the hell Gwen meant by that, but she poofed out of existence right after she'd made that announcement. Literally. There was an actual poofing sound.

I stared at the wolf and slowly slid my way down the wall next to my bedroom door.

"What the fuck is going on with my life?" I looked around at the Princess Bride, Harry Potter, Moana, and Doctor Who posters that covered my walls, but they seemed disinclined to help.

The wolf whined a bit, and tucked its head under the hand that wasn't holding the field hockey stick.

"I have psychos creeping into my bedroom at night, crazy women who can poof in and out of existence showing up to relate cryptic messages…" I hesitated and looked down at the large, amber-eyed wolf currently resting its muzzle peacefully on my leg. "And a giant, friendly wolf that followed me home."

The wolf whined a bit.

"I feel like I'm losing my damned mind."

I looked around my bedroom and realized that I wasn't going to be able to fall asleep here. I was exhausted, but the thought that Edik might come back, or that Gwen would poof in whenever she felt like it… a shiver crawled along my spine and I stood up.

"Come on, wolf. I can't sleep here and you… probably need to get back to wherever your pack is."

To my astonishment, the wolf got up and followed me without complaint.

Until we got to the front door, where it resolutely sat down and refused to cross the threshold.

"Come on, buddy. I can't keep a wild wolf. It's illegal, and you'd hate it. I don't have anywhere close to the acreage you'd need to be comfortable. Surely you have a pack somewhere."

The wolf didn't respond with any sort of noise or gesture, but it remained resolutely in place.

"Right. I'm still talking to a wild animal. Thanks for reminding me that I'm going cuckoopants."

The wolf snorted, far too close to a human chortle for my liking, and then headed for my living room.

"Seriously?" I sighed, shutting the door and locking it, not wanting to let anyone else show up uninvited in my house tonight if I could help it.

I stepped into the living room, just in time to see the wolf disappear on the other side of my couch.

A heartbeat later, Seamus was standing on the far side of the couch, naked, or at least, I was pretty sure he was naked. If he was wearing pants they were… incredibly low.

I swallowed and tried not to scream.

"Do I have a sign painted on me somewhere saying 'please surprise me naked'?"

"Vic, I'm really sorry. My clothes are outside. I can run and get them, but I wanted to show you the truth first."

"The what?" I asked, my foggy brain finally realizing that I couldn't see the wolf anymore.

"The truth. You kept talking about losing your mind and I thought… shit, maybe this wasn't a good idea."

It was taking a lot of effort not to launch myself at Seamus with the field hockey stick, and maybe he could tell that I was struggling, because his face looked pretty concerned all of a sudden.

"You have 30 seconds to explain yourself well enough to keep me from applying this stick to your head."

"Fine. Right. Ok. Look, I'm not supposed to talk about this, but… you're clearly not a non, and… Gwen did magic in front of you, right? So, I shouldn't get in trouble, but… damn it, I've never had to explain this to anyone else before!"

"Start making sense quickly, Seamus, you have 15 seconds." I adjusted my grip on the field hockey stick and settled into a fighting stance.

"I'm a werewolf."

"What?" I almost dropped the field hockey stick.

"I'm not naked because I want to sex you up or anything, and I'm not stalking you, I just… I followed you because I was worried that Edik would try another stupid stunt like the one he pulled at the pool, but you made it clear you didn't want me around, so I tried to just stay nearby and hope I would hear it if you needed help. I must have fallen asleep, because I didn't hear anything until the sirens were most of the way here. I tried to get in, but your doors were all locked, and by the time I'd decided to try breaking a window or something, the cops were already here. Then it seemed like they took care of Edik somehow, because he was out cold and in handcuffs when they dragged him out of here. I waited for them to leave in order to check on you. But then, well you know the rest of it, we heard that thump upstairs and now… well, crap. You seem so… exhausted? Upset? Alone? I don't know, I didn't want to leave you alone, but I was worried you'd try to call animal services on me or something, so I decided the best thing was just to tell you the truth. I mean, you saw Gwen do magic, Edik straight up told you he was a creature of the night, and you smell like one of us, so I figured… crap. You think I'm insane, don't you? Look."

And then suddenly I was staring at the wolf again. He was just standing there, amber eyes and wolfy ears pointed right at me.

"See."

Now I was looking at Seamus again. Right where the wolf had been.

That was about the time my legs gave out.

OK. FINE. WEREWOLVES existed. By the time Seamus had left last night, there really hadn't been any arguing that. I did briefly try to convince myself that it was a truly elaborate prank, but in the end I couldn't figure out how it worked if it was, and, oddly enough, Occam's razor suggested that Seamus actually turning into a werewolf really was the more likely explanation. In the end, the fact that I could run my fingers through the wolf's fur and then be sitting next to a naked Seamus half a second later—and it was a sign of how stunned I was by the whole revelation that sitting next to a naked Seamus didn't phase me at all—well, what other explanation was there?

Of course, the best "scientific" explanation I could come up with was that Seamus was somehow pulling a wolf through an inter-dimensional pocket and trading consciousnesses with it, but that sounded almost as far-fetched as the idea that the whole thing was magic, so I kept it to myself.

Meanwhile, after eventually coming to terms—at least marginally—with the idea that Seamus was actually able to turn into a wolf at will, I kicked him out so that I could finally get some sleep.

Then I'd remembered that the thought of sleeping in my own bed made my stomach turn, and I'd set up camp on the couch. It wasn't rational that I felt in any way safer there, but my brain wasn't looking for reason, it was just looking to not go upstairs and be reminded that some psychotic asshat had shown up in my room in the middle of the night.

Despite how exhausted I'd been, sleep was a struggle. My brain kept turning over the things that Seamus had said. He was a werewolf, and I was…

he wasn't sure, but he knew I was something, probably a were, just not a wolf.

All of which was preposterous. Werewolves were one thing… maybe. Me turning furry at will? Well, that was insane. I'd know if I had an animal form I could call on whenever I wanted. The idea that I'd somehow missed my ability to turn into something with four legs whenever I felt like it was just stupid.

And whenever I'd managed to stop thinking about the ridiculousness of a world where a guy from my english class could turn into a wolf, I'd gone right back to thinking about some douchetart showing up in my bedroom while I slept.

Sometime after the sun started to rise, I drifted off to sleep.

And was woken by my alarm almost immediately afterward.

"Fuck everything," I muttered, rubbing my eyes and hating life.

I debated just skipping school. After all, I would be useless after the negligible amount of sleep I'd gotten… but even as I thought about slinking upstairs and curling up in my bed, my stomach twisted. Memories of head butting Edik came flooding back, and I realized that I wasn't likely to get any more sleep, even if I stayed home.

"I repeat. Fuck everything."

I took a quick shower, scarfed a bowl of cereal, and trudged off to school as quickly as my sluggish legs would allow.

~~~

"I'm actually a vampire."

"What?!" I was trying to whisper, but I was so flustered that freaking Stalky McStalkerson was still my lab partner, despite the fact that he had been taken away in handcuffs the night before, that I was raising my voice more than I'd intended.

He was supposed to have spent the night in prison and not been allowed to attend school today. The cops had told me we were supposed to have a court date on Thursday to establish a restraining order. I wasn't supposed to have to see him until then. But my lawyers (yes, I have lawyers, my parents left me a whole estate, there was a lot of paperwork involved) had called me this morning while I was walking to school to inform me that, despite everything I had told them and what the police had confirmed with them the night before, Edik had been released immediately. In addition, none of the
~~~

law enforcement officials who had dealt with him seemed to recall any sort of violation of my rights. My lawyers were baffled and looking into it.

In the meantime, Sir Creepsalot was sitting right next to me in class with a face that didn't look at all like I had head-butted him the night before.

I felt like I was losing my mind.

Which may explain why I wasn't all that surprised by the words coming out of his mouth.

"I'm a vampire."

I simply stared at him. He was clearly not in the best place mentally. After all, who thinks it's ok to break into someone's house and watch them while they sleep? I tried not to think about how fucked up the night before was, and took a deep breath.

"And why, exactly, do you think you're a vampire?" I asked. I glanced at the front of the room to see if Ms. Rebuke was getting ready to send us both to the principal, but she seemed distracted by some disgusting blob that one of the students had created over one of the Bunsen burners. I wasn't clear why they were using the Bunsen burners in physics class, but I had bigger problems to worry about at the moment.

"I don't *think* I'm one. It's just what I am. It's why I'm different. It's why no one understands me."

My eyebrows lifted towards my hairline and I had a hard time keeping my face from reading as "you're batshit nuts!" when I turned to look at Edik.

"Um… have you considered that no one understands you because it's socially and morally unacceptable to show up in people's bedrooms and watch them sleep without an invitation?"

"No. That's not it. I'm a vampire. I drink human blood. Humans can tell I'm a predator and I make them uncomfortable. But you're different."

"No, I'm not. You *definitely* make me uncomfortable."

"It's not that. It's your smell. You smell different. And I can't tell what you're thinking."

"I have a good poker face and I don't wear gaudy perfume. That doesn't mean anything mystical. It means you should give me my space."

"No. You're special. I can tell. Here, look."

Some form of sheer morbid curiosity had me turn to look at Edik. What I saw was not reassuring. The way that Edik's teeth caught the sun was entirely disconcerting, and it fully explained why I'd never seen him smile with his mouth open up till now.

"You had your teeth encrusted with diamonds? Doesn't that cut your mouth up all the time?" I asked, trying to keep the pitch and meter of my voice level, despite wanting to scream across the room that I was paired up with a lunatic.

"I didn't *have* my teeth encrusted. They *are* diamonds. My whole skull is made of diamond. It's part of who I am."

This was going a bit far for an emo fantasy, or strange divergent cosplay, or whatever the fuck this was. It was too much. Ok, fine, his teeth were sparkly. Disconcertingly sparkly. And he was disturbingly handsome as well. But whatever the explanation was: "I'm a vampire," or "I'm a crazy person who shouldn't be allowed to be in school with the people I stalk," it amounted to the same thing: I was soooo done talking to him.

"Edik, I hate to say this—no, scratch that, I don't hate to say it, I just don't want you to attack me again, but I'm going to say it anyway—I don't believe that you're a vampire. And even if you are, you really need to stop talking to me. I'm working on filing a restraining order against you. I can't believe the cops let you come to school today."

I was agitated beyond tact and well into honesty. I didn't have the emotional fortitude to protect this guy's feelings, and frankly, he didn't deserve to have his feelings protected. I don't have much patience for guys who break into my bedroom and then corner me. Go ahead, accuse me of overreacting.

"The cops can't stop me. I just altered their memories. Same as I'll have to do with the girls who just noticed me showing you my teeth. But that's ok. They're just humans."

"I'm not sure which part of that I find most disturbing, so I'm not going to analyze it much. But seriously. You need to leave me alone. I want nothing to do with you, vampire or human."

"Vampire."

"Ok. Fine. Go away, vampire."

"We're lab partners."

"We're lab partners who are about to try to get each other arrested."

"I wouldn't have you arrested."

"Fine. I'm a lab partner who is going to get you arrested. Either way. Stop. Talking. To. Me."

"But, Vic—"

"Do you need me to knee you in the balls again?"

Edik's mouth slammed shut, and I wondered how he reconciled the idea of being a vampire with the simple fact that he got pwned by me last night.

Not that I wasn't a very competent fighter, I was, but still. Vampires in all the books I'd read were supposed to be hot shit when it came to physical defenses. What kind of vampire gets taken down with a nut shot from a normal human that he outweighs by 50lbs?

~~~

It wasn't my first time being the new kid in school, so I was accustomed to the attention that one generally garners just by dint of being an oddity. Of course, I was usually considered odd enough that I continued to garner a bit of extra attention even after the initial new girl obsession had worn off. But just because I was used to the attention didn't mean that I liked it. It wasn't that I couldn't stand being the center of attention; class presentations and theater performances didn't bother me. It was more that I hated the kind of attention that being the new kid garnered. It was rather like what I assumed it felt like to be in a circus sideshow. The looks were long and leering, filled with a derogatory curiosity that left you feeling like you needed a shower.

Imagine my delight then, when, during my second period class, whilst I blearily settled myself into a seat at the back, I noticed a student I hadn't seen yesterday. More than one person was looking straight at her and whispering in a way that clearly told me she was either new, or a pariah of some kind. Either way, she was taking the spotlight off of me. She sat calmly in the row directly ahead of me, and her dark, tightly-curled hair, pulled into a thick braid down her back, was all I could see. I smiled to myself at the idea of someone else getting stared at for a while, and then instantly regretted it.

"Ms. Marmot! What are you so smug about this morning? Is there something you would like to share with the class?"

What was Rebuke even doing in this class? I'd just escaped first period physics with her and was supposed to be in English with Topaz. She must be subbing again. I sighed.

"No, Ms. Rebuke, I was just smiling after relieving myself of some painful gas buildup. Thank you for asking though."

Oh dear. Filters were down after a night of almost zero sleep and a morning full of stalker. Perhaps she would be distracted by my self-deprecating humor? A chorus of laughter sounded around the classroom, but one look at her revealed that my joke had done little to deflect her ire.
~~~

"Ms. Marmot, are you under the impression that you are funny?"

"Everyone farts, Ms. Rebuke. I believe there was a book about it."

I bit my own tongue after that slipped out. *What the hell is wrong with me?* I didn't usually talk back to teachers, no matter what they said to me. Although, to be fair, I'd never had a teacher dislike me quite as strongly as Ms. Rebuke seemed to. It must have been the cumulation of stress and exhaustion over the past few days, but I couldn't seem to keep my mouth shut.

"Ms. Marmot! Do you *wish* to visit the principals' office again?"

"Actually, yes. I have a number of questions for him." I startled even myself with that one.

It was small consolation that the new kid at the table in front of me seemed to find my little display amusing, as I watched Ms. Rebuke's face take on a deep shade of vermillion. While my brain tried to regain control of my tongue, I drowsily wondered what she would do next. Since I'd just asked to be sent to the principal's office, the threat of sending me there lost much of its weight. On the other hand, allowing me to remain in the classroom would undermine her authority.

I briefly regretted having challenged the woman's authority, until I remembered that I'd never actually done anything to set her off except answer her questions on the first day of class, when she had seemed to hate me instantly for no reason. I wasn't proud of undermining her authority in her own classroom, but I was happy to demonstrate to her that it wasn't a good idea to go around being horrible to people for no reason.

"GO. TO. MR. BUMBLEBEE'S. OFFICE. IMMEDIATELY!"

Her face was so red by the time she spoke that I was surprised not to see steam exuding from her ears like a Warner Bros cartoon. I stood up and shouldered my backpack.

Just as I reached the front of the room and turned towards the door, I heard a voice mutter, "Incidi!" and felt something sting my shoulder. I turned to find the new kid pinning Ms. Rebuke's arms to her sides and... snarling?

I inspected my shoulder, but found nothing wrong with it. The young woman, who looked like a younger version of Zoe from *Firefly*, left Rebuke where she was and came to usher me out the door and take a look at my shoulder.

"Looks like she missed," she said, once we were on the other side of the classroom door.

"Um... I felt something hit my shoulder, but... well, I feel fine otherwise."

I was struggling to string a sentence together. This girl was gorgeous, and everywhere she touched me felt like my skin was on fire. I'd never found a woman attractive before, but my body didn't seem to give a damn about that small detail.

"So she *did* hit you? Why aren't you cut, then?"

"I'm not sure. What did she throw at me?" I asked.

The young woman's eyebrows raised in confusion. For a moment, she seemed as though she were about to reply, but then she looked around the hallway and shook her head.

"Let's just say the fact that it didn't cut you is… interesting," was all she said, in the end.

I nodded, even though I had no idea what I was agreeing with.

"Well, I'd better get to Mr. Bumblebee's office, I suppose." I may have started unexpectedly giving lip to teachers, but I wasn't about to start ignoring direct orders to go see the principal.

The Zoe look-alike tilted her head as though she expected me to do precisely that.

"You really respect *her* authority?" she asked.

I shrugged.

"I need to talk to him, anyway."

It was true. I had been meaning to talk to him sometime today about what I could do to keep Edik away from me, even if the police weren't going to cooperate. Just because either I, or the world, was going insane didn't mean I had to put up with Edik's bullshit.

I turned again and headed down the hall, not sure what had just happened or why it seemed so important. Not to mention why I was mesmerized by the eyes of a woman I'd just met.

"HEY! WAIT!" CAME the voice of the woman whose hands made my skin tingle.

"What?" I asked, turning slightly as I kept walking towards Albert's office.

"We need to talk," she said, her strides keeping pace with mine, even though she was a good three inches shorter than I was. Or would have been, if her black, combat-style boots hadn't had a two-inch heel.

"About what?" I asked, trying to focus on the hallway walls instead of on the warmth creeping up my skin as she drew closer.

"We shouldn't talk about it here," she said, grabbing my wrist.

The surge of warmth that spread up my arm and shot straight to my core was enough to stop me in my tracks. I swallowed, staring at where her hand touched my wrist, expecting to see… something that explained the reaction I was feeling, but it was just her skin touching mine.

"That's… weird," she said, clearing her throat and dropping my wrist.

"What exactly—"

Before I could ask any of the five million questions that jumped into my head, a familiar voice interrupted me.

"Vic, hey! I got to English late and heard you were sent to Bumblebee's office again. Need company?"

Seamus was a surprisingly welcome sight. I wouldn't have thought that seeing someone who had only recently revealed to me that he was a were-wolf would make me feel less anxious, but I had to admit that, after the chaos of finding Edik waiting for me in first period physics and then being attacked by a teacher not five minutes into second period… Seamus' friendly, open expression made a few of the knots in my neck and shoulders relax.

"Go away, pup," the new girl snarled. "I have something important to discuss with her."

"The fuck?" I asked, my brain unable to keep my tongue from spewing forth whatever it conjured. "Why are you talking to him that way?"

"I don't play with dogs," she replied, as if that somehow explained things.

"I have no idea what you mean, but Seamus is my friend and he's walking me to the principal's office, so if you 'don't play with dogs' I guess that means you can take a long walk off a short pier."

I grabbed Seamus' arm, did my best to ignore the heat that coursed through me when I touched his skin, and dragged us both in the direction of the principal's office.

What the fuck is with me today? Has sleep deprivation made me the horniest person on the planet? It's like I can't touch people without wanting to jump their bones.

Seamus looked smug enough that I almost turned back to talk to the new kid. If he was getting possessive, then this friendship was going to be over before it even started. Ugh. I was probably reading too much into it. My brain was still fried from last night. There was too much bullshit going on. It wasn't even lunch time yet, and I was sooo done with this day.

Just as I had that thought, the new kid caught up to us and grabbed my arm again, but this time I ignored the fireworks inside me and kept trucking.

"Wait! Vic, stop walking! I need to talk to you about your brother."

Well, fuck. That did it. I shook free of her arm, let go of Seamus' elbow, turned towards the nearest exit, and ran.

I DON'T HAVE a brother. I don't have a brother. I don't have a brother.

Of course, you'd think, if I really didn't have a brother, that having said non-existent brother mentioned wouldn't be giving me a fucking panic attack. So, then, you'd wonder why I was sprinting—not walking, not running, SPRINTING, as fast as my limbs could propel me— out the nearest exit and into the street.

I stopped when I felt sunlight on my skin, inhaling a breath of clear Northern Arizona air while I took a moment to try to figure out why some new girl bringing up a brother I *didn't* have made me want to run away in a blind panic.

And then I instantly forgot about that, because a wolf and a panther came slamming out of the door I'd just sprinted through and before I could tell my brain not to panic, that the wolf was probably just Seamus, I was sprinting again, as fast I could, towards home.

Part of my brain was taking this moment to remind me that running away from predators was a terrible idea, especially ones that had decent land speed, but it was too late. My limbs were already pumping, my blood was filled with adrenaline, and I was headed flat-out for home.

It belatedly occurred to me that leading wild animals to my house might not be the best idea, and I ducked down a side street lined with tiny wooden houses and lawns in various stages of disarray, hoping to distract or lose them.

They must have slowed a bit, because I didn't see them as I made yet another turn that would take me one more block out of my way before I beelined it back to my place.

By the time I reached my cul-de-sac there were no large predators in sight, and I had regained enough calm to convince myself that the wolf must have been Seamus, and thus it was unlikely that I was in any real danger. Still, try convincing *your* brain of that when you're staring at over three hundred pounds of raging panther and wolf running you down.

I took a deep breath as I approached my house, trying to let its barely familiar teal wood paneling and cedar-shingled roof bring me some kind of calm. I willed the pines that surrounded the property to lend me some strength, and hoped, rather desperately, that I was done with crazy for the day. I didn't even care that I was officially skipping more than half of the school day.

As I neared the front porch, I had almost convinced myself that I could go upstairs and rest for the remainder of the day, when a form appeared on my doorstep that made my blood run cold.

"My darling Victoria!"

"Fuck you, Eric," I muttered, getting ready to fight.

IT WAS PROBABLY childish to take delight in calling someone by a name they hated, but if anyone deserved it, the sparkle-fanged douche-canoe standing on my top step did.

Edik wasted no time in violating my personal space.

"Darling Victoria," he exclaimed again, reaching for me even as I settled into a fighting stance, "I've missed you since this mo—"

He didn't get to finish, because the moment his hand reached my shoulder I peeled it off of me and turned with him so that his weight and my momentum acted to take his center of gravity. Then I leaned with him and dropped my own center of gravity so that he had no choice but to launch head over heels into the scrub oak that adorned my front stoop.

"Victoria, how—"

I never heard what he was going to ask then, because at that exact moment three hundred pounds of black feline fury slammed into him and started tearing him up.

I had been preparing my next round of defense, but the arrival of unexpected feline backup gave me pause. Would the panther attack me, too, if I joined in? Was it here to help me, or just happy to attack whatever looked tasty?

My hesitation dissipated when a familiar snarl came from near my elbow and Seamus-as-wolf launched himself into the panther-diamond-toothed-asshat-melee happening in my scrub oak.

The panther seemed to be doing its best to coordinate its attacks with Seamus', although it was clear that Seamus didn't have much experience fighting with help, or maybe even fighting at all, as he kept getting in the panther's way.

That decided me, especially when Edik took a bite out of Seamus' shoulder and he started bleeding solidly from a gaping wound.

The panther and wolf were both attacking low, so while Edik dealt with them, I went in high, planning to start a series of kicks to Edik's head and shoulders, since he was preoccupied guarding his lower half and wouldn't have a chance to grab my legs. It would have been a solid plan of attack too, if Seamus hadn't lurched sideways and fallen into my planted leg, just after I'd shifted my weight and started the arc of a high kick. Too committed to the move to regain my balance, I toppled forward, and Edik didn't hesitate to catch me and wrap one arm around my throat.

"I do not like your friendth, Victoria," he mumbled into my ear, and I saw out of the corner of my eye that his clear, sparkly canines were entirely too long, and dripping somebody's blood.

I was already struggling against his hold, trying to gain enough purchase to let me knee him in the groin, or administer another head-butt, but he was holding me tight against him with one insanely strong arm, while still fighting the dodging and weaving panther with the other.

Seamus seemed to be losing steam, but he managed to get in one last lunge, causing the panther to shift course at the last second, and me to scream as the panther's teeth found the meat of my calf instead of whatever else they'd been aiming for.

And then the world went insane.

Suddenly my vision was reporting to my brain in a way that did not compute. Everything looked like I'd upped the frames per second rate on my video console, and the world was… not quite the right color. Moreover, my feet were no longer touching the ground.

I tried to scream, because Edik was now actually strangling me, since I couldn't find purchase on the ground beneath me, and I was suspended in his arms by the neck, but all that came out was a strange growl.

The fuck?

Panicked, I scrambled against Edik with everything I had, and was amazed when I felt claws unsheathe and drag against flesh. Edik screamed in agony and jumped away, releasing me, even as I turned and pivoted midair so that I landed on…

…all *four* legs?

Seriously. What. The. Fuck?

I barely noticed that Edik was running screaming into the neighbor's yard. I was too busy trying to figure out what in the seven hells had happened to me.

"Is your door locked?" a voice asked from nearby.

I turned, and saw the gorgeous new girl standing completely naked on my front step.

I tried to answer her, but a purr was all that escaped me.

Really, a purr? I mean, yeah, she was hot as hell, but I was just trying to say the door was open.

When that failed, I swayed my head up and down.

She stepped forward, turned the handle, and gestured inside.

"Come on, we shouldn't let anyone see us like this if we can help it."

Baffled by what the hell had just happened to my life, I followed a naked new girl and a limping Seamus-wolf into my house.

AS SOON AS the door closed behind us I looked from Seamus to the new girl and back again, hoping that my face—whatever it looked like now—conveyed the full weight of my "what the everlasting fuck?!" attitude.

Seamus shifted back to human form and I had to take a moment to regain my composure.

What the hell? Did I seriously just lick my paw?

I stared at it in bafflement, not sure how to process any of this. I had paws. Four of them. They were large, seriously large… they splayed wide when I walked, and they were white, with maybe a hint of grey and some light spotting.

Curiosity getting the better of me, I padded upstairs to my bedroom, pushed my way past the door, and swung around to stand in front of the full-length mirror that hung down the back of it.

I sat down, stunned.

I was a snow leopard.

A snow leopard.

A motherfucking SNOW LEOPARD!!!

This was awesome!!!

I ran down the stairs, taking them in leaps, and landed excitedly at the bottom.

"I'M A FUCKING SNOW LEOPARD!" I screamed.

And then I looked down.

"Damn it. I'm human again."

Heat rose to my cheeks as I looked at Seamus and the new girl standing naked in my kitchen and realized that I, too, was bereft of clothing. I worked hard to tamp down the surge of attraction I felt for both of them. *Chill out, body, now is REALLY not the time!* I turned metaphorical tail and ran upstairs again. Halfway up the stairs I realized that my clothes were probably lying in a pile on my front step, but I was soooo not going back downstairs and *outside* butt naked to get them. I headed to my room instead.

When I came back down I was fully clothed, and I carried a baggy pair of sweats and a t-shirt for Seamus and an extra pair of jeans and a tank top for the new girl.

"You're both welcome to stay naked if you're… er… more comfortable that way, but… well, in case you're not, I brought some clothes down."

I tried not to blush while I handed the clothes out.

"I didn't realize snow leopards were so shy," the new girl said, taking the clothes but not looking like she was in any rush to put them on.

Seamus cleared his throat, and I was relieved to see he'd put the pants on immediately.

"She wasn't raised in a were community," he said, as if that explained everything.

I shrugged.

"Seriously, I have nothing against nudity, I just… I wasn't comfortable, so I thought I'd offer you the same amenities. You're welcome to stay as you are…. What's your name, by the way?"

"I'm Sol," she said, extending her hand to shake mine. "Short for Soledad."

"Nice to meet you, Sol," I said, returning the handshake. "This is Seamus."

Seamus reached his hand out and Sol sneered at it briefly, then looked away.

"Wow," I said, not liking where this was going. "That was shitty. What's your problem?"

Apparently I was all out of diplomacy for the day.

Sol shrugged and walked out of the room holding the jeans and tank I'd brought her. She didn't head for the door, so I didn't think she was leaving. I assumed she had just decided to change out of sight. Why she bothered, when she'd just been standing naked in front of us for five minutes, was anyone's guess.

"What the fuck was that, Seamus?" I asked, as soon as she was gone.

"I don't think she likes me," he said, glaring after Sol's retreating form.

"Clearly not. That's not what I mean. What the fuck just happened out there?!" I gestured wildly to the front door.

"Oh that," he said. "Looks like you found your were form."

"My what? What does that mean?"

"Well, as you so accurately shouted when you got down the stairs, you're a motherfucking snow leopard."

His smile was entirely too smug for my liking.

"What does that mean? How is that even possible? WHAT IS HAPPENING TO ME?!"

Of course that moment, the moment when I was basically falling into full-blown panic mode, was the moment that Sol came back from the bathroom.

"Gatita, don't worry. Nothing is wrong, you're just doing what you're supposed to do. You're a were, just like me, somewhat like your doggy pal here. You have an animal form that you can call on at will. Although, I will admit, it usually takes us a while longer to learn how to call and dismiss our animal selves so quickly. You seem particularly adept at it."

I looked between Sol and Seamus.

"That explains precisely NOTHING. How is it possible that I'm a were anything? How could I not know this?! Didn't you say it was genetic?"

That last one I directed firmly at Seamus. Last night, when I'd been peppering him with questions, trying to convince myself that werewolves didn't exist even with the evidence staring me in the face, he'd explained that the condition wasn't transferred by bite, it was genetic. You were only a were if your parents were weres, and your animal was likely to be the same animal that your parents called on, although there were exceptions.

"You lied to me," I said, staring him down. "My parents weren't weres. I would have known if they were, they would never have hidden that from me, and I've never changed before. Until… until she BIT me!"

I glared at both of them.

"It is genetic, Gatita. My biting you didn't do anything except call your animal to you for the first time. Our animal forms require another were's bite to bring them across. Contact with another were's saliva is like a neon sign calling your animal over. Like calls to like."

"WHAT DOES THAT EVEN MEAN?!"

None of this made sense. Don't get me wrong, I'd spent my entire childhood and early adolescence waiting for my damned owl to arrive and tell me I was special, magical, somehow privy to a different world in which dragons were actually REAL, but this was ridiculous. I was an adult now, or would be in a week or so, and I knew as well as anyone that magic wasn't real, as much as I wanted it to be. I couldn't be a wereleopard. My parents would have told me. Also, physics. I mean, come on. How on earth could I be both a human and a snow leopard at the same time? That just didn't make sense.

Judging by the looks on Sol and Seamus' faces, I must have said some portion of that out loud.

"Gatita, physics is precisely how this whole thing works. I'm not one of the folks who research this kind of thing, but the way you access your were is through dark matter, at least that's what the latest scientific journals are claiming. It's not the kind of thing I pay attention to."

That was a non-explanation if ever I'd heard one, but it was clear that Sol wasn't super up-to-date on the physics stuff. I'd have to ask someone else about how dark matter allowed me to have a snow leopard form. There were plenty of other questions fighting for my attention instead.

"But my parents…" I argued feebly.

"Now that one, Gatita, I can easily explain. Your parents certainly knew you're a were. They were both weres themselves, and they probably told you about it, too, at least early on, but… after your brother went missing…"

"My brother…"

"I didn't know you had a brother, Vic."

"I don't… I didn't… I don't know…"

I suddenly had a raging headache, one that felt like my skull was about to split.

"We're going to need tea, I think," Sol said, fumbling through my cupboards and pulling out the kettle and my assorted tea collection.

"Gatita, I don't know how to say this any other way, so I'm just going to say it," she said, filling the kettle and placing it on the stove top. "Your brother is alive and I know where to find him."

And *that* was when I passed out.

THE TEAKETTLE STILL hadn't boiled when I opened my eyes to find Seamus holding my hand and whimpering at me even though he was in human form.

"I'm ok," I said, shaking him off and sitting up slowly. "Just... I'm not sure, actually, my head feels like I'm recovering from a bender." I'd never actually been on a bender, but the one time I'd gotten drunk at a cousin's wedding it had felt kind of like this the morning after.

Seamus helped me to my feet, despite my best efforts to shake him off, and I couldn't decide if I was appreciative of his concern or peeved by the coddling. Honestly, I was shaky enough that I was leaning towards appreciative. The peeved part of me was probably a holdover from his interference in the fight. Where he'd gotten in my way and wound up causing Sol to bite me. Which had turned me into a freaking snow leopard.

"Did I hallucinate that?" I asked, even as I checked out my ankle and found it devoid of any sign that it had been bitten by a three hundred pound panther. My brain seemed to be ignoring the fact that the run-up to that question had all been in my head.

"Hallucinate what, Gatita?" Sol asked, handing me a cup of Earl Grey. "Drink this, it will help with the headache."

"Did you infuse it with eye of newt or something?" I asked, eyeing the cup warily.

Sol laughed.

"No, caffeine helps with headaches, that's all. I'd make you a coffee, but I don't see a coffee maker, so..."

I shrugged and took a sip of the Earl Grey, not bothering to mention my aero press—which was probably still in my backpack from the weekend anyway—or the fact that there was a coffee pot hidden somewhere in the pile of boxes I had yet to unpack in the garage. Honestly, just doing something as normal as sipping tea helped me let go of some of the tension in my neck and shoulders.

"Me turning into a snow leopard," I asked, trying to get back to the subject at hand, instead of getting sidetracked by home remedies. "Did I actually turn into a snow leopard, or was that just a freaky hallucination? I don't have any signs of a bite on my leg."

"Yes, you turned into a snow leopard. The signs of it disappeared because you shifted afterwards, the bite was small, and shifting speeds up healing," Seamus said. Then he smiled. "See, I told you, you aren't just a normal human."

The look on his face made it sound like it should have been the best news in the world, but even though turning into a snow leopard was basically a childhood dream come true… the whole thing just felt like a betrayal.

"How is it possible my parents never told me about this?"

Seamus looked at Sol quizzically.

"I told you she might not remember," Sol said, making me even more confused.

"What? What am I not remembering?"

"Vic, Sol said there were some powerful mage spells put on you and your parents when you were a kid."

"What?! Why?"

That didn't sound good. None of this sounded good, and my headache was coming back with a vengeance.

"Do you remember what we were talking about just before you passed out?" Seamus asked. His voice sounded gentle, like he was about to pull off a Band-Aid but wanted to lessen the sting.

I tried to think back to what we'd talked about before I'd blacked out, but it just made my headache rage, and I couldn't think through the pain anymore. I cradled my head in my arms and focused on not vomiting.

"This isn't going to work. The spell is too strong. She's just going to keep passing out every time we bring it up," Sol said, though I could barely hear her over the pounding in my ears.

"What if she shifts and we tell her snow leopard?"

"That might work," Sol said, after a pause. "If the spell was only cast on her human form, her snow leopard might be free of it. It won't work if it was a spirit binding, but if it was just a corporeal spell, that should do the trick." She hesitated for a moment. "Nice thinking, puppy."

If I'd been in less pain, I might have given her a talking-to about back-handed compliments. As it was, the headache was still raging, and besides, Seamus could probably take care of himself. I might have heard a growl, but it was hard to tell over the sound of my skull being stabbed repeatedly with a knife—metaphorically speaking.

"Vic, can you hear me?" Sol asked.

I nodded, and then instantly regretted it. Mental note: DO. NOT. MOVE. HEAD.

"Vic, can you manage a shift? Do you have any idea how to call on your snow leopard right now?"

I did not shake my head, but talking seemed like an impossibility with my jaw seizing with pain, so I just whimpered a bit and hoped that got my point across.

"Ok, Seamus is going to talk you through it."

I had no idea why Seamus was being voluntold to take care of me, but I was in no position to argue or second-guess.

"Ok, Vic… just… try to relax, if you can. Can you remember what it felt like to be a snow leopard? Try to imagine it, if you can. What was different from the way you normally move, smell, see, taste, balance? Try to picture those things, and then… sort of… *will* them into being."

Sol snorted, and I wondered if she thought Seamus' instructions were lacking in some way. I tried to do what Seamus said, but the pain was too much for my concentration.

"Vic," Sol said, her voice getting closer to where my head was cradled in my own arms. "If you manage the shift, the headache should go away."

Suddenly, I found the will to concentrate. At that moment, I would have done *anything* to make the headache go away, and damned if I wasn't going to figure out how to turn into a snow leopard right that fucking moment.

I tried recalling the details that Seamus had suggested, but it was hard to come up with things like sight, sound, and smell right then. My brain was overtaken with pain, and those kinds of details were hard to recall even on a good day. So I focused on the parts of me that didn't hurt. The sensation of having four paws, the agility to right myself mid-fall, the balance of a giant, glorious snow leopard tail.

Then, suddenly, I was calling on my tail, paws, and agility to balance me as I slid from a precarious perch on a stool and kitchen island and fell to the floor.

I smiled delightedly when I landed on four paws, and then smiled wider still when I realized the damned headache was gone.

"Is she *purring*?" Seamus asked, his face bewildered.

Sol just laughed.

I looked at them both expectantly. I wanted to know about whatever it was I had forgotten.

"Ok, Vic, *now* do you remember what we were talking about before you passed out?"

Oddly, I still had access to those memories. Which was weird, because those memories were in human form and currently I was a very large feline. I ignored the disconnect and focused on the memories themselves… we had been talking about my parents and them not telling me I was a were, and then Sol had started to explain why and….

I sat down with a thud, my tail flipping angrily around me as the weight of memory hit me. My brother… I had a brother, and he was still alive, and Sol knew where he was.

And then the floodgates opened. Images from my childhood that had been blocked, or that I had repressed. A little boy, my age, my height, similar features, just… a boy, and clever, and mischievous, and we'd had soooo many adventures together, and…

Did snow leopards cry? Or… I shut my mouth and looked at Seamus and Sol, and the horrified looks on their faces confirmed that I had been making a truly terrible noise.

So I focused on the feeling of tears in my eyes, and grief in my throat, and… suddenly I was sitting in the middle of my kitchen floor, naked and sobbing.

"I REMEMBERED HIM!" I cried, standing up and reaching for the kitchen counter, ignoring the pile of my clothes that lay on the floor beside the stool.

"Good. Then the spell is gone."

"No." I shook my head, grateful that the headache seemed to still be gone, even though I was back in human form. "I mean, I remembered him before, when I was a kid. They tried to charm us all, they DID charm us, but… it didn't quite take on me at first. After they took him, my parents tried to get him back, tried and tried, but nothing worked, and then… then we moved, and my parents told me I couldn't talk about Trevor anymore, and then… they had us all charmed, all of us, and… they stopped talking about him. It wasn't like he was dead, they pretended that he had never existed, that I'd never had a brother, that my *twin* didn't even exist, but it didn't work on me… not at first, and I kept trying to make them remember, and they kept telling me I was making up stories, and…"

My breath caught in my chest as the memories hit me, one after another.

"They sent me to see a psychiatrist. They had me treated… and… I stopped. I didn't want them to put me away somewhere, and I didn't want them to be so mad at me all the time, so finally… I just stopped talking about him, and… eventually, I couldn't remember if he was real or not, he felt more like something I had made up…. My mom always talked about the day they tried to take me as though that was all that had happened, as though they'd never taken Trevor, of course, because he didn't exist… and then…"

My breath hitched on a sob before I managed to speak again.

"I forgot about him. I stopped talking about him, and, slowly, I started to believe he'd never existed. Eight years of memories… how could I forget about him? How? How did I forget my twin brother?"

Seamus patted my back, and caught me as my legs started to give out again. I let him support me for a moment before I settled myself on one of the stools. Then I remembered that I was still naked. I ran the back of my wrist across my face to get the worst of the tears and snot, then grabbed my clothes and rushed upstairs to put them on again.

When I came back downstairs, Seamus and Sol were standing on opposite sides of my kitchen island, sharing what looked like an awkward silence.

"So… do cats and dogs not get along in the magic world, either?" I asked, trying to lighten the mood. Sol merely shrugged in response, but Seamus grinned.

"I like *you* just fine," he said.

The sincerity of his smile made me smile in return.

"You're alright in my book too, Seamus," I said, bumping shoulders with him on my way back to my tea mug. "At least for now. Don't show up in my room uninvited or anything."

Seamus growled, even though he was still in human form.

"No worries on that front," he muttered.

I sighed, taking a sip of my tea as I sat down at the kitchen island once more.

"Vic, when you talked about your brother disappearing… you kept saying 'they' took him. Do you know who 'they' is?" Seamus asked, pulling up the stool beside me.

I shook my head.

"Not really. My parents knew, I think, but… I don't think they told me, or if they did, I'm not sure I understood. I was only eight. Sol, you said you know where he is. Do you also know who took him?"

Sol nodded.

"I do. He's in Bolivia, and I know who put him there, and why. Are you ready to hear any of that?"

I took a deep breath, letting the long-suppressed memories of my brother resurface. Letting the kidnapping come back to me was hard. It was difficult to relive the terror I'd felt as an eight-year-old watching my brother get taken away.

"Shotgun!" Trev called, rushing towards the car, the way he always did, as if Mom ever let either of us ride up front.

"Trev, wait up!" I called from behind him, tugging Mom along so she would hurry up. Trev and I were both excited to get home and test out the new gaming console we'd just gotten. No more playing at Frida's house! Wii bowling nights could happen in our very own living room!

"Come on, Mom! This is going to be the best birthday ever!"

Mom laughed as I tugged her along, dragging her feet, probably just to give me more of a challenge.

"GET AWAY FROM ME!"

My head shot up, and Mom and I were both suddenly running flat-out towards the car. Two men had grabbed Trevor and were wrestling him into a nondescript white van. Trev wasn't going without a fight though, he was flailing and kicking like a wild animal. I heard one of the men grunt in pain as we got closer to the car.

Then Mom turned into the biggest bird I'd ever seen, and launched herself at the men holding Trevor.

"LET GO OF MY BROTHER!!" I screamed, over and over again, while the two men holding him shoved him into the back of the cargo van, and my mom screeched and threw herself at them repeatedly. A third person emerged from the front of the van and came running towards me then, and I screamed until my lungs were on fire. Mom dove at the woman, just before she reached me, digging her talons into the woman's face, causing her to scream even more loudly than I had.

The woman turned and ran. Probably because the white van was pulling away.

Mom flew after it, throwing herself at the windows, but the woman turned back in my direction and I ran away from her, screaming for help. I didn't see what happened to her, but I heard her scream as I dove into the elevator that would take me back to the main floor of the parking garage and the entrance to the mall. Mom landed next to me a moment later. As the doors closed, she returned to her human form, naked and sobbing.

I was crying again by the time the memory was over, but I took comfort in knowing that I was about to find out who those people had worked for.

Finally, I nodded, wondering how much time had passed since Sol had asked her question.

"Yes, Sol, I would like to know who took my brother."

Just as Sol opened her mouth to answer, I heard a knock on the door.

I glanced at the clock on my microwave. 2:41PM.

"Who the hell would that be?" I asked, standing up and heading for the door.

"Wait!" Sol, shouted. "It could be a trap!"

"A trap?" I asked, still walking for the door. Who would come to trap me in my own house? Hell, who even knew where I lived?

I walked to the door, worried that it might be Edik, but deciding that, just in case Sol wasn't crazy, I would check the peephole before I opened it.

What I saw made my brain skip so hard that I opened the door before I'd even had time to think about it.

"Hey, Vic," Trevor said, standing with his hands in his pockets, looking for all the world like a six-foot-tall, dark, handsome, unsure puppy.

I could barely see through all the tears, but I launched myself at him before he had a chance to back away, and wrapped him in a bone-crunching hug.

"Trev! Holy shit!! Is it really you?"

I pushed back, still holding his shoulders, and looked into the bright golden eyes that looked so much like mine, except for the color. His eyes looked darker, in a way, like they'd seen a lot of suffering in the past ten years, but… well, they probably matched mine in that respect. So many things about him reminded me of what I saw in the mirror every day. Hell, he even wore his black hair long like mine. I hadn't seen him in 10 years, and he'd changed just as much as I had in that time, but… I would have known him anywhere.

I wrapped him in another hug, and this time, he actually wrapped his arms around me in return.

"I missed you too, Vic," he whispered into my hair.

I held onto him for another minute. I couldn't help myself. It was like the longer I held him, the more real he became. He even smelled right. Eventually, I pulled back again and smiled at him.

"You should come inside," I said, gesturing to the door that still hung open behind me. "This is your house too."

Trev shrugged and followed me inside.

I couldn't let go of him completely, so I kept his hand in mine. It was warm, dry, and lightly calloused.

"Trev, this is Seamus, he's… a werewolf from my English class," I said, wondering when my life had turned into a fucking J.K. Rowling novel. "And this is Soledad, a werepanther from… well, I'm not entirely sure where, but I think she was about to explain."

Trev's grip on my hand tightened, and he drew me behind him.

"She doesn't need to explain," Trev said, his voice dropping. "I know exactly where she's from."

And then my brother burst into flames and threw himself at Sol.

"NO, TREV, WAIT!" I called out, as Sol shifted deftly into her sleek black panther form, all the while dodging and weaving against my brother's fiery attacks.

As my eyes adjusted to the scene, I saw that he hadn't actually burst into flames so much as turned into a phoenix. Which I supposed amounted to the same thing, since a phoenix was basically just a big bird that caught fire.

"TREV! Seriously! She was just about to explain how she knew where you were before you knocked on the door. Can you just give her a chance to talk before you burn her to death?!"

The show that Trev and Sol were putting on was a good one, and it was nice to see that my brother had some impressive weapons at his disposal, but Sol had clearly been trained to fight by someone who knew what they were doing, and she was doing an excellent job of dodging Trev's attacks, countering just enough to give herself space without doing any damage to him.

Seamus took a few steps back from the fiery kitchen drama and stood next to me.

"I really need to learn how to fight," he admitted, as we watched Trev and Sol go after each other. "You and Sol didn't need me in the fight against Edik. I only made things worse."

I nodded. "Yeah, but your heart was in the right place." I sighed. "And anyway, there are lots of ways to be useful without learning to fight. The only reason I've been training for the past ten years is because of what happened to Trev... even though my parents pretended it was because of the 'attempt' to kidnap me…. I can teach you a few things if you want, though. My sensei in Colorado had me helping to teach some of the beginner classes before I left."

Seamus nodded. We both watched the teakettle get knocked off the stove top and go crashing to the floor.

"It's a good thing that's stainless steel," I mused.

Seamus raised an eyebrow at me.

"Are you… going to stop them?" he asked.

I shrugged.

"Trevor hasn't killed her, and if he had been planning a fatal attack I think she would be dead by now. Moreover, Sol has clearly been going out of her way not to hurt him. That can't have escaped his notice. Whatever beef he has with Sol will probably be out of his system in another minute or two."

"You sound pretty confident for someone who hasn't seen her brother in ten years," he said.

I smiled.

"He's still my twin," I said. "The only person I know better is me."

"But if he's been held captive that whole time…" Seamus took a deep breath and ran his hand along the back of his neck. "Don't you think it's possible he's changed in ways you can't understand?"

I nodded, the smile falling from my face.

"I'm sure he has, Seamus, but… I still know that if he were trying to hurt her, this fight would have been over a long time ago. I don't know who the better fighter is, but…" I gestured vaguely at the two figures dodging and weaving in front of us, "they're both clearly good. Which means if they were trying to harm one another, it would be over by now. Instead… no one has even drawn blood."

"Then why are they still fighting?" Seamus asked.

"Because Trev is fucking furious, though I'm not sure why."

When Sol batted at Trevor hard enough that he backed into my cupboard and set my coffee stash on fire, I drew the line.

"THAT'S ENOUGH!" I shouted, running forward to put out the flames. "Damn it, Trev! If I'd wanted it to taste like burnt asshole I'd have bought dark roast!"

Sol and Trevor backed away from each other and looked at me with similar expressions of amusement, even though it was kind of difficult to read flaming bird face.

"Do you two want to explain what the fuck is going on now that you've had your little sparring match? Do you know each other?"

Trev resumed his human form, and I realized that eight years of shared bath time had not prepared me for seeing my eighteen-year-old brother naked. I took a deep breath and stared him in the eyes.

"Do you want to borrow some sweatpants?" I asked, glancing at the charred remains of the jeans and t-shirt Trev had been wearing when he walked in.

He nodded, and I pointed upstairs.

"I'm not going anywhere while she's here to spread lies," he hissed.

I shrugged.

"I promise not to believe a single word she says until you come back downstairs."

Trev glared at me.

Sol shifted to human and smiled. The gesture was decidedly feline, even though she no longer had whiskers. "I promise not to speak until you return, Avito."

"First door on the left," I said.

By the time he came back down, wearing a pair of sweatpants with my old high school's mascot on the leg, Sol had once more donned the clothes I'd given her earlier.

"So, please enlighten me as to why you two couldn't resist pretending to fight the second you saw each other."

Trev scoffed.

"I wasn't pretending… but when I noticed she was going out of her way not to hurt me… I laid off my more devastating attacks."

"And I didn't come here to kill anyone," Sol said. "Although if that damned vampire shows up again, I may change my mind."

I chuckled.

"Only after I kill him first."

Trev glanced between us.

"What vampire is this?" he asked.

I shook my head. "One who isn't even worth the time to discuss right now. Focus power, people. What the hell is going on between you two?"

Trev sighed.

"It's nothing personal… with, Soledad, did you say?"

I nodded.

"We've never met before, but… she smells like MOME."

"She smells like what?" I asked.

"MOME," Trevor said, saying a word that rhymed with "home" and looking at me like I'd said the sky was orange.

"The Ministry of Magical Entities," Sol clarified.

Trev kept looking at me as though I were growing a second head.

"How do you not know what MOME is?" he asked. "That's like never having heard of Congress."

I sighed.

"Yeah, so about that…. After you were taken, Mom, Dad, and I had our memories messed with, and they pretended we weren't…" I gestured between us futilely, "whatever the fuck we are."

"Huh?"

"Vic had never heard of anything from our world until I told her I was a werewolf last night," Seamus said.

"This morning," I corrected. "It was late enough that it was technically this morning."

Trev looked stunned beyond words.

"I have never heard of MOME, and, until about 30 minutes ago, I thought that you didn't exist and that I was a normal human."

Then I smiled, as a single happy thought struck me.

"But I just turned into a SNOW LEOPARD for the first time ever! So, I'm pretty stoked about that."

Trev smiled too.

"Well, that's fun. I had wondered what animal you'd wind up with. Our family has lots to choose from."

"Choose?" I asked.

Trev ignored me and turned to glare at Sol, even though she hadn't made a sound.

"We can talk about that later. She should explain why she knew where I was and why she's even here."

I would have argued, because every damned thing that came out of Trev's mouth spawned about 500 new questions in my mind, but I also wanted to know what Sol had to do with all of this, and why Trev had wanted to kill her because she 'smelled like MOME.'"

Sol cleared her throat and sat down on the stool she'd been perched on before Trev got here, but Seamus, Trev, and I remained standing.

"It's reasonable that you don't trust me right now," she said, taking a sip from one of the tea cups that had miraculously managed to survive the kitchen brawl. "Because I do, as Trevor implied, work for MOME."

That revelation caused Trev to hiss like an angry ostrich and Seamus to gasp, but I was still lost as to what the big deal was.

"Vic," Sol said, as though understanding my confusion, "MOME is the organization that governs the magical community. It's the police force, the legislative force, the bureaucratic branch, everything most governments do, all rolled into one."

"Only where other governments are filled with elected officials, and vary from region to region, MOME is self-selected, and is the self-proclaimed governing body for magical entities all over the *world*," Trev gritted out, between clenched jaws.

I took a moment to put together the few tidbits that I understood about the magical world and realization came slowly.

"And it was MOME that decided to take an eight-year-old boy from his family?" I asked, as the horror sank in. "WHY?!"

Trev snorted in derision.

"Oh, they weren't just after me, Vic. They would have taken you too, if Mom hadn't fought them off so well."

My stomach turned, but I repeated the question. "Why?" I turned to Sol, who looked decidedly uncomfortable. She swallowed.

"They deem certain younglings to be… dangers, to themselves and others. Both you and your brother were on a watchlist. I don't know why, exactly, they decided to take you then, since I've only been working at MOME for about two years, but last night my unit leader put me on a flight to come here and… retrieve you."

Trev squared off, putting himself between me and Sol, but I grabbed his shoulder and pulled him behind me.

"Cool your jets, Trev, I can handle the panther." I wasn't entirely sure that was true. Sol seemed like a pretty accomplished fighter, especially in her panther form, but I knew I could do at least as well as Trev could, and have I mentioned how much I hate overprotective males? Twin brothers were no exception.

"So, why didn't you just nab me back in Rebuke's class and take me off to… wherever it is you're supposed to drag me?"

Sol looked around the room, taking in the ceiling and the windows in particular. Then she shook her head.

"I'm not at liberty to say."

For some reason that didn't piss Trev off the way I expected it to. He turned to me and mouthed the word "bugs."

I nodded, finally understanding Sol's exaggerated inspection of our ceiling.

"Ok. So, what *can* you tell us?" I asked.

"We shouldn't stay here very long," Sol replied.

"Which is precisely what someone would say if they were trying to get us to accompany them back to the bad guys' hideout," I muttered.

At least Seamus laughed.

"Vic, where are Mom and Dad?" Trev asked, after a moment of awkward silence.

I felt like I'd been stabbed in the chest.

"They… they're…" For some reason, I couldn't bring myself to say the word dead. So instead I copped out with, "they disappeared in the Indian Ocean."

Trev's eyes filled with tears, and I moved to him and wrapped him in another giant hug. This time, he didn't hesitate before hugging me back.

I already knew that, but I had to make it sound like I didn't have access to our file, said a voice inside my head that was not my own.

I startled, but Trev held me tight and didn't let me back away.

We both have a lot more magic now than when we were kids, Vic. Don't you remember when we tried to talk to each other's minds back then?

I was about to say no, but then the memories came flooding back to me. We'd tried, over and over again for years, but the best we'd managed was to sense the other person's emotions. Even then, we'd never been sure that it was magic and not just… knowing each other really well.

Are you telling me this really works? I asked.

Trev laugh/cried into my hair.

Hey, try not to snot me too badly. There are hot people watching us.

But of course that just made him laugh/cry harder.

What do we do to get out of this? I want to know what happened to you. Can you talk about that here? I had a million questions, and I wasn't sure I could keep any of them back now that I could just think them at Trev.

Yeah. MOME already knows that, so their listening spells won't tell them anything they don't already know, but when we get to the end of the story I'm going to have to lie, or we're going to have to go somewhere else. Sol's right, though. They'll have figured out that I'm here, which means we need to go somewhere else soon.

Can they see us? Or only hear us? I asked.

It depends on how long they've been monitoring you, but based on the fact that Sol only showed up here today, she probably only had time to set up listening devices.

Wait, she's the one that set them up? Why do we even trust her at all, then?

Well, we don't. But, she might have useful information, and she didn't grab you when she had an easy chance, so…

His thoughts trailed off for a moment and I decided there was nothing for it but to give it a shot.

Ok… I think I have a plan, I replied into Trev's mind, even though I could have easily said that bit aloud, because, why the fuck not? Everything else in my life was completely insane, so why wouldn't I be communicating telepathically with my twin brother who I thought was dead/never existed?

I backed away from Trevor and started miming to Seamus that we should go for a walk to his house. He nodded, and we all headed for the door.

Just as we got to the front step, Gwen popped into existence right in front me.

"Jesus fuck, Gwen! Don't do that. You scared me. What are you doing here?"

Gwen frowned.

"You're all needed elsewhere," she said, before somehow grabbing onto all four of us and then winking us all out of existence.

21

"WHAT THE HELL just happened?" Trev asked, over the howling wind.

"That was Gwen," I said, as if that explained everything. I looked at all three of my companions—Gwen, of course, was nowhere in sight—and realized that Sol and Seamus were just as confused as my brother.

"She's… well… the short explanation is that she's the one who first tipped me off that this was going to be a weird week."

That was probably the understatement of the century, but, well… the long explanation probably stretched credulity even amongst a bunch of were-creatures.

"Where are we?" Seamus asked, beginning to shiver.

I looked around. We were standing on a granite outcropping that kept us above the snow that covered the slope on which we stood, surrounded by steep, rocky peaks covered in more snow.

"The Andes?" I guessed, my teeth chattering. It could have been the Rockies, but… there was too much snow for September in the Rockies. September in the Andes, though… yeah, this looked about right.

"Everyone needs to shift," Sol said. "There's a place we can shelter near here, but this cold works quickly. Follow me."

Without waiting for anyone to object, Sol shifted to her panther form and started off down the hill. As tempting as it was to make a fuss about how we were suddenly in the Andes and why the fuck were we so close to a place that only Sol knew well… it was too fucking cold.

Seamus had already shifted by the time I had wished myself warmly wrapped in the thick fur of my snow leopard fervently enough to feel it suddenly surrounding me.

Being a snow leopard was the coolest.

Seriously. I was so warm. This might be the Andes, but the Andes had nothing on the Himalayas. Suddenly, I was in no particular rush to get to shelter, but as everyone else was trotting downhill at a decent clip behind Sol, I followed.

Of course, Trev caught up to Sol immediately, since he was flying, but Seamus was only a few meters ahead of me and I couldn't resist the temptation to race him down the hill. I nipped him playfully on the shoulder as I ran up alongside him, and then put on a surge of speed to close the distance between us and Sol. I could feel Seamus surge behind me to keep up, and he let out a competitive howl as we both hurtled over the snow-covered rocks that lay between us and our quarry.

Seamus, in wolf form, had much longer legs than I did as a snow leopard, and he would surely beat me in any long-distance race when we were on four legs, but for a short race over mountainous terrain…

He was sooo going down.

The terrain was uneven at best, with surprise boulders shooting up in front of us and small cliffs dropping away beneath us at every turn. I became hyper-focused, aware of every shift in terrain before I even had a chance to consciously process it, my body simply reacting to my surroundings in a way that I couldn't possibly replicate as a human. Sudden shifts of weight and balance were easy, my tail gliding effortlessly behind me to act as a counterbalance whenever necessary, my legs somehow able to shift mid-fall whenever the earth disappeared beneath me, able to orient themselves to whatever surface became my next foothold.

It was as though the earth were just an extension of my paws. I had never been in the Andes before, but every rock, snowdrift, and bit of patchy mountain scrub called out its familiar presence to me, and my body simply reacted.

Before I knew it, I was neck and neck with Sol and about to pull ahead of her. That was when I slowed up to circle back and check on Seamus. It didn't make any sense to try to outrun Sol, since she was the one who knew where we were going. Luckily, Seamus wasn't injured or anything, he was just stranded on one of the smallish cliffs that I had simply jumped over at full speed.

Damn, it was good to be a cat!

I quickly scaled the ledge and sat next to him. He was still in wolf form, staring frustratedly at the cliff, which occupied a large section of the hillside and would take a while to traverse if he didn't want to climb down the face.

I shifted to human and belatedly remembered that my clothes didn't shift with me.

"Want to down-climb it as a human?" I asked, already starting to shiver.

Seamus glared at me with his amber wolf eyes and huffed a bit.

"Well, do you want to follow me down, then? I promise to go slow this time."

Seamus nodded.

I happily shifted back to my snow leopard and started my descent, but this time, instead of running flat-out, I picked my way carefully down the sheer rock wall, making sure to select ledges that were big enough for wolf paws, and only making movements that would accommodate a wolf's somewhat more rigid center of gravity.

This time, when I got to the bottom, Seamus was right behind me. With another playful howl, he took off towards Sol and Trevor in the distance. I let out a yowl of challenge and followed close on his heels.

~~~

When we got to Sol's cabin, we were all a bit out of breath, even Trevor, which was weird since he had been flying and had needed to circle back a few times to make sure he didn't leave us all in the dust.

"It's the altitude," Sol said, after we'd all filed, panting, into a tiny wooden cabin perched precariously on the side of the mountain we'd all just descended, surrounded by nothing more than a bit of mountain scrub and some boulders. "We're at around 6,000 meters. It gets to anyone who's not from here, or even those of us who haven't run at altitude in a long time."

Sol was, of course, naked as she said this, and busy rifling through a closet in the one bedroom that opened off of the living/dining/kitchen area, which constituted the majority of the cabin's square footage, aside from a rather large porch that clung to the top of the cliff ledge opposite the cabin's front door. None of us had bothered to carry our clothes down the mountainside, and we all stood naked and shivering in the common area waiting for Sol to kit us out.

Sol indiscriminately tossed clothing at us from inside the closet. Long wool underwear tops and bottoms, snow pants, coats… nothing terribly comfortable, but plenty that was warm. I grabbed the first thing that looked like it
~~~

would fit and started pulling on layers. In a few minutes, we were all wearing enough clothing to be toasty, despite the lack of insulation in the tiny cabin and the swiftly plunging temperature outside.

Since I was the first one outfitted from the closet ransack, I set about starting a fire in the wood stove that acted as the center of the small living/dining/cooking area. The furnishings in the cabin were sparse—two low wooden couches with blankets piled up on them to make them comfortable and two large chairs. No real table to speak of, but a few small side tables next to the chairs and couches. A battered-looking upright bass leaned in one corner, looking somewhat worse for wear, and bright, woven tapestries hung on the walls, while a large alpaca rug covered most of the floor. Everything centered around the wood stove, as you might expect in a place that didn't have central heating.

Once the kettle was heating on top of the wood stove and we were all settled on the floor around it, Sol spoke again.

"We can speak freely here. MOME doesn't know about this place."

Trev's eyebrow rose, and Seamus and I looked between him and Sol for clarification.

"Why would you want a place that MOME doesn't know about, if you work for them?" Trev asked.

"Because," Sol said, taking a deep breath before continuing, "I have been working for MOME for the past two years as part of a larger plan to help take MOME down from the inside."

For a long moment, the howling wind outside was the only sound.

"Wait, what?" Trev and I said in unison, while Seamus merely stared wide-eyed at Sol.

"I know it sounds far-fetched, but my family… we're a big family, and well connected. My Abuelita has never liked the way MOME interferes with her business, and… well, we have some very personal reasons to want MOME to go down."

Knowing what I already knew about MOME and what they'd done to my own family, I didn't have a hard time believing that, but…

"It strikes me as more than a tiny bit suspicious that you're trusting us with that information when you haven't even known us for a full day," Trev said.

I nodded.

Seamus was silent.

Sol sighed again.

"I know," she said. "This isn't how I'd hoped things would go down, but now… I don't know that crazy redhead who teleported us here, and for the record I was under the impression that a teleport that far was impossible, but here we are, less than ten kilometers away from MOME's South American Headquarters, and—"

"What?!" Trev and I shouted at the same moment, though perhaps for different reasons.

"We're incredibly close to the Bolivian offices. My Abuelita's territory runs right alongside theirs. I don't know why your friend brought us here. I was hoping to have a few days of helping you evade MOME's other agents to help bring you over to my side. I had a tidy little plan all in place, knowing what MOME was likely to throw at us and how helping you avoid it would make it easier for you to trust me…. But here we are, so what's the point in waiting?"

Unable to process everything Sol had just dropped on us, I turned to Seamus.

"Seamus, it occurs to me that you just kind of got dragged into all this. What are your feelings about MOME?"

Seamus shrugged.

"No one I know is a huge fan of them. We hear stories of the kind of crap that they pull all the time, but no one in my family has been personally affected by it…. That I know of, anyway."

Something in his face told me there was more to the story than what he'd just said, but far be it from me to press someone to relive whatever trauma an agency like MOME might have put them through. I took a minute to process what I'd heard so far. It was hard to be thrown into all of this and know how to feel about it. I had very strong feelings about an organization that had taken my brother from me at such a young age, but I couldn't help but wonder if I was missing some vital information. After all, I'd only been part of this world for less than 24 hours.

"If MOME is so unpopular, how are they still in charge?" I asked the room at large.

"They resort to blackmail a lot," Sol said. "And it's not as though they're elected and can be voted out. They're huge, they act like they're in charge everywhere, and… woe betide the people who don't acknowledge their jurisdiction."

"But if they're really that blatantly evil, surely people would just rise up against them," I countered. "They can't outnumber the entire magical population can they?"

"Well, they have a surprisingly good PR branch. They spin their misdeeds in ways that most people buy into. And besides, the average magic user doesn't run afoul of MOME very often. It's people that MOME deems 'dangerous' that get their basic human rights violated left, right, and center. So, most people find it easy enough to tell themselves that MOME is there to protect them, and not question things. Add to that the fact that they actually *do* stop real criminals, as well as people they just don't think should exist, and it makes it difficult for most folks to believe that they aren't as benevolent as they claim. If you told the whole world tomorrow that your brother was abducted at the age of eight and sent to a research facility at the base of an Andean mountain, most people would be outraged for as long as it took them to find out that he's a Phoenix."

"But he couldn't even turn into a Phoenix when they took him!" I objected.

"That doesn't matter. MOME would play up the fact that they suspected he would turn into a restricted creature when he came of age, and ignore the fact that they were playing a genetic long shot to even think that was a possibility. Everyone's afraid of the restricted creatures; they don't know any better. MOME has gone out of its way to play up the possible dangers of shifters who can access some of the rarer creatures, for centuries."

"Ok. Fine. So MOME are a bunch of assholes and have been for a while. Were they ever not assholes?" I asked.

Sol shrugged. "Hard to know for sure. Revisionist history and all. They've been around for a very, very long time."

I sighed.

"Trev, do you feel up to talking about what happened to you? I mean… you know… not like ten years of catch-up right this second, but… maybe a highlight reel?" I tried to smile while I asked it, but I was too worried.

You don't have to talk about it if you don't want to, I silently offered, just in case. *It's fine. Most of it isn't too bad.*

"They came. They took me. I conquered, much later, by outsmarting them with computers."

That reminded me so strongly of the Trev I'd grown up with that it made me laugh out loud.

"Seriously though, Vic. I have a strong hatred for MOME, not so much because they did anything terrible to me, besides steal me away from you guys, but mainly just because they took so *many* of us. They never let us spend too much time together, so it's hard to be sure of numbers, but there were easily a hundred of us in my age group alone. Spread out, there were probably closer to five hundred. Five hundred families destroyed. Five hundred children raised by strangers. It just… it never ceases to piss me off."

"How did you escape?" I asked.

Trev eyed Sol for a moment, as though weighing what he should say in front of her, but then shrugged and started talking.

"I suppose it will all be in my file the next time you go to work anyway," he said to Sol. Then addressing the rest of us he continued, "I hacked the system, set off a bunch of viruses that made it impossible for MOME to monitor what was going on, and crawled out a conveniently overbuilt ventilation shaft. Easy."

"Ha! Really? Could you seriously crawl through the ventilation system without collapsing whatever section you were in? I thought that only worked in movies!" I said, while Sol's eyebrows rose to her hairline and Seamus smiled warmly at my brother.

"It *shouldn't* work outside of a movie, but for some reason MOME built theirs strong enough to hold a grown man," Trev explained.

"That's weird," I replied.

"It's an emergency escape system," Sol said, surprising all of us. "They built the ventilation system that way so that if part of the mountain collapses and the main entrance is cut off, there's an alternate route out of there. Also, ventilation below ground is serious business. You don't want that getting cut off, or people will die, so it's a seriously robust system."

"That makes sense, I suppose," I conceded.

"What I want to know," Sol said, "is why, if you have the ability to shut down the entirety of MOME's security and monitoring systems, you didn't escape earlier?"

Trev's smile faded at that question.

"I could have left anytime in the past, oh… probably eight years, certainly the last five, but I didn't…" his voice trailed off as he looked at me and then quickly away. My heart twisted in pain as I considered what might have kept him from escaping.

"You thought they would hurt us?" I asked.

Trev nodded, and wiped at the corner of his eyes. "For a long time they insisted that they had access to you and could get to you anytime if I didn't do what they asked, or if I tried to escape. I believed them until I was finally able to hack the system well enough to find your file. Then I realized that they didn't actually know where you guys were. That was a huge relief, and it certainly made me more confident in my rule breaking and trouble making efforts, but…"

"Why didn't you come find us?" I asked, my heart breaking all over again for the things my brother had gone through in the past ten years.

"I didn't want to lead them to you, Vic! I had nowhere else to go. What would I have done when I'd gotten out of there? Lived on the streets? I wasn't brave enough for that. At least with MOME I had a roof over my head and food in my belly. But I knew I wouldn't be welcome anywhere in the magical world. What Sol said about the restricted creatures is true. If anyone found out I was a Phoenix I would be ostracized, or worse, and certainly whoever found out would report me to MOME and then I'd be right back where I started. I knew that I would have eventually become desperate and tracked you guys down, and… and I probably would have led MOME right to your front door."

I suppressed a quiet sob and nodded my head. He had a point, damn it.

"So, what changed?" I asked, when my voice was under my control once more.

"Whatever you did to tip MOME off to where you were," Trev said. "The files I had flagged popped up with a new last known location. Which meant that MOME already knew where you were, so I did too. If MOME knew where to find you, then I had no reason not to try to get to you first. But I guess I didn't make it."

We all stared at Sol, but she just shrugged.

"My department found you because of the report filed by the Flagstaff police department. MOME has a database of 'dangerous' individuals that it cross-checks with every police database in the world. I'd been assigned to your file months ago. Knowing a bit about your parents, and what had happened to Trevor, I decided you were likely to see my family's side of things, so I did everything I could to get my superior to send me after you instead of someone else in my department. My family is keen to recruit as much help as we can get, and I thought offering to help you rescue your brother would get you both on our side."

We were all silent for a long moment, while we contemplated what all of that meant. I still had a million questions for Trevor, but I didn't want to make him recount every detail of his entire existence for the last ten years right away. He'd made it clear he wanted to give as few details as possible.

"So now what do we do?" I asked, eventually.

"Now," said Trev, "we go rescue my friends."

TREV?

Nothing.

Trev?

"Damn it." I slapped my hands against the slightly damp rock beneath me and bounced my head off the rock wall behind me. Thankfully, rather than the urine I had feared it would smell like, it just smelled like wet rock and a bit of mold.

Trev, it's fucking pitch black down here. I can't even see my own hands.

I was supposed to be able to reach Trev from here. We weren't sure what the effective range on our telepathy was, but we'd tested it up to a kilometer earlier, and he shouldn't have been anywhere near that far away.

Is the rock messing with us? I asked the void.

And then I snickered. *The Rock doesn't want you to talk to your brother. The Rock will crush you after gratuitously referring to himself in the third person!*

It was a shame Trev wasn't getting any of this, because I was hilarious. Well, Trev would have found it hilarious, anyway. We used to watch WWF reruns with our dad—Mom preferred MMA.

I wondered how the rest of the rescue mission was going, now that I was locked up in this dank bit of dungeon.

It had been harder than I'd expected for Trev to bring us all on board with the rescue plan. To my surprise, it had been Seamus, and not Sol, who had been the most difficult to convince. Considering how often Seamus seemed determined to 'rescue' me, whether I needed it or not, I figured he'd be all for having a chance to play hero. It had only taken Trev explaining how many young kids were still being picked up by MOME every year to convince Sol to join in on the rescue mission. Apparently, while she didn't seem overly worried about how people Trev's age were still held captive by MOME, she couldn't abide the thought that small children were still being abducted. Seamus, on the other hand, objected to the risk to all of us, and I couldn't help but notice and be annoyed at how often he looked at me while he listed the possible 'perils' of taking the offensive and entering MOME territory. I happily informed Seamus that he didn't have to go at all if he was worried about the supposed perils, and he'd seemed half-inclined to take me up on my offer, until Trev admitted that part of the reason he was hell-bent on staging a rescue was to release his 'girlfriend' from MOME's grasp. That had made me want to pepper him with questions and a light hail of sibling teasing, but I refrained, since we had more important issues to address. Suddenly, Seamus was all in favor of the rescue mission, a change in stance that completely mystified me, but which I didn't bother to question at the time. We had spent the next few hours planning the details of our mission.

I sighed, wishing there were enough light to see by. I wanted to confirm that my disguise was still in place.

In what I was coming to understand as "standard Gwen behavior," the woman had shown up just before we were within sight of MOME and insisted that everyone but Sol needed a disguise. She had then turned all of us into pale-skinned, blonde-haired, blue-eyed people. Or at least, that's what she'd done with Trevor and Seamus, so I had to assume it was what she'd done to me. All I could see of my own disguise was the pasty white skin she'd given me. I had to admit that if Seamus and Trevor were anything to go by, no one was going to recognize us from this little adventure, assuming our disguises lasted for the duration. How Gwen had even known where we were, or what we were up to, was still a mystery to me, but I won't pretend we didn't appreciate the disguises.

Of course, when I'd asked her how she'd created them, her reply had just reaffirmed my assumption that she was decidedly lacking in sanity.

"Vic, darling, a goddess can do whatever she wants."

Goddess, right. Sure… I mean, hey, who am I to judge? I just started turning into a snow leopard yesterday… maybe she *was* a goddess.

She sure seemed delusional though.

Trev, when we get back home I need to find some normal friends.

Why do you continue to talk to ssssomeone who issss not resssssponding? replied a voice that was decidedly not Trevor's.

OH SHIT.

Ummm… hello? I'm sorry, I didn't think I was broadcasting this to everyone.

Could anyone else do this? I had honestly thought this was just a twin thing.

I doubt there issss anyone elsssse who can hear bessssidessss me, but that issss only becaussssse no one elsssse issss here.

Well, that was weird. According to Sol, there were close to two thousand people in this facility, and a number of them were supposedly in these very dungeons.

I must have accidentally broadcast some of that thought, because the other voice replied again.

No one who matterssss. There wassss one before you, but he… left.

Well, that sounded ominous.

Have you been here long? I asked, unsure what else to say.

Not long by my people'ssss ssssstandardssss, but much longer than I would like.

Well, that told me precisely nothing.

What are you in for? I asked, wondering if my tone would be conveyed properly via telepathy.

I killed a handful of MOME agentssss who went where they should not have, the voice replied, in a tone that suggested that this was the obvious and rational response to such a scenario. *And you?*

Um… I resisted arrest, I suppose. I doubted that whoever I was talking to was on MOME's side, especially considering why she was here, but I didn't think

I should just go revealing our master plan to anyone who could communicate telepathically with me. Besides, if she had heard me when I didn't mean for her to, who knew who else could be listening in to our conversation?

You are unssssure? the voice asked.

It's complicated, I replied.

Either you ressssissssted arresssst or you did not.

Well, I guess that depends on your perspective. I don't think I resisted arrest. I didn't think anyone was even trying to arrest me, but tell that to the MOME agent who claims that she was arresting me and that I ran away from her and then fought her off when she tackled me to the ground. I didn't know she was trying to arrest me, I just thought she was some crazy woman attacking me. She claims *she shouted that I was under arrest and to hold still, but I never heard her.*

The story was a bit far-fetched, I had to admit, but it amused me, and I was bored, and what the hell else was I going to do down here?

So you both ressssissssted arresssst and did not? the voice asked.

Yep. It was like Schrödinger's arrest. I was both under arrest and not. I chuckled to myself. It was actually a pretty poor Schrödinger analogy, but it still made me laugh.

Sssschrödinger?

Maybe she had been in here a *looong* time.

Schrödinger was a scientist. He's famous for devising a thought experiment to point out a problem that he saw with the Copenhagen interpretation of quantum mechanics. He said that if you have a cat in a box and you cannot see or hear it, the cat is both alive and dead until you open the box, and then it is only one or the other.

And that was an oversimplification of Schrödinger's paradox, but it was enough to explain most of the internet memes on the subject.

Interesssssting, the voice said. *Sssso, you were both under arresssst and not under arresssst until ssssomeone elsssse looked at the ssssituation and decsssided.*

Yeah. More or less.

Like I said, it wasn't the best analogy for this scenario.

And the people here decsssided you were under arresssst.

So it would seem, I admitted.

Doessss that make you the living cat, or the dead cat? the voice asked.

Hmm… if we take the analogy to its full extent, I guess I'm the dead cat, if one is fond of cats, but I prefer to think of myself as the live cat.

That issss undersssstandable, the voice said.

I was about to make a joke about people who don't like cats, when the door to my cell burst into flames and showered me in fiery shards.

"WHAT THE FUCK, Trev!?" I said, brushing the cinders off of myself.

"Sorry. These doors tend to be soundproof, so yelling was pointless, and I tried to warn you to stand back, but it seemed like you couldn't hear me. The rock must be messing with our connection."

I snickered again.

"The Rock will layeth the smacketh down upon our telepathy!"

Trev laughed loudly, and I wrapped him in a hug. As disconcerting as it was to see him with pasty white skin, blonde hair, and blue eyes, he still felt exactly right.

"Thanks for showing up. Where to?" I asked.

"Down," he said, gesturing towards a dark stone corridor lined with flickering torches that angled gently towards the center of the earth. The hallway carried the same scent of moss and damp stone that permeated my small chamber, but with the added flavor of burning pitch.

"Well, that's not ominous," I said, repressing a shudder even as we started down the corridor. "What's with the thirteenth-century dungeon look?"

Trev shrugged.

"Probably original. MOME is pretty old, and why update the dungeon?"

"Isn't it a little sketchy that a modern governing body still *has* a dungeon?"

"Don't get me started," Trev grumbled.

I laughed, but dropped the subject anyway. Trev had made his distaste for MOME quite clear already. He'd done one full tirade about tyranny and the oppression of the magically different during the planning stage of this mission, and we probably needed to focus on the task at hand.

It took much longer than I expected before we reached the next large wooden door in the corridor. I was mainly surprised by just how much solid rock separated each tiny six-foot by six-foot chamber.

Then I was extra surprised when Trev just grabbed the locked metal bolt that secured said door and held the assembly in his hand until it melted.

The door began a slow swing open, and Trev shouted, "Happy Hunting!" before we both booked it farther down the decidedly downward-sloping hall.

"What the hell, Trev?!" I asked, as we hurried farther down into the dungeon.

"What? That was a selkie. She'll have a grand time finding MOME agents and delivering a bit of payback."

"No. I mean the door! What's up with just melting the bolt off? Why did you have to explode mine into a bajillion pieces and shower me with its flaming ruins if you could just melt the bolt?"

"Oh, that. Your door was reinforced with a few spells I didn't recognize. Blowing it up was the best I could come up with on short notice. What did you do to piss them off, by the way?"

"Well, I didn't think it would be convincing if I went down without a fight. You should have seen the giant troll thing they set on me when they found me snooping around Sol's department. It was the size of an elephant."

"Probably Niko," Trev suggested. "Is he ok?"

"Who knows? He probably has a wicked headache. How prone are trolls to concussions?"

"Not very."

"Then he's probably fine. Friend of yours?" I asked.

"Kind of. Certainly not a bad guy. Trolls tend to get roped into doing MOME's dirty work pretty easily. The alternatives that MOME offers aren't terribly pleasant, so I can't blame them, really."

"Fair enough. Well, I tried to avoid permanent damage, but it didn't seem like he was extending me the same courtesy, so I'm not sure how concerned I am, in all honesty."

"Did you find what you were looking for, at least?" Trev asked, clearly ready to change the subject.

I nodded. "Yep. Just where you said it would be. Didn't have time to look at it before handing it off, though."

"Guess we'll have to trust Sol at some point," Trev said.

"True enough. If she were going to screw us over, she probably would've done it by now."

We finally reached another wooden door, and Trev did the same handle-melting trick as before.

"Seriously? What kind of mega-criminal do they think I am?" I asked, when the door popped open as soon as the bolt and handle disappeared.

Trev smiled.

"Trolls aren't easy to subdue," was all he said, before we turned and headed farther into the mountain.

"Dude, how many of these are we going to open? I didn't think they were going to be this far apart."

"My intel shows that the next one is the last occupied room in this part of the dungeon. One more selkie. That last one was a fire sprite."

I took a deep breath. Forty-eight hours ago, I had thought that magic was just something I enjoyed reading about on the weekends. The idea that we were releasing fire sprites and selkies from imprisonment, or that I had fought a troll earlier… it was still a bit much. I took a long look at Trev and suddenly felt a strange pang of longing.

"What's that look for?" he asked, even as we both kept up a light jog down the corridor.

"Just… none of this is new to you. I mean, Mom and Dad never told us about this stuff when we were little and then you were gone, my memory was wiped, and… I feel like a total outsider in this world, but you're sitting there smirking about how your sister brought down a troll, because you know about things like that."

"I'm not sitting, thank you very much, my legs are moving just as fast as yours."

"You *know* what I mean, Trev. This is your world. You fit in here."

Trev grabbed both my shoulders and pulled us both to a stop.

"Vic, you fit in here just as much as I do, you're just not used to it yet. The strangeness will fade pretty quickly, just wait, and… besides, I'm not really sure you get to complain about being the one who *wasn't* kidnapped and separated from your family for ten years."

I smacked my forehead against his shoulder, and then did it again for good measure.

"I'm so sorry, Trev. Of course I don't. What the fuck is wrong with me? I just… I guess I just haven't felt like myself in a long while and you seem pretty… together."

Trev wrapped me in a firm hug and when I felt his shoulders shake slightly, I looked up to catch his gaze.

Nope. Definitely not together. Trev's eyes were closed, but his breath was shaky and there was definitely moisture pooling at the corners of his eyes. I hugged him back even more fiercely than he'd hugged me.

"I'm sorry, Trev. Pity party over. I love you. I missed you. And I'm here for you any time you need to talk about it."

He smiled, stepping back, and we held hands as we started up our jog again.

The final door was just as easily dispatched as the others.

We were just about to turn around and follow the final selkie (a glorious, blue-skinned, green-haired, nymph-like creature whose webbed fingers and toes were visible in the fashionable jeans, tank-top, and flip-flop ensemble she was sporting) when a voice brought us to a standstill.

And what of me, Living Cat?

I turned and looked at Trev, who appeared so startled that I could only assume he'd heard it too.

"She's down here?" he muttered, taking me from zero to confused in no time flat.

"Do you know… her?"

"I didn't know she was in this part of the dungeon. She said… damn it!"

"What is it, Trev?"

"Come on, Vic. We can't leave her here."

"Do we have time to—"

Trev grabbed my hand and started sprinting down the corridor before I could finish speaking, leading us deeper into the mountain once more, this time at full speed.

OF COURSE THERE was another troll guarding this door.

Of course there was.

We had raced past another ten doors like the one that I had been locked behind after releasing the last selkie, but they had all been empty, according to Trev. Now, we reached one that was clearly occupied, even though Trev's reconnaissance had told him otherwise. Either that, or the giant creature that looked more like a swift-moving boulder was just here for his smoke break.

As we neared the door, I shifted to a fighting stance, getting ready to take this troll by surprise. I hoped I could cause enough of a distraction to give Trev time to pull whatever door trick was needed to get to whoever it was we were rescuing.

I was so focused on the rock-like behemoth before me that I almost didn't notice the tiny winged creature that launched itself from his shoulder until it was too late.

That was probably how she got most of her opponents.

Luckily, I saw the brief glint of steel in torchlight out of the corner of my eye just before she reached me, and I shifted to snow leopard just in time to send the tiny, sparkly, winged whatever-she-was flying past my head. If I was going to distract two opponents, especially ones as complementary as a troll and a pixie, for any length of time, I needed maximum reaction speed, and my human self had nothin' on my snow leopard.

Do not hurt them, Living Cat, they are only here under duresssss.

Well, *shit*.

That would have been more helpful to know before I'd provoked the flying warrior into trying to stab my eyes out, because now that she was at it, she was going to be rather difficult to discourage without doing some damage.

The pixie issss more ressssilient than the troll, Living Cat.

Oops. I must be projecting again. I *really* needed to work on that. I also needed to look into how many people could pick up on those projected thoughts, but now was not the time to worry about that. Now was the time to lay the smack down on the fierce-ass tiny warrior who was getting far too close to spearing my head with her six-inch sword for my liking.

The tricky thing was that I was batting her out of the air (or trying to) all while weaving in and out of the troll's legs, in order to make it as difficult as possible for the troll to grab me. The troll was delightfully slow, but if he (curious how I know it was a he? Go ahead, ask! I dare you. No? I'll give you a hint: I wouldn't have known if I hadn't been dancing between his legs looking up occasionally to keep tabs on a damnably fast pixie—and I would've been quite happy to live out my life with the mystery unsolved, let me tell you) grabbed me I was going to be one squished kitty.

The flying warrior dove at me again, at the same time that the troll shifted his weight to try to step on me, and I barely slipped between them without losing an ear. I hissed in frustration while turning around as quickly as I could to resume the fight, and was delighted to find that the winged fighter woman had embedded her tiny sword into the troll's skin and couldn't seem to dislodge it.

I roared in triumph, but before I could leap forward to make a pixie tattoo on the troll's leg, Trev let out his own whoop of victory, and I saw him slip inside the room beyond.

A moment later, he emerged from the dungeon cell with the most startlingly beautiful woman I'd ever seen. Her skin and hair were the color of midnight, covered in a faint iridescent sheen, and her irises were bright yellow, with slitted pupils like a snake's.

"Do not attack the Living Cat, Ssssylvesssstra. She meanssss you no harm."

It was odd to hear that voice coming from the woman standing before me instead of inside my head, but when tallied up with everything else that had happened to me this week, it really didn't rank very high on the Bizarre-O-Meter.

"Vic, this is Rhelia. Rhelia, this is my sister Victoria. We need to go before anyone realizes what we're up to. Especially now."

"Why especially now?" I asked, after shifting back to human.

"Because of Rhelia," he replied, as though that explained everything.

But Trev wasn't joking about being in a hurry. He turned and started sprinting up the corridor, Rhelia following close on his heels for a moment before she did... *something* that sped her past Trev and out of my line of sight. Having resumed my human shape, I started wrestling with my jeans so that I could follow them as soon as possible.

"Well, that was rude," came a voice from behind me.

I turned and saw the small winged warrior holding her sword over her small armor-plated shoulder and tapping one foot on the shoulder of the troll.

"Sorry," I said, as I pulled my sports bra and shirt back into place. "We have a whole escape plan thing we have to keep up with. If you guys need a distraction to get out of here, now might be a good time."

It surprised me that the troll and the winged fighter had listened to Rhelia at all, but I wasn't about to look a gift... whatever Rhelia was, she didn't seem much like a horse... in the mouth.

"I'd better catch up to them," I said, tugging my boots on, thankful that they were zip-ups instead of lace-ups, and then turning on my heel and taking off before they could rethink our truce.

By the time I caught up with Trevor, we were back in the standard institutional halls of the upper levels of MOME and Rhelia was nowhere in sight. I was about to ask him where she'd disappeared to, when all of a sudden he was no longer running beside me.

Instead he was lying on the floor a few yards ahead of me, scrambling to fight off a crazed, sparkle-fanged moron.

"EDIK!! GET OFF of him, you lunatic!" I shouted, launching myself into the fray.

Edik was clearly doing his best to rip Trev's throat out, so I didn't waste time trying to be nice. I kicked him in the head as soon as an opportunity presented itself, and then, as the inevitable shock of my boot hitting his face sent him reeling backwards, launched myself at his shoulders so that I would be between him and Trev.

"Victoria, darling, I do not like this disguise. Where are your beautiful eyes? Who is this pale whisper of a woman?"

I was a little surprised that Edik didn't prefer the blonde that Gwen had turned me into, since that seemed more like his type, but I honestly cared so little about what he found attractive that I skipped right past his comment and continued punching him in the face.

"Ow! Why did you do that, beloved?"

"Edik, seriously. I don't know what you're doing here, but if you ever touch my brother again, I will kill you."

"Brother?" he asked, finally letting his head fall back to the floor.

"Yes. My brother. Not that it's any of your damned business who he is."

As Edik was now lying down and cradling his likely broken nose, I got off of him and stood up.

"If you ever attack me or anyone I care about again, Edik, I swear it will be one of the last things you do. Now, what the hells are you doing here?" I asked.

Edik stared at me with such a strange look in his eyes that for a moment I wondered if he was concussed.

"You can't charm her, vamp, so stop wasting your time," Trevor said from beside me.

"I'm here because I love you. We're meant to be, Victoria, you will come to see it in ti—"

Edik's voice cut off as I wrapped my hand around his throat, picked him up off the ground, and slammed him against the wall. I made a mental note to be shocked later about how I was suddenly strong enough to use only one hand to pin a two hundred pound person to the wall, but for now I just clamped down on his throat with my hand and growled threateningly.

"Let's try this again," I gritted out, so *very* sick of Edik's shit. "Why are you here? And don't pretend it has anything to do with me, asswipe. You may be a moron with no sense of personal space, but you didn't follow me to a MOME facility in the Andes just to profess your misguided amorous feelings for me."

Edik shrugged, after a moment, and then wrenched his way out of my grip.

"Fine. You're right. I suppose I shouldn't have expected you to buy the besotted lover ruse for much longer…. I'm looking for my daughter."

I FELT MY brain scratch like dirty vinyl, but Edik just kept talking.

"I heard you talking about MOME in your home, and then that Gwen person showed up and I decided to hitch a ride."

That had to have been the truth, because it didn't make any damned sense as a lie.

"Daughter? Wait, what? How do vampires even work in this world? And how could you have hitched a ride? We'd have seen you. And how could you have known where Gwen was taking us? We didn't even know!"

"I didn't know where she was taking you, but I was desperate to follow you to MOME, and I had to hope she would get you closer than I could have gotten on my own. And as for you not seeing me there, I am quite capable of shadow walking, thank you very much."

I opened my mouth to ask a hundred more questions, but Trev cut me off.

"We'll do vampire 101 later, Vic. We have to go. Now."

I wanted to argue with that, because nothing that Edik had just said made any sense. Like why he had thought I could lead him to MOME when I hadn't even known MOME existed until a day ago, and he'd been stalking me for three days. But Trev had a point—we were low on time. Besides, that was when we heard a bunch of incoherent screaming from the hallway ahead of us, and Edik jumped up and ran in the opposite direction.

Since we didn't wish to confront the screaming ourselves, we followed him.

I could hear cursing in at least three languages behind us, as well as what sounded like chanting. I might have been new to the whole "magic is real" thing, and no, I wasn't super clear on how everything worked yet, but I certainly wasn't new to the *idea* of magic. And any experienced fantasy nerd, whether gamer, reader, or movie goer, knows that bad guys chanting in languages you don't speak and running in your direction means shit is about to go *down*.

We quickly picked up speed, right on Edik's heels, as we transitioned from vampire-smack-down to runneth-the-hell-away. I didn't have a Holy Hand Grenade of Antioch shoved in my back pocket, and whatever was behind us was definitely in possession of some big, pointy teeth—metaphorically, at least.

We plowed through a few identically bland institutional hallways, turning seemingly at random, but presumably following some sort of pattern that Edik could sense. At any rate, Trev never suggested that we follow a different course, so I just went along with it. Each hallway was the same disgusting off-white lit with flickering halogen lights. I had no idea how anyone kept their bearings in a place like this. I generally had an excellent sense of direction, but I couldn't keep track of where we were in this MOME facility. Perhaps it was because we were too far beneath the mountain, or perhaps it was simply because every damned hallway looked exactly the same.

Then we turned a hard right into a fifteen-by-fifteen foot room, painted in the same disgusting eggshell and lit with the same shitty halogen bulbs as every hallway we'd just gone through, and I was so surprised that I actually ran into Edik's back.

"The fuck?" I asked, finally looking up as I bounced off of Edik's frame, almost knocking both of us to the floor.

"Well, that's a surprise," I heard Trevor mutter behind me, and then I stepped around Edik to see the rest of the room.

I ignored the bland trappings of the place as my eyes were instantly drawn to the two women standing in the center of it. Namely Gwen and someone I'd never met who had mouse-brown hair, brown eyes, and skin that looked like it had never seen the sun.

THE PALE WOMAN looked nonplussed to see all of us there, but it wasn't until I heard Edik scream something incomprehensible in what I thought might have been Russian that the other woman paled a bit. Then she smiled weakly, as though she thought she could smooth things over with the right facial expression.

Edik, however, looked furious. Oddly, despite the number of times I had broken his nose, or otherwise beaten the crap out of him, I had never seen him look angry. It wasn't a good look on him. Too much sneering—facial features all distorted—it ruined the symmetry of his near perfect face. Made him look like the douchetart he actually was.

"WHERE IS MY DAUGHTER?!"

Huh. The plot thickens. I couldn't help but share the thought with Trevor, and he shared a sensation of humor with me, on top of his general annoyance at being held up in our escape. I, for one, was curious how the new person that Gwen was talking to was involved in this latest development.

"I don't know," said the pale brunette who had been talking to Gwen moments earlier. "They took her."

"*They* took her? *THEY* took her!? YOU took her from me!"

"I did not. We left together. Voluntarily. To be with Guille, but he…"

The brunette looked embarrassed.

"B! She's not an adult yet. You can't take her out of the country without my consent, no matter who you've chosen to run away with. You should have left her with me."

"She didn't want me to leave her behind."

"Then you should have stayed."

If flames could have shot out of Edik's eyes I imagine they would have, but luckily that didn't seem to be on his list of skills. By this point, Trev was cursing almost silently behind me. I was waiting for him to suggest that we keep moving and leave Edik to his fate, but it hadn't happened yet. In the meantime, I will admit to being damned curious about what was going to happen next.

B shrugged.

"We were both bored. It's not as though there's anything much to do in that town, and you were so hell bent on keeping us hidden from the rest of the vampires that we felt like shut-ins."

"And tell me, dear B, what happened to you as soon as you made yourselves known to the magical community outside of our family?"

B looked entirely sheepish.

"Well, I won't pretend I'm not disappointed about how things turned out with Guille, but—"

"But WHAT? You're trapped here at MOME, aren't you? This is their primary research center. Did you *know* that? Did you know anything about that asshole before you ran off and handed over our DAUGHTER to him?"

I wasn't a fan of Edik at all, and I thought the yelling was stupidly over the top, but for just a moment I felt sorry for him. The context was clear enough, and while I certainly couldn't blame anyone who wanted to get as far away from Edik as humanly (or vampirely) possibly, the whole stealing away with his kid who winds up in MOME's hands struck me as pretty damned heartbreaking. Then I remembered what Edik was like, and the heartbreak ended.

"I didn't know he worked for MOME. Thanks to you practically keeping us in a damned cage, I barely understood what MOME was! If you had let us talk to *anyone* else I might have known what the risks were. Instead you tried to keep us wrapped in fucking bubble wrap and we had no idea what we were getting ourselves into!"

Yeah. There we go. I should have realized before I even started to feel bad for him that he was likely the bringer of his own destruction.

"It never even occurred to you that people might have a more than healthy fascination with a Dhampir!?"

That was a fair point. Dhampir, huh? I wondered if that word carried any of the meaning it held in certain works of fiction.

Gwen raised a hand and spoke before either of them could continue.

"There are approximately twenty guards headed this way at the moment. The only reason they aren't here yet is thanks to some handy spellwork Trevor left behind for them in one of the hallways, and I don't think now is the best time for the rest of this conversation. B," she said, turning towards the young female vampire, "when was the last time you saw Renata?"

"Guille said he was going to take her for a hike two days ago. They never came back. It took me a day to track them here. I spent the morning sneaking through this place."

Gwen looked impressed.

"They didn't catch you until an hour ago?"

"They didn't catch me at all!" B replied angrily. "I walked into this room and accidentally let the door latch behind me. I couldn't get out again."

"What made you come in here?" Edik asked, looking around himself for the first time.

I had to admit I hadn't paid much attention to the room, aside from the lame paint job, until Edik raised the question, but just as I started to take in the details of the various apparati around the room, and the creepy metal table in the center of it, Trev jumped up on the table, pushed one of the ceiling panels out of the way, and started crawling into one of the vents.

"Where are we headed, exactly?" I asked, climbing up on the table and pulling myself up into the vent behind him, following his feet as they disappeared down the large metal shaft.

"We're headed to the northern slope," he replied. "The ventilation system ends in the middle of a cliff face, so they don't leave much security on it."

I wondered if Edik and B would follow us, or if they had their own way of dealing with the security here. I knew Gwen would just do whatever the fuck suited her fancy.

"Right. Makes sense," I said, taking a deep breath. We were already in the shafts that led to our exit point? I enjoyed a brief moment of feeling hopeful that we were going to get out of here without anyone dying.

Of course, that was when the alarms started going off.

<div align="center">~~~</div>

"And what does this mean, exactly?" I asked Trevor, as we both sped up our snakelike movements along the ventilation shafts.

"It means," said Trev, as he deftly "vaulted" over another of the down shafts that we ran into periodically, which we had to clear by shimmying as close to the edge of one side as we could get and then stretching our arms across and pulling/pushing the rest of our bodies across the gap without sliding into it, "that they finally noticed that we freed up the entire high-security roster."

I nodded, ignoring the fact that he couldn't see me.

"And that's a good thing?" I asked.

"We need the distraction."

"Right. And what about the two vampires and er… Gwen?"

"Your redheaded friend smells like a deity of some kind, so she likely can't be trapped, the vampire who followed you seemed like the kind of asshat we wouldn't mind seeing interrogated by MOME's goons, and as for B and her daughter… could be risky, but they can probably take care of themselves."

"Even her daughter?" I asked.

"No one likes a Dhampir, but she can very likely take care of herself."

"She's a kid, Trev."

He swiveled his head around and stared at me until I realized the ridiculousness of what I was saying. For all I knew, she was our age. Certainly she was likely to be only a few years younger, and if…

"Are Dhampirs the badasses everyone writes them to be in Urban Fantasy books?"

Trevor chuckled.

"Very much Dorina Bassarab style, from the few I've met, though perhaps slightly less… intense."

I chuckled at that. Then frowned, when I realized why he'd likely met any Dhampirs at all, let alone a few, since they were supposed to be incredibly uncommon.

"Does MOME kidnap *all* of them?" I asked.

"The ones they can get to before the vampires kill them, yes."

"For 'research' purposes?"

"Yep. And to 'protect the people,' don't forget that. Same as me, I guess. Although, to be fair, the vampires do try to kill them all, so MOME is providing some protection in the case of Dhampirs."

I scowled at Trev's back but said nothing.

As we'd been talking, we'd turned at one of the intersections and started scurrying slightly uphill.

"Sol and Seamus should be up here somewhere, if everything went the way it was supposed to," Trevor said, as we reached another intersection.

"Well, since everything else has gone so swimmingly, I don't see how they could have run into trouble," I replied, with just a *hint* of sarcasm.

Trevor chuckled, ahead of me, and I decided to stop talking and focus on where I was crawling. I was impressed that he had the whole place mapped out well enough in his head to keep track of where we were and where we needed to be. I still knew where we were pointed in terms of cardinal directions, thanks to whatever directional sense my snow leopard form granted me, but I was lost in terms of these tunnels of ventilation shafts and hallways that all seemed identical and veered off arbitrarily.

I was still contemplating whether someone in charge of MOME might be a wererabbit trying to make this research facility feel like home when Trev stopped abruptly ahead of me.

"I think we found them." His voice sounded… less than optimistic.

"Is that not a good thing?" I asked.

"Not when they've got five high-security mages for company," he replied.

"Does that mean we're fighting our way out?"

"Depends on whether or not you want your friends back."

I smiled. I hadn't had a good fight in… well, not since I left my old dojo, and even that had just been sparring, not a real test of my skills.

"I could use some exercise," I said, to the back of Trevor's head. When he said nothing in response, I added, "I don't have many friends Trev, it'd be a shame to lose these ones."

That seemed to convince him.

"You may want to shift," he said, just before the floor fell out from under us.

I WAS ALL for having the element of surprise, but I generally would have preferred to not be getting surprised right along with my target. Things must have been about to get hairy though, because Trevor went down flaming.

Of course, Trev, who could blink and become an eight-foot-wing-spanned fire bird, didn't think anything of the drop from the ventilation shaft. Whereas I had to do my best to roll through a fall that left me crashing into the linoleum floor eight feet below where we'd started.

Yeah, sure, Trevor had warned me to shift, but I couldn't call on it quite that fast yet, and I didn't know if I was better off in cat form anyway. After all, I had trained for my san-dan in Shotokan as a human, not as a snow leopard.

In the beginning, not shifting seemed like the right decision. The mages who were in that room with Sol and Seamus all started screeching (presumably slinging spells) as soon as the flaming ball of wings and fury that was my brother descended into the room, and they all seemed inclined to take my human-looking female frame for granted. In our planning stages, Sol had mentioned more than once that mages weren't very good at detecting weres, so I supposed now was my chance to take advantage of their ignorance about my powers. The nearest one didn't even throw any spells at me, simply stepping forward with a pair of handcuffs—presumably magic ones, but I never let him get close enough to find out.

I ducked under the arm he swung out to grab me, a horribly telegraphed move that would have ended up with him unconscious at my feet if I hadn't been defending against multiple opponents, and swept my leg out to take his feet from under him while also dodging something sparkly that flew from the hands of the next closest mage.

So, some forms of magic were visible. Useful intel. In the meantime, it also helped that mages, or at least *these* mages, telegraphed their spellcasting like crazy. Maybe they couldn't help it, maybe there was no way to cast without the wild hand gestures and targeted glaring accompanying each spell. I was too new to all of this to know what the rules for mages were, but as it was, I had multiple seconds of warning before each attack came, which was *more* than enough.

The second mage closest to me was still casting her next spell when I punched her in the gut. I would have aimed for somewhere more permanently damaging, but I wasn't sure what the deal with all of these MOME people was. How many of them thought they were doing good in the world? How many of them were there to take things down from the inside like Sol was? How many of them actually thought it was ok to abduct young children for 'research' purposes and keep them from their families?

Whatever the answer was, either Trev already had it, or he just didn't care. The mage who was fighting Seamus—who had shifted to his wolf form and was happily digging teeth and claws into said mage—was reaching into his leather vest (I hadn't noticed until that moment, but three out of five of the mages were dressed like they'd driven Harleys to get here) when he suddenly burst into flames with a bloodcurdling shriek. I caught sight of Trevor's wing clipping him just before he ignited, and wondered what on earth he'd been about to reach for that made my brother decide he deserved a flaming death.

I didn't have time to ask, though, as that bit of pyrotechnics set the remaining mages, who *weren't* engulfed in flames, scrambling to regroup. I decided the safest thing was to render unconscious the one I'd just hit in the gut. I clipped her just under her jaw and watched her collapse.

Just as I was about to attack the mage who had come after me with handcuffs earlier, I felt something hot graze my back and shoulder, and ducked just as something sizzled past my ear. I could smell my hair burning where the spell had grazed me.

A heartbeat later, searing pain jolted through me, as my nerves finally registered whatever had been done to my back and shoulder by the spell.

Some instinct made me reach for my snow leopard form before I could even think twice about it. The pain was gone as soon as I shifted, and I wondered if that was because I was no longer attached to the body that had been hurt, or some other, more mystical reason. I didn't have time to contemplate it for long though, as more spells were slung around me.

And now I realized why Trev had suggested I shift before we'd even hit the floor in this room. While I had been able to see some of the spells being slung in my human form, as a snow leopard it looked like I could see… well, everything. All magic seemed to be visible to me. Not only could I see even more spells whizzing through the air, as my friends did their best to dodge them and take down the mages, I could also see a thin skin of power around the mages who remained conscious. I could even see residual magic along surfaces throughout the room where spells had either hit and bounced off, or passed right through the materials. It was an interesting view.

In addition, my other senses, smell and sound, as well as the vibrations picked up by my whiskers, were so heightened in this form that I found myself reacting to things I would never have noticed as a human. And my muscles… they responded to my call so quickly that I almost felt as though time was slower as a snow leopard. Maybe it was.

I saw Sol take down the mage who had cast whatever spell had burned me, and I almost felt sorry for the bastard as she tore into his arm with her teeth. She was in her gloriously huge panther form, and I was once more impressed with the deep black of her fur and the bright yellow of her eyes. It looked as though she, at least, had decided not to kill our opponents, as she released the mage's arm once he appeared to have passed out from either shock or blood loss.

He was the last to go down. Five for five.

Trev reappeared as a human. He seemed untroubled by the fact that he was naked.

"Don't anyone else bother to shift, unless you have something of dire importance to add. We need to get out of here, quickly. Follow Vic and me through this ventilation shaft now. If we can get to the exit before they realize we're using the vents, we might just make it out before they try to drug us, or worse."

Then he turned into a flaming bird once more, shooting up through the gaping hole that we had crashed through earlier. I didn't hesitate, but leapt through the hole and reveled in how powerful my snow leopard body was. I didn't know if a normal snow leopard could have made that leap—I'd have to do some research on that front—but either because I was a shifter, or because snow leopards were badass, the eight feet between floor and ceiling felt like nothing to me.

Being a snow leopard was so awesome.

LESS THAN A quarter of an hour later, I saw Trev disappear suddenly from in front of me and felt a cold wind slap me in the face as I neared the open vent that waited ahead. The drop beneath me was sheer; climbable, certainly, but far enough down that I wasn't stoked about the idea of scaling it without a rope. Since I didn't see Trev below me, I looked up. There he flapped lazily, a firebird relaxing on a heady breeze. Assuming we were in for a long, upwards climb, I shifted to my human form.

Come on up!

Even though we'd been doing it since Trev had shown up at the house in Flagstaff, it still blew my mind that we could communicate telepathically.

I still can't believe this works! Our five-year-old selves would be so stoked, I thought.

They may have encouraged me to… practice here, Trevor said. That made my mouth go dry. What else had they forced him to do?

Trev, if it's… we don't have to use it. We can just wait till we've both shifted to human again and talk then.

It's fine, Vic. This part was never so bad, and it always made me think of you. Once I started getting it right I got really excited about showing off for you once I found you again.

That made me smile. Typical Trevor, really. Must share all new discoveries with Vic, otherwise they don't count.

You never gave up on us, did you?

Before Trevor could respond, a hand was resting on my back and pushing me forcefully towards the opening.

"Now, now, now. Must go now. No time to hesitate. Go. Go. GO!"

The last go was followed by a shove so firm that I catapulted to the edge of the vent and would have free fallen the 1000 feet to my rocky death below if I hadn't managed to catch the lip of metal that had formerly kept the grate in place.

"Sol! What the—"

The "fuck" died on my tongue as I turned to see a terrifying green cloud of… I didn't want to know what, that was seething behind Seamus' and Sol's fast-moving, now-human forms.

The green cloud was so horrifying that I didn't even notice that Sol and Seamus were both naked, let alone take a moment to appreciate the view, as they burst out of the vent and onto the cliff wall, just barely catching the rock in time to prevent themselves from plummeting to the ground below. Instead, I just angled myself so that I could reach the rock face above and to the left of the hole I'd almost fallen out of and started scrambling for holds as fast as I could.

There are some benefits to growing up in the Rockies. One of them is having access to world-class climbing every weekend throughout one's entire childhood. I was never going to be a professional climber—I spent too much of my time training in martial arts for one thing—but I loved to climb, and could get up and down your average cliff face with minimal trouble. At the moment I was doing my best to "sprint" up the face before me. I don't know if it was some sixth sense provided by being a were, or if it was just a basic human instinct, but something told me that whatever the festering cloud of green slime that was chasing Seamus touched would not come out unscathed, or even recognizable.

Luckily, Sol and Seamus seemed comfortable enough on the rock face we had suddenly all found ourselves scaling, though they were probably highly motivated by the cloud of roiling death that seemed to be dissipating into the clear void beneath us. Still, neither of them seemed paralyzed by a fear of heights, or so unsure of their next move that they couldn't keep going. They were both seeking holds and making use of them with the seasoned motions of people who had done this before.

Thank the gods. This was going to be a long enough climb as it was, we didn't need to add stressed out newbs to the equation.

"What in the hells *was* that thing?" I asked Sol, as we picked our way up the cliff face that towered above us. There wasn't as much left above us as there had been below, but it was still a formidable wall. Thankfully, it was made of a friendly granite composite that had eroded into some relatively positive holds. Of course, the downside of these types of walls is that they crumble easily, but we weren't going to think about that just now. We were just going to climb… and worry about the creepy cloud of whatever-it-was behind us.

"*That,*" Sol explained, as she sought out her next handholds, gingerly testing their solidity before putting her full weight on them, "was a spell that is supposed to be banned. A fucking scrambler that supposedly only the 'bad guys' use. If it touches you… let's just say it turns you into a Picasso, and not in a good way."

"So… we have your MOME buddies to thank for having one tailing us?"

Sol grunted.

"Buddies isn't the word I would choose, but yeah. Three of the five mages we were up against in that room are known for using illegal spells. They are *supposedly* only sent after the most dangerous criminals in the magical world, but…"

"But they sent them after us?"

"Well, first they sent them to 'help' with my interrogation of Seamus. Once they heard me ask him about *you,* they decided I needed backup. When they decided I wasn't being rough enough with Seamus, that's when everything went to hell in a handbasket."

"Ah. So we showed up just in time, then," I muttered. "Shit!" I added, when one of my handholds broke off and tumbled away from me. "Rock!" I cried, even though there was no one below me. Well, no one that I cared about, anyway. Seamus and Sol were both climbing to my right, not far enough beneath me to be in line of any rockfall I might create, and Sol had basically caught up already.

"Yeah, well, I could probably have gotten us out of there," she said. "But not without completely blowing my cover. As it stands now… HQ will probably forgive me for not wanting my captive beat to shit, and then you and Trevor clearly showed up to break Seamus free, and I merely followed you."

"What about the guy you tore up back there?"

"I can write that off as protecting Seamus. Technically, there are laws protecting captives, even MOME captives. It would be very by the book of me to have defended him."

"And will they—shit!"

Another hold crumbled out of my hand, and I was left hanging by my left arm. I had been testing holds before I took them, but some seemed more solid than they actually were. I made a point of not looking down at the over 1000 foot drop below me.

"It's only a matter of time before one of us loses our grip completely," Sol said.

I looked at her and Seamus, both still climbing along steadily. Seamus hadn't said a word since we'd started our ascent. He might have been shitting his pants (figuratively that is) but it was hard to tell. Trev had flown up ahead of us, and I wondered if he was doing general reconnaissance, or had already seen something that concerned him. Then I remembered that I could ask him.

How's it looking up there, Trev?

For a long moment there was no reply. Then, suddenly—

Fuck, fuck, fuck, fuck, fuck! Must fly faster. Vic! Change direction. Now!

What? Trev, it's over 1000 feet to the bottom an—

NOW, Vic! Go, go, go!

"Shit! Downclimb! Now! Trev sounds scared shitless and is telling us to reverse course."

No one argued, though I could tell they didn't like the idea any more than I did.

Downclimbing was always sketchier than going up, especially on a face like this one where anything could crumble out from under you. There was no way to check holds first when you were downclimbing, especially not when you were in a hurry to escape… whatever the hell had Trevor cursing like a Spanish sailor.

All three of us descended as quickly as we safely could, but apparently that wasn't fast enough. A ball of flames and wings shot past me, which I could only assume was Trev, and then there were blasts of magic shooting past me on all sides and Sol and Seamus were both releasing a string of curses as they went.

There was no way for us move faster without greatly increasing our likelihood of falling to our deaths, and there was no way to dodge the spells being slung at us easily either. The best we could do was try to move erratically, but that wasn't exactly easy when trying to scale a cliff in reverse.

"We're so screwed," I muttered, as another spell flew past my shoulder. "At least these mages seem to aim like storm troopers."

As soon as I said it, I felt the rock under my right foot tumble away at same moment that I had let go with my left hand to bring it to the next hold beneath me. I felt my left foot pull back from the rock, as my body swung wildly to the right, and then I began to scream as my right hand held, held,

held, held for all it was worth, hundreds of hours of muscle memory doing their damnedest to save my life, and then I felt the rock there crumbling away too.

The fact that it was probably a spell loosening the rock around me, and not just shitty luck, didn't make much of a difference as I felt my body start the free fall that would end with it splattered all across the jagged boulders below me. Somehow, I suspected that turning into a snow leopard would only leave fuzzier remains spread out across the valley floor. My right shoulder bounced off of the cliff face as I tumbled into the air, knocking the wind out of me, and leaving my arm feeling numb at my side. I'd probably lost a fair chunk of flesh on that rock—naked climbing certainly had its added risks.

I heard Sol shout my name as I fell away from the cliff face, and Seamus let out a bloodcurdling cry as he leapt for my body. He crashed into me, already fully changed to wolf form by the time we smashed together, and I wondered what the hell good he thought he was doing. All he'd managed to do was push us both farther from the side of the cliff face, which I suppose was a good thing if one didn't want to die hitting every damned ledge on the way down, but it left a lot to be desired as far as saving our asses went. We were still going to die horribly when we hit the giant scree pile that was getting closer with every last beat of my frantic heart.

I wanted to thank him for trying, or curse him for throwing his life away with mine, but I couldn't do anything but scream. It wasn't a high-pitched keening or even a crying wail, it was just a sustained emptying of my lungs. Just me raging against the dying of the light.

Then, before the ground could swallow us in its rocky maw, something else hit me hard from the side. I barely managed to keep my grip on Seamus' furry form as everything turned black around us.

I BLINKED AND found myself standing in a small forest clearing gazing stupidly at a tree that looked a lot like a figure in a hooded robe, holding a scythe. Seamus was still clutched in my arms, breathing heavily in wolf form.

"What the —" I had been about to say hell, but I stopped myself. Just in case.

"Where are we?" I asked the clearing at large. This place was familiar. I suppose it had only been a few days since my last camping trip, in the clearing where all of this started, but it already seemed like a lifetime ago.

I looked at Seamus as I gently placed him on the ground in front of me, but he just gave me a wolfy shrug.

"Thanks, Seamus," I said, rubbing his head. "Are we dead?" I wondered aloud. "I seriously hope we're not dead."

YOU ARE NOT DEAD.

"Whoa… who is that?"

I AM THE TREE OF LIFE.

I focused my eyes on the lone oak tree in a glade full of scotch pines and felt a weird tingle go up my neck. It was the oak from the night that I had met Gwen. The one that looked suspiciously like a robed, hooded figure holding a scythe.

"Are you sure you're not Dea—"

I AM THE TREE OF LIFE. MY RESEMBLANCE TO ANY PERSON OR CHARACTER, REAL OR IMAGINARY, IS PURELY COINCIDENTAL.

"Ok. Ok. Sheesh. You don't have to go all legal disclaimer on me. I get it. You are the Tree of Life. Fine. It's just that you look an awful lot like Terry Pratchett's Dea—"

LIFE. YES. THANK YOU. I APPRECIATE IT. I HAVE BEEN GROWING THESE BRANCHES TO LOOK MORE ALIVE FOR A VERY LONG TIME.

I shut up, not wanting to waste any more time arguing with the big tree with glowing eyes. Had they been glowing when we'd arrived? I didn't think they had been, but whatever, I had more important matters to worry about at the moment. I started to stand up and pull my hand from Seamus' fur, but he whined and leaned hard against my leg, unwilling to put any space between us. I dug my hand back into his fur.

"So, Dea— er… Life! It's good to see you. I think…"

I looked around the clearing again.

"Did you just save us?"

The hooded tree figure that *definitely wasn't Death* shook its head.

I DO NOT SAVE PEOPLE.

"Right. Ok. Cool. You didn't save us. Do you know who did?"

ME.

"Umm… didn't you just say that you don't save people?"

GWEN HELPED. ACTUALLY, SHE DID THE SAVING, BUT SHE IS MY INSTRUMENT.

"I'm not a damned violin, you talking tree."

The leather-clad redhead stood in the circle next to Death, and I couldn't help but wonder how much of this they had known about back on that first day in the woods. I mean, that's an awfully convenient setup otherwise. Still, first things first.

"Thank you," I said, meaning it. I really didn't want to die in general, but least of all smashed into a bunch of tiny pieces at the bottom of a mountain in the Andes. Well, ok, maybe not "least of all," I could think of far worse ways to go, really, but damn it. I had a lot to live for yet, and my long-term goals involved dying peacefully in my sleep in my hundreds, or at least dying splattered at the bottom of a cliff when I was a LOT older.

"I can't ever repay you," I said. "I really had no way out of that."

Gwen smiled, and the amount of tooth she bared made me start to sweat a bit.

"You *can* repay us, actually," she said, "now that you mention it."

"Oh?" I asked, feeling decidedly nervous. "How, exactly?"

"Don't look so frightened," she said. "I'm the goddess of good fortune and helping those who help themselves. I don't have any nefarious plans."

"You're the goddess of luck?" I asked. Honestly, if Sol and Trev hadn't independently confirmed that they thought she was a deity back in Bolivia, I doubt I would have believed she was anything more than the delusional woman who claimed to be my narrator.

"You can call me Serendipity if you like, but I prefer Guenhwyvar, and Gwen is easier on the tongue."

"Umm… does that make you a new god, or—?"

Gwen laughed, and suddenly her hair looked like it was liquid fire mixed with rubies, her eyes were molten emeralds, her skin glowed like radioactive gold, and everything about her was moving in its own private wind.

"One of the oldest, actually," she said, with a voice that sounded like seven different voices, each in a different octave, all speaking at once.

"Ok… dramatic effect taken. What can I do to help you that you can't already do yourself?" I asked.

"Well, I can't be everywhere at once, though I do try. There's just not enough belief these days to go around, and my powers aren't what they used to be."

I nodded again. Fair enough, omnipresence was probably a rough deal, really. I was going to have to interrogate someone about how *any* of the gods actually existed, ASAP, but I had a feeling this wasn't the right moment.

"So, I use agents," Gwen continued.

"Agents?"

"Agents of fortune," she replied. "Today, because I was already nearby, I was able to tackle you out of the sky and save you, but if I had been in say… Helsinki, for some reason, I might not have been able to get to you in time. As you can no doubt appreciate from very recent experience, seconds can make all the difference in some cases."

I nodded, not sure I liked where this was going, but unsure how it could be avoided.

"I need agents on the ground," she said. "I have some, spread around here and there, but it's difficult to find reliable people who can meet the demands of the job."

"And what are the demands of the job, precisely?" I asked.

"Pretty straightforward: whenever you see someone in need of help, who has been doing all they can to help themselves but just needs a bit of a nudge, you do whatever you can to help."

"What does that mean, they've been doing all they can to help themselves?"

Gwen shrugged.

"Means different things for different folks, I suppose. Mostly I just meant that they haven't given up. I'm not trying to constrain how you help people on your own time, you're welcome to help whoever you like if it's something you can do on your own, but what you do with the power I grant you… I'd like that only to be for those that meet my requirements."

"And am I only helping *people*?"

Gwen didn't answer, but shifted into a beautiful timber wolf, then an owl, then a snake, then a very uncomfortable-looking dolphin, then back to her two-legged form.

"I wasn't willed into being solely by humans. I help *all* of those who help themselves. Animals are generally first on my list, to be honest."

She took a good look at me and I shivered a bit, wondering what all she saw beyond the human who stood before her.

"Are you willing to assist me?" she asked.

"Dea—er… Life said you were his instrument. What did he mean by that?"

She laughed, looking over her shoulder at the shaped tree behind her, who merely gazed impassively out of two glowing eyes deeply recessed in the hood he'd formed out of his branches.

"Life and I go way back. We're two of the very first gods willed into being on this world…. He was technically around before I was, and some of my powers come from his. I wouldn't call myself his instrument any more than I would call the sun and tides his instruments, but you could say that he uses them when he feels the need."

I thought about that.

"So, Life, if I sign up to help Gwen, are you going to be calling on me all the time to help you out as well?"

It was difficult to tell, but I thought the figure might have shrugged.

I DON'T NEED HUMANS RUNNING AROUND DOING MY BIDDING.

Well, if that was another answer along the lines of "I don't rescue people," it wasn't particularly reassuring, but I decided not to worry about it for the moment. Another, darker thought occurred to me, requiring my immediate attention.

"If I say no, do we go right back to free falling to our deaths?" I asked.

Gwen's face paled.

"Holy shit, Vic. No! What do you take me for?"

I sighed and ran a hand through Seamus' coat for a moment. He hadn't reacted much since we'd arrived here. Certainly, he wasn't frantic, the way a real wolf would be after being thrown from a cliff and then whisked into a random bit of woods. Considering how frantic I felt, I was impressed at his calm.

"Sorry, I just… I dunno. Gods are supposed be tricksters."

"You've been reading too many fantasy books," Gwen replied.

I raised an eyebrow at her. "Oh yeah. Clearly that has been in no way useful at preparing me for my completely normal and straightforward life." I deadpanned that line, and Seamus made a small wolf snickering noise beside me.

Gwen smiled.

"Fine, maybe not *too many* fantasy books, but still. I'm not evil, I just need help. I would have asked you at the end of your 'quest' anyway, but I figured since I had you here, and you brought up the idea of owing me…"

"Fine," I put my hands up in a gesture of surrender. "I'll work for you. I certainly owe you after that last bit, and…well, whatever, I like the idea of helping people anyway."

In retrospect, I really should have asked more about the fine print.

"Great!" Gwen said.

And then a thousand lightning bolts struck me at once.

Or that's what it felt like, anyway. As though I were being ripped apart at the atomic level and rebuilt by lightning. I didn't even have time to scream.

When I could open my eyes again, I looked down at my body, expecting to find myself scrambled into a million microscopic pieces, or glowing, or…something. But I still looked normal, or as normal as a naked woman with a death grip on the fur of a wolf could look.

"Sorry, Seamus," I muttered, releasing his fur. I inspected my hands and arms, but found nothing different.

"You won't notice much… visibly different. And as to the rest… well, my powers affect everyone who takes them on differently, so… you'll just have to practice to find out what you can do."

"Well, that's vague."

Gwen glared at me.

"My power is vast and affects everyone differently. Imagine a list of all the things you *might* be able to do right now. Think of how fun it would be for the reader to go through all of that."

"Good point," I admitted. "Now, how about we go save Trevor and Sol."

Gwen nodded.

"You should be able to get yourselves there now. Just keep a good hold on anyone you need to bring with you and, if you can manage it, bring anyone injured back here."

That reminded me.

"My shoulder—"

ALL FIXED.

I guess Life was still paying attention to us.

"Oh. Cool. Thanks."

Sure enough, trying to move my shoulder and arm wasn't excruciating in any way.

IT HAS BEEN FIXED SINCE YOU ARRIVED AT THE CLEAR-ING. SIMPLY BEING IN MY PRESENCE WILL HEAL ALL INJU-RIES.

"Well, that's useful," I muttered. And then I reached through space and time and pulled us back to Sol and Trevor.

UNFORTUNATELY, SOL AND Trevor were still fighting their way down the side of the cliff.

Luckily, Seamus shifted to human again as soon as we materialized on the cliff face. Oddly, we were both now wearing clothes. Huh. Something to wonder about, when I wasn't busy trying to rescue my friends and family from an onslaught of homicidally angry mages.

Since we'd somehow managed to pull ourselves to exactly where Sol seemed to be, and it appeared to be only seconds after we had been whisked away by Gwen, I suppose I shouldn't have been surprised that we also arrived facing the cliff wall, and in a position to grab hold of it without tumbling to our deaths. Apparently, reality was taking a break for a bit, as I wielded power that made even less sense than my ability to turn into a large, furry predator. Fun times.

Whatever, reality could suck it. I was going to use the hell out of this to save the people I cared about.

Seamus snarled, despite being in human form, as more spells were slung in our general direction, and he made his way toward Sol, while I started gesturing wildly to get Trev's attention.

Trev seemed busy leading the mages' spell-flinging attention on a bit of a wild Phoenix chase, and it took me a good thirty seconds to signal to him that he needed to head my way.

When he finally turned and saw me, I thought he might fall out of the sky—his wings stopped moving for a full heartbeat. Luckily they were still extended outwards, rather than down.

I would love for you to torch these guys, but maybe we should just go, I sent to him, once I belatedly remembered that I could just think things at him instead of speaking or gesturing wildly.

I didn't know how much I could do with the new powers Gwen had given me, but the only thing I was *sure* I could do was the one thing that made the most sense anyway. It was time to get the hell out of Dodge.

YOU'RE ALIVE!

Trev managed to convey his levels of both surprise and elation at the news that I wasn't a fresh serving of human burger all along the valley floor, and I just barely managed to keep his concern and excitement from completely swamping me.

I will happily explain it all in a minute, once we're safe somewhere. For now, we just need to go.

Trevor nodded his flaming bird head, and shared a feeling of affirmation through our twin bond just in case he was too far away for me to see, which, when you added in all the fire and spells flying through the air, he was. He winged his way towards me, and I could see Seamus and Sol working their way closer along the cliff as well. I was certain that if I could touch everyone, or at least if we were all touching each other, I could get us all out of here and back to that forest. I just had to—

Fuck. A giant ball of... something nasty flew over my shoulder and left behind some rather disquieting blisters. Luckily, I still felt like I had most of my skin, and full control of my arm, unlike the last time a spell had grazed me that way. Soon, we weren't going to have much choice about how close we all got before I shifted away with whoever was touching me, and I didn't know if I'd get a chance for round two.

Trevor was almost within arm's reach (although I wasn't sure about how badly he'd burn me if I grabbed him) and Sol and Seamus were only one or two moves away from being within range when I heard the crack of rock breaking high above us. Someone had either wildly missed the mark with one of their spells, or they were simply trying to kill us with rockfall.

I didn't waste the moment it would take to curse the cowards who kept trying to kill us from the safety of the top of the cliff, but I promised myself I would take that moment later. Instead, I leapt for Seamus and Sol, covering the last few feet of distance between us and grabbing hold of each of them, screaming Trevor's name all the way.

I had to hope that Trevor would either dive for me, or just dive away from the wall. We didn't have time to hesitate before the refrigerator-sized chunk of cliff that was coming towards us was here and we were dead. We didn't have time for anything, actually. Only preternatural speed had gotten me to Sol and Seamus before the boulder got there. I willed us back to that circle of trees as hard as I could, and felt searing pain in my hip just before the world went black around us.

I CAME TO looking up at a starry sky through a bunch of pine boughs. The air held the crisp scent of autumn in the mountains; a mixture of fallen leaves, pine needles, and cool wind. Considering the two mountainous regions I'd been flashing between lately, that didn't really narrow things down.

I sat up.

My body objected strenuously to the movement, and made said objections known by forcibly ejecting everything I'd eaten in the past 24 hours.

I lay down again.

"Vic?"

The voice was weak, or maybe that was just my hearing, but I recognized it.

"Trev?" I asked. I vaguely recalled being worried about Trev earlier. He had been in decidedly mortal peril. "You alive?" I figured it wouldn't hurt to check. The afterlife might have stars and pine boughs too.

"Yep. You?"

I tried to nod, but when that small motion almost made me heave again, I settled on whispering a weak little, "yes," before lying completely still.

"What did you do?" Trev asked.

"Dunno." How little could I move and still vocalize my replies? "Gwen gave me some powers. Thought they might work to save our butts."

"I'd say you were right."

I smiled. That, at least, didn't make me feel sick.

"How long have I been out?"

Trev was quiet a moment.

"Only a couple of hours. I'm surprised it wasn't longer, actually, with all the healing you must have done."

That made me want to sit up, but I had learned my lesson. I took a very long time to bring my head up from the leafy ground on which it was pillowed.

"I didn't heal anyone," I said, once I was sure my stomach wasn't going to try escaping through my throat again. "The tree does that."

I looked around for Life. I didn't see the glowing eyes, but we did seem to be in the same clearing, with the tree shaped like a hooded figure carrying a scythe.

"I meant you. You needed a lot of healing."

"I did?"

I finally locked eyes on Trevor. He was sitting on the pine needle covered forest floor a few feet away from me, with his arms wrapped around his knees.

"I might have singed you a bit," he admitted quietly.

"That's ok, Trev." I took in his appearance. He was wearing a simple pair of jeans and a black t-shirt, sensible boots, and a stainless steel watch.

"Where'd you get your stuff?" I asked. As far as I could remember, we'd all been naked the last time we'd been in human form. Or had Seamus and I found clothes somehow? My memory was a bit hazy. "Did you shove your clothes in a dimensional pocket or something?"

He smiled at that.

"I do have a tendency to singe things, so that wouldn't be a bad idea. But I'm not actually sure why I'm dressed this way. We all materialized with clothes on, when we got to this clearing."

Well, that was interesting.

"Was I awake?" I asked.

He shook his head.

"Not in a way that counted, no."

"Hm… I was wondering if it was part of Gwen's power, but if it happened with me unconscious…"

"Gwen's power?"

"Yeah I… it's a long story. So, where are Seamus and Sol?" I asked, before I could get too sidetracked by the question of mystery outfits and meddling deities.

"They went to your place to clean up and make food. They said they'd meet us there. I didn't see any reason for them to stick around and watch you sleep, when I was here to keep an eye on things and light anyone suspicious on fire. They agreed, although the wolf pup howled about it."

That made me chuckle a bit. I didn't find Seamus' overprotective streak attractive or endearing, but it was kind of funny sometimes. He was nothing if not consistent.

"Were they ok?"

Trevor nodded.

"They were all healed up the second we arrived in the clearing. The only one who needed extra time was you."

That was odd. If anything, I would have thought that Gwen's powers would have made healing easier, rather than more time-consuming.

IT IS NOT PHYSICAL HEALING THAT HAS FORCED YOU TO REST.

"Oh hey, Life," I said.

Trevor was looking around the clearing a bit frantically. It looked like he was trying to find anything *other* than a talking tree to attribute that voice to, but he was, of course, failing.

"Trev, this is the Tree of Life. Life, this is my brother Trev."

A PLEASURE TO MEET YOU.

My introduction seemed to confirm Trevor's wildest fears, but at least he seemed to know where to look now.

"Umm… likewise? Thanks for the healing."

YOU ARE WELCOME. VIC, YOU MUST GO HOME. EAT HUMAN FOODS AND REST. YOU CONSUMED ALMOST ALL OF YOUR MAGIC. IF YOU DO NOT REST, YOU MAY INADVERTENTLY TAKE YOUR OWN LIFE.

"Well, that's not on my list of things to do. We'd better get going, Trev."

Honestly, it didn't take much to convince me that I should be at home. In addition to being where I could find both of my friends—was it sad that I could count all my friends on one hand at this stage?—it was a place where I could lie down for a few hours and safely munch on all the pizza I could possibly need to refuel my magic-weary body.

That was a weird idea—that I could be magic-weary—but I was too tired to deal with it at that moment.

Trevor stood up and I turned towards home. Weirdly, despite the fact that we were in the middle of a clearing in the woods that I had only been to twice before, I knew exactly which direction home was.

Just as my body began to protest the mere idea of walking home from here, Gwen popped into existence and grabbed us both.

~~~

I was both relieved and grateful to find that Gwen had taken us to my place rather than… anywhere else in the world. Honestly, with Gwen I never knew what to expect. I was pretty sure her intentions were good, but she and I often had different ideas of what constituted "helpful."

"Rest up for a while, Vic," she said, as she gingerly helped me to one of the stools around my kitchen island. "You're not used to channeling that kind of power, and it's pretty different from what it takes to call your snow leopard in through the dark matter running in your veins, so it'll take you a while to recover until you get used to it, and… well, even then, you can still use too much and do yourself some serious damage."

My brain stuttered over so many parts of that explanation that I didn't even know where to start. Self-preservation took over my mouth for me, though, and I asked, "How long until it's safe for me to use the power again?"

"Whenever you stop feeling like walking across the room is akin to climbing Everest, you're probably on the road to recovery. Honestly, just like with anything else in life, when you feel rested and whole you're good to go, and if you feel ragged and awful, you're not. There's no trick to it, outside of practice."

Well, that was both reassuring and not. Of course, it would have been sweet if my newfound powers were limitless and never strained me, but that would have been too much like some poorly considered fantasy gimmick, where the rules of magic mold to fit the author's purposes, and were only limited randomly, when it suited the plot. Even though Gwen had claimed to be my narrator, and then I had "taken over"… I didn't believe that I was in a book. Or if I was, it wasn't *that* kind of book. My life had never been that easy.

Whatever, I should be stoked that I could suddenly will myself through time and space. It didn't have to be easy. It was already ridiculous enough that I could turn myself into a snow leopard without much strain. Now, I had suddenly added Whovian style powers to my arsenal. I was all for it. Or I would be. As soon as I could have a nap.
~~~

I WOKE UP sometime the next day blinking groggily at Cary Elwes & Robin Wright cutting their way through the fire swamp. It was nice to open my eyes in my own room, staring at one of my favorite posters, even if I was dismayed to find that I had passed out before I'd had a chance to interrogate Gwen. As I slowly stretched my way out of bed, and plodded to my shower, I was relieved to discover that my brain and muscles now moved slightly faster than molasses in January.

Gwen may have left, but Sol, Seamus, and Trev were all present when I made my way down to the kitchen, throwing on the least-dirty clothes piled on my floor.

"Vic!" everyone chorused, as I jumped the last couple steps and skidded into the kitchen/dining area.

They were all perched on stools around the kitchen island, noses buried in mugs of hot beverages, until their heads popped up collectively at my less than subtle entrance.

I waved and then bowed, because what else do you do when you walk into a room full of people happy to see you?

"Hey folks," I said, making a direct line to the half-full pot of coffee I spied on the kitchen counter next to the fridge. "Whichever of you dug out the pot and made coffee is my new hero."

Seamus raised a hand and waved it casually.

"About time I managed to rescue you, instead of the other way around," he said, smiling.

I poured coffee and scowled at him.

"You have done plenty to save my ass in the short time we've known each other. And saving me isn't a prerequisite to being my friend, or anything."

Now Seamus was raising both hands.

"Calm down, Vic. It was a joke. I'm perfectly happy with the number of times you've saved my ass."

I kept the glare going, just for appearance's sake.

"Somebody woke up grumpy," said Trev, waving his mug of green tea at me. I marveled at the fact that I could smell it from where I stood, still five feet away from him. This whole feline senses when not in a feline body thing was both interesting and weird.

"I'm grumpy," I said, as I walked over to join them all at the tile-topped kitchen island, "because I woke up with a thousand questions buzzing through my head, and my primary source of answers is off doing… Gwen knows what."

I chuckled internally at my word choice. Gwen certainly would know what she was doing. Unlike the rest of us.

"We might be able to piece together a bit for you," Sol said, her smile making my stomach tighten again. She was dressed now, and I wondered what she'd done for clothes, as the ones she was wearing didn't look like mine. I guess she'd had plenty of time to head out and buy stuff while I was sleeping. I filed it away as way too low on the priority list to ask about now, and instead listened as she continued talking.

"We've been trying to piece things together all morning."

"Is it even safe to talk here?" I asked.

Trev nodded. "I've taken care of any monitoring 'devices' that were left behind."

The way he said devices made me think that some of said devices might actually be spells.

"How far have you gotten in unravelling our mysteries, then?" I asked, looking around at all three of them.

My heart stuttered for a moment, as I realized how damned relieved I was to see them all here and in one piece. I didn't have many friends. I mean, I'd had a few friends in Colorado growing up, but most of them hadn't known how to act around me after my parents had died, and I had run off to Arizona before they'd had a chance to figure it out. They might be there for me in the future, they might not. But these three people… these three people were my rocks now. It hadn't taken long, fuck, if you considered the fact that I'd only known Trevor for eight years before he was taken from us,

I hadn't known any of them as long as my friends in Colorado. And I'd only known Seamus and Sol for a handful of days… but I already knew I could count on them. I knew that if someone was trying to kill me, they'd try to stop them. That they would risk their own lives to save mine, and that I would do the same for them. I'm not sure there was a higher bar for friendship, and I certainly didn't want to find out if there was. I took a deep breath, blinked until the tears that had threatened to do more than make my vision fuzzy disappeared, and then focused on what Sol was saying.

"Well, luckily, Seamus was around when you got turned all Agent-of-Gwen, so he was able to explain how the hell you managed to flit in and out of nowhere to save our butts back on the cliff."

I nodded, appreciating not having to go through that part again.

"Though," Sol continued, "he never did explain how you managed to find time to get dressed while Gwen had you whisked away to that clearing."

I quirked my eyebrows for a second, unsure what she was talking about, and then remembered that Seamus and I had both appeared fully clothed when we returned to the cliff.

"Probably the same way that all four of us were fully dressed when we materialized in the clearing yesterday," Trevor suggested.

I hadn't been conscious for that part, but I had noticed that Trev and I were indeed both fully clothed when I came to. After thinking about it for a minute, something occurred to me. That first time I'd met Gwen, she'd been naked at first and then had conjured clothes out of nowhere, magically converting them into an entirely different outfit later.

"Gwen's power certainly lets her shift clothing around however she likes. Maybe it's part of my new arsenal of magic."

That had eyebrows raised all around.

"What's the big deal, guys? Wardrobe change is hardly something noteworthy on the list of badass talents a person can have."

They all chuckled.

"You clearly haven't been a werecat very long," Trev said, still smiling.

"Well, duh." I said.

"The rest of us have had longer to get frustrated with always having to carry clothes in our mouths, or stash them somewhere convenient, or just get used to being naked in front of people, which is fine for us, but generally weirds out norms."

"You mean nons?" I asked.

"He means muggles," Sol said, smirking. "And he's right, many of us would trade a limb for the convenience of not having to deal with the clothing fiasco in the modern world."

I just stared at all three of them.

"A limb?"

Sol just shrugged. "Ok, maybe not a limb. After all, sometimes it's nice to just be naked whenever you feel like it, which is certainly how we handle things in a community of weres, but…"

"But it's a pain in the ass if you're surrounded by mages," Trev grumbled. "They're superior gits at the best of times, and add in the necessity of going naked to use your were powers, and you have to burn the crap out of quite a few of them just to keep them from teasing you every time you shift."

That made me laugh.

"Ok, so clearly you three will just have to stick with me forever, so I can always conjure clothes for you. Next item?"

"How about the reports I got from my supervisor last night about a firedrake wiping out most of MOME's Bolivian facility?" Sol asked.

"Wait. What?!" Seamus and I asked, in unison.

Trev just smirked a bit, leading me to believe that he knew something about that.

"Apparently," Sol continued, "after we escaped MOME, a few fire demons and some selkies wreaked havoc in the lower levels, causing a massive evacuation of MOME, which, combined with a massive security breach disarming most of the wards in and around the building, caused all the people being held by MOME to be released."

"Well, that was the plan wasn't it?" I asked. "Didn't we mean to release all of the kids that MOME had taken over the years?"

Sol glared daggers at Trevor.

"We were supposed to be releasing the children, but *everyone* MOME was holding escaped. Some of whom may very well have deserved to be held."

I looked at Trev, wondering what his reply would be. He simply shrugged.

"We didn't have time to be choosy about who was released, and besides, who died and made us the arbiters of all justice? Who am I to judge who deserved to be in MOME's clutches and who didn't? MOME is a dishonest organization from the core. I can't be sure that their reasons for holding anyone are legitimate, so it just made sense to let everyone go."

"But what about the serious criminals?" Seamus asked.

"How could we have determined who those were in any reasonable amount of time? Not to mention figuring out how to release everyone else but them? Besides, it sounds like being caught in the facilities yesterday would have been a death sentence. Did they all deserve to die?"

That left both Sol and Seamus quiet, and I had to admit that I didn't have any answers to Trev's questions. I had a hard time believing that MOME's idea of justice was in any way unbiased, so how could we possibly have discerned who deserved freedom and who didn't, even if we'd had enough time, which we certainly hadn't?

"Ok. Can we get back to this fire-drake business?" I asked, trying to contain my excitement. "Was there seriously a dragon there? Am I misunderstanding fire-drake? What happened?!"

Sol sighed.

"The report I read said that after the building had been evacuated, a large, black-scaled fire-drake began immolating the entire premises."

Trev's smile was so wide that I had a hard time not laughing.

"You know exactly who that was, don't you?" I asked.

He shrugged and I punched his shoulder playfully.

"Ow. Hey! What was that for? You know just as well as I do who it was."

I just stared at him for a minute, until a memory came back to me. A sibilant voice in the darkness. A beautiful young woman with iridescent ebony skin and reptilian irises…

"No way!" I said, punching Trev's shoulder again.

"Seriously, Vic. Ow. Stop punching me. You're a lot stronger than you used to be."

I stared at him, baffled. He'd never used to whine about our sibling arm punches when we were kids, but ok, fine. He certainly didn't have to let me punch him. Honestly, it was a habit I thought I'd grown out of after I'd started actually training in martial arts, but apparently something about having my brother back made me jump back in time to when we'd still spent every day together.

"Sorry, Trev," I said, wrapping him in a hug instead. "So, you want to tell us how you know Rhelia?"

"We're friends," he shrugged, pushing me off of him.

I do not want to talk about this now, he added, just to me.

I sighed.

"Fine," I said. "Be all mysterious about it. What about the kids? And what about Rhelia? Did she escape? Have you heard from any of them? Did MOME not manage to round everyone up again after they took care of the fire?"

Trev chuckled briefly.

"There was no 'taking care' of that fire, Vic. And yes, I put Rhelia in charge of getting the kids to safety, so I'm sure they all got somewhere where MOME will have a very hard time tracking them."

"Well that's a relief," I said, and looked at Sol and Seamus, who also looked satisfied with that response, at least.

Then a thought struck me.

"Wait a second. Is Rhelia… your girlfriend?" I asked. "Is she the main reason we went back there?"

My jaw dropped at the thought that Trev could be romantically involved with a woman as… intimidating as Rhelia had seemed. Not because that would be a bad thing, just because… well, Trev was pretty laid back, and Rhelia seemed pretty no-nonsense to me.

I said I don't want to talk about it, Trev complained mentally.

"Whatever," I hastily added, waving the topic away as if it horrified me—which it absolutely did not—before Sol or Seamus could ask any follow-up questions. "I want to talk about the paperwork I tracked down in MOME, anyway. We still need to look at that together."

"Wait," Sol said, not allowing me the change in topic I was hoping for, "you both know the fire-drake?"

A sharp knock on the door conveniently made it so that neither Trev nor I had to reply.

I looked at Trevor, who closed his eyes for a moment, then nodded.

"Uncle Algernon," he said, his eyebrows rising. "Why on earth is he here?"

"What day is it?" I asked. I'd left my phone upstairs after my shower.

"The 21st," said Seamus.

I nodded.

"It's the day he usually checks in with me," I said, getting up to go to the door. "And you're going to have to explain how you just checked my front porch from the kitchen table without a device, Trev."

When I opened the door, I found uncle Algernon, which I had expected, thanks to Trevor's warning. And a gun pointed right at my chest, which I had not.

VIRGINIA McCLAIN

Victoria Marmot
AND THE
Inconvenient Prophecy

VICTORIA MARMOT BOOK TWO

To Corey, for being a true partner.

"UMM… NICE TO see you too, Algie." My tone may have been less than sincere. As you might expect from someone who found herself with a gun pointed at her chest by one of her few remaining relatives.

"I'm terribly sorry, Vic. I wouldn't be doing this under normal circumstances, but… I'm being coerced."

"Ok. That doesn't really make me feel any better about the hot lead you could pour into my chest at any moment, but I appreciate that it's bugging you."

Algernon had always been cordial with me, and he was, in fact, my great-uncle, not my uncle, though as a kid I'd never known the distinction. He was my dad's father's brother, and even though we'd never spent a ton of time together, I'd never gotten the impression that he wanted me dead before.

"Come outside, Vic, and close the door behind you. I really don't want to shoot you, but I won't have any choice. They put a godsdamned compulsion spell on me."

I nodded, wondering what the point of getting me outside was if the plan was just to shoot me anyway. If they were willing to risk my getting shot due to non-compliance, then what was the end goal? Or was Algernon just trying to get me outside and doing a bad job of coming up with lies? Knowing that no one in the kitchen could see me from where they were, I decided to share some intel with Trev as I stepped out the front door.

Kidnapping commencing in 3… 2… 1.

What?! Trev's thoughts conveyed shock and disbelief. *Vic, what the fuck!? Is*

Algernon taking you somewhere?

But even as Trev's reply entered my mind, Algernon was reaching back with the hand holding the gun, tears streaming down his face as he brought the butt of it down against the back of my skull. Before I could convey anything else to Trev, the world turned black.

"OW."

WAKING UP on a strange floor with your arms bound is probably never fun (this was my first time, so I couldn't really be sure, but it seemed like a safe bet). It's even less fun, however, when you have a raging headache and a goose egg on the back of your head (again, no basis for comparison, but this seemed like another obvious truth).

Embracing the whole "I'm a victim of a recent head trauma" trope, I lay there and moaned for a bit while I waited for the world to stop spinning. As the room settled into a single ceiling with only four walls, instead of the crazy-assed kaleidoscope it had started off as, I began to put my thoughts in order.

Clearly, my warning to Trevor hadn't been quite fast enough. Or, at least, it hadn't been fast enough for them to stop Algernon before he ran off with me. Hopefully, it had at least been enough to keep any of them from getting caught by whoever had Algernon by the nuts.

I decided to remain prone. Besides not feeling capable of the ab workout it would take to get upright with all of my limbs tied behind me, my head was pounding enough to make my gorge rise without putting it through the trauma of changing its elevation. So, even when I heard the unmistakable sound of a door opening to my right, I didn't bother to move much. Instead, I slowly and carefully turned my head to see who had come to torment me.

It turned out to be a pale, thin, elderly-looking man, wearing a pinstriped three-piece suit, who was dragging my uncle Algernon behind him like an unwilling rag doll in one hand and holding a gun in the other. The odd mirroring of two well-dressed older men was almost comical. The man with the gun looked like a faded version of my great-uncle, boasting less hair, less melanin, and less style.

I sighed.

"I fucking hate guns."

I hadn't meant to say it aloud, but it appeared the blow to my head had turned off my filters.

"Wretched things, aren't they?" said the man holding the object in question. He raised it and pressed it to Algernon's temple, looking for all the world as if it disgusted him to do so.

"Nonetheless, they make effective tools."

I couldn't argue with that, so I said nothing.

"I can tell from your silence that you're inclined to agree with me. It's a shame, really. I miss the days when all these things could be settled amicably simply by knowing who held the stronger magic."

"Were you alive for those days?" I asked.

The guy didn't look more than sixty or seventy, but I imagine that the days when guns *weren't* great equalizers between magic and non-magic folks had been a good long time ago.

"Sadly, no. Still, one can dream…"

"I suppose." I tried to shift a bit more onto my side, in order to relieve some of the strain in my neck, but the man turned the gun on me with surprising agility.

"Just trying to get comfortable," I said quickly, hoping to keep us from getting shot.

"Well, don't," he replied testily.

I nodded. Slowly.

"Now then, tell me where your brother is, Ms. Marmot, lest I be forced to shoot your uncle here."

He pointed the gun at Algernon again, and I tried to swallow, but there was suddenly no saliva left in my mouth.

"I don't know where he is right at the moment," I replied. The man thumbed off the safety on the gun. I would have raised my hands if I could, but since they were still tied behind me, I just kept talking. "But the last place I saw him was in my house, just before Algernon here held me at gunpoint on my own front step."

The man glared at me as though I were a level of stupid he had not yet encountered.

"I don't believe that you would be imbecilic enough to bring a known MOME fugitive to hide in your home. Surely you realize it would be the first place we would look."

That had me returning the look he'd just given me.

"Except that, if I'm correct in surmising that your whole goal in holding me here is to find out where Trevor is, then you clearly *didn't* look there. Or maybe you just weren't able to. I think my brother is easily a few steps ahead of… whatever it is you guys use for spying and eavesdropping these days."

He didn't lower the gun on Algernon and continued staring at me.

"Fine," he said, after a lengthy pause, "If you're going to play hardball, we can do that. I didn't want to have to draw this out, but you leave me no choice."

He pushed the gun into his belt, just in front of the pinstriped vest, a move that made me cringe. But my wincing at poor gun safety was cut short as he pulled a six-inch dagger from somewhere inside his vest.

Without pausing to repeat any of his questions, or even explain what he intended to do, he brought up the wrist by which he had been restraining Algernon and rammed the knife into it, all the way to the hilt. Algernon and I screamed at the same time.

"What the FUCK, dude?! I told you, my bother is in my fucking house. It's not my fault if your people are too incompetent to find him there. And it certainly isn't Algernon's fault."

I could feel tears run down my cheeks. Algernon and I had never been particularly close, but after my parents died, or disappeared, or whatever the fuck they did, he was all that I had left until I found Trevor again. We had enjoyed a few companionably silent teas, and shared enough teary hugs that I really didn't want anything bad to happen to him, not to mention that he was just a decent human being who didn't deserve to be stabbed in the wrist by a psychopath.

Mr. Pinstripe looked up at me then, even as Algernon crumpled to the floor, his arm still hanging awkwardly from the other man's grip. He glared at me, but said nothing.

"Use a fucking truth spell if you have one, or whatever you want. But that's all I know about where my brother is. He was at my fucking house when you assholes took me. If you'd done your jobs properly, he would be here right now. So STOP. TORTURING. MY. UNCLE."

"Interesting," said Mr. Pinstripe. "I hadn't expected that you had inherited any of your grandfather's gifts."

I had less than no idea what he was talking about, but as he wasn't driving any more knives into Algernon, I was going to count it as a win.

"What do you mean?"

"You just put power behind your words. I can tell because I feel inclined to stop stabbing your uncle here, which, I can guarantee you, is not my usual mode of operations."

"So, you enjoy stabbing people?" I asked, my voice carefully neutral. "Tell me more about that."

Ok, yeah, so maybe it was a cheap attempt to keep the man talking, but hell, I would play shrink all day if it meant giving my rescuers more time to find me. And yes, I assumed I had rescuers, because, well, damn it all, we had just spent the morning bro-ing it up over how we all saved each other's asses and would do it again. So, yeah, I expected my posse to be coming after me. Assuming they could find me.

It would be easy enough to tell them where I was if I had any earthly idea myself.

I had considered, very briefly, when the man was first pointing the gun at Algernon, just shifting myself away from here. But that would leave Algernon alone, with a man who was very pissed off holding a gun to his temple, and I didn't think that would end well for Algernon. So I had stayed, but if I could somehow convince Mr. Pinstripe to let me touch Algernon… maybe I wouldn't even need a rescue.

Pinstripes just sneered at me.

"I'm not a serial killer in search of validation, or a Bond villain looking for an audience, so I'm afraid your questions about my motivations will go unanswered. The organization I work for has a vested interest in your brother. That is all you need to know, I'm afraid."

He turned toward Algernon and pulled the knife rather slowly from his forearm. Algernon screamed again, and I shuddered.

Pinstripe was just raising the knife to plunge back into Algernon's arm, while I flailed futilely against the bonds holding my wrists, when the door flew open with a bang and Sol sauntered in.

"WHAT THE FUCK are you doing with my assignment, Vince?" Sol asked.

I kept my mouth shut. My body had flooded with relief at the first sight of Sol, but her words made me realize that she might not be here to rescue me. After all, she had a rep to keep with her MOME superiors. She would be risking a lot to break that cover. She was probably just here to assess the situation.

I doubted she would let Mr. Pinstripe, aka Vince, kill me if it came down to it, though. So that was somewhat reassuring.

"Just getting some useful information out of her before she's put down. Seeing as you managed to end her usefulness before it even began."

"You're not going to touch her, and neither is anyone else. I spent MONTHS tracking this bitch, and I didn't do all of that to have you ruin her before we even find out if she's useful."

Well, that was a different story than the one that Sol had been selling us earlier. I wondered how much of the change in tune was for Vince's benefit, or how much Sol had simply glossed over the truth in order to get on our good side.

"She already lost whatever usefulness she might have had when you let her thrice-cursed brother escape. She was only ever good as collateral."

"That's not what my department thinks."

Sol said that last bit with the kind of authority that implied her department was not to be fucked with.

Vince just eyed her for a moment, but before he could do anything else, she turned to Algernon.

"Who's the old man?" she asked, sneering.

"The freaks' great-uncle. He's *helping* us in return for a favor."

"Oh?" said Sol, sounding barely interested. "What favor?"

"Not killing his grandchildren."

"Hmm… they at HQ?" she asked, looking around the room, as though she were more interested in the decor than the question itself.

Vince didn't reply, and Sol just shrugged.

"Well, I have good news, Vince. I have the brother. So you can go ahead and move on with your day."

That made Vince narrow his eyes.

"Why are you telling *me* that instead of HQ?"

"Because HQ sent me over here to find out what the hell kind of shady shit you were up to, and I'm the one who found him."

"Where was he?"

Vince was toying with the knife in a way that was not at all reassuring. He looked like he was just itching to stick it back into some human flesh. Creepy. Vince was officially a creepy fuck.

"In her house," Sol said, turning back to Vince and looking smug. "Dumbest place to hide him they could have thought of. Of course, they didn't even *try* to hide him from *me*."

Apparently, Vince didn't like Sol's tone, or else he decided that Sol's revelation meant that Algernon's existence was no longer useful to anyone. Whatever his motivations, he lunged forward with his knife hand. I shouted a warning, but could only watch in horror from my prone position on the floor.

Just as the knife was about to reach Algernon's throat, a giant, black ball of fury and teeth slammed Vince into the wall behind them both. Algernon whimpered and looked like he might faint, but otherwise seemed unharmed.

When Sol-as-panther stepped back from Vince, the man's head flopped vacantly to one side, a large gash having taken the place of where his Adam's apple used to reside.

"Ew," I said, feeling my gorge rise. "I mean, don't get me wrong, he deserved it, but… yuck. I never realized how gross the human trachea looks."

Algernon held a hand to his mouth and moved to the corner of the room, but he didn't quite make it before his most recent meal came up to visit.

"And, that's even more gross," I mentioned, trying to turn away, but only managing to close my eyes against the image, desperately trying not to think of the smell.

Suddenly, Sol in human form was kneeling over me, doing something with the bonds that held me.

I was surprised by how quickly my nausea fled and was replaced by a very different kind of warmth in my stomach.

"Remind me to stay on your good side," I mumbled to Sol, as she loosened the bonds on my wrists.

She just smirked and continued untying me.

"Is this going to be problematic for you… work-wise? And how did you find me?"

"I'll explain once we're safely out of here," Sol said, as she finally undid the binding around my ankles.

"Should I shift us?" I asked.

Sol shook her head, but didn't say anything, looking pointedly at Algernon, who was still being quietly sick in the corner of the room.

Interesting, and mildly suspicious, that Sol didn't want to discuss things in front of him, but I supposed one couldn't be too careful.

"Ok. What's our exit strategy, then?"

Sol strode to a window that I hadn't been able to see this whole time because of the way I'd been positioned on the floor, and flung open the blinds, then the window itself.

She whistled loudly, and there was a return howl from outside. I had already gone to kneel beside Algernon.

"Come on, Algie. We have to get out of here quickly. We need time to find your family before they have a chance to hurt them."

Algernon stared at me through glassy eyes.

"I can't leave here. They'll kill my granddaughters. I can't risk it. If you can find them, please, help them. Get them away from MOME, but I can't risk doing anything that might seem like not cooperating."

I stared at him in consternation, while gesturing vaguely in the direction of the newly deceased. "Vince over there was ready to kill you because he'd decided that you'd outlived your usefulness. What makes you think whoever else is here won't do the same?"

Algernon simply shook his head.

"That doesn't matter. I have to know that my granddaughters are safe. They can do whatever they like with me, but those girls…"

Algernon's eyes filled, and I did my best to keep from imitating him, not because I didn't think it was an appropriate time to cry, it certainly was, but because I needed clear vision to get out of here fast enough to save Algernon's grandkids.

I took a deep breath.

"Damn it, Algie, if I'd just wanted to leave you to the sharks, I would have abandoned you the second I woke up."

Sol growled softly from behind me, but I didn't bother to turn around to see if it was directed at me or not. I didn't think Algernon was with it enough to put together that I meant I could shift people through space and time, but how did MOME not already know that anyway? I had shifted the four of us out of their clutches not twenty-four hours ago.

"Come with us, please. I'll make sure they can't get to the girls."

He shook his head, and Sol muttered "We have to go," so softly that I doubted anyone without enhanced hearing would be able to even tell that she'd spoken.

I sighed.

"Please be careful, Tio. I'll do my best to get Lucy and Mia away from these assholes. Your part of the deal is to make sure you're around to see them again. Ok?"

Algernon nodded, but still didn't speak. I decided I didn't have time to do anything other than run to the window and follow Sol's lead, reaching for my snow leopard and jumping out of the open frame as close to her furry tail as I could manage without landing us in a tangled heap of cat.

As we hit the ground running, I felt the getting-more-familiar-than-I-would-like flash of heat caused by a spell whizzing past my shoulder, and I began zigging and zagging my way to Seamus, whose wolf form I could just see in the distance. My hope was that the quick directional changes would help prevent spells from turning me into a gooey Picasso or… whatever they were intended to do.

I heard a screech from the sky above us that told me Trevor was close by, and I wondered how long they'd been out here fighting off mages.

Long enough that we're getting tired, Numo.

More spells burst onto the landscape nearby, and I heard Seamus howl once behind me, just as we neared the woods bordering the grounds of the estate we appeared to be on. I hadn't been able to tell much about the house we'd been inside of from my limited perspective tied up on the floor, so this was the first time I was getting any sense of the size and shape of the place.

We had jumped from a second story window and landed in a heavily land-scaped garden, complete with artfully manicured lawn and oddly sculpted decorative shrubs.

Like, seriously, why had I just run past a hedge shaped like a herring? And why did I know what a herring looked like, come to that?

Within a hundred yards, however, stood the edge of a forest that I was willing to bet backed onto the nearest mountain, and might, therefore, provide us not only with cover from spells, but also an avenue of escape.

I risked a look back over my shoulder and saw that Seamus was lagging behind. Just to add to the fun, his slow pace seemed to be leaving him in serious danger of getting hit by more spells.

I turned on my haunches and sprinted back in his direction, before I could think better of it. A plaintive screech from behind me told me that Trevor had seen the move and was not impressed. Oh well. I had too few friends to risk losing any to MOME asshats. Surely, Trev of all people could understand that.

Seamus seemed similarly nonplussed when I arrived at his side, but I ignored his growl of protest, flattening him to the ground just as another spell shot towards where his head had just been.

It seemed as though the mages were catching up.

In fact, for the first time since the encounter where Trev had immolated a MOME agent in Bolivia, I could actually see who was attacking us. The spells on the cliff side had seemed like disembodied magic floating at us without an origin, since all of the mages who had been coming after us had still been on top of the cliff. And, until a few moments ago, the mages coming after us here had been behind the cover of the various decorative shrubs. Now, finally, they were forced to leave the limited protection of the oddly shaped bushes in order to cross the open ground of the estate and reach the forest beyond before we did.

I could smell the coppery tang of blood coming from Seamus, beneath me, and knew that if I hadn't just pounced on him, yet another spell would have hit him, doing who knew what kind of damage.

No time, Trevor sent, from wherever he was, flapping away behind me.

He and Sol had likely turned back to try to cover my tail as I had run for Seamus, but I wasn't sure and it wasn't like I had time to check. I needed to get Seamus out of here. Now. Injured, he wasn't fast enough for this. He needed help.

Without waiting to confirm the plan with anyone else, I thought about the clearing where the Tree of Life resided and reached for that space with my consciousness.

Between one heartbeat and the next we were there.

Seamus lay panting beneath me, but I didn't wait to see how he was doing. The Tree of Life was supposed to take care of him, and I couldn't leave Sol and Trevor in the hands of those mages, no matter how badass each of them might be normally. They were grossly outnumbered.

I shifted back to the exact place I had just left.

I felt a foot connect with my ribcage, just as I heard a human cry out in surprise, and knew that someone must have tripped over me. I could only hope that it was one of the MOME mages and not Sol or Trev.

A flash of flame to my left caught my attention and I ran towards it, desperate to get to Trevor before MOME got ahold of him.

When I reached him, he was diving repeatedly at a mage who kept shooting what looked like nets of magic at him from the end of a wand. He would dodge and attack her all in the same move, over and over again, and part of me wondered if she was just meant to be a distraction while some other mage came at him from a different angle.

Apparently, my guess was spot on. Suddenly, a second net made out of light flew towards Trevor, just as he swooped away from the first mage he'd been dodging. It looked like the second net was about to enclose him, but just before it hit him, the flames that enveloped his phoenix form flared brighter. When they faded back to their normal glow, the light net was nowhere to be seen.

I briefly wondered how many types of spells he could burn through, but then I was close enough to leap through the air and collide with the giant bird that was my brother. I didn't wait for us to land before I shifted us to the clearing with the Tree of Life.

We landed hard in the leaves and dirt that made up the clearing, and I saw that Seamus had shifted to human and was making his way towards the Tree of Life itself. I didn't wait to see how angry Trevor was with me for interfering, I shifted back to the grounds at the house.

I found Sol cornered by three mages, and I wasn't sure how to get to her without getting us both killed. She was backed into an alcove created around an impressive statuary, and she must have just arrived there, because I couldn't see a reason for the mages not to have killed her already, if they'd had the time and inclination.

Not knowing what else to do, I climbed the closest shrub and gained as much elevation as possible. When I launched myself at Sol, it was from the height of about fifteen feet, and I sailed easily over the heads of the three mages that had her pinned into that corner. Unfortunately, I wasn't faster than the mages had been at preparing their spells, and three of them hit Sol at once, just before I did. I didn't wait for the breath to return to my body after the impact of slamming into her from fifteen feet away, I just shifted us to the clearing as quickly as I could.

When we materialized in front of the Tree of Life, Sol wasn't breathing.

I SPRANG AWAY from her, my nimble snow leopard form leaping away backwards even as I pulled on the human part of me and transitioned to walking on two legs.

The lack of my weight on her chest did not make her start breathing.

I instantly fell to her side.

"LIFE!" I cried, as I knelt next to her prone, furry form. Her glossy black coat was slick with blood.

"LIFE!"

Suddenly, the towering form of the Tree of Life loomed behind me. Right now, the scythe was particularly off-putting.

"Heal her!"

IT IS TOO LATE. HER LIFE FORCE IS GONE.

"No. Damn it, Life! What good are you, if you can't save people who have only been dead for five seconds? There are regular humans who can do that!"

PERHAPS YOU SHOULD TAKE HER TO THEM, THEN.

"But she was killed by magic! I don't know what a hospital can even do for her."

Life just stared at me.

"Fuck this!"

Tears streamed down as I turned to the one person who had never failed me yet.

"Trev, please."

He looked at me like he didn't understand at first, but then, slowly, he must have realized what I was asking.

"Please," I begged, unable to let Sol die, for all that I'd only known her for a handful of days. I wasn't sure that he could truly do anything, but clung to the hope that some of the myths were true. I'd spent the past week getting a crash course in living fantasy, and damn it, if the naked lady in the woods who claimed to be my narrator turned out to actually be a goddess, the guy in my English class turned out to be a werewolf, and the guy stalking me in my fucking bedroom turned out to be a vampire, then surely this miracle was possible.

Please, please, dear Gwen, let it be possible.

Trev nodded, though he looked far from confident. He reached down and set both of his hands on Sol's prone form.

And then flames consumed her.

SEAMUS, TREV, AND I watched the flames consume Sol's body, and I struggled to remind myself that she was technically dead, so the flames weren't hurting her. But damned if it didn't look like the flames were hurting her. Her body convulsed repeatedly, and I was extremely thankful that the fire was too bright for us to make out what was being done to her flesh.

Gwen damn it, if all that was left after this was a charred corpse, I was going to feel like a first rate asshole. Not to mention, I would probably never forgive myself for having gotten Sol killed to begin with.

I felt an arm wrap around my shoulder and turned to see Seamus still staring at the flaming body on the ground, but leaning against me as though he needed the support as much as I did.

"She doesn't even like you," I said, unsure about the devastation that registered in his eyes, but mainly just saying the first words that came to mind.

One corner of his mouth turned up.

"She was raised to hate wolves. Someone in her family is an asshole, certainly, but she apologized for all that last night, when we were at the house before you and Trev got there."

"Bonded over almost dying together?" I asked. He nodded.

"You guys make out?" I asked.

"I don't think Sol's into me that way," he replied, still leaning against me, still watching the flames.

"You're using the present tense," I whispered. "You think she's still in there?"

Seamus nodded, his eyes flickering with reflected phoenix fire.

I turned back to the flames, finally letting out a deep breath I didn't know I'd been holding.

As if my breath were a gale force wind, the flames around Sol extinguished.

"Well, that was intense," said a calm, slightly accented voice, from the ground.

"Sol!?" the three of us shouted, jumping forward. I knelt at her side and grabbed her hand, doing my best to ignore the pulse of sexual heat that coursed through me at the contact.

"What the fuck just happened?" she asked.

I looked around the glade at Seamus and Trev, as if to confirm that my mind wasn't fucking with me and that I was really seeing a whole, living, distractingly naked Soledad lying on the ground in front of me.

Seamus and Trev were crying, but also laughing and smiling, so I had to assume that I wasn't hallucinating the whole thing.

"Um… the bad guys killed you, and then Trev brought you back."

I HELPED.

"And Life helped," I added, laughing and sobbing at the same time, not wanting to piss off the tree, even though he'd claimed he couldn't do anything to start with.

Sol laughed, and then sat up. I thought really hard about her being fully dressed, and was somewhat surprised to see her clothed a moment later.

"¿Qué demonios?" she asked.

"Um… I think that was my Gwen powers acting up." I carefully did not mention that I found naked Sol decidedly distracting. For one thing, I was embarrassed not to have more self-control, and for another, I didn't want to weird out my friends and make them think I was objectifying them.

"How did that even work?" Seamus asked, looking between Trev and Sol as though he expected either of them to burst into flames at any moment.

"It has never worked before," Trev said, looking both bewildered and a bit sad. "Maybe having the Tree of Life here was the difference, but… yeah. Phoenix fire is supposed to lead to rebirth, so… it was a last ditch effort."

I took a moment to be appropriately horrified that Trev had needed to try that trick before, and then another moment to mourn the fact that it hadn't worked. Then I got back to the business of being amazed at what he'd done.

"Why did you get all the cool powers?" I asked, giving him a teasing push.

"Dude, Vic, you turn into a snow leopard and can move people through time and space in the blink of an eye," he replied, leveling me with his best "srsly" face.

"Yeah, but only because a goddess decided to turn me into one of her minions. You were born with this!"

Trev shook his head.

"Sort of… there's a lot more that any of us could do. The dark matter inside each of us is more raw potential than a set of genetically predetermined 'powers.' MOME, and everyone else, have perpetuated the myth that people can't access power in ways they weren't born to, but that's a lie. Shifters can use their powers to access spells if they train the right way, and a mage could call on an animal form if they practiced hard enough. Regular humans could probably access a spell or two, if they trained enough. They have to have some amount of dark matter, or else Vampires wouldn't use them for snacks."

And in that one statement, Trev had told me more about the magical world than I'd learned in the past week. I looked to Seamus and Sol for confirmation, but they both had their eyebrows pinned to their hairlines as though Trev had just claimed that vivisecting puppies was a good time.

"Trev, why do Seamus and Sol look like you just kicked them in the face?"

"Probably because no one in our world wants to talk about how similar shifters and mages are, and how our powers are the same at the root."

"And why do you know so much about this taboo subject?" I prodded.

"It's what MOME was training me in, before I escaped."

"And it's the reason we really shouldn't be discussing things here," said a vaguely familiar British voice from the edge of the clearing. I wrinkled my nose at the cloying smell of weed and realized who it must be.

"Mr. Bumblebee?" I asked, turning towards the voice.

"Please, Victoria, I believe I asked you to call me Albert."

"Yes. Sorry, Albert. It's been… a long few days since then."

"Vic?" Trev asked, looking as though he was ready to attack the newcomer at any moment. Indeed, Sol had already jumped to her feet, and she and Seamus both looked ready to fight as well.

"Um… team, this is Albert Bumblebee. He knew my parents."

I had made a split second decision that I didn't necessarily want Albert to know who Trevor was, assuming he didn't already, so I didn't bother to explain that my parents were also Trev's.

You don't trust him? Trev asked, having noticed the exclusion.

I don't know. Maybe? It's hard to say. He hasn't given me reason not to, but… where

MOME is concerned, can we really trust anyone?

Fair point.

"It's only a matter of time until MOME decides to try their luck here. I'm afraid the Tree of Life isn't entirely a secret."

"Vic, can you take us somewhere?" Seamus asked. I could tell that he was doing his best not to share too much about my newfound powers with Albert, but I was at a loss as to how we were going to keep him from finding out as soon as I actually shifted in front of him.

"I think I've got enough energy for one more shift, thanks to Life here, but where do we go? We can't go to my place, that's the first place they'll look now."

"We could try my place," Seamus suggested, but I was shaking my head as soon as he'd said it.

"Too risky. They've probably figured out who you are by now. It's not worth putting your family at risk. We should probably get out of the state if we can."

Sol sighed.

"You know where to take us, Gatita."

I looked at her. She had a point. Assuming that MOME hadn't somehow discovered her cabin since the last time we were there—which didn't seem at all likely, since they'd only discovered that she was working against them in the past half hour or so—I stepped forward and grabbed Sol and Trevor's hands. Seamus took Sol's other hand, and I focused on a mental image of Sol's little wood cabin on a Bolivian mountainside, willing us all to be there instead of here, even as the image came into focus in my mind.

Then an arm wrapped around my chest, and I heard Albert shout, "Damn it all, how did he find us!"

The world went black.

WHEN I OPENED my eyes, we stood on the side of a mountain in a blizzard so thick that I could barely see the small log cabin that stood less than a meter away. Yet I ignored the slashing cold that battered me, as well as the warmth that lay within easy reach, and instead focused on beating the ever-living crap out of the creepy, undead dickwad who had his arm around my chest.

"Victoria, wait!" Edik shouted.

I did not wait. I pulled on my snow leopard form and set about inserting my three-inch claws into his undead flesh.

"Aghhhhhh!!! Victoria, stop!"

Spoiler alert—I didn't stop.

I was so fucking sick of Edik showing up in my life and screwing things up. In particular, I was sick of him touching me as though he had any right to do so, in any way, ever. A rage coursed through me that I hadn't known I was capable of as I slashed at him again and again, slicing through the flesh of the forearms he feebly held in front of his face as protection.

I roared, my whole feline body shaking with fury, and slashed at him again and again.

"Victoria, please! I'm only seeking my daughter."

And what did I care if that was true? His daughter probably never wanted to see him again. She probably hated him with every fiber of her being. Maybe she wanted him dead.

Maybe I was projecting…

That last thought didn't occur to me until multiple sets of arms worked to restrain me, and Trev whispered into my furry ear, "It's ok, Vic. We won't let him touch you again. Maybe let him live. Just for a minute…"

I snarled, and did my best to take another swipe at Edik, but Sol's arms were wrapped around my shoulders, holding my front legs against me, and I couldn't get at him without possibly slicing her up, which I wasn't willing to do.

I shifted back to human form, fully clothed thanks to Gwen's bonus powers, and without saying a word, I turned, brushing three sets of arms away from me, and strode into the cabin.

As soon as I stepped inside my legs gave out from under me.

~~~

"You've overtaxed your magical reserves," said a British accent that I was beginning to recognize.

"What is Albert doing here?" I asked the room, which was still spinning above me.

"He hitched a ride along with Sir Sparkle Brains," Trev muttered.

"I only hitched a ride *because* of Sir Sparkle Brains, as you call him. You'd made it clear enough that you didn't wish to have me with you, but when I saw him latch onto Victoria, I thought I would offer my services at vampire disabling."

I couldn't see Albert, because I was too busy trying to get the ceiling to stop rotating.

"Well, you do seem to have a knack for it," Seamus admitted from somewhere by my feet.

"Where *is* Mr. McStabbyTeeth?" I asked.

"He's outside in the snow, looking for all the world like a miniature statue of David." That was Sol.

"Huh?" My brain really wasn't up to the task of well… probably even basic addition at this point, let alone trying to unravel references to Italian statuary and biblical figures.

"Albert froze him or something, and he's pale enough that he kind of looks like marble anyway. He's out there collecting snow," Trevor's voice added.

"Not that he doesn't deserve to freeze to death, but… I assume that he won't?" I asked.

"Nope. Unfortunately, vamps don't need warmth to survive," Sol replied, sounding truly disappointed.
~~~

I blinked, unsure if I was relieved or disappointed at the news that he would survive the cold. Unable to make up my mind, I took a moment to appreciate that the ceiling was now mostly stationary.

"So, how long before I can shift us again?" I asked.

For a long moment no one replied. Or maybe I fell asleep briefly, it was hard to tell.

"Probably not for a day or two. It depends on how much you've been practicing."

That was Albert's voice again, and I still couldn't convince my head to turn and look at anyone, so I didn't have the benefit of facial expressions to help me figure out if that was meant to be an admonishment or not.

"Considering that I've only had most of these powers for a day or two, it is safe to say I've hardly practiced at all. If it weren't for the Tree of Life I'd probably be dead already. Twice."

Albert began to object, although whether he was going to protest the idea that I'd only had magic for two days, or the fact that the Tree of Life had saved me twice already, I didn't know, because Sol cut him off.

"You need rest, regardless," Sol said, and it sounded like she was fussing with the wood stove while she spoke. "MOME doesn't know about this. So as long as Edik and Gramps here don't turn us in, we should be safe while you rest up."

"And what do we do with Edik?" I asked. "Leave him sitting outside like a statue?"

Sol chuckled. "Sure. The cabin could use some decoration. We can have Albert unfreeze him once you're rested enough to shift us all away if he pulls anything sketchy."

That sounded like as good a plan as any, and before anyone had a chance to suggest an alternative, I fell into a deep sleep.

I WOKE UP to a deep thrum that reverberated all the way down my spine. Not wanting to do anything that might make that pleasant feeling stop, I waited a few minutes before opening my eyes. After a few blissful minutes of just listening, I felt sufficiently awake to realize that the sound was that of an upright bass being bowed. Or at least that was my best guess, since I'd noticed an upright bass in Sol's cabin before, hadn't seen any other string instruments lying around, and knew that whatever it was, it sounded like nothing I'd heard before. I opened my eyes and the sound stopped.

"Don't," I said, sitting up and turning towards the corner of the room, where I found Sol still holding the upright against her with one arm, her other hand loosely holding the bow at her side.

"Sorry," she said. "After you slept through all the shouting, I didn't think this would wake you up."

"Please don't stop," I said, before my brain could process the fact that Sol had mentioned shouting.

She started playing again before I could ask, and I didn't stop her. The sound was entirely too pleasant, and watching her play turned out to be even more pleasant. She was wearing a T-shirt and jeans, since the wood stove was kicking out maximum heat, and the muscles of her arms as she fingered the strings and drew the bow across them was hypnotizing. Damn it. I was going to have to go jump in a snowbank or something. I stood up, suddenly conscious of how turned on I was, and decided it might be a good idea to let my cat out.

Saying nothing, because *Sorry, Sol, I can't stay and watch you play because it's making me want to tear all of your clothes off and I feel that would be disrespectful of both you and the music* wasn't high on my list of things to say to other humans (if I didn't already have permission to tear the clothes off of them periodically), I walked out the small wooden door that led to mountainside beyond and thought about being a snow leopard until it went from memory to reality.

Running over and around snow, rocks, trees, and the occasional cliff was exhilarating and refreshing in a way that nothing else was. I felt free, and truly myself as I never did as a human. It was as though all of the backpacking, trail running, and rock climbing I had ever done had all been a pathetic attempt to achieve the true freedom of being a giant, mountain-climbing cat. I may have let out a few celebratory yowls. Perhaps a feline barbaric yawp.

I didn't run for very long. Just enough to take care of some basic needs out of sight of the house and raise my respiratory rate a bit. I could cover so much ground in so little time in this form that I probably went for what my human form would have found to be a three hour hike, but I ran it in a handful of minutes. The terrain here was a bit gentler than a snow leopard was designed for and, as I headed back to the house, I suddenly had a very strong desire to travel to the Himalayas.

Ha! That was probably gonna have to wait.

I shifted back to my human form as I neared the tiny log cabin that was nestled on what was probably the only remotely level bit of mountainside for miles. I took a moment to once again appreciate that something about Gwen's transfer of power made it so that I was always appropriately clothed in my human form. I was now wearing a pair of fleece lined jeans over long underwear and a soft cashmere sweater with a down vest over it. It wasn't warm enough to linger on the mountainside for long, but it was perfect for the wood stove heated cabin, and adding a parka and some snow pants would make it a solid base for the Andes in springtime. I had no idea where the clothes had come from, but whoever had dressed me, I couldn't fault their taste.

Ignoring Edik's frozen form, doing my best not to look at his slightly anguished eyes, and feeling rather proud that I had managed to resist the urge to pee on him so far, I walked inside.

"Sorry," I said to Sol, as I walked to the wood stove and moved the still-full kettle onto one of the burners there. She still had her head bent over the bass. "Had to pee," I added.

She smiled and looked up from the bass, and when her yellow eyes caught mine my heart almost stopped.

"No worries, Gatita. You'd been asleep for a while."

Which reminded me of her earlier statement and distracted me from the heat spreading through my body simply from having locked eyes with her. What the hell was up with that? "You said I slept through some shouting?"

She nodded and, finishing the last bar of whatever melody she was playing, sheathed her bow in its holster on the side of the instrument and leaned the massive thing against the wall in the corner after collapsing the foot.

"Albert and Trevor were getting into it over something. Not sure what, though. I think it had to do with your parents."

Well, that was interesting.

"You didn't hear any details?" I asked. That seemed weird, if they had been shouting.

"I heard everything, but I couldn't understand most of it. Not sure what language it was, but it wasn't English or Spanish."

"Huh. Weird. Not sure what other language Trev speaks aside from Tibetan, but why would Albert speak Tibetan?"

"Hmmm… could have been Tibetan. I didn't think of that, but I should have, considering the file I was given on you before my assignment. I knew your mom's family was from Tibet. Anyway, it all started after they looked through that file you grabbed at MOME."

"Which is why you assume it was about my parents," I muttered, wondering what that file said. I hadn't had a chance to look at it since stealing it out of the office in MOME, due to subsequently getting shoved into a pitch black dungeon, then participating in a daring escape, then getting kidnapped, then escaping again, and then almost beating a vampire to death and collapsing in a pseudo-coma… it had been a busy two days.

Seemingly reading my thoughts, Sol picked up one of the brightly colored cushions on the couch nearest where she had been playing, then produced a manila folder from underneath it.

"Here," she said, handing it to me. "Thought you'd want to see it as soon as you could. Maybe figure out what the hell they were on about before they come back."

"Where did they go, anyway?"

"Not sure. I kicked them out when they were being too damned loud and I thought they might wake you up. Seamus went off to water some trees not long before you woke up. The other two haven't been gone an hour yet."

I nodded absently at her answer as I stared at the manila folder in front of me, hesitating to actually open it. Would it carry any answers about my parents' disappearance? Would it just confirm my newly budding suspicion that my parents were people I didn't really know?

I think that was my biggest fear, really. I'd already been shocked as hell to find out that I was a snow leopard, and that my parents were a part of the world in which that was a normal thing to be… and yet, they had never told me any of it. As cool as it was to find out you can turn into a giant, badass feline, I did feel marginally betrayed on that front… and I couldn't help but wonder if this folder would tell me a hundred more ways in which my parents weren't the people I'd always thought they were. Was that why Trevor and Albert had been yelling?

Oh well, sitting here staring at the damned thing wasn't going to get me anywhere, and wondering was worse than knowing one way or the other, that was for damned sure. So, I took a deep breath and flicked open the folder.

It took me a moment to adjust to the layout of the forms, as well as the fact that everything was in Spanish, but soon enough I was skimming the file efficiently enough to catch things that stood out. Probably the first thing that caught my eye was the fact that my last name was apparently NOT Marmot.

Ok. That really shouldn't have been too surprising considering what I now knew about my parents and their attempts to hide me from MOME, but… damn it. Was anything I "knew" about my life the truth? Ok. Fine. So, apparently my mom's last name was Milarepa… that was odd, that was a dude my mom used to tell stories about all the time when I was a kid but… ok… and now I was suddenly remembering a grandmother I'd completely forgotten about…. I could feel another headache coming on, and I wondered how much of my life had been erased by my parents' attempts to protect me.

Dad's last name had been McMarten. Boring. Still, according to our file here, my real last name was McMarten Milarepa. Well, bonus points to Mom for keeping her name, but that was a hell of a mouthful.

"I think I'll keep Marmot," I muttered, drawing a slight chuckle from the kitchen, where Sol had taken up the tea-making efforts I had abandoned after she'd distracted me with this manila bundle of angst.

Not liking the pressure that was building up beneath my temples, I shifted quickly to snow leopard and then back to human. It worked, much as it had when I'd first found out about Trev. I came back to my human form with a clearer mind and no pain.

Feeling a bit overwhelmed by the whole new last name thing, not to mention vivid images of a shriveled, tiny woman with white hair and fierce, glowing eyes, I decided to refocus my efforts on the rest of the file. The next gut punch was less personal, but still pretty sharp, and explained, in my mind, why Trev and Albert had been shouting.

"Well, shit," I muttered.

"What'd you find?" Sol asked.

"Albert used to work for MOME," I said.

"What? Why was that in your parent's file?"

"Because he was their instructor."

"Instructor for what?" she asked.

Before I could reply with the "fucked if I know" that rested on my tongue, we heard shouts just outside the door to the cabin.

We both rushed towards the door, but it burst open before we got there. Seamus stood outside, looking out of breath and wide-eyed.

"The fucking vampire is loose," he said, before collapsing to the floor.

HAVING QUICKLY DETERMINED that Seamus' maladies were likely altitude-based rather than injury-based, I left him to Sol's ministrations, rushing out through the door to discover Edik running faster than my eyes could easily track between the low trees and boulders that surrounded the cabin, dodging the spells that Albert was firing at him, and all the while shouting his innocence.

"I'm just searching for my daughter!" he cried, diving behind a large rock as yet another burst of… something nasty looking… shot from Albert's extended hands.

"Yes, yes. So you've said," Albert replied calmly, as though they were having a peaceful conversation in which Albert wasn't trying to kill him. "But we really can't have you running off to tell MOME where we are, can we? If you would just hold still. I'm only trying to restrain you."

Huh. Whatever Albert was flinging at Edik looked like it was meant to do more than restrain, but hell, what did I know? Maybe the fact that it obliterated rock didn't mean it would obliterate vampire… diamond skulls, and all that.

"MOME doesn't have Renata, so I don't have the slightest interest in helping them! You all know where she is! You must!"

He was forced to break in his pleading to dive behind yet another boulder, with Albert's spell missing him by mere inches.

I couldn't help but think that Albert was one to talk when it came to snitching us out to MOME, but as I had absolutely zero love for Edik, I didn't mention it. Trev sat on a rock nearby, seeming completely unconcerned with the proceedings.

Did you find out what Albert was teaching our parents? I asked, since Albert seemed to have Edik distracted. I was more concerned with the possible threat that Albert posed than whatever bullshit Edik was spewing this time.

Trev raised an eyebrow in an expression visible even from twenty feet away.

You know about that? he asked.

I was just reading their file before Lord Sparkle Fang started stirring up trouble.

Albert was training them much in the same way that MOME was training me these past few years. His insistence that it wasn't for nefarious purposes was what started the shouting match. Sorry if we woke you.

Does Albert speak Tibetan? I asked.

Yes. Which isn't reassuring.

Why not?

Because it's a bit of a coincidence isn't it? That he speaks Tibetan when almost no one does. It's not exactly a useful world language.

Does it have any magical uses? I asked.

Trev's face turned carefully neutral, which worried me.

It might, he said. And I wasn't sure if his hesitation was because he thought it unlikely, or because he knew more than he was willing to share.

Pretty sure I don't like you hiding shit from me, I thought to Trevor just as I stepped towards where Albert was slowly blasting away at the last boulder that Edik had disappeared behind.

"Is that not a waste of your energy?" I asked, looking between him and the large chunks of boulder that were cascading to the ground, even as Edik whimpered audibly on the other side.

"That depends on your definition of waste," Albert said, raising one side of his mouth in a decidedly non-cordial smirk. "Is it likely to help us capture him? No. Is it incredibly satisfying after years of putting up with his horse shite?"

He turned and continued to fire wave after wave of… whatever it was at the boulder and Edik.

It may make me a bad person, but I laughed. Edik really was an asshat, and after having dealt with him for less than a week I couldn't blame Albert for wanting to take potshots at him. I can't imagine how I would feel if I'd known him for years.

"Edik," I shouted, over the sounds of spells slamming into rock and sending bits crumbling to the ground. "If you'd like Albert to give up on this whole blowing you to tiny bits thing, you could just agree to be restrained and answer a few questions."

"How do I know you won't just try to kill me as soon as you have me restrained?" he shouted from behind the boulder, without showing himself.

"Maybe because we have better things to do with our time?" I suggested.

Albert scoffed. "I don't," he muttered.

"Ok, fine. Maybe because you were frozen out here for a day already and no one killed you yet."

"How do I know you won't kill me as soon as you have whatever information you want?"

I looked to Albert, and then to Trev.

"I guess you don't," I replied after a while. "But you know that Albert's perfectly willing to kill you if you do anything that makes him think you're not cooperating, so why not give cooperating a try and see if it makes him feel a bit less homicidal, or vampicidal, or whatever?"

Hmm… this whole fantasy world within my normal world was going to need a vocabulary adjustment.

"Is there a Latin root for vampire?" I muttered, to no one in particular, while Edik was silent on the other side of the rock.

"Fine. I'll talk."

Edik stepped out from behind the boulder, but before he'd even gotten a full step away from it Albert blasted him with a spell that sent him careening into the granite behind him.

"Oh. Terribly sorry. Must have slipped!" Albert almost sang, stepping forward to restrain a nearly unconscious Edik.

I couldn't decide if I wanted to laugh, or if I felt bad for Edik. If he'd been someone who hadn't just spent the past few nights terrorizing me in my own home, I would certainly have leaned towards the latter, but as it was…

"Oops," I said. "Well, Edik, you can hope that Albert has had his fun for the afternoon. In the meantime, we need to know what in the seven hells you're doing here."

As I spoke, Edik's form became wrapped in some creepy tendril things that must have been under Albert's control, because they certainly didn't seem to be making any effort to be gentle with their captive. Edik still looked disturbingly handsome, despite being covered in dirt and flecks of granite.

I kinda hated how he remained so aesthetically pleasing despite being such a complete and utter douchetart.

"I already told you. I am searching for my daughter," Edik grunted, as the vine-like things that held him tightened their grip unnecessarily.

"Right. And why on earth do you think we know where she is?" I asked.

"Because she disappeared from MOME on the day that you and your friends destroyed the place. You must know where everyone went!"

Huh… I turned to look at Trevor, who was still perched on a boulder a few meters behind us. It had been his plan, his friends, his nemesis. His escape route…

"I might have some idea where most of the younger MOME detainees were headed, but I have no idea if your daughter is among them, or whether she'll want to see you, if she is."

I smiled. I was glad that was out in the open. It was difficult to imagine anyone being happy to see Edik, even his own daughter. Especially his own daughter, if what the mysterious B had said about him the other day had been true. It seemed as though B and Renata had gone through quite a bit of trouble to get away from Edik in the first place, and I wasn't sure how I felt about helping him find her again. Maybe he was an abusive piece of trash. No, scratch that, he most definitely *was* an abusive piece of trash. The question was whether or not he was an abusive piece of trash with her.

"I'm her father," Edik pleaded.

"I don't care if you created her single-handedly from a piece of clay," I replied. "If she doesn't want to see you, that's it. We will make damned sure that she isn't subjected to your presence."

"But the law—"

"I don't give a flying fuck what the law says, Edik. MOME, human, whatever. No law that forces children into the presence of their abusers gets any support from me."

"I would never hurt her." Edik's tone was the most sincere I'd ever heard from him, but that didn't change the fact that someone who thought that personal boundaries didn't matter, just because he liked someone, probably didn't have a very healthy definition of "hurt."

"There's more than one way to hurt someone, Edik. If she doesn't want to see you, she won't see you. Period. If you can't accept that, then we aren't taking you anywhere near her."

Edik nodded, though the way the blood vessels in his neck were bulging didn't leave me feeling very confident about his willingness to comply. Whatever. I could flash Renata halfway across the world in the blink of an eye if I needed to.

"Whadya, think Trev? Should we take Mr. Sparkle Fang with us?"

Trev shrugged.

"I'd rather not, but… I suppose we probably shouldn't abandon him here in the wilderness, especially with MOME HQ only a few hours' hike away…"

I thought about that for a good minute before agreeing.

"Fine. Pack your shit."

SHIT STARTED TO go wrong the second we hit the streets of Unterberg, but I was too busy being blown away by the scenery to really take notice at first.

The place was like something out of every epic fantasy book I'd ever read. Buildings that resembled the secret love-children of Notre Dame Cathedral and a drippy sandcastle were everywhere, and the streets were crammed with creatures I'd only ever seen in my imagination, along with a few that I'd never run into even there. The whole place was surrounded by steep cliffs that rose into the sky, leaving only a small strip of blue visible above. It made me wonder if we were actually underground rather than just nestled into a canyon.

Sol and Albert had given us a brief rundown on the city before we left, but it hadn't come anywhere close to doing the place justice. They'd described it as a holdout for beings that MOME considered "too dangerous," along with anyone else that managed to piss MOME off, and, as it technically wasn't located on earth, MOME held no sway there. That, and they weren't allowed in the "door," as it were. This small dimensional pocket, which could be accessed from numerous places around the world, but was only about the size of New York City, was ruled by a committee of elected members, all of whom had an equal vote in determining the few laws they bothered to uphold, the most stringent of which was that MOME agents were not allowed within its perimeter for any reason. That was the bare bones explanation we got before we arrived, and it had made me stare at Sol quizzically before she'd shrugged and explained that her Abuela had worked out some sort of deal with Unterberg ages ago and her arrival wouldn't cause a stir.

Even as we wandered down a cobbled street packed with creatures of every description, and some that defied words, I was still unclear on how we'd gotten here, since we hadn't really used my powers to do it. I'd transported us to a sketchy-looking alleyway in La Paz that Sol had shown me photos of and described in detail, a shift that had tired me out substantially, since I'd moved so many of us to a place I'd never been before, and then Albert had used some spell or other to light up a brick wall, which we all then proceeded to walk through as if it were no more than a tepid waterfall. On the other side, we'd been instantly immersed in the busy crowds of a street unlike any I'd ever seen before. I wanted to spend a few months wandering these small, winding, cobbled streets, getting lost, asking strangers for directions, and making friends with some of the amazing people I saw.

I definitely did not want to start a fistfight in the middle of the street.

But guess which of those two things I was now doing?

Yep.

My luck is shit.

The hand that clamped itself across my mouth was cold and calloused, but I didn't wait to absorb any more details about it before I threw my elbow hard into the sternum of the person attached to it. It was a good thing my backpack was nearly empty, or whoever it was might have been out of reach of my elbow, but as it was, I'd only brought along my parents' MOME file and a few essentials, so I connected solidly with whoever had tried to grab me. My heel automatically stepped back on the instep of my attacker and I heard the person cry out before stumbling away from me.

This way, Trev thought at me, as I felt his hand grab mine, and before I could even figure out how Seamus and Sol were faring, or who we were even fighting, Trev and I were running through the densely crowded street, away from Seamus, Sol, Edik, and Albert, and towards… well, I had no idea.

Where are we going? I asked mentally, since I didn't have the breath for speech.

This telepathy thing was seriously handy.

I have no idea, Trev replied. *Just trying to lead those MOME asshats on a wild goose chase.*

Those were MOME agents? I was amazed that Trev had been able to tell who had attacked us at all, since I hadn't had a chance to get a look at anyone before we'd taken off running. *How could you even tell?*

I recognized the guy who grabbed you.

It sounded like Trev was leaving something out, but I didn't have time to press the issue as our mad dash through the streets seemed to be gaining us some attention, and not just from the three (yes, I'd managed one quick look over my shoulder to count) MOME agents chasing us.

Trev's plan, whatever it was, seemed to be working, and we had MOME hot on our tails, even as we ran past carts filled with fruits and vegetables, and a few hot dishes that smelled amazing. The crowd was slowing down the MOME agents, but they weren't giving up. Unfortunately, we also had a number of large, menacing creatures forming a tight line across the street ahead of us, with the rest of the pedestrians who had been filling the streets around us somehow disappearing from view.

Who are they?

Unterberg enforcers, Trev replied.

Friendly? I asked, even as I wondered how he knew anything about what was happening, since he'd claimed never to have been here before.

Not exactly.

Trev turned left so suddenly that I probably would have lost him if I hadn't spent the first eight years of my life running around with him. Ok fine, the fact that he was still holding my hand didn't hurt.

We snapped into a narrow alleyway between two of the palatial drizzle castles that passed for buildings in this city, complete with creepy-assed gargoyle things that stared at us from the crenelated wall that demarcated each property line. The alley didn't look like a dead end, so I assumed that Trev had planned for us to make our escape that way, although how he had any idea where said alley went was beyond me. His plans seemed unlikely to matter, though.

The alley was blocked by a cadre of more of the same menacing creatures that had created a blockade across the street we'd been running through earlier. Now that I had a moment to inspect them more closely, I saw that the creatures were identical masses of what appeared to be roughly shaped clay. They had been molded into more or less human forms, but without any regard for the details.

"Are those golems?" I asked aloud, since we had stopped cold just before we'd run headlong into the oddly shaped creatures that towered before us.

"More or less," Trev assented, still panting from our run.

"Are they going to kill us?" I asked, as the creatures stepped forward in disturbing unison.

Before he could answer, a shout from behind alerted us to the MOME agents careening around the corner of the alley, with their hands readied to throw who knew what at us. I was a heartbeat away from shifting us back to Sol's cabin, when something huge and rough clamped on my shoulder and everything went black.

"OUCH! FUCK. THAT was unnecessary."

I would have rubbed the sore spot on my ass where I'd just been dropped onto a rock-hard surface from golem shoulder height, but my hands were tied in front of me and I couldn't even see what I'd been dropped onto, thanks to the bag that had been tied over my head.

"As is your profanity," said a lilting voice, tinged with an accent I couldn't place.

"No more than your condescending tone and mistreatment of prisoners," I replied.

"Profanity is the mark of the uneducated," said another voice, this one harsher and with a thicker accent that I still couldn't place.

"Ok, Fuckface, tell that to my dad, who had two PhDs and cursed more than anyone I know."

That was followed by a rather drawn-out silence.

It might have been awkward if I'd been able to see, but as I still had a bag on my head…

"What? Too soon?" I snickered, knowing full well that no one here had any right to be more upset about references to my possibly dead father than I did.

I had started cursing way more after my parents had died. It wasn't like I'd started cursing more on purpose, but… I don't know. Maybe it was in memory of my dad, or maybe it was just because I was a bit prickly about becoming an orphan. Algernon had pointed it out a month or two ago, and I had realized he was right, but had made no attempt to correct it.

"Perhaps it should be a privilege earned by those with more experience," said the first voice.

"Perhaps you should keep your bullshit opinions to yourself and quit policing people's use of language so damned much. If you dislike my profanity to such a degree, perhaps you should remove yourself from my presence and return to whatever prudish origins begat you. Then your knavery might entertain those more inclined to partake in it, and the rest of us might be free of your stodgy presence."

"Or you could just fuck off," added Trev's voice, from somewhere nearby.

I couldn't help it, I chuckled.

"Damn it, Trev, I was trying to keep a straight face."

"Enough of this, remove their hoods," the first, more lilting, voice said.

And with that, I was doused in light, as the bag was pulled swiftly from my head. It took a few moments of blinking to bring the room into focus, but when it did, I let out a low whistle.

The entire floor appeared to be made of a dark marble, veined with silver and gold, polished to a high shine, and reflecting the light emanating from hundreds of glowing orbs that hovered at various heights around the ornately decorated walls, all the way up to the top of a vaulted ceiling that looked like the forgotten love child of a three-year-old's sandcastle and Notre Dame cathedral.

"Nice digs," I said, deciding to embrace the sass I'd been rocking so hard, even though I was clearly (now that I could fucking *see*) talking to the rulers of Unterberg. They were all seated around the most intense conference table ever built: a foot-thick marble slab over forty feet in diameter, which appeared to be engraved with glowing runes all around the edges. "Which one of you is compensating?"

That made Trev snort, and I took a moment to look over at him for the first time since we'd been dumped here. He was lying on his side, not having bothered to sit up yet, and he had four menacing looking golems standing directly behind him.

The room we had been dumped in was larger than a football field, but one curved wall was almost directly behind us, and a series of windows appeared to open onto a giant balustrade immediately behind the twenty or so people seated around the massive piece of rock. As impressive as the rock was, it was nothing compared to the array of people seated around it. A few of them looked like elves straight out of a video game, complete with skin tones taken directly from a tipped over Crayola box. Others looked like they might spend their free time lurking under bridges with clubs, while still others looked liked they'd hopped out of Hamilton's *Mythology*. A few more had fur, wings, and horns in arrangements that I would never have predicted, despite a lifetime of reading fantasy and mythology on the daily. One or two wore hooded capes that kept them hidden from sight. None of them looked particularly "human" from where I sat, but far be it from me to deny anyone that label if they want it, so they were all people until they asked me to call them something else.

This whole scene definitely would have qualified as intimidating twenty minutes ago—ok, if I was totally honest, it was still intimidating now—but… in for a penny, in for a pound. It would seem completely two-faced to start being polite at this point and, besides, getting snatched up by golems and dumped on my ass on a marble floor with my head wrapped up in a blanket and then talked down to wasn't exactly on my list of "ways to treat me that will earn my respect" so I was just going to hold my ground and hope that it didn't get us killed.

"You do not seem to understand who you are dealing with," said the first voice that had spoken to me, which I was now able to match to an extremely tall woman who could be described as… reedy. She was even a pleasant green color, with straw-yellow hair and ears that reached delicate points well above her head.

I interrupted her as she was taking a breath to continue.

"Well, my first guess was a World of Warcraft guild meeting, but, even though your ears might back up my initial impression, I'm guessing that you're actually the folks in charge of this little realm."

I could see a few people bristle at the claim that this was a little realm, but damn, people, I had been told it was the size of New York City. Even if it matched the population of New York City, it was still "little" in the grand scheme of things.

"Geographically little, I mean. I'm sure you guys are very big where it counts," I said, through the firmest smile I could manage.

"Vic, you are totally gonna get us killed," Trev chuckled, from his spot on the floor. If he really meant that, I wondered why he was laughing.

"Well, you're no help. You must know more about these folks than I do—any sage advice is quite welcome."

Neither of us bothered dropping our voices. These folks had home court advantage, and it seemed ridiculous to assume that they couldn't hear us, no matter what we did, so there was no point in pretending. If we'd really wanted privacy, we could have spoken telepathically, but Trev hadn't bothered with that since we'd arrived, so I assumed it was either a bad idea, or simply pointless.

"Can we get to the point already? We are wasting time."

That was from the second voice that had spoken when we'd had the hoods on, which I could now see emanated from a person who looked... well, like a minotaur. I mean, a pretty handsome minotaur if such a thing were possible, but he totally had a massive, fur-covered upper body that looked quite muscular, as well as mostly human, although it was definitely holding up a bull's head, or something kind of like a bull's head. Definitely sporting a snout and horns at any rate. Kinda reinforced the whole World of Warcraft vibe, if I was being totally honest. I looked around briefly to see if anyone had snakes for hair, but no one seemed to.

"Yes, please," I replied, once I'd wrapped my mind around addressing a minotaur, "getting to the point would be great. I like you, sir. What's your name?"

Everyone just stared at me for a moment, and then the minotaur, or whatever he was, grunted.

"Torrence."

"Seriously?"

He glared at me.

"Okay... well, Torrence, let's get to the Gwendamned point, shall we? Why have you brought us here?"

"You have brought MOME agents into our inner sanctum and you DARE question why we have brought you here?"

"We didn't bring any MOME agents wi—"

"Silence!" That was the elf lady with the seriously long ears, and she must have put a little something extra behind the words, because my mouth slammed shut before I could even think about it.

"MOME agents arrived here at the same instant you did. Whether they were chasing you or helping you is none of our concern. They are here because of you, and their presence is even less welcome than yours."

"So, the fact that we were doing everything we could to avoid MOME counts for nothing? It's all about consequences, and intentions be damned?"

"The road to hell is—"

"Oh please, don't cliche us to death. Is that the punishment for bringing MOME agents here? What's next? Pun-nishment?" I waited a beat, and Trev was kind enough to fill in with a verbal drumroll. The rest of the room was silent.

"Tough crowd. Look, we didn't mean to bring MOME here. We will happily do all we can to help you rid yourselves of MOME in exchange for some help tracking down a friend of ours and—"

"You are in no position to negotiate," said the minotaur.

"Torrence, I thought we were friends. Look, I don't—"

"As it is your first offense," Elf Lady continued, as if I had never spoken, "you are sentenced to ten years imprisonment in the dungeon of Regnadevarg, with an option for parole at three and six years if you behave—"

"You will releasssse them to me."

My head snapped to the nearest archway in time to see Rhelia, in all her ebon-skinned, reptilian-eyed glory waltz through it, as though no one would dare stop her. Since she was a good head shorter than I was, I found that particularly impressive. I couldn't help but notice the way Trev's eyes lit up when she walked into the room, and I made a mental note to ask him about it later.

"Lady Rhelia, this sentencing hearing is not open to the public. As you are not a family member of the accused, you must—"

"He issss my *mate*," Rhelia said, pointing a regal finger at none other than my twin brother.

"WELL, THIS IS awkward," I said into the absolute silence that greeted that announcement. It had gone on long enough to make me wonder what kind of crazy taboo there was against Rhelia dating my brother. However, as I took in the shocked look that Trevor was working hard to hide, I decided that there was more going on here than Rhelia announcing that she and Trev were an item.

"I'm assuming that means she wins?"

I looked between Rhelia, Trev, and the twenty or so flabbergasted people who ran Unterberg.

Once again ignoring me as though I weren't even there, Elf Lady spoke directly to Rhelia.

"We cannot hold a dragon's kin without their express permission," she said, and then she turned to Trev. "Do you consent to being held in the dungeon of Regnadevarg?"

Trev cleared his throat briefly, and looked like he was trying very hard not to look at Rhelia.

"I do not."

Then Elf Lady turned to me, and I had to assume that if Trev was somehow Rhelia's family, that made me family by extension, because she repeated the question.

"I do not," I replied.

"Then you are free to leave, under the protection of your dragon kin."

Trev stood up, and I moved to where he and Rhelia were now holding hands close to the door.

"Know that if you are ever found here without the protection of your dragon kin, your stay of sentencing will be revoked and—"

Rhelia whipped around to snarl at the woman, who was not only twice her height, but had the command of a massive golem army, "He issss my *mate*, Nethia. Not even death will ssssever that bond. You have no hold over *my* family!"

Nethia (up to now known as Elf Lady) fell silent, and the rest of the room began to murmur quietly.

Rhelia turned on her heel again, marching from the room. Trev and I hurried to follow.

Dare I ask what the fuck just happened? I sent to Trev.

"I will explain it shortly, Living Cat."

"Damn. I really need to work on not broadcasting to the whole damned room."

"Yessss, you do. But even sssstill you cannot hide your thoughtssss from me."

"Well, that's discouraging," I muttered.

"It's kind of her specialty, Vic."

Trev sounded like he was trying to make me feel better, and I snuck a glance at him to find him grinning from ear to ear.

"You don't seem upset about this turn of events."

"We just got out of a ten year prison sentence. What's to be upset about?"

"Nothing, but… were we seriously in danger of going to prison, just for showing up here with some asshats following us?"

It was Rhelia who answered, and I couldn't help but notice that she seemed unable to repress a smile of her own.

"For leading MOME officers through a hidden seam into Unterberg, the council would gladly have killed you, if they thought you'd done it on purpose. As it is, a ten year sentence was relatively light, considering how many MOME agents are still unaccounted for on the streets here now. Plus, your sentence would have had the bonus of luring the MOME agents to Regnadevarg, the most defensible hold in the entire city. The council will be… disappointed that they were forced to let you go. I imagine they will be contacting my Matriarch immediately to ensure that I am not lying."

"I'm not sure that explanation made any sense to me, but if they thought you were lying, why wouldn't they just confront you about it right there, while they still had us?"

Rhelia's smile only grew.

"It will take very careful wording to confirm the truth with my Matriarch without starting a diplomatic incident, as it is. They could never have confronted me openly without risking war with the dragons."

"I have definitely missed a few key details," I mumbled.

"Worry not, Living Cat. You are a dragon ssssissssster now, you will learn all that you need to learn in good time."

I looked hopelessly between Rhelia and Trev.

"Well, at least this answers my question about whether or not Rhelia was the girlfriend you were talking about," I said.

That only made Rhelia and Trev laugh so loudly that the walls almost shook, as we descended an ornately decorated staircase that covered the distance from whatever they called the drizzle palace that housed the council into an open square full of people, pigeons, and…

"Fuck. MOME agents," Trev muttered, just before bursting into flames.

OF COURSE, WHEN Trev bursts into flames it's not as disconcerting as it would be if someone else were to do it. After all, when someone spends half of their time as a flaming bird anyway, random combustion is par for the course. But that didn't mean I was used to it. Still, surprising as it might have been, it was nothing compared to seeing Rhelia become a dragon large enough to fill the entire square.

I tried to shout "holy fuck!" but the words were swallowed as I was dragged involuntarily into my snow leopard form. I didn't waste time being pissed about it, because I was too busy trying to figure out where the dragon ended and the bad guys began, so I could whoop a little bit of MOME ass. As it happened though, Trev and I were surrounded by ebon scales that shone with the same silvery iridescence that coated Rhelia's skin, and I couldn't find a single gap between us and the bad guys.

Of course, Trev, in his fiery, winged form, wasn't hampered by the circle of serpent that enclosed us. He just shot into the sky straight above us and started circling.

Do not engage, little onessss, Rhelia's voice spoke directly into my (and I assumed Trevor's) mind, even as I was trying to gain purchase on her scales in order to launch myself over the heap of dragon tail that lay between me and the MOME agents.

What's up with the overprotective act? I asked Trev, who was now diving for a patch of cobbled square next to me, as a streak of some nasty-looking spell flew through the air he'd occupied only a moment earlier.

There are some rules of dragonkind that make it very tricky for us to fight MOME now that Rhelia has declared us kin, Trev replied, as he landed beside me.

So why'd you shift to phoenix and start calling attention to yourself? I asked, genuinely curious.

Well, now that they've very clearly shot at me, in full view of witnesses, Rhelia can claim she was defending her kin if it ever comes up. They violated the treaty first, so her Matriarch will be forced to acknowledge that she was provoked.

I decided that dragon politics were complicated and that I'd ask more questions later, then tried to focus on what was going on in the square outside of our little circle of serpent. Unfortunately, I couldn't see shit, and all I could hear was what sounded like a jet engine roaring to life periodically, and a few truly agonized screams.

A few moments later the smell of barbecue filled the square, and I tried not to retch as my brain attached the meaning of burning meat smell to the sudden quiet that now surrounded us, and its significance.

"Umm… I think I might throw up," I muttered, not even noticing that I'd returned to human form, along with Trev and Rhelia beside me. I closed my eyes before I could take in the heinous scene that I was sure was waiting for me, and swallowed hard.

"You are so weak of constitution, Living Cat? Do you think the agents of MOME would have spared you from an equally gruesome fate?"

I expected the next breath I took to be laced with an even more disconcerting smell of charred meat, but when it instead came with the smell of crisp, clean air, I decided to risk opening my eyes. There was a giant scorch mark before us, but there was no trace of flesh left, only a few tiny wisps of ash that were already blowing away on the wind.

"Well, that was cleaner than I expected," I said, as the churning that my stomach had been doing earlier was replaced with a leaden feeling instead. The MOME agents were still deader than dead, and I wasn't entirely sure how I felt about that, even though Rhelia was probably right about the fate they had planned for me, but at least I wasn't staring at barbecued human. I supposed the one whiff I'd caught of charring flesh was just what the wind had still carried from the instant in which the deed had been done.

Rhelia stared at me for a moment, as though she were trying to decide whether or not she should be insulted, so I tried to compose my features.

"Look," I said. "I don't think you're monstrous for destroying the people who were attacking someone you love. I just… I'm not used to killing people, and I was expecting to see charred human remains everywhere, so… forgive me if it takes me some time to adjust. And… I can't promise I'll ever be ok with the whole killing people thing, even if they deserve it. It's just… really final."

To my shock, Rhelia smiled, wrapping me in an embrace.

"You will make an exsssscellent dragon," she said, delivering a quick kiss on my cheek before letting me go.

Since I had no idea what *that* meant, I decided to change the subject.

"So, how do we find everyone else?"

Rhelia smiled. "Follow me."

I'M NOT SURE what I'd expected when Rhelia had told us to follow her, then strode purposefully through the large cobbled square that she'd just left half-scorched and drifting in the ash of immolated MOME agents, but her leading us to a meticulously maintained, topiary filled garden that took up as much space as the palace behind us, walking into the center of what appeared to be a solid tree larger than even the biggest sequoia I'd ever seen photos of, and disappearing save for a single ebon-skinned hand that reached out and beckoned us to follow, was not it.

I didn't even have time to take in the details of the green space that surrounded us before Trev pushed me forward and I was stumbling, reaching for Rhelia's hand out of a desperate wish not to fall, more than anything else. Her slender fingers caught mine with a strength that seemed far beyond their scope, supporting me without even dipping under my sudden weight. Trev followed close behind, with a hand still on my shoulder, and I wondered if we were really standing in the middle of a tree, or if we were just in some dark space that could have been anywhere. The faint glow from Rhelia's skin was the only light in the space, but it did nothing to illuminate whatever surrounded us, only made her faintly visible in the darkness and made me able to see my own hand in hers.

Before I could ask where we were, or what we were doing, Rhelia made a strange hissing sound that resembled no language that I had ever heard before, then moved her hands as if she were parting an invisible curtain.

Only, suddenly, the curtain wasn't invisible, it was a giant, shimmering, shuddering thing, like aurora borealis in a tangible form, and she was parting it, and Trev was pushing me while Rhelia pulled me with her other hand and… then it was all gone, and we were standing in the middle of a green meadow dotted with wildflowers, surrounded by snowcapped peaks.

"Where in the seven hells—" I was cut off by a great shadow eclipsing the sun, as a dragon's head filled my vision so completely that I thought the entire sky had been swallowed.

"Child, what in the realms have you done?" The dragon's head—presumably attached to a body, but I couldn't see that far—asked, blinking a reptilian eye so large it could easily have been the moon.

"I thought we were agreed that I wassss no longer a child, Vereneth," Rhelia said, from where she stood next to me.

"I thought so as well, but you have brought strangers into this realm twice today, and I can sense that these two carry something more ominous with them than the mere status of refugees." The dragon sniffed as it spoke.

Its giant slitted nostrils, curving at the top of its enormous snout, flared and smoked, as a second set of eyelids—perpendicular to the first set I'd noticed—opened and closed twice. I tried to take in more details of the giant creature, since I hadn't been able to see most of Rhelia properly the one time that she had shown her dragon form in front of me, but I could barely process what I was seeing I was so awed by its massive eye and cavernous mouth—which contained a deadly array of teeth so large they might as well have been marble columns. It had horns that rose from its head, twisting and curving like the most enormous junipers I'd ever seen. They were similarly silvered, and, indeed, the dragon itself was a deep bronze color, like a mix of aged wood and burnished metal.

"Thesssse two aren't refugeessss, they are dragon kin," Rhelia replied, her chin held high in defiance.

The giant serpent before us turned away and released a gout of flame so hot, I felt my eyebrows singe away, even from a distance of a hundred feet from where it had released its ire.

"That will take some explaining," it said tersely, when it turned back to us. I wondered briefly if I'd soiled myself. I'd certainly felt scared enough, but I must have been dehydrated and underfed, because my pants appeared to be dry.

"Then let ussss meet with the elderssss sssso I do not need to repeat mysssself," Rhelia replied.

~~~

If Vereneth had made me want to wet myself, the circle of elders made me wish I'd never been born. I didn't know if the dragons had some enchantment on them that induced fear in all who viewed them, or if it was just my body's natural reaction to being confronted with a predator that so clearly outmatched me, but I found it difficult to look any of them in the eye, or even stare directly at them for long. The only thing that allowed me to see more than an eyeball of any of the behemoths was my vantage point atop a giant column, or maybe it was a tiny but very tall plateau, it was difficult to say. At any rate, I was at least a hundred feet up on a natural platform, along with Trev and Rhelia, and we were surrounded by about thirty dragons, each the size of a cruise liner, a few of them larger than shipping freighters. I had asked where Sol, Seamus, Albert and the refugees were, as we'd made our way to… whatever this column thing was, but I'd only gotten a few vague assurances that they were nearby and safe before I'd been distracted by the most terrifying sight of my life.

I hated myself for the fear that coursed through my body, because I had always considered myself a dragon person. I mean… every time I read a fantasy book, I hoped there would be dragons in it. And if there were dragons, I wanted them to be good guys, or at least neutral. I hated the stories in which dragons were unthinking menaces. If a fantasy author wanted my money, then dragons needed to at least be thoughtful and compelling villains. Books in which humans and dragons worked together were my favorite, although I wasn't overly fond of the ones where humans treated dragons like horses. I'd never been particularly keen on the idea of dragons being tame and loyal beasts. It seemed unlikely that an apex predator could ever find humans useful enough for that to be a good deal.

So, the fact that I was nearly pissing myself just looking at these creatures made me feel like the world's biggest fraud. After a childhood of imagining how cool it would be to meet a real dragon, back when I was still convinced they existed, my response now made my cheeks warm with humiliation. I mean sure, they were giant and imposing creatures that could kill me with a single bite, or perhaps even an accidental sneeze, but they were clearly beings who could be reasoned with. So there was no need for me to be standing atop a tower of rock shaking like a reed in a strong wind.

"You can sssstop your glamorsssss," Rhelia, still in human form, called out from her perch beside me.
~~~

My head snapped to attention. The thirty behemoths that formed a giant circle around us all grumbled.

"You would dare to frighten my family ssssoooo, without causssse?" Rhelia asked. The grumbling cut off abruptly, replaced by a silence that sounded like it might break with bloodshed.

"Your family?" a thunderous voice from directly across the circle boomed. It came from a dragon covered from snout to tail in glinting silver scales.

Rhelia inclined her head deferentially for a moment before replying.

"Trevor Marmot issss my mate, and hissss ssssissssster issss therefore my ssssissssster."

The uproar that followed that announcement made me long for the silence that had greeted her last statement, but I noticed that the fear that had encompassed me earlier had fled. I was able to stand at my full height and look every one of those giants in the eye.

"Were they enchanting me to fear them?" I asked Trev, over my shoulder.

"Not just you, I was about to poop my pants," Trev admitted, in a stage whisper.

I would have laughed, but Rhelia looked like she was about to go hulk on someone's ass, and I didn't want to miss the show.

"You dare quessssstion my choicssssse of mate?" She didn't shout, but her voice thundered from where we stood atop the raised bit of earth that held us, and I wondered if she was magnifying it magically, or if it was simply the acoustics of where we stood. Regardless, all thirty of the voices that had been grumbling in unison now quieted.

"Rhelia, you are young to make such a choice at all, and… a human? Do you wish to spend so much of your existence alone?"

That was a different dragon, one covered in scales of jade, but almost as large as the silver behemoth that had spoken earlier.

"Not a mere human, a phoenixssssss. And if I am old enough to rissssk my life for our realm, then I am old enough to choossssse whom to sssspend that life with."

"So… you guys are more than just dating, huh?" I asked Trev, out of the corner of my mouth. Communicating telepathically seemed like a terrible idea, since Rhelia could always hear me and I had no idea whether her fellow dragons shared that ability or not. They might easily hear us where we were, but I was tired of not knowing what was going on, and if thirty dragons were about to decide to kill me, I wanted to know why.

Trev chuckled, but it was Rhelia who replied.

"Sssssissssster, I will exssssplain all of the dragon cusssstomssss that you musssst know ssssoon enough, but know that dragonssss mate for life, and we live a *very* long time."

"Yikes," I muttered. "No shopping around first?"

Rhelia smiled, turning to face me fully. I was once again entranced by the way her ebon skin and iridescent sheen caught the light of the sun.

"We are allowed to 'shop around,' assss you ssssay, and often we live our whole livessss without choosssssing a mate, but when we find ssssomeone worthy, we treasssssure it beyond all thingssss."

"Sounds stifling," I quipped.

"No one ssssaid we cannot have loverssss," she replied, smirking before turning back to the elders that encircled us.

I stared at Trev for a moment, but he just shook his head at me and wrapped his fingers in Rhelia's.

Ok. Score one for the dragons. Boy, did I have a million questions about how their society worked. In particular, why it was such a big deal to pick a mate if you could still be polyamorous?

It's mostly about having kids, Trev sent to me.

Well, that just launched a thousand other questions.

"You have served us well, Rhelia, and we appreciate all that you have done for this realm, which is why we would hate to see you squander your-self with a human who can do so little to serve your family," said the silver dragon.

"You act assss though the deed issss not already done," Rhelia said.

I was about to snickeringly ask if "the deed" was what I thought it was (because, yeah, sometimes I have the sense of humor of a twelve-year-old), but then Rhelia slid into her enormous serpentine self, and Trev went with her, transforming into his phoenix form. Both of them launched skyward, leaving me behind on the earthen pedestal as they careened through the sky, dancing together in an intricate pattern that brought tears to my eyes. Trev seemed somehow magnified by the dance, and his phoenix form loomed larger than I had ever seen it, until he appeared to almost match the size of Rhelia in all her ebon-scaled, iridescent glory. They twined round each other, weaving in and out of patterns that looked as though they'd been rehearsed for hundreds of years. If I hadn't known that Trev was exactly as old as I was (give or take a few minutes), I would have thought them ancient partners.

Apparently, I wasn't the only one. When they landed, the surrounding dragons made a low, resonant sound that felt like it was going to reduce the pillar we stood on to dust. Since Rhelia and Trev returned to their human forms and bowed, I took that sound to signify approval.

"Come," Rhelia said, nodding at Trev and me. "Let them prepare the fessssstivitiesssss. There issss much to exssssplain."

I nodded and followed, wondering how much stranger my life could possibly get.

~~~

The answer was a fair bit.

Rhelia spent the next few hours explaining to me the various intricacies of dragon culture, most of which, I won't lie, I didn't fully understand. There was a crazy hierarchy that sounded like it would take years to fully comprehend, and all the cultural subtleties seemed to stem from that hierarchy. The key points were mainly that Rhelia had saved our asses in Unterberg by declaring Trev her mate, because it meant that the Unterberg rulers couldn't touch us thanks to a treaty struck long ago between the dragons and Unterberg. They couldn't touch us because Trev being Rhelia's mate made us dragonkin.

I thought that title was purely superficial when Rhelia first explained it. Like, we were in-laws and it would be a political disaster to mess with us. Rhelia hinted that there was more to it than that, but she said that she couldn't explain what until after the ceremony.

"What ceremony?"

"Your induction," she said.

"*My* induction? What do I have to do with any of this?"

"You are my ssssissssster now. And, assss you are not of age by dragon ssssstandardssss and you have no parentssss, you will need a guardian. Luckily, an older sssssisssster issss allowed to be a guardian if she issss of her majority."

"Umm… what do you mean, I'm not of age? How old do I have to be, to not be under your guardianship? And what the hells does that even mean?"

"You musssst be one hundred yearssss old to reach your majority in the dragon realmssss."

"Seriously? Wait. How old are you?"

"One hundred and sssseven," she replied, placidly.
~~~

"Does Trev know?" I asked, before I could stop myself. She laughed.

"Yessss. He issss not concerned. If I were a human, I would only be a teenager, that issss why my human form lookssss the way it doessss. Dragonssss live a *very* long time."

I nodded and shut my mouth. I mean hey, if Trev knew and was cool with it, then… well, Rhelia seemed like a badass to me. It's not like she was anyone's grandmother.

"So do dragons live to be a thousand, then?" I asked, doing some math and rounding up.

Rhelia laughed.

"No, dragonssss lowered the age of majority after the influxssss of dragon shifterssss during the purgessss on earth. The age of majority ussssed to be five hundred, but with dragon shifterssss not living quite assss long assss full dragonssss, the age was moved to 100."

"So dragon shifters live to be a thousand?"

"Ssssometimessss two thoussssand, it variessss."

"And full dragons?"

She shrugged.

"The oldesssst are… *very* old."

I made myself close my mouth.

"Right, ok. So, were they right about you dooming yourself to a life of loneliness after Trev dies?"

She sighed and shook her head.

"For reassssonssss that are too numeroussss to lisssst at the moment, we think it likely that Trev might outlive *me*, but regardlessss of that, I wouldn't have chosssssen differently. He *issss* my mate."

"You make it sound like it's just a part of who he is, like it's not a choice."

Rhelia sighed and started unbuttoning the silky shirt she was wearing. I considered objecting, but for one thing, I'd already learned that shifters were way less restrained about nudity than most people, and for another, I doubted that Rhelia was just stripping in front of me for funzies.

When she got halfway down her shirt, she pulled the collar open and exposed her chest from the sternum up. Spread across it was the most beautiful tattoo I'd ever seen. In a bright, sparkling white that contrasted starkly with the ebon shade of her skin, the outline of a phoenix in full flame glowed like starlight. It was so entrancing that I began to think it was moving.

"Isn't it considered bad form to get a tattoo of your significant other?" I asked, despite how awed I was by the beauty of the mark.

To my surprise, she laughed.

"It issss not a tattoo. I have carried thissss mark ssssince birth."

"Umm… that's one hell of a birthmark."

"A sssseeer attendssss the birth or hatching of every dragonling, ssssome-timessss they name a child, ssssometimessss they lay a mark upon them, sss-sometimessss they do nothing at all. Thissss issss the mark I wassss given momentssss after I wassss born."

I sighed, not knowing what I was supposed to say, or even believe, for that matter. That Rhelia and my brother were somehow fated for each other? I'd never bought into that concept. I even struggled to swallow the idea when it was wrapped up in a fairy tale or fantasy novel.

"It's beautiful," I said, because that much was true.

"You do not believe in fate?" Rhelia asked, after a long and awkward pause.

I shook my head.

"Good," she said, stunning me enough to make me meet her eyes again. "Neither do I. I do not think that thissss mark meanssss that I *have* to love your brother, or that we have no choicsssse but to be together… but when I met him, it felt like a missssing part of my ssssoul returned to me, and I only later learned that he wassss a phoenixssss."

I could read the embarrassment in Rhelia's face, like all this talk of love made her feel childish. So, I decided to woman up.

"Rhelia, if you love my brother and want to be with him forever, you don't have to justify it to me. And whether it's fate, or just a weird cosmic coinci-dence, or even just a really solid gimmick to get my brother to join some weird cult, you have my blessing."

I paused for a second, and Rhelia just stared at me.

"Ok. Fine, you don't have my blessing if this is just a ploy to get him to join some weird cult."

She finally laughed.

"I'm all for Trev loving a dragon." I continued. "I mean, so far you seem like a badass and, more importantly, from what I can tell, you're a good person. You saved a whole bunch of children and found a place for them here in your secret realm that no one is ever allowed to enter, *and* you love my twin brother, which shows that you have excellent taste in humans."

When she still didn't say anything I added, "Look, it's not like you two need my approval or anything, but for what it's worth, you have it. Now tell me what the hell it means that I have to be your ward until I'm a hundred."

And so she did.

The short version? After a ceremony in which I would swear loyalty to the dragon realm before all others, I would become official dragonkin, and after that I would get to find out all kinds of cool things about the dragons. Then Rhelia would be responsible for me, and if I fucked up at all it would be her fault, as far as all the dragons were concerned. I didn't like the idea of shucking responsibility that way, but she said we didn't have much choice in the matter, and she trusted me not to do anything that might get her banished or killed. Then she gave me a rundown on the things that might do that. The biggest ones were revealing the secrets of how to enter the dragon realm to an outsider, or somehow contributing to the death of a dragon. After that, I was given a basic breakdown on dragon history. It was long and boring and by the end of it my brain hurt. The highlights? MOME treated the dragons just as poorly as they treated everyone else, if not worse. Luckily, dragons have always been good seekers (which I learned was the name for folks who could sense seams—seams, of course, being the interdimensional pockets that let someone get from say, a back alley in La Paz to a hidden kingdom the size of Manhattan or, say, a realm filled entirely with big-assed mountains, fresh air, dragons, and dragonkin).

Before I really felt like I had a solid understanding of… well, anything (and wasn't that just par for the course these days?), I was being ushered out of Rhelia's cave-like, though well furnished, dwelling, and led to the ceremony.

THE VIEW FROM the top of the pillar this time was both less and more intimidating. It was less intimidating in that it looked kind of like a party. That is, if a party consisted of a thousand dragons of all shapes, sizes, and colors, scrambling all around the elder circles making as much noise as a hundred freight trains, and doing everything from slumbering peacefully to flitting about the sky like overexcited bats. Many were decorated with bright jewels and feathers.

I was still wearing jeans and a T-shirt, but had been crammed into an ornate feathered headdress that I was convinced was a rather elaborate prank that Rhelia was pulling on me, which she would spend the next hundred years laughing about.

If I lived that long.

Ok. I was probably overreacting. No one had said anything about the dragonkin ceremony being potentially dangerous. I didn't *think* that the elders would eat me if I messed up somehow, but Rhelia had cautioned me to "Be ssssure that you mean the wordssss of the oath when you ssssay them." In addition to that, I was told, just before Rhelia flew me up to the top of the pillar, that there would be a test of some kind.

"Do not worry, Living Cat," she had reassured me. "I am ssssure that you will do very well."

That was scant reassurance when it was the first I'd heard of any kind of test and it was approximately ninety seconds before said test was scheduled to happen.

I thought over the words in the oath that Rhelia had helped me memorize, not an hour earlier, and thought about whether or not I meant them. I thought I did, but honestly, I'd only been introduced to the dragon realm a few hours ago. What if the whole lot turned out to be a band of deranged miscreants who only sought power over the other realms, or wanted to sacrifice virgins at every full moon, or some such shit? I mean, nothing I'd seen so far made me think that was likely, but whatever, I hadn't pegged Edik as a vampire stalker the first time I'd met him either. Evil lurked behind surprising corners.

I supposed I would just have to trust that Trev's judgment in partners was sound, and that the culture that had created my brother's life mate was a good one.

Fingers crossed.

"Victoria Marmot," boomed one of the thunderous voices that had addressed Rhelia earlier, when she had been declaring her mating to Trev, "are you prepared to pledge your loyalty to the Realm of Dragons?"

"I am," I replied, hoping desperately that I would remember all the words to the oath, and not fuck it up.

"Then you may begin," the voice called, across the now hushing crowd of dragons below me.

"In solemn bond with the blood of wings and serpents, I profess my loyalty to the Realm of Fang and Claw. I swear never to betray its people or its place. I swear to protect my people and my home with everything that I am."

As I said the words, I felt the air around me warm, and a buzz, like the hum just before lightning strikes, enveloped me. I was getting ready to leap from my perch, sure that a freak weather event was about to wipe me out, when the hum ceased abruptly and I was plunged instantly into darkness.

"What the fuck? Why can't I see?" I muttered into the void. I could still feel earth beneath my feet, but I could no longer hear the sounds of the dragon crowd that had filled the circle below me, nor could I see anything, not even my own hand when I raised it up to wave in front of my face.

"Hello? No one told me that going blind was going to be part of the ceremony."

I heard nothing save my own voice, but I… felt?… laughter.

"Who's there?" I asked, hoping I wasn't about to join the ranks of people who say those words just prior to dying horribly.

No one is here, Living Cat, said a voice in the darkness, which I could tell wasn't Rhelia's even though it had used her nickname for me.

"Great. Am I going to be stuck with that name forever because of Rhelia's crap sense of humor?" I asked.

I do not think it is such a 'crap' name, as you call it. It is both amusing and accurate. You should treasure it. Good names are difficult to come by. Besides, the name you use is not your true name, and we need a true name to call you by.

I snorted, not impressed, but I supposed it could have been worse.

"At least it's accurate and not insulting."

Indeed, replied the voice in my head, "sounding" amused. I suppose it was more that I felt its amusement, as though it shed some of its emotion to me, but it certainly didn't "sound" amused, since it didn't sound at all.

"May I ask who I'm speaking to?"

You may ask. Does the answer matter? Do you know who any of us are by name?

"Fair point. How about sending along an image of what you look like? My guess would be that I saw you earlier today at the elder's council."

Smart cat, the voice replied. And then my mind was filled with the image of a behemoth of a dragon, not quite as large as the gold and silver dragon that had questioned Rhelia, but only slightly smaller, and with scales of a brilliant indigo hue.

"You have beautiful scales," I said, without thinking, then hastily added, "I don't know if your culture values physical beauty or not, or what a dragon would find beautiful if it does, but… I really like that shade of blue."

Thank you, child. I am pleased that my colors please you.

I took a deep breath and let it out. It occurred to me in that moment that it had been a bit insane to agree to go through this ceremony in a culture that I knew almost nothing about. Oh well. It was a bit late for cold feet at this point.

"Is this the test?" I asked, when only silence followed the dragon's last statement.

Mmm… it might be. What do you think?

"If it is, I have no idea what I'm being tested on, but then again, since I was only made aware that there even was a test a few seconds before I came up here, that's not saying much."

Tell me, Living Cat, what you see in the darkness.

I refrained from saying that it was a stupid question. I also refrained from making a comment about dramatics, fantasy novels, and plot twists that were driven by surprise tests and challenges. Gwen wasn't here, and she was my narrator, the one I expected to appreciate literary criticisms of my own story. So I swallowed my glib remarks. I saw nothing in the darkness. That was the thing about darkness, wasn't it? It doesn't show you much.

But then, slowly, as though someone were approaching with candle from over a mile away on a moonless night, something began to take shape.

It took me a very long moment to figure out what I was seeing, but when I did, it filled me with the warm fuzzies, almost literally. As though arriving from far away, I began to make out the shape of a snow leopard coming into focus. It was difficult to tell from this distance, especially considering how few times I had actually seen it, but something about it felt instinctually familiar.

"That's my snow leopard form," I said, before I even had time to question the notion myself.

Indeed? Excellent. Now if you'll just—

But the voice was cut off by my gasp, as something much larger approached behind the furry figure, a form that I felt such a deep familiarity with, even though I'd only had a week or so to get to know it.

What is it, child? What do you see?

If I had known what the test was supposed to be about, or how anything in this new world I'd been dumped into was supposed to work, I might have kept my next words to myself, but as it was, I was too awed, and far too unsuspecting, to hold my tongue.

"I… it's… I think it's a dragon. I mean, it's a small one, judging by all the ones I've seen today, but… it's got wings, a long slender body like a snake's, a head… a head kind of like a horse's but with giant horns, covered in scales, and it's… it's all silver. It looks as if it should be embroidered onto a kimono."

The voice was silent for a long time.

Do you see anything else? it eventually asked.

I waited, but nothing else appeared behind the dragon, which swirled peacefully in the darkness above and behind the more familiar snow leopard. I had never seen the dragon before, but something about it felt incredibly comfortable—known, the same way the snow leopard felt to me even though I'd only ever *seen* it once in the mirror and otherwise had been too busy dodging people trying to kill me to get a good look at the form itself. Besides that, there was nothing in the darkness, save a tiny ball of light far in the distance.

How intriguing, the voice said, after I explained that I only saw those two forms and the ball of light. *Let us return.*

And with that, I was surrounded once more by light and sound, and saw the crowd of dragons waiting with quiet anticipation as I blinked away the darkness.

The same voice that had sounded in my head now sounded out loud to the entire crowd.

"The Living Cat has looked into the darkness and seen the light, she has said her oath true, and she has been granted the finding of seams. She will forever be called dragonkin and shall enjoy a true drago—"

I didn't hear what followed, because at that moment a familiar hand grabbed my wrist.

"Seriously, Gwen?" I said, glaring at her. "Now is not a good time."

"Seamus and Sol need you," she said, before she pulled me through time and space.

I HAD *THOUGHT* that Seamus and Sol were safely tucked away in the dragon realm. That's where I'd expected to find them when I'd asked where they were and Rhelia had replied that we should follow her. And then the first dragon that had confronted us had straight up talked about the refugees that Rhelia had brought through earlier. I had assumed Sol and Seamus were busy settling the kids in or something, but I had figured once I was officially dragonkin, whatever that meant, I would be able to see them.

So having Gwen show up saying they needed me and then blinking us out of existence was more than a little disturbing.

Which meant that for the first time in my entire life, I was relieved to see Edik.

Even though he was attacking Sol and Seamus, who had their backs up against Sol's cottage, and was screaming something incoherent while he repeatedly tried to bite them.

I sighed.

Then I shifted directly behind him and put him in a headlock.

"Edik, I give zero fucks about what you are doing here, but you have precisely 30 seconds to make me care enough not to rip your throat from your neck."

When he sagged in my arms, I relaxed my grip just enough to let him speak.

"My darling Victoria, I—"

I cut him off by tightening the hold once again.

"Let me make this part really clear. I'm not your darling anything, and any references to me as such will lose you ten seconds of time to explain. Try again. Twenty seconds. Go."

"These heathens won't tell me where my daughter is! They have hidden her from me, and I can no longer sense her. Where is she!? She is so frail, she needs me, she cannot make her way in this world withou—"

I cut him off again.

"Is she with the others?" I asked Sol and Seamus, who both looked as exhausted as I felt. No wonder, they'd been struggling against raging vampire. They nodded.

"Great. Then she's safe. Edik, your daughter is safe and that's all I can tell you. I've been sworn to secrecy regarding her location, but you're just going to have to trust me. Or I can just kill you. I'm really fine either way, at this point."

That wasn't strictly true. I loathed Edik pretty substantially at this point, but I still didn't know if I'd be able to kill him. Not if he didn't attack me first, at least. I didn't think I had it in me to snap his neck right now, for example, if all he did was beg me to let him see his daughter. Then again, if it had looked like he was really going to hurt Sol or Seamus, he'd probably be dead already. Regardless, I certainly didn't have the time or energy to coach Edik through knowing where his daughter was. If she was still with the other children rescued from MOME, I had to assume that was where she wanted to be. I couldn't imagine Seamus or Sol trying to keep her with the group against her will, and if a teenaged girl wanted to get away from her parents so badly that she was willing to stay in the dragon realm with a group of total strangers, I was not going to get in her way.

I dropped Edik to the ground, stepped forward to grab Seamus and Sol by the wrists, and shifted us all inside Sol's cabin.

Where I almost fell to the floor from the intense heat that rolled through my abdomen, making my toes curl.

Holy fuck, I felt like I was going to burst and the only thing that would stop me was getting in bed with Sol and Seamus right now.

I dropped their wrists like they were on fire and ran to lock the door, hoping neither of them could tell how turned on I was. My whole body felt flushed, and I wondered how it was even possible to be this attracted to two people at the same time. I took a few deep breaths and tried to tell myself that it was just relief at seeing them safe and alive.

When I looked up, they both looked like deer about to be taken down by a Mack truck. What was wrong with us?

"I'm really glad to see you guys," I said, desperate to distract myself from the molten longing that consumed me. "I thought you were back in the dragon realm, though."

Sol swallowed, licked her lips, and then swallowed again. I tried not to watch every move like it set my skin alight, but I failed.

"We were. Rhelia took us there with the kids from MOME, but her matriarch decided that we were no longer needed and offered to send us home. We had no idea where you were, so…"

She trailed off and I couldn't help but notice that she seemed to be watching the rise and fall of my chest. For some reason that made my nipples harden, and I had to swallow a moan. What the fuck? Five minutes ago I had been in the middle of some weird assed dragon rite of passage, three minutes ago I'd had my vampire stalker in a headlock. I had so many more important things to think about than whether or not Sol was staring at my chest. What was wrong with me?

"When we got here, that asshat was waiting for us, screaming his head off about his precious Renata, and then when we refused to tell him where she was, he started trying to bite us. As if his damned vampire venom would even work on a strong were." She sighed, and my own eyes were drawn to the rise and fall of *her* chest in a way that was completely inappropriate to the conversation.

"We'd already fought off five MOME agents today…. It's a good thing you got here when you did," Seamus said, but his voice sounded rough.

Before I could even take a good look at Seamus, or ask what was going on, he rushed to the door, muttered, "I'll be back in a minute, just going for a run," and slipped out so fast I wondered if I'd even locked it.

I should have been worried about Seamus running into Edik, or getting cold, or getting lost, or something, but instead all I could think about was how I wanted him back here so I could have my way with him. Ugh… what was wrong with my brain? Seriously, even teenage hormones didn't explain this kind of single-minded lust.

I almost voiced the question, but then Sol stepped up to me and I could feel the heat rolling off of her body in waves. I hadn't ever been with a woman before, but I now knew deep in my bones that I wanted to be with Sol. I wanted to run my tongue over every curve of her body, and explore… everywhere.

She leaned against me, and suddenly I couldn't think of anything else at all.

"Gatita, I know we haven't known each other very long, but do you…" her voice trailed off, hestitant.

"Want to take you into that bedroom and learn everything I can about how to pleasure a woman?" I finished for her. "Yes. Yes, I do."

FROM THERE A few sizzling kisses quickly progressed to an incredibly hot sex scene that I'm not going to relate to you, because that's not the point of this story. I will say, however, that I was surprised by how good it was, considering that first time sexual encounters with a new partner aren't always very good and also that it was my first time with a woman at all. I had expected more awkwardness. Instead, we both finished at the same time with a pair of mind-blowing orgasms. I didn't think it was that suspicious at the time, but afterwards…

Well, anyway, I had been on the cusp of initiating round two when a familiar voice announced, "I'm afraid the two of you are needed elsewhere."

I nearly jumped off the bed as that voice doused me like a cold a shower.

"Ack! Fuck, Gwen! You can't just show up like that when people are getting it on!"

She was standing just inside the door like it was no big deal.

"You'd be surprised how often I show up like that when people are getting it on, actually."

"What?!"

"Goddess of fortune, remember? For some folks that's all about makin' babies."

"Ugh… Gwen, why are you here?" I asked. Sol had been surprisingly quiet, but unlike me (trying to cover myself with whatever bit of blanket I could grab) she was just lying there casually, as though she spent most of her time naked on a bed, with another woman, expecting random deities to show up and announce things. And hell, for all I knew, maybe she did.

"Seamus needs you," Gwen said, then poofed out of existence.

Luckily, she only poofed as far as the living room. I could hear her rustling around the small kitchen, likely looking for tea paraphernalia. I guess she was giving us some privacy to wrap things up. Sol kissed me in a soft lingering manner that promised all kinds of fun was to be had later, then grabbed her clothes and walked out of the room. I chuckled at the thought of her not giving two fucks about strutting around naked and then put on my own jeans, shoved the ladies back into my sports bra, and pulled on a hoodie. Then I did my best to think of things other than the amazing sex we'd just had, but largely failed.

I took a deep breath and walked out into the kitchen.

Gwen was busily fussing with a teapot and Sol had put on pants and a bra, an outfit I didn't object to in the least, but found incredibly distracting. I couldn't get the feel and taste of her out of my mind, and every time I looked at her, I instantly started replaying everything we'd just done to one another.

That was weird. I didn't usually find sex to be all-consuming. I had thought the way we felt before Seamus had run out was just an anomaly.

I walked over to stand beside Sol, and almost purred when she put her hand on my back and started sliding it under my hoodie. My skin caught fire wherever she ran her fingers, and all I could think of was dragging her back to bed.

Focus power, Vic. Come on.

I mentally shook myself, trying to pay attention to Gwen and her tea.

Sol's hand wandered up the front of my hoodie and began sliding over my sports bra, making me thoroughly ready to pull her back into the bedroom to have my way with her again, when Gwen must have dropped the teapot. A loud shattering noise briefly took my attention away from Sol.

"Damn it," Gwen said, looking between us. "It's happening already."

"What is?" I asked, leaning into the feel of Sol's hand playing over both of my breasts. I ducked my head and kissed her shoulder.

"That damned mating bond!" Gwen said, clapping her hands, presumably to get our attention, but I was too busy kissing my way towards Sol's exposed cleavage to care.

"Mating bond?" Sol asked, sounding vaguely concerned. "Can't be, we're not a mating pair. No testes."

Her hand had never stopped roaming my breasts, and now she was pinching gently at my nipples through my sports bra. Apparently neither of us were at all concerned that Gwen was standing right there, cleaning up fragments of shattered teapot.

I had started running my fingers under the fabric of her bra, and she was leaning her head back in exaltation.

"Well, then how do you explain your sudden inability to keep your hands off each other?" Gwen asked.

Sol snorted.

"Because we just had some of the best sex of my life," she muttered, grabbing my breasts more forcefully and bringing her other hand under my hoodie to join the fun.

"And mine," I seconded, running my tongue along the tops of her breasts again.

"And how common is that between two people who've never had sex with each other before?" Gwen asked.

I shrugged, knowing that Gwen had a point, but not really caring. Sol sat up a bit though, and her hands paused in their task, which made me growl a bit.

"And how often does a woman who has never been with another woman before know every move that will push her partner right over the edge?" Gwen continued.

Sol stopped everything and dropped her hands, and then I really did growl.

"We can't have a mating bond," Sol objected. "Those are for pairs that can procreate. My kind never have them."

Gwen just looked between us. Sol looked at me and stepped back.

"What. The. Fuck. Is. A. Mating. Bond?" I gritted out.

"It's an unbreakable lifelong bond between two weres," Sol replied.

"Two or more," Gwen corrected.

"Multi-way mating bonds are a myth," Sol replied.

Gwen shrugged.

"Suit yourself."

"What are you two talking about?" I asked, through the haze of lust that was clouding my mind. Now that I considered it, thinking was a lot harder than it should have been. All my body seemed to want to do was pin Sol down to the bed in the other room with various forms of pleasure. As I forced myself to think through the fog of lust, I had to recognize that even though she was hot, and we'd just had amazing sex, something was definitely not right about the single-mindedness of this.

"What is going on?" I asked, finally snapping out of things enough to understand how strange this was. I tried to take a step back from Sol, but found it was a surprisingly difficult proposition. My body did not want to move away from hers, no matter what my brain told it.

"Gwen is suggesting that we've somehow become a mated pair," Sol said, still sounding incredulous. "But that's not possible, because that doesn't happen to same-sex couples."

"It does sometimes," Gwen corrected.

"Only in legends," Sol scoffed. "Not in the real world."

Gwen only shrugged again.

"Why would the mating bond snap into place for two women? We can't MATE, not in the sense that Gaia, or whoever decides these things, would approve of, anyway."

"Maybe the gods have gotten more progressive," Gwen suggested.

I laughed.

"You would know if they had, wouldn't you?" I asked, even as I tried to restrain myself from touching Sol again. My hands did not seem inclined to listen, and I noticed that she was subtly raising her arm towards the waistband of my hoodie once more.

Gwen fixed me with a glare.

"Some of us have never cared about such things, and I don't keep tabs on all the other gods and their politics. Gods are slow to change, but some of us do. Gaia might be one who does. Or maybe she never cared to begin with. We don't talk much."

"It just doesn't make any sense," said Sol, even as her hand started to slide up under my hoodie once more. I moaned before her hand even reached my breasts, then shook myself and tried to take a step back.

"What. The. Actual. Fuck." I gritted out, through clenched jaws. I wasn't opposed to wanting to jump Sol a bunch in the foreseeable future, but I was trying to hold a conversation, damn it. This was getting ridiculous.

"Ok. For the sake of argument," I managed to say, while stepping back from Sol and her free-roaming hands, "let's say this is a mating bond. How do we get out of it?"

"We don't," said Sol. "Mating bonds are for life. Or… well, that's what I've always heard, anyway."

"But surely no one lives like this?" I said, finding myself sliding towards Sol again, despite not wanting to. "How do they get anything done?"

"It's only supposed to drive people like this until it's completed."

"What do you mean, completed?"

"Consummated."

"Did we, or did we not, just consummate the crap out of each other back there?"

Sol smiled, then forced her hands to her sides.

"We did. If this were a mating bond it should have cooled down by now."

"Not if it isn't just a two person bond," said Gwen gingerly from behind the teakettle that had somehow reassembled itself.

"WHAT?!" Sol and I chorused together.

"That's not possible!" said Sol. "Those bonds are legends, and nothing more."

"You keep using that word. I do not think it means what you think it means."

I couldn't resist putting on my best Iñigo Montoya voice.

Sol was so angry that she ignored my Princess Bride reference completely.

"There hasn't been a three person bond in… I don't know… a thousand years? It's possible it was just a myth to begin with. Why would there be one now? And who would the third be anyway?" Sol looked ready to tear something up, and I was suddenly glad that her hands were no longer under my shirt.

"Um, three person bond, two person bond, why is ANY of this happening? And why us? Why me in particular? I didn't even know this stuff existed."

Sol turned to me and looked like she was finally taking pity on me. "Ok. The short, short version is this: mating pairs feel a very strong pull when they meet each other—the more time they spend together, the more they are drawn in. If they take too "long" getting to know each other without consummating things, they can be thrown into a frenzy until they finally manage to seal the deal. Once they mate properly, they are mated for life. They will always be with that person."

"Why?" I asked.

"Why what?" Sol's eyebrow rose in what I could only assume was confusion.

"Why any of it? Why mate to people for life? Why stay together after the mating bond is consummated? Just… why?"

"Not a believer in monogamy, are you?" Sol asked, smiling.

"Not particularly." I shrugged. "It's not that I don't believe in it. I just have a hard time buying that it's the default switch for most humans. I think the reason most people become dissatisfied with relationships after a few years is a general human tendency towards genetic diversity and thus towards having multiple partners over the long run. Plus, I think it's lame that we try to get *everything* we need in a partner from a single person. No human can reasonably expect to find someone who gives them everything. That's crazy."

Sol's smile widened.

"Well said."

"So, I take it neither of us is thrilled at the idea of being mated for life?" I hedged.

Sol shook her head.

"Gatita, you're hot as fuck, but I do not want to be saddled with you, or anyone else, *forever*."

"Are we having a sharing circle or something?"

Seamus' voice sounded perfectly calm, and perfectly normal, but for some reason it sent a jolt of liquid heat sliding through me.

"Damn," I said, turning to see him standing in the doorway. He was silhouetted by the afternoon light shining over the mountains behind him, and his long, dark hair was pulled back from his angular jawline and high cheekbones. His amber eyes seemed to glow from the doorway, and suddenly I decided he was wearing entirely too much clothing. I'd crossed half the distance between us before I even noticed that my body had moved. I managed to stop myself before I got to him, though.

"What is happening?" I asked, feeling more lost than ever.

"We may have figured out why the earlier consummation didn't take."

I felt another jolt of heat just standing there, watching Seamus as he took off his coat, and was trembling with the effort it took to keep from jumping him where he stood. I'd always found him attractive, but this was ridiculous, and I'd just spent the past hour shagging the life out of Sol.

Once his coat and boots were off, Seamus was standing in front of me. He smelled amazing, like pine trees, rocks, wind, and snow. I caught myself leaning forward to lick his neck, but stopped. He was already leaning down to wrap his arms around me, though.

"What did I miss?" he asked, slowly enveloping my waist with his arms. His breathing and speed suggested each move was calculated. I wondered if he was fighting the same thing Sol and I were.

"Gwen?" I asked.

But Gwen wasn't there.

"Sol?" I tried.

Sol sighed.

"As a were with a theoretical mating bond in place, I should want to tear his throat out for touching you like that," she said, as Seamus' hand starting running up and down my back beneath my hoodie. "But instead, I find myself wanting to watch him take you. And, I have *never* wanted to watch a man have sex before."

Just the idea of it had me pressing myself against Seamus. Poor Seamus; he'd missed all of this. He'd gone for a run, or whatever he'd done, to try to escape this very feeling, and now he was back and everything was just as bad as before, or maybe worse. What the hell must he think of what was going on?

"Is this a mating bond?" Seamus asked, still only caressing my back. I marveled at his restraint. I wanted him to caress so much more than that.

I nodded, trying not to press myself any harder against him.

"Weird," he said. "I always figured it would be between two people of the same animal spirit."

Sol laughed.

"Yeah, and I thought they were never between *three* people."

"But you're the bridge, aren't you?" Seamus asked, his eyes locked on me.

"If you mean am I bisexual?… I think the answer is a resounding yes," I sighed. It was nice to say that out loud finally, and, certainly, if I'd wanted proof here it was. I was just as attracted to Seamus as I had been to Sol. Was still attracted to both of them… was starting to fantasize about being with both of them at the same time…. Of course, sexual attraction was only one part of the whole equation, but for now it was the part that was jumping up and down waving semaphores at me, so I was going to go ahead and let it have its way for a moment.

Sol laughed and came over to stand beside me. She took my arm and Seamus released me on that side, still rubbing his left hand up and down the right side of my back, while Sol grabbed my left arm and pulled me towards the bedroom.

"You're right," he said, looking at her. "I should feel defensive as hell about you touching her like that if this is a mating bond, but…"

His eyes flashed, and I wanted to sprint all three of us to the bedroom.

"You're just picturing me sitting on her face while you ride her, aren't you?" Sol said.

Seamus nodded.

I moaned.

"Can we *please* make that happen? Like right now."

I didn't wait for a reply, I just pulled them both into the bedroom.

HOURS LATER, WHEN none of us could move anymore and we finally decided that we should break for food before we wound up with permanent damage, we emerged, dressed at least partially, into the living room.

I was grateful that no one was out there.

"I'm glad Trevor and Rhelia aren't here at the moment," I said, making my way to the small fridge that was on the far wall of the kitchen. "Do we have ingredients for sandwiches?"

Sol patted me on the back, then hip checked me out of the way so that she had primary access to the fridge.

"Yes. Now, step aside so I can put them together *quickly*. I am fucking starving."

"Me too."

"Me three," agreed Seamus.

I looked at him and smiled.

The three of us had certainly bonded in the past few hours. It was night outside the windows of the cabin and I wondered exactly how many hours we'd spent fucking each other's brains out. The edge had been taken off by that first round, no doubt. As soon as we'd all finished together (and when does that happen to a threesome?) the driving *compulsion* to have my way with Sol and Seamus had all but ceased, but the fun of pleasuring each other so completely had simply made me want more and more each time. Especially when you threw in the novelty of having sex with another woman *and* a man at the same time. I'd fantasized about threesomes before, but since I'd never met a woman I had been attracted to before Sol, I'd never pursued it. Now… Now I couldn't stop pursuing it. Damn. I needed to think about something else, or I was going to drag them both back into the bedroom before we ate. We needed to eat.

"So, do you think the mating bond is… satisfied?" I asked.

Sol looked up from where she was generously applying mayonnaise and mustard to six slices of bread.

"I should fucking hope so," she said.

Seamus cackled.

"Seriously," he agreed.

I smiled.

"I mean it, though," I continued. "Is it going to do that to us again? Because while I'm a huge fan of the results, I do *not* appreciate the means."

Sol and Seamus both nodded.

Then Gwen popped back into existence.

"Oh goody," I said, sighing. "Are you here to answer questions or just raise more of them?"

Gwen frowned.

"Don't you enjoy my visits?" she asked. "My last one was… instructive, wouldn't you say?"

I just glared at her.

She sighed, as though I never appreciated her. She might be right.

"The mating bond is likely satisfied, to answer your question."

"Eavesdrop much?" I asked.

She just shrugged.

Sol shoved a sandwich into my hand, then turned on Gwen.

"Mind telling us what the hell a mating bond is doing on the three of us, anyway? It makes no sense. I'm a lesbian. I don't care how hot it is to watch those two get it on, I am *not* having sex with a man. WHY AM I PART OF A MATING BOND?"

Gwen shook her head.

"I didn't put it on you, if that helps, and I'm not privy to all the details about why it had to be you three, I only know that it does. The whole concept is stupid, if you ask me."

That had all three of us nodding.

"Are we all going to turn batshit nuts whenever either of the others bats their lashes at another person?" I asked. I really couldn't stand jealousy as a concept, and that idea bothered me more than anything.

Gwen snorted. "Not unless you normally would. To my knowledge, the mating bond doesn't make you insane with jealousy unless that's your natural tendency anyway. It just makes you crazily attracted to the person, or people, in the bond."

"What does that mean for Sol and Seamus?" I asked.

"I think Sol just stated pretty clearly what she will and won't do when it comes to Seamus."

"And what if Seamus becomes overwhelmingly attracted to her?"

"He can take care of it with fantasies and his hand?" Gwen said, sounding baffled. "It's not like any of this gives any of you more rights to each other than you would normally grant. Look, I know the traditions around mating bonds go back millennia and are… well, stupidly patriarchal, but the magic behind it is simple enough. It wants to create a bond between certain people that is unbreakable, and that encourages those people to procreate."

All three of us started to object.

"The magic was around before condoms or birth control were a thing, ok?" Gwen raised her hands to forestall our objections as she spoke. "You have every opportunity to prevent pregnancy that anyone else does. The magic just makes you want to screw a bunch, and ok, yeah, it makes you want to stick with people for life, or so I'm told. If you *didn't* have access to birth control, that would greatly increase your chances of reproducing. Since you do… enjoy shagging a lot. Or don't. It's up to you."

I took a deep breath. It was reassuring to hear that we weren't going to be… forced into anything.

"The storytellers always make it sound like the magic of the bond makes people do crazy things to keep each other from 'straying,'" Sol said, still seeming unconvinced.

Gwen smirked.

"The patriarchy is a long-standing, opportunistic, piece-of-shit mythology that has corrupted so much of history, it boggles the mind."

"So… those people were just being jealous assholes?" Sol asked, sounding relieved.

Gwen nodded.

We all three let out a breath I hadn't realized we'd been holding.

I finally took a bite of my sandwich. It tasted heavenly.

Then the door to the cabin exploded in a ball of flames.

"TREV! WHAT THE fuck?" I shouted, as Trev fell into the living room fighting with… an unfortunately familiar looking vampire.

Without waiting for any kind of reply or explanation, I jumped into the fight, wondering why Trev was bothering to fight Edik in human form, and what had blown cdown the door if Trev wasn't a fiery phoenix at the moment.

The answer rapidly became clear as more spells slammed into the cabin, some making their way through the door and singeing past Trev and I, as we grappled with Edik on the floor.

"Hijo de puta!" Sol shouted. "The fucker led them right to us!"

It was the last thing she said before shifting into her panther form and charging at the first MOME agent to stick his head in past the door.

I didn't have time to pay attention to what Sol was doing, I was too busy trying to keep Edik from hurting my brother.

Why aren't you in phoenix form? I asked him, while I struggled to pin Edik down.

They have a null out there. He touched me just as I was about to immolate this asshole.

I didn't know what a null was in the real world, but in most of the fantasy books I read it was someone who absorbed magic. That made sense with what Trev had just described, and I didn't have time to ask for clarification anyway, because Edik was actually fighting me for once, and the asshat was surprisingly fast. It seemed that whatever creepy romantic notion had kept him from attacking me before had expired. Thank Gwen. I needed him to be distracted by me, because Trev was clearly in no shape to fight for much longer, and I wondered if getting hit by a null was the only thing that had happened to him.

How many MOME agents are out there? I asked, while blocking an insanely fast series of punches of from Edik. Not for the first time, I was sincerely glad that Edik didn't seem to have ever trained in a martial art. Even with the way he telegraphed every single one of his punches, kicks, and attempted bites, his moves were almost too fast to track.

Twenty or so, Trev replied. *Rhelia's keeping most of them busy.*

Well fuck. That was a lot of MOME to fight off when one of our most effective fighters couldn't pull on any of his magic. And of course, we were too spread out for me to grab all of us.

Well, if I couldn't get all of us to safety right away, at least I could start taking out the trash.

The next time Edik threw a punch at me, I didn't block it, I just grabbed his fist.

I shifted us all the way back to the school pool in Flagstaff, but I didn't even give him a chance to get his bearings, I just jumped back from him, laughed at the ridiculous expression on his face as he hit the water, and then shifted myself right back to the inside of Sol's cabin.

Luckily, Sol and Seamus had been successful in keeping more MOME agents from gaining access to the house. Trev looked like he was still catching his breath when I grabbed his wrist, before launching myself at Sol and Seamus. They were fighting the nearest MOME agents coming through the doorway.

As soon as I grabbed hold of them, I shifted us to the top of the rise outside of Sol's cabin, hoping that it would be behind enemy lines.

Rhelia! I shouted mentally, hoping to gain the dragon's attention without bringing any more MOME agents to us. Apparently, Sol had been mid-bite to the wrist of a MOME agent when I'd shifted us, because he had come along for the ride, so Sol continued to fight him atop the rocky outcropping that stood 200 meters above her small mountain sanctuary. I joined her, hoping against hope that Rhelia would make her way to us before any of the other MOME agents did. Sol was limping and Seamus was shaking like a leaf, and I remembered that none of us had gotten much sleep or food in the past few days. The best we'd managed was to shag for a few hours and eat a bite of sandwich. We were all running on empty, and Trev looked like he'd run a marathon or something just in order to get here.

Sol must have decided that we were running out of time too, because she lunged for the mage's throat and the man didn't even have time to scream, though he did manage to light Sol's fur on fire as they both went down in a heap together. Not waiting to see if the man was dead, I reached forward and grabbed his arm, shifting him back to the cabin, which was now more of a smoldering hovel than anything else, as the myriad spells that MOME had launched combined with what must have been dragon breath and brought the house most of the way to the ground. I dropped the offending MOME agent in the flaming confines of the living room before shifting myself back to Sol, Seamus, and Trev. Seamus, now in wolf form, leapt to my side and pressed his head against my leg as soon as I appeared.

A roar like a typhoon shook the earth around us, and then we were all knocked to our asses as Rhelia backwinged herself to a spot a few meters above us on the slope. I was almost completely out of energy, but I could hear MOME agents calling to one another from below us. We didn't have time to climb the 200 meters to Rhelia, not in the state we were in. Not with Trev unable to shift.

"To me!" I shouted, feeling a bit like Aragorn, or Gandalf.

Luckily, cheesy one-liners aside, everyone got up and put a hand, snout, or paw against me.

I shifted us to Rhelia's back, and hoped to hell she wouldn't be offended.

If she was upset with me, she gave no indication, instead launching herself skyward while we all still scrambled to find something to hold onto that would keep us from falling to the earth.

Relief coursed through me as she took us higher and higher, and I realized I wouldn't have to shift us all again.

Then I passed out.

I REGAINED CONSCIOUSNESS fighting off an attack from some evil, furred beast that was trying to smother me.

Or… Sol's tail.

I sat up gasping, swatting the offending appendage away from my mouth. Sol and Seamus were curled protectively around me, both asleep. Sol's tail was just doing its own thing. My hands pressed into the sand underneath me, and my eyes finally took in my surroundings. Aquamarine water and white sand took up my field of vision, the water extending all the way to the horizon, until the sky bled into the sea.

"Where are we?" I muttered.

"Ssssomewhere near Fiji," Rhelia's voice called, from behind me. I turned to see her sitting on the beach a little ways behind me, with Trev beside her. They were holding hands.

"Fiji? Holy crap, how long was I out?" I asked.

"Only about a day," Trev replied. Something in his voice made me look him in the eyes, and I realized that he looked wrecked.

"When was the last time you got any sleep?"

He smiled. "I slept most of the way here."

"Then why do you look like shit?"

"Vic, I—"

"Can someone tell me *why* we're in the middle of the Pacific Ocean?" Sol had apparently been woken by our conversation and resumed her human form. She was clothed in a sarong wrapped over a skimpy looking swim suit, and I had to wonder if my Gwen-given powers were pranksters, or if my subconscious had some sway in how everyone wound up clothed. Then I shook myself out of my pondering, because everyone else was still talking.

"MOME are behind us at every turn," Trev grumbled. "Rhelia thought the safest way to lose them was to fly over the ocean for a long assed time."

That made some amount of sense…

"And?" I asked, sensing that we weren't getting the full answer.

"And Rhelia talked to a seer before we left."

As if that was an explanation.

"Just wondering what your next lotto numbers should be?" I asked, giving Rhelia a hard stare.

"The sssseer came to me, actually," Rhelia said. "She gave me a very cryptic messssage about finding answerssss in the ocean."

"Well, that's pretty vague."

"Indeed," Rhelia agreed. "When I ssssaid assss much to her, she showed me an image of an island, thissss island, I think."

"Did she show you a map? How did you know where to go?"

"No. Thissss island issss on no map."

"Well, then how did you—"

"Vic." Trev cut me off. "You didn't finish your initiation ceremony, so there's a lot we can't tell you yet, especially with two people who aren't dragonkin present. Can you just trust us for a minute?"

"So *you* know what's going on here?" I asked, suddenly a bit peeved at all the dragon secrecy shit.

"Not exactly, but I have a better idea of *why* we might be left in the dark about a few things, and yes, it's annoying, but it's mostly with good reason. Besides, if the vague prophecy was in any way accurate, we're about to get a few answers."

I thought about that for a moment, and then something else occurred to me.

"Where the fuck is Albert?" I asked.

"The old mage?" Trev asked.

"Yeah, I haven't seen him since we hit the streets in Unterberg. Have you?"

Seamus must have woken up not long after Sol, because he shifted to human form and said, "He was with us when we moved the MOME refugees to the dragon realm, but he chose not to come back with us. He said he wanted an audience with the circle of elders."

"Hmm… I hope he's as trustworthy as he seems," I muttered.

Rhelia laughed.

"If he issss not, he will be little more than a char mark when nexsssst we return to the elder cssssircle."

"Right. I suppose the elders can take care of themselves."

"That issss putting it mildly," Rhelia replied.

"So, how exactly is this island meant to give us answers?" I asked.

Rhelia and Trev got very quiet for a moment, and then Trev stood up.

"Come on, Vic. Follow me."

DRAGONS ARE SNEAKY bastards.

Ok. That's an unfair generalization. The seer who approached Rhelia appeared to have been a sneaky bastard. Minus the slur on her parentage, which I knew nothing about. Still, I was beginning to understand why Trev still looked like a train had hit him, even after a full night's sleep. We hadn't even gotten to where he was leading me yet, and I was already a wreck.

Not as much of a wreck as my parents' boat was, though.

Trev had led me through a small stand of palms that reached almost all the way to the water, then onto a long stretch of beach that was completely empty, save for the small husk of a wrecked yacht. A fifty-footer. The mast was gone, no trace of it left but a gaping hole into the galley beneath where it had once stood.

I glanced at Trev, saw the haunting shadows in his eyes, and realized that he'd probably already had a look around.

The whole mass of wood and fiberglass was sun-bleached and deteriorating, as one might expect from something that had probably washed up on this shore months ago, but it seemed oddly at peace; as though it belonged here on this beach, away from everything else in the world, as though it were simply resting after a job well done.

Ok. Maybe my emotions *were* more of a wreck than the boat.

The name was still visible on the stern. The Victor. I had always hated that name, as much as I'd loved the boat itself. My dad had always assured me it wasn't named for me, especially after I had asked him if he'd wished that I had been born a boy. Mixed feeling about the fading name aside, this boat had been my home every summer since I'd turned seven. The place we'd always escaped to when the requirements of school had released me, and my parents had set aside time for all of us to head to the west coast, climb aboard The Victor, and become floating nomads, kings of our own tiny realm for six weeks out of every year.

I didn't bother to swipe at the tears running down my face as I took a few steps towards what was left of my childhood playground.

Trevor put a hand on my shoulder.

"Vic… you don't have to—"

"Yeah. I do, actually."

I gave Trev's hand a squeeze before I pushed it off of my shoulder, stepping towards the wreckage.

Trevor had been on that boat as a kid, I was sure. The memories that had been leaking, and sometimes flooding, back into my brain since Sol had initially helped me break whatever spell had tried to cut Trevor out of my life confirmed that much, but my parents had just purchased it before Trevor was taken. I don't even think we'd had a chance to do more than resurface the top deck before MOME had snatched him away from us. Perhaps that was part of why the boat had become such a big part of our lives afterwards. It wasn't laden with memories of the twin who had disappeared, the child erased from my parents memories in an attempt to spare the last child they had left. Or maybe we spent so much time there simply because it was a project my parents could obsess over, distract themselves with in an attempt to erase the nagging memories that must have been pulling at them, despite the spells that had tried to erase a quarter of our little family from their hearts.

For me, this boat had almost been another sibling. A playmate that filled a hole I knew was there, but had been convinced was only a figment of my imagination.

Just as I drew level with the boat, I felt a familiar presence at my side.

"Thought you might want some backup," Seamus said quietly.

"You worried the Kraken is going to jump out of this thing?" I asked, unable to keep the exasperation out of my voice, even around the tears. Seamus' protective streak was not something I appreciated.

"Nah. Just ghosts."

"Ghosts can't hurt me, Seamus."

"Lucky you," he snorted. "They manage to hurt the rest of us easily enough."

I turned to look at him then, and when I saw his eyes I no longer wondered why Seamus had come to offer comfort instead of Sol or Trevor. The shadows that haunted Seamus' eyes made me reach out to wrap an arm around him.

"One of these days, when no one is trying to kill us, I really need to ask you more about yourself, don't I?"

Seamus leaned into the one-armed embrace, still facing the boat, while I tucked my head into his shoulder.

"Meh. We'll get to it eventually. It's been a busy week. Some things are not exactly at the top of my list of things to talk about, even when no one is trying to kill me." He shrugged.

I chuckled, but the sound didn't hold much humor.

"Yeah. These things aren't my favorite conversation pieces either," I said, nodding towards the boat that had likely been my parents pallbearer. "Still, you shouldn't remain all dark and mysterious just because I've been too self-absorbed to ask you any questions."

"Don't be too hard on yourself, Vic. I'm not much of a talker."

I sighed.

"We doing this?" I asked.

He nodded.

I stepped forward, my right arm still loosely wrapped around Seamus' torso.

I stood before the hole in the galley where the mast had once been, the wooden deck lying almost perpendicular to the beach. I doubted much of the keel was left, but whatever was there was likely ensuring that the boat stayed on its side.

My left hand reached out to the deck, and I could feel the salt drying on my cheeks where the sun was evaporating the tracks of my tears. The sound of the turquoise ocean around us faded, the scenery of this tiny island paradise all but disappearing, as I refocused my attention on the miniature floating world that had once been my home away from home. Even the faded grain of the wood was familiar enough to be a blow to the gut. Gwen knows I'd sanded it enough times, I'd probably recognize it with my eyes closed.

When my hand connected with the deck I felt as though I'd touched a live wire. I tried to jump back and let go of Seamus, convinced that some of the navigation equipment must have managed to electrify the timbers of the deck, but I couldn't move an inch. My arm went rigid and my jaw locked tight, preventing me from even screaming. My eyes rolled into my head, and a series of images, worse than even my most devastating nightmares, cascaded across my vision.

My parents, crying, hugging each other as they watched The Victor sink beneath a violent sea from the dubious vantage of a small motor boat that looked likely to be overcome by the thrashing waves that surrounded them. A man I'd never seen before, with bulging eyes and prominent fangs, pounding against a locked door, rattling the windows and screeching, a half-dozen children huddled crying on the other side as the hinges shook. A wolf, torn limb from limb in a way that no natural predator would ever have left it. A young boy, drawing a picture of that same wolf, and a redheaded woman, tearing the picture into shreds. Six men and women sneaking up on a small wooden cabin under cover of darkness, wands drawn and guns out. Two women in pajamas screaming, turning into wolves and being hit with multiple spells and bullets, eventually falling still.

Suddenly, I was lying in the sand looking up at three sets of legs.

"Seamus?" I asked, hoping he was as not dead as I was.

"I'm ok."

"What the hell was that, Seamus?"

"We have to go, Vic."

"What the HELL was that?"

"Vic, we have to go. We have to get back to Flagstaff!"

"I'm not going anywhere until you tell me what that was!"

"There isn't time, Vic!"

"Fucking make time! What did I just see?!"

"I don't know what triggered it. That's never happened to me before. I saw *your* parents and then I saw… things I've seen before."

"You can start making sense any time now."

I was grateful that the owners of all the feet that surrounded us were staying out of it, for now— maybe because Seamus and I were both clearly alive and conscious. I supposed no one else was shouting questions at Seamus because no one else had just seen a vision of the last moments of their parents' lives followed by… whatever all that other shit was.

"I see the future sometimes, Vic. Sometimes the past, I guess. But mostly that's just me reliving visions I've already had, or nightmares of things I already lived through. The future though… you can understand why I don't talk about it, right? Almost no one believes in seers, Vic. Not even in our world. I was amazed to hear Rhelia talk about what she heard from a seer without a hint of derision in her voice. I guess dragons have their own thing going on, but for humans, mages, weres… it's not like there haven't been a few throughout history, but… it's not a healthy condition, right? People kill you for what you do see, or what you don't see, or what you *might* see. It's not something you go around mentioning to folks, if you want to die of old age. My family doesn't even really believe it—the few who even know about it. Did you… did you see all of that?"

I nodded, too stunned to speak for a moment.

"I don't know if we saw the same things, but… I saw a kid who drew a picture of a wolf torn limb from limb… was that you?"

"Sometimes the visions come when I'm drawing, especially when I was younger, but mostly they come as dreams. They don't come often, regardless, but… Vic, we have to go. My moms. My moms are in danger. That vision. The mages closing in on that cabin. That's my house, Vic. I had that vision for the first time a month before I met you, but it was different the first time. The first time I had it *you* were there. And you saved them. You saved my moms' lives and… they're all I've got, Vic. Please."

Holy fucking shitballs, Seamus was begging me to save his parents. What kind of friend was I? Did he really think he'd have to *convince* me to help him save his family? Even if I was a little worried that he'd only befriended me to ensure I was around to help him, I wasn't going to say no to doing whatever I could to save his moms.

Trev, stay here and find out what is up with this Gwendamned boat.

Then I grabbed Seamus' hand and shifted us the hell to Flagstaff.

THE WOODS OUTSIDE of Seamus' cabin were dark, thanks to being on the opposite side of the world from Fiji. I had been forced to shift us to my place first, very briefly, since I had never been to Seamus' home before, and he'd tried calling his moms to warn them about the possibly impending attack, while I had run upstairs to grab something. There had been no answer at his place.

We hadn't waited after that, I'd just had him bring up a few images of his home on his phone, then I'd reached through space and time and deposited our asses into the middle of the woods 100 meters from the house.

I'd decided that inside a house that might be crawling with evil mages wasn't a good place to appear all of a sudden. Or at all, preferably.

From our vantage point, the house looked calm enough. There was no sign of any disturbance. The porch light glowed welcomingly, but the interior lights were off.

"Could they be asleep?" I asked.

Seamus checked his phone.

"It's 7:30. Not likely."

I nodded.

"Out to dinner?"

"Maybe," he replied. He did not sound convinced.

I kept my eyes on the house and the surrounding wilderness, but could see Seamus texting someone, out of the corner of my eye.

"They're not at Uncle Rom's," he said, after a minute.

That didn't sound like good news.

Just then, a light flicked on in the window of the cabin, and a silhouette briefly blocked out the light that was seeping out between a set of dark curtains.

"Was that either of your mothers?" I asked, fairly sure of the answer due to the dropping feeling in my gut, and the fact that the silhouette had looked pretty much like a dude.

"No." Seamus' voice sounded cold. I reached out my hand and squeezed his.

"Plan B?" I asked.

He nodded, squeezing my hand in return.

I shifted us again.

~~~

"Ow! Fuck!" I whispered angrily, as my head made contact with a low beam.

"Shhh!" Seamus admonished.

In my defense, I had barely vocalized the sentiment, though my head was now throbbing with the impact. If the stooges upstairs weren't weres, then there was no way that they could have heard me, and even if they were, it was was unlikely unless they were already in their animal forms.

This basement was not made for human habitation, and it wasn't just the goose egg on my forehead that proved it. The spiderwebs I was working hard not to inhale were further evidence, along with whatever squishiness was making my boots sink into the… ground? Dead rats? What the hell was I standing on?

"They should be here by now."

Seamus and I stiffened. The voice came from directly above us, muffled by the flooring and insulation that separated us from his moms' bedroom.

I looked at Seamus, but it was clear from the cold rage suffusing his face that the voice had not belonged to someone in his family.

"How many times do we have to tell you—he isn't here, and he isn't coming! He's traveling with friends, and he's too smart for whatever ridiculous trap you—."

The sound of flesh connecting with flesh resounded above us, and I put my hand on Seamus' arm, worried that he might do something rash… like tear through the floor and launch himself at whoever had clearly just hit one of his moms.
~~~

I looked at him, and with the diffuse light that seeped in, I could see his lips pulled back in a silent snarl that very effectively imitated his wolf form.

I wished I could communicate with him the way that Trevor and I did. Anything to try to help calm him. Now was not the time to lose our shit, though I couldn't blame him for the impulse at all.

"Whatever you assholes did to keep us from shifting to wolf isn't going to be enough to keep me from killing you all at the end of this."

That was uttered by a different female voice, one that I thought sounded a bit like a slightly higher version of Seamus'.

But as soon as I processed the meaning of the words, I grabbed Seamus' arm more forcefully and pulled us back to the far corner of the basement instead of worrying about who had spoken them.

Seamus resisted at first, but soon realized where I was headed and probably assumed I was just taking him to the corner so that we could whisper out a plan with less chance of being overheard.

Instead, as soon as we were as close to the wall as I could get us, I pulled on time and space and dropped us in the woods outside the house once more. Only this time it felt like I had to reach through a wall of taffy to find the power that had come so easily to me only minutes before.

"What the HELL, VIC!" Seamus turned on me, teeth bared, as soon as we had fully materialized in the woods.

"Are nulls a real thing?" I asked, stepping back from him, hoping to lead him deeper into the woods in case he decided to yell any louder and let all the damned mages in the world know that we were here.

"What?!"

"Nulls. People, or devices, that absorb magic and keep spells and shit from happening. They exist in half the fantasy books I read. Do they exist in real life? Trev said he was touched by one back in Bolivia and then he couldn't shift."

Seamus thought about that for a long moment.

"They might exist. I don't know any personally, and they would probably be mages, or related to them, but I've heard a story or two with a person that fit that description."

I nodded.

"Well, I think that the mages in your parents' place have brought one along for the ride. One of your moms was talking about not being able to shift, and pulling us out here felt like pulling through a wall of taffy just now, when pulling us in five minutes ago felt as easy as any other shift."

"Couldn't you just be getting tired? You brought us here from Fiji, after all."

"Yeah, but the distance shouldn't matter. If I'm wrinkling time and space to bring two points together, the distance between doesn't matter. The thing that tires me out is doing it over and over again, or taking multiple people on multiple rides. So far I've only brought you on two, now three, trips, while being fairly well rested, although I'll admit I'm damned hungry."

"Here," he said, handing me an energy bar that he pulled from the cargo pocket on his snow pants, leaving me reeling at how quickly he'd transitioned from wanting to kill me for taking him away from his moms to worrying about my well-being.

"I'm sorry I took you away from your folks," I said, biting into the slab of crunchy peanut butter energy bar. "I didn't know where the null was, or if we'd be able to get out of there, or pull on were forms at all if we stayed. It didn't seem like a good idea to walk into that kind of trap without some kind of backup."

"What kind of backup is going to help us when our magic won't work at all?"

"This," I said, holding up the Glock 45 I'd retrieved from beneath a floorboard under my bed.

"I thought you hated guns," Seamus said, grimacing at the handgun I was holding up.

"I do," I said, loading it and stuffing two extra clips into my pockets. "But an ex of mine loved guns, taught me how to shoot, and bought me this thing for Christmas one year."

"And you kept it?"

I shrugged.

"After my parents died and I started living alone, it seemed like a not terrible idea for a bit… but I locked it up with the ammo stored in a separate container, so… not actually all that useful for home defense."

"Why didn't you use that on Edik?"

I shrugged.

"I didn't really expect him to show up, so it's not like I could have gotten the gun loaded fast enough to be useful. And I really wasn't lying—I do hate guns. But we both saw the vision. The assholes in there are going to try to kill your moms, or us, or both, and we can't use magic against them. Of course, that should mean they can't use magic against us, either."

"Which means that they probably have guns too."

I nodded. "Shitty, but better than taking a pointy stick to a gun fight."

Seamus sighed.

He held up his phone and swiped to the lock screen. On it was a photo of two happy-looking women hugging a slightly bashful-looking Seamus in wolf form. One of them looked just like him, but thinner, and with shorter hair. The other was much paler, with freckled skin and long, curly red hair.

I smiled.

"Alexandra is the redhead, Rowan is the one who shares my dashing good looks. Don't shoot either of them, ok?" he said, sounding stern.

I nodded.

"Definitely not."

Then I thumbed off the safety with my right hand, grabbed his hand with my left, and shifted us both to his front porch.

~~~

"Open up, douchetarts, or I come in shooting," I shouted, raising my Glock to chest level on the door and shoving Seamus behind me.

"How did they—"

"SILENCE!"

Both those voices had come from inside. Oh good. Dissension among the ranks, perhaps? That might help us out.

When the door popped open, I had my gun trained straight at the chest of a six-foot-tall man who was holding one of the women Seamus had just showed me on his cell phone homescreen by the throat, with a gun leveled at her temple.

It was incredibly tempting to aim high and put a hole in the pale douchetart's forehead, but I didn't want to risk giving him enough time to shoot Rowan. Which meant that we were at a bit of an impasse.

Luckily, he seemed to come from the Bond School of Villainy. He was feeling chatty.

"You shouldn't play with guns, little girl," the man said, condescension dripping from his voice as he gestured at me with his 9mm.

As soon as he pulled the barrel away from Rowan's head, I pulled the trigger. I didn't aim at his forehead, tempting though it had been. I shot him straight in the chest. Center of mass, so even if I didn't hit his heart, I would likely pierce a lung or something. I wasn't really trying to kill him, though that was a likely outcome, but I needed him down and I wasn't willing to
~~~

risk him shooting any of the people I cared about, myself included.

He clearly hadn't been expecting me to pull the trigger. He didn't return fire. No surprise there. The 9mm he had been holding slid from his hand and he clutched at the newly created hole in his chest, blood seeping past his fingers. His body dropped to the floor in counterpoint to the bile rising in my throat.

I wasted no time stepping forward and using my foot to push the 9mm behind me, towards Seamus, while also pulling Seamus' mom clear of the doorway. I managed not to puke while I did it, but barely.

This is why I fucking hate guns. They are not for screwing around. Mages apparently didn't respect them properly. Or this guy hadn't. You don't wave guns around to try to get your way when you don't know how to use them, or when you think you'll just intimidate someone else who is also armed.

"Anyone else?" I said, gun still raised, finger resting on the trigger guard, stepping forward so that I blocked line of sight from the cabin to both Seamus and Rowan. I could hear her sobbing loudly, but she wasn't screaming, and she hadn't thrown up yet. I was thankful for that. If she threw up, I was certain I would too.

The remaining people in the room were all in various stages of shock, as the tall mage I'd shot lay bleeding, now unconscious, across the threshold. He must have been the one in charge, because no one else seemed inclined to step up.

I quickly assessed the room. There were five more mages, and one woman who matched the other one in the photo on Seamus' phone. They all seemed to be unarmed. Even the woman who was restraining Alexandra didn't seem to have a weapon on her. Perhaps she was the null.

"Anyone else have a gun they want to wave about? Anyone else not understand how easy it is for me to kill you with this?"

I didn't gesture wildly about the room, but I kept the gun up and ready, my finger on the trigger guard, the safety still off.

I was starting to get angry. It might have been the shock of just having shot someone, or rage that I had needed to shoot someone in order to protect people I cared about, or it could have been the fact that this was yet more evidence that MOME didn't give a fuck about justice, and only cared about eliminating threats to its own power. Also, MOME allowed complete douchetarts to lead missions that involved abducting civilians, and Gwendamnit, I really needed to take a few deep breaths before I started to shoot holes in the wall.

"Your null is canceling whatever shields you might normally have against bullets, and on top of that, you can't even fight back with magic right now. We have all the guns, and you have nothing, so I suggest you give me Alexandra there, and I will put this damned thing away so we can all just get back to our lives. If you hurry, you may even have a chance to keep Captain Asshat here from bleeding to death."

No one moved.

"Fine. Alexandra, can you walk?" I asked.

She paled, but nodded and began to stand.

"If anyone but Alexandra moves, I will shoot them," I added, just for good measure.

No one else moved.

See? When you prove up front that you are a) capable of, and b) willing to, shoot someone, people don't fuck around. If you're not willing to shoot someone, don't wave a gun around. Coercion with a gun certainly can work, since enough people are terrified of them, especially if they themselves are unarmed, but then there are the *other* people carrying guns who will just shoot you the moment you hesitate. And in a state like Arizona, where a five-year-old can basically buy an Uzi, why would you risk it?

It seemed like it took Alexandra an hour to cross the small hardwood floor between where she had been held to where the barely breathing body of the man who had opened the door now lay. Without lowering the gun or looking away from the five remaining mages, I sidestepped, so that she could climb over Captain Asshat and out the door.

"I really wish you assholes would just leave me and my family alone," I said, backing myself carefully out over the too-still body of Captain Asshat and onto the front porch. I closed the door, which thankfully had remained unblocked, and finally lowered the gun, putting the safety on. Then I wiped the tears from my face.

"Hold on tight," I said, wrapping Seamus and his moms in a bear hug, after tucking the gun into the holster I'd worn to bring it here. I might have imagined it, but I thought all three of them grimaced slightly when I touched them. I couldn't really blame them, but it still hurt.

I tried to ignore the wretched feeling in my stomach, and reached through time and space for the one thing in the universe that still felt like home.

"TREV?"

I must have fainted after I shifted everyone back to that tiny island near Fiji, but sure enough, the thing that had drawn me there swayed gently in front of my eyes.

"You dead, sis?" Trev asked, his golden eyes dancing in the sunlight, the cerulean sky behind him clear as crystal.

"Yep."

"Well, too bad. I need you in this world."

I smiled, and was pleased to note that it didn't hurt to do so. Nor did it hurt to breathe in the salt-scented air that caressed us. In fact, I just felt a bit tired and mildly sore, like I'd gone for an extra long trail run the day before, on a steeper than usual mountain.

"Is everyone else here?" I asked, deciding it was safe to maybe sit up.

Trev nodded. "Seamus and his moms are over by the fire with Sol."

"A fire in the middle of the day?" I asked, taking another look at the sun glittering off the waves that crashed against the white sand shore stretching away from us in both directions.

"It seemed like a nice enough distraction." Trev shrugged.

"Is everyone ok?"

"They seem pretty shaken, but mostly alright. How are *you*?"

I really didn't want to answer that question, and wasn't sure what to say anyway, so I decided to go with a change of subject. "Any luck with Mom and Dad's boat?"

Trev was sitting on the sand beside me, the lines of concern on his face receding somewhat when I managed to keep my balance while sitting.

"Negative," he replied, sighing. "I don't know what it was supposed to tell us, besides the fact that Seamus' moms were in trouble, but that seems like something he might have gotten a vision about anywhere... doesn't really seem to me like 'answers.'"

"Yeah. That'd be a stretch even for a prophecy, I'd think. We could ask Seamus..." I hesitated. "Maybe you could ask Seamus if that makes sense for a message from a seer."

Trev quirked an eyebrow at me.

"Why wouldn't *you* ask Seamus?"

I sighed and closed my eyes, not feeling brave enough to watch Trev's face while I confessed.

"Because I don't know if he wants to talk to me anymore, after seeing me shoot someone in the chest."

You don't have to hide from me, Vic. I've done a few things I'm not terribly proud of in order to keep MOME from hurting people.

When I opened my eyes and dared a look at his face, he looked sincere, and sounded it too, as he continued, "I know it probably makes you sick, and that's fine. That's healthy, but... it's not your fault that MOME forced you into violence to protect yourself."

"Isn't it, though?" I asked, my voice a bit desperate. "Couldn't I have talked them into handing over Seamus' moms? Offered myself in exchange? Something? What if I hadn't taken a gun with me?"

"If you hadn't taken a gun with you, you would either all be captured by MOME right now, or Seamus' moms would be dead. There's no way that MOME would have negotiated with you and held up their end of the deal. They either would have harmed Seamus' family anyway, or they would have kept you all prisoner."

"And is that so bad? What if we were all prisoners? How bad would that be? At least no one would be dead."

Apparently, my unconscious mind had been hard at work on drumming up all the toughest questions while I was passed out. I wanted to agree with Trev. I wanted to be angry with MOME, hell I *was* angry with them. I was furious with the asshole I'd shot, because he'd made it seem like the only sensible option in a deadly situation... but I was still sure that it was wrong. That if I were a better person, or a more powerful shifter, or *something*, I wouldn't have had to shoot that man.

"There is some possibility that he might not have shot anyone. Maybe he would just have locked all four of you up. I think it's a very slim chance, Vic, since he had a gun pointed at Rowan's head, but for argument's sake let's say there was a chance. What then? What happens after you, Seamus, and Seamus' moms are locked up by MOME?"

I shrugged, as my brain just reminded me over and over again that at least I wouldn't have shot anyone in the chest, but Trev just kept talking.

"Do you think that Sol, Rhelia, and I would have just let that slide? Do you think we would have just left you guys in MOME custody to rot, or worse? We would have come after you, Vic. As sure as the sun rises in the morning, we would have come after you. And how many of us would still be standing at the end of that?"

My head was starting to hurt and tears were pouring down my cheeks, so I didn't say anything, just stood up and started walking, not paying attention to where I was going, just walking, away from Trev. Away from everyone else. Away from all the people who hadn't pulled the trigger of a gun that was pointed at someone else's chest a few hours ago.

Of course I wound up in front of Mom and Dad's boat.

Because the universe hates me.

Because I wasn't fucking crying hard enough as it was.

Because dragon seers are sneaky pieces of shit.

Barely able to see through the tears, and feeling like I was going to throw up and faint all at once if I didn't just sit down, I collapsed face-first against the deck, which lay at a forty-five degree angle to the sand. Unable to comfort myself in any way, I cried.

And cried.

And cried some more.

Because sometimes you cry so long you forget why you're crying, so then you think of reasons you might need to cry, and you're suddenly flooded with things, some small—a stupid comment about how 'exotic' you look, some huge—shooting someone in the chest, being assaulted in your own home, your parents dying—that have hurt you in the past year or more, and you just need to keep crying until you sort of mentally go through the entire checklist and start to feel better.

I don't even know how long I'd been there when I heard footsteps in the sand behind me. It seemed like hours, but it might have only been minutes.

"Feel any better?" Trev asked.

I nodded, using the hem of my shirt to wipe some of the snot from my face.

"I think I had been holding that in for a while," I admitted.

Trev stepped closer and I briefly felt his hand rest on my shoulder as he leaned his side against the boat, and—

It was then that a shriek like a dying banshee tore at my ears, and seemed to tear at the very fabric of time and space. It was followed by a deafening clap, like the end note of a lightning strike.

Then our mother stood in front of us, half hidden in the shadows of the galley, with her right arm wrapped around our father. They both looked… pale.

"Hey Vic," my mom said, her voice sounding tired.

"Mom?!" I stuttered, my voice barely audible.

"Hey Trev." This time my mom's voice sounded ready to break. Trev and I both started to take a step forward to reach for our parents, but Mom's voice was urgent.

"Don't let go of the boat!"

We both stopped in our tracks.

"If you're watching this," she said, taking a deep breath, "then we're dead, which sucks, but isn't too surprising in the grand scheme of things. More importantly, it means you two have found each other."

And here she took a moment to wipe away a few tears.

"Which makes all of this worthwhile, if you ask me."

I looked between them both, my mom and dad, *dead*, I'd thought. Dead, she'd just said. But why was I seeing them? Why did it look like they were standing right in front of me? Was it a hologram? Was it some quirky mage message? What the fuck was going on? And why couldn't I hug my parents?

"Mom," I started, but she just kept on talking, as though I hadn't said anything.

"If you two are back together, then there's literally nothing that MOME can do to us that isn't worth it."

My dad was nodding fervently, but was crying too hard to say anything. I could feel Trev trembling beside me, and I wanted to throw both of my arms around him, but Mom had said not to let go of the boat. Would this message disappear? Would we ever be able to see it again? I couldn't risk it, and I figured Trevor would understand.

"We don't have much time. They've been catching up with us since we left Cape Town and we don't have much longer to try our last gambit, which, if you're watching this, probably didn't work, but who knows. Maybe you'll never see this, or maybe they'll only catch us years from now. There's no guaranteeing that any of this will play out the way we hope it will, even you two seeing this. Maybe especially that. We're counting on Vic's persistence, and MOME's greed, and hoping beyond hope that Trev... Trev, that they left something of you in there, that they didn't erase our sweet mischievous boy.... You're so much smarter than they are, sweetie. We just have to hope that you remember it at all the most important times."

She stopped to wipe her nose and eyes. Dad had already hidden his face in her shoulder.

"I'm rambling," she said, taking another deep breath. "You need to know the truth. Both of you. It'll have to be the Cliff's Notes, I'm afraid, because this storm is picking up and we have to get going, but... they're after us because of what we know. Because we know what they're planning to do, and how they're planning to do it. It's..."

A loud thud sounded on the hull, and my parents both looked at each other.

"Gods damn it!" my mom shouted. "It's an army, Vic. Trevor will likely understand exactly what kind of army, and even how they're making it. It's why they took him. Vic, it's an army of people like you and Trevor. Like me and your dad. They're using all the misfits of the magical world and training them, but they're not training them to help them, they're training them to use them. We think—damn it!"

There was another large noise in the background, and my dad hugged my mom furiously, gave her one kiss, turned towards us and said, "I love you both, and I always have."

Then he turned his tear-streaked face towards whatever lay behind him, disappearing from sight.

"They're here. That's not just the storm anymore. We have to go," my mom continued, tears rising to her eyes. "We suspect that they're also preparing a weapon, but we don't have proof."

She turned to me then, and it felt like she was looking straight into my soul, even though this was by all appearances some kind of recording.

"Vic, you need to find my journals. I can't say more than that, in case... just find them. They'll tell you everything you need to know."

Then she turned and looked to where Trevor was standing beside me, and I could only assume she pierced him with the same stare she'd just used on me.

"Trevor, you could be the key to stopping all of this. With all that you've probably learned... Teach Vic. Teach her everything. Between the two of you, you can make sure this doesn't happen to anyone else. Families shouldn't be torn apart like this, and MOME shouldn't get to take over the world."

She paused, as though listening to something, but whatever it was, I couldn't hear it.

"I love you both," she said, baring a watery smile. "Give 'em hell."

Then she turned and was gone.

Trev and I just stood there, silent and unmoving, for a long, long time, and then one more long time, just for good measure. One of us was shaking, but I wasn't sure which one. Maybe it was both of us.

"How did they know we would find each other?" I asked eventually, still standing with my hand awkwardly against the hull, Trevor beside me, matching my pose.

"How did they know we would find the boat?" Trev asked.

"How did they make that recording? That felt like they were here. I felt like I could have touched them."

"Ghosts," Trevor said.

"What? You're telling me those were their spirits? Are they haunting the boat?"

"No. Well, sort of. They're not haunting it. It was just a message. And it's not their spirits, or not the whole of their spirits anyway. They left remnants of themselves here to deliver the message."

"Remnants? Do you mean they left a portion of their souls here? How does that work? Wouldn't that kill you? Or fundamentally change you? How can anyone do that?"

"It's not recommended, but if you're about to die anyway…"

Right. Intentionally shear off a portion of your soul to deliver a message, instead of risk dying with something important unsaid. Fair enough, I could imagine a few scenarios dire enough to warrant that, and this one certainly counted, but…

"I may be clinging to my Potter lore a little too hard here, but wouldn't that be the kind of thing the bad guys teach you?"

Trev shrugged.

"Maybe. If the bad guys are MOME? Probably. They're more about practicality, and you have to admit it has its uses. Even some old failing countess or whatever could use it to will stuff to people if she needed to, right? I mean, it's not like you're shearing off a part of someone else's soul."

"But wouldn't the principle be the same? I mean if you can shear off some of your own soul, couldn't you shear off someone else's… fuck, why am I clinging to this? It doesn't matter." I took a deep breath. "Was that really our parents, Trev?"

"I think so, Vic. That kind of thing is pretty hard to fake."

And that was when I started to cry.

I think Trev joined me, but I never was sure.

The boat burst into flames before I had a chance to get a good look.

"WOULD IT BE too much to ask that you NOT immolate the last vestige of our dead parents?" I asked, jumping back from the now-flaming wreckage.

"That is *not* me," Trev said. He was looking frantic, and also seemed to be straining, like he was trying to do advanced calculus while taking a shit. "It's not responding to any of my magic!"

I looked all around us, desperate to find a way to stop the flames. The ocean was only a few meters away, but it might as well have been a thousand miles, for all the good it did us without even a bucket to move it.

"Rhelia!" Trev shouted, and I could hear the call inside my mind as well.

She must have been close by; I heard the wingbeats before I saw the dragon herself, and she lay down on top of the boat as though hoping to smother the flames.

Then she hissed and shot skyward again.

It will not bend to my will and is too hot for my scales, she sent, before flapping the short distance to the ocean and squelching whatever bits of fire had adhered to her.

And before we could even look for another method of putting out the flames, the conflagration roared even higher, then suddenly stopped.

Apparently it had run out of fuel.

There was nothing left of my parents' old boat but a few charred coals.

"Gwendamnit! Can't a few hours pass without something *completely* shitty happening to us?!" I shouted at the cloudless sky.

Sol must have walked over while I was too preoccupied with putting out an impossible fire for me to notice, because suddenly she was right next to my shoulder, saying, "Well, we did have a handful of not-shitty hours yesterday."

Her voice was practically purring, and the reminder of how good things had been that day sent warm shivers coursing over my body.

"Hey, Gatita," she whispered, wrapping me in a hug that left me warm in more ways than one. "Te echaba de menos."

I smiled and breathed in the sun-soaked scent of her skin.

"I missed you too," I murmured, realizing that it was true even as I said it. It was strange to think of how much closer Sol, Seamus, and I were than even a few days ago.

"Rowan and Alexandra were just regaling us with tales of your heroics," she said, not letting me go. "I hope you don't feel too bad about shooting that asshat."

I laughed a little bit, and probably cried a bit too, I don't really remember, but it felt good to be held by someone I was intimate with and not feel rejected for all that I'd done today.

"Now," she said, looking between Trev and me, while still holding me close, "Why exactly did you set your old boat on fire?"

~~~

One hour, and a whole lot of fruitless searching of our tiny island oasis, found us no closer to figuring out why the boat had ignited, except that maybe it was set to self-destruct like a secret message in a cheesy spy movie. Which, the way my life had been going lately, seemed just as likely as anything else. Especially when you considered the contents of our parents' final message to us. It wasn't the kind of thing that they'd have wanted MOME to know they knew about. Then again, why was MOME after them to begin with, if not because they knew things they shouldn't? Maybe they were more concerned with MOME finding out that *we* now knew more about their evil schemes.

Sadly, Sol had no answers for us.

"I've only been at MOME for about two years, so I'm not privy to any information about secret armies or secret weapons. I worked my ass off to make it into the special services department just to get higher security clearance, but I still haven't been granted access to anything more than the personal files of people I've been charged with tracking down. You and Trev
~~~

being prime examples. But even then, I was only given partial access to your file. It's the file you rescued from MOME that has all of the real details, and that was something I never had access to."

"Fuck," I said, just barely restraining myself from slapping my own forehead.

"What?" asked Trev and Sol at once.

"The file. It was in my pack when we left Sol's cabin to go to Unterberg…. I never got it back from the council after they took us."

"Shit. So the Unterberg council is in possession of our family's file?" Trev asked, looking a bit paler than usual.

"Yep."

"What are the chances that they haven't taken a look at it?" Trev asked.

"Not good," Sol replied. "They would be looking for anything they could to incriminate you."

"But they can't touch us now, can they?" I asked. "And besides, what about Mom and Dad's file would they find incriminating, I mean it's not like they—"

"They trained with Albert, Vic. Voluntarily. They sought out instruction from a MOME researcher when they were teenagers. The Unterberg council won't find that very reassuring. They'll assume that they were MOME sympathizers."

"But that doesn't make sense. They all seemed bummed when I made that joke about Dad being dead, which made it seem like they respected him."

"Maybe they hadn't found the file yet when they were talking with us, or maybe they respected him anyway, but regardless it's not a good thing that they have that file in their hands."

"Fine. How do you even know that about Mom and Dad? That they trained with Albert by choice, I mean."

"I must have gotten farther into their file than you did. Plus, I talked to Albert afterwards."

"Talked? More like shouted-at-a-whole-bunch," Sol scoffed.

Trev smiled a bit sheepishly.

"Yeah, well, I was a bit mad at our parents for keeping certain secrets from us, and I may or may not have taken my anger out on Albert."

That made me chuckle.

"Well, as the principal to a public high school, I imagine he's fairly used to that by now. So, what do we do now? I think it's pretty important that we figure out what MOME is up to. The idea that they're training an army," I glanced at Trev, wondering if he knew more about that part than he was letting on, "or building some secret weapon… I mean, it sounds like something out of a Bond movie, but Mom and Dad weren't prone to conspiracy theories… I think."

Trev looked me straight in the eyes, as if he knew what I'd been thinking, and who knows, maybe he did.

"I wouldn't be surprised if some of the kids that were taken by MOME were being trained, or brainwashed or whatever, to be used as an army, and it wouldn't be hard to imagine how powerful an army of kids like us would be, but don't worry Vic, if MOME was trying to make me sympathetic to their side, they failed every time they threatened you or our parents."

Sol looked between us both, shaking her head.

"Twins creep me out sometimes. I feel like you two just had a conversation I couldn't hear."

I laughed.

"That was nothing compared to the actual conversations we have that you can't hear," I said, giving her an exaggerated wink.

"Alright you three," Seamus called from a hundred meters down the beach. He had crossed half the distance between us and where his moms and Rhelia were sitting around a small fire doing… who knew what. "Come talk to the rest of us. We need a plan."

When we made our way to the rest of the group, Seamus smiled at the three of us, and the fact that he included me in the gesture went a long way to easing the hurt I'd felt when we'd first shifted back here.

"We have a very important issue that needs resolving immediately," he said, shifting his face to a more somber expression. "I'm hungry."

MY HOUSE WAS untouched since the last time I'd been there, and it felt a bit surreal to be back within its walls. Somehow, traveling between countries and realms in the blink of an eye, learning that dark matter coursed through my veins, giving me access to a snow leopard form and teleportation, and learning that the world was full of what was still best described as magic, (in my mind at least), had made me feel more out of place than I'd ever felt before. Yet, even so, arriving at the house my parents had left me in their will didn't feel like a homecoming at all. I felt as out of place here now as I had anywhere else. It felt like these walls couldn't contain all that had happened to me in the past two weeks.

In the end, we had decided to send Rowan and Alexandra to Unterberg with Rhelia, since they were all unquestionably welcome there still, to see if they could convince the Unterberg council to hand over my family's file and provide a safe place for Rowan and Alexandra to stay until we could be sure that MOME wasn't going to try to kill them in their own home. Unfortunately, at the moment, that seemed likely to be a permanent arrangement. I felt awful that they'd had to leave their home so suddenly, but at least we could be sure that they would have a safe, MOME-free place to hide.

Sol, Seamus, Trev, and I, on the other hand, had decided to listen to Seamus' stomach and head someplace we knew was well-stocked with snacks, not to mention also a potential hiding place for the mysterious journals that my mom had mentioned.

Sol, the self-appointed sandwich-maker-in-chief, had taken on the task of preparing food for us all, while Trev worked on checking the house for sensors, tracking devices, spells, or any other ugly surprises that MOME might have left for us. Since we weren't useful to either of those tasks, Seamus and I, grumbling stomachs and all, started to search the house.

"Hey," Seamus said, after we walked into one of the storage cupboards on the main floor and started opening boxes that looked like they had been here since before I was born, "I just wanted to thank you… for saving my moms."

"Seamus, you know I never would have left you to do that alone, right?"

I turned, still wary of what I might see in Seamus' eyes, but finally willing to face whatever it was… but he was staring determinedly at a half-opened box full of cookbooks.

"That's not what I mean, Vic. I mean… it was really hard for me to see you shoot someone, but… but not harder than it must have been for you to actually do it, and if you hadn't…"

He turned to look at me, finally, and I saw the unshed tears in his eyes.

"He was going to kill them, Vic. I saw it in my visions, over and over again. Every time I had that vision and you weren't there, they died. I thought I would be ok with… with what you had to do, because I'd seen it probably a dozen times in my head by the time it really happened, but… it still shocked me."

He was silent for a long moment, and when I finally reached for him and he didn't flinch at all, I wrapped him in the biggest bear hug I could manage.

"It's ok, Seamus. It was a damned ugly thing. If our situations had been reversed, it would probably take me a little while to get over the shock of it too."

Seamus started to object, but I couldn't bear to hear him contradict me, because I didn't want to know what I already suspected: that if he had been holding the gun, he never would have pulled the trigger, or only would have pulled it too late. So I kissed him, partially to stop him from saying anything, and partially to prove to us both that we were still human. That we were still capable of something as normal and life-affirming as a kiss. I probably should have asked first, but with the way he leaned into it and pulled me closer, I figured my lapse was forgivable.

Of course, it was in that moment that Sol burst through the door to the cupboard that we'd been searching through.

"Oh! Sorry to interrupt. I figured you'd want your sandwiches."

Seamus and I both laughed as we pulled apart.

"Sandwiches sound like a great idea," I said, while Seamus simply replied by taking a giant bite out of the slab of bread and meat offered to him.

I had just taken a bite of mine, and was opening my mouth to exclaim that Sol was officially the one and only sandwich-maker-in-chief as far as I was concerned, when Gwen popped into existence right behind Sol's back and shouted, "They're coming! Hurry up! Get Seamus out of here!"

"Gwen, what!? Who's coming? What the hell is—"

But she was already gone, as were Sol and Trev, as Seamus and I realized as soon as we stepped out of the cupboard and into the kitchen.

Seamus ran to the door to check the lock and look out the window.

"What the fuck?" he asked, taking the words right out of my mouth.

"Did Gwen just nab Sol and Trev?" I asked.

He nodded, crossing towards the living room window, probably to see if MOME was within sight.

I started to follow, in case we needed to make a quick exit.

"I guess we'd better get out of he—"

Then the door exploded in a rain of fire and wood, and I was leaping behind the kitchen island, screaming Seamus' name. I could hear boots hitting the floor and shouts filling the air, so I shifted to where I'd last seen Seamus before the door exploded, hoping that I could shift us out, but Seamus wasn't near the window, he was on the floor next to the couch (which was only reasonable as the air was filled with ricocheting spells of every variety). I reached down to grab him so we could get the fuck out of Dodge, but then something hot hit my back and I was screaming in pain, and Seamus was screaming something, and then the world went black.

"OW. FUCK."

"Thank gods, you're awake."

"Seamus?"

I had to ask, because it was pitch black in… wherever the hell we were. I could feel a hard surface underneath my shoulder and leg, and I seemed to be lying on my left side. Other than that, I had no clue what was going on, except that I could hear Seamus' voice, and half my body felt like it was on fire and/or had been hit by a truck—mostly and.

"Are you ok?" Seamus' voice asked.

"I don't know. I'm afraid to try to move, because just lying here hurts enough as it is. What the fuck happened?"

"MOME got us."

"Yeah, I guessed that much. But what *happened?* How did they find us? Why aren't we dead? And where the seven fucks are we?"

"Do you mean before or after you killed a MOME agent?"

"After. I remember that part. And we aren't sure that I killed him. He could have lived if they got him help soon enough."

I wasn't happy about the reminder of how I had shot a man in the chest at point-blank range, but I was in too much pain to notice the nausea that rose when I thought about it, so that was something… I guess.

"I don't know how they found us, except that we were at your house, so I suppose they must have known where to look. Do you remember Gwen coming and grabbing Sol and Trev?"

"Yeah, it's the stuff after that part that's… fuzzy."

"Well, after that you jumped behind the kitchen island and I dove to the floor, then you shifted to me, I assume to take us somewhere else, but they were waiting for that, or else they had just decided to start firing everywhere at once, and you got hit, and… I don't know why they didn't kill us, but they threw us in the back of a truck and… then they dropped us here. They put bags on both our heads. Not sure why they bothered with yours, since you've been out cold from the moment they hit you with that spell, but all I saw was when they put the hood on your scorched, unconscious form, and since then I have literally been in the dark."

"How long have I been out?" I asked, trying to think past the pain all down the right side of my body, as well as the headache that was quickly taking up residence inside my skull.

"I'm not sure. It's not like they've been coming in to tell me the time and date, but… a few days, at any rate."

"Days?! Was I in a coma?"

"Kinda. I think. I don't know. Honestly, Vic, I seriously thought I was never going to talk to you again."

Seamus sounded like he was about to cry, or maybe like he had been crying for a while already. It was hard to tell. His voice was rough, at any rate, and I couldn't say I blamed him. I wasn't exactly feeling like this situation was made of win as it was, and if he had thought me as good as dead for a few days…

"Any idea what kind of spell they hit me with?" I asked, mainly to get us both thinking about something other than how screwed we probably were.

"No idea. I don't have much experience with mages at all…. Now, if a giant were had mauled you, I could probably be of more help."

I tried to laugh, but it hurt too much.

"Ow."

"Sorry."

"No, it's good. If we don't keep up a sense of humor, then we're fucked."

Seamus chuckled.

"Oh, good to know there's still hope, then."

"There's always hope, Seamus."

"Yeah. If you say so, Vic. Any chance you'll be able to walk soon?"

I took a moment to assess. My right side was still alight with pain. It was an awful combination of the hot pain of a bad burn and the dull ache of a strong impact. I tried to move my right arm, but the immediate response from my nervous system was to abandon ship. I took multiple deep breaths to keep from passing out, then decided that I would wait a bit before I tried my right leg. I needed to rest up first.

"Not likely," I replied, after conducting my little mobility test. "But I don't really need to be able to walk, do I?"

Seamus didn't say anything for a moment.

"Wherever we are, I can't pull on my wolf form."

"Well shit. I suppose there's a null somewhere nearby, then."

"Maybe."

"How long did it take them to bring us here?"

"I dunno. Long enough that they stopped to let me pee once along the way."

"So they brought us by car?"

"Yeah."

"Weird. What did they do about me?"

"Can't you smell yourself?"

Ugh… I couldn't. Either because my nose was just used to it, after however long we'd been like this, or maybe because I'd been damaged somehow. Fuck. I hope I hadn't lost my sense of smell, that would suck.

"I'm just kidding. You're either super dehydrated, or they have a spell for that, or something."

"You ass."

"You said we needed to keep our senses of humor."

"I hate you."

"That's fair."

And then I tried to laugh again, and wound up almost crying, because it hurt so damned much.

"Owwww… ok. No more sense of humor, it's going to kill me."

"Vic, how do we get out of this?"

"I don't know." I thought about that for a long time. I wasn't touching Seamus right now, so I couldn't shift us both, but to be honest, I wouldn't have tried anyway. Beyond the fact that there was a null somewhere nearby, which likely made it impossible anyway, I felt so wrecked by whatever had happened to me that, judging by how much energy shifting had taken from me in the past, I didn't think I would be able to move the two of us for quite some time.

"This must be episode two," I muttered.

"What?" Seamus asked.

"Episode two. You know, in episode one the plucky, brave underdog is pulled into a world he or she doesn't understand, but manages to gain the upper hand somehow. In episode two, everything falls apart, and it looks like our hero is lost."

"And then in episode three the plucky underdog takes it all back and wins the day?"

"Yep. Everyone's favorite fiction trope."

"Right… so, how do we get to episode three?"

"Close our eyes and wait for rescue?" I suggested, half-heartedly.

And with that, I did close my eyes, since having them open didn't seem to make any difference anyway. Seamus remained silent too, and, eventually, sleep took me.

VIRGINIA McCLAIN

VICTORIA MARMOT
AND THE
SHADOW
OF DEATH

VICTORIA MARMOT BOOK THREE

To Cedar, for being a light in the darkness.

I WIPED THE sweat from my brow and tried, yet again, to roll the large block of granite up the side of the cliff, stopping it with my forehead when it finally reached head height, then lowering my wrists to lay against the boulder at my waist. My hands quivered, half with the strain of having pushed the block of granite into place, and half with trepidation. I took a deep breath, trying not to gag on the sulphur stench that permeated what passed for air here, and pulled my wrists as far apart as the manacles would allow. Then I pulled my forehead back, trying not to flinch. I really didn't want to graze myself again. The thumb on my left hand was still numb from the last time, and I was sincerely hoping that my efforts would pay off soon, because if I didn't get to a healer in the near future, I was pretty sure that gash was going to get infected.

The rock collided with the chain connecting the manacles, releasing an earsplitting crack that reverberated through the narrow canyon surrounding me. I almost cried as I felt my wrists fly outwards, the resistance from the steel chain that connected them finally giving way. Unfortunately, breaking the chain wouldn't restore my ability to pull myself through space and time, or to pull on my snow leopard form.

Throwing a suspicious glance at the brooding purple clouds that hovered in the thin strip of orange sky visible from my narrow prison, I scrambled onto the boulder in front of me and began the slightly less cumbersome process of beating the shit out of the shackles holding my ankles together. At least now I could aim the rock with my arms instead of my forehead.

Consequently, I didn't bash the crap out of my legs or ankles, or even tear up the skintight black jeans that had materialized the last time I'd shifted back into my human form (much to my dismay). Also, it meant it only took three good slams of the thirty-pound granite block against my ankle chains before they split.

Since my feet had been splayed as wide as they would go against the force of the chain, and now that force was removed, my legs went sprawling and I landed on my ass between the edge of the boulder and the cliff face. Luckily, I managed to drop the block away from me, so I wasn't pinned by anything. And I finally had four limbs free.

"Fuck yeah!" I shouted, dragging myself up so that I could stand on top of the boulder again and start climbing my way out of this cursed fucking canyon. No more worrying about drowning in the flash floods that swept through here every night. No more dodging rockfall, as whatever huge-assed creatures stampeding along the top of the canyon fled who the fuck knew what. And NO. MORE. GWENDAMNED. SQUIRREL. DE-MONS.

I didn't care that half of my hand left hand was numb and useless, or that I hadn't eaten in days, or that I was pretty sure the water I'd drunk from the pools left behind by the flash floods had made me hallucinate. I was going to get the fuck out of this canyon, magic powers or no magic powers. Help or no help.

I still didn't know how I was going to get back to my own world after I got out of this canyon, but at least I wouldn't be stuck in a place that tried to kill me five times a day. At least I would be able to use my hands and feet.

I was extremely grateful that the canyon wall was riddled with handholds from all the broken rock that periodically tumbled to the bottom. Honestly, the place was surprisingly crumbly for a ravine carved out of granite. Generally that kind of thing was pretty stable, but... well, this wasn't even Earth, as far I could tell, so what the fuck did I know about how rocks should work here?

Anyway, I had no shortage of holds for climbing to the top of this thing. Which was a huge relief, considering that I had about three hundred feet to ascend before I reached the top, and falling would make for a pretty horrific death. I wasn't stoked about doing this without a rope at all, and with who knew how many unstable holds along the way. Especially considering how injured my left hand was. But my options were limited, and dying in a flash flood or getting crushed by rockfall really didn't appeal. Since those had clearly been likelihoods at the bottom of the canyon, I had little choice. I'd already shuffled for days in either direction to try to find a likely place to crush the bonds that held me, hoping that I might also get lucky enough to find a way out that didn't involve scaling one hundred meters of loose granite, but nothing had turned up except the literal rock and hard place I had used to break my chains.

I still didn't know what the damned things were made out of, but whatever it was, they kept me from pulling on the magic (or dark matter, or whatever you want to call it) that I normally had access to. Believe me, I'd tried, and I'd almost knocked myself out a few times over the past few days attempting to access my abilities in order to get out of this place. Especially after the damned squirrel showed up…

Of course, you're probably wondering how the hell I got here, and where the hell "here" is to begin with. The funny thing is: "hell" is my best guess for an answer at the moment. I really don't know where I am, except that MOME dropped me here when they finally got tired of Seamus' and my attempts to escape from the dungeon where they'd shoved us while I awaited my "trial." That's in quotes because I have no doubt that those asshats at MOME have about zero intention of giving me a fair trial. That was made evident on the very first day I regained consciousness in that shithole.

<div align="center">~~~</div>

"You're awake, Ms. Marmot. I'm impressed. I had rather expected to be trying a corpse."

I blinked into the light pouring out of what appeared to be a headlamp. The voice that addressed me was female and southern.

This particular southern accent was muted, and had that cloying condescension that comes from some educated southerners.

"I've been told I'm full of surprises," I muttered, still blinking, and wishing I could move my hands up to rub my eyes. My arms weren't restrained, but one of them was asleep from having been pinned underneath me for days and the other hurt so much whenever I tried to move it that it may as well have been a button labeled "to wish for death, press here."

"You'll have to forgive me," I continued, since I still couldn't see. "I'm not exactly up to speed on the who's who of douchecanoes employed by MOME. Do you have a name?"

"I was told you lacked manners, Ms. Marmot. I'm sad to discover it's true. However, since you've asked, I'm Rebecca Dryer, attorney at law and Magister in the High Courts of MOME."

"Well, how very pretentious of you."

I had to admit, not being able to see the woman, despite all the light she'd brought down here, was starting to rub me the wrong way, and I was already irritable due to the whole trapped-in-a-cell-can't-move-half-my-body-feel-like-I'm-about-to-die scenario, as it was.

I had just now confirmed the trapped in a cell bit, though I had suspected it for a while now. But neither Seamus nor I had been able to see anything since we'd been in here, and the headlamp that Rebecca had brought with her provided our first illumination of the steel bars that separated us from the stone passageway in which she smugly stared at a clipboard.

I could finally see enough of her to make out the smugness and the clipboard.

She had curly hair. I couldn't really tell what color it was, because it was too short to fall in the direct beam of the headlamp, but something on the lighter side, I thought. And the rest of her features were too washed-out in shadows for me to be able to tell much about her. I didn't think it mattered. Whatever she looked like, I doubted she was here to trade fashion tips.

"Well, now that the niceties are taken care of," she said, blithely ignoring my quip about her pretentiousness, "Victoria Marmot, you stand accused of assaulting an officer of magical law enforcement with the intent to kill. How do you plead?"

"The fuck. What's going on?"

"You stand accused of—"

"I heard you the first time. What is going on here?"

"You are being tried for your crimes."

"Oh, that's rich. I bet it will be a fair trial and everything, too. Do I get representation? Do I even get to speak at this trial?"

"As I said, I had half expected to be trying a corpse. I'm sure that since you're conscious now, we can accommodate that. Now, please answer the question."

"Wait. You said that I stood accused of assault with intent to kill. That means he's not dead. The man I shot lived?"

"I am not allowed to share any details of this case with you. Your own magistrate will—"

"But you would sure as shit be trying me for murder if he'd died. So that means he's alive!"

"I can't say."

"You don't have to," I said, and I couldn't help it. I was smiling.

"You sound pleased," she said, after a pause.

"Look, that guy, whoever he was, is an asshole. But yeah. I'm glad he's not dead."

"Don't think it will reduce your sentence, simply because—"

"I don't care about the fucking sentence, lady. I'm glad he's not dead. I didn't want to kill him."

"Then why did you shoot him in the chest?"

"He was going to kill people I care about."

"Our officers only use deadly force in the most extreme circumstances. They would never harm an unarmed person who was in compliance with the law."

Seamus and I both laughed, though there wasn't humor in either of our tones.

"You tell yourself whatever you need to in order get to sleep at night, lady." I wasn't about to waste my breath convincing someone who was clearly going to be directly involved in whatever sham MOME had planned for my "trial" that MOME was the bad guy here.

"Listen here, young woman, you—a family member of a known convict, escapee from MOME's southern holding facilities, colluder with known criminals, and class A fugitive—shot a man in the chest just because he opened a door, before he'd had a chance to say anything to you. So don't you lecture me about sleeping at night."

That angered me enough that I almost tried to sit up, and the pain of it winded me for a moment. When I could speak again, it was very deliberate.

"Try this on for size. That known convict, also known as my brother, was abducted by masked men driving a fucking unmarked white van when we were eight years old. Those men worked for MOME. And why did they grab a terrified eight-year-old boy? Because they thought he might turn into something unsavory when he finally made his first change. Then, when my parents tried to get him back through the courts, MOME told my parents they were lucky MOME had "let" them keep me (who they would happily have snatched too if my mom hadn't physically fought them off). Then they pulled some bullshit to erase our memories and sent us packing. I spent my childhood thinking I was insane because I remembered a brother that my parents didn't think existed. Turns out it was just that MOME's magic wasn't strong enough to erase him from his twin sister's memory. Of course, I didn't learn any of this until you assholes tried to meddle in my life AGAIN. Then, if memory serves, MOME followed me back to my home in Arizona in order to try to recapture my INNOCENT BROTHER, and in their attempts to do that they held my great-uncle's granddaughters HOSTAGE and tried to kill me and my friends. From there I've been stalked, beaten, and threatened by MOME operatives all over the world. So, yeah, when a MOME operative opened the door with a gun held to the head of my best friend's mother and started threatening me--which I'm pretty sure counts as talking by the way--I fucking shot him. In the chest. So he would drop the gun, and let everyone go, and not kill anybody I care about."

I took three deep breaths before I spoke again.

"So, I'm gonna go with not guilty, just on principle."

<div align="center">~~~</div>

"I don't think you were supposed to say that kind of stuff without legal representation," Seamus said, after Rebecca Dryer was long gone.

I sighed. Seamus might have had a point.

"It's not like they were going to give me a fair trial, anyway. They're just going through the motions. If they don't, they just give their opposition more ammo to use against them."

Rebecca Dryer had left without saying anything else, aside from asking me one or two questions about my injuries. Then she'd taken a minute to write a few things down on her clipboard. None of that had felt reassuring to me.

"Doesn't that mean that they have to give you a fair trial?" Seamus asked.

"No. It just has to look like one. I don't even know if the magical courts allow audiences, or what. Hell, all I even know about the U.S. legal system is from procedural crime shows. I'm talking out of my ass here."

Seamus chuckled. "Ew. Gross."

There wasn't much conviction in his voice, though.

Still, I started to laugh, and then tried to stop myself because the pain was too great.

"Are you feeling any better?" Seamus asked.

"I don't know. I'm not feeling any worse, but I still hurt all over. I'll let you know if anything stops hurting."

"It's a shame you're all beat up. This would be a great chance to have tons of sex."

"Seamus, stop making me laugh."

"I'm serious. It's pitch black, there's no one here, we have absolutely nothing else to do..."

"Seamus, cut it out. Laughing is excruciating."

"Well, if you need a distraction, you let me know."

"Seamus!"

The weird thing was, I totally agreed with him. It might have been the damned mating bond talking, but I couldn't help but feel like shagging would have been a much better way to spend our time.

"Oddly enough, I agree with you, but man, I hurt so much it cannot possibly be a good idea."

"To be clear, I'm not touching you with a ten-foot pole until you say you're all better and excited about sex. I am not into pain, certainly not your pain. I'm not suggesting we do anything. I'm just lamenting the missed opportunity."

He was silent for a moment.

"And now that I think about it, there's a good chance that's the mating bond talking, because honestly, I could have proposed that we write a new treatise on women's rights or something. I swear my brain wouldn't normally have jumped to sex."

"It's ok, Seamus, this mating bond thing is a jerk…. Besides, it would be kind of difficult to write a treatise on anything right now. For one thing, we don't have any paper. For another, it's pitch black in here. For another—"

Before I could finish, the sound of hinges screeching in the distance made both Seamus and me jump. I could tell Seamus jumped because the floor vibrated a bit. The sound of boots on stone rang out down the corridor, then more light flooded our cell.

"What the—"

"Victoria Marmot?" asked a voice in the darkness.

"Who's asking?"

I mean, because why the fuck not. I had nothing better to do, and talking was one of the few things that didn't hurt.

"Come to the cell door, please. We're here to check your injuries."

The voice was authoritative and masculine, but that did not add to the total fucks I had left to give.

"So, funny story: I'm not lying here for fun, asshole."

"Get up, please."

"I can't, genius. My injuries are such that moving is excruciating, I haven't even gotten close to trying to stand up without passing out. So, if you are here to look at my injuries, you can come and get it."

There was silence for a moment, then the light from the cell door passed over me and Seamus. I would have taken the chance to check out Seamus and make sure that he was ok, but I was still blinded by the light that had flashed my way. By the time I could see again, the light was focused elsewhere.

"Neutralize the other one."

"What? Wait! Don't hurt him!"

But before I was done talking, I heard the compressed air bang of a tranquilizer gun, a sound I was only familiar with thanks to my summers working in wildlife rescue. I was relieved and upset at the same time. Getting shot with a tranq was, by all accounts, no fun, but at least they hadn't done anything permanently damaging to him.

The cell door opened, and I tried to move so that I could see whoever was coming in, but the pain of adjusting my position was more than I could take and I almost passed out with the effort.

Before I could do any more, the light was shining in my eyes again and I couldn't see who was examining me, anyway. A set of hands started gently exploring the skin on my left side, and I couldn't help but flinch at the touch.

"She looks rough," said a second voice.

"Silence, Flemens," said the first voice that had spoken. The hands didn't waver in their assessment.

"What's the matter?" I asked. "Don't like the handiwork of your comrades? This is all courtesy of whichever MOME operatives came to pick me up at my home."

"Quiet, prisoner. No one asked you to talk."

"Funnily enough, I talk all the time without permission. You should try it sometime. It's very freeing. Might loosen that stick up your ass."

I might have imagined it, but I could have sworn I heard Flemens stifling a chuckle.

"Are you two here to finish the job your colleagues started? Not willing to risk me going to trial and telling the world what a corrupt organization of fascist douchetarts you have here?"

"I told you to be quiet."

"And I told you to pull the stick out of your ass. Oh wait. No I didn't. I just implied that. Sorry. Probably too subtle. Let me try that again. You should really pull the stick out of your ass."

Silence, while the hands continued to gently prod what felt like every bruise I'd ever had in my entire existence come to life at once. The hands were professional and gentle, and I wondered if it was Flemens or StickAss examining me. Whoever it was, he was a consummate professional. I had to give him that. Still, the pain was so intense I had to talk to distract myself.

"So, which of you gentlemen is secretly questioning whether MOME is all that it has always pretended to be?" I asked. "Because I sure could use some help getting the hell out of here, and I don't particularly like the idea of being executed, or locked away for life, just for trying to defend the people I care about from a douchebag waving a gun around."

I was rambling, but I figured it couldn't hurt. After all, MOME seemed incredibly shady as soon as one took a look at it up close. I couldn't imagine how decent people managed to convince themselves that it was a fine place to work. Then again, maybe I could. People lied to themselves all the time, and I was sure that MOME worked hard to keep up a decent front, even on the inside. How many people even saw the authoritarian bullshit they pulled? Still, these two might have seen some of it, and one of them might even sympathize with me a bit. It couldn't hurt to push a few buttons.

"I mean, you can't seriously believe I wound up in this state because I fell down a flight of stairs or something, can you?"

"We were told you came to look like this because you shot one of our colleagues point-blank in the chest, then resisted arrest when they came to apprehend you."

"Sure, that's the story they would tell you."

"Are you saying that you didn't shoot Schreyer?"

"Is that his name? Schreyer? I definitely shot him, and I meant to shoot him. I didn't want to kill him, but he left me with very few choices. I don't consider allowing someone to hold a gun to my best friend's mom's temple until they decide to pull the trigger a choice."

"A MOME operative would never——"

"Shut it, Flemens. You don't know Schreyer. He would have."

Well, that was surprising. StickAss was on my side. At least for a half a second.

"And that is enough out of you, Ms. Marmot," StickAss said, just before I felt a sharp prick in my neck. "You should really rest."

~~~

When I came to, Seamus was sitting up, his back against a low, wireframe bed that was pushed up against the steel bars separating our cell from the next one over.

It took me a moment to realize how strange it was that I could see him.

"Who turned the lights on?" I asked.

The other strange thing was that I was lying on something soft, or at least, quite a bit softer than whatever I had been lying on for the past few days. And I was on my back, with my head turned to the side to look at Seamus. I turned it towards the ceiling and saw what looked like solid rock.

"Old school," I muttered, still too startled by finally being able to look at our surroundings to fully put together the strangest thing yet.

I turned my head to look at Seamus again, who was silently staring at his hands.

"Hey! That didn't hurt. Turning my head didn't hurt at all!"

I tried sitting up, and found that it was painless and simple. It was slightly more tiring than it ought to have been, but it didn't hurt at all. Something did feel strange about it, though—my right arm, back, and shoulder felt oddly tight. As though they were wrapped in plastic, or tape, or something. I was too excited about how little everything hurt to worry about it, though.

"Seamus, did those guys fix me up? I feel about a thousand times better than I did the last time we talked."

Seamus finally looked up from his hands.

"Yeah, Vic. They did everything they could to heal you, actually. I wasn't awake for it, after whatever they used to knock me out, but they've come back to check on you a few times since then and filled me in a bit."

He didn't sound nearly as happy about this as I would have. I mean, damn. I had been worried that I was never going to walk again. The fact that I was no longer in pain, and that I could move all of my limbs easily and well… I was damned near giddy.

"Vic, I'm really sorry," Seamus said. My eyes snapped to his, and just to be sure he wasn't about to tell me I was paralyzed or something, I tried to stand up. It worked. My legs held my weight, and no part of me objected to the action of standing. Except for that tight pull across my skin.

"Why are you sorry?" I asked, now bewildered. My body worked. It didn't even feel as bad as it had after I'd torn my ACL and gotten surgery to replace the damned thing.

"You… umm… shit, why do I have to be the one to tell you this, when it's those MOME assholes who did this to you? Umm… take a look at your hands."

I looked down. My feet poked out from lime green pajama pants, which I could only assume were what passed for prison garb in the magical community. My feet looked like they always had. Dark, calloused, not particularly noteworthy in any regard.

I raised my hands up from my sides.

My left hand looked normal. The same caramel skin that had always covered it was there, all five digits present and mobile. Nothing out of the ordinary. My right hand…. Now I could see why Seamus was sorry, although I couldn't say I was overly concerned. My right hand was covered in bright red scar tissue—the kind that comes from a third-degree burn. It encompassed 90 percent of my hand. Only my pointer finger and thumb appeared to be free of it. I turned my hands over and saw that I was missing three of my fingerprints. The hand moved well enough, aside from that tight feeling, but most of my original skin was gone. I followed the burn to the sleeve of my inmate pajamas and saw that it continued, so I pulled the sleeve up. It kept going.

I flexed my arm. I could feel the tightness all up and down my arm to my shoulder, along my shoulder blade, and back along my right side.

Not even glancing at Seamus, I pulled off the shirt and inspected my arm. The burn was everywhere I could feel tightness. It didn't cover much of the front of me other than the top of my shoulder. My chest was still my old skin. I tilted my head to look at my side, saw that it barely wrapped around to my rib cage at all, and in doing so I noticed the same tight pull on my neck. I ran my left hand along my neck, up to my ear and cheek. Slick scar all the way. It stopped about halfway up my right cheek.

"Huh," I said, taking a moment to register it all. "Is it all this same bright red?" I asked.

Seamus nodded, though I barely noticed the motion in my peripheral vision.

"They said it would take on a more natural tone with time. It's just red because it's new. They did everything they could to improve the… texture. Or that's what they told me, anyway."

I nodded. My left hand was still exploring all the new skin on my right side. It felt strange. Not just because the texture was so different from the rest of my skin, but because the sensation in the skin itself was weird. It felt partially numb, but also some of the feeling transferred to strange places. There were spots where touching the skin there made it feel like I was being touched six inches away, yet in many places the touch felt almost normal, albeit somewhat dulled. I couldn't stop touching it, but I was starting to get cold. I decided to put the long-sleeved lime green prison shirt back on, although my left hand instantly started exploring the skin of my right hand again.

"I'm so sorry, Vic."

Seamus sounded sincere. I just laughed.

"This might just be shock talking," I said, still feeling the skin on my right hand. "But I am so damned thankful that I can still walk that this really doesn't bother me."

I took a deep breath as I considered the thought that I would look… different for the rest of my life.

"That may change the more I think about it but, fuck, Seamus. I really thought I was going to be in pain for the rest of my life, and possibly immobile."

I looked up then, meeting Seamus' eyes, and he sat down on the bed behind me.

"Is it bad?" I asked, wondering how startling the facial scarring was. I didn't think I would care, but I'd be a little bit sad if Seamus and Sol didn't find me attractive anymore.

Seamus took a deep breath.

"You're still hot as fuck, if that's what you're asking."

His smile was so wide, I couldn't even accuse him of lying.

"Well, I'd like to pretend that I'm above caring what I look like, but I'm not sure I'm that zen. I don't know how I'll feel if I'm…"

If I'm what? I thought. Scars weren't necessarily ugly. They were just jarring, because they were usually a stark difference from what our brains expected to see when we looked at a person, and because they were very obvious signs of physical trauma. They were hard to ignore. I'd never worried about getting scars before. The scar from my knee surgery was a damned badge of honor, and despite my surgeons "suggestions" for keeping it from darkening in the sun, I showed that thing off at every opportunity. I had a few others left behind by various mishaps from childhood, some martial arts training incidents, running into a large metal door once, and I'd never worried about a single one of them. But this…

Burn scars were big, they could cover a lot of area, and they typically didn't ever heal fully. I mean, turn-back-into-normal-skin-heal… And this one certainly covered a large part of me. By rights, it still should have hurt like a son of a bitch. The healing magic used on me must have been pretty strong, if I was down to friendly red scar tissue at this point. Just judging by the size of the burn, it should have taken weeks to get this far.

"Ugh… whatever," I sighed. "Surely we have more important things to worry about than whether or not I'm going to have a scar on my cheek for the rest of my life."

And I would, I realized, even as I said it. I would have a scar on my face forever…

Well, boo-fucking-hoo. I was just going to have to suck it up. I wasn't blowing smoke when I said I was happy to be fully mobile. The worry that I wouldn't be able to walk again had been real, and terrifying. The relief I felt at being able to move was like a physical weight being removed from my shoulders and chest. Sure, grieving my non-burned self was probably something it would be healthy to do at some point, but fuck it. Right now I really needed to focus on more important problems. Like how to not get executed for shooting a guy who really deserved it.

Seamus smiled and seemed to be reading my mind. "Right. So, how are we going to get you out of this?"

~~~

Of course, the answer was that we couldn't get me out of it. Despite five escape attempts and a dozen stunned guards, nothing had gotten me out of the farce of a trial that awaited me. Yet.

It wasn't that MOME had us outmaneuvered, per se, it was just that they had us locked up where we couldn't use our magic, and they had finally stopped underestimating me now that I'd shot one of their agents, so the guards had all known how to fight hand to hand, and been armed, and… yeah. We never really stood a chance once they dragged us into that magic-blocking dungeon.

Except, maybe, if I could escape this hellscape and hotfoot it back to Earth without MOME knowing about it. That assumed that I could drag my ass to the top of this canyon without dying in some horrible and unforeseen fashion. Or any fashion, for that matter. Dying would really throw a wrench in my escape plans.

So, I took another deep, sulphur-laden breath, trying not to think about the pain in my hand, or how far I would fall if I missed a hold. Needless to say, I was embracing the "slow is smooth, and smooth is fast" method of climbing.

Keepin' it zen, that's me. Yep.

Right up until a shrieking squirrel demon leapt at my head, releasing the most terrifying series of squeaks and trills that I've ever had the misfortune to hear.

"AHHHHHHHHHH!" I screamed in return, trying desperately to grab onto the hold I'd just inadvertently jerked away from when the squirrel-thing leapt at my head. My first swipe missed, but, luckily, I hadn't thrown my body too wildly off-balance when I'd let go of the rock face, and had been moving up a portion of the cliff that sloped away from me, rather than towards me, so I had time to correct before I went toppling to my death. I managed to snag the hold I'd let go of on my second swipe, then promptly began cursing everything that had ever lived, but mostly the glowing-eyed, red-skinned, giant-fanged rodent that was now perched in front of my face,
~~~

squealing with terror. Or maybe I was just terrified and projecting it back on the squirrel. It was hard to know.

"What. Do. You. WANT?!?" I said, trying to keep my own voice as level as possible. On some level I knew that freaking out was not going to help. After all, what creature ever responded well to being screamed at? But that was a difficult to impulse to control, especially after the number of times this creepy-assed gremlin had shown up and scared the hell out of me in the past week.

The only reply I got was, of course, more unintelligible screaming. Which was no surprise, as this creature had yet to produce any other sound in my presence.

I shrugged.

"Buddy, once again, I have no idea what you're trying to say, but I would really appreciate it if you could stop saying it with… so much volume and… enthusiasm?"

I wiped a fleck of squirrel demon spit from my chin to illustrate this last point.

Unlike everything else I'd ever said to the creature, that last bit seemed to garner some kind of understanding. The creature shifted its ears a bit flatter, cocked its head, and grabbed its own tail (the only part of it that sported any kind of fur) in a way that made me think it might be embarrassed.

Then it opened its mouth and screamed at me again.

"Ugh, dude, seriously. I'd rather have you spit at me than shriek like that. Anyway, I need to get to the top of this cliff without dying, so if you don't mind…" I made a slight shooing motion with my hand, to indicate that I wanted to move past the squirrel, and to my complete astonishment, it responded by moving out of my way.

Loath to lose my one chance at freedom from shrill noises, I resumed climbing, hoping to put as much distance between me and squirrel-thing as possible.

The three hours that it took me to make it to the top were so blissfully squirrel-demon-free that I'd largely forgotten the creature's existence by the time I launched myself, beached whale style, over the final ledge and lay, gasping and barely able to move through the exhaustion, at the top of the deep slot canyon that I had been trapped in for a week.

"Finally," said a high-pitched voice behind me. "I'm amazed you survived down there for so long, and I thought you'd never make it to the top climbing so slowly."

I turned, grunting with the effort of even that simple motion, after what was surely the longest unroped climb of my life, to see who the hell was talking to me.

I shit you not, it was the squirrel. The red-skinned, glowing-eyed, fluffy-tailed rodent-thing that had been tormenting me with its shrieking and random appearances for the past week was moving its mouth and forming words.

"Um… pardon my French, but… what the fuck?"

"That isn't French, kid."

"You can talk?"

The squirrel-thing nodded.

"With words?"

Now it glared.

"WITHOUT FUCKING SHRIEKING LIKE A BANSHEE?!"

And yeah, ok, I might have been mad enough that I sat up abruptly and shouted a bit, despite how tired I was.

"Hey! It's not my fault you couldn't understand me down there. That's the damned magic of the canyon. Or anti-magic, I guess. At any rate, I was talking to you just like now, but you could only hear shrieking."

"What?"

"In this realm there's a spell in place that lets most folks communicate, assuming they use a verbal language. But no spells work down in that canyon—it's an anti-magic void."

"How does that even work? I thought all magic was just dark matter anyway. How can you stop dark matter from working?"

"Beats me, kid. High energy fields, maybe? I dunno. I'm not a physicist or a mage, so… it's not really my thing."

"What are you, then?" I asked, before I could consider the fact that it might be rude to ask.

"Just a local," he replied, sounding a bit shifty.

"Uh huh… demon?" I hazarded.

He tilted his head again, this time locking me with just one glowing eye.

"You gonna run away screaming if I am?"

"Dude," I said, lying down again and staring at the creepy orange sky, finally able to see a good 180 degrees of it. "You are a talking, red-skinned, glowing-eyed squirrel-thing that almost made me fall off a cliff two hours ago. You really think finding out what you're called is going to make me run away?"

"Hmm… alright. Yeah. Folks from other realms call us demons sometimes, especially when they find us here. They sure as heck call us nicer things than that when we travel to *your* realm. Been called an angel more than once, myself."

I stared down one of his beady, glowing eyes, raising an eyebrow.

"What? You wait. If you saw me in *your* realm, you'd think I was quite the sight."

Too tired to argue, and fairly certain that I had no idea what I was talking about anyway, I shrugged.

"So, is this realm hell?" I asked.

Squirrel-thing nodded.

"One of 'em, yeah."

"What's your name?" I asked, not really wanting to get into how many hell realms there might be.

"Azrael."

That got another raised eyebrow.

"Azrael? Archangel of death, Azrael?"

Azrael shrugged.

"Maybe."

"You're a squirrel," I said.

"Squirrel, angel… same same," he shrugged.

"Why do you sound like you're from the south of London?"

"Last time I was in your realm, I spent a fair bit of time there."

"How do I get back to my realm from here?"

Azrael just stared at me for a moment.

"Same way you came in, Luv."

"I was dragged in by MOME agents against my will, through… what is it called again? A seam? I think."

Azrael nodded.

"That'd be it."

"You're telling me I can't leave unless I'm dragged out against my will by MOME agents?!"

"No, no. Nothing like that. But you have to leave by seam. It's the only way in or out of here."

"Well, how am I supposed to find it without my magic?" I asked.

"That would be difficult. Shouldn't matter now, though."

"What does that mean?" I sat up, no longer interested in the orange sky blotted with purple clouds. "Are you saying I have my magic again?"

I looked at my hands and feet, at the metal shackles that still encircled them.

"I didn't think breaking the chain would break whatever was keeping me from my magic. Are you telling me I didn't have to climb that freaking cliff? That I could have just shifted myself up here?!?"

"It wasn't the manacles that kept you from your magic, Luv. It was the canyon itself."

"But the MOME agent said—"

"Well, they're not exactly going to tell you how to escape, now, are they? Mind you, most people never manage to break those chains at all, let alone the manacles. And come to that, I've never seen anyone make it out of that canyon before, either."

I sighed and lay down for a second. I already knew I was too tired to shift myself any distance worth trying, so there was no point in making myself pass out.

"Probably because most people who wind up here grow up with magic," I mumbled.

"What's that?" Azrael hopped over so he was looking me in the eyes again, even though I was lying down.

"I grew up thinking I was a normal human. I've only had magic for a few days, or only known I've had it that long. It amounts to the same thing, anyway. Taking my magic away doesn't leave me as paralyzed as it might someone else. I'm used to having to make do with whatever my body is capable of."

"Whatchoo doin'?" asked Azrael, as my eyes started to close.

"Taking a nap," I mumbled. "Can't do shit if I pass out the first time I pull on my magic."

OF COURSE AZRAEL waited until I'd just drifted off into a peaceful sleep before pouncing on my chest and batting my face with his tail repeatedly.

"Azrael. What the fuck?" I asked groggily, pawing his tail away from my face.

"There's a storm coming, and believe me when I tell you that you do NOT want to be out here when it hits."

I thought of all the flash floods in the bottom of the canyon, and also the sounds of large animals stampeding a few hours before each flood...

"Ok. I will take your word for that. So... where can I go? Is there high ground around here somewhere?"

Azrael shook his head.

"During a storm, the safest place in the realm is the bottom of that canyon."

"Fuck that. I am *never* going back down there. How do they expect any prisoners to survive down there? I mean, I assume they don't particularly care if I survive, but if you've seen other people stowed here..."

"They expect you to get washed down the canyon, I think. That's what happens to most of 'em, anyway. I think they have a collection unit at the bottom. Likely keeps most of them alive. I did try to tell you that on the first night."

That whole thought process, especially the bits in which I was supposed to have let myself get washed down the canyon, with my arms and legs shackled, no less, instead of resolutely climbing to high ground during each flood and eventually finding a way to break my manacles… it kind of made my blood boil.

I took a deep breath, deciding to let that go for now. I also ignored the idea that Azrael had been trying to impart useful information on the first night that he'd flown at me out of the darkness and started shrieking like a dying cat.

"So, what am I supposed to do, then? I don't have the energy to shift myself back to Earth from here. I'm exhausted."

"Luv, you could be as rested as the Queen on her birthday and you'd never be able to shift yourself to Earth from here. You'll have to find a seam. And you'd best get on with it, 'cause the storm will be here soon."

It did occur to me, briefly, to wonder what in the nine hells Azrael was getting out of this whole save-the-human-you'd-never-met-before-finding-her-randomly-at-the-bottom-of-a-canyon thing, but since it seemed likely that whatever nastiness these storms caused was just as likely to kill a squirrel-sized demon as a 150lb human, I decided it didn't really require that much assessment. He was probably just trying to save his own ass.

"So, how do I find a seam?" I asked, eyeing the angrier-looking purple clouds above us, which were beginning to blot out the orange sky.

"How does a dragon not know how to find a seam?"

Azrael's voice was so incredulous that I actually turned to look at him. His face showed as much indignance as I thought was possible from a squirrel, demon or not.

"I don't know what I look like to you, buddy, but I'm not a dragon."

I could feel my eyebrows reaching for my hairline, but Azrael skittered back from me and started gesturing wildly to the ground behind me.

"Have you never seen your Shadow?" he asked.

"Umm… I have, on more than one occasion, looked at the silhouette of my body cast by the sun. I have a feeling that's not what you're talking about, though."

"That's exactly what I'm talking about, Luv, but on this planet the sun doesn't just shine a tiny portion of the electromagnetic spectrum through the atmosphere, and the creatures here are built to actually *see* things properly. Look."

He gestured emphatically at the ground behind me.

I turned to look, but only saw an even darkness spread on the ground.

"Shit," Azrael mumbled. "The cloud cover is too dark, and you'd probably have to call on your snow leopard to see it anyway, but believe you me, your Shadow tells the whole story."

I found it both suspicious and creepy that Azrael knew I had a snow leopard form, and it irked me that there was something different about the shadows here that I wasn't catching. I tried looking at the ground behind Azrael, but I only saw the general darkness cast by the clouds in the sky.

"Never mind," he muttered. "No point now. And you already said you were raised without magic, so I don't know why I'm surprised. Look, just close your eyes and feel around for a break in the ether."

That was a sentence that would have made less than zero sense to me even a week ago, but, weirdly enough, thanks to the crazy turn my life had taken lately, I actually had some sense of what he was talking about.

I closed my eyes, centered my breathing the way I did at the beginning of a training session, and tried to sense any gaps in the energy that surrounded me.

I felt for a rift in the darkness, seeking for the seam. Just as I found an edge between the energy that suffused the world and the nothing between it, I felt something warm and slick stick to my leg. Without waiting to find out what the hell it was, and hoping desperately I would still have a leg on the other side, I pulled.

I WAS BLINDED by a white light and felt the sweep of large wings as I fell backwards against cold, hard rock. By the time my eyes had adjusted to the dim glow of the light around me, whatever had blinded me was long gone. The only thing left was…

"Seamus?"

"Vic?!? Is that really you? They tried to tell me you were dead."

"What? Who tried to—Gwendamn it!"

And that was when I realized I was right back in the same fucking dungeon I'd started out in before they'd shipped me off to solitary. I tried to pull on my snow leopard form, my Gwen-given powers, anything. Nothing worked. I was right back where I'd started.

F. M. L.

~~~

The next day, after a long night of banging my head against the wall, cursing myself, Azrael, and MOME, Seamus and I were both dragged out of our cell and through multiple rock corridors, finally reaching a bland, drywall-covered maze that led us from one shitty, neon hellhole to the next, until we emerged into a grand marble foyer opening onto a set of large, arched wooden doors.

Beyond the wooden doors lay a round room encircled by high benches laden with people in robes. Great. I felt like I'd walked into the Wizengamot
~~~

or some shit. If I saw Dolores Umbridge holding a gavel, I was going to lose my shit.

"You ever been to this kind of thing before?" I whispered to Seamus, who had his hands tied behind his back, just like I did, and who was being man-handled through the room right behind me.

"Nope. Wolf justice… looks different," he whispered back.

"Silence!" That was a voice from somewhere in the darkness that surrounded the circle we'd finally stopped in.

The center of the circle was brightly lit, while the benches surrounding it were dark, leaving us blind to everything but the otherwise empty space we inhabited.

"Lovely set up you have here. I was really digging the antique bleachers. Shame we can't see them anymore."

Apparently, I fought my spiraling fear of death or incarceration with sass.

"I said, silence!"

"Yeah. I heard you the first time. Did no one else mention that I'm terrible with following orders? I'm surprised it didn't come up. The lawyer I talked to found it fairly irksome, and the medics drugged me to stop me from talk-ing. Oh, and you guys threw me into a hell dimension just to keep me out of your hair for a while, so—"

"Siopí!" shouted the voice in the darkness. I felt a slight buzz pass over my skin, and wondered if that meant someone had just cast a spell.

"Is that Greek? Cool! I didn't know that Arizona had much of a Greek population."

Much muttering and gasping followed that exclamation.

"Are you all Greek? Did I just offend you all? I can't see shit past this circle of light, you know, so you'll have to forgive me if I've missed some visual cues."

Seamus snickered behind me.

"What?" I asked.

"I think that was supposed to be a spell to make you shut up."

"And it didn't work?" I asked.

He chuckled again.

"Well, I can still hear you. I'm guessing they can too."

I turned back to the darkness around us, in the general direction of the voice that had uttered the spell.

"I told you, I really don't take orders well. I thought I was supposed to testify, though. I can't do that if I've been silenced." Not that I actually expected to be allowed to testify—I fully expected them to conveniently "forget" about that part—but if they were going to pretend this was a trial, then I was going to keep reminding them of it. Not for the first time, I wished that lawyer had left behind a book on mage law or something.

"You will be quiet, or you will be removed from this court."

"Now that seems counterintuitive. I'm here so that you can ask me questions. Kicking me out for talking would just be silly. That would be hard to explain to your dissenters, wouldn't it? Are there any reporters here?"

That caused another stir, and sure enough, no one repeated the threat. I supposed I'd guessed right about the reporters and the dissenters. I guess they had to at least make it *look* like a fair trial.

"So, now that you've dragged us all the way up here, what did you want to know?" I wasn't feeling at all cooperative, but I at least wanted to get this farce over with. I knew that silence wouldn't help me, but giving the mages time to compose themselves didn't help me either.

"How long have you been working with the Openers?" The question came from a different voice than the one that had been telling me to shut up in Greek.

"That doesn't sound like a formal inquiry, that sounds more like an interrogation. Is this an interrogation? Weird."

"Answer the question!"

"Sure, but hey, is this being recorded? I want a record of this whole trial. Do you mages have anything close enough to due process to grant that, or are you just going to report whatever you like when this is all over?"

"The trial is being recorded. Now answer the question."

"But who has access to the recording? And can it be altered? Honestly, I would feel more comfortable if someone I knew were here, or at least privy to the recordings."

"You are allowed to request a witness," said a third voice.

"Great. How about Albert Bumblebee?"

I had been thinking about it since my first talk with Rebecca Dryer. Of course, I'd been a bit distracted since then, but as soon as I found myself trapped here again last night, I'd decided that the best person to ask for was my high school principal. Naturally, I would rather have requested my brother, or Sol, or anyone else I actually knew well, but all the people I was closest to were wanted by MOME, and none of them could show up on my behalf without getting locked up themselves. To my knowledge, Albert

Bumblebee was free and clear with this court, and also a mage. He seemed to like me, and had tried to help me a couple of times already.

"What is your association with Grand Master Bumblebee?"

"Grand Master?" That was news to me. "Albert's my homie," I said, delighting in the consternation that seemed to be coming from the bleachers. "He's also my school principal."

"You will address Grand Master Bumblebee with the appropriate respect!" demanded a furious voice on the other side of the darkness.

"She is addressing me just as I requested she address me, Master Elfthwin," came a familiar voice from behind me.

Sure enough, a few more seconds produced the unmistakable smell of pot smoke and patchouli that marked the presence of my high school principal.

"Hey Al," I said, as I felt the old man's hand pat my shoulder reassuringly.

"Sorry I'm late," he said. "I got here as quickly as I could."

I just stared at him for a moment.

"Considering I only asked for you about ninety seconds ago, I'd say you were plenty quick."

Albert looked somewhat offended, but before I could ask how on earth I'd managed to insult him, one of the voices from the darkness called for order.

Albert peered into the darkness, then clucked his tongue.

"No, this won't do at all," he muttered. Then he reached inside his robe, pulled out a joint, put it back in his robe, then pulled out a wand and waved it in a circle around us.

Suddenly the entire chamber was lit evenly, and we could see everyone in the bleachers that surrounded us.

"Ugh," I said. "I think I liked it better when we couldn't see everyone."

Albert chuckled, as did Seamus. I was only half joking.

It wasn't like we were surrounded by rows and rows of sea slugs or anything. Everyone in the bleachers looked pretty normal, outside of the fact that they were dressed like a university convocation ceremony, it was just that... well, it was easier to laugh off a room full of people who were hostile towards you when they were just a bunch of angry voices in the dark than it was when you could make eye contact with them and sense their very real hatred for you.

"Grand Master Bumblebee, may we ask why you've chosen to act as witness for this... criminal?" That was a middle-aged looking man wearing a particularly odd hat, which I supposed could have been a symbol of leadership... I mean, I would have expected it to be the symbol of leadership at say… clown school.

"Oh, but I haven't," Albert replied, causing my brain to stutter for a moment, as I wondered if Albert was about to feed me to the proverbial wolves.

"Did you not come here at the behest of Ms. Marmot, to act as her witness?" the man wearing the lead clown hat asked.

"No."

My stomach sank further, each time Albert spoke.

"Then why are you here?"

"I'm here as Ms. Marmot's legal representation."

~~~

After I managed to pick my jaw up off the floor, the trial proceeded… differently than I had expected. Honestly, when I'd requested Albert Bumblebee as my witness, it had simply been because I'd expected him to be my best shot at having a mage who wouldn't ruffle too many feathers in the court show up, and possibly give an honest account of whatever happened to my brother and Sol.

I hadn't even known what the official obligations of a witness were, or that Albert Bumblebee might in any way be some sort of grand poobah in the mage world. I honestly wasn't even sure the dude would be of any use, or on my side. All his previous affiliation with MOME might have hurt more than helped, and I wasn't 100% sure I could trust him. He had been the best of a lot of bad options.

So, when it turned out that he not only commanded the respect of every mage in that courtroom, but also knew the legal system as well as he knew his own pipe collection… let's just say I enjoyed the hell out of watching the rest of the room squirm while they tried their damndest to accuse me of wrongdoing without offending my defense attorney.

And, boy, did he slay as my attorney.

Rebecca Dryer didn't stand a chance, though she sputtered and argued a lot anyway, glaring at Albert with the kind of venom one generally reserves for lifelong enemies and supporters of rival sports teams.

I had entered that courtroom hoping that they wouldn't decide to execute me, or that they would at least spare Seamus, if they were going to kill me anyway. My distant hope was that they would sentence me to something possibly escapable, like life imprisonment.

I walked out of there free to go wherever I wanted, along with both Albert
~~~

and Seamus.

"Well, that was unexpected," I said, as we stepped out of the courtroom into the large marble foyer.

"Was it?" Albert asked. "I'm sorry, dear, I should have sent word that I was coming. There are some useful rats in this place that could certainly have delivered a message, if I'd thought of it. Sorry to leave you expecting the worst."

I shrugged, unsure if Albert meant literal or figurative rats, and not really wanting to think about it too much, either way.

Albert pulled out the joint he'd accidentally removed when he was looking for his wand earlier, and lit it.

"Though I suppose that would have taken some of the dramatic flair from my entrance," he said, as he finally exhaled a lungful of pot smoke.

He offered me the joint with a gesture, but I shook my head. It was damned tempting, after the week I'd had, but… well, after just narrowly escaping life in prison, breaking any law at all was less than appealing. He offered it to Seamus, who just stood there looking awkward for a moment before mumbling, "No, thanks."

"There's no smoking in this building, Cynthia," came a voice from behind me.

I turned to see Rebecca Dryer, the prosecuting attorney, or magistrate, or whatever the hell mage lawyers called themselves, glaring at the three of us.

Albert waved the joint in her direction in a silent greeting.

"Still smarting from your loss, Becks?"

"Fuck off, Cynthia."

"Come now, there's no need to be rude, Rebecca. What will the children think?"

"I don't care what you and your criminal brood think. Get off the damned premises, if you're going to waste your breath on that thrice-cursed human brain candy."

"You should really try it sometime, Becks. Delightful substance, keeps the vamps away—not that you've ever minded the creepy diamond skulls. Might help you relax."

"Oh… sit on it and spin, bitch."

And with that, Rebecca Dryer stormed out of the foyer through one of the three metal doors that led to the neon-lit maze beyond.

"Did she just call you Cynthia?" I asked, not sure what part of that exchange had confused me the most.

"She really has never gotten over the way we treated each other as school girls," Albert said.

"Oh… right." I mumbled, realization slowly dawning. "Well, shitty of her not to call you by your real name, though. That's a stupidly low thing to do."

Albert nodded appreciatively, foot-long white beard brushing his chest all the while, then shrugged.

"Of course, she would argue that Cynthia *is* my real name…. Honestly, if it makes her feel better, I won't hold it against her," Albert said, as we moved towards one of the other metal doors. "Life is too short, and all of that. Besides, I was rather mean to her in school."

Albert pushed open the farthest right of the three doors, and gestured for us to lead the way.

"Shall we be off, then?" he asked.

I had no idea where we were going, but I nodded, and, as Seamus didn't say anything behind me, I could only imagine that he did the same.

Albert grabbed both of our elbows, then the world winked out.

I SUPPOSE I shouldn't have been surprised to find myself standing in the middle of the Andes, on a hillside that was far too cold for my black leather jacket and skintight black jeans.

"Seriously, I need to talk to Gwen about this clothing thing. These boots are solid enough, but why do they need a three-inch heel? And why can't I ever be wearing a parka when we show up in the Andes?"

"I thought your clothes only changed when you shifted from snow leopard to human?" Seamus said, eyeing my outfit suspiciously.

"I thought so too, but that's the third time my clothes have changed just when I've shifted location… and they haven't even been location appropriate. I honestly think it's just that Gwen likes leather."

Seamus swept his amber eyes over my body and smiled.

"It does suit you," he said.

"Yeah, well, it's fucking cold."

I grabbed his arm and pulled him towards me.

"Now you have to cuddle me for warmth," I muttered, burying my face in his shoulder.

What I wouldn't tell anyone, for any amount of money, was how close I was to tears just seeing Seamus eye me with that much longing in his eyes, despite the burn on my face.

I still hadn't seen the damn thing in a mirror, and I'd almost forgotten it even existed, what with the whole life on trial thing happening, but… ugh. Vanity was stupid.

"What happened to consent?" he asked, even as he wrapped his arms around me.

"You said you liked being touchy-feely with your friends," I said. "But you're right, I totally should have asked."

I snuggled closer and he held me tighter. I would be sure to ask next time.

"Now then, you love birds, we need to get to that blasted cabin."

I had almost forgotten Albert was there.

"Right. Down the hill about a kilometer. Do you have some kind of magey way of traveling quickly? It would be easier for us to shift to animal form and run there, but I don't want to abandon you."

Albert smiled.

"I have my ways. After you, Victoria."

I shuddered.

"Please, Albert, call me Vic."

He frowned, then nodded.

"Of course. I'm sorry. I didn't realize that you don't like your full name."

I shrugged, then closed my eyes and imagined what it felt like to be covered in warm fur, racing on four legs down a mountainside. Then, in a moment of awesomeness that I didn't think I would ever get used to, I *was* covered in fur and racing down a mountainside on four legs.

Suddenly, all else was forgotten. Scars, MOME trials, dungeons, cryptic messages left by my parents, escaping a hell realm, none of it mattered. All that mattered was me and the rocks beneath my paws, the balance my tail provided as I skittered down cliff sides, and the clean scent of snow and pines on the breeze, lightly tinged with squirrel.

Before I knew what I was doing, I was veering away from where I could smell the smoke of Sol's cabin, off into a patch of low boulders and scrub oak to my right, which I was now certain housed a small, fat rodent.

My mouth watered, and it finally sank in that I had barely eaten in the past week. They hadn't even offered me a meal before my trial, and food had been more than scarce in the canyon that I'd been trapped in within the hell realm.

I slunk across the rocks, my profile lowered, my nose probing the air to ensure that I was downwind of my prey.

I ignored the howl I heard in the distance, zeroing in on the tiny heart I could somehow hear beating a few meters away. I might have drooled. I wasn't sure. I felt my tongue reflexively clean my lips, at any rate.

A part of my brain recoiled at the vision of my large canines piercing the flesh of some poor defenseless rodent, but most of me was too hungry to care. Besides, even though I was vegetarian in my human form, I had nothing against a snow leopard catching its dinner. Even if that snow leopard was me.

I checked my footing on the snowy, rocky hillside, readying my muscles to pounce onto the hole that I now knew contained the squirrel. One more deep breath, and…

Light brighter than the midday sun now filling the sky flashed in front of me, and I lost all sense of time and space as I scuttled backwards, my feline reflexes just barely keeping me upright as I let out a yowl of consternation.

"I do not appreciate becoming supper, Luv," said a deep voice, which rang a small bell of familiarity in my mind.

I blinked repeatedly, and soon found myself assuming human form around the words, "Do I know you?"

"Damn. What kind of shifter doesn't show up naked after they shift? Poor form, Luv. I was really looking forward to that."

The figure in front of me looked like nothing I'd ever seen before. Actually, that wasn't entirely true. He looked a bit like Rhelia, with the smoothest, darkest ebony skin I'd ever seen, minus the iridescence and plus a pair of giant silver wings.

It took me a minute before my brain stumbled forward with an answer.

"Azrael? Squirrel demon? Is that really you? Were you the squirrel I was about to eat?"

It didn't exactly make sense, but it was the only thing I could come up with.

"In the flesh. Told you I was an angel, Luv. Everyone in this realm loves me."

Something about the way he said it sounded a bit forced.

"Really?" I hazarded. "Everyone loves the archangel of death?"

He shrugged, his handsome features catching the light in a way that made my breath hitch.

"That's all just a misunderstanding, really, and I can tell you're already warming up to me," he said, dropping a wink at me that made my stomach drop a bit. There was something decidedly… compelling about him. And not just because he was the most handsome person I'd ever met.

Then I felt fur in my hand, heard a soft growl, and looked down to see a brief flash of black wolf before Seamus stood beside me. He looked… awed.

"Who is this?" he asked.

"This is Azrael. He's… a friend."

I watched Seamus' expression turn from awe to puzzlement, then back to awe.

"He?" he asked.

I was about to gesture at the very obviously masculine body of the winged creature in front of us—I mean, hell, Azrael was basically wearing a loin cloth. He was chest to the wind, and so obviously male that I actually gasped in shock when I turned back to look at him and saw a person with the same gorgeous features, but instead of a masculinely sculpted set of pectorals she had a set of breasts almost as perfect as Sol's, a slender but athletic waist… everything about her was still muscular, sculpted, beautiful, but now it was all decidedly female.

"Umm…"

Azrael laughed.

"Oh, how delightful, Luv—you're a bridge! One of the lucky few who get to see both of me."

I tried to shut my mouth before I spat out something overly honest, like the fact that I couldn't decide which Azrael was sexier, or the fact that I shouldn't be thinking that either of them was sexy, since we had more important things to think about at the moment, or… yeah. It was really best to keep my mouth shut. Luckily, Seamus seemed to be feeling talkative.

"What do you mean, both of you?" he asked.

"Vic here, as a being who is equally attracted to men and women, can see both aspects of my angel form. Most folks only see one or the other, even if they have some leanings in both directions. Not very many folks find themselves with an even split, and whichever sex they find most attractive is what they see when they look at me. You, for example, will only ever see me as a female. That angry woman, down the hill there, will only ever see me as a woman. But Vic, bless her, will see me as whatever the nearest person fancies, or maybe even see both of me at once, sometimes. That can be a bit confusing for folks."

I was intensely curious about what Azrael was saying, but his comment about the angry woman down the hill had me turning around just in time to see Sol shift to her panther form and come bounding up the hill.

"WHERE THE FUCK have you two BEEN!?!" Sol shouted, once she'd taken a moment to resume her human form and take her eyes off of Azrael's almost-naked body.

"Albert didn't tell you?" I asked.

"No one has told us shit since Gwen abandoned us here a week and a half ago!"

"Well, don't yell at me, I've been locked up in a dungeon and a hell dimension," I said, raising my hands.

"Me too," said Seamus, similarly raising his hands in the universal sign for *please don't rip my head off.* "Well, not the hell dimension, but still."

Sol looked about ready to punch something, but then she looked back at me and did a double take.

I almost flinched when she reached for me, but she instantly wrapped me in her arms and was kissing both of my cheeks, eyelids.

"Damn it, Gatita. I was fucking worried. What happened to you?"

I knew that she meant my scar. I mean, I'm sure she meant my general well-being too, but… I could tell it was the scar that had turned her from righteous ire to concern.

"What do you think happened?" I asked, caught between wanting more of her kisses and wanting to push her away from the skin on my body that still transferred sensation so oddly.

"I will kill the MOME bastard responsible for this," she muttered into my hair, pulling me closer.

"Ah, reunited at last, I see," said a British voice, quite different from the one that had been explaining its dual sex from a nearby boulder only a moment before.

"Albert," I said, looking up from Sol's shoulder, "this is—"

But as I turned to introduce Albert to Azrael, I saw a whole lotta open sky where there should have been an angel, or a least a fucking squirrel.

"Where the fuck did they go?" I muttered.

"Who, Gatita?" Sol asked, pulling back to look at me again.

"Seamus, I didn't imagine the whole angel thing, did I?"

Seamus smiled and shook his head, stepping closer and nudging Sol with his shoulder.

"Can I get a hug too?" he asked.

After Sol wrapped him in a slightly begrudging embrace, he turned to me.

"No, Vic. That gorgeous winged creature was real. Or… if she wasn't, she was a group hallucination."

I sighed.

"I can't believe the shrieking squirrel demon is a Gwendamned angel."

"Angel—" Albert began, just as a new voice asked, "Who am I damning?"

"Oh great." I laughed. "The party's all here."

~~~

I wasn't expecting to burst into tears when I hugged Trev for the first time after getting away from that MOME dungeon, but what can I say? Trev, running at me with his own eyes full of saline, was more than my emotionally beleaguered, sleep-deprived self could handle, and as soon as his arms wrapped around me we became an indistinguishable mass of damp, salty human.

"Thank gods you're alive," Trev muttered, as we laughed and hugged in a more desperate fashion than a week's separation probably warranted, but damned if it didn't feel like longer somehow. I suppose getting captured by the oppressive regime that's trying to kill you and your whole family/everyone that you love will do that to a person.

Eventually we broke apart and turned to find everyone standing behind us looking a bit glassy-eyed.

"Ok. Gushy reunions over. What'd I miss?"
~~~

THE ANSWER WAS, not much, as it happened. After everyone filed back into Sol's cabin and settled into the comfortable couches and chairs that filled up the cozy living room around the delightful wood stove, we swapped tales of all that had happened in the past ten days.

I had suffered the more "exciting" week-and-a-half by far. I had been hit by a lethal spell, arrested, and locked away in a hell dimension until my trial. Everyone else had just been looking for my mom's journals, without much success.

"So… with the Flagstaff house a pile of cinders, where do we look next?" I asked, trying not to let emotion clog my throat. I still hadn't recovered from the shock of learning that particular detail during the trial—of course, MOME hadn't even had the decency to explain how it had happened, they had just claimed that the house had unexpectedly burned down while I was being held.

Seamus and Sol looked questioningly between Trev and me, while Albert sat in considerate silence. I suppose it made sense that neither Sol nor Seamus would have suggestions. They'd never even met my parents, let alone known them well enough to have an idea where they might hide something incredibly valuable. Albert seemed like he might have reason to know what my parents would have done with these mysterious journals, but he remained mum.

Trev just stared at me in silence.

"We have to go back to the house in Colorado, don't we?" I asked.

Trev nodded slowly.

"Vic, you don't have to go if you don't want to. I never lived at the house in Colorado. I can search it and—"

"No, it's fine. I can think of a few places worth looking that you might not think of, or know about. And besides, it seems like the next stretch of my life is just going to be reminder after reminder that Mom and Dad are gone. Not to mention that they weren't who I always thought they were. It can't hurt to start confronting the memories now."

"It could, actually," Sol said, much to my surprise.

When I turned and met her eyes, she looked more haunted than I'd ever seen her.

"I don't mean you shouldn't do it," she clarified. "Only that it might hurt a fair bit, really, when the time comes."

"That's not what I—gods, why have I been so self-absorbed in the past few weeks that I've been acting like I'm the only person in the world who's ever lost someone? You and Seamus have both clearly been fighting some of your own demons, and I haven't even taken the time to ask what the hell is going on."

Sol gave a lopsided smile and said, "Well, if I recall correctly, the last time we spent more than a few minutes in each other's company, none of us were particularly interested in talking. I don't think that's your fault, Gatita."

Seamus chuckled. "And it's not as though we've had much time to discuss anything since then. We keep getting chased off by MOME before we even have five minutes to get comfortable together."

"Speaking of which," I began, taking a good look around the room for a minute, "why is it that we trust that MOME hasn't covered this place with bugs, or whatever the magical equivalent is? Not to mention, why aren't they blowing the place up, or knocking the door down trying to get to us? It's not like they don't know where it is."

"Fair question," said a voice from the doorway.

I swear all of us were up and getting ready to fight before Gwen even took a full step away from the door.

"Damn it, Gwen! Don't sneak up on people like that. Also, what the hell? I thought you were already here, why are you lurking in the doorway?"

The smirk on the red-haired goddess' face made me want to slap her, but I refrained.

"But your question is a good one," she replied using impressively selective hearing. "As it happens, I know the answer to this one. I thought you would be pleased."

I sighed, sitting back down on the couch, where I had been comfortably resting my legs in Seamus' lap and my head in Sol's. Everyone else followed suit, and Gwen glided her way further into the cabin.

"After all of you took off on your last adventure and MOME was left here with a partially smoldering log cabin, Sol's grandmother showed up to fight the fire and save what she could of the property. Luckily, MOME lost interest in the place as soon as they confirmed that no one was left inside. As I found myself in the area while Sol's family worked to save the place, I was able to help. Further, after the fire was put out and the damage repaired, I helped to put some illusions in place to make MOME think that the place burned to the ground after they left, and is consequently of little interest."

Knowing what Gwen was capable of in terms of disguise, not to mention in terms of… being a goddess, I didn't doubt that she'd done a very convincing job of it.

"So, thanks for that," I said, not wanting to sound too ungrateful. "But why are you here now?"

I was always a bit wary of Gwen. Her heart was in the right place, but she had a funny way of "helping" people sometimes.

"Two things, really. One, to check in on how your quest is going, and two, to find out why you decided to bring Azrael, Devourer of Souls, back into the mortal realm."

EVERYONE STARED ACCUSINGLY at me, while I stared slack-jawed at Gwen.

"Azrael is the Devourer of Souls?" I asked, somewhat incredulous.

Gwen nodded.

"That… shrieking squirrel demon thing is… the Devourer of Souls?"

"More *a* devourer of souls—they're really a succubus. Or, at least, that's another name for them, anyway. I suppose they're rather hard to categorize, when you get down to it, but so are most demons, come to that—when you look at them from a perspective other than the monotheists-rewrite-history-to-suit-themselves one. The hell realms are fascinating, when you learn to see past the—"

"So, I didn't kick off the apocalypse or anything, by letting Azrael hitch a ride?" I interrupted, before Gwen could get too caught up in… whatever it was she was about to ramble on about. Probably some "explanation" about how things worked that would inevitably leave me with another million questions about how everything actually worked.

"Hardly! They are awfully frisky, but scarcely about to take out the entire earth singlehandedly," Gwen admitted.

"I'm confused," Trev muttered, while Sol nodded and Seamus smiled nostalgically, in all likelihood remembering the angelic version of Azrael he'd met earlier.

"Azrael sort of helped me escape the hell dimension I was stuck in," I said.

"Sort of?" Sol asked.

"Well, they explained a few things that were clutch in terms of getting out."

"And then they conveniently hitched a ride?" Albert asked, speaking for the first time since we'd entered the cabin.

"Well… yeah. I didn't think anything of it, at the time. It didn't seem like a great place to be stuck, even for demonic squirrel-thing… is it a big deal that they're here?"

Albert shrugged.

"I can think of a few people who will be less than pleased that they're here. I, for one, look forward to seeing them around."

The raising and lowering of bushy white eyebrows that followed this statement left little doubt as to why Albert would be pleased to see Azrael.

"Is there anyone they *don't* try to seduce?" I asked, before I could think better of it.

"Oh certainly! And beware if Azrael ever truly attempts to do more than flirt, Vic. They are called a Devourer of Souls for a reason. They don't *have* to take all of your soul, but they certainly can, if they feel like it."

That certainly took a bit of the shine off of Azrael's sex appeal.

"So… did I answer your question, Gwen?" I said, turning back to Gwen. Only to find her gone. Because, of course she was.

"She didn't even pretend to stick around and ask how my quest was going?" I muttered.

"Cheer up," said Seamus, patting my leg with exaggerated good humor. "We have no idea how long she was lurking around while we were talking. She may have heard everything already, and only interrupted when it didn't seem likely that you were going to bring up Azrael on your own."

Somehow I didn't find that comforting at all.

I LOOKED AT the mountains that loomed before us, taking up more than half the horizon to the west, inhaled the crisp, autumnal, mountain air… and suddenly felt transported through time. I could almost hear my parents' laughter on the wind. Could smell the pine forests that we'd escaped to so often when my school schedule hadn't allowed us to travel farther afield.

"Damn it."

"What is it?" asked Sol.

"We're not even at the house yet, and I'm getting choked up just breathing the air here."

My eyes were full of tears, and I wiped at them, not out of shame, but out of a desperate need to not feel this much pain. This was a big part of why I had leapt at the chance to move into the house in Flagstaff. Everything in this damned state reminded me of my parents, in some way or another.

"It changes," Sol said, after a long silence in which we'd both just stood staring at the mountains. "People say it gets easier, but that hasn't been my experience, really. It just… happens less often. That feeling that you've been punched in the gut and then hollowed out from the inside… it still hits me. Every now and again, I feel like I can't breathe for missing my mom, but… it used to be every day, and now it's just… sometimes."

Afraid to break whatever spell had Sol sharing that much with me, I leaned against her, wrapping her with a single arm without looking away from the mountains that framed the sky in front of us.

"How long has it been?" I asked.

"Almost five years now."

"I'm so sorry, Sol. Do you want to talk about what happened?"

Sol shook her head.

"Not right now, no."

I nodded.

"If you ever… I'm always here. Any time. Day or night. You know that, right?"

Sol smiled, then turned and kissed my forehead.

"We'd better go help those boys. I think they might have gotten lost in the parking lot."

She turned and gestured to the wide lot full of rental cars behind us. It seemed like a sea of vehicles.

"Either that, or they decided not to rent to a bunch of teenagers, after all."

"It's possible. I told you we could use my—"

Sol was cut off by the roar of an engine, and a few moments later a black open-topped Jeep Wrangler, older than I was, came ripping into view with Trev behind the wheel and Seamus in wolf form hanging out the side gleefully, his giant pink tongue lolling out as he stuck his nose into the wind.

I laughed. Leave it to Trev….

"Your dream car awaits, Madam."

"Complete with loyal canine companion, I see."

I couldn't help but be cheered by the blatantly obvious attempt to make me feel better. How many times had I told Trev that when I grew up I was going to drive around in an old beat-up Wrangler, just like Dad, and take my wolfhound with me everywhere? I wasn't going to quibble if the wolfhound had been replaced by an actual wolf. Or a human that could turn into one…

~~~

The house was exactly the way I remembered it. A small part of me wanted to kick the blue-painted, clapboard-clad, two-story bungalow for daring to be unchanged after everything that I'd been through. It had been both eerie and nostalgic, living there alone for the first few months after my parents had gone missing. Now, it just annoyed me that the house didn't show a single outward sign of the turmoil and confusion it had held within it for all those months. It remained nestled peacefully into the mountainside, surrounded by pine trees and a small bit of naturally inspired landscaping.
~~~

Maybe kicking it would dislodge something, even a tiny fleck of paint, and transfer some small amount of the pain I'd lived through.

I took a deep breath, reminding myself that kicking the house wouldn't actually help anything.

Then I stepped forward and kicked the damned door anyway.

The door was unfazed. It remained the same dark red it had been a year ago, the color my mom had painted it, claiming it was lucky, the year that we had moved to the house. I had always suspected that she just found white to be completely boring, and I didn't disagree, so I had never asked.

And there were those damned tears again.

"Want to go a few more rounds with the house, Luv, or can we all go in now?"

That voice… was not supposed to be here right now.

I turned away from the house to find none other than Azrael, standing in all of their barely clad glory, wings tucked neatly against their back as they stood behind Trev, Sol, and Seamus, all of whom had turned to gawk at the scantily clad succubus.

"Hey there, Devourer of Souls," I said, trying not sound too damning. Gwen had made it sound like Azrael got a worse rap than they deserved.

"Oh dear. Someone snitched, did they?"

I nodded.

"Gwen ratted you out, but she didn't sound too condemning, really."

"Oh? Gwen *has* always been delightfully understanding, actually. So, she just told you the name, then? Left all the gory bits out?"

"There are gory bits?" I asked, trying to repress a shudder. I had thought that the name was likely metaphorical, or, if it were literal, that it at least didn't refer to something done physically.

"Well, racy might be a more appropriate adjective, really."

In a weirdly universal show of testosterone, I could feel all three of my companions perk up at this suggestion, and I couldn't help but laugh, especially since I found the idea intriguing myself.

"She didn't give us details of any kind, as usual. Just said enough to confuse everyone and then disappeared."

Azrael merely blinked at this statement, and when I didn't seem inclined to share anything else, said, "Well, are you going to fight the door again? If you're trying to kick it down, there are better ways."

I snorted.

"Well, I would use the keys, but they're lost in a pile of cinders at the moment." I sighed. "Still, I'm mostly just venting my frustration on the door. Why are you here? Dare I ask?"

Azrael sighed theatrically.

"Can't an angel visit their friends just to say hello?"

"Oh? Do you have friends here?" I asked, trying to sound cheerful. "Who are they? Maybe I know them."

"Is that any way to treat someone who saved your life?" Azrael replied. "I could have just let you die in that canyon."

"Seriously, Azrael, why are you here? I appreciated your help in hell and all, but you are not here for the warm fuzzies, so what gives?"

"Maybe I came for a snack?" they said, raising their eyebrows provocatively, and with entirely too much purr in their voice. I think I heard every single one of us gasp a little bit, and I wondered if everyone felt the same pulse of heat through their bodies that I did.

I shook my head, trying to refocus.

"Azrael, knock it off."

Azrael frowned, then sighed.

"You are trickier than the average wereleopard, aren't you?"

I shrugged.

"And if you wanted an easy snack, you would go somewhere full of regular humans, wouldn't you? Like a bar or something?"

Azrael smirked.

"I could… but it requires putting on clothes and *pretending*."

"You mean something aside from hiding the wings, I assume?"

"*And* you're smart… are you sure you don't want to give me a snack? You're entirely my type."

I smiled, trying to pretend that I wasn't tempted by the idea. I had to assume it was something to do with Azrael's magic that made me even consider the thought. I mean, don't get me wrong, their angelic forms were the most physically attractive people I'd ever seen, both the male and female aspects, but… some part of my brain couldn't stop picturing the tiny, red-skinned squirrel demon that had shrieked at me until I'd been willing to climb a three hundred foot cliff with no rope just to get away from it. Meanwhile, all my friends seemed entranced. Looking around, I realized I was the only one who had spoken since Azrael showed up, and the rest of them were all staring, slack-jawed, at the succubus.

"Can you, um… undo whatever has my friends unresponsive?" I asked.

"Oh, they're responsive enough," Azrael said, raising a hand to their own chest and running their fingers down the center. I was currently seeing Azrael's female form, as I assume everyone else was, since everyone here was attracted to females, and the move was… well, it made me rethink my squirrel demon prejudices.

I shook myself again, and looked around to see Seamus, Trev, and Sol all take a step closer to Azrael.

"Seriously, Azrael, that's enough," I said. "This seems eerily non-consensual."

That made Azrael stop touching themself and stand to attention.

"I *never* force people into anything. I never have to."

I quirked an eyebrow at that, as the moment Azrael stood up and stopped touching themself all three of my companions seemed to snap out of whatever had them basically drooling at the angelic figure before them.

"Ok, well, whatever you were doing was distracting them from what we came here to do." Since I didn't actually *know* what Azrael had been doing, I couldn't be sure it actually was non-consensual. "And besides, unless you clarify exactly how it is you feed, and what a person gives up, I don't think you can claim that it's consensual when someone wants to sleep with you. Wanting to have sex and wanting to give away a part of your soul are two different things, in my book. I may want one without the other. Savvy?"

Why I decided to channel a Disney pirate for that particular moment, I don't know, but it seemed to work on Azrael.

"Oh fine, I won't eat you or your friends. Happy?"

I nodded.

"I'm not sure I'm happy," Sol volunteered, raising her hand. "Depending on what's entailed, I might be willing to give up a small piece of my soul for some of… that." She gestured at all of Azrael's currently female form.

Azrael's face turned smug, and I couldn't help but laugh.

"Everyone is, of course, free to do as they please. I just don't want anyone becoming succubus food against their will."

Azrael raised one hand into the air, and placed the other on their breast in a way that was more than a little seductive.

"I vow that I will only take souls from you four when you volunteer," they said.

"Ok, can we finally get back to business here?" I was still unclear on why Azrael was here, but decided it wasn't worth wasting any more time finding out. Seamus and I may have been cleared by MOME, thanks to Albert, but Trev was still on MOME's most wanted list, and Sol was probably working her way up there, at this point. They could still be trying to track us down, and it was entirely possible that they had this house under surveillance. In fact, that was Trev's primary objective, for now. As far as we knew, MOME had no idea where this house was, but that didn't mean that they hadn't figured it out since then.

I turned back to the house. At least Azrael's appearance had thoroughly distracted me from the storm of emotions that looking at this place brought on.

"Trev?" I asked.

I didn't need to clarify. Because, twins.

"I don't detect any spells monitoring the place, but I can't be sure about video and sound without my—"

"Here," Sol said, handing Trev what looked like a small tablet.

"Thanks, but this doesn't have—"

"Yes it does, Avito. I stole it. It's yours."

"How did you—"

"Long story," Sol said.

I turned to look at her, wondering what the hell she'd been doing, going through Trev's stuff, but she just looked slightly embarrassed, shuffled her feet, and shook her head.

Ok. Weird. It appeared that something had gone down between those two while Seamus and I were locked up.

"There's a… no, got it. We're all good. As long as Sol hasn't tampered with this, we should be in the clear," Trev said, with a decided edge to his voice.

"I only took it because—"

"Ok, you two. I get it. There are trust issues. Apparently, we need to do a group session or something, but we might have limited time before MOME catches onto us, so can we please just… do this?"

They both nodded, and I turned back to the red door.

"Here goes nothing," I muttered.

I lifted my leg, and had just angled my body to get the leverage I needed to kick the lock when it exploded in a ball of flame in front of me.

"THE FUCK, TREV?"

"You'll just break your leg," he said. "The deadbolt is probably thrown, so kicking it won't work unless you're strong enough to kick out the whole frame. It's not a college dorm, Vic, it's a house."

I laughed. What else was I going to do? I had really been looking forward to inflicting some actual damage on the house, but Trev was probably right. Enhanced snow leopard strength aside, I was more likely to break myself than the door. Sometimes movies aren't the best guides for real life; true story.

We all plowed inside and I did my best to ignore the actual look of the house. Everything was exactly as I'd left it, from my parents' old coats hanging by the door to the forest green paint on the wall by the stairs. I didn't bother looking in the living areas. I headed straight for the stairs, then turned left to wrap around to the master bedroom. My parents' room.

I had tried packing their stuff up after they'd… when I'd known that they weren't coming back. I thought it would probably be healthy, or whatever, but… I just couldn't do it. Even the one time I went so far as to get a box ready, when I walked it to their room something had just felt wrong about it and I'd turned away at the door.

As I walked towards the door again, I got that same feeling, that something about what I was doing just wasn't right.

Weird, because I had no intention of packing up their stuff. Just one thing in particular, and something they'd sent me to go get, no less.

The closer I got to the door, the stronger the feeling got. I stopped in my tracks.

Just out of curiosity, I took a few steps back.

Sure enough, the feeling of wrongness lessened.

I took a few steps forward.

The feeling of wrongness returned, full force.

"Well, that's quirky," I mumbled, then jumped a foot in the air when Azrael suddenly appeared at my side.

"What is?" they asked.

"Damn it, Azrael, you scared the crap out of me!"

"Sorry, I wasn't trying to. I walk rather quietly."

I looked the towering angelic figure over, trying not to roll my eyes.

"And dare I ask why stealth is on the list of natural traits for a succubus?"

"Easy. Predator evasion," Azrael replied.

I raised an eyebrow at that.

"What predator can possibly be a match for you in this form?"

Azrael frowned.

"We are not the worst thing out there."

I shrugged.

"I never said you were, but it seems like you've got a handful of advantages in this realm that would make it difficult for anything else to make a snack of you."

I had used the term "snack" to be funny, but Azrael shuddered when I said it, and something about the way their skin paled made me wonder what could actually hurt this six-and-a-half-foot tall creature with a physique reminiscent of Greek statuary.

"I'm looking for something in there," I said, not wanting to get too specific, since I still had no idea what Azrael was really doing here. "Mind keeping an eye on the door for me?" I asked. "Just in case anyone from MOME decides to pop in."

Azrael nodded, and I walked to the door to my parents' room, despite the creepy feeling in my stomach forcefully telling me that it was a bad idea.

I WAS FAIRLY certain that the aforementioned creepy feeling was thanks to a spell, or whatever they called instances of magic in this world, my world—fuck, a lifetime of reading fantasy novels *should* have prepared me for this, but so far nothing matched up with my fictional expectations and I didn't even fully understand how magic worked here…. Whatever. I was going to go ahead and call whatever it was that was trying to repel me from my parents' bedroom a spell, because I didn't have a dictionary and no one was offering me free lessons on how this shit worked. Or if they were, we kept getting interrupted by people trying to kill us.

So this spell. It was making me want to turn right around and run in the other direction, but I was determined to get into my parents' room today. Now that I had a guess as to what was making me feel like this, I was amazed that I'd never noticed it before, or rather, that I'd never suspected anything was weird about it. I had noticed it, I'd just thought that it was my gut response to packing up any of my parents' things, or even looking through them. But now… now I was going in with my parents' permission, or rather, at their request. So I shouldn't be feeling the wrenching guilt that made me want to turn around before I even got to the door.

"Hey, Azrael?" I asked, on a hunch. "Would you mind walking towards this door for me and telling me… if there's anything worth telling me?"

"That's incredibly vague, Vic."

"Yep. Trying not to skew the test results."

"Fine. You just want me to walk towards the door?"

"Yep."

"Alright."

So they did. All six-and-a-half feet of winged glory walked towards the door. And stopped about three feet in front of it.

"Odd," Azrael mumbled, then walked all the way to the door and touched it. "Very odd."

"Care to elaborate?" I asked.

Azrael stepped back from the door and returned to the post they'd been keeping at the top of the stairs.

"Mage spells rarely have any effect on me. My own magic in this realm is too strong for them to do much, but… I felt a twinge as I approached the door, and by the time I got to the door, I didn't particularly want to touch it. Which is why I made myself touch it, just to be sure it wasn't a compulsion taking effect. I was able to touch the door, so I guess not."

I nodded.

"That what you were expecting?" Azrael asked.

"More or less," I admitted.

And then I stepped forward, pushed past the feeling that was yelling at me not to go any closer, and turned the handle.

~~~

It was a bit anti-climactic to just find the room exactly as they'd left it. From the old kimonos they'd brought back from Japan with them, to my mom's aging katana, to my dad's old collection of Calvin and Hobbes books—none of it had moved an inch.

I don't know what I'd expected, exactly, but dust collecting on all of my parents' old stuff wasn't really it. And it wasn't even a creepy-haunted-house amount of dust. Just the regular no-one-has-lived-here-for-a-year-or-so's amount of dust.

What *was* strange was that some of that dust was out of place, now that I took a second look at it.

That is to say, there were some fingerprints in the dust over on the bookshelf by the closet. That was weird, but the fingerprints only marked an empty space on the bookshelf. So, all that told me was that someone had been here recently and stolen a book. That was possibly really terrible news, but I didn't know which book it was, and I doubted that it was my mom's mysterious hidden journals. I didn't think those were just going to be sitting out on a shelf. Besides, Mom had said "journals" plural, so there ought to
~~~

be more than one slender volume missing between *The Hitch Hiker's Guide to the Galaxy* and *Good Omens*, if that had been what someone had taken.

Still, I decided it was probably worth investigating. So I squatted in front of the shelf with the missing book and took a good look at the empty space. Then, just to be extra sure of things, I reached my hand into the cavity left by the absent tome.

And hit my fingers against something that made a crunching noise, followed by a whirring, followed by a creepy creaking noise that totally would have fit with a much thicker layer of dust.

And then the whole book shelf popped off the wall and started to recede into the floor.

Because of course it did.

Because my parents had whole secret lives that they'd never told me about.

But apparently had written down.

On paper.

Lots and lots of paper.

Seriously, so much paper.

Like, holy shit, Mom, how many trees did you kill just to document your life?

The entire shelf *behind* the shelf that had just tucked itself away like a prairie dog on ball bearings was just as large as the first and it was filled with journals!

"Nice taste, Mom," I muttered, picking up one of the first volumes and noticing the nicely tooled leather cover.

I opened the cover and was quickly greeted by the date September 7th, 2000, in my mom's familiar handwriting.

I shut the damned thing as fast as I could, but my eyes were still soaked before I could even put it back on the shelf. Barely able to see, I gave up trying and just sat there and let myself have a bit of a cry.

"Vic?" Azrael's oddly British voice called from the doorway. "You alright, Luv?"

I wiped at my eyes so that I could actually see the angel lurking in the doorway.

"I think so. Just… probably haven't finished grieving my parents, you know."

"Ah… you lost them, did you?"

I sighed. Right. Azrael had no reason to know any of this yet.

"Yeah. It's kind of a long story. The super short version is, I'm an orphan as of like six months ago."

Azrael didn't say anything else, but suddenly was seated beside me and enveloping me in the most comforting hug I think I've ever experienced.

Which was weird, coming from a creature I'd only met a couple of days before, who had never presented themself as being entirely cuddly before. Maybe it was the wings that were joining in on the act. Wrapping me up in a warm cocoon. Whatever it was, Azrael had just moved to my "always accept hugs" list.

"Thanks," I muttered, still not letting go. "I wasn't expecting that."

"I'm not entirely heartless, Luv. Besides, I was really just being nosy."

I laughed at that.

"That may be true, but the hug helped. Is that succubus thing?"

"Nah. That's pure squirrel demon, that is."

I laughed again.

"I have a feeling I shouldn't ask…"

"Ask all you like, I'm not telling. A demon has to keep some secrets, after all. Anyway, I'm glad I could help a bit. If only for a moment."

I was about to reply, when I got a distinct whiff of smoke.

"Azrael? Do you sm—"

"Vic! GET OUT OF THERE! THERE'S A FIRE AND I CAN'T—"

Azrael and I were both on our feet before Trev could finish, but he was cut off anyway, and I had a terrified moment of panic before he sent a message to me mentally.

I'm fine, Vic. I was trying to fight the fire with my magic, but it's not working. Just like the stuff back at the boat. I was breathing deep to yell for you and took in too much smoke. Not sure why I didn't just start with this. Can you get out?

By then Azrael and I had reached the door and discovered that the landing was completely engulfed in flames.

Not by the stairs, I sent to Trev. *We'll try the window.*

We?

Azrael's with me.

And then I was too busy trying to open the nearest window in my parents' bedroom to worry about much else.

The damned locks wouldn't budge, and I had to suppose that a year's worth of weather and humidity fluctuation, without any upkeep, had taken its toll on the hardware. Luckily, after my wereleopard strength proved un-equal to the task, Azrael ripped both locks straight out of the wall.

"Not subtle, but functional," I admitted.

"Come on, Luv. You first."

I almost complied, but then I remembered my mom's journals. The whole damned point of this mission, sitting on those shelves, and the flames that were now inside the doorway and not-so-slowly making their way towards the open window, which was now just feeding the fire with every gust of fresh oxygen that came through.

I sprinted to the hidden shelf.

"No time, Vic!" Azrael shouted from their spot by the window.

"I can't just leave them!" I shouted back, because we had to shout over the roar of shit burning like oil-soaked paper around us now. I grabbed the volume that I'd first opened and the one next to it, and tried to grab a few more and tuck them under my arms. Then I got to the window and cursed loudly. Then I coughed a bunch.

"You have to get out of here now, Vic. The smoke will get you soon, even if the fire doesn't."

And the fire was quickly approaching, even if the smoke was going to kill me first, and damn it all. I was going to break a leg if I made this jump in human form.

"I need to shift. Are those things decorative?" I asked, gesturing to Az-rael's wings as best I could while trying to cover my nose and mouth with my shirt and shove journals into their arms.

Azrael just glared at me and took the books, all except one. That one I put on the windowsill just before calling on my snow leopard form, then picked it up in my mouth and leapt from the second story window into a small patch of scrub oaks.

I TURNED BACK just in time to hear a scream come from inside the house and then see Azrael disappear from the window.

"Did she just go leaping through a wall of fire?" Seamus asked, from behind me.

I nodded, but kept my eyes glued to the window. It wasn't worth shifting back to human just to correct Seamus' gendering of Azrael. After all, if he'd only ever seen their female aspect, why would he think differently? Besides, English is a bit stupid about gendering anyway.

It felt like a lifetime, but it was probably only about 90 seconds later when Azrael came flying out the window, carrying an unconscious Trevor, followed by a glorious full-panther-mode Soledad.

I let out an anxious roar, somewhat muffled by the journal still clenched between my teeth, and bounded over to them all, but Azrael just shooed me back.

"We have to get away from this house. I can't stop the fire either, and this place isn't going to be standing much longer."

I swallowed the anguished wail that wanted to rise out of my throat, and instead just turned and ran up the longish driveway to where the trees opened onto the main road. I could already tell that everyone was behind me before I shifted back to human.

"Trev! Trev!" I shouted, running to Azrael's side and putting my hands on my brother's throat, desperate to feel a pulse.

It was there, strong and constant.

"Just too much smoke," Azrael said. "I think he'll be alright."

"As you just reminded me, too much smoke can still kill you. He needs a doctor, or a healer, or whatever. Should we take him to the Tree of Life?"

Sol shifted to her human form.

"Too risky. MOME knows about the grove. He needs his girlfriend," she said.

I raised an eyebrow.

"Rhelia's healing gifts are well known," she said. "If she'd been able to treat you after that MOME spell hit you, there might not have been any scarring."

With Trev lying unconscious in Azrael's arms, I didn't waste time thinking about that, but instead focused on getting Trev to Rhelia.

"Group hug," I said loudly, trying to get everyone within my embrace.

Seamus and Sol both stepped in, and Trev didn't move.

"Probably best if I stay behind," Azrael said, handing Trev to Sol. "I'm resistant to most mage spells. I don't want to mess with whatever you use for transportation."

I nodded, unsure if Azrael was right about possibly messing with my magic, but unwilling to test it when it came down to getting Trev medical assistance.

With Trev in Sol's arms and my hands on both Trev and Sol, I took a deep breath, and instead of focusing on a place, I reached for the one person I desperately hoped could help my brother.

"UGH. OF COURSE I wouldn't get to keep an encyclopedia's worth of information about our parents' lives. That would have been entirely too easy, not to mention too big an info dump," I muttered, flipping distractedly through the pages of the one journal that I had managed to hold onto from my parents' bedroom (thanks to Seamus, who had picked the damned thing up after I dropped it to run to Trev's side back in Colorado). Seamus had handed it to me right after we'd settled ourselves on the floor of Rhelia's Unterberg base of operations. Apparently, she had more than one place to call home in the world.

I was lying on a futon like the ones my parents had brought back from their time in Japan—the ones that are nothing like the thick mattress things you can buy at Ikea (did they even have Ikea in a place like Unterberg?) but more like deluxe sleeping pads, way better than anything you'd take camping, and great once you get used to them, but probably well below what most North Americans would consider comfortable. Sol, Seamus, and Trev were all lying on similar mattresses spread out on the floor around me, and the whole place made me think that Rhelia had probably read Shogun more than once. There were katana mounted on the wall, and the floor was covered in actual tatami mats. I was going to have to ask her about the decor once she finally got back from wherever she'd been rushing off to when we'd first arrived. She'd barely taken thirty seconds to assess Trevor and show us where we could put him, then she'd been running out the door.

"What?" Trev asked, from his futon on the floor.

"Nothing," I said, snapping back to the present. "Just that, since my life has apparently turned into some kind of adventure tale, it's no wonder I wouldn't be able hold onto all those journals that Mom wrote. I mean, hell, they probably answered every question I've had about Mom and Dad, since they disappeared and I found out that they were deep into a magic world I never knew existed."

"What do you mean, info dump? Vic, what the hell are you talking about? Your life is an adventure story?" Trev sounded mildly worried.

"You remember Gwen, yes?"

"Yeah…"

"Well, whatever kind of deity of good fortune she claims to be, when I first met her, she said she was my narrator."

"Your narrator?" That was Sol, apparently joining in the incredulity party. Not that I blamed her.

"Yeah." I snorted. "She showed up naked in the woods loudly describing everything I was doing."

"And you didn't run the other way?" Seamus asked.

I shrugged.

"She was ruining my weekend getaway, so I decided to talk *her* into leaving instead."

"Did it work?" Sol asked.

"Not really," I admitted. "She left eventually, but only after I insisted that I would take over my own narration."

"First person?" Sol asked. "Yuck."

"Why do people say that?" I asked. "What the fuck is wrong with first person narration? It's gripping and immediate."

"It's so… angsty," Sol accused.

"Yeah, well, you and the old goddess can go take a long walk off of the same short pier. I *like* first person narration. Besides, you would have said whatever was necessary to get rid of the creepy, seemingly insane woman who showed up and claimed to be your narrator, too."

Sol's eyebrows rose provocatively.

"Gwen? Naked? I doubt I would have been in a hurry to get away."

That had me laughing.

"Yeah, well, you were the first woman I ever found attractive, so… I wasn't as impressed."

"Well, I like first person narration too," Seamus said. "So, what's the deal? Why do you have a narrator?"

"I don't know, really. Gwen never explained. She just made it sound like 'they' were listening/or reading or whatever, and wouldn't know what was going on if there was no narrator. So I said I would do it, if it would stop her from standing around announcing every single thing I was doing and describing me like food."

"Ugh, I hate that," Seamus said. "I am not a fucking coffee with a touch of milk."

Sol laughed. "I actually enjoy being compared to chocolate, myself."

We all chuckled.

"You are, of course, welcome to describe yourself as all the delicious desserts you like," I said. "But I'm not about to describe you as one."

"Well, I think you're a mocha, anyway," Sol said, playfully running a hand along my arm.

I batted her away.

"It's not nearly as obnoxious when you do it, but *anyway*—"

"Yeah, I want to hear about why you're in a book," Trev interrupted.

"I don't know. And I'm not even sure it's a book. I mean, I honestly thought that Gwen was just nuts when she said all that, but… well, she actually does seem to be a goddess and stuff, so…"

"So, it's possible that you're in a book?" Sol asked, still sounding incredulous, but not quite as dismissive as she had a minute ago.

"I suppose? I mean, the day Gwen showed up was the day that everything started to turn completely weird."

"But if you're in a book, then that means we all are!" said Seamus excitedly. "At least, we are when we're with you."

I laughed again.

"I suppose so…"

"So, you're saying that all of those journals were burned to ash because it would be too easy for the plot if you found everything out from a set of books?" Trev asked, finally returning us to my original point.

"Well, I hope that's not the only reason. That would be lazy writing, and if I'm in a book I'd like to hope it's not one that's poorly written. But yeah, imagine reading a book that's full of fight scenes and chase scenes and stuff and then finding out most of the major plot twists because the character sat down to read something that spelled everything out."

"Ok. Blargh. Yeah, you make a good point," Sol admitted. "Still, if the book is written in the first person, it's entirely possible that's not very well writ—"

"Hey! Don't you start. First person narrative is a completely viable point of view and can be used to great effect. Fuck right off with your implication that it's a cop-out."

Sol raised both hands in a pacifying gesture.

"Please don't kill me, Gatita. I forgot that you read as much as I do, just in some different genres. Look, so if the writing isn't lazy, then we're still stuck with the fact that someone burned your old house down on purpose, most likely to stop you from reading those journals. We need to know who, and why."

"I may be able to help with that," said a voice from the doorway.

We all turned and looked at the same time, to find Rhelia standing on the threshold, holding what looked like a flash drive, along with my backpack.

"YOU KNOW WHO burned my house down?" I asked, before my brain fully caught up with what I'd just heard.

"Not exssssactly, no," Rhelia said, coming in and sitting down beside where Trev was lying. "But, between your file," she elaborated, handing me my backpack, "and what I have on thissss flash drive, we might be able to figure it out."

"Isn't the safe assumption at this point that it was MOME?" Seamus asked, as I began to pull my parents' file from my backpack.

I nodded.

"Sure, that's the easy bet. But if they knew about those journals, why leave that house standing for all that time?"

"Umm… to lure you in and try to kill you, for, like, the hundredth time in the past month or so?" Seamus stated, so matter-of-factly that I had to stare at him for a moment.

"Fair point. Well made," I admitted. "Still, it was a bit roundabout for MOME, don't you think? I mean, they haven't hesitated with the direct approach before."

"Yeah, but you just won your trial, and now if they just straight-up kill you, they will look really bad, even to their supporters."

Seamus was just full of good points tonight.

"I'm still fuzzy on why they care about their public appearance anyway. I mean, since when do dictatorships, or corrupt oligarchies, or whatever, care about public opinion?"

"Historically? Pretty much always," Trev replied. "It's how they keep uprisings down. They need to maintain at least a vague semblance of justice, or else the masses organize and then they're finally shit out of luck. And, if they don't look legit enough to keep the people they hire to dole out their 'justice' in line, then they lose all their power."

"What would Hitler have ever been able to accomplish without Nazis?" Sol added.

"Right. Ok. So, the MOME assholes have to at least *pretend* not to kill me openly. I admit, in that case, a house fire seems like a legit option. 'Oh how sad! The poor, recently exonerated Victoria Marmot was mourning the recent tragic loss of her parents, when a mysterious house fire took her life, and those of her troublesome and law-breaking friends.' Right. Makes sense. Still, I don't know that MOME knew about those journals. After all, if they did, why leave them there? They could have lured me there without the actual journals, just using the mere idea of them. And it still doesn't make sense that they could have found out about the journals anyway. Mom and Dad went to a lot of trouble to keep that from happening."

"Possssibly, but we cannot rule MOME out," Rhelia said, from Trev's side, where she appeared to be doing a Vulcan mind meld or some shit.

"What are you doing?" I asked, when her hand was still spread across Trev's temple and cheekbone few seconds later.

"I'm jusssst checking to make ssssure there issssn't any tissssue damage in hissss lungssss."

I was intensely curious about how that worked, but realized that with my luck, someone was likely to come tearing into the room with a flamethrower to destroy this file and Mom's last remaining journal any moment now. I should really start reading them if I had any hope of getting any answers, like, ever.

A half an hour later I knew a lot of things about my parents that I'd never known before, but I still didn't know who'd set my parents' house on fire.

"Trev, how far did you get in this file before you started that argument with Albert?" I asked.

Trev, no longer under Rhelia's ministrations that I could see, but now sitting up and holding her hand rather endearingly, tipped his head back as if to think.

"I got to the point where I found out exactly *what* they were studying with Albert."

"Ok. I read that part, but it didn't really make sense to me. Expanded

Dark Matter studies? What does that mean?"

Trev took a deep breath and sighed.

"Its what they were teaching me and the other 'misfits' at MOME too. Well, some of us, anyway."

"But Mom and Dad went to learn it from Albert voluntarily?" I asked.

"Yes. Because when they were teenagers, the program actually *paid* them as test subjects, rather than merely kidnapping and then 'educating' them, but they were still more or less lab rats."

"How do you know that?" I asked.

Everyone else in the room seemed to be making a point of maintaining absolute silence, and I wondered what taboo we were getting into that had them all so quiet.

"Albert as much as told me that much, after I confronted him about it, but it was clear enough in the file itself. Besides, no one from our world who had anything left to lose would volunteer to be in a study on Expanded Dark Matter."

"Really? Why?"

"Because most people consider it a myth," Sol replied. "The most respected researchers in the magical world have disproved its existence time and time again. There have been over a dozen articles published to that effect."

Rhelia snorted.

We all turned to look at her.

"Humanssss are sssso limited," she sighed. "Bessssidessss, it hassss alwayssss been in MOME'ssss besssst interesssstssss that no one believe in Exsssspanded Dark Matter theory, sssso why would they let anyone 'prove' it, unlessss it wassss for their own purpossssesssss?"

"So, did Mom and Dad even know what they were signing up for?" I wondered aloud. "Sounds like MOME wouldn't have made it public knowledge."

"Unlikely. Who knows how MOME advertised it back then, but they probably just said they were conducting a study and willing to pay qualifying participants."

"And how did one qualify?" I asked, a chill running down my spine.

"Likely by being on the list of 'dangerous persons' that MOME used to bandy about in those days," Trev replied.

"What does that mean?"

Trev and Rhelia exchanged a look that I couldn't decipher, then Trev stood up, muttered a word I couldn't quite make out, and a ball of light appeared, floating above his hand.

I just blinked at him, but Seamus and Sol both gasped.

Then he muttered something else, and the ball of light disappeared, replaced with a rock.

Sol and Seamus gasped again.

I just blinked some more. I mean come on, Trev could turn into a fucking bird made out of fire—why was this supposed to be impressive?

I must have said that last part aloud, because Sol replied, "Gatita, it's not that those are impressive tricks, it's just that they're mage tricks. A were shouldn't be able to do them at all."

I shrugged, feeling more out of place in the magical world than I had all month.

"Dark matter is dark matter, isn't it? Why wouldn't you be able to use it for whatever?"

Trev smiled, then banished the rock and bent over to hug me.

"That's the benefit of growing up outside the magical world, Vic. You aren't hampered by a lifetime of internalized propaganda. You are absolutely right. Dark matter is dark matter, and anyone who can access it, who has it running in their veins, should be able to pull on whatever aspect of it they like, even if they have a genetic predilection for certain ways of accessing it."

"Makes sense to me," I said, returning Trev's embrace.

"The dragonssss have known thissss for millennia," Rhelia said, sounding a tiny bit smug. "We have tried to tell humanssss before, but you alwayssss wanted proof, and when we gave it to you, you ssssaid, 'but you are dragonssss, it issss not the ssssame.'"

Sol and Seamus both looked dumbstruck.

"It's even possible to access more than one animal form," Trev added, now seeming truly excited.

"Impossible," Sol whispered.

Trev and Rhelia exchanged another glance.

"You guys have been witnessing Vic pull us through time and space for weeks now, and you don't think that it's possible to have more powers than the ones that you're genetically predisposed towards?"

"But a goddess bestowed some powers on her," Seamus objected.

"And how would that work, if one couldn't access dark matter in different ways than the ones we're born to?"

"I don't know. She's a goddess?"

"Look, let's all go into the basement, and we can show you something."

"Well, that sounds ominous," I muttered.

Trev laughed, giving me a noogie, and I wondered what was making him so giddy.

"We could go to the roof, but then the whole city might see, and that could be… complicated."

~~~

So, that's how we wound up in the creepy basement of a giant stone apartment complex in the middle of the night.

I was not reassured when Trev asked me to stand in the middle of said creepy, weeping-stoned room, and then asked me to close my eyes.

"Imagine yourself as a dragon," Trev said.

I laughed.

"What?"

Rhelia replied, "Feel the wind on your facsssse assss you fly through the ssssky. Feel the protection of the ssssscalessss that cover your ssssskin. Feel the raw power you contain within. Feel the ansssscient knowledge that you are an apexssss predator and none can sssstand in your way…"

I decided it would be faster than arguing to just keep my mouth and eyes shut and go along with the exercise, even if it was pointless. I didn't know what they thought was going to happen, but—

Everyone gasped.

"Yessss, very good!"

I suddenly felt… weightier… like I was taking up quite a bit more of the room, and… I could feel the stone beneath my… claws? with four feet instead of just two. What the fuck? Had I pulled on my snow leopard form without meaning to? But that didn't explain how much wider apart my feet felt, and, ah fuck it, I had better just open my eyes.

Um… am I a dragon? I asked Trev and Rhelia.

"Yep," Trev said proudly.

Looking around the room, I couldn't really argue the point.

I was a dragon.
~~~

AS SOON AS I opened my eyes, it became clear why we had done this here, rather than in Rhelia's apartment. When I looked down, everyone was way below me. My head was just shy of bumping the ceiling, and that was only because my dragon form seemed to have entered the world ducking. I couldn't quite see the end of my tail until I made a point of flicking it up off the ground and waving it at myself. I was coiled tightly, but if I had to guess, I was about the length of a soccer field. My scales appeared to be every color of a tropical sunset, from deep crimson to bright orange, and a thousand shades in between. The fact that I could even distinguish that many colors in this dank, candlelit cellar was strange enough as it was.

How am I a dragon? I asked. *It's not like I've spent a lifetime training how to access different paths in dark matter, or whatever you were suggesting it would take to do this.*

"You can do it because one of our ancestors was a dragon, so the pathway is there anyway, no practice needed."

"If it were that simple," objected Sol, "EVERYONE would have access to multiple animals, from birth."

"And to some degree they do," Trev said. "But two things keep them from accessing them. One is years of conditioning to make you believe that you can only access one form, and the other is lack of genetic diversity in were communities. How many non-panthers are in your family, Soledad?"

Sol stared at him for a moment, then nodded.

"Ok. Fine, maybe that's true, but we're not the only were community. You and Vic aren't the only weres in the world with parents of mixed heritage."

"That's true," Trev conceded. "But that brings me back to the first point.

Conditioning. Have you ever *tried* to reach for a form other than your panther?"

Sol shook her head, then Trev turned to Seamus.

"Have you ever tried to reach for something other than your wolf?"

"Nope. I've always been pretty stoked about the prospect of turning into a wolf. Never occurred to me to try anything else."

"Right. Why bother?" Trev agreed.

"So are you saying that MOME actually taught you all of this?" Sol asked, slightly incredulous.

"Well, they didn't teach us the theory behind it, they only experimented on us by trying to get us to access different things. They wanted to see who could learn what, and how much dark matter access you had to have to be able to pull off certain things. All for 'research,' of course. I put together a lot of how it all worked on my own, but Rhelia is the one who brought it all together for me."

We all turned to Rhelia and she shrugged.

"Assss I ssssaid, dragonssss have known thissss for millennia. It wassss eassssy to share with ssssomeone who wassss willing to lisssssten."

I suddenly found myself in human form again, apparently so I could voice the question, "What exactly were you doing in that dungeon again, anyway?"

I was a bit sad not to be standing there as a dragon anymore, but if all it took was remembering the physicality of dragondom, then I was sure it would always be easy. I was never going to forget what that was like.

"We should return to my apartment," she said. "It issss not ssssafe to disssscussss ssssuch thingssss here. Anyone could overhear ussss."

Unfortunately, before we could even question Rhelia's suggestion that this might not be a safe place to chat, a spell exploded over my head and the ceiling started to come down.

"TELL ME WHERE she is!!" cried the crazed voice of a vampire who I was really getting tired of seeing, as I felt the weight of a full-grown man plow into my back, hurling me to the ground.

"Gwendamnit, Edik! If your daughter wants to contact you, she will fucking find you. Now stop trying to get us killed!"

The room had already descended into chaos. I had no idea how many MOME agents were here, but I didn't stop to count. I pulled on my snow leopard form, clawing and twisting my way out of Edik's grasp as fast as I could, taking zero care not to injure him, and possibly throwing in an extra set of back claw scratches as I got myself out from under him.

Of course, you may be wondering why I didn't just flip myself back to my newly acquired dragon form, but there were many reasons for that. One, I wan't sure how to fight in my dragon form. Could I breathe fire? A cone of cold or acid? Ok, I might be leaning a little too hard on my D&D lore here, but I could have a breath weapon, or then again, I might not. And even if I did, I had no idea how to control it in tight spaces and not take out my friends. Plus, I filled up most of this room on my own as a dragon, and I did not want to crush any of the people I loved right now. Furthermore, my snow leopard was light and quick, and I was already very used to fighting with it.

I didn't hesitate to launch myself at the nearest MOME agent. After their attack on Seamus' moms, I no longer doubted that they had the worst possible intentions every time that they engaged with us, and I wasn't about to let them kill any of the people I cared about.

I had my work cut out for me, though. The room was crawling with MOME agents. Luckily, there were so many of them that they were reluctant to fling spells willy-nilly, and they'd brought more shifters than they usually did. This creepy-assed basement was starting to resemble the world's most fucked-up zoo.

A bear was launching itself again and again at Trev in his phoenix form, and Sol was facing off against an honest-to-Gwen Bengal tiger. Seamus was chasing after a giant-eagle-looking-thing that I didn't know the name of, but which was almost the same size as Trev's phoenix. Rhelia was calmly in her human form, deflecting the various attacks of what appeared to be a silverback gorilla, and there seemed to be mage upon mage filing into the room, setting off spells wherever they could get a clear shot that wasn't going to take out one of their comrades.

In short: shit had gotten real.

I heard screams and roars as intense heat flared behind me, and I turned to see Trev immolating not only the bear that had been attacking him, but also half a dozen mages who had been closing in.

Deciding that he seemed to have things the most in hand of anyone, I headed for Seamus and his giant-eagle-thing. Despite the fact that Seamus had the eagle on the run, he didn't seem to be faring too well. The mages all around them kept firing at him continuously, and when I looked more closely, it seemed like he was mainly trying to use the eagle for cover. Which was fairly clever, but not a great long-term strategy when your target has wings and you don't.

I decided to wait until the eagle was on the downswing, trying to expose Seamus to mage fire and not looking in my direction, then I launched all furry two hundred pounds of myself at the giant thing, sinking my teeth into its neck. It collapsed quickly beneath my weight, making a sickening crunch as we hit the floor. I didn't wait to see if it would get up again, but instead put myself between Seamus and the mages that surrounded us. I was pretty sure that MOME would use the excuse of "apprehending" Trev and Rhelia as cover for killing Seamus and me, and it made me wonder why I had ever given credence to the idea that they might have been trying to find a subtler way to wipe me out.

Luckily, the mages decided that hitting their downed eagle friend was too risky for the moment, so Seamus and I had a second. I put my paw on him and shifted us both over to where Rhelia was deftly avoiding the attacks of the eight hundred pound gorilla. I figured that Rhelia was the most likely of all of us to be able to defend someone else at the same time as herself. She seemed to understand this, giving me a slight nod as I deposited Seamus by her side.

Then I leapt over to where Sol was facing off against a half-ton of feline might, the likes of which I had only seen up close at zoos. Since I didn't know of any better options, I went with a standard flanking move, leaping for the tiger's hindquarters and sinking my teeth and claws into his haunches even as he slashed his giant paw at Sol's head once more.

My teeth and claws ripping into his flesh seemed to pull him up short. Indeed, he took a moment to turn and snarl in my direction, either to express his displeasure or simply to exclaim in pain. Either way, it was a mistake he couldn't afford to make, and Sol instantly pounced at the opportunity.

That is, she leapt forward and sank her own teeth into the tiger's throat.

Not that the move did an untoward amount of damage. The tiger was far from going down, even with Sol latched to its throat, but now it was thoroughly distracted by the close proximity of panther teeth to its jugular, and it was my turn to do some damage. So, I scrambled farther up the giant cat's back and spread my claws out into its shoulder blades, hoping to do a debilitating amount of damage.

I had a feeling that the gashes I was leaving in the otherwise pristine orange and black fur would turn my stomach, once I was back in human form, but my snow leopard had no qualms about fighting off a predator that was threatening my mate and family. For the moment, I was thankful for the desensitization, because I really didn't have time to agonize about whether this guy (and yes, I'd approached in a crouch from behind, so I had full confirmation that this tiger was a dude) had a partner, children, or any number of other innocent people attached to him who would be devastated by his injuries. The human part of my brain kept wanting to go there, but I was not in a human body, and my snow leopard didn't give a fuck.

The tiger seemed to give an equal number of fucks as he attempted over and over again to throw me from his back, all while trying to rip Sol's throat out. Luckily, she was tenacious and her jaw strength seemed unshakeable. She had added her front claws into the mix and was deeply anchored on the tiger's neck. I continued to rip and tear, hoping against hope that tigers were built similarly enough to bulls for my efforts to cause his head to drop. I'd only seen one bullfight in my life, and only on television, but that had been more than enough. The memory of the men on horseback spearing the poor thing's neck and shoulders, before the matador even took the field, had haunted me ever since.

If it came in useful now, though, it would be worth it. Worth it to protect Sol, to protect Seamus, to protect Trev…

I was starting to slide off the tiger's shoulders due to all the blood that was seeping from the dozens of cuts I'd spread across its shoulders and neck, and I lost my footing completely when the Bengal swerved wildly from the pattern he'd been following up to now. I rolled gracelessly to the floor, only landing upright thanks to the magic, possessed by all felines, that enables them to essentially defy physics anytime they need their paws under them.

Even with my paws under me, I slipped halfway across the floor, my paws grappling for purchase through the thick coating of blood that covered them. By the time I regained traction, Sol had disengaged from the tiger, who now lay thrashing feebly on the floor, and had charged the silverback that was attacking Rhelia. The choice made more sense when I noted that the gorilla had been joined by a… was that a moose? Crap. That thing was huge.

I was turning to join her when I heard a cry from behind me that sounded too much like Trev's phoenix for my liking.

When I got a good look at him, I saw that they had him in a huge net made of… something that looked like silver, but probably wasn't, because it wasn't melting and Trev burned *very* hot. Silver had a low enough melting point that it would have turned liquid the moment it got within a foot of him, if he was flaring, as he clearly was right now.

Before I'd even fully registered the cry, I had turned in his direction, and now I was racing towards him. I hadn't even covered half the distance be-tween us, and he was surrounded by mages. Over a dozen of them formed a tight circle around him, half of them facing towards him, and half of them facing outwards. I was now dodging and weaving, hoping to avoid getting hit by another spell that would melt half of my skin off.

The barrage of spells that they sent my way was constant, and I soon found myself giving ground, backtracking slightly now and then, in hopes of dodging more of their attacks, but ultimately giving up more ground than I was gaining.

I let out a roar of frustration, then followed it instantly with a roar of agony as one spell hit my shoulder. I crumpled, but managed to keep my eye on Trev, who was slowly being maneuvered towards the same damp archway through which we'd entered. Without second-guessing the move, I pulled through time and space, shifting myself directly on top of him, hoping that I could shift both of us away from the circle of mages. Instead, I shrieked in agony as whatever that net was made out of seared itself into my skin. Trev cried into my mind, *No, Vic! Get away! This net is blocking everything I throw at it. They'll just capture you too. Please!*

The anguish in his voice, and the certainty that he was right, joined with the debilitating agony produced by that net to convince me to listen to him. I rolled myself to the floor, narrowly missing the grasp of a handful of nearby mages, then managed to shift myself away from the circle of mages, but still maintain line of sight to Trev.

So I was watching when Rhelia shifted into a dragon form that was far too large for this space and began destroying every MOME agent within sight. Her serpentine neck swayed, bobbed, and struck with such agility that the MOME agents closest to her never had a chance. I think she swallowed the silverback whole, and I was well beyond furious enough not to feel a moment's sympathy for the creature. They were taking my brother from me. Again. Fuck that!

I suddenly found myself on my feet. I was amazed, because the pain in my shoulder was intense, and I was fairly sure I was missing half of the muscle that was supposed to hold me up on that limb, but I shifted my weight to my other three feet and did my best to limp forward towards Trev.

Unfortunately, it quickly became clear why Rhelia hadn't shifted to her dragon form at the start of this fight. She was trapped by the room, and couldn't advance beyond the archway through which they were dragging Trev. Also, the space was far too small for her to use her fire on anyone, or she risked destroying the rest of us along with them. She was reduced to claws and teeth. Still quite formidable, as the men and women now lying in various segments across the floor had learned all too clearly, but not enough to catch the assholes who were dragging my brother down the narrow hallway. Though she did manage to grab a few of the ones that didn't move fast enough.

They threw spell after spell at her, but nothing stuck. Everything seemed to simply bounce off of her, or hit her and then instantly dissipate. Either she was ignoring the effects of the spells, or they did nothing to her dragon-scale hide. Watching her tempted me to shift to my own newfound dragon form and fight alongside her, but I knew that the two of us in here would crush every last soul that wasn't a dragon, and besides, then I would be just as stuck as she now was.

So, I rushed ahead in my snow leopard form, as fast as my injured right shoulder would allow, and launched myself towards the circle of mages that kept reforming around Trev. As if there were an unending stream of them, as if a new one popped into existence to take the place of each one that went down.

By the time I reached them, I could hear Rhelia bellowing in frustration behind me. Or, more accurately, I could feel it, as the sound shook my entire being, as well as the floors and ceilings all around us. I hoped that my charge forward hadn't gotten in the way of her attacks, but as far as I could tell, she was out of effective range already.

Before I could worry about it much, I was sinking my claws and teeth into the nearest mage and dragging her to the floor. She screamed, but she didn't fight me once she went down, so I leapt past her and towards my next target.

It was then that I felt a rush of fur, as Sol and Seamus both leapt at the mages to the left and right of me. The two of them tore into the mages with as much ferocity as Rhelia and I had, and I felt a renewed sense of hope as we plowed forward together into the circle of mages.

But that hope was short-lived, as they continued to pull along a thrashing, screaming, phoenix-Trev, still wrapped in netting, and their numbers kept replenishing, no matter how many of them we took down. Sol and Seamus both seemed to have taken small hits and we were all nearing exhaustion.

Each swipe of my claws felt heavier and heavier, as if someone were gradually increasing the resistance on a weight machine that I didn't remember strapping to my wrists. Having to rear onto my hind legs repeatedly, just to swipe with only my left paw, made everything harder.

Seamus and Sol were faring marginally better, but Seamus, in particular, looked like he was nearing collapse anyway, and I wondered briefly if he was bleeding somewhere that I couldn't see.

Then an ebon streak of terror threw itself at the circle of mages.

Rhelia's battle cry was soul-shaking, and I half expected the cry itself to shatter the men and women surrounding her mate.

But it didn't. And neither did the series of attacks that she launched at them in her human form, though she did take down mage after mage, until she was practically in the circle of them, whirling in all directions, resembling nothing so much as a character from a modern kung-fu flick.

She even started flinging spells at them, something I'd never seen her do before, but which seemed to make no difference, considering how easily the line of mages replaced the fallen. They must have brought a hundred mages or more with them, keeping them all in the hallway while they sent in their initial force to distract us.

When none of that worked, Rhelia let out a final bellow and then threw herself on top of Trev. I assumed she thought that her weight would bear him down and then… I don't know, she would find some way to fight her way out with our help? Maybe that was her plan, but it didn't matter. The mages had wrapped Trev in as much spellwork as netting, and Rhelia's presence did nothing to dislodge him from their grasp. In fact, before I could do anything about it, they quickly threw an identical net around Rhelia, who screamed one more time before the whole mass of them turned the corner, disappearing from sight.

I put on a burst of speed, despite the protestations of my injured shoulder and aching muscles, almost collapsing when it came time to turn the corner, but they were gone.

"It's too late, Gatita," Sol shouted from behind me. "They'll have had a transport spell waiting, out of sight. They'll be back at MOME HQ by now."

I shifted back to human form, and nearly fell over as the pain in my shoulder flared. Right. I was going to have to remember that my snow leopard form had a much higher pain tolerance than my other half.

I slumped against the wall.

"Then get over here so I can shift us to MOME HQ."

"Not happening, Gatita. They would be waiting for us, and we'd be captured or killed in no time."

"Damn it, Sol! I can't just let MOME take my brother again!"

"I know. But we need a plan."

"Guys," Seamus said, finally joining us, in human form. "I don't feel so good."

I turned to look at him, and indeed, for someone who never wanted to be described as coffee with a touch of milk, he was looking awfully milky.

Shrugging off my own pain, I stood up, covering the distance between me and Seamus quickly. Just as I reached him, he started to slump. I caught him by the shoulders and could feel a slick wetness coat my fingers. Soon I was holding all of Seamus' weight, and my right hand was soaked in blood.

"Sol, he needs a healer. We just lost Rhelia, can we risk the Tree?"

"If I'd been planning this mission for MOME, I would have specifically left a unit there, in hopes that we'd be injured enough to need it."

"Damn it, what do we do?"

"It seems like a slow bleed. A regular healer might be able to help him. Take him to his parents?" Sol suggested.

Unable to think of anything else, I nodded, waited until Sol put her arm on my shoulder, and then shifted us to the small Unterberg apartment on the opposite side of town where Rhelia had arranged for Seamus' moms to stay.

IT WAS WITH no small amount of embarrassment that I learned that Rowan was a doctor. I really needed to work on asking my friends more personal questions. Especially the friends I was sleeping with, and might be fairly romantically attached to. I tried to give myself a break for it, since it had been a particularly trying couple of weeks, but it still bothered me that I didn't know the professions of my best friends' parents. At least I could console myself that I knew just as little about Sol's family…. On second thought, that didn't really make me feel any better.

Fortunately, since Rowan was a long practicing ER doc, I felt quite confident leaving Seamus in her care. Unfortunately, since Sol and I were likely to bring down a horde of MOME agents on any location where we were present, as far as I could tell, we decided it was safest to leave Seamus with his moms and try to find somewhere else to regroup, despite Rowan's protestations that she should really take a look at my shoulder before we went anywhere.

Of course, I couldn't really think of a place less likely to attract MOME attention than the place where Rhelia had hidden Seamus' parents, but, even still, we had a couple of errands to run before we could settle down anywhere anyway.

I shifted us directly to the middle of Rhelia's apartment, in hopes of avoiding whatever surveillance might have been left at her place. We didn't stay long at all. Just long enough to grab the journal, the file, and—thanks to Sol, who spotted it on the floor just as I was about to shift us out of there—the flash drive that Rhelia had been carrying when she'd first come back to the apartment. It was ridiculous to think that had only been a few hours earlier.

I sighed as Sol grabbed my arm and I rallied to make another shift. I had a feeling this would be the last one I was going to be able to manage until I was able to rest, and/or get my shoulder healed. As such, I had one specific destination in mind, even if it was risky.

So it was that a certain creeptastic vampire managed to hitch one final ride back to Arizona with us. I didn't see or hear him, but I felt his creepily cold grasp on my shoulder as I was already reaching for the small, familiar glade that had saved my life so many times already.

While I was somewhat unsurprised to see Edik as we landed in a tumble in the middle of the glade that held the Tree of Life, I was completely in shock when I stepped back and an ebon-skinned hand clamped down on his pasty neck, ripping it from his shoulders before I'd even had time to scream my rage at him.

I half expected to lift my eyes and see Rhelia, since she certainly had plenty of reasons to wish Edik dead, but aside from her being currently locked up by MOME, the skin of that hand was missing the iridescence that suffused Rhelia's skin. My brain had almost filled in the blank by the time I looked up to see Azrael, once more in their feminine form, grasping a very surprised looking Edik by the shoulder while his body slumped to the ground.

Then Azrael threw the head into the woods. My stomach turned at the sheer violence of the whole thing, but I couldn't get my brain to drum up any sympathy for the vampire.

"Umm… dare I ask what he did to you?"

Azrael shrugged. "I loathe vampires."

When neither Sol nor I said anything for a very long moment, they added, "It's a succubus thing."

"Right. Ok," I agreed eloquently, just before passing out.

WHEN I WOKE up, I felt infinitely better than I had in a long while.

"Dare I ask how long I was out?" I queried… possibly no one. I was staring at a beautifully tiled ceiling, but since I hadn't looked around at all yet, I had no idea if anyone was here with me. Something told me that I wasn't addressing an empty room, though.

It was Sol's voice that answered.

"Only a day, this time. Not bad, really, considering how many times you shifted us while missing a third of the muscles in your shoulder."

I sighed.

"Did Life heal me up? Or did we have to flee another herd of MOME agents?"

Sol laughed.

"No. No one was there besides Azrael and the Tree. Life healed you up, as usual, as soon as I took you over to him. Azrael ran off before I could ask any more about why they felt the need to decapitate the vamp, and then Gwen showed up out of nowhere and shifted us to Rhelia's apartment in the dragon realm, claiming that the dragons would be angry if you weren't turned over to their care."

"Huh. At least I didn't miss anything interesting."

Sol laughed again.

"I appreciate your sense of humor, Gatita. One of these days you're going to need a really good cry, though."

I chuckled, trying not to think about how right she was. I didn't feel like sobbing right now. I needed to—I knew that. I could feel it building up, threatening to tear my lungs apart if I let it, but… not yet. I needed to come up with a plan first. I needed to get Trev back. Get Rhelia back. Then I could sob for a while.

"I wonder why Gwen really dropped us here," I muttered, even as my eyes began to drift shut again.

"You think she has ulterior motives?" Sol asked.

"I think she's a goddess of good fortune who 'helps those who help themselves.' So she, at least, thinks that we have something to gain by being here. The question is, what?"

"Indeed, that is an excellent question to ask, youngling."

That was decidedly not Sol, and I snapped my head towards the voice's origin just in time to see a woman who looked like she could have been Rhelia's sister walk into the room. Sol inclined her head respectfully as the woman came in, then left the room.

"Weird," I said, as the woman approached the bed on which I was lying. I now saw that it stood in the middle of a colorfully decorated room, tiled from floor to ceiling and draped with vibrant tapestries all over. "Sol isn't ever that subservient, in my experience. You must be Rhelia's grandmother, or some shit."

I liked the dragons quite a bit more than I liked the folks who ran Unterberg, but something about authority figures made me flippant, and this woman simply oozed "elder in charge of important shit," even though her human form looked no more than five or ten years older than Rhelia's.

"Ha! Rhelia said you were irreverent to a fault, little one. I like it. I'm not a fan of obedience, myself. And I can assure you that your friend didn't initially react to me with that amount of deference…. Though, I do hold a certain amount of respect for those who are old enough to have witnessed the beginning of the civilization from which I crawled."

She added that last bit with just a hint of reproach.

I laughed.

"It's not my fault that you're really fucking old, lady. I just got here. Do you have a name?" I asked, in a hurry to figure out who she actually was so I could be flippant without blatantly shoving my foot in my mouth every other sentence.

"You can call me Grandmere," she replied.

"Why would I use French to address you, and why would I call you Grandma, anyway? Are you actually Rhelia's grandmother?"

"More or less. And, as you are her ward, I am essentially your grandmother as well."

"First of all, weird. Second of all, I'd prefer to call you by a name. I already have a handful of grandparents."

After a long pause, I added, "Thank you for the offer, though. I appreciate how welcoming you've been."

She sighed.

"You can call me Siara. And, as to being welcoming… well, you are dragonkin in more ways than one, as you no doubt understand by now."

"Right, the whole turning-into-a-dragon thing… so that's really a genetic thing, and not some special power conferred to me by the whole my-brother-married-a-dragon thing?"

"Correct. I believe your maternal grandmother had a dragon form as well."

I thought about that for a moment, trying to remember if I'd ever seen Momo turn into a dragon, and when I couldn't come up with anything, decided to file it away under the giant-assed list of crap I was going to have to figure out later, after I rescued my brother and discovered what had happened to my parents.

"So, when you came in, you hinted that you might know something about what we stood to gain by being here."

"Did I?" she asked, with more than a hint of mischief in her eyes.

"Look, you don't seem like the type that allows for coincidental timing. We were discussing why Gwen brought us here and you waltz in, saying, 'that's an excellent question.' Don't pretend you don't have the answer. I'm not the type of person to underestimate you just because you come in a petite, feminine human package."

"Quite so," she admitted. "Well, Soledad has informed me that my granddaughter and her mate have both been taken captive by MOME. That is a crime we do not take lightly in the dragon realms. They have been warned before that they are not permitted to interfere with our people. Rhelia's previous capture was affront enough. We won't stand for it again, no matter what manufactured crimes they accuse her of."

As understanding began to take root, I sat up.

"What exactly are you saying?" I asked.

"We have reason to believe that MOME presents a threat, not only to dragon kind, but to everyone inhabiting the human realm you know as Earth, and all of its associated seams."

"So…"

"So, when you go after your brother and my granddaughter, you will do so with the full might of the dragon realms at your back."

SOL AND I spent the next day searching through every scrap of information we could piece together about what secret weapons MOME might be working on. It wasn't like we needed any more reason to go after MOME, as it was. We had more than enough. And with the dragons behind us, we might even have enough firepower to succeed. But that was the problem, *might* wasn't good enough for the dragons. It also wouldn't be good enough for the leaders of Unterberg, to whom Siara would shortly send an envoy, attempting to persuade them to join us. It would be difficult to persuade anyone to aid us, if we didn't have an accurate prediction of what we were up against. A possible army of misfit soldiers like Trev was one thing. A secret weapon that we were completely unaware of the nature of… that was something else entirely.

Thankfully, it didn't take too long before we found a few clues in the material that Rhelia had brought back to her apartment. My family file provided our first clue, buried in a note scribbled on the margin.

Both subjects present during incident 72197, but not directly involved. Subjects' exit interviews suggest they chose to leave program after incident due to rumors and in protest of research tactics used.

It was an oddly worded note, and I wasn't sure what it meant, but the fact that it was the only note in the margins of the entire file made me feel like it was worth looking into. Besides, we'd found precious little that stood out in their file up to that point. I mentioned it to Sol as something to keep an eye out for, which paid off a few hours later when she found another tidbit in the files that she was sifting through on the computer—the ones that were on the flash drive Rhelia had brought back.

Sol dragged me away from my mom's journal, which I'd just started on, after carefully going through the family file first, and plunked me down into a comfortable leather chair in front of a twenty-four-inch computer monitor. I hadn't realized that she and my brother had quite so much in common, until I saw her computer set up. From what I saw in this room, Rhelia was an accomplished hacker. Which probably explained where she'd gotten ahold of the files Sol had just been looking through.

Special investigation: Stripping Incident 7/21/97

After carefully considering patterns of destruction in the lab, the amount of damage overall, and the few notes retrieved from the site, we have determined that the explosion was a direct result of the stripping experiment. We recommend a full cease and desist for all experiments related to this research for the foreseeable future. The risk of another such incident is too great, and the results of the first experiment have clearly demonstrated the practice to be entirely inhumane.

That was a decidedly short and vague report, all things considered, but the thing that had me dropping my jaw and grabbing Sol's shoulder was the fact that it was signed, ***Albert Bumblebee & Evelynn Keeler.***

Sol turned, caught my eye, gave me an emphatic nod, and I was gone.

~~~

Sol had probably wanted me to bring her along for the ride, but I wasn't sure that I had enough energy to take us both from the dragon realm to wherever Albert was, and back again. Especially since I had zero idea where Albert was. My Gwen-given powers hadn't failed me, though. I had focused hard on Albert's presence and then, sure enough, wound up plopped into the seat of his red velvet wingback chair, complete with hissing, disgruntled iguana.

"Vic! What a delight to see you here. I don't suppose you've come with good news?" he asked.

I stared at his earnest face, partially covered by the thick white beard, bushy white eyebrows, and flowing long hair that made me wonder if he'd once looked up "wizard" on the internet and done his best to cosplay the whole thing. He was really nailing it. I still wondered if the whole thing was
~~~

an act, though.

"Like what?" I asked. "Like, oh hey, found my parents' killers, overthrew MOME, NBD? Just wanted to let you know? That sort of good news?"

"I'm afraid I'm not familiar with NBD."

"Don't worry about it," I said. "Not really what I'm here to talk about."

Albert only smiled beatifically and took a seat in the wingback across from me.

"Do tell," he said encouragingly.

"I'm here to ask you about the 'Stripping Incident.'"

Ah. There was the reaction I had been hoping for. Albert's face darkened, and his mouth turned down at the corners. I hadn't wanted to upset him, but based on even the vague description I'd read in his report, I could only assume the subject would be a bit of a downer. Still, I was relieved not to see blank indifference.

"What do you wish to know about it?"

"Everything you can tell me. I think it could be very important."

"It undoubtedly is, but I'm afraid I can't tell you about it if I don't know what you plan to do with the information."

I frowned. If that was true, then this was even bigger than I suspected. But if I told Albert the truth, would he still tell me what was going on? I didn't think he held any love for MOME anymore, but I didn't really know the guy. He could still be a MOME sympathizer, for all I knew. Still, I didn't think I could come up with an overly convincing lie, and besides, he might have some way to tell if I didn't tell the truth. If he was truly on my side, the truth would weigh heavily in my favor, and if he wasn't, then… well, I doubt I could trust anything he said anyway.

"I plan to use whatever you tell me to help take down MOME and get my brother and his mate back."

Albert smiled the smile of a hunter closing in on its prey, which wasn't completely reassuring until he said, "Right answer."

Then, of course, he took out a joint, lit it, took a long drag, offered it to me, shrugged dismissively when I turned it down, and then exhaled just before starting his story.

"I worked for MOME for many years, as I believe you now know. I worked in research for most of that time. That was how I met your parents. They both joined a study I was running in the mid-nineties. It wasn't long, however, after meeting your parents that I realized they were more than mere research subjects. They were both powerful enough to be at the cutting edge of dark matter theory, if they were willing to work with me. However, I already had reason then to be suspicious of some of my colleagues, so I didn't publicize their talents, nor did I change their status from that of research subjects, even though it would have been far more fair to call them colleagues. I didn't want them attracting attention from some of my less scrupulous workmates. We continued to work together to research expanded dark matter theory. Are you familiar with the concept?"

I nodded, not wanting to interrupt, but added, after Albert left an expectant pause, "Trev gave me a brief explanation and demonstration just before he was taken by MOME."

Albert looked dour again for a moment, but took another drag on his joint before continuing.

"Very well, if you're familiar with the basic concept then at least I won't need to prove it to you. So, your parents were already well versed in the concept of expanded dark matter and its possibilities by the time that the Stripping Incident occurred. Consequently, when they left the program immediately afterwards, MOME wished to keep an eye on them. That's only relevant later. First the incident itself. I can't be entirely certain *why* my colleagues were exploring it, but the evidence I found in the aftermath of the experiment left little doubt as to *what* they were experimenting with. They were attempting to strip a human who possessed dark matter in their blood of said dark matter."

Now it was my turn to frown.

"How does that work? And what would that do? Could you make someone non-magical? Why would you do that to someone? As punishment? That seems fucked up."

Albert only nodded, taking another drag on on his swiftly dwindling joint.

"All good questions, and indeed, it does seem fucked up. Unfortunately, I only have answers to some of your questions, and the rest is mere conjecture. I don't entirely know how they accomplished it, though I have a few guesses, and none of them are pleasant. Still, regardless of how they accomplished it, its effect was to destroy the entire laboratory and all of the people within it. It was only contained because of the way those laboratories are built. It wasn't the first time an experiment has ended in an explosion, after all. However, the destruction was thorough, and clearly unexpected, because all of the researchers for that experiment were in the laboratory, along with the recording equipment. If they'd thought that anything remotely like that could happen, they would have left all of the recording tools and at least some of the research team out of the room. So, we can assume they expected the potential effects to be contained within the test subject himself. Clearly, they were as wrong as it is possible to be, on that front. My suspicion, based on the resumes of the people involved in the study, is that, yes, they were attempting to find a way to make someone non-magical, quite likely as punishment, or simply as a weapon against MOME's many enemies. However, I have no proof of that. I do have proof that they were trying to strip the subject of his dark matter, although I destroyed that proof long ago, for fear that someone might decide to pursue the project's goal again. And, as I was put in charge of the investigation into what happened, I became more and more suspicious that the people who had ordered the experiment done were keen to take up the research project again. Eventually, they asked me if I would be willing to head up the group attempting to discern what happened, so that they could replicate the experiment. I declined, and that was when I retired from MOME. Your parents left immediately after the explosion. It was the final nail in MOME's coffin for them. They'd never particularly trusted MOME to begin with, but after all they'd seen while involved in my study, they decided to quit while they were ahead. They'd gained each other, and I vowed to destroy most of my notes on our research in hopes that MOME wouldn't take too great an interest in them. Unfortunately, everyone registered for my research was already marked by MOME for a certain level of surveillance. Especially if they were likely to procreate."

My frown had been deepening throughout Albert's account, and now it reached a point where I was worried my mouth was going to break off my face.

"So that research is why Trev and I were MOME targets to begin with?" I asked, putting everything together as quickly as my brain could keep up. "Because my parents had been red flagged somewhere, so as soon as MOME put it together that they'd had kids, MOME came after us?"

"I'm sad to say that, yes, that is likely the entire reason that MOME attempted to kidnap you, and successfully kidnapped Trevor, all those years ago."

I felt a lot of emotions run through me at that news, not least of which was rage, but I reminded myself that this was all a ten-year-old hurt, and that I had more pressing things to focus on.

"But why do they want him now? They sacrificed dozens of agents to get him last night. I mean, I get that they want him back because he might know too much, but… that's a bit extreme."

"I cannot say, for certain."

"That sounds like an evasion."

"It is."

"Why?"

"Because I fear the answer might drive you to extremes."

"What can you tell me about MOME's secret weapon?" I asked, hoping the quick change of subject might elicit an honest response.

"What weapon is that?"

"I'm not sure. That's the problem. My parents left a… message, suggesting that MOME had been working on a secret weapon, but that they didn't know what it was. They also suggested MOME might be creating an army of people like Trev."

Albert pulled on his joint until the flame reached his fingertips, then winced as he extinguished what was left in a large ceramic ashtray on the small table next to his chair.

"Well, I can confirm that they've trained up a few hundred people like your brother over the past few decades, but I doubt any of them can match your brother in raw power."

"What? What do you mean?"

"Your brother, and you as well, come to that, possess the most raw access to dark matter of any human I've ever encountered."

"How can you tell?" I asked, a small warning bell starting to go off in the back of my mind.

"I've developed a spell that can detect dark matter in others. I cast it on most everyone I meet."

"Would MOME be able to tell the same thing?" I asked, more warning bells joining the first.

"They have their own methods, though I haven't shared this particular spell with them. They've likely run every test imaginable on Trevor, though. Over the years that they had him in custody."

"Albert… how powerful was the man they stripped of dark matter in that experiment?" I asked, despite being terrified that I already knew the answer.

"Not very powerful. He barely qualified as magical at all. I imagine that's why they started with him. They assumed it would be easy to strip him of what little power he had. And it's a good thing, too. If he blew apart the room with barely any dark matter within him, imagine what someone with any real power might do. Why do you—"

I didn't have to interrupt Albert. He cut himself off mid-sentence. Then he leapt to his feet.

"Oh bugger."

"Yes. Bugger about covers it."

"Vic, we have to get your brother back immediately."

"No shit, Sherlock."

"Wait—did you say they'd taken his mate, as well? Who is his mate?"

"Rhelia. How did you not—"

"Oh fuck. Vic, take me to the dragon realm immediately. Please."

Since that was where I was headed anyway, I didn't hesitate.

I SHIFTED US back to the room where I'd left Sol, ostensibly Rhelia's office, but Sol was gone and the lights were all off. Only the cool, dusty scent of a unheated home in fall greeted us.

Albert cursed.

"Where is Siara?" he said.

"I have no idea. I've only met her once, and she came to me. I don't even know where everyone else lives, in relation to where we are right now. I haven't had much time to explore."

"Right. Then follow me."

He had conjured a largish ball of light and was halfway to the entrance of Rhelia's home when the doorway flooded with light, outlining the petite shape of Siara before us.

"Albert, always a pleasure."

"Siara, I hate to be rude, but we have urgent matters to discuss. I believe we know what MOME's secret weapon is."

Siara stepped through the doorway into Rhelia's home, waving a hand, which somehow set all the lights ablaze.

"What is it?" she asked.

"My brother," I replied.

~ ~ ~

"Explain," Siara said, as Sol pushed her way into the house through a crowd of what must have been weredragons. They were peering curiously through the door, making me wonder what exactly Siara had been on her way to do before we'd shown up with news about MOME's weapon.

"They plan to turn Trevor, and possibly Rhelia, into a dark matter bomb."

"There is no such thing as a dark matter bomb," Siara said decisively.

"There is now," Albert replied. "I'm afraid all of our worst fears about Rebecca have come to pass, Siara."

"Wait, Rebecca?" I turned to Albert, my eyebrow raised in disbelief. "Rebecca Dryer?" I suppose it could have been some other Rebecca, but how many Rebeccas worked in the higher echelon's of MOME?

"Indeed," Albert said, turning away from Siara to confirm my suspicion. "She is the head of MOME's Department of Justice, and she has finally taken full leave of her senses. I have questioned her morals for nearly a century, but this is too far by half. She is risking the stability of the entire world. Or worse."

"Wait. What?"

Don't get me wrong, I was already prepared to put everything on the line to stop anyone from turning my brother into a weapon of mass destruction, but the entire world being at risk? I hadn't made that leap yet.

"Beyond the devastation that you would personally experience, and of course the annihilation of whatever location Rebecca decides to target, my own research has led me to believe that these kinds of explosions might cause irreversible damage to time and space, the effects of which might be worse than that of a black hole."

"Wait, you've been studying these kinds of explosions? Does that mean you've created *more* of them?"

"Heavens, no, Vic. That would require killing innocent magical beings, which I would never do on purpose. No, I've spent the years after I retired from MOME searching out natural occurrences of similar phenomena. Mostly through a telescope. That's why I relocated to Flagstaff. Excellent skies there, not to mention the observatory. Easy to track interstellar phenomena."

"I'm afraid we don't have time for an astronomy lesson, Albert," Siara interrupted. "We have to get Trevor and Rhelia out of MOME's grasp before it's entirely too late. The question now is, where do they intend to strike?"

"Who benefits if they blow something up?" Sol asked, speaking for the first time since she'd entered the house, albeit after she'd given me a quick hug and a gentle punch in the arm for leaving her behind.

"Rebecca's goal has always been to gather as much power as she can get her hands on," Albert said, with a sigh. "In that, at least, she has always been consistent. At least, since her parents died. Before that, she seemed hell bent on doing whatever would please them most, but after… it's as though they left a hole that she could only fill with power."

"That's weird," I blurted out, before I could stop myself. "I mean, hey, don't get me wrong, everyone grieves in their own way, but… 'I'm grieving and the only thing that will make me feel better is oppressing everyone around me'… seems like a slightly wacky way to do it."

Albert shrugged.

"I'm not even convinced that it's grief. It may just be what she chose to do with her newfound freedom. We don't have time to analyze her motives, I'm afraid. We simply need to predict where she will strike."

"Well, if she wants power… who does she most need to take it from?" I asked.

"She's already largely in charge of MOME. There's no branch more powerful that the Department of Justice, and she has all the other leaders there in her pocket, either through bribes or blackmail. So, she doesn't need much help controlling the magical world on Earth."

"So Unterberg, then? Or here?" I asked, wondering how in the hells she planned to mount an attack through a seam. Although she had just attacked us in Unterberg two days ago, and we still hadn't figured out how, exactly, other than the fact that Edik had led all the MOME agents there somehow.

"Her biggest threat is muggles," Sol said. "Non-magical people," she clarified when Albert and Siara simply gave her blank looks. "They have guns, tanks, biological weapons, and nukes. Magical power can do a lot against those, but the magical world never had their own nuclear equivalent until now. If she wants to be in charge of ALL of Earth, then she needs to get the muggles in line. Which, in her mind, she can only do by showing them that she has something stronger than a nuclear bomb."

"Would stripping Trev of his dark matter really cause an explosion *worse* than a nuke?" I asked, chilled to my core at the very thought of it.

It was Albert who answered.

"Undoubtedly. Although Rhelia would cause an even more devastating swath of destruction, so it's difficult to tell which one they would use first."

I felt like sitting down, all of a sudden, but I put a hand on Sol's shoulder to steady myself instead.

"Trev," I whispered. "He would be the demo. Worse than a nuclear blast, but still not as bad as what they could do if people don't comply. Save the big guns for long-term threat."

I wanted to vomit, even as the words passed my lips.

"Where would they set him off?"

Sol jumped almost a foot in the air, then put her hand in her back pocket.

"Oh fuck," she said, as she lifted up her phone and the blood left her face.

"What is it?" I asked.

"Apparently they're planning to set him off in La Paz," Sol said.

"What? Why La Paz? How do you even know that?"

Then she handed me the phone.

"From my abuelita," she added, her voice barely more than a whisper.

Her screen showed a picture of Trev, tied to a statue in the middle of a circular plaza I'd never seen before. He was surrounded by a bunch of marble buildings and some nice landscaping, but his face was one of pure pain, and he was still tightly bound in that damned metal net that they'd captured him with.

"Perhaps they chose La Paz because—" Albert began.

"I wish I knew what that shit was," I muttered, passing the phone to Albert and Siara, who were already hovering anxiously over my shoulder.

"What shit is that?" Albert asked, looking closely at the photo and seemingly forgetting whatever he'd been about to say before I cut him off.

"That weird metal netting they used to capture him. It repels magic, or something. It was excruciating to touch, and it wouldn't let me shift us when I tried to grab him."

That had Albert zooming in on the photo, and I was surprised to see how easily he dealt with the tiny supercomputer he held in his hands. I didn't usually expect folks with white hair to have a firm grasp of cell phones.

"That, my dear, is Technetium—assuming they found a way to stabilize it—a metal not naturally found on earth. And I would bet dollars to doughnuts that is precisely what they are going to use to strip him."

"WHAT?" everyone else in the room asked at once.

"Non-magical scientists believe that it breaks down too quickly to remain anywhere in the universe, other than in the stars in which it forms, and that is why it does not exist outside of said stars, though copious amounts of it are created on Earth as a part of the nuclear fission process. However, I have a different theory as to why it does not occur here naturally. I believe that it reacts with dark matter in a rather… dramatic fashion. I believe that is why it is never found outside of the stars in which it is created. I believe that as soon as it is ejected from the stars that create it, it reacts with the dark matter available, creating the dark energy that is pushing our universe apart. When this happens in the vacuum of space, it is largely unnoticeable, certainly by most human forms of detection. When it happens around other matter, however…. It's the only thing that might possibly, if put in direct contact with the dark matter inside an individual, be able to accomplish what Rebecca wishes to do to your brother. They would need to inject it to cause that kind of reaction however, and in the meantime, she appears to be torturing him with it externally in the form of that net."

"WELL, FUCK," I summarized, for the room. No one had moved from where we stood, in the center of Rhelia's beautifully decorated living room, a setting that now seemed a strangely cheerful counterpoint to the rather horrific topic at hand. We were surrounded by comfortable looking couches that no one seemed inclined to make use of, and colorful tiles with bright patterns and warm lines.

"Yep," agreed Sol.

"Indeed," added Siara.

"We need to break Trev free, like, yesterday," I said.

"Could you?" Albert asked.

Everyone returned their shocked expressions to Albert's serious visage. This time, I really wasn't sure what he was talking about, though.

"Could I what?"

"Could you break Trevor free yesterday?"

"You mean, like time-travel?" I asked.

"Precisely."

"You got a time turner hidden in your sweater?" I asked, nodding to the grey cable-knit he was wearing, baggy enough to look more like a bathrobe than anything. "Looks like you could hold a whole horde of treasures in there."

Part of my brain was shouting at me that we didn't have time for stupid jokes, but part of me insisted that none of this was real. That the entire thing had to be some kind of stupid joke, so why not throw some humor around?

"I do not know what a time-turner is, though the name is rather descriptive, but I would say that *you*, my dear Victoria, are the time turner to which you refer."

"Gwen gave me powers that let me reach through time and space to move around, but I've never—"

"Never tried moving only through time? If the power takes you through one, it can take you through the other. They are merely coordinates on a map."

Weird. Despite the fact of always thinking about how Gwen's power let me reach through time and space, I'd really never considered the time aspect. I mean, I may have had my world turned upside down in the past few weeks, learning that werewolves, leopards, dragons, and every other damned mythical/fantastical creature existed, but… time travel? Surely that was a bridge too far.

"But, if time travel were possible, surely everyone would be doing it? I mean, wouldn't someone like Rebecca Dryer be using it to go back and put herself in charge of every major government in the world? In the realms? No one would ever die, because everyone would be going back and saving them/curing them, discovering the secret to living forever, and then going back and administering it to everyone they loved? I mean, come on."

"Certainly that might be the case, if everyone could do it, or if more than a tiny group of people could do it. But I'm not sure you realize quite the gift that Gwen has given you. She has only demonstrated how to use the power by traveling from place to place, and by the way, to my knowledge, you are the only non-deity who can travel between the realms without using a seam. Something I didn't realize until you brought me directly to see Siara. I had expected you to take us to the nearest seam, then teleport us to her from there. You—"

"Albert! Seriously. My brother is tied to a fucking post in the middle of a square, waiting to be blown up, along with an entire city!"

"My point is, Vic, that if you can jump through points in space, you can do the same with time. It shouldn't even take much more effort, just some flexibility of mind."

"Surely there are a ton of risks inherent to that? Couldn't I destroy the space-time continuum, or something?"

"The space-time continuum is, by nature, self regulating. Hence the 'continuum.' It is an oft worried about piece of fiction, but in reality there should be no possible way to ruin it. If you change the past, the future automatically alters itself, and if you create a paradox you must inherently ruin that timeline, but it will likely snap to the nearest available alternate timeline, or create a new one."

"Ok. THAT. Right there. Sounds terrifying."

Albert shrugged.

"It's all theoretical, of course, but my point is that while you can likely ruin things for yourself, in your own timeline, I doubt very much that you have the power to destroy the whole universe entirely, even if you destroy the universe in a single timeline."

"How does that even make sense? Doesn't the universe include all available timelines? I—" I stopped talking, shaking my head to force away the cascade of thoughts that wouldn't let me get to the important part. "Look. I don't think I can do that. I'm pretty sure I wouldn't be able to figure out what to do in time to save anyone, so can we go with plan B, or whatever? I need to save my brother."

PLAN B, IT turned out, was to just go in with guns blazing. Siara sent someone else to appeal to Unterberg for help. Meanwhile, she brought a hundred dragon shifters with her to the street in front of Rhelia's home which we'd chosen as our base of operations. The hundred she brought with her would go in the first wave, and she'd left instructions for reinforcements to follow behind us should they be needed.

We had to hope that MOME didn't know that I could shift that many of us from one realm to the next without going through a seam first. Honestly, we had to hope for a lot of things. If this went wrong, we were about to get a whole lot of people killed, ourselves included.

~~~

In order to maximize our element of surprise, we decided I would shift us all into a spot in mid-air and everyone would shift into dragon form upon arrival. The main reason for the plan was that my brain couldn't handle the idea of shifting a hundred dragons through time and space as easily as it could fathom shifting a hundred people. Apparently, everyone from the dragon realm who had signed up for this mission had no qualms with being dropped into the air a few hundred feet above La Plaza Murillo.

The sky was a cerulean blue and there was not a cloud in it. The air was crisp and fresh, despite being in the middle of a city of half a million people. I barely had time to notice any of that, though, or even take note of where Trev was, before I was free-falling through the sky and trying to call on my dragon form.
~~~

Thankfully, it responded quickly to my call and then I enjoyed a crash course in flying. I snapped my wings out, and they caught the wind with a deafening crack that shot me upwards at a terrifying speed. Panicking, I tried to drop my wings, but found them buffeting in and out awkwardly as I tried to lower them slowly, so I snapped them shut instead. Of course, that caused me to plummet towards the ground again. Terrified of hitting the ground, I spread my wings wide again, and this time, apparently clear of whatever updraft had grabbed me before, I began to glide in a gentle arc towards the ground instead. By the time I circled back around to where everyone else was, I was rather enamored of flying and vowed to practice it more often, assuming I survived everything that was about to happen.

Or… everything that was already happening, I corrected, as I looked at the scene unfolding in front of me.

The dragons were mowing into the MOME forces that lined the plaza, and the only thing that seemed to keep them in check was the fact that there appeared to be some non-magical people wandering nearby, as if they'd been curious to see what all the fuss was about. As a result, the dragons were mostly using teeth and claws to destroy the MOME agents that surrounded the plaza, the majority of spells flung their way simply ricocheting off of them, and the attacks of the few shifters present hardly grazing their hides.

It was easy to see why MOME had considered the dragons a big enough threat to try to eradicate them, even though the mere thought of doing so was completely despicable. One had to appreciate just how much damage the dragons could do when provoked. Of course, one also had to take into account just how far one had to go in order to provoke the dragons to begin with. They had spent centuries in peace with everyone else in the known realms. It had taken the abduction of two of their own and threat to the entire world, before they'd been willing to bring this down on MOME.

I looked around to see if I could spot Sol in the fray. She had come in on the back of one of the weredragons who was better at flying than I was (which is to say, ANY of the other weredragons), since I hadn't been confident that I wouldn't send us both crashing to our deaths. I barely caught a glimpse of a tiny (relatively speaking) black figure darting in and out of the mass of dragons and mages clashing on the ground before I refocused on my primary objective.

In the quick plan that we had hashed out before embarking on this whole endeavor, I had been given a very clear assignment: do whatever I could to free Trev before Rebecca Dryer, or whoever else she'd put in charge of the task (of course whoever applied the syringe would likely be killed in the blast unless they were able to make an incredibly fast escape, so there was little to no chance that it would be Rebecca), could inject Trev with liquid Technetium. Or, barring that, kill whoever was going to inject him.

He was exactly where he'd been in the photo sent by Sol's abuelita, tied to a somewhat phallic statue in the middle of a small, nicely landscaped circle in the middle of the plaza. He'd clearly been tied there in order to draw the maximum amount of attention from the camera crews that now crowded around that center circle. Indeed, we'd realized during our planning that the only reason Rebecca hadn't set Trev off immediately, before we'd even known what they were planning to do, is that she intended to gain maximum visibility before doing so. After all, her threat would be that much more effective if she had the eyes of all the world leadership on her for her demonstration. And only a live feed would work, because any and all equipment close enough to get footage would be entirely destroyed by the blast. If she wanted any long-lasting record of the event, she would need to have coverage from afar. I wondered if she had cameras placed miles and miles from here, to try to capture a video of the explosion from a distance.

Of course, even if she did, they wouldn't be all that helpful if she managed to take out the entire earth with her. She had grossly underestimated the effectiveness of her own weapon, or was willfully ignorant of the additional risks—either way, she had to be stopped, regardless of the cost.

I still wasn't caught up on all the physics behind how it worked, but essentially the introduction of unstable Technetium into blood that contained large amounts of dark matter could easily cause a wave of dark energy strong enough to destabilize any nearby seams, thus potentially sucking our realm into another realm, and possibly destroying both of those realms in the process. And that was *on top* of my brother and half a million innocent civilians being killed. Not to mention all the dragons that I'd just shifted in here to help kick MOME's ass.

So, when I saw a person in a white hazmat suit approach my brother, with one arm outstretched, I didn't hesitate. I dove as fast as the wind would allow me, wings tucked tight to my sides and nothing between me and my target but thin air. I really hoped that I wouldn't take Trev out in my attack, but he would be dead either way, if I didn't get to this asshat before he got to Trev, so it was a risk I would just have to take.

I crashed into the earth hard, even though I flared my wings a bit just at the last second, and plowed through the grass and stone of the circle surrounding the statue that Trev was tied to. Before I let myself even register the pain of the stone impacting my scales, or the features of the person underneath the hazmat suit, I shoved my head forward, pushing past the line of stone that had finally stopped my slide forward, and snapped my jaws around the person whose arm was still outstretched to Trev.

"NOOOOOO!" Trev screamed, his face contorting with more pain than I'd ever seen on a human face. "RHELIA!!!"

For a moment I thought he'd somehow mistaken me for Rhelia, even though our dragon forms looked nothing alike. Even though there was no way my brother would ever have made that mistake.

And then my brain caught up with the truth, and I opened my jaws to allow the person in the hazmat suit to fall to the ground. The small window in the face of the suit showed an unmistakable visage. Ebon skin, ebon hair, and yellow, unblinking eyes.

"NO," I WHISPERED, amazed to find myself in human form again, my arms wrapped around Rhelia's waist, though I couldn't remember moving. "No! NO! It can't be her! Why is it her? WHY? She would never have agreed to inject you. She wouldn't! It can't be her. It can't be—"

Rhelia, why? A whisper in the distance.

I looked down and saw the syringe on the ground, which she'd most assuredly been about to inject into Trevor, but it still didn't make any kind of sense. Why would she have volunteered? Why would they have let her? She would just have died with Trevor, while causing an even larger catastrophe. Did she not know that? Had they told her something else? Did she think that her dragon's scales would save her from the explosion? Or did she just want to die with her mate?

My brain couldn't land on any explanation that made sense, and I couldn't fathom how a single bite from my dragon's teeth had been enough to end her. That didn't make sense. Rhelia was invincible. She was death on wings. She couldn't be killed, least of all by me. She could kill me a thousand times before I would ever get close to her, I was sure of it.

"Trev? What happened? Why is it her?"

But Trev was sobbing uncontrollably, and wouldn't answer. I was sure it was that he wouldn't, and not that he couldn't, because he could have spoken to me through our twin bond, but all I felt through that bond was despair. The worst kind of pain that a human could experience, as though I'd torn a part of his soul away from him.

"What do I do, Trev? What do I do? How do I make this right?" Tears were streaming down my face and my voice was barely audible around the grief that choked me, but I didn't know what to do. My brother was going to die because of a thing I had done, and I didn't know how to make it right.

Could you?

Could I what?

Could you break Trevor free yesterday?

The memory surfaced like a bubble in a pond, clear, and shiny and destroyed with the mere swipe of a hand… but it was there. And before I could think of anything else, before I could say anything, before I could even take another breath, I was reaching through time and space, but in this case, mostly through time.

I HAD MOVED entirely on instinct, or what I thought was instinct, using some tiny backwater of my brain that understood better than I did what was going on. Or maybe it was just that the thing I wished to see most in the world right then was a living, breathing Rhelia. One who hadn't just had the life crushed out of her by my dragon jaws. One who wouldn't stare blankly at me as I screamed her name over and over again.

"Rhelia!" I gasped, mostly in surprise, as I found myself staring into her eyes once more. Her living, seeing eyes.

Before she could even acknowledge my presence, I threw my arms around her and held tight, hoping desperately that she wouldn't find the personal contact an invasion of her space.

"Living Cat, are you well?" she whispered, returning the embrace, much to my surprise and relief. "You sssseem disssstresssed."

Yeah. You could say that. Or well, someone could. I couldn't, because I was too busy sobbing into Rhelia's hair.

When I could finally breathe clearly again, I said, "'Well' is not the word that I would choose to describe myself at the moment, TBH."

"TBH?" she asked.

"Oh, come on. I know you spend as much time on the computer as Trev does, you must know that acronym."

She laughed, then.

"Ssssomeone hassss been sssnooping while I've been locked away," she responded, then stepped back a bit and took a good look at me. "Why are you here? You cannot hope to resssscue me from thissss placsssse, ssssurely?"

I took a deep breath, noticed said breath was full of dank, moldy smell, and finally took a look around.

"What, does *every* MOME headquarters have its own dungeon?"

"Mosssst of them were built long enough ago that they do, but in thissss casssse, we are in what wassss left of the Bolivian HQ. Ssssomething about not wanting to rissssk anymore officesssss, in casssse our friendssss wanted to come get ussss? The guardssss were a bit all over the placsssse with their thoughtssss. They sssseemed nervoussss."

Indeed, we were standing in the middle of a dank stone cell, surrounded by solid rock walls and thick metal bars. At least they'd left enough light in here for Rhelia to see by. It was a nicer accommodation than my last MOME visit. I reached out to touch one of the metal bars and instantly recoiled. It burned the way that the netting surrounding Trevor had.

"Technetium," I muttered, as I checked my hand for damage. "I'm amazed I was able to shift myself here."

Rhelia nodded.

"Indeed, I did not exsssspect to ssssee you. Where did you come from?"

Ah yes, that was a legitimate question, but how to answer it? And what good would that answer do? Could I shift Rhelia and myself out of here? And even if I could, would that save Trev? What would happen in the future if someone else were holding the needle? Would I kill them in time? Would they inject Trev sooner? How could I be sure I wasn't going to make this whole thing worse? There was no way to predict what would happen if I changed things, unless…

"Unlessss what, Living Cat?" Rhelia asked.

I ignored the reminder that my thoughts tended to be an open book for Rhelia and the other dragons, focusing on the thought that had just tickled the back of my mind.

"Unless the person holding the syringe in the future knows exactly what's supposed to happen and plays along," I said, realization dawning on me. "Albert was right, time does fix itself."

Rhelia gave me the kind of smile that would have terrified me if I'd thought I were her prey. Luckily, we both had bigger game in mind.

IT DIDN'T TAKE Rhelia and me very long to come up with a plan, especially after I asked her a few pointed questions about how they were being held. Perhaps unsurprisingly, they were each being used as collateral against the other. If one attempted escape, the other would be killed, and vice versa. It wasn't particularly creative, but it was effective. Of course, once I informed Rhelia of MOME's true intentions (which, thankfully, she had suspected already—thus cutting my explanation time in half), she was more than willing to take the necessary risks. I just hoped I was right about how this was all supposed to play out.

The reason I was able to shift in and out of Rhelia's cell, it turned out, was that the cell was not lined completely with Technetium, so I was able to shift through the rock bed instead of the areas where the bars covered things. Meanwhile, for Rhelia and Trevor, who were unable to shift through time and space as I was, the prison was quite effective. They didn't have time to dig through the rock bed before a guard would come running, and the Technetium kept them from even touching their bars, let alone somehow manipulating them out of the way.

I probably *could* have shifted Rhelia out of there with me, but I discovered not long after I settled into her cell that I was truly exhausted from everything I'd already done that day. Not only had I shifted myself to the past, and straight to Rhelia's prison, I had also shifted an army of a hundred weredragons straight from the dragon realm into the human realm, then changed into a dragon, taught myself to fly right quick, and attacked and killed one of my new friends. It had been a rough day, by any stretch of the imagination.

So, I wasn't going to shift Rhelia anywhere before I got some rest. Instead, Rhelia and I talked for a long time, switching to our mental-only channel for all of the important bits. To an outside observer, it probably looked like two really tired people just staring at the walls and each other for a long time. Then it probably looked like I fell asleep for a few hours.

Probably because I did.

I woke to a quick slap across my face.

"You musssst go. They are coming."

I nodded and, without another word, I shifted, hoping against hope that the next time I saw Rhelia she would be alive and well, not a blank-eyed rag doll hanging limply in my arms.

~~~

When I arrived in front of Siara, she damned near dropped the ceramic bowl she'd been drinking soup from.

"I do not appreciate being surprised, youngling," she said.

I smiled, though I doubt the gesture reached my eyes.

"Then you're not going to like anything I have to say."

I looked around the room we were in, a modern kitchen by all appearances, complete with tile backsplash and a fancy kitchen island with a butcher block counter, and I wondered if she had brought all of this back from an Ikea in the human realm and installed it herself, or if she had somehow transported a fully finished home from the human realm to here, or somehow managed to get human contractors to come work on the place in the dragon realm. The last seemed particularly unlikely.

"When you have finished admiring my home decor, would you mind telling me why on Earth you are here? You are supposed to be discerning what weapon of MOME's devising your parents were attempting to warn us about."

At that reminder, I took a moment to look at the clock. Then I sat down at the nice, lightly stained pine table that held Siara's bowl of soup.

"Hmm… right. I suppose that makes sense," I muttered.

It was only an hour before I would be back with Albert, and Siara clearly wasn't in the middle of rallying her troops, even though she should be, at least according to how things had played out in my earlier timeline. (Earlier? Ugh, talking about time once you'd started messing with it was hard. The
~~~

last first time I did this? Maybe. Maybe that.)

When that vague statement and my wildly shifting thoughts simply earned me a cold stare from Siara, I tapped my fingers against the table for a moment, then added, "Siara, how quickly can you assemble a unit of 100 or so weredragons who are good at changing form mid-air?"

~~~

It was the next hour, watching myself (which was fucking trippy, by the way), Sol, Siara, and all the weredragons assembled outside of Rhelia's home, that was the most trying. I had tucked myself into the darkened doorframe of a house across the path from Rhelia's, as there was almost nothing I could do at this juncture. There was no point in shifting myself back to "the present" (an arbitrary distinction really, but one that I had to cling to for the moment, because I lacked a better term), when that would just exhaust me and I knew that I would need the energy soon. And the only thing that showing myself now would do is confuse the hell out of the me that was already here, along with all of the other people that me was already talking to. And I didn't think it would do any good anyway, although a strong part of me wanted to take the me that was already here and tell her in advance what was about to happen. Just to spare her some of it… but I shook that thought away, and huddled close in the stucco archway of the tastefully designed home that sat quietly in the night across from Rhelia's. One thing was for certain; if everything went as planned, I really needed to spend some time exploring the dragon realm. It was a truly lovely space, and I was extremely curious as to how and where they managed to design and build their homes.

~~~

In the final minutes before we were all about to group together and launch our attack, I saw a strange shadow on the house next door to Rhelia's. Unable to discern what was causing it, I began to edge closer, but when I was halfway across the path, I ran into Siara.

"You should ride with me," she said, pulling on my arm.

I gave her a puzzled look. The me that was already here was supposed to fly on her own because she needed to learn to fly without risking anyone else's life, and so she would have the freedom to strike hard and fast against whoever was going to inject Trev. Siara knew this, she'd given me the damned assignment.

"I'm supposed to be on my own. I need to—"

"I'm certain the other you has that covered," she replied, before I could finish.

My mouth was doing a solid impression of an oxygen-starved fish when she gently took me by the arm and led me away.

"I can drop you where you need to be," she said, as we joined the ranks of weredragons circling up to be shifted by my earlier self.

I nodded dumbly, following after her, and didn't bother to ask how she'd figured out that I was a future me, deciding that the less we discussed it the better, most likely. By the time earlier-me was ready to shift us all to La Paz, I'd forgotten entirely about the odd shadow.

SIARA LANDED QUICKLY and cleanly in a shadowed corner of La Plaza Murillo, depositing me without comment and taking off again almost in a single graceful movement. It made quite the contrast to the sunset-colored hot mess of a dragon who was currently banking wildly in the sky, trying desperately to learn how to fly in a brief handful of seconds—which is to say, me. Earlier-me, I guess. Though we were both getting pretty close to being present me, and I wondered what the hell was going to happen then? Would there be two of us forever, now? Did one of us have to die? Were there going to be infinite mes throughout the universe now? Were there already infinite mes throughout the universe? How the fuck did this shit work? Time travel was complicated.

It was also freaky as hell.

Here I was, crouched in the shadow of a large shrub, out of sight of most everyone, watching myself in dragon form—which, can I just say that I make a beautiful fucking dragon? I looked like somebody's Pinterest board for the coolest possible dye jobs, but instead of just my hair my entire body was covered in gorgeous, shimmering scales that ranged from deep crimson to bright yellows and blues, and every shade of purple in between. Anyways, here I was, watching my dragon form career wildly through the sky, knowing what it had felt like to go through every moment I was watching, but feeling like it was a distant memory, because so much had happened in between. I think I had only gone back a single day, but it felt like a century had passed since I'd held Rhelia, limp and lifeless, in my arms.

And now my stomach was churning as I watched myself dive steeply towards the ground, aimed straight for the person in the white hazmat suit. I'd been too busy watching my former self's seemingly drunken flight pattern to even notice her appear at first, but she was there, and reaching out for Trev, even as my dragon form speared through the sky right for her.

Watching me hit the ground, and her, at such high velocity almost made me throw up, and I was weirdly grateful that I hadn't eaten much in the dragon realm.

"NOOOOOO!" Trev screamed. "RHELIA!!!"

And then I was running forward, without making a conscious decision to do so, my legs pumping me out of the bushes and towards the spot where a hurt and confused earlier-dragon-me stared incredulously at a limp figure in a hazmat suit. And, suddenly, I was filled with the worst kind of dread. Had Rhelia lied to me? Had she volunteered for this because it was the only way we could figure out to keep Trev from dying?

A cold knot formed in my stomach, heavier than any lead ball, as I sprinted the last few steps between me and Rhelia. Then she was in my arms, and I was leaning over her, sobbing, and dragon-me was gone, and there was no other me here, which means I must have caught up to myself, but Rhelia still wasn't moving.

"No," I whispered, once more staring into her too-blank eyes, dread coiling through my entire body.

No! NO! It can't be her! Why is it her? WHY? She would never have agreed to inject you. She wouldn't! It can't be her. It can't be—

"Rhelia, why?"

She wouldn't have done this. We had a plan. The plan made sense. She wouldn't have lied to me. Why would she have lied to me?

Trev? What happened? Why is it her?

Could I go back and fix it again? How many redos did I get? What would it take to fix this?

"What do I do, Trev? What do I do? How do I make this right?"

How could I be here again? How could I be holding onto this limp, bleeding—

No, wait. I took better stock of my hands—they were dry. She was wearing a hazmat suit, but still… dragon teeth are huge. Could it all have been pooling inside?

I took a better look at the body of the woman I was holding. There were tears in the suit. There should have been holes throughout her entire body, but there was no blood. No blood anywhere.

Rhelia? I sent the tiniest whisper.

*Convincsssse them, Living Cat, they musssst **believe.***

I sobbed. I let all the tears come. I could tell, somehow, that Rhelia had directed that thought only to me. She must have done something to cut herself off from Trevor…. Shit. Poor Trev. But for some reason Rhelia wanted everyone, even Trev, to think that she was dead, and she had sounded desperate. I didn't know what her plan was, but the least I could do after all of this was help her out. So I let the tears come. All of them.

A year of grieving over parents who had turned out to be people I didn't really know. Ten years of mourning a twin everyone else pretended was never there, and letting them make me forget. Shooting a man who was holding a gun to the temple of an innocent person. Being held captive by people who wanted me dead. Having a fucking lowlife vampire show up in my bedroom uninvited and having to fight him off. Watching that same vampire get decapitated by a vengeful succubus. Losing the only homes I'd ever known. Losing everything I owned. Seeing a woman I admired, respected, and liked die at my own hands, or at least believing that's what had happened. It hadn't been a great year, really, and I let it all come out. I mourned it all. Right there, in front of a hundred television cameras that had been brought to witness some devastating event, I cried like my soul had been torn out. I cried harder than I'd ever cried in my life.

And then had to pull myself together, because shit was about to hit multiple fans, and I couldn't even keep track of them all. MOME agents were rushing towards us. Probably coming to inject Trev anyway, but they were going to have to race Trev, who was straining against his bonds, reaching for the damned syringe which had somehow managed to land barely a foot away from him.

Trev, no! It won't just kill you, it will kill everyone in this city!

But Trev either wasn't listening or didn't care, and he was straining like a madman against the netting that held him in place. Damn it if he wasn't inching his way closer and closer to that fucking space metal that was likely to kill us all and take the whole damned world down with it. I tried to scrabble sideways, with Rhelia still in my lap, but she was a lot heavier than a five-foot-nothing petite woman looked, and I wasn't going to get there before Trev, damn it, unless I dumped Rhelia on the ground. If I did that, MOME might get to her before I did, and then we were just as screwed as if Trev got the syringe, because Rhelia would make an even bigger bang than Trev, and Gwendamnit, I needed some help!

Which was right when Sol pounced onto the backs of the two closest MOME agents and I decided I had enough time to drop Rhelia and launch myself at Trev, who already had his fucking fingertips on the syringe—and how did he even get down here, when he was supposed to be tied to the fucking statue? Did I knock him loose when I crash landed?

But I didn't have time to figure out how he'd loosened his bonds enough to slide down to the ground, or to worry about anything at all, except diving at Trev to make sure that he didn't jab anyone with that damned syringe.

And now we were fighting for the syringe like the Gwendamned climax in a freaking Bond flick.

TREVOR, DON'T DO THIS. I PROMISE EVERYTHING WILL BE OK, TREV. PLEASE, YOU HAVE TO BELIEVE ME.

I really hoped that no one else could hear me mentally shouting at Trev, but damn it, I had no other choice. He might have been restrained by that fucking Technetium netting, but he was thrashing like a madman. Probably in hopes of just accidentally spearing himself with the syringe, which, to be fair, there was a fairly high chance of at the moment.

Finally, I clamped my fingers around the syringe and pried it from his hand. For a brief moment, I was grateful that he was weakened from being trapped in that netting for days.

Then I took a good look and realized I wasn't really all that grateful. His face was as pale as Albert's, and he looked like he'd lost about twenty pounds. If I didn't know any better, I would have guessed he'd been doing multiple rounds of chemo for the past six months.

"Take him and go, I've got the rest of these douchewhips."

Sol was standing over Rhelia and assessing the next squad of MOME agents that were quickly approaching.

"You can't take them all on your own," I said. "Besides, I don't know how to get him out of this netting, and I can't shift him anywhere with it on."

"Perhaps I can be of assistance with that," said a British voice I hadn't really been expecting to hear anytime soon.

"Albert?" I asked, looking up to find the grey-bearded man stooping over Trev's other side. "Does this mean that you've already dealt with Rebecca?"

"I'm afraid not," he replied, while doing something I couldn't see to Trev's bonds. "May I have that syringe, my dear?"

I hesitated. I won't lie, I didn't really trust this thing in anyone's hands but my own. How could I be sure he wouldn't just turn around and use it for something else? But then I heard MOME charging us in the background, Sol's snarl as she resumed her panther form, and the battle cries of a few dragons as they dove to engage the enemy.

I handed Albert the syringe.

"If I am correct," he said, taking the syringe and carefully removing the plunger so that the liquid within could be poured out, "pouring this liquid form of Technetium onto these bonds will make them at least partially malleable."

"And if you're wrong?"

Albert's eyebrow arched, even as he remained focused on the task his hands were attending to.

"Then we might all die horribly, but what else is new, eh?"

I laughed. What can I say? My tolerance for dark humor had grown substantially over the past year.

"Ah there we are," he said gently. And, before I could really tell what he was doing, he had somehow unwound the netting that surrounded Trev's whole left side and then begun to pull him out.

I jumped up to help, grabbing him from the right, and in less than a minute we had Trev clear of the remains of the netting.

"Take them both, Vic. Take them both and go. We will deal with what remains of MOME here."

This time I didn't hesitate. I grabbed Trev by one arm, bent us both down to grab Rhelia with the other, and pulled us all to the safest place I knew, my heart breaking slightly at the knowledge that I was leaving Sol here to fight alone.

No, not alone. Backed by a hundred weredragons.

I saw her leap at a mage and tear into his shoulder, just as La Plaza de Murillo faded to blackness.

THE GLADE WAS quiet when we arrived, and I must have put us right in front of that scythe-holding oak tree that I had come to know as Life, because I could feel myself healing the moment I arrived. Indeed, I could see the color returning to Trev's skin even as I reached past him to start getting Rhelia out of that damned hazmat suit.

"What are you doing, Vic? Leave her be. Can't you just leave her in peace? Haven't you done enough?"

Each of those words cut me like a physical blow that the Tree of Life could never heal, but I didn't let them stop me.

"No, Trev. Not nearly enough, yet."

The hazmat suit tore surprisingly easily. It made me wonder if it had really served the purpose it advertised. Of course, it would make sense that MOME wouldn't have been too worried about actually protecting whoever they sent to inject Trev with that shit, as no amount of hazmat gear would stop that person from being atomized along with everything else in the vicinity, or worse. Still, it was weirdly harrowing to see how thin the suit was, and it crumbled as if it were cheap plastic that had been left in the sun too long.

YOU CAME JUST IN TIME.

I jumped, and sat up from where I'd been peeling at Rhelia's suit to see that Life had decided to take his ambulatory shape and come for a visit.

"Did you need us?" I asked.

NO. IT IS THE OTHER WAY AROUND. YOU NEED ME. AND YOU HAVE CUT IT VERY CLOSE, AS THE HUMANS SAY.

"What do you me—" I started to ask, just as Trev collapsed beside me.

I AM DOING ALL I CAN FOR HIM, BUT IT WILL BE DIFFICULT. THE RADIATION HAS BEEN ATTACKING HIM FOR DAYS, IT WOULD SEEM.

"Radiation? But I thought the syringe was—"

IT WOULD HELP IF HE WERE NOT FIGHTING ME.

"Fighting you? He's trying to keep you from healing him? Fuck. Trev!!!" I collapsed beside him and held his hands. "Trev, please. Don't go. She's not gone. She's not, I swear. Please, you have to listen to me!"

But Trev's eyes were closed, and his face, while pained, seemed absent. Like he wasn't quite there. Not knowing what else to do, I turned to Rhelia.

"Rhelia, now would be a great time to come back. We're going to lose Trev. He thinks you're dead."

YOU MEAN THAT ONE IS NOT DEAD?

I looked panicked between Life, standing over my brother, and Rhelia, lying prone on the ground.

Rhelia! You have to come back now. Trev is dying and he thinks you're gone, so he's not trying to save himself!

I am sssstuck, Living Cat. I did not craft thissss enchantment. I asssssked her to leave a channel in placsssse sssso I could sssspeak with you. You will have to convincsssse Trev that I am sssstill here. Or elsssse remove thissss blassssted sssspell.

If you didn't put it in place, who did? Who managed to visit you in there who was interested in helping?

Your Gwenhwyvar. She wassss very eager to be of asssssissssstancsssse.

"Gwen! Gwen, we need you!"

SHE HAS BEEN RATHER BUSY TODAY. WHAT IS GOING ON IN THE WORLD, THAT SO MANY PEOPLE NEED GOOD FORTUNE AT ONCE?

I could think of a few things that would qualify, really. Of course, of course she was off helping with a battle to save half a million lives and overthrow a tyrant, rather than here with my entire world crashing down on me. That only made sense.

It still pissed me off, though. I knew Trev wasn't going to believe anything I said now. I'd heard the pain and contempt in his voice when he'd accused me of "doing enough" to Rhelia. He blamed me for her death, not unreasonably, and he wasn't about to listen to anything I said about her being alright until he could sense her living presence on the other side of their bond.

I realized, perhaps belatedly, that he and Rhelia shared a bond similar to the one that he and I shared. It was different, in that it wasn't a bond forged since conception and reinforced through eighteen years of life, but it was a bond of love, and a mate bond, and being mated as a dragon, whatever that meant. It was strong, and Trev thought it was broken. Until he felt it in place again, there was nothing I could say that would convince him Rhelia wasn't dead. And until he believed that, he was going to let radiation poisoning eat away his life.

So I did the only thing I could think of. I grabbed Rhelia's hand, and I followed our own bond. The one that she'd left open, so that she could contact me—the only person who was supposed to know that she wasn't really dead. I was her ward, and apparently that meant something too, because I could feel a place for her inside me, a place that I had thought was shattered when my teeth had sunk into her flesh less than an hour ago.

I followed that bond with… I'm not sure what. My essence? My magic? Some part of me that was transferable. Something that was me, but that I could manipulate and move outside of myself. Was that dark matter? Whatever it was, I moved it. I sent it flickering along the bond that held us, and I pushed it further, searching for Trev within Rhelia. I wasn't sure that made any kind of sense, and I sure as shit didn't know what I was doing, but that felt right. There must be some part of Trev inside of Rhelia, the same way that there was a part of him within me. It was what formed the bond, I figured. Tendrils of one person anchored inside of another, and then they were always connected, even when they were apart.

I could sense the parts that were Trev now. The ones inside of Rhelia. They weren't quite the same as the ones within me, but they were unmistakably Trev. Fiery. Fierce. Loving. Kind. Goofy. Fun. They held all of that, and more. Stubborn and reckless, too. It was all there. But they were blocked. There was something between me, between Rhelia, and that part of Trev. Not knowing what else to do, I pushed some of the bits of Trev that were within me against the ones inside Rhelia. At first I thought nothing was happening, but then, slowly, the parts within Rhelia started to writhe, as though they could sense their own kind and wished to reconnect. So I pushed them further, and also added a bit of the Rhelia that I had been surprised to find within me as well, and now the parts of Trev that were within Rhelia were jumping like a live wire.

I had a brief sense of misgiving as I pushed further, worried what it would mean that I was crossing these lines. These bonds that were so personal might never be the same, after what I was doing, and I didn't know how to undo anything that I did, but Trev was going to die. I couldn't let that happen. I couldn't. I'd lost too damned much lately to lose him again too, and… damn it, even if I hadn't, he was my twin. He might never forgive me for what had happened with Rhelia, but if he never lived long enough to hate me and love her, and do whatever he was going to do with his life, then I would never forgive myself, for any of it.

So I pushed again, mixing my own Trevor-bond with Rhelia's and my Rhelia-bond with Trev's Rhelia-bond, and this was fucking weird to put into words, but the words didn't matter. What mattered was that after a few more moments of this strange mingling, I felt a flash of energy, like touching an electric fence, and then I heard Trev cry out.

When I opened my eyes, still holding Rhelia's hand, and now holding Trev's as well, though I wasn't sure when I'd grabbed it, I saw Trev's face, streaked with tears, a faint smile curling the corners of his mouth.

He can ssssensssse me.

THE BOY HAS STOPPED FIGHTING ME. AT LAST HE BEGINS TO HEAL.

So, now tears were streaming down my face, too.

Rhelia's face was still the mask of death, including the blank, staring eyes that had chilled me so the first time that I'd seen them, but I now understood that all of that was simply part of the enchantment that Gwen hadc placed on her.

"What a touching scene," said a voice I had been certain I would never hear again.

"FUCK, EDIK, YOU'VE really let yourself go," I said, standing up and putting myself between my brother and the vampire, who was really channeling his inner Walking Dead right now. His head looked like it had only loosely reattached itself to his neck, and his body was coated in mud, dead leaves, and what looked like a few forms of fecal matter from various woodland creatures. His face was in only marginally better shape, and looked like an owl had crapped on it.

"It took me a rather long time for my body to find my head, but thanks to the healing properties of this glade, I was able to survive."

I gave Life a rather judgmental glare, but the tree merely shrugged.

I CANNOT SIMPLY SWITCH IT OFF, YOU KNOW.

"Now, Vic, I believe you have some information that I am in need of, and I am no longer in a forgiving mood."

And, with that, he charged, not at me, but at my still-prone brother, lying on the ground at the foot of the Tree of Life. Which is how Edik learned what my bad side was really like.

Even I was surprised at how quickly I was able to shift to my dragon form, but only Edik was surprised at how quickly I used those giant jaws to snap down and remove his precariously attached head.

Which I then promptly spat on the ground.

Then I opened my giant maw, and learned that dragon breath gets up to over 900 degrees Celsius in a matter of seconds.

IMPRESSIVE. I DID NOT KNOW YOU COULD DO THAT. DIAMOND IS NOT EASY TO MELT.

"Neither did I," I said, returning to human form and getting thoroughly sick all over the leaves next to the charred remains of what had been Edik's skull less than minute ago.

IF YOU ARE WONDERING, HE IS DEFINITELY DEAD THIS TIME. I AM THE TREE OF LIFE. I WOULD KNOW.

I laughed, threw up a little more, and said, "Yeah, Life, I'd guessed as much this time. But thanks."

And then I passed out.

ONE OF THESE days I was really going to have to get tested for anemia or something. I mean, who passes out this much? Of course, with the number of times I had been healed by the Tree of Life, you would think that I couldn't have any diseases left. Which made one wonder what was wrong with my life, that I kept fainting. Something to think about another time, I guess.

"Is she going to be ok?"

It sounded like it was time to open my eyes.

"There she is," Seamus said, as I blinked him into focus before me.

"Gatita! Nice of you to come back so soon," Sol added, from next to Seamus.

They were sitting on chairs, side by side to the left of the bed I was lying in. Which was a bed I didn't really recognize, though the style of it seemed familiar. When I finally looked at the walls and took a deep breath filled with cool, dusty air, I realized that I recognized where I was.

"We're at Rhelia's house?"

They both nodded.

"Gwen showed up with you, Rhelia, and Trevor a few hours ago, and dropped you here."

"Are they alright?" I asked, my voice cracking even as the words came out.

Sol and Seamus didn't say anything.

"Seamus?"

"He said you killed Rhelia, and… is she really dead? She looked dead."

"It's true. Well, sort of true, I guess. It was true, briefly. Or maybe it was never true. Maybe you can't really ever change the past, I don't know. But, at any rate, as far as he and I were both concerned, there was a brief period of time in which I definitely killed Rhelia."

"I assume it was an accident," Seamus said.

I thought about that for a long moment.

"It was, I guess. The first time, anyway. I mean, I didn't know it was her, but… honestly, even if I'd known, I don't know what I would have done differently. If she'd injected him, we all would have died. Not just us, but a half a million people who had no idea what was going on and just had the bad luck to live in the city that Rebecca Dryer decided to use as a testing site, and…" I trailed off when I saw that both Seamus and Sol were staring fixedly at their hands.

"What is it?" I asked.

"Dryer got away," Sol said.

I looked at them both again.

"That's not all," I prompted, taking in the pallor that tinged both of their faces. "Go on…"

"They… MOME captured Siara and two other weredragons."

"Fuck. Fuck. Fuck. That is sooo not good. So very not good. Where are they? What are we doing to get them back?"

Sol was quiet for a long time, while she stared at the wall. Then she said, "We just got word that she injected one of them in Sucre."

I felt the urge to faint again. To disappear into some kind of void and never return.

"How bad is it?" I whispered.

"It must have been a weaker weredragon… it took out a few city blocks. They're not sure how many people were killed yet. In the thousands, likely. Luckily, Albert says he hasn't detected any tears in spacetime yet."

"Luckily." The word felt so flat in my mouth I wanted to spit it out. Instead, I could feel my stomach start to turn.

"Have we already lost?" I asked, not really expecting an answer. "How do we get them back?"

Sol and Seamus just stared at me. Right. How would they know? And what could I even do?

"Did Gwen say anything about Rhelia?" I asked, needing desperately to cling to the only thing that had gone right so far today. Rhelia and Trev were alive. They had to be. I had done everything I could to save them, and they had to be alright.

"Gwen said she was dead, Vic," Sol said, her own voice cracking.

I swallowed. I didn't think I could handle pretending that it was true with Seamus and Sol. Especially if Trev…

Trev? Trev. I know you can't forgive me, but… will you talk to me? Is… is Rhelia alright?

The silence that followed gutted me a hundred times over. I considered reaching out to Rhelia myself, but something stopped me, maybe just a desperate need to know my brother would still talk to me. Even though it was seeming more and more like he wouldn't.

She's alright, Vic. We won't have to keep this up for much longer. Gwen just said that the more people who thought she was dead the better, and Rhelia agreed.

It felt like a hand had finally stopped squeezing my chest when I felt Trev through the bond.

All will be well, Living Cat. You should ressssst.

I wanted to ask them both a million questions, not least of which was why we had to pretend Rhelia was dead, but I didn't want to bother them right now, and I wasn't going to argue with them even if rest was the last thing on my mind, and nothing was going to be "well" anytime soon.

There were two weredragons out there who were in desperate need of rescue, not to mention all the people who would die if they were weaponized.

"Rebecca Dryer has declared war against… well, everyone who isn't MOME, really," I said, to no one in particular.

Sol smiled then, and grabbed my hand, and Seamus piled his hand on top.

"Well, she really picked the wrong people to fuck with, didn't she?"

"I DIDN'T EXPECT to see you again," said a south London accent, somewhere behind me.

I jumped nearly a foot in the air. I hadn't expected to find them so easily.

I turned, my vision sweeping past the strange orange sky dotted with purple clouds, lowering to a low grey rock as I took a reluctant breath of sulphur-tinged air. My eyes settled on a small, ugly rodent with red skin and glowing eyes.

"I can see why you wanted to return to Earth so badly," I said, smiling at the small creature, that sat on the low stone in front of me. "But I'm not sure why you came back here so soon after you arrived."

Azrael huffed.

"I wasn't exactly keen on returning here, but it was better than the alternative."

"Which was?" I asked.

"Continuing to spy on you and your mates," they replied.

I wasn't sure if they meant my friends, or my romantic-partners-as-decided-by-Gaia, but since they were largely the same group of people, I decided it didn't matter.

"And sabotage us?" I guessed, thinking of the fire at my old house in Colorado.

Azrael shrugged.

"If necessary. MOME wasn't specific about the particulars, but that angry woman with a stick up her arse wanted to know what you were up to and wanted you out of the way if possible."

"Sounds like Dryer," I said. "So why'd you come back here?"

"I only agreed because she sicced a mob of bloody vampires on me, and threatened to do the same again, if I didn't cooperate."

I considered that.

"Vampires don't seem to pose much trouble for you," I offered.

"Not a lone vampire in the woods who isn't expecting me, no. But a damned bunch of trained ones, yeah. Vampires are—never mind. I don't owe you an explanation."

It was my turn to shrug.

"I suppose not, but I still don't understand why you're here and not on Earth, tailing us and stirring up trouble. Setting houses on fire, or whatever—"

"I didn't—" Azrael let out a long sigh and then started again. "Look. I was fine with the idea of keeping a couple of kids out of Dryer's way, yeah? But I am not interested in blowing up cities full of humans, or stripping people of their dark matter to do it, alright? Dryer crossed the line, and I'd rather starve here in the Wastelands than help with that kind of thing. You may hate me for what I've done already, I wouldn't blame you, but even a succubus has morals."

That made me smile, and I remembered the shadow I had almost followed in the Dragon Realm, just before we'd gone to La Paz the second time.

"Besides," Azrael continued, "I saw what you were doing to help, and I suspect you might be the only thing standing between Dryer and full control of the realms we know."

"Well," I said, reaching out a hand towards the creepy demonic squirrel body that offered such a stark contrast to the angelic forms Azrael could take on Earth, "if that's how you feel about it, I have a proposition for you, Az."

"Oh, and what's that?" The squirrel asked, sniffing my hand skeptically.

"I need help taking down Rebecca Dryer, and everyone who supports her," I said.

"Oh, is that all?" Azrael said, frowning their little squirrel mouth at me.

"That's the short version, yeah."

My hand still lingered in the air between us.

Azrael leapt, clung to my arm, and then ran across my shoulders to perch beside my head.

"Well, go on then."

VIRGINIA McCLAIN

VICTORIA MARMOT
AND THE
DRAGON'S RAGE

VICTORIA MARMOT BOOK FOUR

To Mom, for never giving up.

THE ALLEY WAS as dark as an elephant's asshole. I mean, not that I'm super familiar with an elephant's asshole or anything, but you know… it'd be dark, probably, and wet, and smell like feces, so… pretty close to the alley I was currently standing in. Although I'd wager that the elephant would have to be in extremely ill health to have as much standing water lying around inside of it as this alley did. Ok, the simile falls apart at some point, so sue me. I'm not a writer, I'm just a teenager.

Well, "just" may not be the best qualifier for someone who can turn into a snow leopard and also a dragon but… Gwendamnit, narrating is hard.

Look, the alley was dark and wet and I was standing there, surrounded by concrete and refuse, looking around like a dazed meerkat, wishing I had a wand or some shit, so that I could just tap a brick and disappear into Diagon Alley or whatever, but no. Nothing in my life was that easy. There was no wand, there was no half-giant to show me the ropes, there was just me and elephant-ass alley, and a weird tingly feeling in the skin of my hands that got stronger in certain directions and weaker in others. Hence, why I was doing a slow-motion, arrhythmic version of thriller.

As I stepped in yet another puddle and my nostrils informed me that it was a puddle comprised almost entirely of human urine with perhaps a sprinkling of vomit, I decided that I really wasn't a city person.

"Any luck, Gatita?" came a voice from farther down the alley.

"Depends," I said, trying not to retch as I took in enough air to speak, "on what you mean by luck. If you mean have I found the seam, then no. If you mean have I stepped in a statistically disproportionate amount of human excrement? Then yes. Yes, lots of luck."

Sol laughed, and I smiled at the sound, even if nothing else about this scenario was amusing to me.

"You're awfully squeamish for an outdoors-woman."

"Fuck that," I said, turning to glare in Sol's direction, even though it was too dark to see her from where I stood. "I will pick up scat and rub it in my hands to tell you how long ago the nearest mountain lion passed by, sew a gaping wound shut with nothing but a hotel sewing kit, and make a tourniquet out of sticks to set a protruding bone back in place, if I have to. But humans in the city are fucking gross."

For some reason that made Sol laugh even louder.

"I won't argue with that, but I think we're gross everywhere. It's just that there are more of us in the city."

Which was a fair point, and really, La Paz seemed to be no grosser than any other city I'd ever been in—if anything it was cleaner than a few I'd visited—but that wasn't a point my urine-coated self was willing to concede at the moment. Sol had grown up in La Paz, and had an easy confidence here that I envied at times. I could lead us through the remote parts of the Andes that sheltered her family cabin, and the Colorado Rockies might as well have been my backyard, but I was… less useful in the hustle and bustle of just under a million people.

"La Paz isn't even that big," Sol said, walking over to stand between me and yet another nondescript stretch of concrete wall. "It's about the same size as where you lived in Colorado, isn't it?"

I shrugged.

"I'm pretty sure it's got more people than where I'm from, but even if it doesn't… the Front Range is more like a giant suburb. There isn't much urban center. The population is all spread out. This is different," I explained, gesturing at the narrow alley that contained us, a dumpster, and too many pools of urine. Seeing Sol start to look defensive, I quickly added, "Don't get me wrong, La Paz is beautiful. What little I've seen of it outside this alley is charming, and I'm really looking forward to seeing more of it, but… I'm not a fan of dark, stank alleys, I guess."

Sol ran her hand along my arm, or the black leather that covered it, anyway. I wasn't always in agreement with the style choices of whatever Gwengranted magic was in charge of supplying new clothes to me (and all the shifters in my immediate vicinity) every time I shifted, but at least it had taken into account that spring in the Andes was no time to leave me in less than a thick leather biker jacket, a pair of lined jeans, and some sturdy boots. The outfit struck me as fairly cliché given that I was standing in a dark alley, could turn into an animal, and occasionally fought vampires, but at least it was warm. All thoughts of my wardrobe fled when Sol leaned in to purr at my ear, though.

"There's a lot that can be accomplished in a dark alley," she whispered, licking my neck and making my skin ignite.

The heat was quickly quelled by the stench of human feces and urine that permeated the place, but it was a testament to how attractive I found Sol that she was able to turn me on even for a moment in those conditions.

"I'm afraid my nose is entirely too sensitive for that to be a pleasant prospect," I replied, disappointed that it was true. "But once we get out of this place I'd be keen to take you up on the offer."

She bit my earlobe playfully.

"Excellent. We haven't had nearly enough time alone for my liking," she purred.

I took a deep breath and tried to swallow. The stench of the alley was becoming less and less of a deterrent the more Sol's breath caressed my neck, and for a moment I was oddly glad that Seamus had decided to go check on his Moms today.

It wasn't that I didn't want Seamus with us on this mission. It was just that I was glad he would be safe for once. He wasn't much of a fighter, after all, and well… at this exact moment… I was ok with Sol having me all to herself.

"Yeah, saving the world is a real buzz kill," I muttered, as I felt my back push up against the concrete wall behind me.

"Yet one more reason that Rebecca Dryer deserves to die," Sol replied, the corner of her lush mouth turning up on one side.

I laughed, because the alternative was to have a full-on panic attack triggered by thinking about how close we were to losing everything.

A few hours ago, when Sol and I had been getting briefed by Trev on what little he could tell us about Rhelia's mission—basically that Torrence was a potential contact and that she had gone dark earlier after her morning check in—we'd been interrupted by a series of newsflashes about demands being made from the "unknown terrorist organization in Sucre."

Apparently, Rebecca Dryer wasn't feeling patient, and she was already making demands that the U.N. cede power to her, along with all the nations that weren't members of the U.N. She was threatening to set off more "weapons of mass destruction" if her demands weren't met in the next 48 hours. That had been eight hours ago, and, unfortunately, Dryer wasn't saying *where* she was planning to do her mass destruction. Con-sequently, we were left without any leads, despite Trev and Rhelia having gone sleepless hacking and monitoring every bit of MOME security footage they could get their code on for the past two days. None of the backup footage they'd managed to access had turned up anything useful regarding our two missing weredragons yet.

The people we loved, our homes, the Earth… maybe even the whole universe were at stake here, and we were out of time for anything but drastic measures. To top it off, Rhelia had been following a desperate lead when she'd suddenly gone dark.

Which had me swallowing for an entirely different reason, trying to keep the emotion at bay. Everyone I had left, which was a pretty short list these days, had come far too close to death already in the past three weeks for my liking.

For some reason—sympathy, empathy, a sudden need to remind us both that there was still some good in the world—Sol took that moment to pull me close and kiss me deeply. For the span of a few heartbeats I was consumed by the fire of that kiss and everything else was swept away; it didn't matter that the Ministry of Magical Entities was trying to kill us, that they were holding the world hostage with a potentially Earth-annihilating weapon, that my brother was still barely talking to me after it had looked like I'd killed his mate two days ago in order to save all of our lives. Those thoughts had consumed me five seconds ago, but in that moment they ceased to exist.

Elephant asshole and all, I *really* didn't want to pull away from that kiss, but the tingling in my hands wouldn't let up and, eventually, I pulled back just enough to say, "I think I can tell where that seam is."

"REMIND ME WHY we think this is a good idea, Gatita?"

I lowered my hands from where I'd raised them to Sol's shoulders, and stared at her as she leveled her gold-green eyes at me, the graffiti-tagged alley fading away as her eyes caught mine.

"What in particular do you mean?" I asked. "I'm pretty sure my entire life has been one bad idea after another for the past three weeks."

Sol's lips quirked up at the sides, but her gaze remained implacable.

"I mean, why do we think that going to Unterberg is a worthwhile use of our time? I still think that we'd be better off waiting for a lead from your brother or—"

"My brother basically admitted that he was out of leads, Sol, not to mention out of options, as soon as Rhelia didn't check in this afternoon." I reminded her, before she could get caught up in the same argument she'd had with Trev before we left. "If all the surveillance he's doing isn't getting us anywhere, then whatever long shot Rhelia is taking is the only chance we've got right now. He's trying to sort through security footage from five different MOME HQs and who knows how many smaller outposts. Even if he had a whole team working for him it would take days to find anything useful. We just don't have the time."

"But Dryer could use Siara as her next bomb at any moment, and we don't even know what lead Rhelia was following when she left this morning."

Sol's voice was marked by the frustration we'd all been feeling since we'd sat helplessly by and watched a whole section of Sucre get razed to the ground three days ago (or in my case, watched the news reports of it after I'd regained consciousness). That frustration had started leaning heavily towards terror as we'd watched the morning news flash headlines about demands from the mysterious terrorist organization that was responsible for the attacks. Of course, we knew exactly what the "mysterious" terrorist organization was, but that didn't help anything. The fact that we knew that the organization was MOME, and that we knew that MOME was being led by Rebecca Dryer in this particular mission did us little good since we didn't know where Rebecca Dryer was, or, more importantly, where she was holding the two weredragons that she was intending to use as her next weapons of mass destruction.

"We know Rhelia thought whatever lead she had was our only chance to find Siara and Emil before they wind up turned into Hiroshima and Nagasaki times a bajillion, so I'm inclined to think that her mission, whatever it is, has become priority number one," I said, trying to keep the irritation out of my voice. I didn't succeed.

"But Dryer could use anyone as a bomb now. Why are we even going after Siara and Emil when Dryer could explode any of her own agents if she felt like it? Shouldn't we just be planning to take out all of MOME now? I know the dragons supposedly make the biggest bang, but does that really mean that they won't use someone else even if we manage to get Siara and Emil back from them? Gatita, I know you trust your brother and Rhelia, but..." her voice trailed off and she shrugged, leaving me to fill in the blanks.

I bristled. I understood perfectly what she was getting at, and I didn't want to hear it.

"You think it hasn't occurred to me more than once that Trev was in MOME custody for over a decade?" I hissed. Just because it was a possibility I'd considered myself, didn't mean it was one that I wanted to talk about. Something Sol had assuredly picked up on when she'd brought it up while I was still recovering from my own injuries. Rhelia had still been pretending to be dead to everyone but me and Trev, and Trev had seemed oddly distant. He still did. It was disconcerting to all of us, especially me, but what did any of us expect when it had basically looked to him like his sister had killed his mate right in front of his eyes?

"You worked for MOME for three years," I said, latching on to whatever I could to avoid talking or thinking about the idea of not trusting my twin. "You could be loyal to them just as easily as Trev could."

Sol's eyes flashed and her lips formed a hard line, all hints of humor vanishing in a breath.

"They killed my mother, my aunt, and my cousin," she said, her voice a harsh whisper. "Do you think that made me loyal?"

I took a deep breath, but it still felt like I'd been punched in the stomach. Sol had been more than a little reluctant to talk about what MOME had done to her family, and who she had lost. This was the first time I'd heard her say who was killed. I was suddenly swamped with sadness, not just for Sol and her family, but for Trev and everything he'd been through, for all of us who MOME had fucked with and tried to destroy.

Taking a deep breath, I reminded myself that we'd all been under a metric shit-ton of stress lately and that neither of us was in a great headspace right now.

"And they killed Trev's parents, abducted him as a child, and have been trying to kill him, me, and his mate, ever since he finally got away from them," I replied. "What loyalty do you expect him to have for them?"

I had hoped that the grief I was feeling for all of us would show through my voice enough to disarm Sol, but I should have known better. Her voice was still icy when she spoke again.

"You said yourself he was a child when they took him," Sol began. "He was more susceptible to—"

"And how old were you when they took your family from you?" I was losing my patience despite everything Sol had just admitted to me.

"That's different!" she countered. "I wasn't trapped with MOME after that, I didn't have a chance to develop Stockholm Syndrome or to—"

"Look. Even if you think that Trev would betray us, do you really think that we're so crucial to the dragons' resistance plans that misdirecting us is going to bring the whole thing crashing down?" I couldn't believe I was having to have this argument for the second time today.

"We may not be, but Rhelia is one of—"

"Rhelia left this morning to go on this mission despite Trev's best arguments against it, because she was convinced that she knew something the rest of us didn't that would help us find Siara and Emil, even if she couldn't tell us what that was. If Trev was secretly trying to help MOME, he either wouldn't have tried to stop her, or he wouldn't be sending us to help her now. You can't have it both ways, Sol."

"It just seems dangerous to head to Unterberg right now, considering everything that happened to us the last time we went there. And the time before that."

That was hard to argue with, but I tried anyway.

"Is there anywhere in the universe that's safe for us right now?" I asked, almost ready to collapse against the brick wall behind me. I probably would have, if I hadn't been convinced it was covered in human urine.

Sol finally laughed, and I could only stare at her as though her head had suddenly grown horns.

"You're right, Gatita," she sighed, running a hand along my arm again. It felt like a magnet pulling all the tension out of my body. "That's probably why I'm feeling so combative. We aren't safe anywhere, and we haven't been for so long, I'm starting to feel a bit frayed around the edges. I kinda desperately wish we had time to spar."

It was difficult to keep myself from angling my head at Sol like puppy that had just seen a large hoppy bug.

"WHY HAVEN'T WE BEEN SPARRING!?" I asked, grabbing Sol by both arms.

She laughed again and this time I joined her.

"Maybe because we've been fighting real bad guys nonstop since we met?" she suggested.

"Yeah, good point. Fine, but when this is all over, we're definitely sparring."

"Maybe once we find Rhelia and use her secret plan to retrieve our missing weredragons."

It was a sobering reminder that we rather desperately needed to be elsewhere, not here, making out and debating our orders, surrounded by human waste.

I sighed.

The last seam we had used to sneak into Unterberg had been compromised immediately after we'd used it, so we had to assume MOME was watching it. The dragons had a secondary seam that was safe enough for Seamus to sneak in and visit his Moms, but it let out in a public square and was still too public for a top-secret rescue mission—or whatever this was. We needed a new seam that wasn't monitored by MOME, but also dropped out somewhere a bit more circumspect.

Luckily for us, there were a lot of seams to Unterberg. Unluckily for us, most of the ones MOME didn't know about were little more than rumors in dark bars. It had taken us all day to find a trust-worthy(ish) source in a dingy cafe in La Paz. Then it had taken us a few more hours to find the nondescript back alley our less than sober source had described, let alone the seam itself.

Rhelia had mentioned to Trev that she might need some backup not long after she'd arrived in Unterberg, and then she'd missed her midday check-in. Trev couldn't go, because he was knee deep in security feeds from all of MOME's bases of operation, trying to find our missing weredragons, and the only person qualified to do the job instead of him was Rhelia. Despite that, he'd practically begged to come with us. He'd been a wreck ever since Rhelia had failed to check in, and the only way I'd convinced him to stay behind was to remind him that if Rhelia headed back to the Dragon Realm while we were gone he'd miss her, and if he missed a chance to locate Siara and Emil while we were gone, Rhelia would tear him in two.

So he'd stayed, and we'd left, and you, dear reader, (assuming I buy Gwen's whole, "I'm supposed to be your narrator, you're in a book," line) caught up with us making out in an alley in La Paz.

But just before we'd started arguing, the Marco Polo game my hands had been playing with whatever it was in seams that made my skin vibrate had come to an abrupt halt as I had been running them up Sol's back. As I had reached her shoulders, I'd suddenly realized that the reason I'd been going back and forth through this urban shit funnel without finding anything was that the pull I kept feeling wasn't coming from in front of me or behind me, as I'd initially suspected, but from directly above me, instead.

And, indeed, when—deciding that Sol's laughter and dropping of the topic of Trev-as-Traitor meant that she'd agreed we could move on with our mission—I finally stretched my hands into the air, I felt like I was parting a curtain.

"If you don't think Unterberg is too dangerous," I said, with as much scathing sarcasm as I could muster, "grab on."

Then I dropped into a crouch, and Sol complied, asking no questions, but throwing me a startled look.

Not nearly as startled as I probably looked when I fell on my ass a second later, after attempting to hop into the air with a hundred and twenty pound person on my back, and instead collapsing in a small heap of pain, embarrassment, and unfortunate bodily fluids.

"What were you trying to do, exactly?" Sol asked, as we attempted to brush the dripping human excrement from our clothes.

"The seam is above us. We need to launch ourselves upwards."

"And you thought you were going to launch us both six feet into the air using nothing but your human form?"

I muttered something indecipherable and shuffled my feet, staring fixedly at a patch of filth on my jeans.

"How about we shift first?" Sol suggested, rather politely not mentioning how idiotic my initial plan had been.

"How will you hold onto me?"

"You know I don't actually have to hold you to pass through a seam, right? That's why we're using a seam instead of having you use your Gwen-given-power to shift us there, remember? So you don't tire before we even know what we're up against."

That was news to me. I mean, it shouldn't have been. We'd talked about using seams instead of me shifting us to save energy, I just… had we talked about how anyone could use a seam if they already knew where it was? The more I thought about it, the more I suspected we had. Because I was now remembering Sol telling me how sometimes even non-magical folks walk through them by accident and that's where you get your Narnia and Wonderland type scenarios. I clearly needed more sleep. It hadn't been an easy… month.

Not wanting to drag out what was quickly becoming a thoroughly embarrassing conversation for me, I decided to focus on shifting. I imagined what it felt like to have a tail for counterbalance, a much lower center of gravity, and whiskers wide enough to help me navigate swiftly through cracks in rock. Then, almost instantly, I felt myself take on my feline form.

Damn, it feels good to be a snow leopard.

At the same time, Sol took shape as a large panther beside me, and I gave her one quick nod before launching myself at the magic I had sensed with my fingers. A magic that now took on a full-body, physical sensation, as my furry form collided with what felt like a large velvet drape lined with hot taffy.

~~~

"Woah," I whispered, as we shifted back to human immediately upon hitting the cobbles of a very different alley in a very different city. La Paz's 16th century colonial charm (if we want to call colonialism charming—which was not at all high on my list of things to call colonialism; I had some other choice words for colonialism that were far less complimentary—but if we're just talking architecture, sure, the buildings were cute) had been left behind
~~~

and replaced with a sort of melted glass meets Sagrada Familia look that was so impressive it left me with the vocabulary of Keanu Reeves learning Kung-fu.

The last time I'd been in this city we'd been instantly set upon by MOME agents and then apprehended by the Unterberg security golems (who had promptly put bags over our heads), so I hadn't had much time to look around, even though I'd been just as entranced with the view then as now.

Instead of the scent of alley sewage (thankfully shed along with our clothes, which had been replaced due to our brief stint in feline form), the air here was filled with something warm and slightly floral, as though fruit-bearing trees were in bloom nearby—albeit no tree I was familiar with. Indeed, peeking above a high wall nearby, visible even in the moonlight, their blossoms were a riot of colors rarely seen in my world, striped and polka dotted as though they were more fashion show that flower. The buildings looked almost organic, aside from the fact that they followed patterns that looked so intricate and symmetrical it was difficult to imagine that they weren't created by sentient beings. The color selections also seemed too vibrant and contrasting to be naturally occurring. While most of the architecture seemed to be made of stone or clay, every building was adorned with giant sections of glass—windows and sometimes entire walls—forming a vibrant display that reflected even the moonlight with enthusiasm.

As we walked from the cobbled alley where we'd arrived into the larger, cobbled street beyond, it was difficult for me not to stare. The streets, which had been packed with people headed to market the last time we had been here, seemed no less crowded now that the sun was down. The people were almost impossible to describe, and encompassed beings whose skin colors ranged from lime to aubergine, jet black to glittering silver, and who sported a startling array of hair, fins, wings, and horns, not to mention a variety of limb numbers that often exceeded four. I couldn't help but smile, as I turned to Sol and reached for her hand.

"Unterberg may not be safe, but at least the sightseeing is good when you aren't instantly forced to run for your life," I said.

Which was, of course, when a large, black ball of fur launched itself at me, tackling me against the nearest decorative window before I could even make out where it had come from.

"WHAT THE FUCK? Seamus?" I said, as the black ball of fur disengaged from my chest to shift back to his human form, complete with a jeans and T-shirt combo appropriate for Unterberg's warm summer nights. Unfortunately, I was too flustered from having my back abruptly slammed into an ornate stained-glass window to appreciate the way the aforementioned T-shirt clung to his swimmer's body, the way he smelled slightly of fur and cinnamon, or the way the moonlight glinted off his amber eyes.

"What are you doing here?" I asked.

"It's uh… a long story," Seamus said, looking somewhat abashedly from Sol to me. "I was worried about you two."

I took a deep breath and tried not to let out an exasperated sigh. We'd all been worried about each other lately, but Seamus had been safely tucked away with his Moms for once, and I had been mildly relieved to think he wouldn't be risking his ass with us today.

"Seamus, I thought we talked about the over-protective male thing," I began, but Seamus cut me off.

"It's not that, Vic. Fuck's sake, you're here with Sol. I know you two can take care of yourselves better than I can."

Seamus' eyes darkened and I wondered if he was angry or jealous about that fact.

"So, what's going on? Is everyone ok?"

Seamus took a deep breath.

"My Moms are fine, if that's what you're asking, but…"

To my surprise it was Sol who took Seamus' arm and turned him so that she could look in his eyes and speak to him with a level of concern I hadn't heard from her before.

"Did you see something?" she asked.

Seamus looked like he might cry with relief as he nodded, and I kicked myself for jumping to the assumption that he was here to play the overbearing male in a story that had far too many alphas in it already. I should have known better. Seamus might have a protective streak from being a wolf raised by wolves, but he had little interest in dominance. He must have had a vision.

"Do you want to tell us about it?" I asked, belatedly trying to match Sol's level of concern.

Seamus shook his head and took a deep breath.

"I don't think I should. Not all of it, at least. First, because we don't really have time, and second…" Seamus looked between both of us, as though he was searching for an answer to a question he hadn't asked aloud. I didn't know what answer he was looking for, so I just smiled as reassuringly as I could while Sol squeezed his arm a bit. "Don't freak out, but Rhelia needs our help. Which I suppose you guys know if you're here already, but… I need to be there too, and… this is gonna sound weird, but… we can't trust the green lady."

He flinched after he said all of that, as if ex-pecting us to say or do something that would hurt him, now that he'd said it. I just looked between Sol and Seamus and wondered what my life had become that vague prophecies not only didn't surprise me anymore, but kinda made sense. I mean, I didn't know who the green lady was, but whatever, we were in Unterberg, where every color in the Crayola box was a perfectly normal skin tone. Still, I was guessing she'd be pretty obvious when we ran into her. Meanwhile, I was adding to the mental list of questions I needed to ask Seamus when we finally had time to talk like normal humans. Like why he looked like he expected to be punished for telling us about a vision.

"Alright, noted. We won't trust the green lady. Anything else?" I asked.

Seamus shook his head, but there was still a haunted look in his eyes.

"Seamus, are you… are you sure you need to come with us? We have no idea what we're up against here and…"

I trailed off as I realized I was being a colossal hypocrite, after I'd just accused Seamus of being an overprotective git, but… he already looked scared enough to crap his pants, and we all knew that he wasn't a very effective fighter. Maybe I was just trigger shy after almost losing everyone I loved three days ago, but it seemed irresponsible to let him join us on this particular mission if he didn't absolutely have to be there.

Seamus rolled his eyes, and I cringed, expecting him to tell me off for being an ass. Instead he said something completely reasonable.

"Vic, I know I'm not the best fighter. This isn't about that. I just… I have more information than you do, and I can't convey it all in a reasonable amount of time. There are too many variables, and… look, let's just say that when I tried to run alternate scenarios for the future, all the ones without me in them ended… unacceptably."

The amount of times Seamus hesitated in that little speech had me incredibly wary of what he'd seen, but I barely got a chance to pick one of the thousand questions it raised (to start with: Seamus' Moms' new place was on the other side of the city from where we were, and Seamus shouldn't have known where to find us—because we hadn't told anyone how we were getting to Unterberg or where we'd come out; then there was the fact that he could apparently sift through possible futures to see which ones worked best, and the implications of that were off the hook) let alone voice one.

"Seamus, how did you even get—"

I was cut off by a large, heavy hand falling onto my shoulder while a voice said, "You should not be here, Ms. Marmot."

UNFORTUNATELY FOR THE body attached to that hand, I don't take kindly to being touched without permission and, unlike a minute ago when I'd been bowled into by a close friend at high velocity, whoever had their hand on my arm was not someone I recognized immediately. Nor did they move fast enough to prevent years of training from kicking in.

Which was how I wound up looking down at the profile of a very large, fur-covered, irate person with a bull's head pressed sideways into the cobblestone street. I was still holding his wrist and twisting it in a way that was designed to be in-credibly painful, which, combined with the impact from rolling over my shoulder and hitting the ground from a few feet up, probably explained the "irate" part of that description.

"Sorry, umm…. Torrence, was it?"

Don't ask me how my brain supplied the name of a minotaur I'd met once in a room full of other fantastic creatures during our first visit here, but… well, to be honest, Torrence is a pretty memorable name. Especially for someone with a bull's head.

Since I remembered him now, and he didn't appear to be trying to kill me at the moment, I released my hold on his arm and helped him to his feet. It took almost a minute before he was able to speak again, though. I guess I'd knocked the wind out of him.

While we waited, I looked to Seamus and Sol, and found that Seamus looked weirdly calm, as though large bull-people regularly put their hands on his friends and wound up lying on the pavement for it. Sol, meanwhile, looked rather like she'd have preferred it if I'd pulled a knife on the guy instead of helping him to his feet.

I shrugged and took a second to look around the crowded street, worried we might have drawn someone's attention and would shortly wind up with a bunch of the council's golems chasing us down again, but it looked like the nighttime hustle of Unterberg remained content to ignore our existence.

"I am sorry if I startled you," Torrence said, when he had finally caught his breath.

I blinked a few times as my brain caught up with what I was hearing. Judging by how pissed Tor-rence had looked when I'd flipped him, I really hadn't expected an apology.

"Apology accepted. For the record, I do not appreciate being touched without warning or my consent."

Torrence tipped his large bull's head, and the red-brown fur coating his highly sculpted, shirtless upper body glistened a bit in the moonlight.

"Duly noted, Ms. Marmot. I regret the breach of personal space. I was… upset, and not thinking clearly."

I nodded, totally at a loss for words as this mysterious semi-bovine person replied to me with the kind of respect I would hope to get from a 21st century modern human who had overstepped their bounds. Of course, he was a 21st century modern bovine-person. After a moment's consideration, I decided I probably shouldn't let the elements of this place, which reminded me of so many fantasy novels, movies, and MMORPGs, lead me to unfair assumptions about its residents' standards for decency.

As part of my brain reassessed where Torrence (and perhaps all of Unterberg) stood in terms of modern ethics, some other part of my higher functioning raised a more pertinent issue.

"As dragon kin I have the freedom to wander Unterberg in safety," I said, eyeing the minotaur (or tauren, or whatever he was) with a bit more suspicion. "You and the rest of your council left us free to go. Why shouldn't I be here?"

"It isn't safe to discuss out in the open," Torrence whispered. "Would you and your partners be willing to accompany me to a safe location?"

I looked at Sol and Seamus. Sol shrugged, still looking suspicious but not quite as stabby as she had a minute ago. Seamus gave me the kind of nod that told me he had expected this turn of events. I swallowed the questions that sprang to my lips. Now wasn't the time to grill Seamus on how his visions worked, or how much of the future he actually saw, especially considering the fact that Torrence was here, but I made a mental note to ask Seamus all about it the next time we had five minutes to ourselves.

"Fine, Torrence. After you."

"It would be easiest if you would allow me to transport you there."

Honestly, if Rhelia hadn't mentioned Torrence as a contact in her missive to Trevor I never would have agreed, but Seamus had the composed face of someone who wasn't the least bit surprised, and outside of hoping we'd find Rhelia in her apartment, we didn't really have much of a plan now that we'd made it to Unterberg. Whatever info Torrence had would probably be useful, and either way, we certainly didn't want to discuss our mission out in the street.

The bull-man (minotaur? Tauren? I seriously needed a couple minutes with no one trying to kill me so that I could figure what all the major species in Unterberg were called) nodded, straightened himself out while wincing a bit, threaded one of his arms through mine, and then grabbed onto both Sol and Seamus by the forearms, all while saying something guttural that sounded suspiciously like an expletive.

Then the world disappeared.

"UGH… SHIFTING HAS never made me want to throw up before," I muttered, even as my stomach came entirely too close to re-leasing itself on the highly polished marble floor in front of my face.

The floor was in front of my face because I was bent over at the waist trying to hold my dinner in place. I barely registered that it didn't match the cobbled streets we'd been standing on moments ago, because the sounds of Sol failing to keep her own meals in place threatened to overwhelm me. Seamus was also making retching sounds, but as far as I could tell he wasn't actually evacuating his stomach yet. I was doing my best not to breathe through my nose, but a hint of vomit and floor polish trickled in regardless, making the retention of my most recent meals seem less and less likely.

"Strange," said the deep voice that I now associated with the bull's head and heavily furred and muscled torso known as Torrence.

I supposed there were probably some legs in-volved in the equation, but I really couldn't call them to mind in that moment, as I stared at a particularly shiny vein of marble and tried to think about anything but vomit. That might've been because Torrence was shirtless, or… yeah, ok, maybe be-cause of the bull's head. I mean, the overall effect was pretty distracting. Half because he was surprisingly attractive, bull's head and all, and half because he was a bit disturbing. I mean, don't get me wrong, I can turn into a snow leopard and a dragon, so who the fuck am I to judge someone for having a bull's head, but… it was the transition from what was essentially a very furry human to a full-on bovine head with horns that threw me off, ok? I was trying not to be judgy about it, but it was something I'd only ever seen in video games and movies up to now and… well, seeing it in real life took some getting used to. For me anyway, but hey, add it to the pile, right? What wasn't new to me these days? And Gwendamnit, I must've been desperate to think about anything other than being sick all over this fancy marble if I was this obsessed with Torrence's appearance.

Torrence was mid-way through a sentence my brain hadn't processed at all when he danced out of the range of Sol's latest splatter and straight into my line of sight, drawing my vision from the sparkly, gold-veined marble tiles to some very shapely furred calves and…

"Hooves," I muttered, even as Torrence continued speaking. I had to drag my eyes away from the badass leather kilt that stopped just above Torrence's knee and circled his waist, which was muscular enough that I could make out his six pack even through all the fur. I shook my head and made a stronger effort to tune into what Torrence was saying.

"Most magic users find shifting planes to be both exhausting and nauseating in the early days, and shifters spend their entire lives feeling adverse effects from it. And yet you claim you do not feel it?"

"Nope. I do not claim that at all. I'm just barely not covering your pretty little hooves in the last 24 hours' worth of meals I've eaten. But whenever I shift us, I don't feel this way." Torrence's hooves weren't little, actually, but they were well-kempt and even a bit shiny, so I felt like pretty covered those bases nicely.

Sol kicked me, belatedly, from where she lay crumpled on the floor, and almost toppled into her own vomit. Consequently, I straightened up and went to grab her, hoping to prevent the whole scene from devolving into one of my worst nightmares. No way was I going to keep any food down if she tumbled into a pool of vomit. Just the smell of what was already there was pushing my limits.

Ugh.… Time for a subject change.

"So, what exactly did you just do to us?" I asked, deciding that if Sol wanted me to stop talking about my shifting power, asking my own questions was as good a distraction as any. Not that I thought Torrence would fall for it, but I was genuinely curious anyway.

"He cast a spell, Vic," Sol muttered, her voice still ragged from her recent escapades in food relocation.

"I used my own access to dark matter to pull us through a pocket dimension that paralleled both the location we were in and this location."

"Like lining up stitches in a crochet pattern and then pulling through all three at once?" I asked.

Torrence hesitated before saying.

"I do not crochet as much as I once did, but that is an apt comparison, yes."

Sol's mouth dropped open a bit, and Seamus snickered.

"You used to crochet?" she asked.

Torrence only smiled. I think. I mean, on a bull's face that could easily have been gas.

"I'm liking you more and more, Torrence," I added, before Torrence could take offense at Sol's question, or Seamus' laughter. I doubt either Sol or Seamus meant to offend—Sol hadn't sounded condescending at all, just surprised, and I think Seamus was more amused at Sol's surprise than the fact that Torrence crocheted. Seamus' Moms had shown me a quilt he'd made last summer, and he basically never stopped drawing, so I didn't think he found arts and crafts to be degrading activities.

"I spend more time in the community gardens now, but when I first moved to Unterberg I became quite an avid crocheter," said Torrence, without a trace of defensiveness in his voice.

There was definitely a smile on his face now. I mean ok, if I'd seen a bull on Earth doing that I would have assumed it was about to vomit or something, but knowing that the brain behind the bull face was in full control of its expressions, and that it functioned in a bipedal society where facial expressions were a thing, that had to be a smile.

"So, why does traveling through a pocket dimension tend to make most magic users, and especially shifters, nauseous?"

I was trying to bring us back to our original digression, even as I reminded myself that we were in a damned hurry, because, honestly, I needed a minute for my guts to realign themselves, and I would take any information I could get that I didn't have to wrestle out of people. It had been an uninformative few weeks and easy answers felt like a milkshake going down right about now.

"The theory is that shifters have a difficult time bringing both of their selves along, as their animal form is in its own dimensional pocket, so bringing both along for one of these trips requires leaps of physics that aren't particularly comfortable. As for most other magic users, no one is sure why it affects them adversely early on, but most of us grow used to it with practice."

"Interesting… I wonder how much of that is because most magic users probably have alternate forms they could reach for if they had the time and focus to access them. Maybe they get more comfortable with the shift as they grow more and more distant from their other forms." Trev had explained the bit about all magic users having access to alternate forms in an attempt to fill the awkward silence while we had waited at Rhelia's bedside after I'd felt well enough to get out of my own recovery bed. It may also have been his attempt to address our Mom's suggestion to "teach her everything." I won't pretend I didn't miss some of the content, because I was distracted by how distant Trev had felt ever since the whole accidentally-killing-his-mate incident, but the gist had been what I'd just explained; people were limited by their perceptions of how their own magic worked, not actually by their DNA.

The ensuing expression on Torrence's face made me think that cows must be really good at poker.

"I'm surprised that you've been exposed to that theory. You have only been aware of our world for a few weeks, no?" he asked.

I nodded.

"I'm getting a crash course, I guess you could say. So, does that mean you subscribe to the theory that all magic users can be shifters, and vice versa?" I asked.

When Trev had explained it, he'd made it sound as though that theory was not widely accepted in the magical community. Most folks still held with the idea that you only had access to whatever magic you had "inherited." Technically, they were right, it was just that when you looked back through every single ancestor you'd ever had, you really had just about the entirety of human (and magical) diversity to choose from. Thanks to the unique intersection of epigenetics and dark matter, all you had to do was focus long enough to unlock it. Apparently, when you ignored your pre-conceived notions and focused on what was actually in your DNA, you got… near infinite possibilities.

Still, not knowing how Torrence felt about that idea, I tried to put my own poker face in place. I wasn't sure how well I did. I probably just looked constipated.

Torrence tilted his head noncommittally, but said nothing.

Then a voice from somewhere beyond the foyer asked, "Torrence, are you going to bring our guests out of the entryway at any point this evening?"

The vaguely familiar voice set tiny warning bells jangling in my mind.

A moment later, a willow of a woman with yellow hair, long but elegantly pointed ears, and green skin barely visible underneath her off-white tunic and calfskin pants, walked through the hallway, stopping short of us by a few meters and wrinkling her nose in obvious disgust. Her violet eyes pulsed momentarily, and then we were all relieved of the smell of Sol's rejected meals. I glanced cautiously at the floor, and confirmed that the mess was gone.

That was when I first really took in our surroundings—aside from the shiny marble floor and the various bits of bull-person in front of me, that is. It was like my fear of taking too good a look at Sol's opening volley (which I was still un-comfortably close to copying) had given me a kind of tunnel vision that blocked out everything but the furry face in front of me.

Now, with the threat of witnessing someone else's lost meal removed, my vision opened up to encompass a marble hallway that featured some rather bland painted landscapes trussed up in heavily gilded frames, along with a mirror large enough to serve a small rugby squad who all wanted to check their teeth at the same time.

It was quite spacious and, despite the fact that it could easily have con-tained Sol's entire mountain cabin, it appeared to be only the foyer.

"Soledad, Seamus, Victoria, please come in," said the woman, who I now recognized as Nethia, the one who had given the impression she was in charge of the Unterberg council the last time we'd been here.

"Um… not that it's any of my business, but are you here just to talk to us, or is this your home too?"

"You're correct. It's none of your business."

I nodded.

"Fair. Only, if anything, it looks like you live here rather than Torrence. I mean, stale art, flashy mirrors, marble… a general sense of trying too hard," I continued, my tongue deciding that sass was appropriate even though Nethia could probably make me disappear from Unterberg with the sort of finality and discretion that it was generally unwise to provoke.

"Will you come in?" she asked again, ignoring my commentary.

I turned to look at Sol and Seamus, and caught Torrence rolling his eyes in a way that made me think that one of us was being ridiculous, but I wasn't sure who.

I looked at Sol, who, despite still being a bit off-color, looked like she was ready to bite Nethia for her condescending tone. I shook my head subtly. Pissing Nethia off verbally was one thing, sinking your teeth into her was another. We didn't need an incident. In fact, from what little Rhelia had told us in her communique, Torrence might be one of the few people who could help us, and our current situation suggested he was unlikely to do so without Nethia's say-so. When I turned and caught Seamus' eye, he was staring fixedly at Nethia with something like awe. Or it might have been fear, it was hard to tell.

"Look, we were in a bit of a hurry before we got sidetracked by Torrence here. We'd like to get back to what we were doing, but Torrence made it sound like some top-secret shit was about to go down, so… here we are. Want to tell us what the hell's going on?" I asked.

"That thing you're doing here," Torrence began, exchanging a glance with Nethia, "Would it happen to include searching for your dragon sister?"

I shrugged.

"My dragon sister?" I replied, deciding to play dumb. I wasn't feeling overly generous now that Nethia had shown up. After all, Seamus had warned us not to trust the green lady, a description that fit Nethia all too well. And our whole mission with Rhelia was entirely secret—so secret that we didn't even know exactly why she was in Unterberg—and I wasn't convinced these two needed to know any of it yet. Rhelia had mentioned Torrence was a contact, but she didn't say if he was someone she trusted.

"The dragon sister everyone else believes is dead," Nethia clarified.

"What makes you think that she isn't?" I asked.

"The fact that she's unconscious in the next room," Nethia replied.

And for some reason that was when Sol decided to shift to her panther form and launch herself at the willowy green woman's throat.

"SOL! ¡NO LA mates!"

It was the best I could do in the time it took for Sol to turn into 300 lbs of snarling black fury and pin Nethia to the golden-veined marble floor. Sol's jaws surrounded the all-too-delicate-looking green neck of the Unterberg council member, and for a moment I was certain that I was already too late, that the woman was dead, and that we were definitely going to Unterberg's prison for this, or worse.

Then I heard Nethia grunt.

"Get this blasted beast OFF of me!"

Sol growled, but didn't move, and Torrence and I stood frozen where we were.

Seamus was smiling, with his hands in his pockets, as though his friends habitually launched themselves at green-skinned, pointy-eared foreign dignitaries. Come to think of it, it was possible that they did. I didn't really know what Seamus' other friends were like, or how most werewolves interacted with other magical creatures.

Meanwhile, I only had one guess as to what had prompted Sol to act like a man-eating cat from a cheap horror flick, assuming it wasn't solely based on Seamus' warning about Nethia—which was a possibility—but this situation was too precarious to do anything but go with my gut.

"I think…" I began, even as I started edging my way towards the open archway that Nethia had been gesturing towards when she mentioned our unconscious friend, "…that I'm just going to go make sure that Rhelia is alright, while everyone else holds perfectly still."

Sol's tail flicked in an enthusiastic twitch that repeated three times, making me think that I was onto something, and Seamus nodded like I had the right idea.

"I really do suggest that you not move at all, Nethia, and I have a feeling the same goes for you, Torrence."

"Agreed," Torrence said quietly, as I passed through the archway into what looked like a large living room.

The room was furnished with daybeds, ornately carved to look like they were naturally occurring shrubberies that just happened to have soft cushions in them, and surrounded by walls full of more elaborate paintings in even more ornate frames, all circling a medium-sized raised koi pond covered with a plate of glass that turned it into a functional coffee table, with the added zing of some lazily circling koi fish.

On the daybed directly across from me (leaving the koi pond between us, and the other daybeds to the left and right of me) lay an unconscious Rhelia. For a moment, the sight made my breathing hitch. I was in no state of mind to see Rhelia lying inert, so soon after her feigned death, but, luckily, after only a heartbeat or two, I saw her chest rise and fall. The sight broke the hold of whatever had been keeping my lungs and limbs from moving, and I ran to Rhelia's side.

Her pulse was normal, her breathing even, and her ebon, iridescent skin looked the way it usually did. Aside from the fact that she didn't wake up when I touched her, or even when I shook her—gently at first and then more vigorously—she seemed fine.

"She won't wake up," I half shouted across the room.

Sol's hearing was excellent in panther form, and Seamus had followed me as far as the entrance to the living area, but was still within view of Sol and her prey. I probably didn't need to yell, but tell that to my barely-not-panicked brain.

I heard a small yelp from Nethia's direction and then, "I can wake her if you get this infernal cat off of me."

That was followed by another yelp.

"I think you'll have to figure out a way to wake her now, Nethia. From under the 'infernal cat,' if you really want to keep your throat," I called back.

I hoped Sol wasn't drawing blood yet. I didn't want to go to Unterberg's prison, and I had no idea how Torrence would side in this thing if we wound up in front of the council again.

Then I heard a gasp at my side, and all thoughts of the council were forgotten.

Rhelia's eyes blinked open, and instantly narrowed at the archway across from us.

"Careful, Ssssol! She'ssss a Dragon Hunter!"

"SHE'S A WHATTY-what now?" I asked, before my brain caught up and reminded me that the name was fairly self-explanatory.

"Dragon Hunter. A group of people reviled by my own, assss you might imagine."

Rhelia had already gotten up and started crossing the room back to the ornate foyer, where Sol was hopefully not yet tearing out Nethia's throat, so I was following her even as I asked inane questions.

Seamus nodded, smiling, at Rhelia, and then stepped in behind me as I followed the irate weredragon into the foyer.

"That seems like a really dumb hobby," I sup-plied, as we walked through the archway and took in the tableau of Sol, still enveloping Nethia's throat with her teeth, while pinning her to the marble floor with the entirety of her 300 pounds of feline fury. In other words, right where I'd left her. Torrence, good as his word, hadn't moved an inch.

Nethia looked as though she'd tried to move at least once, but had eventually learned the error of her ways. There was now a disturbing amount of feline saliva, along with some ugly looking scrapes, visible just to the sides of Sol's jaws.

"That issss an undersssstatement, Living Cat."

Rhelia's use of my nickname caused some of the tension to leave my shoulders. As though her calling me something silly meant that maybe we weren't necessarily watching our mission completely unravel in front of us. After all, she was the only one who knew exactly what our mission was.

"So… dare I ask what kind of moron takes up Dragon Hunting?" I asked, glaring at Nethia in a way that I hoped conveyed my full disapproval.

"Thesssse two moronssss," Rhelia replied, ges-turing in a way that encompassed both Nethia and Torrence. To be fair, that gesture encompassed Sol as well, but I thought it was safe to assume that was just positioning, and not because Sol was secretly a dragon killer.

"That's a lie!" Nethia shouted, or tried to shout, from between Sol's jaws. "The Dragon Hunters were never more than a myth," she said, with less force, thus sparing herself more scrapes from Sol's teeth.

"You rendered me unconsciousss assss ssssoon assss Torrencsssse told you I wassss inquiring about Dragon Huntersss," Rhelia countered. "And your magic may not be assss sssstrong assss you think it issss, becausssse I heard you asssssking Torrencsssse why he revealed the truth to me even assss I wassss losssssing conssssciousssssnessss."

"Ugh, you can turn off the accent, dragonling, it tires me," Nethia grumbled from the floor.

"All the more reasssson to keep ussssing it, then."

"You can turn off the accent?" I asked, completely derailed from the more important topics at hand.

Rhelia just leveled a gaze at me that made it clear we were not talking about this right now.

"I believe we owe you an explanation," Torrence said, finally breaking the silence he'd kept since Sol had first pounced on Nethia.

"No shit," I replied, turning my gaze from Rhelia to him. "Better get started. I don't know how long Sol can hold her jaws open like that."

Sol growled and flicked her tail. I wasn't sure if she was agreeing with me, or objecting to the insult to her stamina. Either way, Torrence seemed to take it as his cue to get started.

"I think we would all be more comfortable in the living room," he hazarded, but Sol growled again at the suggestion, so he began talking even as Nethia whispered, "Torrence, don't."

"Nethia and I were both members of the elite Dragon Hunters. We each have our reasons for not wanting anyone to know of our past, not least of which is that we all took oaths of secrecy when the Dragon Hunters disbanded. Just talking to you now may render our lives forfeit, but the alternative is taking your lives, and that is something I will not do. Though you should know—what we tell you now may make you targets for whatever members of the Dragon Hunters remain."

Rhelia and I exchanged a glance with Seamus, and Sol flicked her tail from her place atop Nethia.

"Well, they can get in line," I sighed. I mean, it wasn't like it would matter, if we couldn't stop Rebecca Dryer from blowing up the entire world.

I looked at Rhelia again. "You think it likely they can help us?"

Rhelia shrugged, but her face was as hard as the stone her skin resembled.

"Unfortunately, I cannot think of anyone better suited to help find a missing cadre of dragons than those who used to make such their livelihood. It is why I came here. Though I admit that I did not expect to find out that Torrence and Nethia were Dragon Hunters themselves, I was merely hoping they could point me in the right direction."

I nodded, and worked very hard to swallow my comment about Rhelia's sibilant accent disappearing.

Torrence looked between us and then down to Nethia again.

"Soledad, if I can extract an oath from her not to harm you or your friends, will you release Nethia?" he asked.

Sol's tail flicked, in what I took to be an affirmative, and Torrence must have taken it as one too.

"Nethia, will you swear on your blood and mine not to harm these four individuals?"

Nethia glared at Torrence with such vehemence that I half expected him to burst into flames.

"Or do I need to bind you here and take them to my own apartments so that you cannot interfere?" he continued.

Nethia sighed, and then nodded. I wondered what "binding" actually meant, if it was bad enough to make Nethia concede, but at least my question about living arrangements had finally been answered.

"Your word, Nethia," Torrence prompted.

"I give you my word, Torrence."

Torrence just glared at Nethia for a long mo-ment, then she took a deep breath and tried again.

"By your blood and mine, I give my oath that I will not harm Rhelia Wyvern, Soledad Sierra Oscura, Seamus Hunter, or Victoria Adelaide Marmot."

I felt a warm buzz in the air, while a smell like a desert thunderstorm permeated the room before fading suddenly.

In a blink, Sol was standing in front of us wearing a tight fitting pair of jeans and a soft cotton shirt. She looked down at herself and smiled.

"You're so useful, Gatita."

I smiled in return.

"I don't even try."

Rhelia looked between the two of us with some-thing like exasperation before turning to the green-skinned elf now cradling her neck, and the poker-faced tauren standing next to her. If she'd been in her dragon form, I would have expected the two of them to be cinders in another heartbeat, but instead of fire, she seared them with words.

"Now that Soledad is no longer about to kill you, we have no more time for idle chatter. You will help us, or we will reveal your past to the Unterberg council as well as the Elder Dragons. I don't have to remind you what that will do to your lives as you know them. You will lead us to the missing drag-ons right now, or you will die horribly by the hands of those who owe you justice."

THE ROOM THAT we stood in was dimly lit and heavily warded—at least, that's what I assumed was making it feel like a contained thunderstorm was right on top of our heads even though the circular space was entirely indoors, and not large enough to contain any actual weather events. That didn't stop the air from smelling like salt and ozone.

As I took in the flickering torches that lit the dark stone walls, I mused at how my actual magical knowledge was severely limited, but the fact that I'd read a lot of fantasy books and played a fair few role playing games somehow had trained my brain to interpret the feeling as indicating the presence of wards. I'd made a few gut decisions based on my fictional expertise in the last few weeks, and so far they'd all paid off. So much so that I was starting think that all of the nights I'd stayed up playing WoW or reading fantasy books instead of doing homework weren't the waste I had originally suspected them of being.

Anyway, aside from a giant salt circle etched out around the room, encompassing all of us standing within it, and the intense non-weather-related pressure that filled the space, this room could have easily been someone's sunroom. That is, it could have if any of the walls had been windows instead of heavy-looking, unpolished black marble. As it was, it felt more like a tomb.

Five of us stood on the points of a star while Nethia stood in the center of the whole thing. Rhelia stood at the top point, facing the center, and I stood to her right, while Sol stood to her left and Seamus stood to my right, with Torrence standing to his left on the final point of the star. It was extremely tempting to ask Sol to switch to her panther form so I could start making Sabrina jokes, but I restrained myself. Barely.

The urge to break the tension that had been mounting since we'd left Nethia's apartment in Unterberg was strong, bad jokes aside. After Rhelia had made it clear that Nethia and Torrence had no choice but to help us, Nethia had said little beyond explaining that if we wanted their help she would need to conduct a blood ritual (whatever that meant) in whichever realm we suspected the missing weredragons were being held. Which had meant a really awkward trip through the shadowed streets of Unterberg as we made our way to a seam that led to Earth, and then another stomach-churning teleport thanks to Torrence. This time, Seamus threw up. Sol probably had nothing left, and I had decided that I was just going to accept that multiple "me"s needed to make it through the trip and try to relax into it. Weirdly, that seemed to have worked, and I didn't feel nearly as sick this time as I had the trip before. I didn't bother to question why my own method of shifting through time and space didn't seem to make anyone sick, but filed it away to ponder another day.

Meanwhile, once we'd all finished being ill, or barely ill, or barely not ill, depending on who we were talking about, Nethia led us deeper and deeper into what appeared to be a subterranean lair, judging by the earthy smell, the lack of natural light, and the stagnant air that filled the passageways. Torrence had teleported us directly in-side the wherever we were, so we had no points of reference for where we might be in the world, which I guessed was on purpose.

Certainly, if I'd had Rhelia glaring at me with the degree of hatred she was leveling at Torrence and Nethia right now, I wouldn't want her to be able to find me later either.

"So, if you despise Dragon Hunters so much, why are we here?" I had whispered to her, as we'd all filed down a long earthen corridor behind Nethia and Torrence.

"These people slaughtered my people in droves, for centuries, allegedly in service to MOME's crusade against us, but in reality simply for the coin they were paid. They were mercenaries who took hundreds of missions against any creature too difficult for MOME's own elite squads, but they specialized in destroying us at any cost. I would as soon wipe them from the face of the realms as work with them."

I stared at Rhelia, wondering if she even realized that she hadn't answered my question, or that she was still speaking without her sibilant accent.

Then she turned to me and sighed.

"But there will be no realms left, if we do not find my brethren quickly. We have used every trick that we can think of, and none have worked. My people like to pretend that the Dragon Hunters are as much a myth as most believe them to be. It is better for us if no one believes they exist, but we know better. They found us, unerringly, whenever we wandered outside of our own realm during the Dragon Genocide. If anyone can find Siara and the others, the Dragon Hunters can."

After a moment of silence, I finally asked a question—the question that was ringing loudest in my brain.

"Ok. I have a feeling this was mentioned in my dragon orientation, but… what was the Dragon Genocide, exactly?"

Rhelia stopped to stare at me for a moment be-fore resuming her stride and pulling me along with her through the stone corridor.

"It was MOME's attempt to kill us all. They claimed it was because we were too dangerous, too difficult to hide from the non-magical humans. But really, it was just that they were frightened of us."

"So they tried to wipe you all out? If they were afraid of you, why would they do something likely to start a war with you?"

"That was precisely it. They could not risk a war with us. We are too powerful for a full-scale assault. Instead they sent assassins after us, and only when we left the safety of our own realm. We did not know who was re-sponsible, at first. We were not even sure the attacks were connected, for a long time.

"But later, centuries after it began, we captured some MOME operatives who knew what was going on, and discovered the truth. The cowards never even came after us themselves, merely spread anti-dragon propaganda— attempting to set the rest of the magical world against us—and then sent Dragon Hunters after us whenever we stood in any realm but our own."

The way her mouth had formed the words "Dragon Hunters" made it look like she was about to be ill, but she clearly held a grudging respect for their ability to track down dragons. And I had to agree with the reasoning that had brought us here. We were out of time and options. If there was a shortcut to finding Siara, we had to take it, even if it was risky as hell and involved a centuries-old enemy.

Which is why we had all blithely followed two people we barely knew into the bowels of Gwen-knew-where, so that we could trust one of them with something called a blood ritual that was supposed to tell us exactly where the weredragons that shared Rhelia's blood were being held.

From the looks on everyone's faces when Nethia had said there would be a blood ritual, that shit was a big magical no-no. No one had explained why yet, so I just filed it away with the three thousand and one other things I didn't understand, but would have to ask about later when we weren't fighting the clock.

And here we were.

I looked around the circle again, and vaguely wondered what we would have done if Seamus hadn't been here. Did we have to have a person on each of the five points of the star, along with some-one in the middle, or could Nethia have completed the spell from one of the points? Did any of us need to be there besides Nethia and Rhelia? Or would this whole thing be impossible if Seamus hadn't shown up? I fought off the shudder that precognition triggered in me, because Seamus couldn't help seeing the future, and everything he'd told me about it so far made me think he hated it.

When I heard the sound of metal singing through air, my head whipped up just in time to see Seamus leap in front of a blade that had clearly been heading directly for Torrence. I almost screamed, as I thought it had hit Seamus in the center of his chest, but he'd leapt with his arms crossed in front of him, and I was suddenly, desperately glad for his abilities as a seer. Nethia was already pinned under the giant panther that was Soledad, and Rhelia had drawn two daggers from somewhere, placing one at Nethia's throat, somewhat redundantly. I didn't really notice how any of that had happened, be-cause my body was too busy moving me to Seamus' side.

The dagger that Nethia had thrown had impaled his forearm, and it looked like it had pinned it to his chest, but not deeply enough to pierce any vital organs, I thought.

"Rhelia, we're going to need you over here," I said, noting the unnatural pallor of Seamus' face. It was a serious wound no matter what, but I didn't like the sweat that was beading on his forehead already.

There were sounds of movement behind me, but I couldn't tell what was going on, and didn't turn to find out.

"Seamus?" I asked, as his eyes started to close. "Seamus!"

"Allow me to help, Victoria," said Torrence.

"Why would I trust you to help? Your friend just tried to kill him!"

"She was trying to kill me, I believe."

Right. Seamus had been jumping in front of Torrence to save his life. Why would he do that?

"Seamus? Why?" I asked, not letting him go.

"I have some healing ability, Victoria, and I believe Nethia's daggers are poisoned. Seconds matter."

"Rhelia!" I shouted. Rhelia was supposed to be one of the best healers in all the realms, and I would be damned if I let a Dragon Hunter "heal" my friend/boyfriend, whatever Seamus was.

There were more sounds behind me, grunts and thuds, and metal scraping stone.

"Living Cat, let the cow heal him. He is bound by blood," she called, her voice not getting any closer.

I looked at Seamus' face, tight with pain, and then leveled my gaze at Torrence, who, I was surprised to see, was looking at Seamus with tears in his eyes.

"If he dies, Torrence, I swear to everything that I hold dear, I will make you wish it had been you instead," I hissed, before letting go of Seamus gently and allowing Torrence to collect him in his arms from his place on the floor behind him.

"Believe me, Victoria, I already wish that it had been."

LUCKILY, TORRENCE WAS not trying to kill Seamus. Indeed, in a few short minutes, Seamus was no longer sweating, overly pale, or bleeding. By then Rhelia was approaching and I finally looked over at what she and Sol had been up to, which apparently was trussing Nethia up like a holiday hog, even though she appeared to be unconscious.

"Is she dead?" I asked, glancing at her still form again.

"I am not certain," said Rhelia. "But we did not kill her, if that is what you are asking."

I looked at Rhelia, then over to Sol, who was also coming over to check on Seamus.

I pulled farther away to make space for Rhelia. I hoped she would confer with Torrence about Seamus' healing.

"How can you not be sure if she's dead?" I asked Sol, since Rhelia was busy.

Sol looked over at Nethia and frowned.

"I don't know. Before I could reach her she collapsed and her eyes rolled into the back of her head. I think she still has a pulse, but… it's not strong."

To my surprise, it was Torrence who spoke next. He stood up from where he'd been tending Seamus, leaving him in Rhelia's care to come stand beside us and look at the green-skinned woman who'd just tried to kill him.

"It is the oath," he said, after a moment. "She was likely trying to kill me so that she would be free of it. She swore on both of our blood, and the only way to be free of an oath like that is for one of us to die. However, when Seamus jumped in front of the blade, she broke her word instead, so the blood oath took her. There may not be anything left of her now."

"Fuck," I muttered, looking at Nethia again. "What about the spell she was going to cast?"

Torrence took a deep breath.

"I can cast it, though it will not be as strong."

"What does that mean?" I asked.

"It should serve us well enough, but it won't last very long or be portable. If Nethia had cast it, we could have tied it to an object, a weapon, a jewel, whatever you like, and it could have led any of you on your search. The version I know… well, I cannot tie it to anything but myself. I'm afraid you'll be stuck with me until you find your weredragons."

"Considering the fact that we have less than 40 hours to find them, I think I can live with that."

I looked over to Rhelia, assuming that she was going to be less than pleased at this turn of events, but she was too caught up in whatever she was doing to Seamus to have noticed. Either that, or she didn't care.

Not having anything else to do, I looked around the room, and my eyes inevitably fell to where Nethia lay at Sol's feet once more.

"Not that I'm objecting or anything, but… if Nethia is as good as dead, why did you bother to truss her up like that?" I asked.

I almost jumped when Rhelia's ice-cold voice replied, "So that she can pay for her crimes against the Dragon Realm."

When I turned to look at her, she was standing, supporting a groggy but mostly-conscious Seamus, and faint wisps of smoke were twining up from her mouth.

UNFORTUNATELY, RHELIA'S RAGE was go-ing to have to wait a hot minute, because we had to start the whole damned spell-casting thing over again.

"What does the pentagram actually do?" I asked, as we scattered salt in the same pattern on the black marble floor that it had formed just before Nethia caused a scene by trying to kill people.

There was a moment of silence before I looked pointedly at Torrence and he answered.

"Sorry, I did not think you were asking me. I am not generally the magic casting expert in any given crowd. I forgot that you are all shifters. As you've no doubt guessed, a pentagram is not required for mages to access their magic."

I snorted at that, since, yeah… not a single person of the magical persuasion who had tried to kill me in the past few weeks had bothered to draw any-thing on the ground in salt first.

"But," continued Torrence patiently, "the magic that Dragon Hunters use for tracking is… despised. It is also easily noticed, and tracked, if it is cast out in the open. Hence, we are here in a heavily warded chamber, and cast-ing it in the middle of a pentagram. Blood magic and demon summoning are the primary reasons you would use a pentagram. Otherwise, they can help if you are afraid of harming those around you with unwieldy magic. They act as containment for spell work."

"So, beginners, blood mages, and warlocks, got it."

Torrence looked up from where he was pouring salt onto the floor and raised a bovine brow.

"Indeed, that sums it up nicely."

"Warlocks?" asked Seamus from where he was leaning up against the wall.

"Anyone who summons demons for magical pur-poses," Sol clarified.

"Why else would someone summon a demon?" Seamus asked.

"Well, now that I've met Azrael, I could think of a couple reasons," I muttered.

Sol chuckled, and Seamus' cheeks reddened.

"For anyone with their own dark matter, sex with a succubus would still qualify as magical purposes. It amplifies power," Torrence explained. "Now, if a non-magical person summoned a demon in order to have sex, that might qualify as non-magical purposes."

"How would a non-magical person summon a demon?" Seamus and I asked, at the same time.

"You only need a demon's name to summon them," Torrence replied mildly, as he finished the circle on the floor. "Keeping the demon from killing you for interrupting its nap, on the other hand, might require a fair amount of magic. Succubi are often the exception to that rule, if you're polite in your requests, since they benefit from being invited to feed."

Then Torrence took a deep breath and turned towards Rhelia, who had been staring broodingly at Nethia's unconscious form, where it lay on the floor outside of our newly recast circle.

"I'm ready to begin, if you are," he said.

Rhelia shook her head, as if clearing her thoughts, and turned towards Torrence. Her golden eyes still burned with something like hatred, but whether it was for Nethia, for Torrence, or for what she was about to do, I wasn't sure. Perhaps all of the above.

"Assss ready assss I'll ever be."

I wondered what it meant that her sibilant accent was back.

"I will do my best to make it painless," Torrence said, stretching out his fur-covered, but otherwise human-looking hand.

"You know it issss not the pain that botherssss me, Hunter," she replied.

The way she said "Hunter" made it sound like the basest insult, but Torrence didn't even flinch. I was having a very difficult time sorting out what made him tick.

As he took Rhelia's hand. though, I heard him offer the barest explanation.

"I have not performed this ritual for centuries. I abandoned my position in the Hunters when I finally realized that, despite all of MOME's propaganda, your people were as innocent as any other, and more so than many. It does not excuse what I've done, and I will willingly go with you to face the punishment of the Dragon Elders once we have found those you seek, but I wish you to know that I do not lightly take on the burden of blood magic once more."

And then he slashed open her palm with a dagger.

Rhelia had clearly been expecting it, even if I hadn't, and barely winced at the pain.

To my surprise, she also did not stab him repeatedly or take on her dragon form and incinerate his head, which was kind of what her facial expressions had been telegraphing ever since I'd woken her up on Nethia's couch.

Before I could even come up with something to say (sorry, you're bleeding, do you need a bandage or anything?) Torrence cut an identical slash into his own palm. Then, slightly more hygienically than I'd expected, given how this whole thing had started, he gently tipped Rhelia's palm until the blood that had been pooling there ran into the open wound in his hand.

Torrence grimaced, and Rhelia's eyes flared in the low light of the stone room.

"If you usssse thissss for any purpossssse but the one we've requesssssted, I will end you sssso painfully you will wish you had never exissssted."

Torrence nodded, but said nothing, his eyes drifting shut in apparent effort and concentration.

The rest of us just stood there awkwardly for a few minutes, while he did his secret blood magic thing.

Is this going to take a while? I asked Rhelia eventually.

Did you have ssssomewhere better to be, Living Cat?

Nope. Just have to pee.

Rhelia's eyes flashed again, but this time I thought it was with contained amusement. Good, that's what I'd been hoping for.

I have never sssseen a blood ritual performed before. It issss a forbidden art in both the dragon realm and the human one.

Is that just because it's super creepy, or…?

It issss consssssidered a violation. From my undersssssstanding it requiresssss the casssster to project their own dark matter into the blood of another. Thisssss issss almosssst alwaysssss againssssst the other'ssss will.

And how does that help us?

It can be usssed to track people. I share ssssome of my blood with Ssssi-ara, and thussss my blood, in the right handssss, can be ussssed to find her. It issss how the Dragon Hunterssss tracked ussss and alsssso how they bound ussss. It issss the only way they were ever able to defeat ussss. Or ssssso the ssssstoriessss sssssay.

Let me guess, the dragons did whatever they could to make sure those stories didn't get around.

We had little to do that the Dragon Hunterssss themsssselvessss did not do for ussss. They had cornered the market, if you will.

The thought of Torrence and his allies using the dragons' own blood against them made my stomach turn. Especially when I considered that if I'd been born a few hundred years earlier I certainly would have made the list of acceptable targets. The thought hit me a little bit harder than it should have. I still hadn't fully wrapped my brain around the idea of being a dragon.

Finally, Torrence's eyes opened, and his hand glowed a dull red.

"I believe this will work. As I said, it would be much stronger if Nethia had cast it—she was our expert blood mage—but this will suffice to let me lead you, as long as we are quick. I am sorry that I could not attach it to some sort of talisman, and thus free you of the burden of my company."

Rhelia rolled her eyes, and the rest of us just stared at each other in be-wilderment.

"I'm hungry," Seamus said from the floor. "Is anyone else hungry?"

~~~

We arrived in the Dragon Realm a few moments later.

In a display that seemed to fit no one's mood, the moon was full and shin-ing in a cloudless, star-filled sky, as we stepped out into the same valley where we'd arrived the very first time Rhelia had brought us here. I took a deep breath, filled with the scent of earth and wildflowers, and then almost choked on my own saliva when I saw Torrence basically prance through the aforementioned wildflowers and then fling himself down on the ground to stare at the sky.

Ok. Maybe the clear sky and moonlight fit someone's mood.

Rhelia was looking at the bull-man as if he had two bovine heads instead
~~~

of one, and I almost lost my shit at her expression.

"I think he likes flowers," I offered.

Rhelia turned her baffled gaze to me, then rubbed her eyes.

"Can you pleasssse take Nethia to your brother to deal with, and collect whoever issss available to help usss?" she asked. "We do not have time for all of usss to walk there, and you should ssssave your shiftssss with multiple people for when it countsss."

"Sure," I said, grabbing the still-unconscious Nethia by the arm, and picturing Rhelia's home in the small main drag that constituted the weredragon portion of the Dragon Realm. "Does Trev know a good dungeon to throw her in?"

Rhelia's smile was cold, and didn't reach her eyes.

"More or lessss."

I decided I didn't really want to know, so I left Rhelia, Seamus, and Sol to keep Torrence in line. Or in flowers. Whatevs.

We'd debated rendering Torrence unconscious for the duration of our visit to the Dragon Realm, and Torrence hadn't objected, but he'd admitted that he couldn't be sure that the spell would hold up if we had to knock him out and revive him. He seemed to sympathize completely with Rhelia's reluctance to take a known Dragon Hunter into the Dragon Realm—one that she wasn't planning to throw into prison immediately, that is, she'd been more than happy to bring Nethia along—but we couldn't figure out any way to avoid bringing Torrence along, awake, without devoting way too much time and energy to what was likely to just be a quick respite on our way to a very difficult rescue mission. We had to come to the Dragon Realm to drop off Nethia, debrief Trev, and see if we could recruit a few more people for the next part of our plan. Not knowing how much MOME knew about our movements, and not being sure when they were planning their own attack against the non-magical world, we couldn't afford to waste time keeping Torrence away from the Dragon Realm right now. I needed to minimize my shifting so I would have enough energy for our rescue operation, and any other iteration of the plan split the group in too many ways to make sense. In other words, we were stuck with him. But that didn't mean that Rhelia wanted to drag him into the middle of the residential portion of the Dragon Realm. So, we'd decided the most efficient thing for conserving my energy and keeping Torrence as much in the dark as possible was for me to do in-world shifts only, to avoid shifting between realms, and to take as few people with me as possible for each shift. Hence why I was leaving everyone in this field of wildflowers out of sight of town, while I took Nethia off to be delivered to justice.

Nethia, or her barely living body, and I arrived directly in front of the door to Rhelia's office, skipping past trivialities like front doors and the rest of the house, and I knocked before pushing it open to find Trevor staring intently at one of his two enormous monitors (not to be confused with Rhelia's even larger set of monitors, which took up the other half leg of the giant L desk covering half the walls), scanning through lines of code.

"Vic!" he said, sounding surprised to see me, even though I was pretty sure Rhelia had been communicating with him telepathically as soon as we'd hit Dragon Realm soil. I hadn't tried to get in touch because I'd been too wary of a cold reception.

"Hey," I said, wrapping him in a hug when he stood up to greet me. "I'm playing Hermes today. You've won a mostly dead Dragon Hunter, and a request for all the backup you can spare for a covert rescue operation."

Trev hugged me back with enough enthusiasm to erase some of the distance I'd felt between us in the past 48 hours, and then he looked at Nethia behind me (I'd left her in the doorway) and sighed.

"I'll have the Dragon Elders come collect her. Best if we don't let General Aira know she's here just yet," he said.

I didn't particularly want to know what they were going to do with her, or why General Aira should be kept in the dark, so I didn't ask. I just reminded myself that she'd tried to kill Torrence, almost killed Seamus instead, and had likely been trying to take out Torrence in order to kill ALL of us, so… whatever they were going to do with her was fine with me.

"And my backup?" I asked.

"We don't have much we can spare from the twelve reconnaissance ops that General Aira is running. She's not willing to sit around and wait while we find Siara and Emil. Not to mention, she's unwilling to send any more big booms into MOME territory."

I raised an eyebrow for a moment, then my brain caught up.

"Right. No dragons or weredragons for this mission."

Trev nodded.

"In fact, Rhelia is probably going to be pissed at me, but…"

Trev's voice faded, and I wondered if he didn't want me to know that he was about to tell Rhelia she couldn't go, even though that had been obvious as soon as he'd mentioned the no weredragon thing. I assumed the only reason I was allowed to go was that I was just a baby weredragon, and a baby everything else, and… well, we needed my emergency escape powers. I was just about to ask Trev if the cat had his tongue, when that train of thought was derailed entirely by the sound of feathers brushing wood.

"Hullo, Luv," said a familiar voice behind me.

I turned to see a dark figure with silver wings blocking out most of the door frame, just as Trev said, "I suppose I can spare Azrael, though."

"WHAT IS SHE doing here?" Torrence asked, in a voice somewhere between turned on and put out. He was no longer lying in the meadow flowers gazing at the night sky. Instead he was standing in the meadow flowers, swaying gently, as though he were a flower himself and the wind had taken him. Somehow, he'd found time to make a crown of daisies and drape it between his horns in the few minutes I'd been gone.

I tried staring into the moon to keep myself from laughing unnecessarily. I really didn't want to discourage anyone embracing nature, and it was honestly awesome that a giant bull-person like Torrence was super into flowers, but some visuals are just too striking to do anything but conjure mirth.

"Azrael was invited, because Azrael is part of our strike team," I replied, doing my best to gesture towards the succubus without looking directly at them again. Though it might have been an excellent way to avoid laughing at Torrence, I wasn't in the mood to be distracted by my own hormones, and Azrael was nothing if not distracting, when they weren't a demon squirrel.

Seamus, Sol, Torrence, and even Rhelia all took a moment to stare at Az, which made me work all the harder not to. Trevor stepped out from behind the succubus and made his way to Rhelia to wrap his arms around her, a gesture she returned in full as soon as she pulled her eyes away from Az. It didn't seem possessive at all; Trev had spent the whole day worried about her, and it showed.

"Please try to focus, people," I said, wanting to shove Azrael behind me or something. Not that it would have helped. They were a foot taller than I was. Maybe if I'd had a blanket or something, I could have done something effective, but as it was we were just going to have to push on through.

"Not even going to look at me, Vic?" Azrael's voice asked from behind my neck, apparently having closed the distance between us while I wasn't looking.

"You give me a headache," I replied, looking resolutely forward.

"I can fix that," Azrael said, running their breath along my shoulder in a way that left little confusion about how they would fix it.

"Yeah, maybe, but we don't have time for that, and I don't trust you not to steal my soul."

"Ugh, so tetchy."

"What do you mean she gives you a headache?" Torrence asked, seeming genuinely curious.

I normally would have insisted it was none of his damned business, but since I wanted to focus on anything other than the breath running over my shoulder, I threw a light elbow behind me and stepped forward without looking back, taking no small amount of pleasure in Az's muttered "ow, not nice."

"Azrael gives me a headache because I can see both of their forms at the same time, unless we're surrounded by people who all find the same form attractive."

"Interesting," said Torrence, looking me up and down in a way that made me wonder what assumptions he'd made about me, and how he was rearranging them.

I shook my head, reminding myself that I didn't really care what the giant tauren thought of my sexual orientation, and hoping to get us all back on target. Azrael had a way of making everyone in the immediate area unnaturally horny and that was actually the larger portion of why I wasn't looking at them.

It was true that it gave me a bit of a headache to see a six foot tall, gorgeous man with giant silver wings superimposed on top of a six foot tall gorgeous woman with giant silver wings, both of whom were largely naked and who moved at exactly the same time and said the same things. But more than that, I found both of them incredibly hot, and it was distracting, obnoxious, and felt really awkward because part of my brain still recognized Azrael as a red-skinned, largely furless, demon-squirrel thing.

"So, about this mission," I tried to get everyone's attention, which had once more wandered back to Azrael. Trev was staring too now, his pupils wider than normal and his hand clenching Rhelia's even tighter than before.

"Damn it, Az, can't you put on more clothes or something!?"

"She's wearing a suit," Seamus said, still sound-ing awed.

"Really?" I almost turned around to check, but stopped myself just in time.

"Didn't want to be a distraction," Az said.

"Right. Thanks, I guess. So, then why…"

"Well, I'm still me, Luv. Can't turn that off."

I chuckled. "Not on this planet."

I felt fingers pinch my side, hard, and I shot another elbow behind me, this time without hold-ing back at all, but the elbow connected with nothing but air and then, suddenly, Azrael was standing directly in front of me. Both of them.

The pinstripe suit that both forms were wearing just made the headache worse. The two outlines of the feminine and masculine atop each other were extra dizzying with the added barcode of the stripes.

"Can you just choose one?" I asked.

"Can you?" they replied.

"Touché."

I blinked and held the sides of my head.

"Seriously, does no one else have to put up with this?" I muttered.

Rhelia chuckled. "Once you said that you could see both, I started seeing the female form, but for me it flips all the way from one to the other."

I decided to close my eyes.

Azrael sighed dramatically.

"Alright, I will spare you. Vic, give Seamus a kiss."

I tried to glare at them with my eyes closed.

"I promise it'll help," Azrael said.

I opened my eyes and turned towards Seamus, who looked perfectly happy to oblige, and even did me the favor of nodding visibly, so I didn't have to ask.

Not wanting to drag this out any longer, I stepped over to Seamus, wrapped my arms around his waist and planted a kiss on his mouth. It was quick, and fairly chaste, since we were surrounded by people and about to head out on a potentially lethal rescue mission, but it was enough to wake up the mating bond within me and get my blood going. I stepped back quickly, before the mating bond could get too excited about anything, and looked around the field.

My eyes were instantly drawn to Azrael, who was now very decidedly a man wearing a pinstriped suit with no wings, silver or otherwise, in sight.

"Weird. You did mention once that my attraction varying could change how I saw you, but I didn't really believe you."

Azrael shrugged.

"I meant what I said. If you ever need to stop seeing double, try pushing your attraction more to one side or the other."

"But what if no one else is around?" I asked, before I could stop and think.

"Well, if no one is around, I'd prefer you were focused on me, Luv," Azrael said, with a grin that did strange things to my insides.

"If you weren't so damned good at killing vampires, you would be off the team right now."

"Oh, is that why the succubus is here?" Torrence said. "I had wondered."

"Doesn't everyone know that succubi are renowned vampire hunters?" I asked, looking from Sol to Rhelia, to Seamus, to Trev, to Torrence.

Judging by the blank stares I was getting, I was gonna have to go with "no."

"Huh, I just assumed that would be common knowledge. I mean, since when do I know anything about this world that you guys don't?" I shook my head. "Ok. So, we have our vampire take-out 'squad,' we have our intel, we have our hackers, we have our muscle and we have…"

"Our bait?" Seamus suggested, with a small frown.

"I was going to say decoy, but yeah. We have our bait."

In truth, the lines of our team weren't nearly that clear cut. Except for Seamus—he really was our bait.

"Now, can we please talk about the freaking plan? We're down to just over 36 hours before Rebecca Dryer makes good on her threat."

Everyone nodded and I took a deep breath, about to go over the details that Rhelia, Sol, Seamus, and I had sketched out as we'd made our way out of Nethia's underground spellcasting lair.

"Perhaps I can be of some use?" asked a familiar voice that had me spinning on my heel before I could even begin to speak. Of course she arrived from an angle that left her backlit by the sun—it wouldn't be dramatic enough otherwise—but eventually I made out a curvy silhouette, which was making its way closer and closer to our little posse.

"Hey Gwen," I said, sighing as the redheaded goddess of fortune came into full view. "I have a feeling you could be useful, yeah."

"BECAUSE WE CAN'T risk them using you as a bomb," Trev said for what seemed like perhaps the 20th time.

I stared at the blue sky, took a deep breath of sun-warmed flowers, and wished that I'd walked off with the rest of the group when this argument had started. For some damned reason I'd wanted to show solidarity with my so-recently-estranged brother. Now I was wishing I'd just let him dig his own grave.

"They were more than happy to use you as one, Trevor! They could use any of us!" Rhelia's sibilant accent had dropped away for this argument, and I couldn't tell if that was because she was angry, or just impatient and the extra sibilance took too long. Maybe a bit of both.

"But dragons make the biggest bang," Trev replied. "Rhelia, we've been over this. MOME must have wanted to start small, or maybe Dryer was just in a hurry to get rid of me because of how much I know about MOME's inner workings, but you are made of much more dark matter than I am. You know that."

"And what of your sister? Victoria is a dragon and more, Trevor. How can you risk her becoming a weapon if you cannot risk me?"

"Vic has an emergency escape method that none of the rest of us do. She's probably the least likely to be captured of all of us," Trev said. His voice sounded firm, but I could tell Rhelia was wearing him down. "Vic, help me out here."

I stared at him for a moment, though my gaze had nothing on Rhelia's glare.

"Why on Earth, or any realm, would I help you keep a grown-assed woman from going on a mission she wants to be on? Especially when that woman spends half her time as a walking, flying, fire-breathing tank?"

"Because they could try to use her to destroy everyone?"

"How is that different from what they could do with any of us?" I asked.

"It's damage control," Trev insisted. "It's trying to make sure that the fewest people—"

"It's you being overprotective because you thought she was dead three days ago," I said, not willing to listen to the excuses anymore.

Rhelia actually laughed as all the fight went out of Trev in that moment, and then she was hugging him, and he was crying a bit, and then I thought I heard kissing, and that was lovely, but I didn't need to watch it, so I headed over to the huddle of all the sensible people who'd left that argument as soon as it started.

"You finally realized there was no way to win there?" Sol asked, as I wandered over to the group. Azrael and Gwen stood facing me already, but Sol and Seamus had both turned to see me as I approached.

I sighed.

"My brother probably hates me now," I muttered.

"Ah, so you stood for the side of reason?" Azrael asked.

"If Rhelia gets so much as a scratch on this mission, Trev's gonna blame me, personally."

"Ha! Only if he wants Rhelia to take his head off," Sol chuckled. "I can understand the reaction based on recent events, but if your brother is always that protective, Rhelia is going to find someone else to be her partner, 'mate' or no."

I sighed.

"I don't think he's that much of an idiot, but I haven't spent that much time with him in the last decade, so…" I shrugged.

Seamus tentatively wrapped one arm around my shoulders, and I leaned into him and wrapped my arms around his waist to let him know the touch was welcome.

"Don't ever let me be that much of an ass, ok?" I pleaded.

"You mean like earlier today when you tried to tell me I should go home?" Seamus asked.

I was reassured by the fact that he didn't let go of me, but it was a painful reminder of my own crappy reaction earlier.

"I'm sorry about that. I get nervous sometimes, about how little training you've had in combat. That's no excuse, though. You're as much of an adult as I am, and you can put yourself at risk as you see fit. Plus I need to remember that you have a much better idea of what risks lie ahead than most people." I almost kicked myself for that last part, not knowing how much of his abilities Seamus wanted the rest of our group to know about.

Seamus ignored the reference to his abilities as a seer, though, and kissed the top of my head in what would have been a patronizing way if I hadn't so richly deserved it.

"Lucky for you I was raised by wolves and have been conditioned to see protectiveness in all family and friends as a sign of affection."

I laughed then, thinking of all the wolves I'd known in my summers volunteering at the wildlife rescue. Seamus was spot on, they were all inherently protective of their pack.

A cough sounded behind us, causing half of us to turn around and the other half to look up. Seamus and I both turned at the same time, dropping our hold on one another, because the cough was directly behind us.

"I am going to sssstay behind and ssssift through ssssecurity feedssss from here, assss well assss run some additional code that might be helpful later," Rhelia said calmly, her arm wrapped around Trev's shoulders in almost the same way Seamus' had been wrapped around my own moments ago.

A few of us raised our eyebrows at that.

"And I am going to apologize profusely for being an overprotective git, and then be the one to patch Rhelia into the computers at MOME in order to let her run everything from her apartment on Earth," Trev said, sounding more than a little sheepish.

"How is it that you are apologizing and also getting your way?" I asked, when no one else seemed inclined to question this.

To my satisfaction, it was Rhelia who answered.

"Becausssse, while I may be a better hacker, Trev issss more familiar with MOME'ssss protocolssss and he will be able to quickly inssssstall a proxsssy devicsssse that will allow me to monitor the necsssesssssary ssssecurity feedssss. And I am better equipped to ssssearch for two weredragonssss than he issss. In addition, Trev has promissssssed me that he will not interfere when I abssssolutely demolish MOME oncsssse we have gotten all of our people out."

I swallowed, because I didn't think Rhelia was joking, and I hadn't known that was on the "to-do" list for today.

"Do not worry, Living Cat. We have people behind MOME'ssss wallssss other than the prisonerssss you will resssscue now. Today issss not the day that MOME will burn."

I glanced at Seamus, saw him shudder, and wondered if he was just reacting to the violent glint in Rhelia's yellow eyes, or if he had seen something.

"We should go."

It was the first time Gwen had spoken since I'd walked over from Trev and Rhelia's argument, and I'd almost forgotten she was still here. I had half expected her to simply disappear while we were all distracted. It wouldn't have been the first time.

When we all looked at her expectantly, she just stared back for a moment.

"Oh fine. I suppose I can give you a lift," she muttered, before corralling us into a group hug and blinking us out of existence.

THE WHOLE THING about gods of serendipity is that they're really good for short cuts. Apparently, the way the tracking spell that Torrence had cast worked was that it more or less turned him into a walking compass—a compass for which magnetic north was always Siara. So, while our original plan had been to head to Earth via the seam in the dragon realm and then have me shift us in the general direction Torrence's compass pulled, Gwen showing up cut what might have been a longish game of Marco Polo down to two jumps. We first touched down in a nondescript alley in La Paz (blissfully devoid of human fluids, this time) with the idea that we should start with the last place we were certain MOME had held Siara and Emil. In addition, it was where Rhelia's Earth apartment was—a fact that had some of us raising eyebrows, since we hadn't known she'd had a place here until just before we'd left and Gwen asked us where we'd like to head first.

After Rhelia left us, a quick consult with Torrence and his Siara compass had us aiming NNW, and then in a single blink through space and time we were in front of a large, nondescript concrete building in downtown Phoenix, standing on a brightly lit piece of sidewalk that was still baking with the day's heat despite a darkened sky, the gathering clouds in the distance, and a wind that carried the scent of impending rain.

The good news was that I was fairly certain that we were standing in front of the same place where they'd held Seamus and me back when we were awaiting my sham of a trial, and that meant this wasn't just some random stop on the way to Siara and Emil, but rather was quite likely where they were being held. A quick look at Torrence con-firmed it. He nodded and pointed inside the building.

"They are inside and down, I believe," he con-firmed.

We'd done it. In a handful of hours we'd done what days of searching every bit of external MOME security footage couldn't do.

The bad news was, it was a mass of drab concrete with a giant parking lot beside it nestled in downtown Phoenix, a city that held over four million people. Meaning that if things went sideways, the very least that would happen was four million people going up in smoke (assuming we somehow avoided the whole "tearing a hole in time and space and imploding the universe" piece).

Luckily for me, our plan didn't leave me time to think about how terrifyingly wrong things could go.

Gwen added a few finishing touches to every-one's disguises—which she accomplished with a single wave of the hand that could just as easily have been a gesture of farewell, especially since she disappeared as soon as she finished the gesture—and then I was being dragged along just above the elbow, courtesy of a very stern-faced almost-Sol. Whatever Gwen had done made her look like a stranger, though she was a stranger who shared the same basic skin tone, hair type, and facial structure as Sol. She pulled Az along on her other side. We both did our best to move mechanically, imitating the way that Sol had described the motions of someone under a MOME arrest spell. Torrence, meanwhile, seemed to be doing his best to injure Seamus and Trevor as he dragged them by their collars into the building through the double set of glass doors that was so common for desert office entrances.

Watching him play the role of a violent enforcer who considered his four captives to be just so much shit under his boot was an education in acting. Either that, or he was totally going to kill us.

Torrence had slipped into the skin of a pissed off, unthinking muscle cop so well it was hard to believe he was actually the Unterberg council's lead intelligence officer. Trusting him made me more than a little nervous, but he'd had plenty of chances to kill us or let us die today, so I just had to hope he was actually on our side.

You'd think that after our last few MOME rescue initiatives, having Torrence and Sol pose as MOME officers wouldn't really be an option, but Sol had confirmed that more than one tauren already worked for the North American branch (bonus: she confirmed that tauren was the right word for what Torrence was) so he wouldn't look out of place despite being a large bull-person who looked like he could have just stepped out of a Greek myth. In addition, Trev had confirmed a few days prior that no major security protocols had changed in MOME's online database. Which meant that, while our Bolivian rescue ops might have caused a few word of mouth warnings for folks to keep an eye out for anyone strange, nothing had changed so much that two officers who looked familiar (thanks to Gwen's hastily applied illusions) bringing in a handful of nondescript law-breakers was going to attract undue attention, as long as we didn't stick around too long.

Not sticking around too long was going to be key.

And, yeah, ok, maybe Torrence was actually doing too good of a job of playing the asshole cop, or maybe Seamus was playing up the battered prisoner thing too much, because we'd only made it past the second security checkpoint—courtesy of some fake IDs Trev had cooked up for Sol and Torrence, and which Gwen had further modified—when an actual MOME security officer approached us. She was dressed in a grey pantsuit which, combined with her light skin and brown hair, made her completely unremarkable. I assumed she was a mage.

The expression on her face made it seem like one of us had stepped in dog crap on the way in, and only reinforced my guess that she was a mage. My brief experiences with MOME had taught me that mages in this line of work didn't think much of their shifter counterparts. Then again, maybe she just took issue with the man-bull who was dragging Seamus by the collar. Sol was holding my elbow instead, along with Az's. I tried to look at Az, but they had done something to themself to prevent anyone from more than glancing at them (it was the best way to keep them hidden in a place like this, because covering up the fact that they were a succubus was nigh impossible, no matter what kind of illusion one used), so I couldn't get a good look at their expression. Still, I didn't think they were too happy with the new scrutiny we were under either.

"Bullard, I'm going to need to talk to you for a minute," she said, addressing Torrence. I couldn't read his fake ID from here, but I doubt the mage could either. Apparently, Gwen had done a good enough job that this woman had mistaken him for some other tauren jerk, though.

"What, now?" Torrence asked, exuding the kind of disdain that spoke of either a personal history or a deep dislike of women in power. Torrence held firm to Seamus, shaking him angrily even as he spoke. But, at the same time, he pushed Trev towards me in a way that forced him to lightly jostle the grey suited mage. The glower she directed at Torrence intensified, but she didn't give Trev a second glance as Sol let go of Az's elbow to take Trev's instead.

Given my previous interactions with Torrence, his acrid tone was a bit of a shock, but apparently it was exactly the reaction that the grey-suited officer was expecting.

She nodded to Sol, dismissing her quickly, before rounding on Torrence.

Sol didn't hesitate. She turned on her heel and continued on down the hall with her three prisoners as if everything were perfectly normal.

"This is the third time this week that I've had to talk to you about the way you treat the people you're bringing in, Bullard. How am I supposed to…"

The security officer's voice faded out of hearing as Sol kept us moving down the hall.

Even so, I was deeply glad when Trev pulled us down a side hall leading to a closed, windowless black door. Trev swiped a keycard down the access panel next to the door and I had to restrain a shocked exclamation as I recognized the grey-suited mage in the photo ID attached to it. Trev had mentioned that the fake IDs wouldn't get us to the cameras he needed, he'd just never told us exactly how he'd planned to get ahold of a real one, only that he'd "handle it."

Probably a good thing. If I'd known that his plan had relied on mugging a real MOME agent, I might have objected.

For now my objections were put on hold, as, the moment the door swung open, we were faced with a small, dark room, full of security video feed—and vampires.

FORTUNATELY, WE HAD Azrael with us.

Before the two closest vampires could even react to our presence, Azrael swooped in and dealt with all seven of them. It was really quite something to see Az work. The succubus moved so fast that it barely registered as motion. From the looks of things, all Az needed to get the better of a vampire was to get one hand on their bare skin. When I'd asked them to explain to the group about their vampire fighting superpowers, they'd said that their succubus nature simply pulled all the vamp's stolen energy away, and then they collapsed like rag dolls. Apparently, vamps were so easily drained because the energy wasn't theirs to begin with.

"Are they dead?" I asked, even as Trev stepped over the limp vampires to get to whatever controls he needed to access. "'Cause they seem dead."

Az looked at me, hand on their chest as if hurt, and they must have dropped whatever spell they'd used to keep my gaze away, because I was able to look back at them.

"You asked me not to kill them," they said.

"Yeah, well. Not everyone does what I ask, you know."

"They are vampires, Vic. They technically were dead before we started. However, these ones will regain themselves in a few hours' time."

Trev had gotten to work as soon as the vamps were down, and he was already immersed in pulling apart a few control panels and messing with wires.

"We have to go," said Sol, pulling on my arm.

I hesitated. We were going to need to leave Trev here to run things while we made our way to the dungeon, so he could keep security off of our tails for as long as possible. I hated it.

Az touched my arm.

"I'll stay here with him," they said. "I am an excellent defense against more than just vampires."

I nodded. That hadn't been the original plan, but it sounded a hell of a lot better than leaving Trev here by himself. Especially now that I'd seen how heavily guarded MOME was leaving their security feeds. It no longer seemed likely that Trev wouldn't have someone else from MOME drop in on him while he was trying to tell us how to get to Siara and evade more security personnel.

So, we left Trev to set up whatever relay he needed for Rhelia to do her thing, along with Az to help keep MOME security off of his back.

Meanwhile, I continued on with Sol.

I still didn't like the fact that Trev was here, and that we were leaving him behind, but I'd be doing the same thing to him that he'd tried to do to Rhelia if I attempted to stop him. I still hated having him so close to MOME again after everything they'd done to him, all that they'd tried to do him, had wanted to do to him. It made me pretty ragey just thinking about it, but I pushed those thoughts aside and focused on looking like a frightened prisoner. It wasn't a big stretch, to be honest.

Even without the extra help from Torrence, getting into a MOME headquarters never seemed to be a problem for us. Getting out was usually the challenge, and this time I couldn't shake the feeling that we were going to be caught at any moment. If things went badly this time around the results would be catastrophic, not just for me and the people I loved, but for the entire Phoenix metro area, possibly the world, and if we were especially unlucky, maybe even the universe. So… no, acting wasn't really required to get my palms sweating and my stomach feeling like it was about to jump out of my mouth to parachute someplace safe.

Except if we failed today there might not be a safe place, like, anywhere, and I was really just going to have to stop thinking about failure, because it was doing me no damned good.

Sol was clearly dragging out our walk as we waited for Trev to patch Rhelia through so that she could confirm that the dungeons were indeed where Siara was being held, not to mention tell us how the hells to get there.

Seamus and I had been here exactly once before, and we'd been blindfolded and unconscious on the way in, and too nervous to see straight on the way out. We were about as helpful as a service dog with a sinus infection. Apparently, the only thing Sol could think of to draw things out was to shake me while talking smack periodically. This seemed so unlike her that it was almost humorous.

Except that her cuffs up the side of my head were getting difficult to ignore. I was just considering ways to retaliate the next time she hit me, when I heard Trev's voice in my head.

We're in, Vic. Rhelia has the location. Head southwest to the next major intersection of corridors, then turn right.

Roger that.

"Are you taking me to the dungeons or what?" I said aloud, as Sol readied another blow. "You're a lot of talk for someone who isn't even taking me to interrogation."

"Shut up," Sol grumbled.

Basement, sub-section six, Trev relayed mentally.

I tripped then, and Sol had to bend down to catch me, so that her face was right next to mine.

"Basement, sub-section six," I whispered, while she was there.

Hopefully, with no one right next to us, and Trev dutifully pointing the security cameras elsewhere, no one would notice.

I let Sol drag me down the hall, while my brain wandered for a moment to how strange it was that Gwen always showed up just in time to cast a major illusion spell for us before any major mission. I mean, seriously, she almost never missed the chance. This was the first time I'd thought of it, and I would bet money that if I tried to PLAN on Gwen showing up at the last minute to cast such a spell it would never work out, but still, it was weird how consistent she was.

I am the Goddess of fortune, my dear.

Odd. That had sounded like Gwen's voice, but I'd never had Gwen's voice in my head before.

I hear you whenever you think of me, Vic, but I rarely answer. You seem unusually troubled, though, so I thought I would check in.

Strange that she thought I was more troubled than usual. I mean, I was just thinking about her consistently random timing for saving our butts, she was a literal deus ex machina, and that was kind of funny when you thought about it.

You are so desperately trying not to think about what you are about to do, that I can sense your distress even from here.

Well, I think I'm doing a pretty good job coping, all things considered, I thought reproachfully.

Yes. You are admirably placing one foot in front of the other and marching directly into the lion's den. It is to be respected. I should warn you, though, I'm rather busy at the moment. There are many threads being pulled right now. I can't promise to be there if you need me. I strongly recommend solving this one yourself, if at all possible.

There was something more important than Rebecca Dryer possibly destroying the entire universe by injecting an incredibly powerful weredragon with technetium right now? Hot damn. The shit must really be about to hit the fan on a global level.

You have no idea, dear. There's a reason that I have one of my best agents assigned to this mission in my place.

Oh? Who did you send?

I could feel relief wash over me as the meaning of Gwen's words sank in. Someone with Gwen's powers would be here. Someone Gwen trusted. Gwen didn't always get the little things right, like personal space, or freedom of choice, but she had yet to screw up any of the big things, like letting us die. I sensed some of the tension in my shoulders release for a moment, until Gwen's voice in my mind said, You, Vic. I sent you.

Me? What? How am I possibly your best agent? I just started. I have no idea what I'm doing, I—

Have managed to keep everyone you love from dying on multiple occasions. I have complete faith in you. Must go, there's a Russian leader that is in desperate need of being knocked off his horse.

Gwen?

Hello?

Did you seriously just ditch me to knock Putin on his ass?

Gwen didn't reply, and I wondered if she was just deflecting my curiosity with a weird story, or if it was actually somehow important to maintaining the fabric of the universe that she knock Russian dictators on their butts. Honestly, with Gwen it was impossible to know. One thing was clear—I was on my own.

I took a deep breath as Sol shoved me into an elevator, mashed in a security code I recited to her via Trev's voice in my mind, and then hit the button for the bottom.

Gwen believed in me. That had to count for something. Besides, our plan wasn't completely crazy. The things that could go wrong were fairly unlikely at this point, and even if things went wrong, the chances that events would lead to Siara getting injected with technetium here inside the MOME facility were pretty low. The people guarding her would have to be incredibly stupid for that to happen.

"NO, NO, NO. Put. That. Down. You won't just kill her, you'll kill all of us, along with everyone in this whole city, and possibly the entire earth. Seriously. Stop freaking out. Just put the needle down." I was doing my best not to shout, but I was going to fail any second now.

"You're lying! MOME wouldn't risk that! Why would they give us these suits if that were true? This suit wouldn't protect us against what you're describing. They wouldn't protect us at all."

I decided that shouting, "No shit, Sherlock! They don't care about you, and killing you is just part of their fucking evil scheme," wasn't going to help defuse the situation. Instead, I opted for putting my hands at my sides, palms out, and trying to use my calmest voice possible. I tried to look the shaky young man in the eyes, even through the thin rubber hazmat suit that enveloped him, but it was hard to see him behind the flickering light that reflected off the clear part covering his face.

"It's possible that MOME have decided to sacrifice a few for the sake of the many," I hedged, hoping that the dude an inch away from killing us all wasn't completely devoid of reason. "But let's say I'm wrong. Let's say all it's going to do is kill the woman you have your arm around. Does she really deserve to die right now? Is that really your call? Do you really think your bosses want her injected right here without any witnesses? Didn't they order for her to be taken up for a public execution?"

Dude just blinked at me for a full ten seconds before shuffling backwards again, as we both heard the shouts and scuffling of Sol fighting the other guards farther up the passage. With Trev and Rhelia's help, we'd managed to avoid every single MOME employee on the way down here. Then, not long after we'd descended past eggshell painted walls, linoleum floors, and cheap fluorescent lights into coarse stone everything and torch sconces, we'd basically smacked face first into Siara's entourage, which had appeared to be in the process of taking her to the surface in order to inject her somewhere more public than the dungeon below a secret facility. We must have come upon them right after they'd grabbed her, because I could see the metal bars that marked the very same dungeon I'd been kept in during my "stay" here, just behind the guy who had a needle three centimeters from Siara's neck.

Trev had warned us that they were coming up, but not with enough time to hide before they reached us. Regardless, we didn't want them making it out of here. It seemed unlikely that their reinforcements would come from inside the dungeon, and as long as we were still inside these stone walls, no one could use their dark matter. Sol and I had both been trained to fight without magic, but past experience suggested most MOME officers weren't.

So, pressing what little advantage we had, Sol had engaged the guards at the front of the line and I had sprinted to the back to try to get Siara away from the two MOME agents in hazmat suits who were dragging her shackled form through the dark stone halls. If I hadn't known for a fact that Rhelia wasn't in Phoenix I would have had a brief panic attack thinking that she had somehow been captured. I almost did anyway, until I remembered that Siara was a dead ringer for her granddaughter, down to the iridescence of her ebon skin. The only difference between them that I could see was that Siara's eyes were green instead of yellow. I tried to calm my breathing even as I ran down the tunnel. There were no other prisoners in sight, so I had to assume that Emil wasn't a part of today's entertainment.

I had a fair bit of momentum going when I skidded to a stop in front of Siara's guards, so I'd used that to turn and kick the first guard in the head hard enough that he bounced off the wall and slumped to the ground before he'd even really known what was going on. The second guy had pulled Siara in front of him like a hostage and put the needle uncomfortably close to her neck.

Now, as I watched this panicky minion who apparently had never bothered to question his evil overlords before, the needle's point dipped dangerously close to Siara's skin. I wondered if he'd been the one assigned to inject her with technetium once they reached the surface, or if they'd all been equipped with syringes just in case things went south. The latter thought was truly terrifying, but I couldn't imagine how else this trembling cowpie of a human being could possibly have reached the conclusion that he ought to inject technetium into a weredragon inside of his own employer's U.S. headquarters.

My palms were already sweating from resisting the urge to launch myself at this rubber-wrapped asshat, but I dug my nails into my palms as I did my best not to raise my arms and shout threatening things at him as well. One false sway of the wrist and that needle would be in her neck. From there, all it would take would be—

Oh. Fuck.

In the blink of an eye, all my worst nightmares were realized. That needle entering the skin of one of the most powerful weredragons in the world was going to erase everything. Everything. Everyone I loved most in the world was right here in this building, and injecting Siara with a dose of technetium would likely destroy the entirety of the Phoenix metro area. Almost five million people gone in the blink of an eye, along with maybe the entire earth, but especially my brother and my two best friends. I didn't have time to process what I was doing. Didn't really have time to think anything, but the options were pretty simple: Option 1: Do nothing and let everyone I care about, including myself, die horribly, along with many people I didn't even know. Option 2: Launch myself at the asshat holding the needle and the woman he was trying to kill, reach for whatever magic I could, and hope it made things better. I didn't really see how it could make anything worse.

I heard multiple people yelling as I leapt the short distance between me and my target, but I couldn't really process anything that was being said. My eyes were focused on Siara's pupils, which told me all that I needed to know, and I saw them dilate with the shock of the needle puncturing her skin, and perhaps the feeling of technetium entering her veins. I barely noticed as hazmat moron pushed himself away from her, as if that would somehow save him. As if the flimsy rubber that covered him could serve as any kind of protection from what he'd just done. I certainly didn't process any of the shouts from around me. I did my best to ignore Trev's mental cry of my name, as I threw myself on top of Siara and reached with everything in me for what I hoped would be there.

Just barely there. Just the edge of time. A fold in the fabric of space. I pulled.

Blackness took over.

WHEN I OPENED my eyes, lying on my back in the sands of a narrow red canyon, looking up at a small stretch of orange sky, I almost cried with relief. Instead, my body did one weirder and I started laughing hysterically. I guess thinking you were about to die, along with everyone you love, and then not, can do that to you.

"How are we alive?" Siara asked.

I almost countered that I wasn't entirely sure that we were, but then I rose up to my elbows and took in just how rough she looked—raven hair a curled, matted mess, skin a shade of charcoal rather than the deep ebony it normally was, reptilian irises still dilated and sclera red from… well, from the shit we were still going through, I supposed.

"How do you feel?" I asked. When Siara simply stared at me, I realized that maybe she really needed an answer to her question before she could answer mine. "I'm not 100% positive, but my understanding is that there is something about this canyon that completely suppresses dark matter. Not just mostly, like the dungeon at MOME, but completely."

"But why would that stop the Technetium from blowing me up?"

"Well, keep in mind I didn't really plan this, I just dove at you and hoped like hell my subconscious brain knew what it was doing. But now that we're here and I can think about it, my best guess is that the Technetium can't react with the dark matter because it's being so suppressed it might as well not be in your blood stream."

"So… I'm trapped here?"

I shrugged.

"Maybe. Sure beats dying and taking the whole world down with you though, doesn't it?" I said, collapsing to the floor of the canyon again as I realized just how fucking lucky I'd been.

I giggled again.

"You find this funny?" Siara asked, allowing her own legs to give out and joining me on the sandy canyon floor.

I shook my head as the giggles turned into raucous laughter once more.

"Nope," I said when I could manage enough air. "I just think my body and brain are freaking out about how close we came to dying just now."

Siara lay down and looked at the sky.

"Why is the sky orange?" she asked.

"No idea. That wasn't part of my orientation. And before you ask, no, I have no clue why it smells like sulphur here either. Or why the sun is purple, not that you can see the sun right now. Also, we probably need to get on our feet as soon as possible because the floods here happen every few hours and we need to find somewhere for you to not drown while you're here."

I got up and started brushing the sand off of my legs.

Siara remained lying down.

"Now isn't a great time for a nap, Siara," I said.

"Perhaps I should simply remain here and let the waters take me," she replied.

I sighed.

"Right. I guess living in this canyon for the remainder of what is likely to be a few more centuries of life probably doesn't appeal much. I get that."

"Do you, child? Do you understand the eternity that faces most of dragon-kind? Rhelia and my family are not just weredragons, we have ancestors who are pure dragons as well. That is why we look as we do, and not as you do. We are likely to live for millennia, if nothing brings us down before then."

I forced my mouth closed and tried to breathe through my nose.

"Ok. Did not know that, but it explains a lot, thanks. However, it doesn't change what I was about to say."

"Which was?"

"Which was that if you let the flash floods carry you to the bottom of the canyon, I have it on good authority that MOME has a net or something that catches people and zaps them back to the facility we just left."

"Which means that I would be returned to a place where my dark matter would once more engage with the Technetium in my blood?"

"Yep. And then you're right back to killing everyone in Phoenix and possibly the world."

Siara sighed and then stood up and punched the canyon wall. The resounding crack, and the shudder that reverberated the canyon, was even more startling than the revelation of the lifespan of dragon kind. I looked up to see if we were about to be killed by rock fall, but luckily, aside from the cracks that radiated away from the impact point of Siara's fist, everything looked stable.

"What are the chances that being dead would prevent the Technetium from having its desired effect?" she asked.

I wondered when I had suddenly become an expert on Technetium and its reactions with dark matter, or why Siara thought I knew more about it than she did, but then I remembered Trev talking about how some of the oldest magical beings had the hardest time coming to terms with the science behind dark matter manipulation. For them, the powers they wielded had always been innate and natural. You could do what you could do, and you couldn't do what you couldn't do, and you didn't question the gifts you'd been given or lacked. You simply lived your life breathing magic and sweating spells, and didn't question how any of it all fit together. According to him, anyway. I wasn't sure that Siara was particularly tied to tradition, or even averse to knowing how dark matter worked. Still, it made sense that after however many centuries, or millennia she might have already lived with magic just working without having to worry about the how and why, she might want help sorting out how these new ideas worked, and more importantly, what they meant right now.

"I mean, again, I'm just guessing here, but I would think that the moment your blood, laced with Technetium, returned to a place where the dark matter was no longer suppressed, the two would mix and react, annihilating… everything within a very large radius, possibly taking the whole universe down with it, especially considering how close this seam would be when you exploded."

"You don't have to preface everything you say with the fact that you are just guessing. I have internalized the fact that you are not an expert in this particular subject, but you are the closest that I have to an expert at the moment."

I nodded and sighed. That was still a lot of pressure, but at least Siara acknowledged that I was mostly talking out of my ass.

"Look, I don't know what the long term solution is, but there must be something other than, 'Live here in this canyon for the rest of your very long existence.' We just have to figure out what that is. In the meantime, we need to find you a place that won't let you get swept away with the next flood."

"Where did you go when you escaped?"

"I climbed to the top of the canyon after removing my manacles and shit," which made me do a double take when I looked at Siara. "Where are your manacles, by the way?" I asked.

She looked at her wrists and ankles and then tilted her head to one side.

"No idea. They have not been here since we arrived. Though they were certainly keeping me from destroying that dimwitted MOME agent in the dungeons."

"Weird."

"How did you arrive here the first time?" Siara asked.

"A MOME agent brought me here and left me in the canyon," I said, thinking back. "Come to think of it, that lady brought me here and put a new set of manacles on me as soon as we arrived, saying they would keep me from using my magic."

"And did they?"

I considered for a moment.

"Well, I thought they did, because my magic wouldn't work, but after I got to the top Azrael said that was the canyon and not the manacles."

"So she probably brought them simply to make certain that you were restrained," Siara surmised. "Certain seams will not allow people through if they are restrained, others remove the restraints."

"Really? How does that work?"

"I do not know, youngling. I only know that it is true."

"That makes seams sound sentient," I said, feeling decidedly creeped out by the idea.

Siara shrugged.

"Many things in the universe have a form of consciousness. Perhaps seams do as well."

And with that, Siara stood up and started walking away from me.

"Siara," I said, causing her to turn and look back at me over her shoulder. I was about to tell her that she was headed the wrong way, that she had started walking in the direction of the "trap" that MOME had set for anyone caught in the floods, but those words died on my tongue.

"What in the hells is that?" I asked instead, as something blotted out what little portion of the orange sky could be seen from the bottom of the narrow canyon in which we stood, and a horrible screeching filled the air.

"YOU BRILLIANT, BRILLIANT, genius of a woman!"

That was what I chose to believe Azrael was screeching at me as their red-skinned, fluff-tailed body came flying at my head from the sky. But of course, since we were once more in the canyon, and Azrael was in their demon form, I could only hear what sounded like a banshee and a demented cat having a screaming match.

"What is that?" Siara asked, her nose wrinkling as though Azrael had brought more of the sulfurous stench with them, while the creature collided with my torso and knocked me back into the canyon sand.

"It's Azrael," I said, once I could breathe again. Siara only a raised a single eyebrow at me. "The succubus who was helping us back on Earth?" I clarified. "They helped us find you. They were keeping the vampires busy while we came to your rescue."

That didn't seem to do much for Siara in terms of a memory jog, so I just shrugged and returned the manic embrace that the squirrel demon had me in.

"I think I saw that whole shadow thing you were talking about, Az," I said, not knowing what else to talk about. "You blotted out the sun completely, and it wasn't just lucky positioning. You were HUGE."

Azrael nestled up against my ear and then pulled emphatically on my ear lobe. I didn't know what that meant, but decided it was supposed to be affectionate and patted their head in response.

"Where is everyone else?" I asked, after a brief pause for squirrely affection. And then I wanted to smack my head against the wall of the canyon because the response was, of course, a heinous shrieking directly into my ear.

"Never mind!" I shouted. "You can tell me later. Maybe we can play charades for now? Please remember that I can't understand you down here."

Azrael nodded once and shrugged. Then they leapt from my shoulder and ran off down the canyon.

"Az, wait!" I shouted, but their four legged form was hustling away from me with a hustle that seemed less than casual. "We'd better follow them."

"Don't you mean, him?" she asked, gesturing at Az's retreating form. And yeah, Az looked decidedly male in their naked squirrel demon form, but…

"I should ask if they want me to change pronouns when they're in demon squirrel form. Az has never expressed a preference, actually. They never correct anyone who chooses he or she, but they seemed pleased when I started using 'them.' Still, I should really ask."

It wasn't as if I'd had a ton of time to kick back with Az and talk preferred pronouns, but even so, it was only polite. I needed to make time.

Siara looked at me briefly, then shrugged and hustled after the red-skinned squirrel demon. She moved quickly and with purpose, but there was something about her gait that seemed off. I wondered if she was injured from her time in the dungeons, or if perhaps the reaction between the Technetium and dark matter was only slowed down by the canyon, and not completely stopped. That was a terrifying thought. Deciding there was nothing I could do about it either way, I hurried after Siara and the quickly fading shape of Azrael the squirrel demon.

~~~

"This isn't working, Az."

I shook my head again, as I failed, for the hundredth time, to turn Az's jerky, random motions into some sort of coherent meaning.

"A cat is being mangled repeatedly in a washing machine?" Siara guessed for the third time.

"If that wasn't right the last two times, why would it suddenly be right this time?" I asked.

She shrugged.

"That's just what it looks like."

She wasn't wrong.

"Az, seriously. We have no idea what you're trying to say. How can you be
~~~

this bad at charades?"

Az leveled their gaze at me and gestured their tiny squirrel hands up and down their red-skinned squirrel body.

"Ok. Fair point, well made. You aren't exactly built for the human game in this body," I admitted.

Azrael collapsed in a heap on the tiny rock ledge that formed the "balcony" of the small cave (cave was a generous term, it was more of a slight indentation in the cliff side) that would be Siara's shelter for the foreseeable future. Since Az had led us up here and then proceeded to shoo us inside the small depression, I didn't think they were trying to warn us of some terrible fate. But I couldn't for the life of me figure out what they were trying to tell us.

"If I am going to marooned here with that creature, I am likely to fling one of us from this cliff ledge."

That garnered cold looks from both Az and me.

"That squirrel is more difficult to communicate with than General Aira, and she is a dragon who speaks in three word sentences and acts as though emotions are things that only plague other people."

"I'm starting to get the impression you're not a huge fan of your general," I offered, happy to talk about something other than the ways in which she was annoyed by Az.

Siara sighed.

"She is very good at her job. However, she is blinded by her prejudices and her own past."

I chuckled a bit.

"She sounds pretty human," I offered.

Siara's mouth curved up, on one side only.

"Do not tell her you think so," she advised. "She is entirely dragon, though she has a human form she takes often enough when it suits her."

I wasn't sure I'd ever heard of full dragons taking human form before, but given what I'd just learned about Siara's ancestry, it made sense. Dragons mating with humans in dragon form sounded… awkward. I shook my head, and decided to add it to the pile of things I would ask about later. Right now I needed to do my best to keep Siara safe and alive.

I took a deep breath, looking between the exasperated squirrel demon and the overwhelmed weredragon. I had a feeling I was going to regret this later, but…

"Siara, are you ok if I leave you here for a bit?" I asked.

Siara looked pointedly down at the bottom of the canyon and then up towards the top.

"Where exactly do you think you're going?"

I sighed.

"Unfortunately, I think the only way we can figure out what Az is trying to say is if I climb out of here and let the translation magic that normally works in this realm kick in. Then I'll have to climb back down here and tell you whatever it is."

At my words Az sat up and began nodding enthusiastically.

"This had better be as important as you're making it seem," I muttered to them.

Siara looked at me as though I'd started growing a second head.

"What?" I asked, not entirely sure I hadn't started growing another head. My life had been so batshit nuts lately, and this realm was so much weirder than most, that I would hardly have been surprised.

"It seems a great risk to take," she said, and I could tell she was leaving something unsaid.

"If you think I shouldn't take the trouble to go up there and come back down, because you're planning to just die down here and save everyone the trouble, then we are going to have to have words when I come back," I said, channeling my own mother as best I could, an effort I had never made before, but suddenly found all too fitting. "You're Rhelia's family, and mine, now. If you think I'm just going to leave you here to rot, you've got another think coming."

Siara turned away and stared at the back wall of the cave for a moment.

"Victoria, I would not forgive myself if something were to happen to you while you were trying to assist me."

I shrugged and stood up.

"And I won't forgive myself if I don't find out what Az is trying to say and it winds up being information that could save your life. So, we're at an impasse and, as only one of us can leave this place without taking the whole universe down with her, I guess you'll just have to hang out here while I try not to die. Ok?'

Siara smirked and nodded.

"You are more like your mother than I first supposed," she said.

Which felt like a punch directly in the gut.

"You knew my Mom?" I asked, sitting down again without really meaning to.

Siara raised an eyebrow.

"You didn't know that?" she asked.

I put my head in my hands.

"My parents never told me anything about this world, about magic or shifting, or any of it before they… disappeared." I was going to say died, but I found the word harder and harder to form these days, as everything about their death—and lives, for that matter—seemed less and less clear.

"I knew that, but… surely Rhelia or Trevor mentioned—" she looked at me and started shaking her head back and forth, as though trying to shrug off some insect that buzzed her head. "Those children… honestly… they are far too used to keeping secrets for my liking. I understand the necessity at times, but this? Why wouldn't they tell you?"

No longer having any clue what we were talking about, I just stared at her, wide-eyed, reminding myself to blink.

"Your parents sought refuge in the dragon realm for a time, in their attempts to evade MOME, before they… disappeared."

I noticed that she used the same word I had, but more cautiously, as though she wasn't sure what its exact meaning was.

"How long before they disappeared?" I asked, wondering how much more of my parents' lives I knew nothing about.

"Months. The dragon realm is barred to anyone who isn't led there by someone who is dragonkin. My ancestors chose it for that purpose eons ago, or so the stories say. It makes an excellent hiding place for those trying to avoid an association like MOME—one that is decidedly unpopular with all dragon kind. Unfortunately, your parents eventually decided that their presence in our realm was too great a risk. I am not clear on their exact thinking, but I got the impression they were worried that MOME would figure out a way into our realm and hurt us in an attempt to get their hands on your parents. I never understood how they thought such a thing was possible, but I believe it is what led them to abandon the dragon realm and continue their circumnavigation."

I really wanted to ask a hundred other questions, but Az was jumping up and down like a kangaroo on a pogo stick and gesturing wildly at the top of the cliff.

"We need to continue this conversation," I said, looking between Az and the top of the canyon, or at least the line between the rock and the sky. "But apparently I need to get my ass in gear."

Az nodded emphatically, and Siara merely sighed and nodded towards the cliff face.

"Good luck, Victoria."

"I'll be back soon."

If only I'd known how big a lie that was.

THE CLIMB TO the top of the canyon was substantially less exciting this time than it had been the last time. For one thing, the red-skinned squirrel demon did not launch itself at my head this time. For another, I wasn't completely haggard from days without food or water, exposure to the elements, and breaking out of my bonds. Instead, I was just a bit tired from our master escape plan of the night. My whole body felt somewhat heavy with exertion and my scars pulled periodically as I stretched for some of the farther holds on the way up but, for the most part, the climbing was smooth and steady. Also, perhaps most importantly, I knew what awaited me at the top, so I wasn't constantly checking the horizon to make sure nothing was trying to kill me from above.

In retrospect, that might have been a mistake.

Regardless, I made much better time than my previous ascent, and reached the top only partially exhausted, though not at all looking forward to the downclimb that would return me to Siara's ledge.

"Ok, Az," I huffed out, as I collapsed a few feet from the edge of the cliff it had taken me two hours to ascend. "What the fuck is going on?"

"First of all, can I just say how bloody brilliant you are for thinking of this canyon? I don't know if I would have come up with that on such short notice, and I live here."

"Thank my subconscious. That was a blind leap for me, I reached for the seam and hoped for the best. I guess some part of my brain remembered that the canyon suppresses dark matter, but honestly, that wasn't a conscious thought of mine when I grabbed Siara. I was just desperate to keep every-one I loved from dying."

Azrael poked his long, red nose in my face from above where I lay.

"Are you telling me that you grabbed her, expecting to die, and just did your best to take her somewhere else so that she might not kill the rest of us?"

I grimaced and nodded. It had been one of the dumbest things I'd ever done, but I hadn't seen any choice really, and then I'd been incredibly lucky. Or maybe part of me had suspected what would happen. Who knows.

"You absolutely moronic, lovely, brave, mad individual!" Azrael was bouncing up and down on my chest now, too light to knock the wind from my lungs, but not particularly comfortable either. They were rather large for a squirrel. I sat up when they latched onto my shoulder in a way that I assumed was supposed to be a hug, but it was difficult to tell, and one small squirrel hand was far too close to my boob for my liking.

"Thanks? I guess. Look, I'll admit it might have been mad, and was prob-ably stupid, but what else was I supposed to do?"

"Nothing! Die horribly, I suppose? I dunno. But I'm very glad that you did what you did."

"Look, Az, I appreciate the love fest and all, but what were you trying to tell us earlier? It seemed important."

Az blinked for a moment.

"Oh yes, that. Mostly I just wanted to get you up here to talk to you, but I was trying to say that the spot Siara is in could be good for the long term, as the next time there's a stampede it will likely provide her with some much needed food. Quite a few of the folks who run from the storms fall into that canyon."

I stared at them for a moment and blinked.

"You made me climb to the top of this canyon to mention that there might be falling snacks?"

"Well, yes. It will be enough to keep her alive and keep her from attempt-ing to leave the canyon before it's safe for her."

"But... I climbed for two hours, Az. TWO HOURS! So you could tell us about snacks? What if I'd fallen? What if I'd fallen and wiped out Siara on my way down? Seriously? How could you be so bad at charades that you couldn't manage to sign FOOD?!" I held up a hand and made the Earth-wide accepted gesture for food—sandwiched fingers towards a mouth mak-ing eating motions. Then I sighed, thinking about how far I'd climbed and how much farther I'd have to downclimb just to deliver the message: beware of falling snacks. "I can't believe you brought me up here just for that."

Az's squirrel form frowned, and it booped its elongated red nose against mine.

"I brought you up here so I could tell you that you'd better start workin' out how to get yourself home, 'cause everyone thinks you're dead, Luv."

I just stared at Az for a moment.

"You didn't tell them where you were going when you left?" I asked.

Az shrugged.

"I came here on a guess, Luv. After the world didn't explode, and we made our way back out of that damned concrete dungeon."

"Thought I left you on the upper floors?"

"The whole bloody building's a dungeon, love. No better word for that many cubicles."

Az's whole squirrel body shuddered and I was forced to laugh.

"I did join the fray in the basement, though," Az added, after a moment.

"Oh?"

"Well, Trev was screaming his bloody head off as soon as you disappeared, and then it was only a matter of time before the jig was up, so we ran to meet Sol, and the bull and wolf joined us on the way down. Everyone was cryin' and fightin' and determined to find Emil before they left, but... I ran to the seam and decided to test a theory."

"So, they really think I'm dead?"

Az nodded, somberly.

"I had a hunch, though. Thought that you might have headed here and that you might need my help. Didn't want to get anyone's hopes up, though, so I just told them I'd be back when I could."

I was quiet for a bit as I considered all the implications of that. I didn't like the idea of my friends thinking I was dead. I knew firsthand how painful it was to lose someone close to you. I didn't want them feeling that kind of grief, if they didn't have to. But for now I had other things to worry about.

"Az, what am I going to do for her? Just because she won't starve thanks to your falling snacks, that doesn't mean she'll survive... or want to. How can we fix this?"

Azrael's long nose twitched a few times before they spoke again.

"I honestly don't know, Luv. This is all new to me. I'd never heard of Technetium until you explained things to me after that first time MOME blew a bunch of folks up. I don't know how to reverse that kind of thing, but at least she won't die right away and take the whole world down with her, eh? Nice if we can put off the end of the universe for a little while longer, innit?"

"Why do you sound more human in your squirrel form?" I asked, unable to miss how Azrael's accent had thickened the more we'd sat talking at the top of this cliff.

"Dunno, could just be your perception of me. After all, you're not even listenin' to me speak really, just a translation of what I'm saying in demon. Maybe I jus' seem more human to you now?"

"But you aren't actually from South London, so the accent is put on anyway, at least it is when you have vocal chords, so why on Earth would I—oh fuck it, who cares? Is that all you had for me? I suppose I should be getting back to inform Siara about her meal plan."

Az began to nod, then turned, eyes growing wide with horror, as an ominous thundering rolled in from the distance.

"Az? What is that?"

"That, Luv, is our cue to leave."

I shuffled myself towards the cliff ledge, getting ready to climb down to Siara's cave again.

"Not that way, Luv. We need to get through the nearest seam and get out of here."

"I can't leave Siara down there," I said, turning towards Az for a moment, mentally preparing myself for the climb down, all the while.

"Vic, stop! Don't be ridiculous! You can't get to her before the stampede gets here, and you'll never make that climb without taking a falling demon to the head. You'll just get killed and have nothing to show for it."

"I can't just leave her here, Az!" I said, lying down and dangling my feet over the edge to start my descent.

"You can come back!" Az shouted. He had to shout now to be heard over the distant rumbling. A rumbling that was getting terrifyingly less distant with each second. "You can take the seam out of here and come back in an hour and they'll be gone! But if you stay here, you'll die. Siara has that cave for cover, the demons won't kill her unless she's too dim to duck in when she hears the stampede. She doesn't seem dim to me. Please Vic, believe me, you do not want to be stuck on that cliff when they get here."

Az's face was so earnest, such a tiny, squirrelish vision of concern, that I had to take his words seriously for a moment. Then something occurred to me.

"Are you just saving your own ass, Az? Because I know you can't get out of here without help."

Their eyes widened, but before they could protest, the wave of sound that had been slowly approaching crested a hill behind us and I saw a black sea of… writing life? Demons? I couldn't tell what it was exactly, but it was moving towards us far faster than I would have believed possible. I couldn't make out individual shapes in the mass, but it was quite clear that nothing in the path of that wall of living creatures would be spared.

Before I could think about it again, I pulled myself up from the ledge, snatched Az from the ground in front of me, and reached for the nearest fold in spacetime.

I'm sorry, Siara. I'll try to be back soon. Watch out for falling snacks

I HAD EXPECTED to find myself back in the same MOME dungeon I'd snatched Siara from. After all, the last time I'd used the seam at the top of the canyon in Az's realm, that's where I'd wound up. Instead, I found myself standing in a giant green field, waist deep in waving rows of a grain I wasn't familiar with, but which could easily have been wheat.

The sky was blue again, so we definitely weren't in Azrael's realm, but beyond that I had no idea where we were. The air smelled of earth and plants. The sun was warm on my skin, and the only thing I could see, as far as the horizon, was grain.

"Well… this is new…" I muttered, as I turned to look from the landscape to Azrael, who had been in my arms as we'd arrived. They were no longer in my arms. They were also no longer Azrael. Or rather, instead of a red furless squirrel or a winged humanoid, I now stood a few feet away from an enormous death omen.

Since no one else was around, I was pretty sure it was Azrael.

"That's different," I said, taking in all of maybe-Azrael's latest body.

Maybe-Azrael seemed to be a raven, except they were a raven that was at least a head taller than I was, and proportioned accordingly.

Caw.

"Let me guess," I said, still staring at the feathers that were so deep a black they had a blue sheen to them. "There's no translation magic in this realm."

Caw caw.

"Well, at least you don't sound like a dying cat every time you open your mouth," I replied with a sigh. The giant raven's feathers ruffled, and it snapped its beak angrily, making me fairly certain it was indeed Azrael who stood before me.

"One of these days, you'll have to explain to me why your form manifests so differently in every realm," I said, as I turned my head to the sky to take in our surroundings more clearly. It was going to be damned annoying that Azrael couldn't explain things to me here. Which made me even more certain that Azrael was now a giant raven, because of course they would be. This is my life we're talking about, and if it ain't inconvenient and weird, it's trying to kill me.

I had no idea where we were, but as long as nothing terrible happened, I supposed we just needed to wait an hour and then I could just find the seam that had brought us here and take it back.

"I suppose I should just make sure I know where that seam is," I muttered, mostly to myself, as I stretched my hands out in front of me and felt for the fold in space and time that would get us out of here. "Just to be certain we can get back easily once we've waited out the stampede."

CAW CAW CAW CAW CAW!

I turned to look at Azrael, even as I felt my fingers hum with the energy of the seam that had brought us here.

"What?" I asked, concerned by the frantic tone to Azrael's cawing.

Caw.

Azrael's last caw had contained a finality that sent a shiver down my spine, and when I turned to look at them, their eyes were gazing skyward at a spot in the distance.

A spot that was getting larger.

"Az... what's that?" I asked, even though I knew the raven couldn't answer me, at least not in a way that I could understand.

Caw.

Az hopped to my side, collapsing a swath of wheat in their wake, and hunkered down in a gesture that made it all too clear that I should get on their back.

I scoffed at that, and reached for my dragon form instead. Az wasn't the only one with wings here. I closed my eyes and imagined the rush of air beneath my wings, the feeling of a mouth filled with fangs that could rend an entire cow in a single bite, a belly full of fire hot enough to melt a vampire's skull, and...

Nothing. Nothing happened. Nothing changed.

Caw, caw, CAW.

Az was sounding more than a little bit anxious. I looked up and saw that the distant spot was now much larger, and I decided that having my own wings wasn't worth getting caught by whatever was coming for us. I climbed onto Azrael's back and clung on for dear life as the giant raven's wings flapped in an ever more hurried attempt to get us airborne.

After a few heartbeats, Az shot us skyward. For a second I worried that I would slide right off their back, but then they evened out and we were aloft, streaking over the great field of grain and then over a forest that must have been just out of sight from the field we'd started in. Az put on a burst of speed I would never have though possible for a raven. Of course, I'd never seen a raven this large before, so it could just have come down to the physics of a raven about fifty times bigger than average. Though, when I thought about it that way, I wondered if it should be physically possible for a raven that size to actually fly. I quickly abandoned that line of thinking, however, since Az was clearly flying whether physics liked it or not, and whatever had been coming for us was beginning to catch up.

As I looked over my shoulder I could see the shape of what had once been a burgeoning black dot on the horizon materialize into a cloud of wings and glinting metal behind us.

"That looks bad," I admitted, even as I hunkered closer to Az's shoulders. "Any chance you can go faster?" I asked, trying to keep the panic out of my voice. I didn't know if it would faze Az at all, but panicking generally didn't help anything and I knew it could be as contagious as a bad STI.

Caw.

It was a grumble that I wouldn't have been able to hear at all over the sound of the wind in my ears, but as I was pressed tight against Az's avian form, I felt it in my chest.

Panic or no, the vocalization made it clear I wasn't helping.

And soon enough I didn't have to worry about panic, or Az, or anything else except how I was about to die, because something large, winged, and screaming like a squirrel demon hopped up on cocaine dove from the sky and collided with me, knocking me off Az's back and sending me tumbling through the air.

AZRAEL DOVE FOR me. Since I was falling to my death back first, I could see them tuck their wings to their sides and plunge away from the attacking winged warriors that were encircling them as I fell, but I knew enough about physics to know that they wouldn't reach me in time. We hadn't been that far off the ground—only a couple thousand feet. Not the tens of thousands of feet needed for Az to have time to reach me before I hit the ground.

I tried to reach for my dragon form, my snow leopard form, some random magic that might keep me alive or help me save myself, but nothing responded. It didn't quite feel like being in the canyon in Az's realm, but I couldn't place how it was different, and didn't have the fucking time to worry about it, anyway. I was about to die, and I couldn't use my magic, that much was clear. Then, out of the corner of my eye, through the hair that had been ripped from its holder and was now flapping blindingly against the sides of my face, I saw… something. I wasn't sure what it was, but I didn't care, honestly, because I was about to die, and dying wasn't something I wanted to do. Whatever it was might not help, but it wasn't likely to be worse than dying by hitting the ground in another couple of seconds, so I reached for it. Grabbed at it. And felt somewhat gratified when my hand snagged around a feathered appendage. Then something shrieked like an angry eagle.

My momentum wrenched. I had been prepared for it, hoping for it even—not falling was my goal right now, so it didn't actually tear my arm out of its socket, though it sure felt like it was going to.

Beneath my grip I could feel feather, muscle, and bones shift, as my hand clutched the limb of whatever it was I was clinging to. Then I felt something sharp and awful tear at the skin on my upper arm, but I refused to let go, because FUCK that. I held on as tight as I could. Whatever I'd just grabbed onto WAS NOT FALLING. And not falling meant not dying, maybe, at least for a little while, and I was not about to let go of that.

Unless it cut off my arm.

Which it was clearly trying to do.

I screamed, and looked up again through a flash of flapping hair to see that the thing I had caught hold of was the thing that had been attacking Az and I. The same type of creature that had charged into me and Az to begin with. Possibly even the same one that had knocked me to my narrowly avoided death, but I couldn't be sure as I hadn't gotten a good look at the time.

I got a good look now, though; eagle wings and eagle legs from the knee down, but the upper body of a woman who clearly didn't think much of clothing and who definitely had a thing for weapons. Honestly, she seemed like the kind of person I'd have gotten along with pretty well, if she hadn't been so obviously trying to kill me. Call me cold, but I take exception to people trying to throw me to my death.

The eagle-woman had multiple blades sheathed on her person in thick baldrics that crossed at the center of her chest, more than one scabbard belted to her waist, and possibly another over her shoulder blades—she almost looked like a pin cushion with all the sword and dagger hilts poking out of her—but not a stitch of cloth or armor covered her breasts, waist, or head. I managed to get a good look at her, despite the blood splatter that was flying in my face from where she was trying to hack through my arm with a spear. Honestly, there wasn't much I could do other than stare at her while gripping her eagle leg for dear life, trying to grit through the pain of having my arm sliced repeatedly.

It must have been a terribly awkward angle for her. The spear was pretty long, and she still had it gripped for a more distant opponent, so she missed as often as she caught me, and rarely hit the same place twice. Perhaps she was just hoping to make me let go, rather than cut me all the way through the bone, but I wasn't planning to let go before I bled to death or she landed.

She cried out again, and this time some of her compatriots must have heard her, because I could hear answering cries from somewhere nearby. It was almost a surprise to be able to hear anything but the rush of wind in my ears, but as my "ride" seemed content to maintain altitude instead of plummeting us to the ground, or racing off across the countryside, other sounds were starting to filter in. Like the sound of metal slicing flesh every time the eagle-woman caught my arm with her spear, the subsequent gritted screams from my own lips, or the sounds of the other eagle-warriors' angry shrieks getting closer.

I had just begun to wonder why she wasn't just trying to spear me in the throat, when I saw the weapon drive towards my face. I barely managed to get my other arm up in time to block it. Of course, that arm took a deep gash as it deflected the spear tip—why wasn't I wearing bracers? I really needed to invest in a good pair of bracers—but the harpy, or eagle-woman, or whatever she was, was also slow enough in retracting the spear that I managed to get my hand wrapped around the shaft before she could pull it out of my reach.

And that whole exchange probably explained why she hadn't been aiming at my throat earlier.

You can bet your ass I pulled on that spear with all the force I could spare, which wasn't much, considering what my other arm was doing to keep me alive (holding my entire body weight, bleeding profusely, etc.), but apparently she had a bad grip on the thing to begin with, because my weak-assed yank was enough to pull it out of the harpy's hands.

"HA!" I yelled, as the spear came free of her grip. I was still in a damned precarious position, but at least I was now armed.

I twisted the grip of the spear as quickly as I could, flipping the shaft around in a single hand as if it were a bo, trusting in years of martial arts training to keep me from dropping the damned thing, so that the pointy end was now angled towards the harpy. She didn't seem to approve of that development, and she was damned quick to demonstrate her disapproval, because she met the spear point with the blade of a short sword she'd pulled from one of her many sheaths.

I don't know if she thought I'd actually intended to stab her—which would be a stupid move on my part, since she was the only thing keeping me from plummeting to my death right now—or if she was just still working on killing me, but either way she was clearly ready to cut me any way she could.

We'd barely had time to exchange a few blows, mostly me using the shaft of the spear to parry her attempts to cut my arm off, before something huge, black, and feathered crashed into both of us and knocked me loose.

"GwenDAMNit!" I screamed, as I began to fall again.

I'd barely dropped for more than half a second though, when a taloned claw grabbed me around the middle and I realized that what had barreled into us had been Azrael.

"Ok. Ow, and thank you," I half said, half screamed, as Azrael started a steep dive towards the forest that lay beneath us.

Something swished past my ear, and I turned to see a cloud of harpies flying above and behind us, launching various weapons in our direction.

We were so screwed.

Az was rocketing towards the trees below us, and I began to wonder if they were planning on slowing us down before we hit the trees, or the ground, or the whole cloud-of-harpies-below-us-fuck! Apparently, the dive was partially in order to blow through the harpies that had amassed between us and the tops of the trees. Trees that seemed much closer now than they had only five seconds earlier. Suddenly, my vision went almost black and my world became a haze of wings, talons, and branches. I couldn't see what I was doing really, but I swung out blindly with my newly acquired spear a few times, just in case any of the harpies tried to attach themselves to us as we dropped. The cries that I heard even as we plummeted through the cloud of winged warriors gave me a sense of grim satisfaction. I still had no idea what had sparked the ire of these people to begin with, but I did not take kindly to people trying to kill me, no matter what their reasoning might be.

Just before we crashed into the forest floor, Az spread their wings and cut our speed by at least half, but we still hit with a jolt that shook every bone in my body, especially since Az had needed to drop me before slamming their feet into the ground. I rolled away from the massive raven, over soft earth and a thick layer of pine needles, and stood up, shaken, dirty, and bleeding, but already brandishing the spear I'd somehow held onto through our entire crazed descent, ready for whatever came at us next.

Which was, of course, more harpies.

Despite everything we'd just gone through, we'd only disabled one or two of them, and that left more than a dozen who were still all too eager to take us down. Thankfully, the dense tree-tops slowed their descent, and spread them out.

Sadly, that didn't leave us any less outnumbered.

Az seemed to be stuck in raven form, and as far as I could tell, they didn't have access to any of the powers that had allowed them to kick so much vampire ass on Earth. I had nothing more than ten years of martial arts training and a spear I'd never used before. From what I could make out in the shadows of the dense pine forest, we were up against more than a dozen armed warriors, and we would be totally and completely fucked once they had us surrounded.

Which would be in about 30 seconds.

"Well, Az, it has been a pleasure knowing you," I said, shifting my stance so that we were back to back. "Shame we couldn't enjoy a longer association."

Caw.

I couldn't be sure, but that had sounded like it held a sincere tone of regret.

The harpies—my years of reading fantasy novels made me want to call them harpies, and eagle-women was getting tiresome, so, accurate or not, I was going to call them harpies—were landing all around us, and though they didn't seem to be as nimble on the ground as they were in the air (they hopped awkwardly to move themselves forward rather than walking like any biped I was familiar with), they still seemed more than adequately equipped to kill us both and have time for coffee after.

"We'll take as many as we can with us, though, right?"

Caw.

It was nice not to be alone, in one's final moments. I took a deep breath and widened my stance. I was going to make these assholes come to me.

One of the harpies shrieked, in what I took to be a battle cry, but then the one immediately in front of me, the one closing in that I had assumed would be my first opponent, turned to look at whoever had cried out.

I didn't hesitate. I lunged forward with my spear, taking the opening to stab for the harpy's chest. She turned back just before I connected, and brought her sword up in time to deflect the spear into her shoulder. I was shocked when the spear tip simply bounced off of her bare skin as if it were actually platemail.

My assessment of how screwed we were went up a few notches.

At least, it did until the shrieks that I'd been hearing all around us, shrieks that I'd assumed were harpy battle cries—you know, getting pumped to destroy two unarmed combatants who had no idea why they were even under attack, as you do—abruptly fell silent. I had just enough time to find that totally eerie before the harpy standing in front of me was no longer in front of me, but instead pinned to the nearest tree by what looked like nothing more than a grey haze.

"Did you want this one?" asked a raspy voice I didn't recognize.

I blinked, and the outline of a small figure came into focus in the midst of the haze. I said nothing, and the voice must have taken that as a "no," because the next thing I knew there was a sickening crack and the harpy collapsed to the ground.

In the sudden silence of the forest, I blinked and looked around. Harpy bodies lay everywhere, and not one of them was moving. Whatever the grey haze was, it had taken out every single one of our opponents singlehandedly.

UNSURE OF WHETHER or not we were actually safe now, I turned to look at Azrael. They stood abnormally still beneath the hulking pine trees, which cast us in enough shadow that it was difficult to be certain it was still daylight, even though it had clearly been close to midday when we had been up above the trees less than three minutes ago. Amid the smell of pine needles and some sweet-smelling sap, Az stood blinking their large raven eyes, as if they were still trying to adjust to a change in light.

I was about to laugh with relief when Azrael's legs seemed to give out from under them. I ran to their side.

"Az, are you alright?" I asked, kneeling beside the enormous raven.

Caw.

I was not reassured by the weakness of Az's voice.

"Its wing is hurt," said the same raspy voice that had asked me if I wanted the final harpy.

I turned and found what looked like a twelve-year-old girl staring at me from a meter away. She was lithe, and had long flowing hair, but that was all I could really see about her. She was enveloped in a continuously shifting haze, or maybe she was just standing in her own personal sandstorm. I couldn't see all of her at once, and everything about her was an uncertain shade of grey. Despite that, some part of her seemed eerily familiar.

"I wasn't quite fast enough," the girl said. "One of the harpies got to the raven before I could stop her."

Caw.

Azrael seemed to be agreeing with the girl.

Could this petite creature actually have killed over a dozen harpies in a minute? I wondered. I shook my head at that line of thought. Whatever she looked like, she was dangerous. Looks were deceiving enough, even back on Earth, and here? Well, Az was a giant raven instead of a squirrel or an angel, so… I had no clue what the rules were like here.

"Thank you for your help," I said. Then, turning to Az, "Can you show me where it hurts?"

Az turned a bit towards me and I realized that the wing they had been facing away from me was all but snapped.

"Shit," I said, sucking in a breath. I immediately began to search for splinting materials on the forest floor, and was exceedingly grateful, not for the first time, that I had taken more than one wilderness first aid course since I'd started high school.

Luckily, the forest floor was littered with long, straight branches from the tall pines that surrounded us, and it was warm enough here that I felt comfortable shedding the black leather jacket that had materialized with me the last time that I'd shifted. It was just barely large enough—when tied to one of the leather belts I'd taken off of a fallen harpy—to make a supportive sling and splint combo for Az's wing. I'd had to use my T-shirt as a bandage for my own arms, both of which were bleeding quite a bit more than I would have liked.

"Well," I said, looking between Az's ramshackle sling and my recently reduced ensemble. "Neither of us is going to be winning any fashion contests today, but at least you won't be in quite as much pain, and I still have a sports bra on."

Caw.

"You're right. I could do a decent Lara Croft cosplay right now."

The raspy voice chuckled, and I looked at the warrior girl who'd just saved our lives. As the hazy grey that shrouded her swirled around, I briefly caught a good look at her eyes. Then I felt a gasp escape me, when I realized what looked familiar about her. I'd seen those startling blue eyes before, more times than I cared to remember, most recently just before they'd been engulfed in flames.

"Renata?" I asked, amazed that my mind could conjure up a name I'd only heard mentioned once, in a conversation that felt like it had happened a year ago, though it had only been a matter of weeks.

Before I could take the breath to form a follow-up question, I found myself pinned to a nearby pine tree, with no idea how I'd gotten there except that there was now a small hand holding me by the throat and a swirl of grey mist in front of me.

"Did he send you?" the raspy voice asked from within the mist.

I wouldn't have known who the hell she was talking about except that the entire reason I'd recognized her was because she had her father's eyes.

"No, he didn't send me," I replied, as calmly as I could given my position. I was impressed that I was still able to speak over her grip around my throat, especially since I was also pinned to the tree. How strong was this creature, that she could hold me up by my throat without crushing it?

She eyed me for a full minute, while Azrael let out a series of startled and pleading caws, and I felt fairly certain that if this tiny person decided she didn't trust me, I would be dead and there would be nothing anyone could do to stop it.

"Why are you here, then?" she asked, eventually.

"Look, Renata, I'm not even entirely sure where here is, but Azrael and I were just trying not to get killed by a demon stampede when we landed in a field of wheat not far from here. As to your dad… when was the last time you had any news about him?"

I would have swallowed after asking, but Renata's grip tightened on my throat after I mentioned her father.

"Weeks ago, right after your friends deposited all of us in Unterberg."

So, she had recognized me from our rescue at Bolivia's MOME headquarters. I tried to take a deep breath, but mostly choked on my own spit. Renata loosened her grip marginally.

"If you know who I am," I began, once I'd stopped coughing, "then why would you think I was here at your dad's behest?"

Renata snorted and then spat on the ground.

"You wouldn't be the first beautiful woman whose head was turned by a vampire."

I laughed, and then choked a bit more, because it's hard to laugh when someone is holding you by the throat.

"You really don't know who I am, then," I said, still coughing. Renata dropped me and stepped back from both me and the tree.

"Explain yourself," was all that she said.

"First of all, before you worry about me being here on Edik's behalf, let me be the first to inform you that he is dead."

I wasn't one hundred percent certain that sharing that news with Renata would help things. It could turn out her love-hate relationship with her father was complicated enough that she would be quite upset to find out he was no longer among the living, but I got the distinct impression she wasn't going to be too cut up about it.

"Are you certain? Vampires are very difficult to kill," she said, and I could have been imagining it, but I thought her voice sounded… hopeful.

"Yeah, I learned that the hard way, but I am quite certain. He's dead."

"What happened to him?" she asked.

"Well, first a succubus ripped his head off," I explained. "But he was close to the Tree of Life when it happened, so it didn't stick, as it were. The next time I saw him, he attacked my brother, so I ripped his head off again and then had a dragon hit it with fire."

It was basically the truth. I was the dragon that had hit it with fire, so it was slightly misleading, but… well, I wasn't sure I wanted Renata to know all of my tricks. After all, I had no idea who, if anyone, she reported to.

I was bracing myself for some rage, or at least some verbal abuse for killing her dad. It even occurred to me that she might just straight up kill me, as she'd done with all the harpies who still littered the forest floor.

Without warning, I felt myself pushed against the base of the tree again, heard Azrael's startled caw as I felt the bark carve into my back, and expected that to be my final moment of existence.

Instead, I found a pair of lips pressed enthusiastically up against my own.

WHEN THE LIPS finally pulled away from mine, I dropped back to the forest floor and coughed again, mainly to cover the flush that had gone to my cheeks. I was not at all sure how I felt about being kissed by a woman who looked like a twelve year old, even if the chances were good she wasn't what she seemed. Icky probably summed it up, but damned if I was about to say that to Renata. So, I inspected the pine needles at my feet and coughed some more, while she gave me some space.

"I am free," she said, her voice full of wonder. "I am finally, truly, free of him. Thank you. I am in your debt."

I brought my eyes up and waved my hands in the kind of gesture one might make to calm a rearing horse.

"I don't think you owe me anything for killing your dad," I said.

"I humbly disagree. You have no idea what a nightmare he has made my life for the past few decades. Please, allow me to accompany you to the citadel. That's where you're headed, isn't it?"

I looked between Renata and Azrael. Azrael gave a slight nod, which I took to mean they thought we should accept the offer, but truth be told, I didn't particularly want to travel with Renata. She was… disconcerting at best, and… well, I didn't think there was anything I could do to stop her from kissing me again, or killing me, if she wanted to, and I didn't like feeling defenseless. So, I shrugged.

"I mean, we had planned to just take the same seam that brought us here and go back to the realm we came from, so—"

"Ah, no wonder the harpies set upon you! You cannot use any of your magic here without express permission from Hel."

"Hel?"

Renata quirked a smoky eyebrow at me and for the first time I wondered why she constantly looked like she was walking through a grey and swirling mist.

"Are we in another hell dimension?" I asked.

Renata shrugged.

"All the realms seem like hell realms if you ask me, but this one is ruled by a being named Hel."

"Like the Norse goddess?" I asked.

Renata shrugged.

"Perhaps? My Earth folklore is not what it could be."

I sighed.

"So... are you saying we wouldn't be able to use the seam, even if we managed to get back to it without being skewered by a bunch of harpies?"

Renata nodded.

"It is not that you cannot use it without your powers, since one does not need powers to access a seam, it is that Hel will not allow anyone to access the seam without her express permission. The same is true of using your own power. If you wish to return to where you came from by seam or by magic, then you have to go to the citadel. Hel awaits everyone who comes to her realm there."

Renata seemed to sense my hesitation and she rushed to reassure me.

"I was headed there anyway, it is hardly any trouble. I would be more than happy to ensure that you arrive there safely."

I sighed. I felt terrible enough for Azrael having a broken wing, just because it must've hurt like a bitch, but now I was doubly upset that the giant raven couldn't simply fly us to this citadel.

"How long will it take?" I asked, thinking of Siara sitting alone on that cliff, waiting for us. Thinking of Sol, Seamus, Rhelia, and Trev, all of whom probably thought I was dead, and knowing that every minute I was gone and they hadn't heard from me probably only confirmed their worst fears.

"Only a handful of days!" Renata said brightly, before flickering out of sight just as an arrow hit the ground where she'd been standing.

"Run, Victoria!" called the raspy voice in the mist, as more arrows thudded into the trees around us. I knew there was little I could do to help, and that Renata was clearly more than capable of taking care of herself. I would probably just get in her way. So, I did the only thing that made sense.

I ran.

OF COURSE, I didn't get far before realizing that Azrael was going to need my help to get anywhere without taking more than a healthy dose of arrows, so I slowed my own escape and focused on supporting the giant, hopping raven as they bounced between trees and over rocks, and generally tried to avoid tumbling ass over teakettle down the steep slope we suddenly found ourselves descending.

The terrain in this realm changed so abruptly that if I didn't know better I would have thought it was altering just to spite us. I didn't have long to contemplate it, though, because even though we weren't running amid a hail of arrows anymore, the footing on this hillside was the exact combination of steep, rocky, and muddy that meant watching my footing was going to be key.

I'm not entirely sure what we would have done if Renata hadn't been there, but I'm pretty sure that the short answer is "died."

As it was, I kept an arm around Az to help them keep their balance on the side where their wing was tied up, and we ran/hopped as fast as we could down the slope while Renata killed all the things that were trying to attack us from behind.

I was becoming more and more curious as to just what a Damphir could do, as the sound of flying arrows faded and we came to a somewhat sudden stop. Unfortunately, I had other questions that I needed to address first.

Such as, "Where the fuck did this canyon come from?"

"My best guess would be erosion," replied the raspy voice behind me.

I would have laughed, but I was too busy being dumbfounded by how a canyon as large as the one that spread before us could have been impossible to see in the distance when we were in the air fifteen minutes ago and had a literal bird's eye view of the place. And I must have been dumfounded enough to say part of that out loud, because Renata replied in short order.

"It could be enchanted to be invisible from the air, or possibly even to move at Hel's discretion. This is a very strange realm."

"I thought this place suppressed magic. I can't access any of my powers," I said, my brows furrowed as I looked between Renata and the giant gap in the landscape that looked at least a kilometer wide.

"You cannot access your powers, but not because magic is suppressed here—simply because Hel does not permit its use."

"Well, how in the hells does she regulate that? It's not like you can take people's magic from them."

Renata quirked an eyebrow at me.

"Well, I cannot speak as to what anyone else can do, but in this realm, Hel absolutely takes people's power from them. She alone has the discretion to use her powers or not, as she sees fit, in the Realm of the Dead."

She looked out across the canyon and sighed.

"Regardless of how it appeared here, we will need to find our way around it. It may add some days to our journey."

A million questions swam in my head in that moment. How could anyone take someone else's power, how could anyone hide a whole fucking canyon, what did it mean that this was called the Realm of the Dead, and did it mean that I had died somehow? Also, how in the name of Gwen was I supposed to convince Hel to let me use my powers to get out of here? I took a deep breath and stilled them all, because in that moment only one thing really mattered. I looked out across the canyon again, and then bent over and crawled to the nearest ledge to check out our options.

"The fastest way past this thing is going to be across it rather than around it," I said. "It could take weeks to bypass it, but down and through… it should just take a couple of days."

I looked at the sun.

"We should descend almost to the bottom today, but not quite all the way. If days are the same length here that they are back home, or close to it, then we don't have enough sunlight to make it all the way across, and we don't want to risk sleeping on the bottom in case it rains in the night. Could be prone to flash floods. Tomorrow we hopefully cross the whole thing and then make our way up and out on the other side."

Renata looked at me, then at Azrael, then at the canyon one more time.

"What makes you think we can even cross it?" she asked. "There is no trail. No suggestion that other humans have been this way."

I smiled.

"No, but there is a goat trail, just over there." I nodded in the direction of the faint trace of a path a few meters away. "And we ought to be able to make that work."

Renata frowned.

"Goats are excellent climbers," she said.

"So am I," I replied, just before hopping over the edge to the aforementioned goat trail and offering a hand back up to Azrael.

Azrael looked at Renata, then at me, let out a non-committal caw, and extended their good wing down to where I waited on the rocks below.

Renata looked at me and shrugged before jumping down beside me.

THE NEXT FEW days were difficult. Az's wing was causing them all kinds of pain as we made our way down the loose, steep choss field that was the canyon wall, and every slip, stumble, and fall seemed to wear heavily on the poor, feathered mess.

Renata seemed as unfazed by our descent into the canyon as she was by everything else in life. She helped with Az sometimes, but mostly she just trailed behind us, silent, weaving in and out of the grey mist that surrounded her constantly.

Alone, crossing this canyon would have been a challenge, but with a giant injured raven in tow, the whole debacle felt like one monumental obstacle after another. And yet… and yet, for the first time in three weeks, I felt like I wasn't spinning completely out of control. I felt… grounded, solid, real. After weeks of being thrown one new magical conundrum after another, after trying to solve problems I hadn't even known existed before I was pushed head first into this crazy-assed ocean of magic in the midst of a fucking hurricane… it felt really good to just be in charge of getting three people from one side of a canyon to another.

Like, so good.

Like, even when I was trying to shove a busted raven over a four foot high ledge that was crumbling quickly all around us, or when I was traversing a twenty foot shelf that plummeted into a pool full of scummy water but which would allow me to meet the injured raven in a place that would help them overcome the next bit of cliff face with a much lower chance of dying, or while I was cleaning and cooking trout that Azrael had snatched from the river with their beak in order to feed us all, or building a fire with nothing but two sticks, a large piece of bark, some dry leaves, and a shit-ton of elbow grease, or falling asleep in a heap of raven feathers each night so exhausted that even the scars on my shoulder and face throbbed with it, even then, my days in the canyon seemed a thousand times more manageable than this whole take-down-the-corrupt-magical-government-before-it-takes-everyone-else-down-with-it schtick.

I mean, fuck, why couldn't more of my problems be solved just by managing to survive in the wilderness? This was what I was good at. This was what I had trained to do since I was a tiny kid. This was where I felt like, not only did I know my ass from a hot rock, but I could defend a doctoral thesis on the ways in which my ass differed from a sun-warmed piece of basalt.

So perhaps it should have been no surprise to anyone that when we finally clawed our broken, tired asses up to the top of the cliff on the far side of the canyon and saw a giant fucking mountain range full of jagged, snow-capped peaks in front of us, I just laughed, turned to help pull Az up over the ledge behind me, and kept on plowing ahead.

IF YOU'RE NOT familiar with traversing mountain ranges, you may not be aware that, unless you're on a trip with the specific goal of bagging a summit, you don't generally want to go over any mountain tops. You want to go between and around them as much as possible. Mountains can come in many shapes and sizes, and some of the really old ones can be pretty mellow, but young upstarts like the Rockies, Andes, and Sierras do not fuck around. The mountain range between us and this "Citadel" Renata kept referring to was new to me, but it looked young. Stark, steep, devoid of plant life from about two-thirds of the way up. It was an imposing line of stone sentinels that ran the length of the horizon, and stretched from the ground beneath our feet to the cloud cover that kept its peaks invisible.

In other words, it looked a lot like my old backyard.

Unfortunately, my old backyard regularly kills people. The Rockies aren't a great place to drag an injured friend around, and the pass we were going to need to clear here in the Realm of the Dead was not nearly as friendly as I would have liked either. The pass would keep us from having to summit any of the nearest peaks, but only by a few hundred meters. We still had quite the climb ahead of us. Unlike the canyon we'd just traversed, the pass at least did us the favor of having a trail winding up it. Sadly, that didn't help as much as one might hope. We still wound up having to scale a handful of giant boulders that lay across the switchbacks winding up the steep slope. We couldn't skirt the boulders without risking rolling a few hundred meters down the scree pile that called itself a mountainside here, so up and over we went.

All that scrambling made me extremely grateful that my arms had been healing well; the cuts and bruises that I'd entered the canyon with had stayed clean enough that they'd scabbed over well and could now withstand a bit of exertion. Even still, I had to grit through quite a bit more pain to get myself and Az up over those boulders than I would have liked.

The trail, such as it was, also meant that the aforementioned scree pile wasn't completely covered in a season's worth of cracked and shifting snow for every step of the way. Only half of the way. What can I tell you? Trails aren't always as useful as everyone wants them to be. Sometimes, all they do is tell you that someone else was once stupid enough to make your same mistakes.

On the other hand, the trail also did sweet fuck all to keep us from freezing to death as we fought gale force winds, driving snow, and ice-slicked crenellations on our way to the top of the saddle. As I shoved my hands under my armpits and jumped up and down in place while Renata helped Az over the last crusted rise that should lead to our descent, I reminded myself that this was better than the peaks to either side of us—which definitely would have killed us if we'd tried them—but it wasn't much better, and I was close to hypothermic by the time I'd dragged my own ass over the top.

Sadly, no matter how much I bitched under my breath, the weather didn't seem to be interested in our epic human vs. nature narrative thread, and the wind, clouds, and blowing snow kept the view at the top hidden from us. I could smell the ice-tinged air that often accompanied high altitude ascents, but I did not get to enjoy a sweeping view of the land below us, and I would have been pissed about it, but I was too busy trying to stay warm now that we were no longer climbing.

I had to do a lot of skipping to keep my blood pumping, and Az kept stopping to wrap me in their good wing periodically, shoving me up against their warm, feathered, bird body. Then, when we were about halfway through our descent, the view opened up. I might have missed it if Renata hadn't been there.

As it was, I had my head down and was grumbling, "What the hell is the point of being in a damned book if the clouds don't clear to let you enjoy an epic view from the summit of a mountain you just dragged a giant busted bird up, anyway? If I have to keep performing rescues that almost get me killed and I have to be rescued half the damned time even though I've been granted a bunch of ridiculous magical powers that are straight out of a completely predictable chosen-one narrative, shouldn't we at least get to enjoy the fucking view? Even the fucking hobbits got to enjoy the view, every now and again."

And then, suddenly, I ran into Renata, who had stopped dead on the narrow trail in front of me.

"What…" but as I raised my eyes from where the trail met Renata's mist-covered boots, I saw precisely what had made her stop. The sun, which had been hiding in the clouds for the past few hours of our journey, was now peeking out from behind its grey curtain to entertain us with a glorious orange, red, pink, and purple display splattered across the clouds. And the light show silhouetted the peaks and valleys of an enormous citadel that rested at the foot of the mountains we'd just crossed.

"Well, fuck me."

Caw.

"It is rather splendid in this light," Renata admitted.

"THAT'S ONLY A few hours away," I said.

Renata nodded, or I thought she did. It was difficult to see a motion that subtle through the swirling grey mist that constantly surrounded her.

As we descended the remainder of the mountain in silence, half taken by the glorious sunset glowing ostentatiously behind the city in the distance, half consumed with thoughts of what getting to the citadel meant for each of us, I considered Renata's figure moving silently before me and wondered if the mist was some kind of magic, and, if so, how she managed to use it. After all, Az and I were unable to access any of our powers.

"It is not magic," she said, over her shoulder in front of me.

"You can read minds now?" I was starting to wonder how much Renata wasn't telling us.

"You were going to ask me eventually," she said, as if that was a perfectly reasonable explanation.

"Care to explain how you know that?"

"The mist, how quickly I move, even my strength, all come from one simple thing," she explained. "I am only half in this realm, and always half in my own realm."

My brain stuttered.

"How does that work?"

"I am not entirely sure of the science behind it. It is not widely studied, as my kind are incredibly rare, but something about my existence creates a permanent portal between my realm and whichever other realm I choose to travel in. However, time in my realm runs… differently, and… I can move back and forth in other realms' timelines with some flexibility. Which is why I appear to move faster than should be possible."

"And your strength?" I asked.

She shrugged.

"The gravity in my realm is considerably higher than in most other realms. Most realms leave me feeling feather light and as strong as a titan."

Caw.

I jumped forward to keep Azrael from running into me, and started walking again. My feet had apparently been unequal to the task of keeping me moving while my brain processed the information it had just gotten.

"How do you manage to exist in two places at once?" I asked, once my feet had started moving again.

"I am not sure. As I said, it is a little studied phenomenon."

Something about Renata's voice made me think she wasn't quite telling the truth, but maybe it was my imagination.

"It is why MOME was so desperate to capture and study me," she offered up after a long pause. "It is also why my father was so desperate to keep me near. He was…a peculiar vampire."

That sounded ominous enough that I was pretty much afraid to ask, but apparently I didn't need to. While Renata had been almost entirely quiet on our journey up to now—despite my many questions about this supposed "Realm of the Dead" and what it meant that we were here—she was suddenly all too willing to share. The drastic change was welcome, in a way. I knew so little about how this world worked that any new information seemed incredibly valuable to me, although it also made me a bit uncomfortable.

"I believe you are familiar with my father's obsession with me?" she asked.

"Sort of," I said. "He was very keen to get ahold of you. It was why he kept trying to give us over to MOME. Or at least, he was always asking me where you were whenever he showed up with a bunch of MOME asshats trying to kill us."

"And you did not simply tell him where I was and leave me to my fate?"

I thought about that for a minute. It would have been easier to tell Edik where we'd left Renata and let them have their own showdown, but…

"All I knew about you was that you had been rescued with the rest of the 'child' captives held with MOME and that you clearly hadn't tried to get in touch with your dad after getting free. I knew we'd left instructions with the folks caring for all the children to put them in touch with their families if they wanted them. I figured if you hadn't tracked down Edik yet, there was a reason. And, after my own experiences with him, I wasn't keen to force him on anyone else."

"Most people on Earth would have insisted that a child should be reunited with their parents," Renata commented, seemingly without ire.

"Well, I'm not most people. There are good reasons for kids not to want to be with their parents. If you'd been younger, I might have arranged a meeting or something. I think that's what they did for all the youngest kids we busted out of MOME, but older ones…"

Renata laughed, a dry sound, at least in this realm.

"I am certainly older. I am likely twice your age, at least in your world. However, in my world… I do not seem to age in my world. And as I spend more than half my time here… I do not seem to age very quickly at all. I believe that is why my father wished to find me. He was rather… obsessed with his own mortality."

"Uh… wasn't he a vampire?"

"Indeed. He was. But did you know that vampires aren't truly immortal?"

That had me stopped in the trail long enough for Az to smack into my back.

Caw.

"They aren't?" I asked.

Renata laughed again.

"Oh, they are so close as for it to make no difference to most of them. With food in abundance, they will live for thousands of years. No one is entirely sure quite how long. But eventually, their bodies can no longer support the constant energy transfer, so they age and die, just like anyone else."

"So… you're telling me Edik was afraid of dying?"

"Indeed. So much so, that he was willing to spend as much time as possible in my realm with me. He was convinced it would stop his aging."

"Woah, so he was going to what, move in with you?"

"In a sense…. I do not think that would have worked, for many reasons. But he was determined to try. I could never be near him but he would find a way to latch on to me and make me take him into my own realm."

We were all silent for a long time, as we resumed our slow plod down the steep hillside.

"I do not enjoy having other people in my realm. It… feels wrong."

And sure, I could see that. I mean, I didn't have my own pocket realm that I could visit at will, but… I didn't even like having most people hang out in my room for too long. If I had a whole realm that was unique to me, and I was forced to share it against my will?

I shuddered.

I decided not to ask too many follow-up questions on that one, though. Honestly, I was amazed with how much information Renata had just volunteered. No one else in the magical community had been this forthcoming with me. Then again, maybe this was just the first chance I'd had to spend time talking to someone about how any of this stuff worked. It seemed like ever since that first night that Edik had attacked me, the night when Seamus had explained a bit about being a werewolf and I'd first learned that magic was more than something to read about in books, I'd been constantly on the run, trying to preserve my life and the lives of everyone I cared about. It had all been running, evading capture, dodging death, helping people, getting rescued, almost dying.... None of which left time for lectures about how magic worked, what everything was called, or who got which powers, and why.

Which reminded me...

"Hey, Az, I've been meaning to ask. Do you have different preferred pronouns for your different forms?

Caw caw.

On our first night camping in the canyon, we'd decided two caws would be no. One would be yes. Charades was even harder for Az in crow form than it had been as a squirrel demon.

"So, if I use they/them for all of your forms, that's ok with you?"

Caw.

"Is there any time you'd like me to use different pronouns?"

Caw caw.

"Cool. Sorry I didn't ask earlier. Everyone just keeps trying to kill us and then I forget."

Caw.

Az's beak lowered to my shoulder and they nipped very gently at my earlobe in what I took to be an affectionate motion. It still hurt. I tried to be surreptitious about rubbing it after they let go, though.

I looked out at the citadel in the distance again, and the excitement I'd felt at first seeing it—knowing the end of our journey was in sight, that I'd soon have my powers restored and be able to get back to fighting MOME and stopping Rebecca Dryer from blowing up the world—faded, as I realized that as soon as we reached that citadel, we'd be out of the wilderness and I would be back to feeling like I'd stumbled into the chat room for a MMORPG as a level one character, while the only other people logged in were level 70 and all in a different guild than me.

"Do not worry, Victoria," Renata said, ignoring the hundred times that I'd asked her to call me Vic. "You will not feel like a fish out of water forever. Soon you will hit your stride."

I laughed awkwardly, deciding that even if what Renata could do wasn't mind reading, it was close enough to make me uncomfortable.

This time when the citadel caught my eye, I began wondering how different things would be there compared to all of the other magical places I'd been so far. It looked… like the silhouette of a life-sized Duplo construction—as though a mountain-sized toddler had spent hours perfecting their sprawling structure, half blocky towers, half single-story sprawls, none of it particularly artfully put together, though still striking when haloed by the setting sun from a great distance.

"It does not improve upon closer inspection," said Renata, putting the final nail in the coffin of "I'm not mind reading."

"But I am not," she said. "It is only that once I have responded to something you were going to say in a moment, you will not say it anyway, and so you believe you only thought it."

"So what about the times where I do speak first?" I wondered aloud.

"People are often disturbed by this habit of mine, so I try to keep myself in their time stream as often as I can," she replied. "But I am scouting ahead to make sure that we aren't running into trouble, and I cannot help what I overhear when I return."

"Ugh…" I muttered. "Time travel makes my brain hurt."

Renata turned to me then.

"It is not time travel, it is two realms moving at different speeds through the universe and occasionally touching. Time travel is—"

"If you're going to tell me time travel isn't possible I am going to laugh in your face," I said, before she could finish.

The petite young woman—I had rather resolutely decided that no matter how young she looked, someone who had killed as many people as she had couldn't be considered a child—stared at me with blue eyes that reminded me far too clearly of her dad, and a shiver went down my spine despite my best efforts to look resolute.

"You sound awfully certain for someone who is so new to this world of magic," she said, in a tone that suggested I was insane.

"I may have only just joined this world where dark matter can bend reality, but… let's just say, I've been getting a crash course in what's possible."

Renata considered me for a moment, walking backwards down the trail as she did so, and causing me no small amount of angst as I worried that she'd take a step too far to either side and go tumbling down the side of the mountain.

Then she simply turned on her heel and continued on in silence.

Caw, said Az.

"Caw indeed," I mumbled.

~~~

By the time we reached the citadel my dislike of this realm had gone from mild to emphatic. Aside from the harpies that had tried to kill us right after we'd stepped through the seam to get here, the changing landscape that seemed custom designed to slow us on our journey, and the fact that Az and I couldn't access any of our powers, the city itself had slowly resolved into precisely what it had appeared to be from afar.

It was a life-sized Duplo construction designed and executed by a toddler. Only it wasn't the vivid primary colors that a Duplo set boasted, but rather a combination of concrete and plastic blocks in a dull series of greys and tans that gave the impression of a sepia photograph of soviet Russia.

Consequently, I wasn't even surprised when, as we tiredly stumbled our way up to a tall grey wall topped with medieval looking spikes that had no business in a Duplo set, a horde of harpy guards descended from atop the wall, rushed us with spears, and informed us that we were to be taken straight to Hel.
~~~

"AH, YES. WELCOME back, Renata, darling. You've done well."

I glared around the massive hall that we'd just been prodded into. Harpy spears, as I'd learned on my first day in this shitty realm, were quite sharp, and I cannot tell you how little I appreciated being jabbed at with them for the entire three kilometer long walk that stood between the wall where we'd been apprehended and the hall that housed the ruler of the Realm of the Dead.

So, while I normally might have been quite impressed with the vaulted ceiling that crowned a chamber that had been studiously transformed from concrete block (which it had clearly been on the outside) to cavern-like structure of hedonistic pleasure, I was decidedly not in the mood by the time we got there.

There were steaming pools in every direction I looked, all filled with naked people of every variety. The diversity of bodies on display (in terms of size, shape, skin and fur colors, numbers of horns, eyes, and extra limbs) was equal to that of the crowded streets of Unterberg. Here, however, there was decidedly less clothing involved in the equation, and quite a bit more steam. The misty pools of naked people were spread evenly about the room/cavern/whatever this was, but terraces gradually raised the elevation a half meter at a time until the whole thing plateaued at a terrace covered in a series of boulders shaped into a throne. Atop the throne sat a scantily clad blue-skinned woman with eight arms.

"I thought you hailed from Norse mythology," I said aloud, before I could think better of it. We had been dragged before the eight-armed figure, on the next terrace down, and forced to our knees by the harpies who had wrangled us this whole way, and my tendency to fight emotional overload with snide commentary seemed to be as strong as ever.

I was pissed about a few things, not least of which was that it sounded like Renata had been working with this blue-skinned deity to bring us here, and when I'm angry, I get surly. You may have noticed.

"Tsk, tsk, Victoria, I'd been led to believe you were intelligent," replied Hel.

The silence that followed was clearly meant to give me time to piece together all that was wrong with my assumptions, so I stared at the goddess for a minute before shrugging.

"My Hindu pantheon is pretty limited, sorry."

In reply, the blue figure stuck out her tongue, long and red with blood, and then she shifted to a form that was similar to the first but entirely black instead of blue, and added quite a few more heads and arms than I could count in the few seconds she held it. Then she shifted back to blue, with four arms. Which was when my world religions class from sophomore year poked my brain a few times, and it finally clicked.

"Oooh! Kali! Nice. I guess that makes sense. I'm not super familiar with the mythology, but there's something in there about the realm of the dead, isn't there? So you and Hel…" my voice trailed off as the deity shifted to a tall, lithe, fair-haired, blue-eyed white lady.

"I am Hel, and many others besides," she said, filling the silence that I'd left, and indeed, filling the cavern with the resonance of her voice.

"Cool. Well, whatever you wanna call yourself is fine by me, but I am mainly concerned with getting the Hell out of here (pun intended), so if you could just give me my powers back…"

The woman laughed and shifted back to the blue-skinned, four-armed version of herself, and I blinked hard to keep the dizziness at bay. It was kind of like looking at Azrael when I couldn't get one form to hold, but there must have been something else about Hel's power that made my head spin, because she was only taking one form at a time.

"You are in my realm now, Victoria, and you will do as I require," she said, placing one set of hands on her hips and crossing the other set in front of her chest.

"Look, I appreciate that this is your place, and I really appreciate the hospitality of a few dozen harpies trying to kill me the moment I arrived, but I'm going to have to pass on whatever else you're offering."

I held the deity's gaze, even though her eyes were difficult to focus on, and I knew I was pushing my luck a lot farther than was wise. What can I tell you, my fear response is sass.

"No one leaves this realm without my consent, and none may use power save at my discretion," she hissed. "Everyone completes a task for me. Renata here retrieved you and brought you to my doorstep, as she was bid."

She gestured towards the ball of grey mist that obscured Renata, now quite a bit thicker than I had ever seen it, almost thick enough to block out Azrael's giant crow form standing behind her, but I still managed to make out that Renata's hands were no longer bound. The thought that Renata might have set us up angered me, but right now it was taking a back seat to a hundred other rage inducing thoughts, so I quickly turned back to the four-armed woman in front of me.

"Look, I appreciate that you enjoy a good power trip. Totally understandable, especially if you live forever and get bored easily, but if I don't get back to my own realm as soon as possible, there may not be much of this realm or any other left, and I don't have time to—"

"You will do as you are told, or suffer the consequences!"

And with that, all four of Hel's hands snapped their fingers and two people were suddenly standing beside her that I'd never expected to see again. I recognized them even from afar, even with clouds of steam wafting between us. I would recognize them anywhere.

"Vic?" asked my mother.

"Vic?" echoed my dad.

"MOM?" I ASKED, my legs buckling beneath me as I looked from her to the man she was clinging to as if her own legs could barely hold her. "Dad?"

My world tunneled down to enclose only the two of them, the rest of the cavern's steaming pools and dark architecture fading from view, the smell of warm bodies and wet rocks dissolving as well.

My voice was barely a whisper now, but it echoed through the rocky chambers and I knew that they'd both heard me call them. My parents and I both lunged towards each other at the same time, but the harpies holding me pulled my rope-bound wrists backwards and I sank back to my knees even while Hel made a mere gesture that held my parents by some invisible force.

"What are my parents doing here? Why did you take them?" I growled, turning back to Hel.

"They came to me of their own volition, I assure you," Hel said, her smile curling into something almost feline, and in no way amiable. "They met the criteria, so they were permitted entry. What better place to hide, after all, than the Realm of the Dead?"

It felt like being stabbed, seeing my parents so close, yet completely out of reach, and hearing that they'd left me voluntarily. I looked at both my parents and saw the truth there. The flash of guilt in my Mom's eyes, the sadness in my dad's. Hel wasn't lying. They had come here of their own accord.

"Now," continued Hel, that same smile still curling the corner of her blue lips. "Everyone who comes to my realm must pay the price of admittance. You and your crow both meet the criteria, but that is not enough. You must complete a quest of my choosing, and then we will discuss the return of your powers, and the possibility of your being permitted to leave this place."

I still don't know if it was the surprise of seeing my parents alive, the torment of having them so close and yet not being able to hug them, ask if they were ok, and take them home, or just the blind rage at how fucking unfair everything had been for so long, but something inside of me simply snapped.

"No."

I said it quietly, but in that moment it might as well have been a scream.

"No?" asked Hel, the predatory smile falling from her lips. "What do you mean no? Do you realize what I could do to you?"

And as she asked, fire leapt to life all around me, scorching my skin and hair, and beginning to burn the rope that bound my wrists. It was hot, painfully so, but I was beyond caring. I just glared, and let the rage consume me in even greater measure than the fire.

"I don't care what you do to me," I said, realizing the words were true only as I spoke them. It wasn't that I wanted to die, far from it, it was just that I was so consumed with rage that I wanted to destroy everything, and didn't care if I took myself down with the ship. "I have been doing my damnedest, for weeks, to save Earth, the people I love, and the rest of the universe from a lunatic, and I do not have time for your bullshit quests. I do not have time for your weird ego trip, for your power hungry kleptomania, for whatever bullshit made my parents run to you, or whatever you want to threaten to do to them to try to gain my compliance."

I took a deep breath, ignored the heat that singed my nose hair, and got ready to speak again. It was like I'd broken a dam inside me and now nothing could stop it but getting the rage out. And there was… just so damned much of it. Who knows, a few weeks ago I'd probably have kept it all to myself and just played along. I'd certainly let everyone else tell me what was what ever since I'd learned that the world didn't work the way I thought it did. This rage in me had been building up ever since my parents had "died," and even more since I'd learned the truth about Trev, my powers, and everything else, but I doubt I would have let it loose like this—on someone who could probably destroy me with the snap of her fingers, no less—if I hadn't spent the past five days remembering that there were a few things in the universe that I did understand. A few things I'd worked hard to become competent at, and damn it all, I'd just led an injured raven the size of a small car through a canyon as big as the largest on Earth, and then between two mountains big enough to sit comfortably in the Rockies. I'd dealt with more shit than was reasonable already, and I was fucking bone tired of being told what to do by mystical people who called themselves gods, whether they were on my side or not.

"My parents fucking lied to me for ten years and then disappeared without me to save their own skins. I don't fucking care if you set them on fire right now. I've believed them dead for most of a year now, it won't be that much more crushing to see them actually dead. I have been tested, again and again, over the past few weeks, playing by a set of rules I've never been told, with a hand I can't even stop to look at, and I have no fucking clue who you are or why you think you have a right to anyone else's dark matter just because they wind up in your realm. But I will fucking tell you this right now, if you try to make me go on another fucking quest I will fight you with every Gwendamned thing that I am, and I don't care if it destroys me, your entire realm, and my parents too. There will be no quest. I have saved the world twice in the past week and I need to get home so I can do it again. And if that's not enough for you, then you deserve to go up in flames with the rest of the universe when Rebecca Dryer implodes it all in her misguided attempt to bring the non-magical world to heel."

Then I sat down on the ground, cross legged, in the ring of fire that was licking violently at my entire body and added, "and I will sit here and slowly burn to death until you make up your mind about how you feel about that, and everyone else can just fuck right off."

I WASN'T BLUFFING, exactly. I was so damned angry in that precise moment that I really didn't care if the whole world burned, and by the time I was done talking, the rage inside of me was burning so hot that I barely felt the ring of flames that licked at me as I collapsed into a lotus position on the floor of the cavern. I was even numb to the cry my mother let out when I sank down into the flames. In fact, hearing my mother's despair only fueled my rage. If she was so damned concerned for my well-being, why had she abandoned me, abandoned Trevor, left everything behind and just disappeared? What the hell were my parents playing at? They'd been dead to me for months, and now they were back and I was supposed to care enough about them to abandon the people back on Earth who had NEVER LEFT ME BEHIND just to save them?

Fuck that.

Fuck all of this.

"You are foolish, human, if you think your tantrum sways me at all," said Hel, although the flames surrounding me died away as she said it, so I wasn't sure how much truth was behind those words.

But then the same ring of fire enveloped my parents, and it took every shred of self-control I had not to launch myself at the blue-skinned goddess holding them hostage.

"If your own wellbeing doesn't convince you that your will is mine, then perhaps you need some external motivators."

I was still angry with my parents. Furious, really, even though part of me thought that might not be the most fair response to everything they'd likely gone through. But I pushed thoughts like that aside, focused on the rage instead, and stilled the part of me that was begging to be unleashed in some heroic attempt to save them. An attempt that would probably get me killed, or at the very least leave me stuck completing some stupid, arbitrary, waste of time, just to appease the whim of a goddess who got her jollies by stealing power and making people do things.

I didn't have time for that kind of bullshit.

So, I focused on my anger and ignored the part of me that still wanted to run to my parents' arms, or tear off the extra arms of the woman who was using them as bait.

I sighed and stood up again, not easy from a lotus position while my hands were bound, but I was still so angry I barely noticed the effort.

"You don't get it, do you? There will be nothing left for you to hoard if you don't let me get back to my friends. Your existence is as much at stake as mine. The weapon Rebecca Dryer plans to use will take out the entire universe. There will not be any realm that is spared. Anything that can be reached from Earth, or from an Earth-adjacent realm, all of it could be wiped out by a single use of this weapon. I have already wasted precious days scrambling across your ridiculous realm, dodging harpies, traversing canyons, and climbing mountains, but I refuse to waste another minute for your overinflated ego. And, I may be in a book, but damn it, I refuse, flat-out re-fucking-fuse to go on a side quest just because you have a hard on for pushing people around. If this damned author needs more words or something, they can fucking well figure out a plot twist that works, instead of sending me on a random adventure for no reason."

I took a deep breath and reminded myself that throwing insults around wasn't likely to get me anywhere. Egomaniacal tyrants didn't enjoy being insulted any more than most people did, probably quite a bit less, actually. Besides which, I probably wasn't convincing anyone of my sanity with the whole book rant. I tried changing tacks.

"I mean, look, it's not like I even know what the fuck I'm doing, really, when it comes to this whole saving the world business, but I just learned something that the folks on Earth really need to know if we're going to stop the madwoman with the evil plan, and I've already wasted…"

My voice trailed off as an idea struck me. Silence followed, probably because I sounded batshit nuts, not that I cared.

"Hel… How exactly is it that you take people's power here?"

Hel glared at me as if the question were incredibly rude.

"That is not an answer you've earned, human, that is—"

"Renata said you can choose who has their powers and who doesn't? Is that true?"

"No one accesses magic in this realm without my permission," Hel replied coolly.

"Right, so you can take away someone's power. Is it permanent?"

"That is none of your—"

"Could it be permanent?" I asked. "Could you strip someone of their power forever?"

Hel shrugged.

"All of this?" I gestured around the cavern that surrounded us, my brain putting things together, even in the face of Hel's reticence. "This was accomplished with the power of others, wasn't it? That's what feeds your power, right? Stripping it from everyone else here?"

Hel glared at me, but she didn't deny it.

"Look," I said, holding up my bound wrists in the best imitation of a gesture of surrender I could muster. "I don't care what you do with it, really, as long as it's possible that you can make it permanent."

Hel said nothing.

"I believe," I continued, hoping I was on the right track, "that if you assign me the quest of my choosing, I can bring you a power you might find quite useful."

Hel raised a single sculpted eyebrow and I decided now was my chance.

"In return for my completing a quest at the end of which I will deliver to you a mage of great power, all I ask is one favor in return. Deal?"

"And what quest would you choose, human?"

"Oh, you know, just overthrowing MOME, taking Rebecca Dryer permanently out of the game, and saving the universe."

I BLINKED AND rubbed my eyes, sure that I was imagining what I was seeing.

Because what I was seeing looked like every Gwedamned dragon in the dragon realm mustering for battle in the middle of a sun-soaked valley, and that… that didn't seem like the best idea, considering each and every one of them could be weaponized and used to take out… the world.

"What in the devil is going on here?" asked Azrael from beside me. They seemed relieved to be back in their succubus form, flaring their silver wings in the sunlight atop the pillar of earth on which we now stood, looking out over the dragon meeting grounds. Once Hel had agreed to my terms she'd been almost eager to get me out of her realm. She hadn't even let me say goodbye to my folks.

"I don't know, but I think we'd better find out before 'bad things' happen."

"Bad things?" Azrael raised an eyebrow, and I blinked hard as both of their forms tried to take up the same space in my vision. "Worse than the usual?"

"The same as usual," I replied.

Azrael just smiled and took wing—both of which were healed in their current form—and I was about to issue a complaint about them flying off without me, when I remembered that they weren't the only ones with wings.

I closed my eyes, calling to mind the feel of wind rushing over my scales, gravity defied by aerodynamics, and the faint trace of fire in my belly. Then I leapt off the ledge, spread my giant scaly wings, and joined Azrael as he spiraled down to the center of the frenetic bustle happening on the ground.

I shifted to my human form the moment we landed, and there was a moment of awkward silence before I was wrapped in more arms than I could easily count.

"Vic!"

"You're alive!"

"We thought—"

"When Az didn't come back right away—"

"No one knew—"

"How did you—"

I couldn't keep track of all the things being said at once, but tears flooded my eyes as I registered the familiar feel of everyone I'd thought I would die saving. Sol, Seamus, Trev, Rhelia… all there, all embracing me.

I'm so sorry, Vic, for everything before, about Rhelia.

I was too overwhelmed to reply, especially because something about Trev reaching out telepathically felt like regaining a limb I thought I'd lost, but all I could do was lean even harder into the group hug. It was probably minutes before any of us let go.

"Oh man," I said, wiping at my eyes. "I really missed you guys."

"You missed us?" Sol asked, sounding oddly surprised. When I turned to look at her, probably with confusion displayed in a twist of eyebrows, she smiled and shook her head. "I mean, that's fine, it's great that you care enough to miss us in a short period of time, but we were the ones that thought you were dead, Gatita. You knew you weren't dead. Why would you miss us? You've only been gone for a few hours."

I looked around at all of them, trying to catch the light in their eyes that would tell me Sol was fucking with me. I looked for Azrael to confirm that I wasn't losing my Gwendamned mind, but they were a few meters away talking intently with one of the dragons.

"Ok, this isn't funny," I said, my eyes snapping to Seamus, who I figured was the least likely to keep a joke running if it was clearly making someone uncomfortable, but he just looked at me with his head tilted to one side, as though waiting for an explanation.

"You guys, I was gone for like five days! What are you talking about?"

"Five days?" asked Trevor, looking concerned, but not nearly as incredulous as I would expect if I had seriously been gone for only a few hours here on Earth. "Which realm were you in?"

"Hell," I said, looking desperately between all the faces of the people I loved most in the world. "Or, well, the Realm of the Dead, not really Hell

I guess, and not even really the Realm of the Dead, but that's what Hel called it, so…"

I trailed off, realizing that I was rambling. Sol looked curious, Seamus concerned, Rhelia looked… her face was oddly blank. Like blank enough that I was suddenly certain that she was hiding something, but before I could ask what that might be, Trev distracted me.

"Did you… meet anyone interesting there?" he asked, and the question snapped my attention back to him. As soon as my eyes met his, I knew. I knew in my bones, and the knowledge made me want to throw up.

"You knew they were there. This whole time. You knew."

The way Trev blanched, the tightness in his jaw, he looked almost like I'd punched him in the gut, and he didn't deny it, not even a little bit.

"Gatita, what—"

But I couldn't. I couldn't decide if it was worse that my parents had left without telling me where they were going, but had for some reason told Trev, or that Trev hadn't told me after he found out. It was hard to weigh betrayals that way.

I couldn't look Trev in the eyes, and I couldn't cope with feeling like I'd just gotten Trev back and then lost him again a few heartbeats later.

I wasn't really thinking of a destination when I reached through space and time, but I just didn't want to be here anymore, and I really hoped Azrael had been paying attention enough to fill everyone in on the pertinent details, because all I wanted to do was disappear.

Turns out that's a not a good mindset to have when one is reaching through spacetime.

When I opened my eyes, I was no longer surrounded by my friends, or hundreds of dragons preparing for battle.

I was no longer surrounded by anything at all.

Oops, I thought, as darkness enveloped me.

VIRGINIA McCLAIN

VICTORIA MARMOT
AND THE
ROAD TO HELL

VICTORIA MARMOT BOOK FIVE

To Dad, for always having a sense of humor.

THE NOTHINGNESS WAS absolutely terrifying.

I would probably have shit my pants, except I didn't appear to have any pants, let alone an intestinal tract with which to shit them. In fact, even the sensation of terror felt slightly off, because I had no heart to race, no pulse to quicken, no breath to catch.

An instant ago, I had been surrounded by friends in a world I recognized. Then Trev had admitted he'd known about Mom and Dad being alive, I'd freaked out, reached through time and space while only wanting to disappear, and now…

I had nothing.

I could see nothing. No light, no shadow, no hint of shapes in darkness, just… nothing.

Even that would have been manageable, I think, if I could have felt anything. Anything at all. But for a moment, for as long as it took me to register that I didn't seem to have a body, or anything at all to contain me—whatever qualified as "me" in that instant—I was nothing.

Nothing but thoughts.

And then, as suddenly as the thought occurred to me—in the instant in which my mind wanted my body to be there—it was. I still couldn't see it, or anything else, but I could feel my hands, feet, heart beating, lungs breathing, all the little twitches and ticks that make up a body.

And the moment that I longed to see that body, if only to confirm that I wasn't somehow hallucinating it, I could.

There was light, though it was the strangest light I'd ever experienced, since it seemed to have no origin, and lit nothing but my body. There was no source, and my body cast no shadows. The light wasn't coming from within me, but a glow surrounded me like a tightly wrapped blanket.

It was just enough to confirm that I had eyes to see and a body to feel. A naked one, for a heartbeat anyway, until I thought that I'd rather not be, and was suddenly covered in some galaxy leggings and a soft t-shirt with "i^2 (keep it real)" emblazoned on the chest.

"Better than what my Gwen powers keep choosing," I said, into the nothing. Because even though I now had a clothed body that I could feel, there was still nothing around me. So much so, that I wondered how I was speaking aloud. I supposed there must be oxygen, since I was still alive and didn't even feel out of breath, but there was certainly no motion of air around me, or even a sense of what was up or down. I felt as though I were floating in space, only without all the freezing to death, having all your blood vessels burst, and asphyxiation.

Then I wondered if the reason that I wasn't dying was simply because I was already dead.

What else would cause me to be suspended in nothing, as a string of thoughts that seemed to be able to will myself into being?

Beginning to panic, and now with a body that latched fully onto the sensation of a tightening chest and more rapid breathing, I closed my eyes and tried to shift back to the dragon realm. I reached for it with every fiber of my being. Stretched desperately for that field in the sunlight, where I'd just reappeared in front of all of my friends after my crazy trip through hell.

And got nothing but the mother of all headaches in return.

That did not help the rising panic situation.

I tried to take some deep, calming breaths and focus on lowering my heart rate.

To my amazement, it worked.

Although I wasn't sure why I was surprised. If I'd just managed to think galaxy leggings into existence, why not calm my breathing with a thought too? Which sort of just reinforced the idea that none of this was real. Which brought me back to being convinced that I was dead. And…cue chest tightening.

"Damn it! Calm the fuck down, Vic."

And ok, apparently yelling at myself worked too. As soon as I said the words, my heart rate returned to normal again.

I closed my eyes again, and tried reaching for every location I could think of: the glade of Life, Sol's cabin in the Andes, the ruins of my old house in Arizona, the ruins of my older home in Colorado, Uncle Algy's place, Flagstaff High School—nothing worked. I remained surrounded by nothing.

"This is getting kinda old," I informed the nothing.

"I would really prefer it if I had someone to talk to," I added, hopefully.

Since I'd been half expecting to conjure another person out of thin air, I should not have nearly jumped out of my skin when I heard a soft thump to my right. I did anyway.

But when I turned to inspect the blackness there, I didn't see anything.

"I would love to be able to see the someone I can talk to," I clarified, and immediately gasped, finding myself confronted with a very large, very toothy snow leopard.

"Please don't eat me."

Of course, right after I said it, the giant snow leopard's jaw snapped shut in the final throes of what, now, was clearly a yawn, but that didn't make my ass unclench, or keep my stomach from feeling like it was doing somersaults for a while. Instead, it blew a huff of air out of its nose and twitched its expansive whiskers, before stepping past me and into… a room that hadn't existed a second ago.

Dark hardwood flooring stretched beneath a throw rug, low coffee table, and some plush leather couches. There was also a fireplace, complete with a crackling fire and the smell of cedar smoke. Given that the place looked and smelled like a cozy combination of my parents' Colorado living room and Sol's Andean cabin, someone was trying to make me feel better.

Belatedly, it occurred to me that someone was probably me.

The excessively large snow leopard waltzed past me, past the coffee table, and onto the dark leather sofa. There, she twitched her large, fluffy tail a few times before pressing her furry head into the sofa cushion and blinking sleepily at me.

It was then, gazing into eyes that weren't the dazzling grey exhibited by most snow leopards, but instead ringed in a bright green like my own, that I realized exactly who I was staring at.

"You're me, aren't you?" I asked, unsure if that was the right way to phrase it. "Or, me when I'm a snow leopard, anyway."

Feline me merely blinked at me again, then shut her eyes and began purring softly.

"Well, fuck. I was kinda hoping for someone to talk *to*, you know. Not just someone to talk *at*."

Snow leopard me said nothing, but the large oak door to the room, which hadn't been there a moment ago, suddenly reverberated with a deep and echoing thump.

"Well, that's not terrifying," I said, reluctantly turning away from snow leopard me and heading towards the newly existent door.

If STARING DOWN snow leopard me had been disconcerting, staring into the plate-sized eyes of a dragon was as terrifying as the nothingness of death.

"You can turn off the 'make the human shit her pants glamour' any time now," I said, by way of introduction.

"I am not using my glamour, Vic. It's just that dragons are terrifying up close. Even when they're you."

That voice wasn't mine. Or, at least, it didn't come from my human mouth. What qualified as "mine" in this place was getting stupidly more complicated by the second.

"I suppose we're all here?" asked the dragon, poking her head, which was about five times the size of the average horse head, into the room. "Hey, Kit!" she exclaimed, addressing the still sleeping feline, whose tail flicked in a semi-conscious gesture of welcome.

"Mind making the room bigger, Vic?"

The dragon turned her giant head in my direction again, and I realized she was talking to me. I had been too stunned by her overall appearance to really listen to her. Unlike my snow leopard form, which I had at least seen in the mirror once, I'd never gotten to look at any part of my dragon form for more than a few fleeting seconds while I was inhabiting its skin. Or its scales, I suppose I should say.

"Room, be bigger," I said, not sure how to make things adjust intention-ally without voicing my requests, and finding myself too distracted by dragon-me's beauty to even notice how much larger the room and door got. Instead, I stood mesmerized, as dragon-me pushed her enormous, scaled body into a room that was now large enough to encompass her in all of her sunset-colored glory. I'd forgotten just how stunning those scales were. Perhaps not surprising, considering I'd never gotten more than a peripheral glimpse of them. Seeing them full-on, and from the perspective of a human, was completely entrancing. Almost hypnotic.

"I know, we're lovely, aren't we?"

I blinked, distantly noticing that the voice wasn't mine.

"Why have I never noticed that I can speak aloud in dragon form?" I asked, suddenly embarrassed.

"Yes, well, you're rather new to the whole being a dragon thing, aren't you? And I… well, I don't exactly have more experience—I haven't existed any longer than you have, since we're the same person really, but without human thoughts to distract me it all just sort of… works. You'll need practice, of course, but dragon vocal chords are incredibly versatile. There's little we can't do with them. Anyway, I didn't mean to show off, but since you were already speaking aloud with Kit, I thought it was only polite to do the same."

I took a deep breath and decided to focus on the last thing dragon-me had just said.

"You heard me speaking to her?"

"More or less. I was you while you were speaking to her, so I heard everything."

"And you're not me now?" I asked, starting to wish I were sitting down. As soon as the thought formed, I was sitting on a large, dark leather sofa perpendicular to the one where feline-me slept.

"Ok, this place is freaking me out," I admitted.

"Yes, I'd noticed. I suppose that's understandable. You're never conscious when you're here, after all. None of us are, usually."

"Where, exactly, is here?" I asked, trying not to wince.

"Well, that's complicated, but the short answer is… the extradimensional pocket where you keep all your dark matter."

"Isn't my dark matter inside me, spread throughout my blood?"

"Yep."

"So, I'm inside myself?"

"Sort of."

"That doesn't seem like a place I ought to be able to go," I said, feeling my mind trying to bend around to understand dragon-me's explanation.

"It does seem implausible," she agreed. "But here we are."

"How could I possibly have gotten here?"

"I'm guessing it had something to do with your Gwen-given abilities, but I'm not entirely sure, to be honest."

"And if you're me... how do you know anything that I don't already know?"

"Oooh! That's a good one. The answer is that I'm a dragon. Which is to say, you're at least part dragon. And I don't know anything that you don't technically know."

"What?"

Dragon-me stared at human-me and blinked her giant, green eyes.

"You know everything I do, technically, but dragon brains and human brains don't work the same way, so it would be difficult for you to know the things that I know when you aren't in dragon form."

"And how on earth do you know things that I don't know regardless of what form you're in? Were you... did you..." I swallowed, feeling suddenly ill. "Did I steal a dragon when I—"

"No, no. Good heavens no. Nothing like that. I'm a part of you, accessed through your well of dark matter and a bit of epigenetic gymnastics. You didn't steal an already existing dragon, but... dragons, even weredragons, are a bit of an odd case in the grand scheme of things. Dragons have very large brains, and cerebral matter that is unlike that of any other creature's. It grants us a few advantages. For one, we have genetic memory. Very strong genetic memory, unlike most species, so we keep all the knowledge of our species alive even without an oral or written history (though of course we have those as well). Full dragons are born knowing everything that every single one of their ancestors knew. They are born with dozens, or hundreds, of lives in their memories. Weredragons only get a sort of distilled version of that, since they originally come from a human and dragon pairing up while the dragon is in its human form. But even that little bit of human DNA makes the genetic memory less detailed than a full dragon's memory, since half or more of their ancestors don't have the genetic memory to fill in the blanks. And whatever memories they have, they can only access them when they're in dragon form."

"Holy shit."

"Indeed."

"So... because you're currently in our dragon form, you know that stuff, but I don't?"

"Well, in this space you might actually be able to access my genetic memory without me being in dragon form, but it might be difficult to visualize, and it's hard to look for something you don't know you have. Since you wished for company, and then company that could talk, here we are."

"My head hurts, and it's not from trying to shift myself out of here," I muttered.

Dragon-me looked completely nonplussed, inasmuch as I could distinguish facial expressions on her scaled mien, and feline-me let out a low noise that sounded suspiciously like a growl.

"What?" I asked, glancing between the two of them.

"Aren't you concerned about the fact that shifting out of here didn't work?" dragon-me asked.

I didn't like her tone. It was far too cautious. Like she was worried she'd hurt me if she spoke any louder.

"Of course I am. Weren't you there for the near panic attack I had? What's your point?"

I sounded too shrill even to my own ears, but I couldn't help it. Just bringing it up again made me feel jittery.

"It shouldn't be possible for you to be here," dragon-me said, lending an extra calm to her voice that had the opposite effect than she was probably going for. "All three of us being here means there is no part of your consciousness outside of this space, and thus no tether to shift back with."

"Does that mean that all three of us are actually separate parts of my consciousness?" I asked, wondering if what I actually had was a multiple personality disorder.

Feline-me growled at that suggestion.

"Look, as far as I can tell, our situation here is unique," dragon-me offered. "No dragon in our ancestry had a clear understanding of how dark matter pockets worked, because most of our ancestors were more of the "magic is magic" mindset. But even the one draconic scientist whose genetic memory I possess was never able to access her own dark matter pocket, even after she'd theorized that it existed. She actually tried, of course, scientist that she was, but she only managed to bring out her human form or send it away. She never managed to travel to the pocket herself. Which, of course, only cemented her hypothesis."

"Which was?"

"Her hypothesis? That it was impossible to access one's own dimensional pocket. All her research confirmed it."

"Yeah, well, I doubt any of her test subjects had access to Gwen-given powers."

"True. I've never heard of anyone pulling people through time and space the way Gwen does, or the way that you do."

"Yeah, I didn't think that much of it—I mean aside from thinking it was badass—until Torrence started explaining how mages jump through time and space."

I sighed, almost feeling queasy at the memory of how stitching multiple pocket dimensions together had made Sol throw up. Then I sat up abruptly, as an idea came to me.

"What if I tried it the old fashioned mage way?"

Dragon-me blinked a few times.

"I don't know why that would work when the Gwen-given shift doesn't. If anything, it's just more complicated and—"

"I have to at least try," I interrupted.

Dragon-me didn't argue, but the look in her giant reptilian eyes wasn't exactly encouraging.

I closed my eyes, reaching for a nearby pocket dimension, and... and realized I had no idea what pocket dimension paralleled the dragon realm. Or anywhere. Or how I was supposed to reach for a pocket dimension rather than just reaching for the place I was trying to go.

"I believe it takes mages years of practice and study before they can shift through multiple planes," dragon-me explained.

I sighed, my headache returning with a vengeance.

"And I doubt you'd be able to shift away from here that way even if you'd had years of practice. After all, this pocket dimension lies within you. Without a piece of your soul anchoring you to the world, you have no tether to follow. No way to—"

"Wait. What did you say?" I asked.

"I said—"

"Never mind, I know what you said."

I hated to be rude, but my brain had finally caught up with what my ears had processed.

"Anchor, tether, soul," I mumbled.

Then I closed my eyes and searched my soul. I wasn't sure I really believed in a soul, as such. Agnosticism was about as far as my spirituality had ever gone, and I was pretty firmly in the atheism camp these days, but if dark matter had taught me anything, it was that there was more to human life that our current science could fully explain. I didn't doubt that we'd get there with time, but…let's just say, I was more open to ideas that didn't meet with current scientific scrutiny at the moment. So I closed my eyes and tried to visualize what my spirit might look like, if I could see it. At first I pictured a semitransparent version of me, but that just made me think of low-end special effects from the 90s, so I decided to switch tactics. I pictured a glowing green sphere instead, one that matched the color of my eyes in all three of my forms. Didn't someone once say that eyes were windows to the soul? So I went with that. When I pictured the glowing green ball of energy at my core, I searched it for the various tethers I might have to the place I wanted to return. I found three of them. Two were tiny, new, and barely large enough to notice. Some instinct told me they wouldn't help me get anywhere. But the third one was at least a third of the size of the whole ball. It was large, and bright, and I knew exactly who it led to.

I also knew that I wasn't going to be able to use it unless I forgave him. The whole reason I was here was that I'd been so distraught at the idea of my brother keeping secrets from me, namely the secret that our parents were both alive and in touch with him, that I'd felt a need to run away so strong that I hadn't even picked a place to run away to. I'd wound up here instead. The thought still rankled, but I took a few deep breaths and tried to think about things from Trev's perspective. Then I realized that I didn't even know what Trev's perspective was. I hadn't given him a chance to explain. I'd just felt hurt, hopeless, and bitter, then reached into the void. That was hardly Trev's fault. I owed him a chance to explain himself. I owed him enough empathy to try to understand why he hadn't told me our parents were alive. And even if I didn't owe it to him, I didn't want to withhold it. I wanted my twin back. We'd been separated for so damned long, for reasons out of our control, and now I was voluntarily walking away from him, just because he'd done something I didn't understand.

That didn't feel right.

That felt awful.

In that instant, I wanted nothing more than to be by my brother's side.

And then I was.

I LOOKED UP and found myself staring straight into Trevor's eyes. The hurt in them, the fear, made me look down at my own body just to be sure that I was actually in one piece.

I looked reassuringly whole.

"Vic?" asked Trev and Sol, at the same time.

I looked between them, and realized, with more than a little bit of shock, that they were standing exactly where I'd left them. We were all standing in a field full of dragons preparing for war, the grass was thick beneath my feet and the sky shone clear and blue above us. Azrael was still off a ways discussing Gwen knew what with General Aira, and I was standing encircled by all of the people that I'd held most dear. Standing in the exact spot I'd tried to will myself back to a hundred times from that little dimensional pocket. Standing in front of all of the people I'd tried to will myself back to. But the only one I'd been able to reach had been Trev. People said a lot of weird shit about twins and the ties that bind them. I'd always thought some of it was true. After all, Trev and I had spent the past three weeks communicating mind to mind, but…well, maybe more of it was true than I'd thought.

"Well, shit," I said, trying to will my legs to continue to hold me, even though they both felt like poorly formed jello. "How long was I gone?"

Sol, Rhelia, Trev, and Seamus all exchanged glances.

"You did not go anywhere," Rhelia said cautiously.

"It kind of looked like you shifted," Seamus admitted. "But at the end of the shift, it was still you, in human form, albeit in different clothes."

I looked down again and barely registered that I was still wearing galaxy leggings and my nerdiest t-shirt.

"You're saying that no time has passed?" I asked, feeling the same headache that had been plaguing me ever since I got to the dimensional pocket coming on once more. Everyone shook their heads.

"You ssssaid, 'You knew they were there. Thissss whole time. You knew.' And then you ssssort of phassssed in and out, and now you don't look quite well," said Rhelia, in a matter-of-fact tone.

I nodded, thinking that my life was one of the most ridiculous strings of events I'd ever heard of—causing me to wonder briefly if the author of my story actually existed, and if so, if she got paid very well—and then I promptly passed the fuck out.

WHEN I OPENED my eyes next, I was gazing into the bright silver gaze of the most beautiful person I'd ever seen. I had to blink a few times to realize that it was Az.

Their face was close enough that I could feel their breath on my lips, which felt warm and wet—as if they'd just been kissed. I was somewhat startled to find my arms wrapped enthusiastically around Az's neck. "What happened?" I breathed.

Every fiber of me positively buzzed with the need to continue whatever Az had started. My brain felt muddled, but the headache was gone, and my vision was quite a bit sharper than it had been just before I'd passed out. Sharp enough that I could make out the dragon army still marshaling for war around us, along with my friends standing much closer and looking far more concerned than I would have expected.

"You passed out, Luv. I caught you before you planted your face in the mud, and did what I could to transfer you a bit of energy. Didn't want to do too much, since you weren't awake and I like my partners consenting, but I figured you'd prefer it to sleeping for the next three days. Though that's still an option, if you choose not to seal the deal."

Az winked, and I couldn't decide if I wanted to punch them or kiss them again.

I decided instead to just push myself out of their embrace.

"Hang on, Luv, you probably don't have enough—"

Az didn't get to finish whatever they were saying before I'd pushed myself out of their arms and promptly found myself in a heap on the ground.

"Ouch," I muttered.

"I didn't give you much energy. Like I said, I wanted your consent. So I figured if I gave you enough of a boost to wake you up, we could talk, and you'd be in a better state of mind to say whether or not you'd like my help."

I tried to get up off the ground, but found myself completely unable to move. I could twitch, at least. Enough to let me know that I wasn't paralyzed, but it was as if all of my muscles had shorted somehow, and there was no more strength in any part of my body.

"The fastest way to heal you up would be to get completely intimate, but I remember you expressing your doubts about my trustworthiness as a succubus the last time that came up, so I rather thought you'd appreciate a discussion first."

"How does me letting you steal my soul help me, exactly?" I asked, baffled, from my prone spot on the downtrodden muddy grass.

"It's not stealing your soul. Well, it can be, if I'm using myself as a weapon, but a real exchange is precisely that—an exchange. It's give *and* take, and we'd both benefit from it."

I thought of the glowing green ball I'd just discovered while locked in my own dimensional pocket; the idea of siphoning off a portion of that glow to give to Azrael, even in exchange for some super-duper energy boost, did not particularly appeal. I cringed from where I lay, wondering why none of my other friends were coming to my aid.

"This is ridiculous," I muttered. "I'm just going to shift to Life's glade and get him to heal me up."

I closed my eyes and pulled on space and time, barely hearing the cries of "Vic, no!" from around me, as darkness reached up and snatched me from the living.

I REGAINED CONSCIOUSNESS in a darkened room, surrounded with low-burning, spice-scented candles, and some soft orchestral music playing in the background.

Then I heard the shuffling of feathers, and my gaze caught on a set of glinting silver eyes very close to my own.

"Why have I never noticed that your eyes are silver?" I asked, feeling a surge of guilt as well as wonder. Az's eyes were the most startling metallic silver I'd ever seen, and they practically glowed in contrast with their ebon skin. I leaned back, putting a bit more distance between us, and took in Az's hair. It was all white, in a glorious set of braids that fell well past their silver wings, all the way to their waist.

"It's part of my magic, Luv. Difficult to blend into the human population like this, even if I hide my wings. So, I sort of repel the gaze from my eyes, hair, wings, and ears."

"Ears?"

And then it was like my eyes finally registered the entirety of Az's face. Their ears were ever-so-slightly pointed, nothing like the dagger tips of the few elves I'd met, but pointed enough not to pass for human. I stared at Az and realized that, while I'd already considered them to be possibly the most beautiful person I'd ever seen, the eyes, hair, and ears took things to an ethereal level. I wasn't much for biblical literature, but I thought maybe I understood where the concept of angels had come from.

"Why can I see you properly now?" I asked, mesmerized.

"We're alone, and I'm rather interested in having you see me as I really am, at the moment. I'm sorry for kissing you without your consent, but I couldn't get your consent when you were unconscious, and I wanted you awake and alive to either rip me to shreds or accept my proposal. If we weren't about to go to war, I'd never have done even that much without your enthusiastic agreement."

Az stood up then, and as I focused on the rest of their body, my pulse quickened. My body was enthusiastically prepared to consent to anything Az wanted. They were wearing a gorgeous emerald green brocade corset with black edging and some light-absorbing gems studded periodically around the edging. The corset was gorgeous, but it alone wouldn't have stolen my breath away, even coupled with the supple leather pants that hugged tight to Azrael's legs. It was the fact that I could see both of Az's forms, and that they both wore the same outfit—though it was clearly tailored to suit their very different figures. The overlap made me dizzy, as usual, but I closed my eyes and focused my mind for a moment before opening them again.

I'd never seen a man in a corset before.

Az was gorgeous in both forms, and I obviously had a difficult time deciding a preference, as evidenced by how often I saw both of them, but I really wanted a moment to savor the novelty of the male corset before I went back to seeing double, or maybe just enjoying the female aspect. I swallowed, desire pulsing through my body, and then winced when I realized that my body was in an almost overwhelming amount of pain. The fact that I could feel any desire at all in that moment spoke to Az's powers as a succubus.

"You look awful, Luv," Az said, from the spot where they now stood encircled in candlelight. I blinked as my vision shifted and I saw both of them again. Apparently, it took more energy than I had to keep them separate.

"Thanks. Wish I could say the same about you," I wheezed, letting my head fall back against the pillow behind me. That was the first moment I noticed that I was in a bed. I could feel the scarring on my neck, face, and arm pull tight as I tried to lower myself into the mattress, and the reminder of their presence did nothing for my self esteem, but I tried to brush the thought away.

"I thought you wanted my consent," I added, feeling a bit salty about having been placed in a bed surrounded by candles, even as I let my eyes close against the pain.

"I do, Luv. I won't do anything without your permission. Seamus and Sol helped me bring you here, and I only gave you one more kiss, enough to help you regain consciousness, nothing more. I don't want you to do anything you don't want to do, but we've got work to do, and a universe to save, and if you've any interest in being able to help, you need this."

I thought about that for a moment. Az's power scared me, but how much of that was simply that I didn't understand it?

"Are they still launching the attack against MOME?"

Az's expression went from sultry to troubled.

"Yes. I explained everything we'd learned to General Aira, but they aren't planning to hold back against MOME. Albert wants to talk to you—he has a lot of questions, but Seamus and Sol said you were in no condition to answer them, and they were right. You weren't even conscious, and you still wouldn't be right now if I hadn't given you a bit more of my power to help you out. With everything you've gone through, you'd be lucky if you woke up in a week."

I laughed, or would have, but it only came out as a agonized huff.

"You don't know the half of it," I whispered.

"We don't have much time if we're going to try to stop Dryer, Luv. You and I both know that a full strike on MOME isn't going to stop this if she keeps going. We need to go after Dryer herself, and we need to do it before she can go to ground. I know you don't trust my power, but… after all we've been through together, can't you believe that I would never hurt you?"

I raised my head just enough to look Az in the eyes, and realized that what I saw reflected back at me was pain. Damn. That stung. Az had, despite plenty of reasons not to bother, always tried to help me. They'd saved my life more than once, and we'd literally walked through Hell together…

"Tell me how your power works," I said, knowing that information was likely to be the only thing that would calm the fear coiling inside me, even if we didn't really have time for it.

"The short version is that anytime I'm intimate with someone, I have two choices: I can just take, or I can give and take. Oddly enough, I can't just give. I've tried. It never works. I'm a succubus. My power comes from life energy, but specifically in the form of sexual energy. I generate lust in people simply by breathing, generally, and if I siphon that off, it's enough to sustain me, but a succubus becomes more powerful by taking more than lust. It only sticks if I give back, though. I can only make permanent changes to myself or others through a full exchange."

Azrael sighed.

"If it makes you feel any better, I almost never offer a full exchange. I can get by quite nicely just siphoning off a bit of lust here or there, or consummating with a normal human and skimming a bit of their unused energy in the course of events. That's enough to keep me going. A full exchange gives a part of my strength to the receiving party, just as it takes a bit of their strength for myself. It's not something I do lightly."

"Demons are weird," I chuckled, realizing that the fact that Azrael's biology was so incredibly distinct from my own was just something I was going to have to accept. I couldn't think of a simple energy exchange between humans that would make one noticeably more powerful, but Az insisted that I would benefit from it too, and honestly, it was clear from the fact that I wasn't still completely unconscious that Az wasn't lying about that part. I was beyond exhausted, my body ached with it. I could feel my brain trying to shut things down, even now. One kiss had been enough to bring me back from unconsciousness, and I didn't feel like any part of me was missing. Az was talking about making me stronger… and they had made it perfectly clear that if they just wanted to take my soul they didn't need my permission. Az wanted to help me, and damn it all, I needed help.

"Does it hurt?" I asked, finally willing myself to admit that I might have to do this if I wanted to be a functional person anytime soon.

It was Azrael's turn to laugh then.

"Oh, Luv. Quite the opposite, I assure you. I am widely regarded as one of the best lovers in *any* realm, and I come by that reputation completely honestly. I guarantee you that not only will it not hurt, but it may well be the most pleasurable experience you've ever had."

The smile that accompanied that statement was enough to have me almost panting. I was seeing both Az's again, but I closed my eyes for a moment and decided to focus on the female Az. I opened my eyes and felt my pulse race and heat flood my body. There was no denying that the idea of getting *much* closer to Az was entirely appealing whenever I didn't think about the whole "taking part of my soul" piece.

"So, I get an energy boost and some healing out of it, and what do you get?" I asked, trying to shed the last of my hesitation. If I was going to do this, I wanted to enjoy it, and not be hung up on my random fears of the metaphysics behind it.

"Oh, Vic, Luv, you'll get quite a bit more than an energy boost, but I can't say what exactly, as we've never tangled before. Similarly, I can't tell you exactly what I'll get out of it either, outside of some fun with a person I respect and find very attractive. We will both take a piece of each other away with us. It doesn't bind us, if that's what you're worried about. We exchange energy, and a bit of… spirit, if you will? But nothing that marks either of us as a possession. It's important you understand that; this isn't like vampirism, or any of the more sordid demon exchanges. It's an even trade—the give and take must be equal. I know I'll give you enough energy and healing to make you fit for immediate action, but beyond that I can only guess based on our respective powers. Those will mix and come out magnified, possibly changed, on the other end, but it's anyone's guess as to how. I'm afraid there's really only one way to find out."

I took a deep breath. When it came down to it, I trusted Az. They'd had plenty of chances to do horrible things to me if they'd wanted to, and it sounded like they could have just forgone my consent if they wanted to be underhanded, and taken my energy without me ever knowing or caring until it was too late. I thought of the vampires that Az had dropped so easily when we'd rescued Siara, and a shiver went down my spine. If they were just here to hurt me, they'd be done by now. They weren't doing that, and ok, that alone did not make them a hero, but I trusted them. And I was willing to give up a little bit of spirit if it meant I could get back to making sure my friends didn't die while attempting to save the world.

"Alright," I said, trying to smile as I took in the glory that was Azrael in any form; ebon skin, silver wings, white hair, silver eyes, and in this case, their deliciously feminine form. "Come show me why they call you the best succubus in all the realms."

Az's smile sent heat spreading through my whole body, and their approach was enough like that of a stalking cat to make me giggle nervously. Their eyes were so alight with heat and attraction as they approached the bed that all self consciousness fled me, scars, spirit, and exhaustion all forgotten.

"I promise you will never regret this choice, Victoria Marmot," they purred, as they spread their wings and bent down to envelope me in a kiss so electric I was fairly certain my hair was standing on end afterwards.

<div align="center">~~~</div>

What felt like hours and a hundred climaxes later, when we came back to reality, we were both glowing. Literally. Silver light radiated from both Az's skin and my own, and I watched in fascination as the air around us trembled with unspent energy. I felt alive. I felt like I'd just climbed a 14er and simultaneously gotten twelve hours of solid sleep. This was somehow more than that, though. I felt like I could almost see time. My senses were sharper than they'd ever been, as though I was part snow leopard, part dragon, and part myself all at once. So much had happened in the short time that Az and I had been intimate that it all sort of melted together, but there had been a few key moments when I'd felt like we had ceased being two separate entities. It was every trite romance novel description of a climax, except it was more than a metaphor, it had felt like our bodies, and our perceptions, had actually become a single unit for a series of heartbeats. At the time, it had seemed like the only logical outcome of the way we'd joined our bodies, but afterwards it was clearly more than that. Something in me felt altered. I was more than I had been at the start.

"Wow."

Az's voice caused my head to snap up from where I'd been staring at my own hands and contemplating the difference I felt.

"I thought you'd done this a hundred times," I said, watching them flex their wings and stare at their own hands on the bed next to me.

"This is…different than the last few exchanges I've done," Az admitted, still staring at their hands.

"Is the glowing not normal, then?" I asked, suddenly worried.

"Not exactly," said Az. "It's cool, though. I can't wait to see what new tricks we've picked up."

"New tricks?" I asked, now nervously watching Az's wide-eyed expression, as they inspected their own skin.

"Yeah. I did mention the part about growing stronger, didn't I?" Az finally met my eyes with an expression of genuine puzzlement.

"Yes, you said you'd get stronger, but—"

"Not just me, Luv. You too. This was an exchange—couldn't you feel it? We've both gained something. I just can't tell what yet. It will be truly delightful to find out."

I took a deep breath. Right. For Az this was a neat science experiment. For me, it was a healing I desperately needed and… well, boy howdy, had it ever worked. I not only felt like I had the energy to get up and walk, I almost felt like I had enough energy to fly without my dragon wings. It was… mildly disconcerting, but only because I felt like I needed to go run a few miles before I burst at the seams.

"Shall we go kick some MOME ass, then?" I asked, unable to contain myself any longer.

Az smiled widely and nodded.

"Oh yes. Let's."

T HE LAST PERSON I had expected to find waiting outside the room in which I had just had very vigorous and probably quite vocal sex with a succubus was Albert, but if my life randomly started meeting my expectations now, I was going to get incredibly suspicious.

Az and I walked into Rhelia's living room to find the white-haired mage enjoying a cup of tea and a magazine on Rhelia's largest sofa.

"Everyone feeling better now?" he asked, without preamble.

I felt the blood run to my cheeks and ears, and tried to remember that what we'd just done had been the only way to get me back on my feet in time to be useful to our plans, though it was difficult to remember that now, after however much time we'd spent decidedly *not* hurrying the experience.

"Yes," I said, my voice clearer and stronger than I'd expected it to be. "I'm ready to get to work on stopping MOME and Dryer. Have the dragons already launched their attack?"

Albert shook his head.

"No, they agreed to wait the ten minutes I assured them it would take to have you in fighting shape."

"Ten minutes?" I asked, looking between Az and Albert with my eyebrows shooting up to high five in the middle of my forehead.

"Yes, I managed to put that room into a brief temporal distortion. Azrael assured me that three hours would be enough, and I managed to slip you out of time enough for that to take only a few minutes. We wouldn't have needed the full ten if we hadn't had to carry you over here. Still, we'd best get back to the field if we are going to launch our attack in time to catch Dryer unawares."

If I hadn't just spent Gwen-knew-how-many hours or days trapped in my own pocket dimension, and then come back to the exact instant I left, I would have assumed that Albert was making a very bad joke, or had simply lost his mind. As it was, I understood exactly how he could have used his dark matter to keep us suspended in our own timeline outside of this one, and so I simply nodded and reached my hand out to take his proffered one. Az took my other hand, and then I blinked us into existence in front of General Aira.

~~~

I was almost giddy with how little energy it had taken for me to move the three of us from Rhelia's home to the middle of the dragon council's plateau. Granted, it was a tiny distance, relatively speaking, but still, yesterday it would have been a noticeable drain on my energy to carry the three of us that far, and now it felt like I'd barely blinked. I wanted to laugh at how little it had cost me. If this was what getting busy with Azrael did for me, I was going to have to seriously reconsider my 'no giving part of your soul to succubi' stance. I felt like I could move a mountain with nothing more than my big toe.

Instead I tried to arrange my face into something resembling a grave expression. General Aira was going over her attack plan with Albert, as he suggested how we might maneuver our strike team to take out Dryer.

"She'll be hiding, in all likelihood," Albert explained. "It's unlikely that she'll be among any of her people at MOME, least of all wherever she plans to set someone off using Technetium next. She won't want to be in the line of fire. Hers, or ours."

"So how do we find her?" Azrael asked.

I remained silent, but my brain started to throw together a number of puzzle pieces, even as Albert began to speak.

"We'll have to hope she's at one of her known hideouts and send multiple strike teams timed exactly with our other attacks."

General Aira was shaking her head.

"We don't have time for that. We can't assume that she won't hear about those strike teams before one of them actually reaches her, so we would risk putting her on high alert instead of taking her by surprise. We can't take the
~~~

risk that she'll predict our movements and take out our best people after the first strike force is discovered."

"We can't just do nothing," Albert said, voice rising, as though this wasn't the first time General Aira had rebuffed him. "Dryer is the linchpin to this whole operation. If we don't remove her, none of this will ever stop. We've got to—"

"Albert," I interrupted, my brain taking over my mouth before any other part of me could think better of it. "Do you have any way to get some of Rebecca's blood?"

Albert and the general looked at me, their faces almost humorous mirrors of surprise, but Azrael smiled, as though they knew what I was thinking.

"I am not in the habit of keeping the blood of my enemies on my person," Albert replied, calmly.

"Well, do you know where we might find a relative of hers? One that's not under the same kind of security that she is?"

Albert thought for a moment.

"I might be able to find a cousin of hers. We were friends in school, and we've kept in touch over the years."

"Excellent," I replied, unable to keep the smile off my face. "Then if you'll just give me a few minutes, I believe I have a plan."

STANDING ON A very narrow ledge with a three thousand foot drop behind me should have been terrifying. Even years of rock climbing, and my latest forays into free-climbing, hadn't changed that. What *had* changed was that I now felt exhilarated by the height, the danger, and the energy pulsing through me that was practically urging me to jump and see if I could really fly without wings right now. That little voice was terrifying, so I closed my eyes against the view of distant green meadows dotted with needle towers and embraced by a hazy mountain range, took a deep breath filled with clean late summer air, and then turned towards the whole reason I'd come here.

The cell in front of me was bare stone, fronted by iron bars as thick as my arm, and sparsely furnished. It contained what looked like a recently cleaned latrine in one corner, a small bookshelf covered in withered paperbacks, and a low, but clean and comfortable looking, pallet. Atop the pallet was what looked like an enormous pile of stacked cowhides.

"To what do I owe the pleasure, Ms. Marmot?" asked a baritone voice originating from the center of the pile.

"I've come to ask a favor," I replied.

The pile of cowhides sat up, revealing itself to be a single cowhide draped across a large, muscular man covered in short brown fur and topped with a bull's head.

"I am listening," Torrence replied.

"Is Nethia…" my voice trailed off, unsure of how to word the rest of my question.

"She has not woken since you last saw her. I have been informed that she is being kept somewhere comfortable yet secure, and if she ever wakes, she will stand trial for her crimes."

I swallowed. I wasn't sure which was worse, honestly, an unending magical coma brought on by a broken blood oath, or whatever the dragons were likely to do to her when she was finally put on trial.

"I'm sorry," I managed to say after a moment. "I know you were…friends."

Torrence sighed and stood up from the pallet, walking over to the bars beside me and leaning against them.

"Once, perhaps. I am afraid Nethia and I haven't been friends for a long time now. The bond of the Dragon Hunters was all that held us anymore, and she made it clear that even that meant little to her in the end. I thought, hoped is perhaps more accurate, that she had seen the wrong in all that we had done, as I had."

Torrence stared into the distance. The view through the bars was unencumbered, and certainly good for contemplation. Leave it to the dragons to put their prison inside the tallest cliff in the realm. Maybe they were hoping the view would inspire their prisoners to lead better lives. Or maybe they just wanted to terrify people. With dragons it was hard to know. Maybe I just needed to spend more time as a dragon to figure it out.

"I was wrong, regardless. She was very good at convincing the world, or at least the Unterberg council, that she believed in the values that Unterberg strives for and—"

"Look, Torrence, I don't want to keep you from mourning Nethia in your own way, but my favor is kind of…time sensitive."

I grimaced. I really hated to interrupt the dude while he was processing this, but I'd barely managed to convince General Aira to hold off her attack while I enacted my "plan," and I'd never told her what I was planning to do, just that I had a way to get to Dryer that would let us keep the element of surprise. She'd reluctantly agreed, with Albert's added prodding. I'd only gotten away with not telling her the details because she wanted it done fast, and didn't want to waste time on planning sessions. Luckily, with my particular skill set, I didn't really need her to know what I was up to.

"If I could get the dragons to reduce your sentence, would you be willing to help me track someone again?"

"Is it to aid in stopping MOME?" Torrence asked, his large brown eyes on me now, instead of staring into the distance.

"Yes," I replied.

"Then there is no need to ask the dragons to reduce my sentence. I will gladly help."

My mouth snapped shut in surprise. I'd been about to admit I wasn't sure how much I could do. I didn't really have the authority to do anything for Torrence's sentence, I was just banking on the hope that speaking for him when his trial came would help reduce his sentence.

The more I got to know Torrence, the more I realized that I didn't understand him at all. Who the fuck just volunteers to help the folks who have them imprisoned and refuses to get their punishment reduced? He'd said before that he regretted his past, but hell, lots of people said that, and some of them meant it, too. Meaning it and embracing retribution seemed like two vastly different things to me, though. Still, whether or not I understood Torrence, I was starting to like him. He seemed…honorable. Plus, how could you dislike someone who frolicked in wildflowers at the drop of a hat?

So I smiled when I reached out a hand towards his.

"Shake on it?" I asked.

He tilted his large, horned head to one side and eyed my hand suspiciously before reaching out his own deep brown, furred one.

As soon as his skin hit mine, I pulled us both through time and space.

WE BLINKED INTO existence at the bottom of the valley, not far from where I'd left Albert and General Aira only minutes before. Indeed, General Aira was seated a few meters away, in her human form, her legs folded beneath her and a rather elaborate tea set spread out before her. She was alone, which I supposed I should have expected. After all, I knew that Albert needed to track down the blood we'd talked about. But it was probably the first time I hadn't seen General Aira swamped by dragons in all forms, asking her questions and giving reports, as she orchestrated what she had informed me was the largest fighting force of dragons assembled in over a century. I hesitated before approaching her, since she seemed to be enjoying the uncommon moment of calm.

Then I noticed Trev, Rhelia, Sol, and Seamus all huddled up a few meters away from Aira's tea ceremony. The group turned as one when we moved towards them, and Seamus and Trev immediately came over to us to give Torrence a quick fist bump and say hello.

My eyebrows must have arched in curiosity, because Trev communicated silently, *We all wound up fighting together once you and Sol made it into the dungeons. Torrence fought like a master. He's kind of a badass.*

Oh. Right.

Of course there had been a whole battle after we'd managed to rescue Siara. It only made sense that they'd have to fight their way out after I had whisked Siara to the only place I could think of where she wouldn't blow up the entire universe. So much had happened to me since then, I almost forgot that everyone else had been rescuing Siara just yesterday. For me, it had been a week, several worlds, and a dimensional pocket ago. For every-one standing around me, it had been last night.

I restrained a sigh, and longed for, of all people, Az. They, at least, had been with me for the bulk of what happened after Siara's rescue. Mean-while, I hadn't even had a chance to tell everyone else what had happened, except in the broadest terms.

While I stood there feeling strangely isolated, even while surrounded by my friends, Torrence seemed genuinely concerned about everyone's health and well-being. He was even asking Seamus about how his Moms were set-tling into life in Unterberg.

Which is probably why none of us noticed the sound of steel being drawn. Or the sound of a blade cutting through air. Until the blade was buried in Torrence's chest, and his legs collapsed beneath him.

Trev and I were instantly at Torrence's side, while Rhelia turned, yellow eyes flashing as she sought out the enemy.

Which turned out to be the petite dragon General a few meters away, glaring at our group as though we were all demons of the worst kind.

"How dare you remove a prisoner from their cell?!" she shrieked. It was a sharp contrast to the calm tones she'd maintained through every conver-sation I'd heard with her yet. Even when she completely disagreed with people, her tone was, at worst, calmly dismissive. Now she was shouting at full volume, and when I took a brief moment to glance her way, I saw her eyes wide, whites showing prominently, and spittle flying from the corners of her mouth. "What would possess you to release that kind of menace on my realm? Have you lost your minds? Do you know what he could have done to us? Do you have any idea what his kind are capable of?"

I barely registered the words, because I was too busy fighting to keep Tor-rence's blood in his body. It was a battle I was losing rapidly. The wakizashi that had been launched though his chest had been aimed with uncanny precision. His heart had been skewered. His eyes were already closed, and I could feel no pulse.

Trev, I sent silently, because if what I was about to do didn't work, he was my best chance at plan B. *Grab on.*

I was already holding Torrence, and as soon as I felt Trev's hand hit my shoulder, I reached to the one place that had always been there to save my ass in the past.

IN AN INSTANT, we were both blinking in the dappled light of a small clearing in the Northern Arizona woods.

"WHY ARE YOU BACK SO SOON, VICTORIA?"

"Life, can you save him?" I asked, skipping past all preamble, ignoring the fact that Life's definition of "so soon" and mine were probably vastly different, and hoping against hope that Torrence wasn't already dead, at least not the level of dead that Life couldn't fix. I didn't know if Trev's phoenix fire would be enough to work on someone I barely knew. I had a feeling it had only worked on Sol because we'd already gotten close enough for me to use our mating bond to help call her spirit back, but I'd be damned if I wouldn't try it anyway, if it came to that.

"THE BOVINE IS ALREADY HEALING," Life replied, tilting his hooded head to one side. "HE WAS BARELY ATTACHED TO HIS LIFE FORCE, HOWEVER. A FEW MORE SECONDS AND HE WOULD HAVE BEEN BEYOND MY HELP. WHAT DID YOU DO TO HIM?"

I looked down at Torrence and saw that, indeed, the wakizashi had been ejected from his flesh and the wound was already knitting closed in its wake.

I sighed, collapsing to the ground. The shift from the dragon realm to here hadn't taken anything out of me, really, even with Trev and Torrence in tow—thank you, Azrael—but the adrenaline leaving my system left my legs shaky, even without the drain on my power.

"I didn't do anything to him except bring him here," I said, as I caught my breath. "A pissed-off dragon threw a sword at him."

Life didn't have a face that I could see, beyond the two glowing orbs that marked his eyes within the wooden hood of his cloak, but I could have sworn he was frowning anyway.

"FRIENDSHIP WITH YOU APPEARS TO BE A VERY HIGH RISK FACTOR FOR THE HEALTH OF OTHERS."

I laughed, though a part of me wanted to cry.

"I can't argue with that," I muttered, leaning back against one of the nearby trees.

After a few deep breaths of fresh mountain air tinged with the sweet scent of butterscotch pines, and a moment of staring in silence at the woods that surrounded the small open clearing of the Tree of Life, I looked at Trev. As soon as our eyes met, I felt a pang of guilt; it was probably the first time I'd *really* looked at him since I'd come back from my own dimensional pocket.

"Hey," he said, sitting down against the tree beside me.

"Hey," I replied, eloquence escaping me entirely.

He reached his hand out towards mine, but hesitated before our fingers met. I looked at him, frowned, and grabbed his hand from where it hovered a few inches from mine.

"I'm sorry," we said in unison. Then we both laughed.

"Yeah," I said, giving his hand a squeeze. "I don't know why you kept Mom and Dad a secret, but I'm going to go out on a limb and guess that it was for some noble reason."

"I didn't want them kicked out of the Realm of the Dead," he said quietly.

"You think Hel would boot them, just because I knew they were alive?" I asked, one eyebrow arching incredulously.

He shrugged.

"They said the only reason it was safe to tell *me* where they were was that I was dead to the people who had known me."

I stared at him.

"They sent me an e-mail, Vic. I don't even know how they sent an e-mail from a different realm, but they did, and that was the only communication I had from them for ages and then…. Well, after everyone thought Rhelia was dead, she was able to go visit them, so…I found out a bit more then."

"You couldn't go visit them?" I asked.

"I probably could have if I'd gone back before I found you, but… after that I was alive again, at least to the people who loved me, and maybe even as soon as I replied to Mom and Dad. I don't know exactly how it works. But no, I couldn't go see them. But Rhelia *could,* even though you and I technically knew she was still alive… it seems like a weird set of rules, if you ask me."

I shrugged. "We might have known she was alive, but we'd doubted it for a bit, and EVERYONE else thought she was dead. I mean, a large number of people believed that very firmly, and still do. Maybe that's all it takes."

"Did Mom and Dad tell you why they left?" Trev asked, his voice quiet.

"Not really," I said, leaning my head back farther against the tree. I was too embarrassed to explain that I hadn't given them a chance to explain anything. Although I wasn't sure Hel would have let them talk to me, even if I'd been more cooperative.

"Well, we should—"

"We should be getting back to Albert's office," rumbled a very deep, now-becoming-familiar voice.

"Torrence!" I said, launching to my feet. The large tauren was standing up, looking decidedly healthy for someone who had basically died a few minutes ago.

"Vic, Trevor, I am deeply indebted to you both. I would not have survived that attack were it not for your quick thinking and incredible facility with teleporting."

Trev waved his hands up as though fending off the praise.

"I didn't do anything," he said. "I was just here as plan B."

Torrence looked slightly puzzled, but nodded.

"And you don't owe me shit," I said, smiling and giving him a hug. He stood awkwardly still for a moment, then wrapped his large furry arms around me in return. "I'm just happy you're alive."

"Regardless, I owe you my life."

"Ugh, fine. You owe me your life. I'll try to figure out a way for you to pay me back without dying, 'kay?"

Torrence simply stared at me.

"You need to lighten up, Torrence."

Torrence frowned.

"YOU ARE DISTURBING MY PEACEFUL GLEN, VICTORIA AND FRIENDS."

Honestly, that whole day was almost made worthwhile by the sight of Torrence nearly jumping out of his skin at the sound of Life's voice.

"Sorry, Life. We'll get out of your hair. Life, this is Torrence. Torrence, Life. Life is really the one you ought to be thanking, Torrence. I just brought you here. Life did the hard part."

"DO NOT LISTEN TO THE HUMAN. I CANNOT HELP BUT MEND THAT WHICH STILL HAS LIFE TO LEND IT. I WOULD LITERALLY HAVE DONE THE SAME FOR ANYONE. I EVEN HEALED THAT OBNOXIOUS VAMPIRE THAT KEPT COMING BACK HERE UNTIL VIC IMMOLATED HIS HEAD. THEN I COULD NO LONGER MEND HIM. THAT WAS SATISFACTORY."

Torrence, not seeming nearly as composed as he'd been a moment earlier, sketched a formal bow towards the large talking tree, and then quickly turned back to us.

"May we go now?" he asked quietly.

I decided to take pity on him, since Life can be a bit much when you're not expecting him, and I grabbed Torrence and Trevor by the wrists and blinked us to where I hoped we would find Albert and a vial of blood.

ALBERT'S OFFICE WAS empty when we reached it, save for two disgruntled-looking iguanas who hissed angrily at us when we popped into existence in the middle of their lair. The place looked pretty much exactly as it had the last time I'd been there, including the faint smell of weed permeating the elaborate throw rugs that sat beneath Albert's desk, and the two wingback chairs.

"Where are we?" Torrence asked, after a moment.

"Albert's office," I replied. "He said he'd meet me here after he got ahold of what he needed, so—"

"Ah. Vic, Trevor, lovely to see you. Torrence, it has been…some time."

We all turned to see Albert standing just in front of the door that led into the Flagstaff High School main corridor, though I was fairly certain Albert hadn't used the door.

"Indeed it has," Torrence replied. There was something oddly delicate about the way that they were addressing each other, which made me curious about how they knew each other, but there was no time for that now.

"Did you get it?" I asked

In response, Albert pulled a small vial of red liquid from a pocket tucked away in the thick, robe-like overcoat he always wore.

"Rebecca's cousin seemed all too happy to help, when I asked. Seems they aren't on the best of terms these days."

Yet another topic I would love to ask more about, but we really didn't have the time.

"Can you two complete the ritual without us?" I asked, gesturing between me and Trev, who hadn't said a word since we'd arrived here. Albert and Torrence both nodded. "Albert, Torrence will have to stay with you. Nethia could have cast this spell on an object, but Torrence can only make himself a compass. Is that ok?"

Albert shrugged, as if he would make do with what he got.

"We should probably be getting back to see what the hell is wrong with General Aira," I added.

"Why should anything be wrong with General Aira?" Albert asked.

I sighed.

"Because she threw a wakizashi through Torrence's heart without so much as saying hello first. Still not clear on why, since we were too busy taking Torrence to Life to make sure he didn't die. Maybe… consider not returning him to the dragon realm when you two are done."

"I will return to the dragon realm to face my crimes and receive justice," Torrence declared.

"Ok…your call. We have to go. Good luck finding Dryer. I'll tell General Aira that you two are on the mission we'd planned, and she can yell at me all she wants. Hopefully without any swords, though."

Then, before Albert or Torrence could object, I grabbed Trev's hand in mine, felt a rush of warmth from the thought that things were mending between us, then closed my eyes and reached for a sunny valley filled with dragons and wildflowers.

BUT THE SUNNY valley filled with dragons and wildflowers appeared to be in absolute chaos.

I had taken us back to the spot where I'd last seen General Aira, hoping to find her in a calmer mood. General Aira was there, but so was everyone else, apparently. Twenty people or more surrounded the dragon general, all trying to speak at once, while the troops still massed on the field around us shifted anxiously, as though awaiting the final order to attack. I was honestly surprised that General Aira, currently in her dragon form, hadn't started biting people's heads off, just so she could actually hear people over the din.

I won't lie, after what had happened with Torrence, I hesitated to approach the General in her dragon form, even though all the evidence suggested she was just as deadly in her human one. I scanned the crowd around Aira, hoping to find backup in the form of Rhelia. I didn't see her.

Trev and I were still holding hands when I picked two other familiar figures out of the crowd, though, and that may have been the only thing that kept me upright.

"Is that…?" Trev asked, squeezing my fingers in his.

"Yes," I replied, my voice cracking slightly.

And then we were both running for our Mom and Dad.

In that moment, I forgot about the lies, forgot about the abandonment, pushed aside every negative thought I'd had about my parents in the past year. They were here. They were alive, and in front of me, and not trapped in some strange dimension that I could only visit if everyone thought I was dead.

Trev and I ran, and for a moment, in the middle of a crowd of people trying to organize a war, our world narrowed to a tangle of arms and chests as we somehow managed to all hug each other at once.

"How are you here?" I asked, between hugs, trying to look at both my Mom's and Dad's faces at the same time. "How did you get away from Hel? I thought she was planning to keep you as collateral until I got back?"

"You managed to convince her that the fight against MOME was more important than whatever petty plans she had for a power grab," my Mom replied, hugging me again, crushing my face to her shoulder and then holding me out at arm's length. "After you left, we told her that we had to get to you as soon as possible, that if you were going to succeed in stopping MOME you had to know what we knew."

Dad finally let go of Trev long enough to talk, even as he wiped away the tears from his eyes and cheeks.

"We have to get Albert and General Aira to listen. You can't go after Dryer."

"Dad, we have to go after her. If we don't stop her, we don't stop any of this. MOME will just keep coming after us," I said, exasperated. "Besides, Albert is already gone."

"True, but I don't mean that no one should go after Dryer, only that *you* shouldn't. Let Albert handle Dryer, he can handle her alone. *You* need to go after the Technetium itself."

"Why issss that?" asked a sibilant voice from behind us.

We turned to see that General Aira, and all of the various commanders who had shown up to complain, demand, and wait, had gone silent and turned to look at us.

"Respectfully, General Aira, if we don't remove the Technetium before Dryer knows she's under attack, she'll just make sure we never find it. If she does that, we'll never be able to neutralize it, and this fight will go on forever."

"Are you saying you can neutralize the Technetium?" I asked, my voice flat with the shock of it.

Mom and Dad both nodded, looking around at the assembled group.

"It's why we disappeared, the whole reason we faked our own deaths. We've been looking for a way to neutralize Technetium for decades, but we finally realized that the answer didn't exist in this realm. Once we realized that we needed to go to the Realm of the Dead to finish our research, we knew we would have to fake our deaths and have *everyone* believe it."

Mom and Dad both turned to look regretfully at me, and I stamped down hard on the anger that started to surge up inside me. I could be angry with them later—right now I was going to have to listen to what they had to say, so that we could all live long enough to be moody with each other tomorrow.

"We do not have time for thissss," said General Aira. "We musssst ready our attack before word of our preparationssss reachessss the Minisssstry of Magical Entitiessss."

Mom nodded, but kept talking, "Right. So we won't go into how we figured out how to neutralize Technetium, we'll just tell you that we did, and that we've brought enough serum to neutralize what we hope is the entirety of MOME's stock."

"Even if we neutralize all the Technetium they have, what's to stop them from just making more?" asked Trev, looking skeptical.

It was Dad who answered.

"How about a bunch of dragons completely destroying their labs and all of their research?"

A gleam appeared in General Aira's enormous eyes as she said, "Indeed, that may jussst do the trick."

"As long as we can find all of their research and storage facilities," I said, trying to rein in the hope that was starting to surge through me. Could we really do this? Could it be this easy?

"We already know where they are," said Mom.

OF COURSE, WHEN Mom said they knew where the Technetium stores were, what she really meant was that she had a highly educated guess as to where they were, because, of course, she had been trapped in the Realm of the Dead for the last year (at least according to our timeline—according to their timeline, Mom and Dad had been in the Realm of the dead for more like five years, a number that didn't match up exactly with my own experience of time there, but at least was similarly distorted) and thus they hadn't been able to confirm their hypothesis.

Still, as I stood in the dank tunnel leading down to my "favorite" dungeon, breathing in the unfortunately familiar scent of stale water, moss, and burning torches, I couldn't fault their reasoning. Technetium was deadly, if given half a chance to mix with dark matter, and dark matter was damned near everywhere, so the only safe place to store it was in a place that suppressed dark matter. And MOME had access to a handful of such places, namely the dungeons beneath all of their major headquarters. (I guess it shouldn't be surprising that an organization that claimed responsibility for policing all magical entities would have a bunch of dark matter suppressing dungeons, but it still seemed like a weird architectural quirk to me.)

The trick, of course, was getting to all of those places, as well as the research facilities, and Dryer, all at the same time. It didn't have to be down to the second, since we figured it was unlikely that Dryer was so well prepared that a single second of notice would ruin our attempts, but by our best calculations we couldn't allow for more than a minute of lag between all of the attacks, or else we ran the risk of one location warning all the others and giving them time to clear out before we could do what we came to do. Which was why I had zipped back to Flagstaff as soon as General Aira had agreed to the wait, and thankfully caught Albert and Torrence right after they'd finished the blood magic ceremony that would allow them to track Dryer. I'd told them just enough to make sure our timing would work out, and then I'd gone straight to MOME's Phoenix HQ dungeons. Trev and Rhelia insisted that now that they had a device inside of the security system (they'd confirmed it was still there after our adventure rescuing Siara), they could make the system ignore the breach my shifting in would cause. They could turn the alarm trigger into an error message, buying me enough time to get past the security feeds before we started blowing shit up.

It was an intense plan, and I hated the fact that it required all of us splitting up. I'd been tempted to transport everyone into position by using my newly supercharged powers. I still wasn't feeling any noticeable drain, despite all the shifting I'd done today already, but my parents had, rather sensibly, insisted that I should save whatever stores I had for the mission, rather than wasting it all on setup. After all, we were lining up attacks in seven major cities around the world, all of which we suspected held sufficient stores of Technetium to blow up the world several times over, and I was probably going to need my A-game just to get through this. We had other mages that could shift people, and dragons that could fly, and one or two magical objects that rendered folks invisible. It would be unnecessary for me to take all of my friends to the places they were needed.

Fair enough.

I was in position, keeping an eye on my phone for timing while simultaneously working on calming the panic that threatened to well up inside me as I contemplated the last time that I'd been here.

A few deep breaths helped, as did imagining what Sol, Seamus, Trev, and Rhelia would be doing. They should each be reaching their targets about now. Seamus had been given the task of tackling the now "abandoned" Bolivian HQ, on the assumption that it would be the least heavily guarded. Even still, he'd been given a few weredragons for backup. Sol, meanwhile, had been placed at the European HQ, in the hope that her intricate knowledge of MOME's workings might get her well into the facility without attracting notice before she drew attention by wrecking the place. Trev and Rhelia had been sent together to take on the MOME HQ in Shanghai, because Rhelia thought she had a contact there, but none of us were sure enough about that to risk her going without backup. Albert had been sent with Torrence (who we were referring to as "the compass" in front of General Aira, until further notice) to go after Rebecca Dryer, wherever she wound up being, and Azrael and General Aira were both coordinating troops to attack the research facilities as soon as we cleared the Technetium stores. Because, of course, most of the research facilities were in the same compounds as the storage facilities for Technetium, since they all required dark matter suppression to function without blowing everyone up. 'Cause my life has never been easy enough that we wouldn't have to worry about roasting me and all of my friends alive, after we neutralized the Technetium, if we didn't get things exactly right.

The timing was going to be delicate, to say the least.

I, for one, had been all in favor of just blowing up the Technetium stores, along with everything else, but it had quickly been pointed out to me that doing so risked exposing the Technetium stores to dark matter, thus *causing* the very giant, world-ending explosions that we'd been worried about to begin with.

Nothing's ever easy, is it?

So, now, after checking my watch and seeing my start time tick by with my heart in my damned mouth, I was sneaking my way down into the dungeons on foot, hoping that I didn't run into enough guards to set off the alarms before I got to wherever the Technetium was hidden. I couldn't rely on Trev and Rhelia to help, now that the start time had passed. They had remote access on their phones, but there was no guarantee that they wouldn't be busy with their own problems, or lose signal.

The first guard was pretty easy.

She didn't see me coming. She was busy wrestling with her keys, and didn't even have her footing properly when I hit her in the back of the head. I managed to catch her before she collapsed, and then I very carefully and respectfully took her out of her uniform (thankfully she was wearing shorts and a T-shirt underneath, so I didn't feel like too much of a creeper—even still, I laid my clothes on top of her out of a weird sense of "fairness"), and then I donned the stolen jumpsuit, complete with belt, keys, and baton, before tucking her into the first empty cell I could find. And ok, just because I did it respectfully doesn't mean it was cool, because obviously I didn't have her consent, but I was trying to save the world, and we were both going to have to just live with it. I hadn't had her consent for knocking her out either, but I didn't have time to convince everyone at MOME to join the side of reason before they blew up the world. It was going to have be enough for now.

Even wearing a MOME uniform, I had to hope that I wouldn't run into many other guards. I didn't think my disguise would get me very far if I ran into anyone who worked with her.

I'd made it to the third cell down the ramp when I saw two faces I'd never really expected to see again.

"Sylvestra?" I thought hard, but couldn't come up with the Troll's name, and wasn't sure I'd ever heard it before. I decided it was safest to just skip ahead. "What are you two doing here? I thought you were free of MOME after La Paz."

Sylvestra flew up to the bars that enclosed the cell, and I noticed that the whole cell front had been lined with some sort of mesh, probably meant to keep the pixie contained, since she was more than small enough to fit between the bars.

"You're Rhelia's friend, yes?" said the large troll who leaned against the back wall of the cell.

"Yeah. What happened to you two?" I asked again, completely baffled as to how they'd wound up here, of all places. The last time I'd seen them they'd kindly ignored us (after a brief misunderstanding) as we rescued Rhelia from the MOME dungeons in the Andean HQ. Unless they'd stuck around for some reason, they should have been free and clear of MOME and their shenanigans. We'd certainly left the place in enough turmoil for everyone who'd been looking for an excuse to slip away.

The troll shrugged.

"MOME tracked us down for guard duty again. We thought maybe they didn't know how the last one ended, so we said yes. Turns out it was just a trap."

He said it with the kind of tone that suggested this was just the sort of thing that happened in his life. Nothing to be worried about. Sylvestra, meanwhile, just buzzed angrily in the air in front of me. I shook my head, reminding myself that I was on a seriously tight schedule. Before I even started speaking, I began sorting through the keys on my belt.

"Well, my friends, today is your lucky day, as long as you can restrain yourselves from wreaking havoc until you get clear of this place entirely. I'm afraid that this time through we're shooting for stealth, and we're on a tight schedule."

"Do you spend all of your time breaking in and out of MOME headquarters, then?" asked the troll.

I couldn't help but chuckle.

"It kinda feels like it, to be honest. Some days, it really does."

It didn't take too long for me to find the key that worked on their lock. As soon as the door popped open and I shifted it on its enormous hinges, Sylvestra drew her sword and charged me.

"Hey, what the fuck!? I just let you go, what's your problem?"

She sheathed her sword, but glared at me.

"You are my problem, human."

I blinked and looked between Sylvestra and the troll.

"Don't mind her, she's just cranky," he said. "She hates getting captured."

The troll held out a hand to me.

"Name's Cronk, by the way."

"Nice to meet you, Cronk. Call me Vic."

His handshake was firm, but for someone whose hand covered my entire arm, it was impressive that he managed to be so gentle. Then he turned away with a nod, beckoning to his miniature friend.

"Did they really just set you up to capture you?" I asked, somewhat befuddled as to why MOME would bother.

"Seems that way," Cronk said, still waiting for the pixie to fly away from me and towards the tunnel that would lead them out of here. "Guess we must have gone up the charts of 'most wanted' after we helped you lot escape the first time. The arse who locked us up kept muttering about us joining the right side, whether we wanted to or not."

He shrugged, then dropped his hand and glared at the pixie.

"Come on, Sylvestra. Let's get out of here before our new friend blows the whole place up."

Sylvestra shot me another haughty look, then turned to fly after the already departing troll.

"That reminds me," I called, as they hurried up the slope. "We really are blowing the place up this time. On purpose, I mean. I recommend hustling out of here and not making a fuss, if you can help it. We've got a lot riding on this one. Fate of the world, yada yada."

Cronk waved a giant hand to show that he'd heard and continued up the stone steps back towards the tunnel entrance I'd just come down. I turned and headed farther into the depths, hoping that I hadn't just ruined our entire plan by releasing a cranky pixie and a thoughtful troll.

IT WASN'T UNTIL I got past the tenth dungeon cell—all of which were now empty, even though three of them had been occupied before I came clanking down the tunnels with my stolen keyring of potential freedom—that I began to worry that there was never any Technetium stored in this particular dungeon after all.

The dripping stone walls of the steeply descending hall seemed to only be getting narrower and darker, and the smell of moss and wet stone was getting more and more overwhelming. I was officially farther into the dungeons than I'd ever been, and I had a hard time imagining that there was some kind of recently used storage facility below me. If anything, it seemed more likely that any door I might find would hide a centuries old cellar filled with gunpowder and wine casks, but none of the doors I'd opened on the way down here had contained stores of anything other than people that MOME considered criminals, so I'd continued to play Robin Hood and plough onwards.

Finally, I came across a low iron door that only came up to my chest, tucked awkwardly under what looked to be a natural arch in the rock. The hall continued on, but I could no longer see any torchlight flickering in its depths, and I wondered if anything lay in that direction. I kind of hoped not, although it would be strange for the hall to continue to nothing. Maybe it was just an emergency exit? Regardless, I really wanted this door to be the door I was looking for. I didn't want to have to keep going, or risk getting blown up when the dragons took out the research facilities above me, because I'd taken too long freeing captives along the way or…

I took a deep breath and decided to stop thinking about all the things I didn't want to have happen.

Instead, I set about finding the key that would fit the lock in front of me.

I was still on my knees, struggling to fit various oddly shaped pieces of metal into the dangling padlock that looked at least a hundred years old, when I heard a shoe scrape the stone behind me.

"Oh good, you're already on your knees. That should save us some time."

The voice sounded vaguely familiar, and the southern accent set my teeth on edge, so I wasn't entirely surprised by the view when I turned around and found Rebecca Dryer standing in the middle of the tunnel directly behind me.

I was, however, a bit taken aback to find that she had a gun pointed at Albert's head.

SHIT, SHIT, SHIT, shit, shit.

This was not good. This was very bad. This was on the list of worst things that could go wrong at this point in the plan. It might have even been at the top of that list.

Because standing before me was evidence that we were completely screwed. Not only had Albert *not* taken out Rebecca Dryer, indeed, Albert seemed to have had his ass handed to him by Rebecca Dryer, Torrence was nowhere in sight, Dryer clearly knew what we were up to, and she seemed all too willing to stop it. And even if all she did was slow us down too much, we were all going to get blown up if we didn't get out of here in about seven minutes.

And just to top everything off, she had a gun. And I did not.

"Well, fuck," I said aloud, raising my hands above my head and turning my whole body to face her, while standing up slowly.

"Indeed," Rebecca replied. "This doesn't seem to be going well for you. Though I must say, I'm impressed with how far you've come. I didn't think our security would be that easy to bypass. I'm really going to have to have a "talk" with my people after this."

She was smiling as she spoke, as if we were just catching up over a cup of coffee instead of having a showdown in the middle of a centuries-old dungeon. I wasn't sure if that was a southern thing, or a lawyer thing, but I wasn't a fan either way. Still, it could be used to my advantage.

"How did you find me?" I asked, hoping she came from the James Bond school of villainy. Honestly, it seemed like decent odds she would want to talk. After all, a truly efficient villain would have simply shot me in the back of the head and capped Albert the minute she'd gotten the upper hand on him, so clearly she needed one, or both, of us for something.

"Oh, I didn't, sweetheart. I mean, I just stumbled upon you, really. Once I caught this bitch snooping around my office, I knew something was wrong, but I really only came down here because I needed a dose of Technetium for our mutual friend here."

She gestured towards Albert with the gun and I winced, watching the barrel dig into the skin above his ear.

"Gwendamnit, I hate guns," I whispered.

"What's that, dear?" Dryer asked.

"I said, I hate guns."

Dryer laughed, still keeping the tip of her Glock pointed at Albert's temple.

"That's rich, coming from someone who shot and almost killed one of our best agents."

"Hating them and knowing how to use them are two different things, Rebecca," I gritted.

"Tsk, tsk, so angry. Guns have their uses. Too many of our kind get caught up in *only* using magic. They are unable to see the bigger picture. After all, think of the long term benefits. Why, if we adopted non-magical weaponry *as well* as magic, we could easily be the dominant force in our realm. Think of how many people could be spared, if we didn't have to prove our might without modern weapons. A single nuclear warhead, and we would never have to waste another dragon on something as banal as bringing the non-magical humans in line. Can you imagine? But it was all I could do to convince the damned council that it was time we asserted our dominance over the humans *at all.* They'd never have given the idea a second thought if I had tried to force them to accept human weapons on top of everything else. Luckily, I was able to find a purely magical solution to the problem, and now everyone is on board. That said, I'm going to need you to move, Deary. I need to get into that storage unit. This one has a date with some Technetium."

Before I could even react to her strange monologue, she was marching Albert forward, and then, in a move that would make any Bond villain proud, she took a moment to point the gun at me while insisting that I step aside. I was so horrified to have the barrel pointed my way that I didn't react to the fact that she'd pulled it away from Albert's temple for a heartbeat. If I'd had a gun myself, that would have been the window I'd have used to shoot her, but as it was I could only watch in awful fascination as Albert raised his right elbow and sent it shooting hard and fast into Rebecca's nose. As soon as I'd seen Albert's momentum shift, I'd started to dive out of the line of fire, which probably saved my life, but it did not prevent the hot, awful pain of having a bullet drive its way into the flesh of my left shoulder.

"FUCK!" I exclaimed, with no small amount of feeling. "Does *anyone* at MOME ever learn proper gun safety?"

I was mostly shouting to distract myself from the pain, and to keep myself from passing out. Deciding I really didn't want to get shot again, I launched myself at Dryer's knees, hoping to tackle her to the ground before she could get around to pulling the trigger again. I connected and she collapsed, something she had been half on her way to doing anyway, thanks to Albert breaking her nose with his elbow.

Albert snatched the gun from the floor and pointed it at Rebecca, whose arms I was working quickly to pin behind her back. Unfortunately, she seemed to have no interest in going down easy, broken nose or no. She bucked and kicked beneath me, and I was struggling to keep both of her arms pinned. The pain in my shoulder was spiking every time she moved. I was honestly amazed I could pin her at all, and had to assume my ability to grit through this was entirely thanks to the boost from Azrael.

Boost or not, though, it wasn't enough to keep me from screaming when Dryer somehow managed to buck her head up into my left shoulder, directly against the bullet wound. I managed to keep hold of her with my right arm, but my left arm went numb when she hit the wound, and I dropped her left arm as a result.

Before I could recover from the pain, she turned and jammed her thumb into the hole in my shoulder, causing me to scream once more. I didn't drop her right arm, though, and managed to use it to drag her off-balance and head butt her in her already-broken nose.

Dryer let out a scream of her own, then, but I had to give her points for tenacity when she just dug her thumb even farther into my shoulder wound and screamed in my face. I went down, and she took no time in launching herself at Albert.

Which was probably her biggest mistake.

Because Albert had apparently just been waiting for an opening in which he was unlikely to shoot me. And I was now a heap of pain on the floor.

The shot was deafening, somehow louder than the one that had hit me in the shoulder, or maybe it was just the stillness that followed that made it seem so loud. I tried not to let my stomach heave as the copper tang of blood mixed with the overwhelming stench of gunpowder in the tunnel around me.

"I d-didn't mean…" Albert stuttered, from where he stood. "I d-don't have much experience with guns."

"It's her fault for leaving the safety off," I said, trying to get my legs to respond to my brain. Which was kinda true, because honestly, what else did she expect was going to happen?

I didn't want to look at Dryer to see where she'd been shot, but I needed to walk past her to get to the storage unit, because we were even closer to getting immolated by dragon fire whether Dryer was dead or not. We were surrounded by dark matter suppressing stone, which, not surprisingly, also suppressed cell signal, and we had no way of letting General Aira know that she shouldn't light us up when the time came.

So, I shuffled past, and tried not to notice how still she was lying, or the pool of blood beneath her. I had to assume it was a head shot, since she'd stopped moving so quickly, but I really didn't want to find out. I kept my eyes on the old oak and iron gate, and the padlock that held it closed.

It didn't take long to fumble the lock open, but it felt like ages all the same.

The crate that sat in the middle of the long, arched storage room looked incongruously small, considering how much potential disaster it held within it.

"Is that it?" I asked, almost deflated. I don't know why I'd expected there to be more, but some part of me had thought the room would be packed wall-to-wall with the stuff.

"That's more than enough to take out Earth several times over, if injected into powerful enough recipients," Albert reminded me.

I cringed, remembering how a single dose given to a single, not yet fully developed weredragon had taken out half of a city block and killed a few thousand people, and then my brain stuttered.

"Albert, dragons and weredragons are some of the most dark matter heavy beings in any of the realms, right?"

"Yes."

He was already getting out the small vial of Anti-Technetium Serum (we'd decided to call it ATS for short during our brief planning session) that he'd been given "just in case" when we'd sent him off to track down Dryer, and was prepping it to apply to the vials of Technetium that sat in the small wooden crate in front of us.

"So, how is it that when they set off the weredragon in Sucre they didn't wind up taking out the entire city and a good chuck of the rest of Bolivia?" I asked.

Albert blinked, his hands halfway to the crate in front of him.

"It was a young weredragon. It wouldn't have had the reserves to cause an explosion much larger than—"

"Would it have reserves bigger than Trev's?" I asked, lacking patience for the long calm explanation that Albert seemed determined to give.

"I would imagine they would be similar, although your brother is a bit of a special case and has been training to access even more dark matter than—"

"MOME seemed to think that blowing up Trev would take out the entire city of La Paz, or more. Why wouldn't a young weredragon do similar damage? Or, at least HALF the city, instead of half a city block?"

"I don't know, Vic. Are you saying you wish they'd done more damage?"

I ignored the annoyed edge to Albert's voice and pushed on.

"No, Albert, I'm saying that maybe they didn't inject the other weredragon they took. They must have switched her out for someone else. They could have used some kind of illusion to make whoever it was look like the weredragon they took, so when we only found Siara and one other, we thought we had rescued everyone. So, where is the other weredragon?"

"Vic, we don't have time for this. The strike force is going to take this place out in a matter of minutes, and we have work to do."

I sighed, thinking about how Cronk and Sylvestra had been lured here and held captive in the dungeons, told they'd be forced to join the "right side," and how that explosion in Sucre hadn't been large enough to match the firepower that Albert, Siara, and everyone else had been predicting, based on how much dark matter a dragon had. Then I thought about the kind of person Rebecca Dryer was, or had been till a minute ago, and I thought about how the tunnel that led to this door kept going down and down, but didn't have any more torches on the wall. And a memory of the message my parents had left us with an abandoned boat niggled at the back of my mind.

"Damn it," I muttered. "Here, Albert, take my ATS supply. This should be more than enough to get you through this box."

"Vic, what are you doing?" he asked, even as he took the serum from me.

"We're about to level this place to the ground, and I can't live with the idea that there might be more innocent people trapped in here."

Albert stared at me for a long moment before saying, "Be careful." He nodded slowly, as though the action troubled him, and then handed me back one of the four serum vials I'd given him. "Between the two of us, we have extra, and you might need this down there. Good luck. I'll try to get out of here fast enough to tell them not to blow you up."

"I appreciate that, Al."

I winked, and Albert's eyes teared up a bit, and then I was turning and running out the door, hurdling over the lifeless body of Rebecca Dryer, swallowing the bile and guilt that rose in my throat, and hoping beyond hope that I wasn't about to get myself killed for no reason.

IT HAD BEEN a few weeks since I had run for longer than it took to escape a deadly situation, and even though running is usually a favorite activity of mine, I wasn't used to running with a bullet in my shoulder. It officially sucked. I doubted I would have managed it at all without the benefits of recently getting busy with a succubus suffusing my…everything. I'd briefly glanced at the wound after I'd started jogging and it had painfully and emphatically reminded me of its presence. The bullet appeared to have passed all the way through my shoulder. I had no idea if that was a good thing or not, but I was definitely worried about blood loss. Or I would have been, except that the wound was barely bleeding at all now and I didn't even feel faint. So, yeah, I was gonna have to give Azrael one hell of a high five later, because succubus power exchange seemed to be like gaining multiple superpowers at once, one of which was speedy healing or some shit.

Even still, the damned thing throbbed with every step, and I rather desperately wished I could shift into my snow leopard form to make the whole trip pass more quickly.

"Stupid dark matter dampening rocks," I muttered, as I ran deeper and deeper into the ever-darkening dungeon.

I was left to enjoy the dank dungeon air in my human lungs, and try to ignore the smell of decay that seemed to only grow stronger as I hurried down the dark, rough stone corridor, occasionally splashing myself with enough water that I wondered if this tunnel ultimately led to a pool or underground river, rather than the missing weredragon I was hoping to find.

The puddles became more and more frequent, and I was more and more convinced that I must have passed through a doorway to an alternate realm at some point, because since when is there this much water in the middle of the Arizona desert? But alternate realm or not, the steep tunnel floor was getting more and more slick, and I would have fallen multiple times as I descended if a faint light hadn't started to flicker up ahead, reflecting off of the various puddles that streamed across the stone, thus warning me to watch each step as I wended my way farther and farther below ground.

By the time I'd reached the source of the light, I'd had to slow to barely more than a jog. Trying to make as little noise as possible, all while keeping my footing and not landing my ass in a puddle, was taking most of my attention, despite the clock I was racing to try to keep myself, and everyone else who might be down here, from being incinerated by the dragon strike force that was supposed to follow up on our Technetium neutralization run. So, yeah, I was more than a little tense as I rounded the last curve of the tunnel.

Which was about when I heard voices, and my legs slowed to an extremely cautious walk.

Between the pounding of my heart, the sounds of my own breathing, and the constant drip that had accompanied me for the past half kilometer or so into the tunnel—which had lately surged into the sound of steadily running water—I couldn't understand any of what was being said.

Someone was shouting, and many people were… moving.

A series of boulders strewn haphazardly around the area where the tunnel ended and something else began muffled the sounds from the other side, in addition to blocking my view. The burble of running water that had followed me for the past few minutes suddenly materialized in the form of a splashing creek. It must have been flowing underneath the tunnel I'd descended, but now it emerged to tumble over rocks and sand, running around the larger boulders that obscured my view. I had to hope its rushing would be enough to cover the sounds of my approach from whatever was on the other side.

I absently wished again for my snow leopard form, and even tried to call on it—my human feet could never match its padded paws for stealth and agility—but my attempts brought me the same nothing they'd gotten me the whole way down here. *Fuck this rock.*

For now, at least the boulders were lending me cover, as I tried to figure out what was going on beyond them. So there was that. *Thanks, rocks.*

This may sound like a stupid thing to say, but climbing with a bum shoulder is hard. Super-healing aside, my shoulder still throbbed every time I used my arm, and topping out an oddly shaped boulder to get a better look at the other side definitely counted as using my arm. On top of that, all the rocks leading up to the boulder were slick with water from the no-longer-underground creek, which made my feet slick when I finally reached the boulder I decided to scale. In other words, I felt more like an asthmatic whale floundering on the beach than anything else by the time I was able to see what was going on beyond the tunnel entrance.

So it was no wonder I nearly shit my pants when I heard a shout to my left. I was lucky I didn't just let go and immediately splash ass first into the creek, because I was certain I'd been spotted.

But the shout hadn't been directed at me. It had probably been directed at one of the hundred or more armed soldiers milling about in front of the giant underground lake that extended a few hundred meters ahead of me.

"SHIT, SHIT, SHIT," I whispered, as I dropped back behind the rock I'd been climbing and let my brain process what my eyes had just taken in. Over a hundred people, armed, marching in formation, apparently following shouted orders from a handful of MOME operatives wearing the same uniform I'd stolen earlier.

I took a deep breath filled with damp tunnel air and buried my head in my hands, trying to figure out how I was going to rescue these people, and… well, whether or not I should.

I mean, look, don't get me wrong, I'm not a fan of added casualties, but if everyone in this cavern was a MOME-trained soldier, did I really want to keep them from getting caught up in the dragon's strike force attack? Wouldn't that mean rescuing a bunch of people who were just going to try to kill me and my friends later?

I'd come here hoping to find the missing weredragon, who I suspected hadn't been turned into a weapon back in Sucre, but I wasn't even sure what I'd just seen. It had looked like an army. Was this the fighting force that Mom and Dad had tried to warn us about in their goodbye message? It sounded like an army, too… or did it? I took another deep breath, and did my best to listen over the sound of running water.

"Stop that!" shouted someone, followed by the unmistakeable sound of flesh hitting flesh. A shrill whistling sound pierced the air, then someone yelled, "Pick that up and try again. Don't test me. There's plenty of time to send you back to the vamps."

That… sounded a little weird.

I sighed, realizing I was going to have to sneak closer if I was going to figure out what was going on here, and I cringed, because every second I spent here was one second closer to getting torched by whatever the dragons had planned for the MOME facilities after we'd neutralized the Technetium inside them. Albert would probably be done soon, and as soon as he was clear of the building… hopefully he'd have time to tell General Aira I was in here before she lit the place up.

I couldn't think about that. One thing at a time.

The more I paid attention to the sounds on the other side of that rock, the more convinced I became that I wasn't listening to the training of a willing army. And I knew I would never let myself walk out of this place if even one person down here was an enemy to MOME. Hell, I even had second thoughts about leaving voluntary MOME employees behind.

I climbed back up to the top of the nearest boulder, grateful that my shoulder was starting to hurt less and less, careful to keep as close to the rock as I could, barely bringing my eyes high enough to see the spread of people below me.

Yes, lots of them were marching in formation and following orders, but… dotted throughout, especially in the group with the highest concentration of MOME guards spread out among them, there were… outbursts. The majority of the shouting, and all of the physical outbursts, were coming from that one group. A group in which the "recruits" kept dropping their weapons, sitting down in the middle of drills, and… attacking the MOME agents?

This shit was getting complicated, and I was running out of time. So I did the only thing I could think of. I dropped back down to the tunnel and prepared to swagger into the cavern looking like I had every right to be there.

Then a hand clamped across my mouth and I stifled a scream.

"Shhh… it's me," whispered the hazy grey figure, turning me around after pinning me single-handedly to the boulder I had just descended, before I could even shift my weight to throw them.

I really hated how fast Renata could move sometimes.

"What the fuck are you doing here?!" I rage whispered, as soon as she removed her hand from my mouth.

"I believe you need help," she replied, in a much calmer whisper, as if that explained everything.

"Ok, but—"

"Ms. Marmot, can I be of assistance?" asked a deep voice that I hadn't expected to hear again anytime soon.

"Torrence?" I asked, looking up at the looming bovine who suddenly, impressively, appeared right behind Renata.

"Where the hells did you come from? Is there a party down here I wasn't aware of?"

Both Renata and Torrence blinked at me for a moment.

"A party would be inappropriate at thi—"

"No, I came from Hel—"

I held up my hands to forestall both explanations, throwing a glance over my shoulder and hoping that no one beyond the boulders had heard or seen the growing crowd out here.

"Yeah, yeah, yeah, sarcasm fail. I get it. Ok. Torrence, seriously, where did you come from? I had half assumed you were dead."

"I am not dead. Albert insisted on entering Dryer's office alone. I waited for him to return, then watched as Dryer dragged him into the dungeons, following from a distance."

"Wait. Does that mean you just watched us fight Dryer, without helping?"

"My assessment led me to believe that 'helping' would only end in one or more of us getting shot."

My mouth dropped open. I wanted to argue, especially since one of us *had been* shot, but he made a fair point. Dryer had been wandering around with the safety off on a gun pointed at Albert's head. Surprising her would likely have ended with Albert's brains decorating a wall.

"But you followed me down here without making yourself known because…?"

"I was following at a distance when I noticed the grey haze behind you. As I didn't know what it was, I thought it would be prudent to wait until the haze made itself known as friend or foe before I made anyone aware of my presence."

I did my best not to sigh, because we were making too much damned noise already.

"Which brings us back to the grey haze. Renata? Why *exactly* are you here again?"

"Hel sent me to follow you. Tracking you here was quite difficult, and I did not arrive until after the woman in the tunnel was dead. I assume that is the woman Torrence did not help you fight. I passed the cow man on the way down, but he did not seem threatening, so I left him alone. Hel did not say that I could not help you, but it was not clear at first that you needed help."

I stood there, waiting for more, but I should have known better. Renata just stood there blinking at me, as if she'd given all the explanation necessary for someone who had recently betrayed me, Azrael, and my parents to an out-of-realm deity. Maybe she had. What did I know? Is there an etiquette for that? A certain number of days before you send flowers and a card that said, "Sorry I sold you out to the reigning monarch of the realm we met in," or something? Whatever. *So* not the time.

"Ok… well, we don't have time to sort through how weird it is that both of you are here right now, so I'm just gonna roll with it. Torrence, you said you owe me your life. Now might be a good time to pay that debt. To be clear, that does NOT mean that I want you to die— far from it. Renata…

I'm still not sure I trust you, but whatever, if you were here to kill me I'd be dead already, so I'm going to have to assume you're cool for now."

I took a deep breath.

"We need to get close to the guards before they shoot us, so just… follow my lead."

I took a deep breath and steeled myself for the batshit thing I was about to do.

"Oh, and try not to kill anyone," I added, before I turned, grabbed my two accomplices, and stepped out from behind the boulder.

~~~

The first part of my plan worked. No one asked us questions until I'd dragged a subdued-looking Torrence and a more solid-seeming than usual Renata right up close to the nearest set of MOME guards. They were still far enough away that we had a decent chance to get a look at the cavern that surrounded us. The air still smelled of damp rock and stale air, and the underground lake that extended from the back of the cavern went on farther than I could see. The "troops," such as they were, responded to barked commands, attempting to drill with AR-15s and basic marching patterns. They all practiced on the hundred or so meters of "beach" that stretched from where we'd entered the cavern to where the lake began. For every group of 25 "soldiers" (if soldiers was the word for folks who repeatedly ignored commands and periodically attacked their leadership) there were three MOME guards dressed just like the one I'd knocked out earlier.

The nearest three guards were milling about in the center of a group of grunts who were repeating a basic marching drill for—judging by their vacant expressions—the thousandth time.

"Where's Amy?" asked the first guard I nodded to, thus utterly ruining the rest of my absolutely piece of shit plan with a single question.

"Lying unconscious in the tunnel where I left her when I took her uniform?" I replied, before my brain could stop me.

You could say I panicked a little bit.

To be fair, this plan had never been much of a plan, and everyone but me seemed to have a gun, so I was kind of shitting my pants (only metaphorically for the moment, but possibly literally if someone pointed an AR-15 in my direction).
~~~

In defense of my not-actually-a-plan, it's worth noting that dudeface was probably expecting me to say "getting coffee while I process these yahoos," or something similar. After all, even MOME assholes tend to be maze rats just showing up to work every day. No one really expects a security breach, and even if they do, they don't expect the classic I'm-Harrison-Ford-and-I-just-stole-this-uniform-what-now-punk approach to security breaches. Which… might explain why the dude who'd just asked about Amy exhibited full-on, cartoon-level surprise when I punched him in the mouth and took his rifle from him. (Not sure why the guards all had bolt action rifles, while the training troops held AR-15s, but hey, it wasn't the first time I'd thought MOME was a bunch of idiots, so I didn't think much of it.)

Of course, stealing the gun would do little to keep the other guards from turning on me and opening fire with their own weapons, which is why I grabbed Where's-Amy as he was still reeling from the sudden punch to the face and pulled him in front of me as a human shield, making use of a really fabulous headlock I'd learned from my Krav Maga instructor a few years ago that left one arm free for gun wielding.

It was also why I'd brought friends.

Before the nearest guard could do more than jump back in response to me decking Where's-Amy, Renata had dropped them to the ground. I hoped she'd remembered the bit I'd added about not killing folks, but now wasn't the time to worry about it. Torrence, meanwhile, had the third guard in a very painful but non-damaging looking arm lock, and was dangling the woman's gun in one hand like a dirty set of underwear.

"Right," I said, looking around. "That could have been worse."

"Hey!" called someone from one of the other platoons. "Why do you have Gerald in a headlock and—"

The voice cut off abruptly, and a quick scan of the immediate vicinity suggested that Renata might be the cause, as she was no longer anywhere near us.

"Nice," I muttered, turning to see if any of the other guards had noticed what we were up to. "This might actually work."

Then a high pitched whistling noise rent the air, and a cold shiver went down my spine.

"Troops, attack the intruders!" someone in the distance yelled.

Then over a hundred people holding AR-15s suddenly turned on us as one.

"OH. FUCK."

My mouth didn't have time to drop open in shock, because I was too busy swinging Gerald around to block any potential gunfire while Torrence dropped into a fighting stance immediately behind me. I would have to do the whole shock thing later.

I noticed the guard Torrence had been holding lying suspiciously still on the ground in front of him. I had to hope he was heeding the whole "don't kill anyone" suggestion and simply rendering them unconscious, but, again, no time to check. 'Cause we were being rushed by everyone in our immediate vicinity.

The nearest of the trainees lurched towards me in an almost mechanical motion, and I wondered if androids were a thing in the magical world that I had yet to learn about. The woman looked human enough, but if I'd learned a single damned thing in the past three weeks, it was that that meant less than nothing. At any rate, I was trying to focus on how she moved, not what she was, because she was clearly going to be the first person to reach me.

I was doing my best to position the still-struggling Gerald in between me and her, assuming that she would raise her gun as soon as possible and open fire the moment Gerald wasn't in the way.

I was giving her entirely too much credit.

Maybe because I expected her to fight like someone with free will.

Maybe because I didn't realize that her gun was made of solid plastic, rather than the multiple moving pieces that are supposed to make guns work. Something that became entirely too clear when she raised the gun up over her shoulder and tried to clock me in the head with it, instead of firing any bullets. Thankfully, I was able to duck, and get my not-Gerald-holding arm up in time to block the strike.

Which hurt like a baseball bat, since solid plastic training weapons don't skimp around on the heft. I was lucky it didn't break my arm. I had to drop the rifle that I'd stolen from Gerald in order to make the block, which was less than ideal, but I wasn't super stoked on the idea of shooting anyone, now that I knew the guns the grunts had weren't real. But it meant that I had to hold on extra tight to Gerald, because I didn't want him getting ahold of his rifle again.

Since he was still struggling with every move I made, I was contemplating switching to a choke hold until he passed out, but I didn't have time. The lady who'd nearly broken my arm hadn't decided to stop, just because it hadn't worked the first time.

I watched her hips and shoulders, waiting for her core to telegraph where her next move would come from, but I didn't have to bother. Whatever they were training these folks in, it wasn't hand to hand. She just lifted the fake gun up in her hands and brought it back down again in a hacking motion. This time I turned Gerald into it, letting his side take the hit as I pushed back into Torrence, who seemed to be using the first person who had approached him as a broom, swinging them so that they took out the legs of everyone else who came at him. I didn't have time to be impressed, but I made a mental note for later.

Meanwhile, the other twenty people who had been approaching behind the first woman finally caught up. And, since this wasn't a movie, they all decided to attack at the same time.

Thank Gwen it was the most uncoordinated attack I'd ever witnessed. Half of them tripped over each other, falling in a sprawl that blocked everyone behind them from making it to me. Which still left me fighting a half dozen people at once, but… they were awful. I mean, they moved with almost zombie movie jerkiness, and telegraphed every move as if they were holding up signs saying "kick," "punch," "stomp." I was beginning to think that I was trapped in an old school Batman comic.

I smiled as I managed to block a few kicks with Gerald's legs, and then use him to sweep the legs of two of my nearest opponents who hadn't already tripped themselves. But any humor I might have felt at my opponents' lack of skill faded as I realized that the people attacking me were still managing to injure themselves, and they were eventually going to overwhelm us in enough numbers to also hurt me, Gerald, and probably even Torrence.

Ok, that last one might be a long shot. Torrence—likes to frolic in flowers and make daisy crowns in his free time Torrence—appeared to be a seventh degree blackbelt in every martial art I'd ever heard of, and a few I hadn't. He was taking down swaths of oncoming opponents, and barely working up a sweat. He took down incoming attackers almost as efficiently as Renata had dispatched the harpies in Hel's realm, but he didn't appear to be shifting between dimensions or anything, as far as I could tell.

Even still, the initial wave he'd been dealing with was apparently just the tip of the grunt troop iceberg, because the next wave of people attacking was so thick I could no longer see the lake behind them, or the entrance to the cave we'd come through, or anything but the wall of people that surrounded us. And even though they tripped over each other, and even trampled each other to get to us, we were *so* not going to make it out of here in one piece if they all came at us at once.

Plus, they were probably killing the people on the bottom of the pile, and that was kind of the opposite of what I'd come down here for.

"Gwendamnit," I muttered, as the crowd surged closer.

"What am I damning?" asked a familiar voice, from behind me.

I didn't look, because I didn't have time. I also didn't need to look to know Gwen was now standing behind me.

"Thissss issss a troublesssssome ssssituation, Living Cat," Rhelia's voice commented behind me.

I was too busy dodging the three different training guns that were being bludgeoned in my general direction to express my utter astonishment that Rhelia was here too. I finally had mercy on Gerald, who'd been clocked in the head by one of the last attacks anyway, and was now hanging limply in my arms, and launched him into the closest attackers, hoping they would ignore him, since he hadn't been one of the "intruders" they were ordered to attack.

"You will need the whissssstle," Rhelia said from behind me. Her voice sounded mildly strained, and I had to assume that meant she'd joined in the fight.

"Do I even want to know how and why you're here?" I asked.

"Thissss wassss my ssssecond guesssss for where MOME wassss ssssstowing their newesssst army."

That sentence held so many layers of implications, I didn't even know where to start, and besides, I had to keep fending off the wall of limbs and torsos encroaching on my space.

"Is this the whistle in question?" asked Renata's gritty voice, from somewhere close by. I was too busy grabbing my nearest attacker and pushing them back into the oncoming throng to notice.

"Perfect. Thank you," Rhelia said, before a high pitched trill cut through the air around us.

"Cssseasssse fighting," Rhelia called loudly, after the whistle cut through the crowd.

To my relief, and horrified fascination, everyone around us came to a grinding and eerie halt at the exact same moment.

"Now, ssssleep," Rhelia called.

I almost threw up when the whole crowd collapsed to the floor as one.

"That's going to give me nightmares," I muttered.

"It will be nice to have a bit of variety, won't it?" asked Gwen, from behind me.

"What would you know about my nightmares?" I asked, before I could think better of it.

"Goddess, remember? Besides, I was briefly your narrator, remember?"

"Thought you didn't have access to that info anymore?" I asked, turning to glare at her, despite myself. It was amusing to find Torrence staring bewilderedly at the red haired goddess, even though they'd met before. Or maybe he was more surprised to see Rhelia here, seemingly having popped in out of nowhere.

"That doesn't mean I don't remember the few pieces I had to narrate already," said Gwen.

"Would you two ssssstop bickering pleasssse? We have more pressssing isssssuessss."

"Are the dragons still planning to raze this place?" I asked Rhelia.

"Yessss. Though General Aira agreed to wait until we emerged, before beginning the desssstruction."

"Well, at least she knows we're here. So…" I took a deep breath and looked around the cavern that was now the (hopefully temporary) resting place for around a hundred and fifty people. Renata was a grey haze in my peripheral vision, and looking around the room I had to assume that she was the one responsible for taking out all of the MOME guards. I didn't think the whistle had worked on them. "We still have to figure out a way to get all hundred and whatever people out of here, don't we?"

"Unlessss you wish to ssssacrificssse them for the greater good, yessss."

"Could have saved myself the detour, if sacrificing them had ever been the plan," I replied. "I know we don't really have time, but seriously, how did you know to come down here?"

Rhelia sighed, "You ssssstill know very little about what I wassss doing when MOME captured me in Bolivia. Did you never wonder what misssssion I might have had that would have enabled MOME to detain me?"

I shrugged.

"Seriously, MOME has captured, detained, or killed so many people close to me that I honestly just assumed it was because you were a part-time dragon."

Rhelia laughed, but the mirth didn't reach her eyes.

"That issss cssssertainly the reasssson they put on paper. However, them catching me ssssearching their dungeonssss for ssssecret training facssssilitiessss may alsssso have been a factor."

Right. Ok. Sure. I'd known Rhelia worked for the dragon realm's intelligence gathering. I was just… way behind on a few pertinent details about her work.

"So… you eventually realized they weren't in the Andean office, and then?"

"My nexsssst besssst guessss wassss Shanghai," Rhelia added calmly.

"But when they didn't have training facilities, you realized it was here instead, and asked Gwen to drop you off?" I guessed.

"Oh, they had the facsssssilitiessss, they were merely empt—"

"There is something wrong with your redhaired friend, Victoria."

That was Torrence, whose shoulder appeared to be the only thing keeping Gwen off of the floor. To say that Gwen was looking unwell would be the understatement of the year, but I didn't know how else to describe it. Her skin was dripping sweat and had taken on an unpleasant yellow tinge. Her hair, normally a mane of fiery curls, now clung limply to her face and shoulders, and looked brittle enough to snap if I so much as breathed on it too hard. Not to mention, her legs didn't look like they were holding her weight at all.

"Gwen?" I asked, unable to formulate a more specific question.

"M'fine," she mumbled. "Jus'need t'get out'vehere."

Then she collapsed entirely, or would have, if I hadn't reached forward to grab her. Torrence looked as though he would have grabbed her in the next second, but I happened to be standing in the direction she collapsed, so catching her was all but required.

"Living Cat?" Rhelia asked, sounding startled.

"Gwen's sick or something," I muttered. After a few moments of shifting my balance, I managed to lever Gwen up onto my shoulder. She didn't weigh nearly as much as she should have; lifting her felt like lifting a small child. I suspected that was a bad thing. She already looked like a patient in palliative care.

When I finally reached a standing position, with Gwen draped over my shoulder in a fireman's carry, I found Rhelia and Torrence frowning at us.

"She is a creature of dark matter, so this dungeon is probably killing her," Rhelia said, her accent dropping away. I really wanted to ask her about when she chose to keep it and let it go, but now was definitely not the time.

"How could she have gotten here, with all the dark matter suppression going on?"

"She likely had a single chance to bring us here, and was then stuck. For someone as powerful as she, the getting here was perhaps not that difficult, but she would be even less capable of leaving than the rest of us, as the dark matter suppressors restrain all that she is, not just her magic."

I let my jaw drop, as I considered why on Earth Gwen would have found that to be a worthwhile risk. I couldn't imagine getting Rhelia here as backup was worth it, but maybe I underestimated how screwed we'd been before she mentioned the whole whistle business.

Which reminded me that I hadn't seen Renata recently, and just as I opened my mouth to voice the question, she stepped out of the shadows and stood beside us.

"It should be easy enough to lead the mind control victims out of here, but I am unsure of what to do with the MOME guards."

We all simply stood and stared at each other for a moment.

"I may be good, but I cannot convey all of these unconscious individuals to safety alone before the dragons would destroy us all."

"It's true," Rhelia agreed. "Even if we were to emerge and inform General Aira that she must wait a few hours while we remove innocents, I doubt she would hold her attack. She… is not fond enough of non-dragons to risk the delay."

"Right," I said. "Rhelia, how does the whistle thing work, exactly? Can anyone give directions, or just the whistle blower?"

"There is no magic to it, else it would not work here. I believe the first person to give directions after the whistle blows will be heeded."

I nodded towards the whistle she held in her hand, and cleared my throat for a moment.

She blew the eerie signal that had blown twice already today, and I struggled to keep my stomach in check as all the eyes of the sleeping troops opened as one.

"Everyone, please wake up and make your way to the tunnel in a calm and orderly fashion, helping those around you who need it. If there is an unconscious person nearby, please work with the people near you to carry them. We must all exit this facility as quickly and safely as possible." I tried to use my best theater voice, hoping the acoustics of the cavern would help where my own vocal chords faltered.

A moment passed before, adding fuel to a lifetime of nightmares, almost everyone on the cavern floor rose as one, beginning to calmly progress to the tunnel behind us.

"So. Damned. Creepy," I muttered, before turning to follow them with Gwen on my shoulder.

It was hard not to feel a giddy sense of relief as I led the march of over a hundred captives out of the heart of MOME's North American dungeons and up towards light, air, and freedom. I was leading the pack, because I felt guilty allowing anyone else to risk encountering MOME resistance on the way out.

Luckily, all the MOME mind control victims seemed to be more inclined to follow a leader rather than push ahead, which meant that the glacial pace I was keeping, thanks to having an unconscious goddess slung over my shoulder, wasn't pissing off anyone behind me. Still, about halfway up the tunnel leading back to the top of the dungeon, I passed Gwen off to Torrence, because I felt like my legs were about to give out, and the place where Rebecca Dryer's bullet had gone through my shoulder earlier was starting to feel like it was on fire. Also, with Rhelia and Renata engaged in a whispered conversation just a few meters away, and no guards showing up to be defeated, Torrence looked desperate to have something to do. When I asked if he'd mind carrying the unconscious goddess, he practically jumped with glee.

As soon as Gwen was draped over Torrence's shoulders, Rhelia pulled away from her conversation with Renata and dropped back to keep pace with him.

With zero fanfare, Renata appeared beside me.

"You must be careful with them," she said, coming slightly more into focus through the shifting haze that always seemed to surround her.

I could guess who "they" were, since there was an army of zombielike people still trundling along behind us, but as for being careful…that could mean about a hundred different things at this point, and chances were good I didn't even know what most of them were.

"What do you mean?"

"They are all still under a compulsion placed by the vampires. If we encounter anyone who—"

"Wait, *vampires?*"

"Yes. How else did you suppose they were managing mind control?"

"But I thought vampire mind control only worked on non-magical folks."

"Normally, that is correct. However, it seems that MOME has discovered that even magical beings are vulnerable to vampire persuasion when their dark matter is supressed."

"How does that work, though? Don't the vampires need their dark matter to use persuasion? And then, how does that do any good? I mean, then you have an army of people who can't leave the dark matter suppressing rocks, or whatever—"

"That is what the aquifer is for," Renata interrupted, perhaps growing impatient with my continued divergence from her initial message of caution. "The water that wells there suppresses dark matter as effectively as the rocks it has filtered through. Once ingested, it stays in the system for days. Long enough to move the victims to where a vampire could manipulate them. And long enough to be forced to fight after they'd been 'trained' sufficiently."

My stomach turned at the thought.

"They made everyone drink that stuff?"

"That is what both my and Rhelia's observations would suggest."

"Renata… what are you actually doing here? Did Hel seriously tell you to follow me all the way here?"

It was difficult to see through the haze, but I thought she might have shrugged.

"My father provided MOME with his services on more than one occasion, in his attempts to pursue me. I was… concerned about the legacy that would leave behind. Ever since you informed me of his demise, I have been wondering what wrongs of his it is possible for me to right. When Hel dismissed me and suggested that I could maintain my usefulness by seeing what you were up to, I thought perhaps I could… what is the term, murder two birds together?"

I swallowed, unsure whether or not she was joking.

"Close enough," I admitted. " So, you're telling me that Edik had something to do with the MOME brainwashing scheme we're now up to our ears in?"

Renata met the question with silence, but the look on her face was answer enough.

"Great. Edik is still fucking with me, even from the dead."

"We are nearing the surface," Renata continued, ignoring my jibe at her dead father. I looked around the tunnels and realized that she was right. We'd almost made it to the top of the dungeons. Soon we'd be out of the dark matter suppressing rock.

"You must understand that the vampire charms holding these people will not break simply because we leave the dungeons behind us. They will be in danger of falling under MOME control again, should we meet anyone that has one of those whistles."

"Right. Got it. Dewhistle the whistle holders ASAP."

I glanced at Renata and decided she wasn't done.

"Anything else?" I asked, warily.

"It will take them days to break free of the compulsions, and they will need help to break them. Until then… they may need assistance getting through their daily needs."

I stared at her for a moment.

"Are you telling me I have to babysit a hundred zombie people so they can all eat, sleep, and shit properly?"

Renata shrugged.

"You do not have to, but if someone does not… it may be unpleasant for them."

Ugh. I did *not* want to be in charge of these people's wellbeing until MOME's hooks were out of them, but leaving them to the side effects of MOME's latest shitty plans to take over the world was unacceptable.

"Why did they even *want* a zombie horde? It's not like they could use their magic, with their dark matter suppressed. They would just be cannon fodder."

Renata's mist-shrouded form merely stared at me for a moment, while I wondered what I had said that was so stupid. Then it hit me.

"Gwendamnit. That was the whole point, wasn't it? Horrifying cannon fodder created out of our own allies."

Renata only nodded, mutely.

"Ugh… and by the time we figured out we were killing people who weren't voluntarily fighting for MOME, it would be far too late."

I had kinda felt like throwing up ever since I'd encountered the whole mind control thing in the cavern, but now I could feel the bile rising in the back of my throat. I swallowed, because I hated vomiting in general, and right now I thought it would be exceedingly inconvenient—even though the idea of leaving vomit on MOME property was kind of appealing. Then again, so was lighting the whole place on fire. And, since that was part of the ACTUAL plan, I decided to save my petty bodily fluid revenge, and work on getting all these innocent people out of the way so that a few dozen dragons could torch MOME's North American headquarters as originally discussed.

If only it had been that simple.

As soon as we hit the top of the dungeon, the place where the dark matter suppressing stone ended and the normal prison began, Gwen seemed to regain her full weight. At least, that was my best guess as to why Torrence had suddenly collapsed under the unconscious redhead.

A guess that was confirmed when Torrence muttered, "How can *anyone* be that heavy?"

Considering that Torrence was nearly seven feet of pure muscle, that seemed like an odd question, but when I hustled over to grab one of Gwen's still limp arms to try to help pull her off the giant man-bull, I could see what he meant.

"Holy shit," I said, dropping Gwen's arm. "Could this be some kind of MOME trap?" I asked, looking between Rhelia and Renata, who had hustled over to check on the trapped tauren with me.

The four of us were the only people out of our entourage who were actually looking at anything. Everyone else seemed to be staring blankly into space, after shuffling to a halt behind us. I shuddered, trying to ignore the zombielike horde that had somehow become my responsibility until they recovered themselves. My eyes snapped to Rhelia's, since Renata's were half hidden in the "mist" that seemed to constantly shroud her.

"I do not think sssso. I think thissss may be how much ssssshe normally weighsssss."

"She feels like she's cemented into the floor, Rhelia. How can she walk, if that's how much she normally weighs?"

"She's a goddess, isn't she?" Renata asked. "That means she is *mostly* dark matter. Rather the reverse of the rest of us; we are blood and flesh that contain some dark matter, she is dark matter that has been molded to appear as blood and flesh."

"It would exsssssplain why sssshe weighed nearly nothing when we were in the dark matter ssssupresssssing partssss of thissss facsssility. It issss likely that sssshe can control how much sssshe weighssss when sssshe is conscioussss."

"So what the hells can we do to make her light enough to carry?" Torrence asked wheezily from the floor, even as he managed to push Gwen a few inches to one side. It wasn't quite enough to free him, but it was probably helping his breathing.

"Carry who?" asked a muffled voice, from atop the brown, furred chest she was currently pinning in place.

The four of us all stared at the still-unmoving redhead on the tile at our feet.

"Gwen?" I asked, unsure if I'd imagined the source of the voice.

"I'll be fine in a few minutes," the voice said. "Just leave me here for now. I'm afraid I won't be able to make myself lighter for a bit, but by the time I can do that, I should have no trouble walking on my own."

"Uh…" I looked between Torrence, Rhelia, and Renata again, hoping one of them would have some idea of how to respond to that. "Gwen, we're… kinda still in the middle of the MOME HQ in Phoenix. I'm not sure we should just leave you here."

"Oh, don't worry about me. There's really not much those asshats can do to me. In my current state, they can't move me back to the one part of the facility where'd they'd actually be able to harm me, and as soon as I can make myself light enough to walk, there won't be anything they can do to touch me."

She sounded completely casual, as though she were explaining why her cinnamon buns needed a little more time to rise before she could put them in the oven.

"You sure abou—"

"You really should be going, Vic. There is much to be done still, and not much time to do it in. The fates don't like to be kept waiting."

"The fates?"

"I'll tell you all about it later," she said, her voice now muffled by the tile flooring that her face was pressed against. Torrence had finally managed to slide her off of his chest and onto the floor. "If there is a later. There won't be, if you continue to linger here."

"Right. Cool. That's not ominous at all," I muttered.

"Go, Vic. Seriously. You need to go, or there won't be anything left to be sarcastic about."

I was never sure how seriously to take Gwen, because she'd first shown up in my life as a naked crazy woman claiming to be my narrator. But ever since she'd revealed she was a goddess, it was difficult not to feel like there was a certain gravitas to everything she said. And when she said twice in one conversation that there was a chance there wouldn't be a "later" if I didn't get my ass in gear, I was going to listen.

"Gwenspeed," I said over my shoulder, as the four of us turned and headed farther up and out of the MOME prison complex, our hundred shuffling mind control victims in tow.

"Cute," said the muffled voice from the floor. "I see what you did there." I didn't hear if she said anything else, because I was too busy running towards the exits.

It wasn't that I didn't find it suspicious that we didn't run in to a single MOME operative on our exodus from the building, it was just that I was too busy trying to figure out what Gwen could have meant by suggesting that there wouldn't be a "later" if I didn't hurry up. I mean, I got that we had a lot to do before MOME was completely out of business in the "accidentally/on purpose gonna blow up the universe" department, but I had been under the impression that we'd had most of that sewn shut by the time I got into the dungeons and found the cases of Technetium that I'd needed to neutralize.

If everyone else had found the stores of Technetium they'd been looking for, then we should have been golden. Rhelia and I hadn't exactly had a chance to debrief, but when I'd asked about the cache of Technetium in Shanghai, she'd said she'd got it. If all our other agents had been as successful as Rhelia and I, we should be pretty much Technetium free by now... which is why what Gwen had said made me nervous. So nervous, that I didn't think much of the fact that we didn't run into any regular security or staff members as we ran through the halls of what had been a fully operational MOME facility not thirty minutes ago. Although, even if I had thought of it, I might have brushed it aside as Dryer having tipped everyone off to our whole "burn it with dragon fire" program when she realized we were there.

I certainly would not have guessed it meant we were about to be ambushed.

By what looked like the entirety of MOME's fighting forces from across the globe… led by a short, balding mage with a wand aimed right at my heart, the moment I stepped out of MOME's main entrance and into the way-too-fucking-hot-for-September Phoenix sun.

I had barely enough time to register the entirety of the force raised against us—over a thousand people arrayed around the paved parking lot that stretched outside the double set of glass doors we'd just plowed through, including clusters of folks wearing far more leather than was appropriate for the climate draped over parked cars, concrete barriers, and at least one tank, and a frontline of people holding actual AR-15s with an eerily familiar vacancy to their eyes—before I heard the word "fire" issue from the mouth of the short guy holding the wand.

And instantly felt myself tugged to my right, and into a grey lanscape where the world around me seemed to be separated by a thick veil of water, and everything but me and Renata moved in slow motion. I didn't have time to wonder what the fuck was going on—though a vague memory of Renata shuddering while talking about pulling people into her dimension came to mind—because, slow motion or not, the bullets that had started spraying towards me and the hundred or so stragglers I'd just pulled from MOME's brainwashing basement were still moving as fast as a ball thrown by a professional pitcher, and dodging them was the focus of my entire existence. The spells being slung were moving considerably slower than the bullets, but they were still rolling inevitably towards us, and as far as I knew, no one in our entourage was bulletproof. Or spellproof.

"I can't save all of you," Renata said, her voice sounding pained. "There isn't enough time."

And she was right. Unless she had a few more tricks that I hadn't seen yet, there was no way she could move fast enough to move us all out of the way of these bullets. And the people behind me, the brainwashed innocents who were still compelled by the command I'd given them to follow me, were still coming out the heavy glass doors, and would keep coming until I gave them a contradicting order that they could all hear. Which was never going to work with all the gunfire and shouting going on. Gunfire that had already torn a hole in my sleeve and the skin of my arm, as I tried to dodge a hail of tiny obstacles that were coming at me in the fastest game of dodgeball I'd ever played in my life. Renata was busy dodging as well. She hadn't let go of my hand yet, but I could already tell this was never going to work—we were going to have to dodge in different directions soon. She couldn't even save me. Not to mention Torrence and Rhelia, or all the nameless folks we'd just pulled from MOME's dungeons. Not without getting herself killed. She needed more time.

And then I remembered that we were free of the damned dark matter suppressing powers of MOME's dungeons, and I didn't have to try to solve this one with nothing but a stolen uniform, my winning smile, and the apparently unsuppressable powers of a dhampir.

I also didn't have time to plan anything, so I did the first thing that came to mind. I held tight to Renata's hand, and reached through time and space.

25

AND WE DIDN'T go anywhere. Not really. Because I hadn't reached through space all that much. Just a few feet to the side of where we'd been. Mostly I had reached through time. Not far, only thirty seconds into the past or so. Just long enough to turn and watch myself, Renata, and Rhelia come plowing towards the doors that would lead them out into the open, only they were plowing in a strange slow-mo, while Renata and I seemed to be the only ones moving at full speed. I guessed this was what she'd meant when she'd once told me that time in her dimension moved differently than it did in others. Our hands were still linked, and Renata immediately began pulling me towards our earlier selves, but I resisted.

"Wait," I whispered.

Thankfully we were still in her liminal space, and I didn't think anyone could see us. Certainly, when I glanced over my shoulder, the short bald guy who'd fired a spell right at my chest wasn't doing anything but watching the door with the kind of manic anticipation generally reserved for toddlers and serial killers.

"We have to warn ourselves," Renata hissed.

"No, we can't warn ourselves, or we wouldn't be here. We have to stop the folks who never made it out the door, and send them somewhere else."

I might have only been doing the time travel thing for less than a week, but I was already pretty clear on the fact that you couldn't really change the past, you could just nudge the future a little bit. Because when I finally had talked to Rhelia about it, it had been clear that at no point had she experienced a reality in which we hadn't been working together to save Trev. She had never died, no matter how much it had looked like it, felt like it, to me the first time I'd seen it. But if I hadn't gone back in time, we never would have had the plan to begin with. You couldn't change the past, but if you didn't time travel the past would have turned out differently. So, I already knew that we weren't here to warn past me, or past Renata, or even past Rhelia and Torrence, because damn it, they'd made it out the door, and we couldn't change who left the building before the shooting started, even if we tried.

I hadn't noticed who had made it out besides the four of us, honestly, so as soon as the doors opened, and past me came storming out in slow motion, I pulled Renata along, and the two of us slid past Renata from 30 seconds ago, past Rhelia, who Renata seemed to make a concerted effort to bump into, and past Torrence. Then we plowed into the hallway, where most of the horde of mind control victims were making their way towards the doors at a slow but determined plod.

A few of them had moved more quickly, and were already blasting out the doors, even as we reached the main group. There was nothing I could do about them now. If they were outside, they were beyond my sphere of influence. I had to help the folks standing in front of us, before it was too late to save them. Then we would go back and save Rhelia and the others. We had to. There was no way that Trev was going to forgive me for getting his girlfriend killed for real. He'd barely forgiven me for when it hadn't actually happened.

But first Renata whipped out the whistle, which I belatedly realized she must have stolen off of Rhelia as we walked past her, and she let go of my hand, so that she could blow the thing where everyone could hear it.

The hundred-ish group of magical beings, which I now noticed covered every being, including trolls, pixies, elves, human mages, human weres, and an assortment of other folks I had no name for, came to an abrupt halt.

"I need everyone to hold hands," I said, nodding my appreciation to Renata. I had kind of assumed that I could just give new orders to the mind controlees, but that probably wasn't how this worked. "Hug if you have to, but I need everyone connected right away."

I shuddered, as I heard the army behind us open fire. It wouldn't be long before bullets and spells started making their way through the heavy glass doors into MOME. I had to hope they'd been magically reinforced, or something, because otherwise we weren't even going to have time to get us out of here without casualties.

Luckily, the folks who'd had their minds altered still seemed inclined to listen to whistle-given commands, and within a few heartbeats of asking, we had a group of a hundred or more people of every variety, including all the folks who still had unconscious MOME guards draped over their shoulders, all holding onto one another. It could have been a Coke commercial—f we hadn't all been about to die in a haze of bullets and spells, that is.

"Hold on tight," I said, grabbing the arm of the nearest person, an orangish-toned elf, slightly taller than Nethia, but similar enough in appearance that I assumed he was from the same realm. His eyes were as blank as any of the others, so I didn't bother engaging him in conversation. Even asking someone's name when they were in this state felt like a violation. They couldn't resist any question I asked them, so I didn't want to ask them anything. I was going to stick to saving their lives if I could, and if they felt like telling me about themselves once they were better, that was their business.

As soon as I gripped the orange elf's arm, Renata slipped the whistle back into her pocket and grabbed onto my other hand.

"Here goes nothing," I said.

And pulled over a hundred people through time and space.

AND SUDDENLY, I felt so drained that if I hadn't been holding onto two other people, I would have collapsed to the… cactus and yucca strewn ground? That wasn't right.

"The fuck?" I asked groggily, blinking at the high desert sun shining through a cerulean sky, baking away at the pink-tinged ground as though it were mid-July instead of early September. Because the desert didn't really give a fuck about things like seasons. Or at least, not a piddly season like fall. It gave a little bit of a damn about winter, at this elevation, but September was just an excuse to have pretty sunsets, as far as the desert was concerned. That was fine. I got that. High deserts made sense to me in their own way. What I didn't get was why we were in the rocky scrubland that smelled faintly of mesquite and juniper, when I'd been aiming for a certain grove of pine trees surrounding a singular oak tree just outside of Flagstaff.

"You did it," Renata said, holding me up while looking at me quizzically. "You got them out."

I blinked some more, and saw that she was mostly right. I seemed to have brought us all away from MOME.

But I should have been able to shift us all back to the grove. It wasn't that far away, and this was a lot of people, sure, but I had moved way more people than this back in Bolivia. Of course, that had almost killed me, but this group was like a tenth the size. I should have been able to make it all the way there, and I shouldn't feel so damned drained.

"I was trying to take us to the Tree of Life," I said, absently, as I took stock of where we were. I had also been trying to take us five minutes into the past, to make sure that we would have enough time to get back to the fight as soon as the shooting started. Maybe that was what had drained me so quickly. It was a problem I was beginning to ignore, as I started to wonder what the fuck these folks were going to do out here in the middle of the desert without any mode of transportation.

Renata shrugged.

"They are clear of the hail of bullets that MOME wished them to die in, so I think we can call this a success."

"But they can't stay here. The desert is no joke. September may as well be the middle of summer here, and they don't have supplies. Even if they did have supplies, they can't—"

"They will be fine," Renata said. "At least until we can make it back to them."

"You don't understand how quickly dehydration and sunstroke can take out the unprepared."

Renata shrugged.

"They are much better off than they were. You took them from certain death to a plausibly distant one that we have a decent chance of rescuing them from, *after* we have rescued the others."

I sighed. She had a point. And I didn't have the energy to argue. In fact, I didn't have the energy to do much of anything.

I put out my hand, and was glad that Renata placed the whistle in it without even a question between us. I blew the pattern that I'd heard Rhelia and Renata use, then cleared my throat.

"Seek shelter from the sun, try to find water if you can. Don't drink anything stagnant, only the moving stuff. Take care of yourselves and each other. If you can use your magic at all, do it. We'll be back to find you as soon as we can."

Then I turned and grabbed Renata's hand, and once more reached through time and space.

AND PROMPTLY FELL right on my ass. Thankfully, I missed the two specimens of yucca and prickly pear that were hanging out nearby. Not so the tiny barrel cactus that was now mostly embedded in my right thigh, nor the pointy rock that had stabbed me in the left butt cheek.

"Ow," I said, mainly to vent my frustration. It didn't hurt *that* badly. If anything, it was a bit of a distraction from the still-throbbing bullet wounds in my shoulder and upper arm. As I stood up, both the barrel cactus and the rock released me. Barrel cacti were relatively friendly, as far as cacti went—the thorns were robust enough to hurt, but they mostly stayed in the cactus when I pulled away and stood up. It was a fact I was grateful for at that moment, since I really didn't have time to pull a bunch of cactus spines out of my ass.

"I can't shift," I said to Renata, who was looking at me as though I were an untrained dog whose behavior she couldn't begin to predict.

"Can you reach your magic at all, or did shifting so many people full of dark matter suppressant drain you entirely?" she asked, looking nonplussed. I wondered if she was calculating how long it would take her to run us back to Phoenix in the liminal space she occupied.

I started to reach for my snow leopard form, but then thought better of it. I didn't know how much energy I had, and couldn't be sure I'd have enough to shift again, but if we needed to get from here to Phoenix in a hurry, without me shifting us through space and time, there was really only one useful thing I could do.

Renata smiled, from far below me, as I spread my wings and lowered my neck enough for her to hop aboard. I didn't know exactly how long it would take to fly from here to Phoenix, but it couldn't be more than a few minutes, could it? It would have to be enough. I refused to think that we couldn't make it back in time to save Rhelia and the others.

There had to be some advantages to being a dragon, damn it.

Like getting to light up the asshat who had given the order to fire on a bunch of unarmed brainwashing victims.

~~~

Fun fact: apparently, if you are a dragon with a dhampir on your back, you can fucking *fly* in liminal space, and thus turn what should have been a ten minute flight into a thirty second one. Honestly, with a trip that short, it was almost as fast as using Gwen powers.

And it was WAY more satisfying to dive at the head of MOME's forces from a few thousand feet and release a spray of molten fire right in the bald fucker's face.

Go ahead, ask me how I know.

And look, I am not a fan of killing. It made me physically ill to shoot that one MOME jerk, and it had even made me feel awful to incinerate Edik's diamond cranium, honestly. But all evidence suggested that dragon-me was way less worried about violence in defense of one's friends, and bald-manic-mage-dude had just unleashed a haze of bullets on me, my new dhampir friend, the tauren I was coming to think of as a battle buddy, at the very least, and my dragon sister-in-law, not to mention the hundred brainwashed MOME victims who he didn't know I'd been able to remove from the line of fire.

So, yeah, I wasn't feeling too guilty about roasting the dicktart.

He deserved it, and dragon-me let out a roar of vindictive rage and triumph when his body was immolated in dragon fire.

Unfortunately, having their leader incinerated didn't miraculously get the rest of the troops to immediately cease hostilities. It did, however, serve as enough of a distraction to get Renata on the ground without getting her riddled with bullets. She proceeded to weave through our reality and her own, picking up the dozen or so hapless mind control victims who had managed to follow us out of the door the first time, and had since been standing awkwardly in a hail of bullets. As far as I could tell, Renata and I had arrived
~~~

almost immediately after we'd left, mainly judging by how few bullet holes were riddling the brainwashing victims we'd had to leave behind. Sadly, it was a number greater than zero, but not by much. Most of them were still on their feet. And now they were getting sucked out of my field of vision, one at a time, faster than I could keep up with.

I didn't see Rhelia anywhere, but I didn't actually search for very long, because I was no longer in Renata's liminal space, and therefore suddenly presented a very large stationary target. I was alerted to this fact by the hail of bullets that abruptly began raining down on me.

I needed to focus on saving my own ass for a minute.

~~~

Damn, I was learning a lot in this battle. For example, did you know that dragon hide is basically bulletproof? True story. The slugs raining down around me in the bright September sun simply bounced off, falling harmlessly to the ground. The few that bounced back towards the troops who had fired them at me seemed to ping against the shields that the mages had set up. Shields that my dragon eyes saw as a light glow encircling certain troops. Certain troops. But not all of them. And my dragon brain, for all that it was excited to wale on some enemies, was also a bit faster than my human brain, I guess, because it came to the conclusion that those unprotected folks were very likely to be even more of our brainwashed MOME victims. Perhaps dragon me could actually smell that dark matter suppressing water in them, or perhaps part of me simply realized that the only folks not likely to have shields would be the folks who MOME thought were expendable. So I pulled up before I could accidentally torch any of the folks who were shieldless.

Then I learned that dragon hides are bulletproof, but they aren't completely spellproof. Many of the spells that the mages hiding behind shields slung at me bounced off as harmlessly as the bullets did. Many, but not all. Someone threw another one of those creepy-ass acid clouds outward and I barely dodged it (dragon memory in action is awesome, and it warned me that the acid cloud wouldn't just bounce away), but I was too focused on dodging the acid cloud to successfully dodge the barrage of spells that followed in its wake, and one of those spells was nasty, and stung like a cat on fire. I didn't even get a chance to see what spell it was, but luckily whatever it was had only grazed my tail, and while the pain was sharp, it didn't seem
~~~

to be slowing me down. I roared off the pain and focused on a bit of retaliation.

Which led straight to the next fun fact of the day, namely that while many mage shields protect against bullets, you know what they don't protect against? DRAGON FIRE. Seems like nothing is dragon fire proof, at least insofar as my recent experiments had shown. Which probably explained why, after charring one tank full of vampires and mages, and a few of the mages hiding behind the front line of AR-15 wielding, shieldless mindcontrol victims, Rhelia swooped in to nudge me away from the enemy.

I was pissy about it at first. Dragon-me still wasn't done wreaking havoc on MOME's troops, but Rhelia pushed and pushed with her iridescent ebon muzzle, and once I backed up far enough it was clear what the problem was. The dragon fire I'd unleashed on the tank was… well, it was spreading, quickly. And nothing the mages and vampires were doing seemed to be able to stop it.

Well, shit.

I mean, don't get me wrong, decimating MOME's ranks with dragon fire seemed like a fine idea. Right up until I remembered that those same mages, vamps, and probably weres, were highly unlikely to do anything to stop the fire from consuming the same mind control victims that I'd been trying to spare in the first place.

At least the conflagration that had once been a tank—and damn, I hadn't thought metal could burn like that, dragon fire was some seriously badass shit—was keeping most of MOME's frontline forces busy for the moment. But that wasn't going to stop the fire from taking out the mind controlled grunts, nor was it going to stop it from taking out most of Pheonix, if given enough time.

Ugh…I hate being an adult sometimes.

If it makessss you feel any better, Living Cat, you are sssstill a child by dragon ssssstandardssss.

Then why am I here fighting bad guys instead of playing in someone's yard?

Rhelia made no reply, and it wouldn't have mattered if she did.

As I took in the flaming scene before me, I was tempted to try to remove all of the mind control grunts from the equation and just let MOME deal with the fire, but there were too many for me to remove them without getting a bunch of them killed, and MOME seemed to be having zero luck with the fire, despite having all but stopped fighting in order to put it out.

Right then—time to put the boost that getting busy with Az had given me to the test.

THE TANK THAT I'd originally torched had started setting off small explosions that lit up not just the MOME troops that surrounded it, but also the pavement it was on, and… everything it touched.

MOME had basically stopped fighting, though it wasn't entirely clear if that was in order to try to put out the fire I'd started, or because they only had a handful of people to try to kill left. Renata had removed all of the remaining mind control victims that we had led out, and now I couldn't see her in the fray. Had she taken Torrence with her? I couldn't see him at the moment either. Rhelia was certainly here, and a very large target, but no other dragons appeared to be present, and I didn't even know where Albert had wandered off to.

At any rate, it was handy that they were distracted. But less handy that they were trying to put out the fire by sacrificing mind control grunts carrying spelled blankets.

In fact, that ruined just about everything that was useful about the fire to begin with.

Which is how, seconds after I'd stopped spraying the very fire that had become such a threat, I found myself diving down through the smoke that now clogged the air above MOME's Phoenix HQ, shrieking, talons extended—because I feel like there's a certain expectation of fury with wings that needs to be upheld—towards the flaming wreck that had been a tank only a minute ago.

It was more flame than not, and with my quick descent I didn't have much time to assess where a safe place to grab it might be. Rhelia's warning about dragons not being immune to dragon flame was still fresh in my mind, but honestly, what choice did I have? MOME had decided to use the people they had unwavering control over to douse the flames, and they seemed to have given them some kind of spelled blankets to do it with, but that didn't change the fact that the flames were consuming the blankets almost as quickly as they were applied, and then leaping to the folks holding the blankets, with zero fanfare besides the screams of the victims.

So, yeah, I didn't have time to look around for the best place to put my talons.

There was something that looked like a small hatch open on the side of the vehicle, and while flames consumed every available surface around it, there didn't seem to be any flames inside of the hatch yet, so I aimed for that spot, hoping to grab the inside edge.

It would have been a different story if I'd had to carry the damned thing anywhere, but as it was, I just latched onto the inside edge of the damned thing and did my best to picture a familiar hellscape where it would fit in nicely.

But nothing happened, and I could feel my scales begin to singe.

I let out a roar of frustration, and then saw the flap of feathered wings at my side.

Azrael? Where the hells did you come from? I asked, with far less irony than I should have.

But Az didn't say anything before they kissed me. And I had just about a half second to think of how weird it felt because I was still a *dragon*, so Az was basically just making out with a small portion of my lip, but damned if that didn't get my dragon blood going, and then bam, I felt the power transfer initiate. Apparently, there were a few perks to having *already* gotten busy with a succubus. And I didn't have time to question how any of that worked, because suddenly, still gripping the flaming tank that was now causing the skin beneath my scales to smolder, my power finished the reach I had tried to initiate a moment ago, and then I was in hell.

BOTH LITERALLY AND figuratively, that is. Because of course, with Az's help, and considering how close we were to the seam that ran near here, I'd pulled myself into that damned canyon of dark matter suppression, complete with orange sky barely visible between towering cliffs, purple sun, and air tinged with sulphur.

Which was actually great, because it seemed to be the only thing that could suppress the dragon fire (and wasn't *that* interesting—did dragon fire run on dark matter, then? It must, and that would explain why it was so damned hard to put out, and also why it would eat into dragons as well), but I only had half a second to consider the implications of all of that before my whole world narrowed to one of excruciating pain.

I didn't think it was the naked red squirrel thing that was sitting on top of my chest causing the agony, but I couldn't really tell. I'd fallen to my ass as soon as I'd landed in this damned canyon, and I couldn't see much of what was going on.

I could see that the fire on the tank had been put out, which was great, and I had to assume it meant that no part of my body was currently on fire, but apparently turning human and having human nerve endings to experience the remnants of whatever burning I'd just experienced was the opposite of fun.

And then Azrael started screaming at me.

Maybe they were trying to reassure me. How were you supposed to tell what a red demon squirrel was saying when the translation magic didn't work and all you heard was the sound of a thousand tortured cats every time they opened their mouth?

All of which ceased to matter for a moment, as I passed out from the pain.

When I came to again, Az was staring into my face, looking concerned. I wondered how long I'd been out, but decided it could't be more than a minute or two, because everything was exactly as it had been before consciousness escaped me. Also, Az hadn't abandoned me yet.

"Are we really going to have to climb out of here to get back?" I asked Az.

Who looked at me as if I were a very slow child, for a moment.

I decided to lie down for a bit and let my brain catch up to reality.

Had we come through a seam? I had shifted us here, this time, but used the seam as a guide, because it made the whole thing more energy efficient. What about the last time? The last time I'd used the seam in the dungeon from MOME. Which, Sol had reminded me a few days ago, didn't require any special powers to do. Nons (muggles, normal humans, whatever you wanted to call them) occasionally stumbled through seams, right? So… that meant that I should be able to go back through the seam here. The first time I was brought here, I was dropped off by MOME, tied up, and had no idea how seams worked, so it hadn't occurred to me I could get back from here, besides, I would have just wound up back in the dungeon, so that wouldn't have helped me. But this time, I had no real reason to care about going through the MOME dungeon. Sure, it might slow me down, but not nearly as much as climbing the cliff would.

Part of me wanted to climb up just to check on Siara, but for one thing, I was still largely a ball of agony. For another thing, I still had a battle to fight, and even though it was tempting—so Gwendamned tempting—to just lie down here and take a break for a minute because damned if I wasn't covered in burns, and just generally beat to shit, and felt like I deserved a break after saving everyone's asses from dragon fire…

Of course, I'd been the one to set the damned fire to begin with, and there were still people I loved back on Earth, possibly fighting MOME, and possibly in mortal danger, and if anything happened to one of them because I wasn't there to help, I—

I was suddenly on my feet, Az perched on my shoulder, doing their best not to gouge me with their little sharp-assed squirrel claws—which I sadly was in too much damned pain elsewhere to even feel, but bless their little squirrel heart for trying—and feeling around in the air for the edge to the seam.

"Here goes nothing," I said, hoping that this seam really did lead back to the MOME HQ in Phoenix and not to some other dimension where some other freaking monster was going to swallow me whole before I could even get my bearings

.

Did I seriously jinx myself? I wondered, blankly, as I reached the front door of the MOME compound, only to grind to a halt in horror, my arms and ribs aching with the burns they'd received earlier. Had I *actually* come through the door to another dimension? I wasn't sure what I was seeing, but it was something out of a nightmare inspired by Cthulhu and an oyster having terrible messy sex and then producing… whatever this was.

"What the ever-loving hells is that?!" I asked Az, who was now standing beside me in their winged human form.

"Hmmm?"

Az sounded distracted.

"Az, what *is* that?" I repeated.

"That, Luv, is someone you would do best to avoid if you're able." Their voice was calm, but they were twitching in a way that was anything but. I couldn't say I blamed them.

I'd basically sprinted here after pushing through the seam in the dungeon, burns or no burns—and thanks to Az kissing me rather thoroughly, as soon as we'd made it out of the dark suppressing stone of the dungeons, the burns were barely noticeable anymore. I'd shifted to snow leopard form right after that, in order to move faster through MOME's sterile, fluorescent-lit interior design nightmare, and then I'd shifted to human as we'd reached the heavy glass doors, apparently for the sole purpose of interrogating Az about the hellscape that lay before us. Technically I supposed it was just the one hell-creature, and not a whole hellscape, but… clam shell, tentacles, giant fanged maw, lots of writhing, and dripping… it painted quite the scene.

And whatever it was, it was using suckered, dripping tentacles to grab… everything around it. As I watched in a sort of fascinated horror, it shoved everything into its maw, from people, to gear, to the one remaining tank. It was even grabbing up pieces of flaming pavement and choking them down.

And…

"Oh…" I muttered.

Az turned their silver gaze in my direction.

"What?"

"I still don't know what it is— your explanation was no help at all, BTW—but I think I know why it's here," I said, watching as the thing grabbed an AR-15 out of the hands of a human and swallowed it whole, followed immediately by another chunk of flaming concrete that some of the MOME mages had launched in the creature's general direction after managing to sever and lift it using some form of telekinesis.

"I think someone brought it in to do cleanup," I clarified.

I winced as it grabbed one of the mages that had been manipulating the section of flaming concrete, swallowing him down too.

Az stared at the thing again, and shuddered.

"I'm not sure that's an improvement on the fire, really," they said. "Thanatos does ingest dark matter in any form, but he's… not the most agreeable demon on most days, and… he rather despises being summoned against his will."

And yeah, I could kinda see that. The thing was eating things and people as indiscriminately as the dragon fire. But then something caught my eye that made me realize that whoever had brought it here had probably intended to kill two birds with one stone. My spine straightened in terror, though, as I realized that they were likely to kill a whole lot more than two birds.

"Shit, Az, we have to stop them," I said, pushing the doors open and deciding that I was going to have to brave the monster, no matter how pants-shittingly scary it was.

Az started to object, but then they must have seen what I did, and they were sprinting alongside me.

Someone was trying to sneak up on the creature with a syringe—filled with something that looked an awful lot like Technetium.

UGH. THAT THING, Cthulhu-Oyster hybrid, whatever the fuck—Thanatos, I guess Az had said—was huge. And the closer I got to it (shooting past Az on my much larger wings), the larger it seemed. Not just from the perspective change, but like it had actually grown since I'd started watching it. Maybe it had? After all, if what Az said was true, the damned thing consumed dark matter, and maybe that was the kind of thing that made a creature gain mass quickly? I mean, why the fuck not? Everything else about it was horrifying, so why not add getting visibly larger every time it ate to the list?

Racing towards it, even shifted to my dragon form, made my stomach feel like a solid cold lump of terror. I hoped that, as a dragon, I was too big for the creepy thing to swallow, but I was not particularly reassured. At any rate, I wasn't aiming for the damned creature. I was aiming for the idiot with the Technetium.

Because injecting Technetium into something that was basically a dark matter repository seemed like a terrible idea. Or just a really good way to kill everyone and everything in this whole city… and possibly the entire universe, as previously discussed.

And damn it, I knew that had been Dryer's master plan, but I didn't think the rest of her minions were so stuck on it that they would still be working towards it even after her death. I mean come on, who is *that* committed to taking out the whole universe? I mean, I'd even flambéed the short asshat who had seemed to be in charge of this whole regiment, so who was going around ordering people to blow up the world *now*?

But all of that would have to get filed under "shit to worry about when you're not about to die," because right here and now I had to worry about preventing the end of the world. Again.

And dude with the syringe knew how to hustle. He wasn't wearing any of the useless radiation gear that might slow him down and—

Shit.

I wound up slamming into both him and the clam-Cthulhu love-child demon, because fuck if he didn't reach the tentacled menace before I did. And not *one* of the damned tentacles even *tried* to grab him. Which could not be said for me. I was half-wrapped in one, even as I reached forward with my scaled snout—ignoring all the pain radiating out from my sides and forelegs, where I'd been burned—and tried to nudge the syringe-carrying fool out of the way. But the dude was moving with the kind of determination reserved for sprinters and zealots, and I could do little more than nudge him to the side, as the tentacle of the monster clam tried to pull me into its maw. So I slapped the monster clam with my tail, reaching my neck forward again to crash into the Technetium wielder, but I was too late. I watched in horrified silence as the syringe plunged into a waving tentacle.

I didn't even think, I just shifted with every Gwendamned thing I had.

And I caught just the briefest glimpse of an orange sky with purple sun, before blackness took it all away.

I BLINKED MYSELF awake to a purple sun in the orange sky, almost exactly where it had been the last time I was here.

"Gwendamn, I really need to get some tests done," I muttered, to no one. Or maybe to the small, electric blue rabbit that was sitting on my chest. It, unlike Az in squirrel form, had plenty of fur. It looked downy soft, was almost small enough to fit in my palm, and had eyes the size of nickels. It was practically an anime character.

"Hello there," I said. Since, you know, this was a hell realm, and the shrieking squirrel that I knew as Azrael was also a talking angel back on earth, so, this guy could be anyone. There was no reason to be rude.

"Hello, human/dragon female," the bunny replied, blinking mildly.

I tried to sit up, without really thinking about it, because, even after everything I'd been through, a talking blue bunny was a bit startling. Only I couldn't, because the damned thing felt like it weighed at least a hundred pounds.

"Oh, pardon me," the bunny said, hopping down beside me and causing a tremor in the earth. "Still digesting," it added, as though that explained why it weighed about a hundred times what it should have.

"Do, uh… do you know how long I was unconscious just now?" I asked, wondering if it would be rude to ask the bunny how the hell it spoke English aloud, when translation magic didn't work down here.

"From the moment we arrived here, until just now? Only handful of minutes, by your reckoning," the bunny said.

"Spent time in England?" I asked, wondering why all the demons I was meeting sounded like they'd spent time in the UK.

"Yes! Devonshire. One of my favorite haunts when I've been visiting your world. Although there are many other places I've enjoyed. Earth is a lovely world all around, but Devonshire was where I learned to speak English. I've always loved the accent, though of course I try not to emulate it—very difficult for some folks to understand."

Sure. Why not? And then my brain let go of the fact that the bunny had a British accent, and was producing spoken English from vocal chords that shouldn't have been able to manage those sounds, and focused on the fact that it had said "from the moment we arrived." We arrived. *We.* I was pretty sure that I had only been touching one thing when I'd shifted us here. I swallowed, but tried not to let my newfound fear of the tiny blue bunny show on my face.

"Did, uh… did anyone else show up with us?" I asked, blinking and trying to look around.

"The unpleasant fellow who stabbed me with a syringe arrived here with us, but he took off running immediately after we landed. Thank you for shifting us here, by the way. I don't think I would have been able to reach the seam before the Technetium took effect, and I rather prefer not becoming disassociated atoms."

I swallowed again, but this time the emotion I was trying to contain wasn't fear exactly, it was the overwhelming sense that the universe was just going to keep fucking with me until I died.

"Do I even want to know how you know about that?"

The small bunny twitched its nose as though it might be offended, so I tried to look apologetic.

"I mean, I know shit about shit when it comes to the magical world, and I really don't know who you are, so forgive me if this is something you're a well-known expert on, but I was under the impression that it wasn't widespread knowledge that Technetium reacted poorly with dark matter, and that MOME was weaponizing it."

"Hmph… perhaps it wasn't widespread knowledge before that little power play Dryer pulled in Sucre last week. But you can bet your hat that everyone whose existence relies on dark matter is talking about it now. Perhaps my people are more sensitive to the news than others might be, but you can be sure we started the process of changing our names as soon as we heard."

Which just left me blinking at the bunny, as my brain tried to put all of that together.

"My dear, I'm a demon; I can be summoned by anyone who knows my true name, and, if they've drawn a powerful enough circle, I can be held and made to do as they wish. Surely you've heard of this?"

"You mean outside of paranormal romance books and horror movies?" I asked, not sure what the bunny expected me to say. It blinked at me in a way that was decidedly unbunnylike. Then again, he was also a giant dark-matter-eating clam/squid of doom that could talk, and that shouldn't have been on the list of bunny-approved activities either.

"It might be worth mentioning that, until a few weeks ago, I didn't really know that magic was a thing," I added, just in case.

"Ah, well, I suppose I will have to forgive your ignorance, then, but suffice it to say that even those of my kind who had never visited Earth began the arduous task of legally altering their names here in the realms. Unfortunately, the process takes days, even under normal conditions, and every demon in the realm applying at once is hardly normal conditions. My own paperwork hasn't gone through yet, and some clown at MOME must have had a file on me, because the next thing I know, I'm being summoned into the midst of a battle where some heathen has unleashed dragon fire into the ranks and—"

I tried to cover up my rising embarrassment by interrupting.

"Do you have a way of purging the Technetium from your system?" I asked. "This canyon isn't the best place to hang out long term."

The bunny eyed me again as if I were slow, but then seemed to relent.

"I do not need to purge it. It will leave my system in due time, just as any other substance would. My body clears such things the way that your own clears alcohol, or any other toxin that doesn't kill you first."

"Oh?" I asked.

The blue bunny nodded.

"I don't mean to be indelicate, but the substance will pass through me with the rest of my food. I must say, I'm glad I was able to feast so nicely just before you brought me here, as it will, ah…. it will help move things along, if you take my meaning."

Right. Cool. The bunny-demon was going to poop out some Technetium in…however long it took bunny demons to digest such things.

Well, fine, that was actually awesome, because, yeah. I didn't want the bunny demon to die, just because of my hasty fire breathing in MOME's general direction.

"Look, it has been very educational meeting you, and thanks for not killing me earlier, but I need to head back to that damned battle."

I stood as I spoke, and the bunny nodded again.

"Thank you for your assistance, Miss…"

"Vic. You can call me Vic," I said.

"Indeed, Vic. It was a pleasure. Thank you for saving my life. I hope to see you again in better circumstances."

I laughed, and the bunny looked taken aback.

"Sorry. It's just that my life seems to be one disaster after another, lately. I would love to see *anyone* again in better circumstances."

"Ah, yes. Well, best of luck, and do keep an eye out for the one who summoned me."

"Who summoned you?" I asked, even as I felt around for the seam in front of me.

"If I knew the chap's name, I dare say I wouldn't have let him order me about. He'd never have had a chance to…" The bunny seemed to realize he was mumbling, but quickly refocused. "Tall gentleman, older, white beard, white hair, long nose."

"Shit," I breathed, just as I stepped through the seam and back into the dungeons at MOME.

As I RAN up the dank stone stairs, pulling in lungful after lungful of stale air laced with moss, old urine, and traces of even worse refuse, I desperately hoped that Albert hadn't betrayed us. After all, summoning a demon to clean up a mess of dragon fire wasn't necessarily an evil act. Thanatos had seemed all too happy to eat up a bunch of dark matter, and it had only seemed mildly ruffled at having to be emergency shifted to the demon realm to poop out some Technetium. So it wasn't unthinkable that Albert had summoned it, and then some MOME assholes had done their usual trick of ruining everything by trying to blow people up. That was just MOME being MOME, really.

But Blue Bunny had seemed pretty convinced that whoever had summoned him was someone to keep an eye on. That didn't bode well. Of course, it would be easy enough to mistake the jerk who summoned you from the hell realms as someone who worked for the corrupt government that was trying to kill everyone. Alternatively, it could be that there was another tall, white-bearded, white-haired mage summoning demons at this battle. I really hoped it was the latter. Because if Albert had somehow turned on us...

I didn't want to think about that one, and I didn't have time to, as I finally noticed that I'd already burst into the hideous, fluorescent-lit hallways of MOME's upper levels and was quickly sprinting towards the exit, somehow ignoring the burning aches that still permeated my arms and sides. I reached the glass doors that showed me the parking lot, and ground to a halt once more. I wasn't sure what I'd been expecting. As far as I knew, I'd only left a handful of allies behind to battle the remains of MOME's forces, but maybe something in me had somehow expected Renata, Torrence, Rhelia, and Az to miraculously overcome that whole force with just the four of them. Or maybe I'd just expected the reinforcements to arrive, and for the dragons to be kicking the ever-loving crap out of everyone else.

And maybe something like that had happened. There were more of my allies outside than I'd expected to find. A lot more, actually. I barely had time to register them all, but they ranged from the usual suspects—Seamus, Sol, Trev, Rhelia, Renata, Torrence, and Az—to folks I had never really expected to see again like Mr. Topaz and Ms. Rebuke from Flagstaff High, a surprisingly large portion of the Unterberg council, Sylvestra and Cronk, Seamus' Moms, Sol's Abuelita—accompanied by a half dozen giant panthers, and last but not least, my Mom and Dad.

Yet the tableau before me was anything but hopeful. For one thing, the sky above it wasn't full of raging dragons, and it really should have been by now, since we'd clearly gotten everyone out of the MOME building. Where the fuck was General Aira? For another thing, just outside the building, on the too-hot pavement baking in the September sun, surrounded by an absolutely still ring of mages, mind control victims, and the surreal roll call of all the people I had met in the past few weeks, stood Albert, with one arm wrapped rigidly around Trevor. All eyes were focused on the two of them, and filled with varying degrees of terror.

Their posture could easily have been mistaken for a casual one-armed hug, if it hadn't been for how limp Trev's form was, and how Albert's normally easygoing face was transformed by a severely locked jaw, and a wild gaze that looked anything but sane.

It was an expression I'd seen before somewhere, but I didn't have time to try to place it, because Albert was in the process of raising a syringe in his free hand, all while shouting something I couldn't hear through the quadruple-paned glass doors.

Until suddenly I could hear it—though I didn't have time to make out what it was—because I'd shifted myself outside, right in front of them, so close that my momentum carried me between them, almost knocking Trev out of Albert's grip, even as I felt the prick of a needle at the base of my neck.

I didn't wait for the tingling sensation that accompanies a liquid being injected into the bloodstream before I pulled on the seam that was becoming as familiar to me as the curtains in my old bedroom. And I didn't wait until I'd pulled that seam open by hand, either. I just pictured the one place that I knew could save me, made sure I had a firm hold on Trev, and shifted.

~~~

"Fuck. This is getting old," I muttered, as my legs decided they couldn't hold me up anymore. *At least I'm not fainting,* I thought, as I sank to my knees. I was tempted to go all the way down; to let my head rest against the rocks and take in the orange sky with its purple sun, inhale a few lungfuls of disgusting sulphur-tinged air and relax for a minute, but a small part of my brain reminded me that now wasn't the time. I was going to have to enjoy the view and wonder why I kept ending up here some other time.

Trev had collapsed right along with me, not stopping at his knees as I had. Probably because he'd been unconscious before I'd even arrived on the scene. He was breathing normally, so I wasn't too concerned, for the moment.

Which is why I felt I had time to turn and look at the bastard I'd started to consider a friend, or at least an eccentric and somewhat flakey ally, and who was now shouting obscenities at me as though I'd killed one of his beloved pet iguanas and was wearing its skin as a hat.

"RUINED EVERYTHING. AGAIN!! WHY WON'T YOU JUST DIE, AS YOU'RE SUPPOSED TO!? THANATOS SHOULD HAVE DEVOURED YOU, ALONG WITH EVERYTHING ELSE! THE SEAM SHOULD BE RIPPED OPEN BY NOW! I SHOULD BE KNEE DEEP IN BODIES, WITH THE INVASION IN FULL SWING!!! HOW DO YOU KEEP SURVIVING?!?"

With all the yelling getting shriller by the second, until it seemed that Albert might start to levitate by dint of sound waves alone, I probably shouldn't have been surprised when he launched himself at me, while I was still on my knees, crushing me into the dirt right next to where Trev had gone down. I probably should have been even less surprised that he started to try to strangle me and repeatedly bash my head into the ground. I say try because, well, regardless of what had possessed Albert to start acting like an angry teenager who'd never really learned how to fight, I was a teenager who *had* learned how to fight and, exhausted or not, I was not about to let someone mush my head into the dirt.

So I rolled out from Albert's trembling grasp and pinned him beneath me, slapping him, because part of me was really struggling with the whole
~~~

"your mentor-type-person has betrayed you and lost their mind, maybe you should consider knocking them out" thing, and I thought maybe a few reminders of why he couldn't take me in hand to hand combat (which was his only option, since we were in everyone's favorite dark-matter-suppressing hell canyon) were in order.

"How do you do it?" Albert asked, after I'd slapped him a second time, then stood up to place myself between him and Trev. I didn't think there was much he could do to Trev in this place, but I also hadn't thought he would try to inject Trev with Technetium and wind up injecting me with it instead, so what the fuck did I know?

"How do I do what, Albert?"

"How do you survive? How do you keep refusing to die, no matter how many times you should be killed? How do you *always* manage to stop me from turning this abomination into the weapon he was meant to be?"

He gestured towards Trev as he said it, and a chill went down my spine as I watched him get up from the red dirt of the canyon floor. There was something *off* about the way he did it. It was clumsy, like he was drunk, or like everything about his body wasn't quite where he'd expected it to be.

I was distracted from assessing the movement, though, as a different movement caught my eye in the shadows behind Albert, a brief flash of blue—so quick I wasn't sure if I'd imagined it—in between the puddles of darkness.

I locked my eyes back onto Albert, now warier than ever.

"What do you mean, Albert? As far as I'm aware, this is the first time you've tried to blow Trev up. And I'm a little shocked that you decided to do it in person, since that would have killed *you*, along with everyone else in the greater Phoenix area, not to mention, you know, maybe the universe."

"Ha! You ridiculous human! Don't you know anything? Do you really think your precious *Albert* would try to harm you monsters? The bitch would adopt every magical misfit in the world given half a chance. 'Albert' isn't here, and can't stop me!"

Then whatever it was, which sure as fuck looked like Albert, but apparently wasn't, launched itself at me and resumed trying to strangle me, and for just a moment I was so startled that I let it.

"Did you really think a bullet would stop me, you pathetic, backwater mistake? I am the daughter of two of the most powerful mages to ever grace MOME's training grounds. I am the backbone of a centuries old organization meant to protect magical people from the idiocy of humans and the taint of mixed-breeds like you. I am more powerful than you can even imagine, and I. Will. End. You."

That last sentence was punctuated with the fervent shaking of my neck, which got old real fast, shock or no shock.

I brought my hands down in a move I'd practiced thousands of times over the years, forcing Albert's arms down and breaking the stranglehold. Then I headbutted him, with a silent apology to the real Albert as I heard the nose break.

"Damn it, Rebecca," I wheezed, as Albert's body stumbled back. "Don't hold back. Tell me how you really feel."

Rebecca Dryer, or whatever form of her was here looking like Albert, didn't reply, perhaps *finally* having learned the value of not monologuing in the middle of a fight. Instead she used Albert's body to charge me again.

And, look, Rebecca Dryer might have been a powerful mage—I wasn't sure how those things were measured, and I'd never had to fight her with magic, since she'd always sent other people to do her dirty work for her—but she sure as shit wasn't any good in a fight *without* her magic, and especially not in a borrowed body. I still had zero clue how she'd done it, and whatever it was, the fact that it still worked even with dark matter suppressed was terrifying. But she'd clearly managed to take over Albert's body sometime after he'd shot her. And yeah, three weeks ago that would have been mind-bogglingly creepy, but now it was basically just Thursday.

I had no trouble sweeping Albert's legs out from under him when Rebecca forced his body to charge me, but that left me in a predicament. I knew a ton of ways to put Albert down permanently, but I didn't want *Albert* to die—assuming that Rebecca forcing her spirit into his body hadn't killed him already, that is. I didn't really know how this worked, but I was pretty sure that fucking Albert up physically wasn't going to do much to Rebecca's spirit in any permanent sense. It would probably seriously mess up Albert, though. Which meant that Rebecca would be more than happy for me to fight him.

"Fuck," I muttered, hesitating to follow up my leg sweep with anything more damaging, while Rebecca got Albert's body to its feet and then grinned with a creeptastically manic facial expression.

"You've realized you don't want to hurt your precious mentor, haven't you?" she asked, sneering at me. "Well, you're about to lea—"

I never got to hear what I was about to learn, because Albert's body collapsed then, limp and lifeless, to the ground.

A large belch sounded from behind Albert, as a small blue fur ball hopped over his prone form.

"Thanatos?" I asked, unsure if I should be glad to see the tiny (in this realm) demon.

"I did not like that woman," Thanatos said in an aggrieved tone, "but she was very tasty."

"Uh… how did you… uhmmm, I mean, don't you usually eat dark matter?"

"Me? Oh certainly. I'd rather feast on the stuff. But there's no dark matter here in the canyon, you know."

"Ummm… yeah. I know that. The rock suppresses it."

"Indeed! Well, I was growing rather peckish, and this form isn't an ideal one for scaling cliffs to seek out food."

"Right… but what did you eat just now?" I wasn't 100% sure I wanted to know the answer, but I figured it might be important.

"Why, that mage's shadow, of course."

"Of course," I said. Because, yeah sure. Why not? But what did that even mean?

I must have said some part of that last bit aloud, because Thanatos answered me.

"Surely you've been here enough times to know that shadows in this realm are the souls of those who cast them?"

"They are?"

"Of course. Why else would yours be part dragon, part snow leopard, and part… that other thing?"

I turned my head slightly, trying to actually focus on my shadow, and then promptly looked away. It was kind of nauseating to see that many different creatures trying to take up the same space. Then, out of morbid curiosity, I glanced at Thanatos' shadow, and looked away even faster. The clam-Cthulhu hybrid was not a fun thing to see, even as a two dimensional shape, and it looked especially strange melded with something like a winged human.

"Ok," I sighed, deciding that I shouldn't even try looking at Trev's shadow, all things considered. "So does that mean you ate Albert's soul, as well?"

Thanatos shrugged his tiny blue bunny shoulders. A strange motion on a rabbit, but whatever. He wasn't really a rabbit, when it came down to it.

"I only tasted one…flavor, if you will. So I don't think he was in there. Not that that helps, mind you. If he's not in there, then you may not have any luck returning him to his body before it dies completely."

"I… what?"

"I would recommend getting that body back to earth as quickly as you can. If your friend is still able to reclaim the body, you have very little time for him to do it. It may already be too late."

WHICH IS WHY, a few seconds later, I was slapping Trev awake (or trying to) in the middle of MOME's dank Phoenix dungeons, trying to ignore how many times I kept repeating the same damned loop in favor of focusing on more pressing issues.

Unlike a dark-matter-suppressed Gwen, Albert was a full-grown man, and didn't seem to be any lighter thanks to the dungeon's special properties. I was gonna need help carrying him.

"Gwendamnit," I cried, slapping Trev again, and really starting to worry.

"Now what?" Gwen asked, causing me to almost drop Trev in surprise.

"Damn it, Gwen, you shouldn't be down here, it can hurt you!"

She shrugged, then glared at me.

"I'm a goddess," she said, tossing her ridiculous red curls at me.

"This place almost killed you last time," I said, and something about my tone, or maybe the panic in my eyes, must have gotten her attention, because she put a hand on my shoulder.

"We're almost clear of the dark matter suppressing rocks here, Vic. It takes more than this place to cut me off from my power. It hurts, but it won't do anything terrible unless I stay here for a while. I assume we're not planning on staying?" she said, nodding at my two unconscious companions.

"We need to get Albert back to wherever Dryer left his soul," I said, as if she should just know what that meant.

Gwen looked at Albert, then back at me.

"I don't think that's how this works, Vic," she said, and the gentleness in her voice made my blood run cold in my veins.

"Gwen, you have to do something. We can't just let him die. Dryer possessed him and then a demon ate her soul and…" my voice trailed off, but Gwen's eyes just looked sad.

"Fine," I said, not having patience for whatever she believed was going on here. "Just get the three of us out of this damned dark matter suppressing dungeon and *I'll* fix it."

"Vic, I don't think—"

"Just GET US OUT OF HERE!"

Gwen didn't reply. She just grabbed my arm and Albert's (I was already holding Trev's), and shifted us.

~~~

The next moment we were in one of the horribly lit linoleum hallways of upper MOME. They were, as they had been the last few times I'd traversed them, abandoned. I looked at Gwen, and she looked at Albert and then at Trev.

"Want me to take your brother to his dragon mate?" she asked.

I nodded, not sure I could speak without screaming or crying. Trev was still unconscious, but he was breathing normally, and I didn't think there was much I could do for him aside from getting Gwen take him somewhere else. Rhelia could heal him if he needed it, and would protect him, or ask Gwen to, if necessary.

"Souls don't just come back to bodies, Vic."

"What if I take him to Life and—"

"Life can't fix anything without a soul in residence, and that's Albert's only problem right now. Otherwise he's uninjured."

She was gone as soon as the words left her mouth, Trev in tow.

I stared at Albert's inert form for a moment, hoping beyond hope that Gwen was just wrong. That being possessed meant that Albert's soul was just kicking it nearby somewhere, and would return to him soon. But the seconds ticked by, and his body just got paler and paler and…

Suddenly I was on my knees next to Albert's body, with my forehead pressed to his.

"How do I fix this, Albert? How do I help you? Where is your soul!?"

Of course he didn't answer me.
~~~

But something did.

A memory. My memory. I closed my eyes, trying to relax and let my brain get the message through. Three versions of me sitting around a room that didn't exist in anything but my imagination. Or else, didn't exist outside of my dark matter. Albert wasn't in his body anymore, but that didn't mean he was gone completely. He could just be stuck. I had been stuck once.

And before I could consider what a terrible idea this probably was, before I could remind myself that only luck and my connection to Trev had saved me the last time, before my brain could explain that what I was about to do should be impossible anyway, I was holding onto Albert's shoulders for dear life and reaching into time and space, not following my own dark matter, but reaching for Albert's instead.

~~~

"How interesting," said a voice that filled me with an enormous sense of relief. "By all accounts, this should not be possible."

I looked up into the friendly grey-blue gaze of Albert Bumblebee.

"Yeah, Gwen tried to tell me I couldn't save you. Still not sure this is going to work," I replied.

Albert simply stared at me for a moment.

"But your body is dying, so we should probably get a move on," I added.

"This space is generally devoid of time," Albert replied, still blinking slowly at my sudden arrival.

The room we were in looked an awful lot like Albert's office at school, with a few major differences. It had windows that looked out onto a decidedly English-looking countryside, and there were no iguanas draped over the backs of the red velvet wingback chairs here. I kinda missed them. To my amazement, as soon as I longed for the sight of one, a six-foot-long iguana appeared, already draped languidly across the back of a wingback.

Albert blinked at it for a moment, before turning to me again.

I figured it was best if I didn't ask, so I just replied to Albert's last statement about time.

"That's been my experience with my personal dimensional pocket too, but you came here without your body as an anchor this time, so I'm not sure that's true anymore. I mean, you were a lifeless corpse when I left you. Luckily, you've been that way for less than two minutes, but we are starting to push the boundaries of 'how long a body can survive while technically
~~~

dead,' and I really don't want to get back from here and find out we're too late."

Albert smiled.

"But, my dear girl, you've brought the tether with you already. I can feel that I'm once more connected to myself."

"Seriously? It was that easy?" I looked around bewildered.

"I would not call it easy," Albert said, arching a white eyebrow in my direction. "I've never heard of anyone accomplishing such a task before. Besides, we've yet to make it out of here. I can feel that the tether to my body is restored, but I've no idea what to do with it. I'm not supposed to be in this place."

"So you've never been here before?" I asked.

"No. I've placed other things here, but I cannot venture here myself without becoming trapped. I rather thought this was simply what death was. Rebecca pushed me out of my body rather forcefully, when I wasn't expecting it. I was certain this was to be my afterlife."

"Ok. Weird. If our afterlife is getting trapped in our own pocket dimension, I really don't want to die."

Albert shrugged.

"There were plenty of good books," he said.

I looked around at his shelves and considered it.

"Only ones you'd read before, though, right?"

Albert looked at his shelves for a moment.

"Fair point. Let's get out of here, shall we?"

I nodded, reaching out a hand to Albert. If he didn't know how to get out of here, I was probably going to have to help. I suppose it made sense, as Albert didn't have any experience shifting into animal form by reaching for a body that was familiar to him.

Reminding myself that I had gotten stuck before because I'd been in a dimensional pocket with all of my own forms, I figured the easiest way out of here was probably going to be shifting to one of those. I closed my eyes, even though that was arguably unnecessary, and thought of being coated in thick fur, having a hefty tail to check my balance, and padding along on four padded feet that could run over snow and rocks.

I returned to the awful fluorescence that was the MOME hallway I'd just left, and blinked.

Then I jumped back and hissed when I was confronted with a six-foot-long iguana.

And no Albert.

"Umm…" I had apparently shifted back to human for the sole purpose of speaking. Because, holy shit, what had I done?

The iguana looked at me and blinked a few times, seemingly undisturbed and unsurprised by my presence, both as cat and human.

"Albert?" I asked, wondering if I was hallucinating, or somehow still stuck in a pocket dimension. Or maybe just a very odd hell realm.

The iguana opened its mouth, as though to speak, but it merely wheezed and hissed a bit before snapping its mouth shut again.

A moment later, Albert stood before me where the iguana had been.

"Well, that was educational," he said, before his legs gave out and he slid to the floor.

<p style="text-align:center">~~~</p>

"Albert!" I shouted racing to his side. "Are you ok?"

Albert blinked a few more times, his gaze distant and unfocused, and his tongue darted out for a moment before sliding back into his mouth.

"I am alive, and I am not permanently an iguana," he answered.

"True statements," I replied, waiting for actual confirmation that he was ok.

"I believe that means I am ok. However, when this day is over, I have…a few questions for you, Vic. Everything that has happened in the past few minutes should not be possible."

"Ha! Welcome to my life," I said, giving Albert a hug, which he dazedly returned before getting back to his feet with a little help from my shoulders.

"Indeed," he said. "Let's go finish this, shall we?"

As soon as Albert was steady on his feet I shifted to dragon form, clutched Albert in one set of talons, and then shifted my dragon ass out to the front of the building, because running through those damned fluorescent hallways again could fucking die in a fire.

If I ever got ahold of the jackass who was supposed to be in charge of this story, I was going to slap them. Honestly, if I were a person reading my life right now, I would be losing my shit. How many times can one person run out the same set of doors into mortal peril, only to have to go right back to the same fucking hell dimension to avoid destroying the world, in one day? It was too much.

And whoever was writing this damned story must have thought so too, because when I broke through the doors this time, no one was trying to tear the universe into tiny pieces with an ill-advised magical bomb.

Nope.

They were just trying to kill all of my friends and family with regular old gunfire and spell-slinging.

It looked like things hadn't gone all that well after I'd left with Dryer/Albert and Trevor. MOME was still clearly trying to kill everybody I cared about, just not with any world-ending weapons. I took a moment to wonder who was leading this whole thing, with Dryer deposed, but I honestly wasn't sure that it mattered. In all likelihood, she had more than one lackey, or even a few other MOME higher-ups, who were probably all too happy to see all non-magical humans subjugated, magical entities becoming top dogs, and MOME themselves running the whole thing. Honestly, based on what I'd heard Albert and Sol say about the biases of the magic-wielding world in general, it probably hadn't even been that hard for Dryer to get people to see her "side" of things. In fact, now I was wondering if she'd actually faced more than token opposition.

So it probably shouldn't have been a surprise to find that the asshats I'd left behind when I'd tackled their leader into another dimension were still hard at it, trying to kill the rest of us. After all, a bunch of us had shown up to make it clear that we weren't in favor of the whole "subjugate all humans" piece. And, now, with all of the reinforcements that the Unterberg delegation seemed to have brought along, we had almost half as many fighters as MOME did, even without our suspiciously absent dragon reinforcements.

We'd clearly thrown a wrench in whatever attack plan MOME had for today. An invasion of some kind, if Rebecca Dryer's raving ghost was to be believed. So, yeah, they were probably more than a little pissed off at us.

And that was fine, really. I mean, what the hell? This was something we were all more or less equipped for, unlike ripping holes in the universe. I put Albert on the ground. He nodded and ran off to do whatever badass mages do in a fight, and I launched myself skyward. As I rose into the cerulean Phoenix sky, I took stock of the battle below.

The reinforcements from Unterberg were spread out, not far from where they'd been when I'd grabbed Trev and Albert/Dryer from certain doom, and many of them were flinging spells at MOME's leather-clad mages. They were doing a fair bit of damage, though their own shields were also taking plenty of hits. In addition, the Unterbergers seemed to have a number of shifters, ogres, trolls, and other large hand-to-hand combatants, whose forms and names I was unfamiliar with, and they were giving the MOME mages one hell of a time, as they did their best to defend against a simultaneous magical and physical. Seems like MOME hadn't brought as many shifters to this battle, and they'd lost the advantage as a consequence.

As I rose higher, I caught sight of a huddle in my peripheral vision that included Seamus' Moms and my parents, along with a recently arrived Albert, all of whom seemed to be involved in a hurried discussion. I had to assume that it was a strategy meeting, but soon I lost sight of them in the fray and decided that I was needed elsewhere, anyway.

Rhelia, in her glorious dragon form, was tearing into a troop of mages with her talons and teeth, looking as furious as I'd ever seen her. And, as I dove down to join the fray, I saw Sol streak past in her panther form, knocking the guns from the hands of the few remaining mind control victims who were still running on instructions to kill us, deftly dodging bullets as she went. Rhelia must have spread the word about not killing the front line grunts.

Seamus, much to my surprise, was tearing around in wolf form, dragging something long and wet from his mouth and sneaking up behind troops to hit them with it. I had no idea what that was about, and I didn't have time to figure it out before I reached the fight and started tearing into a line of mages at Rhelia's side.

I gave Rhelia plenty of space, assuming that her attack radius would need to include her tail, and trying to account for how much larger she was than me. Of course, I hadn't really accounted for how she would react to me coming back without Trev. Thankfully, she didn't actually tear into me, the way her shrieking dive in my direction made me fear. Instead, she stopped short and turned on the mages to my side.

Where issss he? He issss not ressssponding to my call.

I batted a few MOME mages aside with my tail as I replied, *He's safe, but I can't get ahold of him either.*

To be honest, I hadn't even thought of communicating with him mentally until Rhelia had started diving at me, and it had occurred to me that she might want an answer about where Trev was. But he hadn't replied to my very urgent suggestions that now would be a great time to wake up, you know, *before* his girlfriend/soulmate/partner eviscerated me. So, I wasn't lying when I told Rhelia that he wasn't replying to me either.

Rhelia turned aside briefly to literally bite a MOME mage in half, and I was grateful that I was in my dragon form, because dragon-me wasn't nearly as squeamish as human-me, and I was pretty sure human-me would have tossed her cookies at that.

Wassss he harmed? Her mental voice was surprisingly calm now, despite how anxious she'd seemed just a moment ago.

Not after we got to hell, I replied, casually swatting a few more MOME mages away with my foreleg before they could launch their spells at me. Damn, it was handy to be able to see magic. It was even more handy to know that the majority of it was just going to bounce off of my scales. *I have no idea what Dryer did to him before I grabbed him, though. I didn't get there until just before she tried to inject him.*

I thought sssshe had merely put a ssssleep sssspell on him, but that sssshould have worn off with her demisssse.

She turned and roared in the faces of a group of about six mages who were trying to sneak up on her, and I swear more than half of them soiled themselves as they retreated. I tried not to take too many deep breaths, as I didn't really want to confirm that one.

Where is he? Rhelia asked again, after the mages had retreated.

I gave him to Gwen. I didn't know what else to do with him. I couldn't leave him unconscious and alone in the hell realms, I replied, trying to keep the annoyance out of my voice.

It hadn't really occurred to me to leave him behind. I didn't consider Thanatos, who could apparently eat people's souls even in his blue bunny form, to be a safe person to leave my unconscious twin with, and there hadn't been time to do anything else.

My thoughts must have leaked to Rhelia anyway.

I am sure Gwen will keep him safe.

I couldn't help but notice that Rhelia's accent was slipping again, and I wondered if it slipped when she was annoyed, or just when shit got serious enough that she didn't want to waste time on the extra sibilance.

We were both momentarily distracted by a barrage of spells that included a few of the nastier, dragon-scale-breaching variety, so we dodged in silence for a moment, before resuming our own attacks and our conversation.

A small part of me just wanted to end all of this nonsense with dragon fire, then bring Thanatos in to do the cleanup and call it good, but something told me that if it were as easy as I thought it was, someone else already would have suggested it.

I'm not sure where Gwen took him, but it's got to be safer than here, right? I said, after charging, bull-style, straight into about a dozen mages and sending them flying. I saw a few of their shields wink out on impact, and I wondered if that meant they would stay down. Human-me was worried I'd killed them. Dragon-me, honestly, wasn't. I brushed aside the worry that there seemed to be a distinction between the two mes as something that I could figure out later.

I can try calling Gwen and ask her to bring him to you, I added, since I could tell Rhelia was still a bit tense, and I didn't want her to think that I didn't understand just how worried she was about Trev.

Rhelia snorted a few tendrils of smoke.

I trust her to care for him. I am merely upset that he is missing this fight. I believe he will be upset not to have participated.

I laughed, accidentally incinerating the mage who'd been charging at me with an actual, honest-to-Gwen, flaming sword.

Luckily, it was only a short burst of flame, and somehow managed not to light anything else on fire. Weirdly, the sword continued to burn, even after the charred top half of the mage disintegrated and the legs toppled awkwardly after it.

Good shot; that sword would have pierced even the thickest dragon hide. Rhelia's praise was casual, albeit sincere, as if I'd done that on purpose. As if I'd somehow known that the sword was deadly to dragons, and not like I'd accidentally just laughed and killed a man. The human part of me felt a bit queasy, but the human part of me was decidedly not in charge right now, so maybe I *had* known. Maybe that hadn't been as much of an accident as I'd thought.

And then I didn't care whether it was an accident or not, because something had just shanked me in the shin. Or rather, I discovered as I looked down, someone had just bitten one of my forelegs. The "someone" was a vampire, that was clear enough, and apparently vampire teeth were another thing (besides flaming swords) that could pierce through dragon hide. Not that it felt like it was doing much damage, since vampires are quite a bit smaller than dragons, even a baby dragon like me.

I reared up on my back legs and shook my foreleg fiercely. The vamp did not let go.

I turned and battered him against the side of one of the concrete parking barriers nearby.

He still didn't let go.

I slammed my foreleg into the ground.

He was still there.

The whole thing was starting to piss me off. It barely hurt, but having a vampire stuck to my leg was not going to help this fight, and besides, I'd felled a vamp in my human form before with a solid knee to the nuts. What the hell was letting this vampire cling to me like the world's angriest Corgi in beast mode?

I didn't know how he was doing it, but I'd just decided I was going to show him who was running this show, when I felt a few more sharp pains along my back legs and sides.

The fuck?

I craned my long neck around to stare down at a good dozen vampires sticking to me, even as I began dancing around trying to shake them off. Those damned diamond skulls must give them the jaw strength of snapping turtles. They. Weren't. Coming. OFF!

I had just taken in a breath to douse the one on my arm in dragon fire, when I remembered the burns on my sides and arms from the damned tank I'd lit on fire. They were still sore, despite my Az-boost and sped up healing. So I shot a bunch of smoke out of my nostrils, instead of the burst of fire I'd been considering releasing.

Fine. If these assholes wanted to leech onto me, they could just try to stick around while I—

My legs collapsed beneath me like jello.

What. The. Fuck?

My eyelids started to droop, my head dipping slowly towards my chest, leaving my neck closer to the ground, though none of the vamps let go of their holds to take advantage of it.

Help, I sent out to Rhelia, or whoever was close by that could hear mental communication. For once, I was *trying* to broadcast.

Rhelia must have been busy.

No one replied.

My eyelids drooped a little bit more. My head sank lower to the ground.

Then my vision began to tunnel, and all the sounds of battle dropped away.

Then silver feathers, and the faint sounds of someone screaming.

Huh. Sounded painful.

I'm not sure how I'd managed to forget how efficient Azrael was when it came to killing vampires. I mean, they had taken out Edik in about ten seconds. And ok, yeah, that hadn't stuck, but they'd also managed to incapacitate a room full of vamps in about 90 seconds.

Whatever. A lot had happened since Az had said they loathed vampires, and I'd kinda forgotten it in the insanity of everything that had happened afterwards, but I wasn't likely to ever forget it again.

My eyes popped open after the first few vampires released me, and I got to watch, in stunned awe, as Azrael took out the remaining vampires. Az was stunning to look at normally, no matter which of their forms they took (as long as it wasn't red naked squirrel form), but now, as they swooped from vamp to vamp, draining the vamps' energy so that each one collapsed to the ground looking like nothing more than an attractive corpse, they were positively glowing. No, literally. Az was exuding light like an exuberantly decorated Christmas tree. Or maybe a lightning bug hopped up on coke, since they were zigging and zagging faster than my eye could track, and vibrating with…something. Souls? Life force?

That was the only thing I could come up with, because I knew Az fed off of people's souls, and the vamps that were now falling like moths that had gotten too close to a flame seemed…drained, empty, colorless.

Of course, that was probably how any animated corpse that had lost its animation looked, but still.

Az was exuding power like a flying torch.

Something about the vamps releasing me had returned enough energy to me to let me open my eyes and turn my head, but it wasn't until all the vamps had dropped, and Az swooped past me to plant a steaming kiss on my scaled snout, that I felt strong enough to stand up.

That kiss felt like a living flame. I wasn't just restored. I was on fire, and I realized that a dozen vamps worth of energy must have been quite the power hit, because Az had glow to spare and they were more than happy to share it with me.

I felt the energy spread through my body like a wildfire, and I flapped my wings in exultation, looking around the field of battle for a new target.

But then an orange streak in the sky caught my eye, and I looked up just in time to see Trev, in Phoenix form, dive-bomb another group of MOME mages who had been about to take aim at Rhelia.

Well, damn. I had no idea what had finally woken Trev up, but he seemed to be fine. I felt something untwist inside me, and realized that I'd been more worried about Trev than I'd let myself admit, even once he was safely under Gwen's protection.

Az had already flown away and returned to the fight before I could even utter a thank you.

Time to get back into the fight.

I didn't see any more conscious vampires anywhere, so dragon-me's intense desire for vengeance was just going to have to wait for a bit. Meanwhile, Az's brightly glowing form was flitting all over the place wreaking havoc wherever they went.

Rhelia was tearing into the mages with abandon, with Trev's assistance, and I was about to join her.

Meanwhile, every now and again I saw what looked like wisps of smoke appear around a person carrying a gun, and then that person seemed to disappear. Which explained why I hadn't seen Renata lately, and why there were very few mind control victims left.

We were still outnumbered almost two to one, despite having wiped out a good portion of MOME's mage forces in the past few minutes, and even with two dragons on our side, that still seemed like a lot.

I could only assume that the main reason they hadn't attacked en masse again was because we'd killed the majority of the leadership. Which raised the question of why they were attacking at all.

And also made me wonder why we still *only* had two dragons.

General Aira has refused to issue reinforcements. Rhelia's mental voice sounded pissed, and I couldn't honestly blame her. *She is keeping herself and our army hidden in a pocket dimension until ready to be deployed.*

Did she give a reason for that? I asked.

She claimed to be holding our forces in strategic reserve. Rhelia's mental communication managed to convey all her disdain for that plan, without any additional words.

Do you think she's betrayed us, somehow? I asked, not sure how she could have, or if she would have, but feeling like that was just the way today was going.

Rhelia sent the mental equivalent of a shrug.

Right. Ok. Super reassuring.

But then I didn't have time to think about all the shitty potential consequences of betrayal by the commander of our own reinforcements, because I was busy batting away another handful of mages who had decided to consolidate their power and send something truly nasty my way. Except, I sent those mages flying before the spell finished forming, causing their half-formed spell to ricochet off the spell of a second set of nearby mages and scatter everyone in a three-meter radius. The first spell had still been just an amorphous blob, and it latched onto one of the mages and sent him screaming, thrashing, and running away from the group. The other spell showed a striking resemblance to Thanatos in his Cthulhu/clam form, and it started devouring the nearby mages indiscriminately. It looked like I had knocked both groups out of their containment circles, which was great for distracting the mages and perhaps getting them eaten by demons, but I kinda doubted that whatever demons had been summoned were going to just call it a day after they'd devoured the mages who'd summoned them. Especially when the thing that looked like Thanatos expanded to its full size, which, yeah…either there was more than one clam/Cthulhu-dark-matter-consuming-demon in the world, or that *was* Thanatos.

Although, since he hadn't exploded and taken us all down with him, I was willing to consider that it was maybe just Thanatos' cousin or something.

Then the thing turned its crazy, protruding eyes at me, and waved a tentacle in my general direction.

Huh, maybe it was Thanatos after all. Or maybe…

Maybe that was just a distraction to keep me from launching myself at yet another MOME recruit, who was busy stabbing the amorphous blob with a syringe on the far side of the parking lot. Far out of my reach.

Pushing the plunger in before I could so much as take one step forward.

MUCH TO MY surprise, I wasn't dead. A quick look around the area proved that most everyone I loved also was not dead. I still didn't understand why the few MOME lackeys I'd run into who had tried to inject people I love with Technetium seemed to think there was even the slightest chance that a hazmat suit might protect them.

Because what I'd just witnessed was horrifying, and had definitely killed the guy who injected the blob with Technetium—who had *not* been wearing a hazmat suit, not that I thought it would have helped—but at least it wasn't the insane, world-ending event that I had expected.

The blob had exploded in spectacular fashion. It was more a light show than an explosion really, like someone had put a billion microscopic Christmas lights into a piñata and then shot it with a Death Star. It absolutely incinerated the MOME guy with the syringe, as well as everyone else in a radius of about ten meters of the demon who'd been injected. Which, as far as I could tell, had consisted solely of more MOME agents.

It was difficult to tell, if only because I was still blinking away the blinding points of light. And also because the dozen MOME mages weren't the only casualties of the event.

Time and space seemed to have taken a hit as well.

Because, holy shit, as if my ears had suddenly come back online after a brief delay, there was a brain-shearing sound, like the rending of a million sheets of tinfoil all at once.

And then I could see an orange sky with a purple sun, still framed by our blue sky with its white-yellow sun; a sight that was enough to make me feel nauseous on its own, but it didn't end there. Nope. It did not.

Because out of the desert under the orange sky with the purple sun poured hundreds, possibly a thousand or more, demons.

And, ok, maybe now I understood what Dryer had meant, when she was raving about being knee deep in bodies thanks to an invasion…

It was difficult to tell how many there were, because they were all changing shape as soon as they tumbled through the tear in the seam and onto Earth. Beings that started out as furless squirrels, furry bunnies, tiny goats, poofy owls, fuzzy otters, strange ducks, and a whole host of other mostly harmless looking animals poured into earth as creatures straight out of nightmares, bringing the pungent scent of sulphur with them.

A small handful, perhaps the other succubi, appeared angelic as they flew through the bright Phoenix sky, giant feathered wings on the backs of gorgeous humanoids, but the majority took on forms that had too many limbs, tentacles, or proboscises to count, all of which were attached to giant, fang-filled maws, or horrible suctioning mouths, or, ew, honestly, it was getting too gross for me to keep track of.

"Well, fuck," I was startled to hear myself say aloud.

I was back in human form, though I'd made no conscious decision to switch. I would have liked to take the time to wonder about that: had the rip in the seam knocked me into my human form? How did that even work? But the creatures were stumbling through the tear in the seam in droves, and immediately setting upon, well, everyone. They were attacking MOME's forces, they were attacking our Unterberger allies, and in a moment I would love to scour from my retinae, but probably never will, I even saw Ms. Rebuke tear off her shirt and launch herself into the arms of a succubus, just before it took off into the sky and left the site of the battle entirely.

The demons were attacking our ranks, but they were also spilling away from our ridiculous battle and out into the streets that surrounded us, taking eager hold of the human population that I hadn't even noticed had been cowering behind whatever cover they could find in the area.

I'm not sure why the non-magical people nearby had felt that was a good idea—perhaps because we'd been very clearly focused on our own little battle and hadn't been making a point of ransacking the city or anything. People like a spectacle, and we sure as shit counted as one. Maybe they thought we were making a movie.

They were learning the price of that choice now, though, as the demons spilled forth and made no attempts to organize their attacks. In fact, they seemed to be plowing into the streets with reckless abandon, grabbing humans and throwing them into waiting fanged maws, or just throwing them into the sides of buildings, where they landed with sickening cracks.

'This is bad," I said to no one.

"No jodas," replied Sol in her standard monotone.

My relief at seeing her alive, in one piece, and well enough to make dark jokes was short lived. The demons just kept coming. The rip in the seam was as wide as the parking lot that it filled, and there were dozens more of them pouring through every second. We had to do something.

If only I had the faintest clue what.

"What do we do?" Seamus asked, appearing beside us and echoing my thoughts.

And ok, I couldn't help myself, I threw my arms around them both, unaware how much I'd missed them until they were both back in my sight again.

"We fight," Sol said, after a brief embrace, even though her face showed what a bleak prospect she thought that was.

I nodded, and Seamus' face paled, but his chin dipped with mine. What choice did we have? The demons were going to tear this place apart, and I didn't know how on Earth we were going to stop them, but I was starting to think some dragon fire might be in order. Just because Thanatos could eat it, that didn't mean it wouldn't kill most of the demons who had just poured through that tear.

So we stood, shoulder to shoulder, facing the horde of demons who had, for whatever reason, maybe because they'd been invited by MOME—*that* would be entirely like Dryer—or maybe just because they could, decided to take out Phoenix, and together, as though we shared an internal count, we pulled on our animal forms.

And came out on the other side as something entirely new.

Vic, Sol, WHAT THE HELLS IS GOING ON?

Um…I have no clue, but we don't really have time to—

And then we were charging into the fray as one because… well, we were one.

There was a horde of demons charging straight for us, so we didn't have time to sort out why the fuck we'd just shifted and come out as a giant dragon body—as big as any of the adult dragons we'd seen in the dragon realms—with three fucking heads, only one of which was a dragon's. The other two were, perhaps predictably—if you could ever *predict* turning into a giant, three-headed monster right out of someone's nightmare mythology without meaning to—a wolf and a panther. But I didn't even have time to process all of that before a few dozen demons reached us at the same time and started throwing various appendages and powers at us at once.

We responded to that as you might expect a giant three-headed monster to respond.

We burned the shit out of them.

Turns out crazy-assed pseudo-chimera-Vic-Sol-Seamus could breathe dragon fire out of *all three* mouths.

Fuck yeah!

I wasn't sure which one of us thought that. Maybe all three of us had. Because in addition to body slamming the front line of demons that had charged us, we'd just used all three of our heads to light up the majority of the ones that were still standing (as well as quite a few of the ones who'd gone down).

We let out a roar that actually shook the pavement where we were standing, and shattered a few office building windows in the block around us.

That was about when the demons decided to take us more seriously.

At least, I assume that's why a surge of demons all attempted to attack us at the same time.

I couldn't count how many tried to overwhelm us, but my field of vision was nothing but demon. Tentacles, claws, fangs, tongues, arms, legs, and a hundred other appendages I had no name for.

We were in an ocean of demons, and it felt like we were about to drown. The sheer press of that many other bodies on top of us, many of which seemed to be trying to drain our energy, was nearly overwhelming. We snapped our jaws and roared our defiance, but the press just kept coming. Pushing us down, down, down, against the hot concrete, under the bright September sun. A wave of dizziness swept us and our legs started to buckle.

But we weren't having that. Oh no. We were not.

Rise. One voice inside us, and our legs tightened against the strain.

These demons were going to learn what it meant to invade Earth.

Rise. Two voices in unison within us. Legs straightening against the horde, and three heads rising above the press.

Yes, they were going to learn, and MOME was going to learn what it meant to try to subjugate humans. And damn it all, this was going to stop.

Rise! Three voices together, and three heads raised to the sky, roaring in defiance and turning to spread flaming death wherever it was needed.

Our thoughts had largely melded, and I really couldn't tell who was thinking what, but none of us were objecting to any of the decisions being made. And our legs pushed against the onslaught of demons and our teeth started rending any flesh nearby that wasn't already in flames. And we drove ourselves forward, cutting a swath of destruction with each step, until the demons were scrambling to get out of our way.

Then our legs carried us towards the largest demon of the lot, which—you guessed it—was the one that looked like Cthulhu and a clam's gory love child.

THANATOS!!! We roared mentally, along with another physical roar that broke glass somewhere in the neighborhood.

And, apparently, Thanatos understood we were coming for him, because he turned his two creepy proboscis-like eyes towards us, and then dropped the tank he had been about to swallow (and yeah, he was as big as some of the buildings around us now, but that was ok, because we were even bigger) and I guess he decided that we would be an even tastier snack, because the next thing we knew, a giant tentacle was trying to wrap itself around our enormous midsection.

So we sprayed Thanatos with three heads worth of dragon fire.

Which *he* seemed to think was like bathing in chocolate or some shit, because he basically just rolled around and basked in it—absorbing it through his skin somehow—his hold around our midsection only tightening.

Which was when we decided to see how his tentacles held up against dragon fangs, wolf fangs, and panther fangs.

The answer was: not well.

He may have been used to fighting creatures with sharp fangs at a much smaller size, because, sure, when you grew to the size of a city block, a regular-sized panther wasn't going to do much but feel like a mosquito bite. But when the panther jaws in question were as large as a semi truck, that shit was going to sever your tentacles, no matter how much dragon fire they could absorb.

Which was when Thanatos' Cthulhu/clam-ass started to look nervous. He was down three tentacles now, and while he seemed to have plenty more where those came from, he did not have an infinite supply.

Meanwhile, we were not running out of teeth anytime soon.

He released our midsection and tried a new strategy, namely wrapping each of our three necks in tentacles. Admittedly, that would probably have been a good move, but he wasn't fast enough. Each of our necks and jaws snapped at the tentacles wending their way towards us, severing them each time before they ever managed to grab hold of us. We had taken off another five tentacles before Thanatos started backing away, using his largest remaining tentacles to help move things along, while its creepy clam tongue pushed it back towards the tear in the seam.

And that, of course, was when General Aira finally decided that we were worth reinforcing after all. I could hear the roar of a hundred dragons behind me, followed quickly by the terrified sounds of a few hundred demons freaking the fuck out.

Suddenly, Thanatos wasn't the only one beating a hasty retreat.

The tear in the seam, orange sky framed by blue, loomed larger than ever, now that we'd gotten quite a bit closer to it, and I/we could finally see that it was outlined by a faint red glow that flared and faded in certain areas.

The red glow actually looked like a shredded curtain, if curtains were made out of shimmering red light, instead of fabric. Bits and pieces of it hung from above and below in tatters.

Then we were distracted from the rip in spacetime by watching Thanatos get closer and closer to the tear between the two worlds, along with all the demons who'd been close enough to him to notice his retreat. It didn't seem like any official retreat had been called, though. A huge host of demons were still plowing their way through the torn seam into our realm, even as half of those that had arrived in the earlier waves were viciously attempting to push their way back through the crowd, most showing little regard for the well-being of their fellow demons who hadn't made it through the tear yet. I saw more than a few limbs, tentacles, and mandibles go flying in various directions as the two throngs collided.

I was relieved that some of the demons were retreating, but it was becoming increasingly clear that if we couldn't close this seam, we had no way to ensure that the whole host wouldn't be back as soon as they'd had a chance to regroup.

With surprising unanimity, we launched ourselves skyward sharply and then dove with single-minded fury for the clam/Cthulhu creature getting ready to slither back into his home realm.

Thanatos apparently hadn't been expecting that, or else he'd been too focused on pushing his way back through his fellow demons to notice our approach. We snapped down around him with a force that shattered a few car and office windows nearby, and sent many smaller demons tumbling away from us. I don't think we stepped on any, but I didn't really check.

Where ya headed, Bunny? we asked, hoping he understood this form of communication. I wasn't entirely sure how he was going to reply, since clams didn't exactly have vocal chords, but...

Please! Don't attack! I wish to negotiate!

Looked like we didn't have to worry about tentacle sign language after all.

Funny, it looks like you want to run away, not negotiate.

Yes, well, I had hoped to run away, but if you're going to pin me here and threaten to rip off all of my remaining limbs, I'd rather negotiate.

And, yeah, I could kinda see where he was coming from with that.

Do you surrender? we asked.

Yes! Most emphatically.

Then call an official retreat. Order the rest of the demons back into the hell realm you came from.

Well…I'm not technically in charge of them, you see, I'm more like—

All three of our heads snapped at Thanatos' proboscis eyes, roaring.

I suggest you exercise your leadership skills, we growled.

Erm…yes. Quite.

Thanatos' tentacles waved manically for a bit, then he made a series of strange trumpeting noises, and… well, not much changed. At least, not immediately. Some of the nearest demons piling through the seam stopped and tried to turn around, but the ones behind them just plowed into them and pushed them through. However, the roar of dragons increased behind us, and soon it wasn't just Thanatos' cries that were egging his fellows on. He made the same weird bugling call again, and that, accompanied by the fiery death being rained down behind us, seemed to seal the deal. The demons who were trying to push their way through to our realm finally noticed that our realm was no longer the free buffet they'd likely been promised, and those who hadn't already been leaving attempted to disengage with whoever they were fighting and make their retreat. An attempt that was aided by the fact that MOME's forces were quickly becoming overwhelmed by our newly arrived dragon army.

Is that acceptable? Thanatos asked, still doing his best to shrink back into his shell.

We didn't release him, but I nodded the dragon head, while the wolf and panther remained within close range of a few of his tentacles.

Now promise that you won't be returning here.

You cannot cut my people off from Earth! We would starve if we could never venture here.

I'm not saying your people can never come here, if they stick to whatever rules bound them before today. I'm saying, never come here as an army. Never another invasion. I don't care how wide a hole some asshat tears in your seam. You stay back and enjoy the view without sending in an army.

And what if some "asshat," as you call them, decides to invade our realm?

If that happens, and it's an unprovoked attack, you are welcome to defend yourself. You can even call on me for backup.

That response got a few warning rumbles from Sol and Seamus, so I decided to clarify.

And when I say "me," I mean Vic. I can't promise that Sol or Seamus will answer your call.

I couldn't fault them for not wanting to jump into a cordial relationship with Thanatos. I was wary of it too, but I had a feeling that Thanatos—as cunning as I was sure he was capable of being—hadn't been the master-mind behind this plan. He seemed to have gone out of his way to attack MOME wherever possible, plus he'd eaten Dryer's soul at the first chance he'd gotten. I didn't know much about how demon summoning worked, but I had a sneaking suspicion that he'd done what he could to help me today, and while I didn't particularly like the guy, I didn't think making an enemy of one of the most powerful demons in the hell realms was a good plan either.

My offer of help made Thanatos cease his constant twitching, for a moment. Then, to my eternal shock, the clam/Cthulhu hybrid beneath us blinked out of existence and was replaced with an imposing winged figure, very much like Az's, but only male (as far as I could see), and with golden skin and charcoal colored wings. Thick black hair fell in curls around his shoulders, and his eyes shone gold in the sunlight.

"You continue to surprise me, Vic," the nine-foot-tall winged man declared, flapping his wings until he was hovering more or less at dragon snout level.

I snorted a bit of smoke out of my nostrils, not wanting to incinerate anyone at the moment, and gave the dragon equivalent of a shrug.

Join the club, I projected to this winged Thanatos, hoping he could still understand me. *I hardly know what I'm going to do or say, half the time.*

"Ha! That may be true, but it is not your choice of words that surprises me. You have had multiple opportunities to destroy that which you did not understand today, and yet, every time, you have chosen… to treat me and my people with respect."

Um… did you miss the part where we wiped out a few dozen demons? I asked, cursing my own honesty. I mean, if Thanatos had somehow missed that part, I really shouldn't be the one to point it out to him.

"You did what anyone would do when their home is attacked. But you also offered us more mercy than we deserved, given the circumstances, and you didn't attempt to kill a small blue rabbit when you had the chance, even once you realized what I was."

I didn't really have a response for that. It was true, though I hadn't done it out of some higher sense of honor, I just… why would I kill someone who wasn't trying to kill me?

You should have seen how long it took her to get fatally pissed off at Edik.

And, ok, it seemed like Seamus could project our thoughts too in this form. I guess that only made sense.

Thanatos merely chuckled.

"Do you require any assistance in restraining the remaining forces from MOME?" he asked, casually, like he was offering to help clear the dishes after a potluck.

Nah, I think we've got this, I replied, before an idea struck me. *Unless… unless you know who has been leading the MOME forces since we got rid of Dryer? That would save us a whole lot of time.*

Thanatos smirked, nodded, and then shot up into the sky and out of sight.

I HAD JUST enough time to wonder if I'd made a terrible mistake when Thanatos shifted his angle, pinned his wings back to his sides, and dove through the mildly hazy Phoenix sky with alarming speed. He flared his wings just in time to avoid colliding with a flaming set of concrete barriers that appeared to have been turned into some kind of command post, and then fluttered gracefully inside it.

A few moments later, he popped back up with a screaming, flailing, balding man, who I was quite startled to recognize as the short dude who had been aiming a wand at me when I first pushed out the door of MOME at the beginning of this fight.

Which should have been impossible.

Because I had burned that man to ash.

A fact that was quickly explained when Thanatos brought the screaming, flailing man into our hearing range.

"WE HAD A DEAL! THAT WITCH KILLED MY BROTHER! YOU CAN'T DO THIS TO ME! I'LL DESTROY YOU ALL! I'LL MAKE MORE TECHNETIUM AND TEAR THIS WORLD APART! I—"

I was fairly certain that the man would have kept going for as long as we let him, but Thanatos shifted his grip on him, one of his hands venturing to the man's neck, performing some technique that caused his eyes to close and his head to loll to one side like a doll.

"This is what's left of MOME's security council—at least, of those who were bold enough to join the battle. I believe you'd already met his brother. Where would you like him?"

Again, Thanatos' tone was polite and casual, as though asking if I'd prefer this pile of dishes rinsed in the sink or placed straight into the dishwasher. And I was at a loss as to how to reply, because… what was I supposed to do with a prisoner of war? I wasn't part of any governing body. I didn't think I had permission to admit people into the dragon realms' prisons, even if Siara was technically my grandmother now, or whatever. Apparently, Sol and Seamus didn't have any great ideas either, and the silence was just getting awkward when Gwen materialized in midair, arm in arm with Albert.

"Oh good," she said, smiling. "You figured out the chimera trick."

Before I could react to *that* interesting tidbit, Albert spoke.

"Vic, Sol, Seamus, excellent to see you all in such fine form. Thanatos, I am less pleased to find you here, but I am… pleasantly surprised to see you corralling the vermin."

Nice to see you alive, Al, I projected, eliciting a small smile from Albert before he turned his full attention to Thanatos and the man he was holding.

"I think it would be best if you both came with me," he said, gesturing back towards the MOME building behind us.

I was honestly a bit surprised that the place was still standing. It was weird to think that so much destruction had been wrought since the start of this battle, but that most of it had missed the nondescript concrete building behind us.

"Vic, Sol, Seamus, you may, ahh…relax, if you feel the need," Albert said.

"Nice work saving the world," Gwen added, before she turned away with Albert's arm still linked in the crook of hers.

Then Thanatos flew off with the prisoner, whose name I hadn't even caught, and Albert and Gwen (and how could Gwen even fly?) floated off towards the front of the MOME building where Siara (who, last I'd checked, had been stranded on a cliff ledge in hell) was also waiting for them in her human form, along with the green-skinned, large-tusked woman from Unterberg, who I hadn't seen since we'd first been taken before the council there (who, for all I knew, was now in charge of Unterberg council, since Torrence and Nethia had been… otherwise occupied for a while now).

As our eyes scanned the battlefield, we realized that the fighting had completely stopped. The dragons arriving en masse had cowed even the most dedicated of MOME's forces, and now the field (or giant parking lot, as the case happened to be) was clearing to show the bodies of the fallen and the injured. Some people/demons were being carried off in various forms of restraint, and others were slinking back through the tear in the seam to the hell realm. A few bits of dragon fire smoldered away still, but there was another demon clam, much smaller than Thanatos, but similar in shape, sliding around eating the various flaming bits that littered the parking lot. As it was one of the only demons not retreating, and it seemed single-mindedly interested in dragon fire, I wasn't planning to argue. It was a harrowing scene, despite the relief I felt at seeing that the fighting was over. So much damage had been done, from the cars and buildings destroyed, to the people lying still all around us, some of whom must have been purely human, though you couldn't tell now who had been were, mage, or non, from the still forms that littered the ground.

And then, as suddenly as we'd become one, we stood next to each other in our human forms, three separate people, huddled against each other for comfort, reaching for one another with our arms even as our bodies regained their autonomy.

"Let's never do this again," Seamus muttered quietly.

"What, become a giant fire-breathing monster?" Sol asked, smiling.

"Nah," Seamus countered. "That part was badass. I was more talking about the whole war thing."

I laughed, and then choked on a sob.

"Yeah," I agreed, my voice cracking. "Let's skip that part next time."

THE NEXT FEW days, hell, the next few weeks, were a mess. A serious, life-altering mess for a lot of people.

To start with, I didn't know where Rhelia and Trevor had gone off to. I also hadn't seen Torrence lately, and a quick scan of the area around us didn't help. Az hadn't shown up since ridding me of a dozen vampires, and I couldn't see Seamus' parents, or mine, either.

Sol's Abuelita showed up to envelope her in a spine-crushing hug, and I decided that was my cue to sidle away, though Seamus gave me a wave that suggested he would stay and look for people.

I didn't particularly want to follow Albert and Gwen over to where a group of people who'd *actually finished high school*, not to mention actually understood most of the workings of the magical world, were about to make a bunch of decisions that would affect a huge number of people for a very long time. After all, I'd just fought, and bled, and risked Gwendamned eve-rything, to save the world, and part of me thought I deserved a damned rest, and that those folks didn't actually need me. They could sort it out, and I could finally go take a nap. That part of me might even have been right, but a more vocal part of me insisted that I should at least make sure they got all the information they needed from me before I let myself relax. I had seen a bunch of shit that no one else had, and it might be relevant to figuring out how we should move forward from here.

As I gave Sol and Seamus one more hug, before turning towards the warded piece of concrete where our present leadership stood, I promised myself it would just be a few more minutes. That I would go debrief with the remaining leaders of the magical community, and then I would go home and take a three day nap.

If only.

The first thing I did when I reached that group of magical leadership was throw my arms around Siara. Judging by how stiff she went in my embrace, she hadn't been expecting the move, but before I could back away and apologize for invading her space, she relaxed and returned the hug.

"How did you get here?" I asked, when I finally stepped away from her.

She laughed. "I'm afraid it's not a terribly exciting story. I waited until I felt my body had passed the Technetium from my system, and then I climbed out of the canyon."

"How could you tell that the—"

"Then," Siara continued pointedly, before I could finish my question, "I found a mass of demons collecting around a rather unremarkable piece of desert near the top of the canyon, and decided it was suspicious enough to be worth my attention. It would appear that I was right."

It would also appear that Siara's return had been the only reason that the Dragon reinforcements had finally come to our aid. She had tracked Aira down as soon as she was through the seam, then insisted that her dragons join the battle.

"General Aira has much to answer for," was all that Siara said about that particular infraction, after describing her arrival. I got the feeling she didn't want to talk about it in front of the non-dragon folk. That was fine with me.

"What do you wish to do with this?" Thanatos asked, as if anticipating the need for a change in subject, holding up the still-unconscious, balding mage that he'd routed out of MOME's forces.

That had seemed like a pretty significant tack away from the topic of demons amassing for an invasion to me, but everyone else let it slide, and I was too tired to bring it up myself. Besides, I was more pissed off at the MOME shitchip that Thanatos was holding than at Thanatos himself, so if he wanted to deflect, I was happy to let him.

"We need to interrogate him," Lizzie proclaimed. I hadn't seen the woman with olive skin (and I meant that literally, not as an unclear reference to Mediterranean heritage, but, like, actually the color of a green olive) enter the fray earlier, but I'd been distracted, and she was covered in enough blood and... dark goop that had probably come out of a demon, that I was fairly certain she'd been battling her heart out with the rest of us.

"He can explain how they ripped open that seam, and how they made a deal with those demons in the first place!"

She sounded pretty angry for someone who helped run Unterberg, which was basically the Switzerland of the magical world and usually stayed so far outside of these types of conflicts that we'd had to essentially beg them to get involved in this one. Or rather, we'd tried and failed to beg them to help us. I thought they'd turned us down, but they were here now, and they'd definitely fought with us, so…

"I can speak to both those points, I'm afraid," said Thanatos.

It still startled me to see him in such a human guise, giant feathered wings notwithstanding. Granted, I'd only known him for an hour or so (less than that, if we only went by Earth time, instead of whatever weird timeline my life represented), but I'd seen him so often as an electric blue bunny or a giant clam/Cthulhu monster that the implacable angel look was definitely throwing me off.

"It is my understanding that the Ministry of Magical Entity officials had originally planned to inject an entity who possessed a surplus of dark matter with Technetium near the seam in La Paz, in order to attempt an invasion on Unterberg, the closest seam there being a relevant one. When that failed them, they tried to do the same thing on a smaller scale in Sucre. They succeeded, marginally. They managed to tear a small hole into one of the more icy hell dimensions, or so my subordinates reported at the time. Whatever they managed, they failed in finding a useful force for an invasion, and found nothing worth invading themselves. Our ice-dwelling brethren are often reluctant to leave their own world for any but the coldest regions of this one. They are… rather susceptible to any amount of warmth."

Those of us that weren't demons all exchanged looks. I, for one, wondered if Thanatos was really about to give us all the answers, and if so, why.

"Regardless," he continued, "they decided to try again, as I'm sure you're all aware. I was not truly cognizant of their intentions until word of their little attempted coup made its way even as far as my own realm." Thanatos turned his attention to me. "I did not lie to you when we first met, Vic. Their apparent plans for Technetium terrified my people. So, when a MOME representative offered my people freedom from such attacks in exchange for a small invasion—one which basically amounted to a free buffet lunch for my people—I accepted at once."

He took a deep breath, returning his attention to the whole group.

"However, MOME made it clear quite quickly today that they weren't planning to stick to their original offer. Rebecca Dryer—wearing someone else's skin—summoned me from my hell realm, even as my people marshaled for invasion. Then she injected me with Technetium, and only failed to destroy me, in the very way her people had vowed not to, thanks to the efforts of Vic, here. I believe I was summoned the second time in hopes that the Technetium would still be in my blood, but thankfully my metabolism is rather quick. However, I wasn't the only one summoned. As you all no doubt witnessed, another demon was summoned and injected. And we must all be grateful that the pour soul was rather starved, for they did far less damage that they might have—even less than a weak magical human would have, in all likelihood. The explosion must have been right on top of the seam when it happened, however, as it was sufficient to cause the rift MOME was hoping for. And... I believe you all know the rest."

"Why did you bother helping MOME at all, if Rebecca had already betrayed you once?" I asked, more than slightly baffled at Thanatos' casual explanation.

"It seemed her side was the winning one," he replied easily, as if it were just a simple truth and anyone else would have done the same. And maybe any other demon would have. I only knew one other, and it wasn't difficult to believe that Az might be an exception to the rule.

Thanatos smirked before continuing, "Although you quickly made it clear to me how wrong that assumption was. I corrected course accordingly."

I laughed. I had to. I mean, Thanatos was remarkably consistent in his self-preservation tactics, I had to give him that. And with so much evidence as to the duplicity of humans confronting him, I could hardly blame him for not holding out any loyalty to me, after I'd refrained from killing him gratuitously one time. That was a pretty low bar to pass, really.

"We will still need to confirm that story with Agent Elgby," Albert replied, gesturing to the unconscious mage. "I'm sure you understand."

Thanatos nodded, not seeming the least bit offended.

"But where can we store him in the meantime? Not to mention all the injured MOME agents being pulled off the field right now," I asked. "It's not like we can trust that the MOME folks don't know a bunch of tricks for getting out of their own dungeons. Even if we could, it's not like we'll have locked them all up. And if any of them remain free, they could easily break the rest of their buddies out."

Albert and Lizzie nodded, though I noticed that Lizzie wasn't offering up storage options in Unterburg. Thanatos said nothing. And Gwen. Damn it all, Gwen had left again.

I almost groaned in frustration. I had so many questions for her, I couldn't even tally them all up in my head. I wanted to find out where she had taken Trev, why she had showed up so many times without just fixing everything, since she was a freaking goddess anyway, and why she couldn't have warned me about any of the damned things I'd had to deal with lately, like, I don't know, turning into a dragon and then, more recently, a chimera.

And, oh boy, did I have questions about the chimera form. How was it even possible? Was that the whole reason that Sol, Seamus, and I had been thrown into this weird mating bond? Or could anyone do what we'd done? If it had been the reason for the mating bond, were we going to stop caring about each other, now that this whole thing was done? And that was just the tip of the iceberg. I had big plans for interrogating Gwen, hells yes, I did.

But all of that was going to have to wait.

"You could stow everyone from MOME in Hel's dimension, maybe. She owes me one, I think. Or maybe my parents could talk her into it. You should ask them, be—"

As if on cue, Gwen chose that moment to show up with both of my parents.

And I didn't know what to do or say to them, so I started backing away, so I wouldn't have to say anything at all. They could sort the rest of this stuff out. My parents knew more about the Hel realm than I ever would. It was possible they knew even more than Renata did, so, yeah. That just about ate up my reasons for needing to stick around this debriefing. They *really* didn't need my help.

But then my hand went to my forehead, as the thought of Renata reminded me that there was another group of people out there who really did.

UNFORTUNATELY, MY BODY didn't seem to care that a hundred people were barely going to be able to take care of their most basic needs without me. I managed to reach for my Gwen-given powers and use them to transport myself to a familiar bit of abandoned desert in Northern Arizona, but as soon as I arrived my legs collapsed and my vision tunneled ominously.

A set of hands shrouded in mist caught me, before I hit the ground.

"Thanks," I muttered to Renata, while inwardly cursing the demons who'd tried to drain us at the end of the battle. I'd known I was weak, and second-guessed shifting my way out here instead of flying in dragon form, but I didn't see what choice I'd had. There was a whole group of people here who were going to literally be stumbling around the desert without me, and the longer I left them, the harder it would be to find them all.

So, here I was, and Renata's grip held me firm as I blinked the scrubby red desert and clear blue sky back into focus.

"I was hoping you'd be here," I said, trying to fill the silence while my body finished silently screaming at me to stop using my power.

Renata's voice was its normal sincere monotone.

"I assumed you had the battle under control."

I really couldn't tell if she was joking or not, but I laughed anyway.

The puzzled arch of her brows when I finally stopped, and stared at her, suggested she'd been serious.

"Did you not leave the battle victorious?" she asked.

I chuckled again, because I couldn't help it, then finally admitted, "Yes. Technically, I guess you could say that, but… I wish I had, at any point, felt even half as confident about my ability to pull that off as you seem to."

"You have many powers and many allies. There was little reason to think you would not succeed."

"Sure, except for the part where I have no idea what I'm doing, and where I was up against an entire army of mages and demons, and—never mind. You're right. We won, I guess, and I'm here now."

Renata smiled, as though I'd finally said something that made sense.

"Yes! Are you here to give me the whistle?" she asked.

I frowned.

"I hadn't planned to ditch you with over a hundred mind control victims," I said.

Finally looking at our immediate vicinity, after attempting to look into Renata's eyes through the continuously shifting mist that enveloped her started to give me a headache, I noticed that all of the aforementioned MOME victims seemed to be clustered nearby in various blobs of shade thrown by the occasional boulders. I also noticed that there were far more of them than we had initially dropped off here. Renata must have somehow wrangled the ones who had been on the opposing side back up here during the remainder of the fight…

"Did Gwen help you collect these folks?" I muttered, looking at the crowd huddled in the bits of shade they could find.

"It is noble of you to wish to continue to care for those you led from the dungeons," Renata said, ignoring my question about Gwen. "But how exactly were you planning to help? You can barely stand."

As if to prove her point, she released my arm, and my legs instantly rejected the idea of holding me upright any longer.

"Damn it," I mumbled, sparing myself from landing on my ass by kneeling with one hand on the ground to keep my balance.

I used the hand that wasn't keeping me from toppling face-first into a cactus to wrestle the whistle from my pocket, and shoved it in Renata's general direction. I felt it slip from my grip, but my eyesight had gone dark around the edges again.

"Is there a place that you would like me to take you, so that you may rest?" Renata's voice asked, from somewhere above me.

"Have you ever met a tree named Life?" I asked, shortly before passing out.

~~~

YOU REALLY SHOULD TAKE BETTER CARE OF YOURSELF, VIC.

I blinked a few times. The dappled light of the sun filtered through tree branches, softly warming my face, but also making it almost impossible for my vision to clear.

I sat up. I was delighted to find that I didn't pass out again, or even feel lightheaded.

YOU HAVE BEEN HERE FOR AN HOUR, NAPPING. YOU SHOULD BE IN FINE FORM NOW.

"Thanks, Life," I mumbled, even as I pulled myself to my feet.

I was wearing a pair of yoga pants, a well-worn sports bra, and a very soft T-shirt. For once, I was completely happy with the Gwen power's choice of clothes, although I didn't remember shifting forms at all, so I wasn't exactly sure why my clothes had shifted.

"Am I clear to use all my powers?" I asked, turning to see the glowing eyes sunk into the trunk of a tree that was shaped a little too much like the grim reaper for someone who went by the name of Life.

I WOULD NOT RECOMMEND USING THEM IN THE MANNER YOU HAVE BEEN, CONSIDERING HOW CLOSE YOU CAME TO BURNING YOURSELF OUT *AGAIN*, BUT YOU SHOULD BE FINE OTHERWISE.

"I'll do my best," I said, waving another thank you as I closed my eyes, thinking hard about the one place in the universe I really wanted to be.
~~~

ONLY TO BE hijacked by a red haired Goddess and snapped into the void.

I had been reaching for a specific destination this time, so winding up suspended in inky blackness with a red haired, green eyed, pale-skinned deity floating before me was more than a little disconcerting.

"What the actual fuck, Gwen?"

"What? I wanted to talk to you and I didn't want to keep your friends waiting."

"So, let me guess, you pulled us outside of time and space to have a chat?"

Gwen's smile made an almost glowing line across her face, and her emerald eyes glittered strangely, for being in a place that appeared to have no source of light.

"Yes! You're getting the hang of things now, aren't you?"

I laughed, though I almost felt like crying.

"You mean, now that we saved the world, am I finally getting a grip on how magic works? Yeah, I guess. Though I still have about a billion questions for you."

Her smile faded a bit, but she didn't disappear.

"Fire away," she said, her arms spread wide.

I cocked an eyebrow at her. This seemed suspiciously easy.

"Really? Ok… if you're really a goddess, why didn't you just swoop in and stop all of this from happening, instead of just randomly showing up to save our butts when it suited you?"

Gwen laughed, and spun in a circle that seemed to almost stir the inky blackness that surrounded us.

"A delightful question. Deities are willed into being by living things, not the other way around. As such, none of us are omnipotent, and we are all limited by the forms we are willed into. I am dark matter made into serendipity. My powers allow me to flit around any realm inhabited by earthlings, and help those who are already helping themselves. My powers won't allow me to directly affect any outcome."

My eyebrow rose again.

"Then how have you managed to save my ass, directly, on more than one occasion?"

Gwen clapped.

"Oh yes, that's a fun one. There are no written rules, per se, so I don't know exactly what we aren't allowed to do, but some of us seem to be permitted avatars, and we are allowed direct actions to save our avatars!"

"But the first time you saved my ass, I hadn't agreed to help you yet."

Gwen shrugged.

"The universe isn't as into consent as a lot of folks are these days. You were marked as my avatar the moment I decided to ask you. I waited to transfer my powers to you until you said yes, but the universe isn't as picky about that sort of thing."

Right. I supposed something older than time might not care about that sort of thing, if it cared about anything at all. As usual, Gwen's explanation was leaving me with way more questions than I'd started with, but at least she was answering me.

"Why did you send me on a quest to find out what happened to my parents, when what you actually wanted me to do was overthrow a magical authoritarian regime?" I asked, after a long pause.

That had Gwen cackling, for some reason.

"Oooh! This is so much fun," she squeed. "Why do you think?"

I just glared in response.

"Oh, come on, do you really want me to just tell you?"

I glared harder.

"Fine, fine. Sheesh. Way to take the joy out of it. If I had shown up and said, 'Hey, Vic, I need your help to take out an authoritarian regime that's making people's lives miserable, because I'm a deity that can't manipulate things directly,' would you have said yes?"

I wanted to just keep glaring, but instead I sat down on nothing, and crossed my legs while sighing profoundly.

"So you sent me on a personal quest that was almost guaranteed to help you get what you wanted, because it would put me in direct conflict with MOME?"

"YES! Oh, see, it is more fun to guess!"

If I could glare any harder, Gwen's hair would have been on fire.

"In the times that you showed up to help, sometimes you barely did anything. Sometimes you just made things harder, like when we had to haul your ass out of MOME's dungeons. What was up with that?"

Now Gwen just scoffed, and did a bit of her own glaring.

"Honestly, Vic, keep up. Outside of transportation, I generally can't affect things directly, unless it's down to saving just *your* ass. To make that battle go the way it needed to, you had to walk out those doors at *exactly* the right moment. The stakes were too high not to nudge you."

I thought about that for a moment, and was glad I was already sitting down in the void, so my legs couldn't give out on me.

"You mean, you… that… Dryer would have taken out the whole Earth if we had arrived earlier or later?"

Gwen nodded.

"The universe likes to remain intact. It pushed me very hard to go interfere with you. Luckily, Rhelia needed a ride anyway, and the dungeons suppress dark matter enough to make me a useless lump. Thanks for not leaving me there, by the way."

I sighed, rubbing my hands over my face and feeling like all the fight had left my body.

"I still don't get why you chose me, of all people, to help you out."

Gwen cocked her head to one side, raising an eyebrow at me.

"That's simple, Vic. You're one of the most naturally lucky humans I've ever met."

And, as I finally shifted myself to the place I'd been aiming for when Gwen hijacked me, I found it difficult to disagree.

It turned out that place was more of a person than anything else.

Or people, if you want to get technical.

A week ago, I was pretty certain that person had been Trev. A year ago, the people would have been my parents.

Instead, I found myself materializing in the middle of a cozy living room in the Andes, where Seamus and Sol were leaning casually, back to back, apparently laughing at something one of them had said.

The second I appeared, they both jumped to their feet, smiling and throwing their arms around me. I threw my arms right back around them. Sol's lips found mine first, and the kiss just about set fire to my skin, but we pulled apart after a moment, and when I turned to Seamus, I found a longing I couldn't name in his eyes.

"Are you always going to ask first?" I asked.

He nodded.

"My Moms really drove that lesson home," he said.

"Well, the answer is an enthusiastic yes," I replied.

And then Seamus' lips were lighting me on fire just as Sol's had, but with a bit more tenderness. Sol's affection was always a bit more assertive than Seamus' and… I found them both just as enticing.

When Seamus' kiss broke off, the three of us all still holding each other, part of me wanted to retreat to the bedroom with them, but a larger part of me just wanted to collapse on the couch and talk. Maybe have a couple of Sol's amazing sandwiches.

Judging by the fact that nobody stopped me from swinging my weight towards the couch, and the fact that they both collapsed with me when I did, I suspected the suggestion might be a popular one.

"Should I make us sandwiches?" I asked, honestly willing to make them, even though I was fairly certain I knew what the answer would be.

"Absolutely not," Sol replied, jumping up. "The thin abominations you call sandwiches are not allowed in my kitchen."

I laughed, though I didn't think my sandwich skills were that low.

"Fine," I agreed, starting to get up from the couch. "I'll make tea to go with the sandwiches."

Seamus leapt to his feet before I could get up, and pointed emphatically back at the couch.

"You will stay and rest. I can make tea. If Sol lets me."

He glanced sidelong at the kitchen, but Sol made no objection, so he headed into the small portion of the cabin that housed the teapot and tea collection, and then quickly returned to the "living room" in order to put the kettle he'd just filled on top of one of the burners that crowned the wood stove heating the whole place.

I sat on the couch and watched them both at work. I considered reading, but didn't think I'd be able to focus on printed words if I tried right now. Instead, I watched Sol sway expertly through her tiny kitchen, moving plates, bread, and sandwich fixings in a graceful dance. Periodically, I would glance at Seamus, who was also watching Sol, with a look I didn't quite understand in his eyes.

"Did you guys ever sort things out?" I asked. He had said something to that effect once, but I never really got the whole story. Not that it was entirely my business. We were all in a relationship, but that relationship was as open as it got. With the ground rules we'd laid out, none of us were beholden to each other for anything, really. Not now, at least. The relationship could change as we did, but we'd basically just decided that we were all too young and restless to offer each other more than sex and friendship. It was the friendship piece I was wondering about now.

I had intentionally asked the question loud enough for Sol to hear. I was asking both of them, although I'd directed the question mostly to Seamus. Sol had been… slow to warm up to the idea that he was a canine half the time.

"If you're asking if Sol apologized for being a bit of a bigot when we first met, the answer is yes."

I looked at Sol, who was smiling, and decided that was probably a good sign.

Probably.

"Why are you smiling like a bag of poop is about to drop on my head?" I asked, after a moment.

Sol actually cackled.

"Because I decided that to truly atone for my pigheadedness, I would introduce Seamus to my family as the man I was in a relationship with."

I could feel my eyes widen and I stared back and forth between them, wondering if I should laugh, or cuddle Seamus to protect him. The grin that went all the way to his eyes told me I needn't bother.

"And… why was that a good thing?" I asked.

Sol laughed again.

"My family, 100% werepanther for generations, according to Abuelita, considers themselves very progressive. No one batted an eyelash when I told everyone I was only interested in women. To be honest, I wasn't even worried about telling them, because I knew they wouldn't care. Tio Javi is married to Tio Rico, and Abuelita herself married a woman after she lost her husband in the war. But being involved with a wolf…"

I frowned.

"So how did that help?" I asked.

"Gatita, they *consider* themselves progressive. I led with the fact that I was in a poly relationship, and Abuelita just nodded like it was perfectly normal. Tia Rosa made one little huffing noise, but Primo Carlos actually applauded, and said 'That's only sensible in this day and age.' So how would they all look if they said anything negative when I introduced Seamus, and said he was one of the two people I was with? I could see Abuelita's face turn red, even as she smiled and welcomed him to the family. It. Was. Glorious."

This time Seamus laughed, and I finally felt the tension drain out of my shoulders. I was worried that Sol had put Seamus through an awful experience just to make a point, and maybe she had, but Seamus' eyes were glittering with mirth when he turned to me, so I didn't think so.

"Oh, don't worry, Vic, it was fine. Her folks are lovely. Her Abuelita was raining compliments on me by the time we finished dinner. Said I was a delightful young man."

"Did she add 'for a werewolf?'" I asked, with a barely restrained growl. People could compliment you all day and still insult both you and your heritage. It happened with damning frequency.

"Not once," Seamus said, looking earnest enough that I decided he wasn't just trying to placate me. "And I don't even believe she was thinking it, by the end. And even if she was, they've clearly been raised with a shitty mindset, and every single one of them was doing their best to just talk to me, actual me, and not their idea of what a 'werewolf' was."

"Like I said," Sol continued, "we consider ourselves progressive. Luckily, my family is actually progressive enough to admit to their own bullshit when they are called on it."

She paused for a moment, as she picked up a tray laden with some truly epic-looking sandwiches and brought them over to the coffee table that took up most of the space between all the couches and pillows.

"To be honest, I'm pretty damned ashamed that my family has believed that shit about wolves for so long, and that *I* believed it at all. I'm not sure who in my family had a falling out with a wolf at some point, but I sure as hell want to go back in time and slap them."

Then she looked up into my eyes and said, "Holy shit. Could we do that?"

And that had the three of us laughing uncontrollably as we dug into a feast of tea and sandwiches of historic proportions, and began a conversation about the myriad dangers and complications of time travel.

AFTER TWO MORE languid days of R&R with Sol and Seamus, I didn't really want to go visit my parents. Not only was I reluctant to leave Sol and Seamus—after all, those two days were the first time in our entire relationship when we'd had more than 24 hours without anyone trying to kill us, and it had been a wonderful haze of delicious sex, deep conversations, and ridiculous laughter. To me, the fact that were able to spend that long in a one bedroom cabin without wanting to fight each other (quite the opposite, in fact) was proof positive to me that our relationship was about more than just the crazy three-way mating bond that had kicked things off.

Nothing about those two days made me want to leave the quiet coziness of Sol's cabin and the stark beauty of the Andes that surrounded it. Part of me was quite certain that I deserved much longer than three days of solace, after everything else that I'd been through.

But another part of me was worried that my parents were going to slip quietly back to Hel's realm before I could talk to them, despite Trev's reassurances via e-mail that Mom and Dad were planning to give me all the time that I needed before I spoke to them again.

That rankled too, to be honest—the idea that Trev was close enough to my parents that after ten years of abandonment and a few hours' worth of catching up, he could confidently proclaim to me that they'd still be there when I was ready to talk to them. Especially in place of them getting in touch themselves. As if Trev had some special insight into both their minds and mine? Even if he did, even if my parents were just respecting my boundaries by getting in touch via Trev…. The whole thing just felt contrived and stupid and… THAT was why I was shifting myself into Rhelia's home in the dragon realm, interrupting what looked like a perfectly boring round of Hearts.

"Vic!" Mom and Dad exclaimed together, dropping their cards in unison and standing up from the small, square folding table.

For a moment they looked like they were going to rush to me and embrace me, and then they stopped, at the last second.

I knew it was because they were worried it wouldn't be a welcome gesture, the rational part of my brain *knew* that, but it still hurt. The hesitation hurt, and maybe it was just a year's worth of pent-up grief and anger talking, but I lashed out.

"What, don't like the scars?" I asked.

It was an odd choice to bring them up; I'd rarely noticed the scars in the weeks since I'd gotten them. Sometimes they caught me off guard when I saw my reflection in passing, or when the skin on my shoulder felt tight when I pulled on a shirt, or did certain poses in yoga, and yeah, I was a little self-conscious about them when I was getting intimate with people—things that had really only come to my attention in the past few days, because honestly, my life had been way too much about running to survive another day and stopping the destruction of the known universe lately, and that didn't leave time for noticing well-healed scar tissue. So it was weird to use that as a barb against my parents, but it must have been a barb that caught, because their faces crumpled.

"How could you think that?" Dad asked, his voice a low whisper.

"Oh, I dunno," I said. "Maybe because you couldn't be bothered to come see my face in person after I risked my damned life *again* to save everyone, and was recovering in a remote mountain cabin."

Mom still looked hurt, but she'd regained her steel a little bit faster than Dad. "Trev told us you were healed, uninjured, that you just needed time to rest and spend time with your…friends."

"You mean my partners?" I asked, starting to feel anger on behalf of Sol and Seamus now. Hoping my parents were going to hand me an argument about being in a poly relationship instead of me taking everything else they said and using it against them. "The ones you haven't officially met yet, because you wouldn't come to visit? Those ones? Has being dead for a year set your thinking back twenty years, as well?"

It hurt to see Mom and Dad flinch with every accusation that passed my lips, but there was so much anger inside me in that moment that I felt like shifting to my dragon form and incinerating half the countryside.

"Vic, sweetie, what is this really about?" Mom said, as Dad just stood there and silently held her hand.

Oh good, at least they were in solidarity against me.

"What do you think it's about, *Mom*? You *left me*. You pretended to be dead to get away from me. You abandoned me for a year and left me alone to pick up the pieces. Do you have any idea what that was like for me? Do you? I was alone. With no one but Uncle Algy for a guardian, and an empty fucking house in Flagstaff as my inheritance. What did you expect when you decided to end the charade? A fucking party? Welcome home, Mom and Dad! We sure are glad you're back from your one year vacation of not giving a shit about your child!?"

Mom and Dad just stood there, silently, their throats bobbing, but no noise escaping them, as I continued.

I noticed that Trev and Rhelia had discreetly abandoned the card table and they were standing quietly a few meters away. I couldn't blame them, really. I was fuming, and even letting all of this out didn't feel like it was helping—I was only getting angrier.

"Of course, I suppose I should be grateful that you only abandoned me for a year, shouldn't I? At least you didn't do to me what you did to Trev. Abandoning him to MOME for a decade!? Forgetting he even existed!? Making *me* forget him!? My own brother? My twin? How could you?"

Tears were pouring down my cheeks and I was so far past caring that I didn't even swipe at them. I wasn't sure if they were from anger, or grief, or some horrible mix of the two—probably all of the above. I hadn't come here to yell at my parents. That really hadn't been the plan, but I was suddenly full of so much rage it felt like it was going to swallow me whole.

I didn't say anything else, because I wanted answers. None of the questions I'd posed had really been rhetorical, but Mom and Dad just stood there, gripping each other's hands like two people shipwrecked, afraid that their floating logs would be torn away from each other if they let go for even a second.

"How could you?" I repeated, since they didn't seem to understand that I wanted an answer. A real fucking answer.

When they remained silent, I turned and walked out the door.

To my surprise, it was Rhelia who came to find me. I mean, I had reached for my dragon form and flown away the moment I'd cleared the door to Rhelia's house, so I guess I shouldn't have been too surprised. But Trev had wings too, and he was learning his way around the ragon realm, so I'd kind of expected him to show up.

Plus, you know, he's my twin.

"Your twin is unssssure of hissss welcome, at the moment, Living Cat," Rhelia said.

She was speaking with her human voice, probably because I had flown myself up to the cliff ledge that topped the dragon's prisons, then shifted back to human form in order to drape my legs over the edge and stare forlornly into the middle distance.

Somehow it just didn't seem appropriate to stare forlornly in dragon form.

I guessed she thought it was only polite that she talk to me in the form I'd taken. She stepped up beside me and gestured to the ledge to my right, as if asking for permission to join me. I nodded. She sat down.

Then we both just stared at the deep blue sky of the dragon realm, watching a few small wisps of cloud scuttle by. The drop beneath our feet was over a thousand meters, and the valley stretching out below us was unlike anything I'd seen on Earth. The grassy swath stretching out from the cliff was dotted with giant pillars of land that stood up like nails tacked into the green valley below. They were topped with tall grasses, just like the land behind me, but the pillars themselves were composed entirely of an almost yellow stone. Each pillar was the same height as the cliff that I sat upon, but while the ledge I was on stretched out to either side of me, running into the horizon, the pillars were just small islands of land, most of them no bigger than a small dragon, some as large as football fields, but all of them balancing precariously on single cylinders of stone. Hundreds of them dotted the valley that stretched a few kilometers in each direction, and ended on the other side with a cradle of low, sloping mountains that embraced the majority of the dragon city. I had no idea what lay beyond that view, but the whole thing was entrancing enough to keep me from thinking about anything else for a while.

It was Rhelia's voice that brought me back to the very thoughts I'd run away from.

"I am your family now, Vic, but I ssssensssse that I am not the perssssson you wissssh to ssssspeak with."

I chuckled.

"I like people I can just kick back and enjoy a view with."

Rhelia smiled, her yellow eyes glinting in the sunlight.

"I alssssso apprecssssiate comfortable sssssilencsssssessss with my companionssss."

Then she sighed.

"But I am concsssserned that sssssilencsssse issss not what you need, at the moment."

I sighed and lay back, my legs still dangling over the cliff ledge and my eyes gazing straight up at the sky.

"I don't want to yell anymore, Rhelia. I don't want to be this angry. It's… painful."

"Yessss, but will keeping it insssside you feel any better?"

I groaned.

"I take it back, you're no fun. I was really enjoying this bit of literal escapism. It's more direct than just reading a book at people, you know."

"Can you read a book *at* ssssomeone?"

"I don't know if *you* can, but I definitely can. It's a developed skill, really. Passive aggressively delicious."

Rhelia laughed, and hearing her laughter loosened a bit of the knot in my chest.

"Wanna call Trev over?" I asked, after a moment.

She nodded, but didn't move.

I wasn't sure why I didn't just call Trev myself. I could still feel him there, on the other side of our bond… but talking to him through it didn't feel right yet, somehow.

Maybe because I was actually furious with him.

Which was something I didn't realize until I sat up and saw him winging his way across the valley in phoenix form. He was beautiful, a giant, flaming bird of doom flying with the grace and ease of a lifelong predator. He may as well have been a bald eagle or a falcon. And yet, while part of me appreciated that beauty, and another part of me was relieved to see my brother on his way to my side, still a third part—currently a larger part than either of the other two—was filled with an almost incandescent rage at the sight of him.

He hovered in front of us for a moment, before swooping down to my left side and dropping into his human form exactly at the same time as he sat down beside me.

"Neat trick," I said, trying to find a smile for the twin I'd missed for more than half our lives.

"You don't look happy to see me," Trev said.

I guess my smile hadn't covered up the rage.

"I am. I'm happy that you're alive, and I'm happy that you're willing to talk to me again. I just… I'm really angry, Trev."

"And part of that is my fault."

It wasn't a question, so I didn't say anything.

The three of us stared into the distance for a while, as I searched for the right words for what I was feeling. It was particularly difficult because I was barely clear on why I was angry. For perhaps the first time, though, I was grateful to all the counselors I'd been forced to visit when Mom and Dad had "died."

"I don't think I'm actually angry with you—well, maybe a little bit, residually, for the whole knowing-about-Mom-and-Dad-being-alive-when-I-didn't thing—but mostly I'm angry *for* you. I'm angry for both of us. I know why they left you with MOME. I understand that they thought they had no choice, but… I feel like they decided protecting me was more important than saving *you,* and I'm not sure I can ever forgive them for that. How could they, Trev? They made that choice for both of us! I know that's not the choice I would have made, if they'd asked. I would have told them not to worry about me, told them that the three of us should have broken you out and then gone on the run together. I've been evading MOME for months now, and I'm a freaking teenager! I'm sure we could have managed it as a family."

Trev reached out for my hand, and I gave it to him, our fingers lacing together in a reassuring knot.

"Are you mad at me for forgiving them?" Trev asked.

I considered that, for a moment.

"Maybe. I don't know. That's your choice, obviously. But… it's going to take me a long time to forgive them, Trev. I know they were trying their best, but damn it… if four teenagers can break into MOME and bust out everyone there, why couldn't *they*? Why did it all have to wait until we grew up and could do it ourselves?"

"Honestly, Vic, I am still amazed that we pulled that off, and it only worked because I knew how to hack into the system from the inside, and Sol had worked there, and even then we might have died if you hadn't had a friend who was a literal goddess… I'm not sure anyone else *could* have done it. And would you seriously recommend to a grieving set of parents, who had just lost one of their children, that they should risk the other child in a desperate attempt to save the one who was taken? I mean, they would have been risking losing *everything*. Leaving you in MOME's clutches, as well as me, and getting themselves locked up in prison, or worse. Missing both of our childhoods entirely."

I sighed.

"You've given this a lot of thought, haven't you?" I muttered.

Trev laughed, though the sound held little humor.

"I had ten years to think about it, didn't I?"

"Ten years that you could have spent learning to hate your parents," I whispered. "I'm sure MOME would have liked that."

Trev squeezed my hand again.

"I think MOME would have *loved* that. In fact, that's probably a big part of *why* I wound up forgiving Mom and Dad. MOME made every effort to turn the kids they'd taken against each other, and to turn us against our parents and families. They did everything they could to convince us that the people who loved us most hadn't cared enough to take care of us 'properly.' That we were a risk to everyone around us, and that if our families had truly loved us, they would have voluntarily handed us over to MOME for safekeeping. Lucky for me, they took me right around the time when I was starting to question adults. I didn't trust them from the start, and them telling me my family didn't take care of me properly? They couldn't have done anything to make me decide to forgive Mom and Dad faster. Once I was in my teens, it was like everything MOME did made me just want to come up with more reasons that Mom and Dad weren't to blame. MOME really should have invested in some child psychologists, if they'd wanted to succeed at turning us against our families. Instead, they had a bunch of guards and research scientists try to prod and bully us into it."

It was horrifying to think of, but also somewhat reassuring that MOME had been so bad at that particular job.

"So, yeah, I forgave Mom and Dad a while ago, and… look, I'm sure we'll have our differences yet. What family doesn't have their disagreements? But, we have parents, Vic. Unlike so many of the people I knew growing up with MOME, we still have our family, and they still love us. Shit, they love us a lot. They haven't seen me in a decade, and I can *still* feel the love rolling off of them every time we hang out. They're pretty desperate to make things up to us."

I squeezed Trev's hand again and leaned back against the tall grass behind me. He and Rhelia did the same.

"I don't want to hate them. I don't hate them. I just… I grieved them for *a year*. The first few months… I was sure it wasn't true, that they weren't actually dead. The stories I made up in my head as to what had happened to them were almost as bizarre as what *actually* wound up being the truth. If they had shown up then, I think I could have shaken the whole thing off. I would just have been *relieved* that they weren't actually dead. Relieved my denial proved true. I would have been so damned grateful to have them back, grateful that the nightmare was just that, a nightmare, a farce, not reality. But that didn't happen. I eventually accepted that they were *dead*. I raged against it, I cried for hours, days, weeks, months, about it, but it was true. It had to be true, because they hadn't come back. I was certain they had loved me, and if they loved me and were still alive, they would have come back. When they didn't… it was finally, horribly true, and… it's not like I was over it, or anything, but I was growing into it as my new normal. Episodes of deep grief followed by mostly normal. Going whole days without thinking about them, or at least without feeling the searing pain of losing them. It was getting better. Tiny bits at a time, it was getting better. And *now* they're back. Now, *surprise*, they're not dead. And I'm glad they're not dead. Of course I am, but… they put me through that. They weren't really dead, but they put me through losing them. I know that they thought they were protecting me by leaving me behind, but they didn't even give me a choice. I'm not a child anymore, and they didn't give me a choice. I'm not sure I can forgive them for that."

Trev was silent for a moment before saying, "Makes sense to me."

I turned to look at him, his face so close to mine that I couldn't really focus on anything but his eyes.

"What? That's it?"

Trev stared back at me, but said nothing.

"You're not going to make their case for them? Tell me I'm being unreasonable?"

Trev smiled.

"First of all, emotions aren't reasonable, but they're natural, and there's nothing we can do about that. Second of all, I don't think you're being unreasonable at all. Your emotional response doesn't need to be grounded in reason to be valid, but, I mean… everything you just said is true, and if it were me, I'd be pissed at them too."

I just blinked at him for a moment.

"But *you've* forgiven them for far worse!"

Trev shrugged.

"I've had more time, for one thing. And for another, I'm not sure it was worse, Vic. Mom and Dad were trying to protect both of us as children, and that's what parents are supposed to do. MOME *stole* me. It's not like Mom and Dad just handed me over—they fought it as hard as they could, legally, but MOME threatened to take you, too, and it's kind of a miracle they didn't, really. It's not like they'd asked permission to take *me*… and then Mom and Dad, rightfully not trusting MOME to keep their word after they'd wiped all of your memories of me, disappeared, to keep you safe. They couldn't do that and try to bust me out at the same time. And honestly, if they'd been able to ask me, I would have told them to protect you too."

He must have seen the horror cross my face, because he frowned and continued, "Don't look at me like that. The whole reason that you're pissed at them on *my behalf* is because you feel the same way about it that I do. If given the choice of protecting your twin or yourself, you'd choose your twin. Right? You're angry because they chose to protect you over me, but if our situations had been reversed, I know you'd expect them to take care of me."

Ugh. He was so right that I didn't even say anything, I just turned to stare angrily at the sky.

"So, yeah," Trev continued, even though I wasn't looking at him anymore. "I get it. What Mom and Dad chose makes sense to me, and I have had years and years to process the whole thing. But what they did to you? You're right, they were protecting you by disappearing. And while you were still legally a child, they probably should have given you a choice, or at least given you some idea of what they were doing. I understand why they didn't, but I'm pretty sure it would piss me off if they'd done the same thing to me. I *know* it pisses me off that they did it to you. So, no, I don't think you're being unreasonable."

Rhelia hadn't said anything for a while, but she was still lying there, silent in her solidarity. And I found I took a surprising amount of comfort from her presence. She was starting to feel like a sister in more than just name. The three of us just lay there for a while, eyes to the sky, sun on our faces.

"So, what now?" I asked eventually.

"Musssst you forgive them in order to sssspend time with them?" Rhelia asked quietly.

I considered the question.

"I suppose not, as long as they know how I actually feel."

"So, let's go tell them how you feel," Trev said, giving my hand another squeeze.

"And then?"

Trev chuckled.

"How about a game of Hearts?"

I toss the keys into the small bowl by the door and kick off my shoes before hanging my backpack from the coatrack. Then I reconsider, and put the bag containing over fifty pounds of textbooks on the floor, because the coatrack is solid, but it isn't invincible. The smell of fresh coffee pulls me down the hall into the brightly lit kitchen, and I wrap my arms around Seamus' waist as he distributes the pot evenly between three mugs.

"Is this ok?" I ask. The embrace is habitual now, but so's the question, and the answer isn't always yes. Usually, but not always.

"Quite," says Seamus, and he turns to hand me a mug of coffee.

I gesture at the two remaining mugs.

"Is Sol home yet?"

He shakes his head.

"Nope. We have a visitor."

I raise a questioning eyebrow.

"Check the living room," he replies.

I take my coffee mug with me.

Draped across the leather sofa that I'd bought to replace the one that had burned down with the rest of this house, over a year ago, is an ebon skinned, silver winged hottie who probably only looks male because I have just been hugging Seamus.

"Az!" I exclaim, placing my mug a little too hurriedly on the coffee table and jumping forward to embrace them.

"Hullo, Luv," they say, getting up and returning my hug with enthusiasm.

"You here for socializing, or research?" I ask, reluctantly letting them go and retrieving my coffee before settling myself into an adjacent IKEA chair.

"Can't it be both?" they ask.

"I suppose it has to, now I think about it," I reply, trying to keep the warm feeling creeping up my neck under control.

I am a big fan of the research that Az has been doing lately on behalf of the Council of Dark Matter Adjacent Peoples, or CODMAP, as I like to call it, much to Albert's annoyance. (Hey, it's better than MOME.)

And it is. Unlike MOME, which had been a regulatory body that was so corrupt it was essentially an authoritarian regime, CODMAP is a research and outreach program. It's doing its best to repair the centuries of damage that MOME has done to the magical (and non-magical) world, and it's trying to include as many previously silenced voices as possible.

"How are your studies going?" Az asks.

"They're interesting. I'm still hopeful that Earth biology will be a solid platform to start a xenological studies branch once I graduate."

"Haven't your parents already started that branch?" Az asks.

"Nope. They're too singularly focused on dark matter to qualify. My current hope is to start cataloguing everything that lives in other realms, not just the things that interact with dark matter to function."

"Fascinating," Az replies, and the glint in their eyes makes me think that they're possibly just saying that because they're hoping to use me as a research subject again tonight. It's unnecessary. I'm always happy to participate in Az's research, anyway.

They are studying the various methods of ingesting and modifying dark matter. It's related to my parents' research, but Az is in charge of their own sector, a fact I'm truly glad of, since I don't really want my parents having intimate knowledge of the experiments that Az and I are running.

Seamus comes into the living room with the remaining two mugs of coffee, and hands one to Az.

"Is tonight's experiment with all three of us?" he asks, sitting down on the far side of the couch from Az.

Az shrugs.

"If you'd like to see if we can bring on the chimera event again, that could be useful to the next phase of my—"

"Who didn't make me coffee just now?!" Sol's voice calls, as she enters the living room, carrying the now-empty coffee pot. "That's just cruel. Hi,

Az. No chimera tonight. And Vic, we should probably reschedule our sparring. We have guests."

That has all of us looking interestedly behind Sol, and sure enough, my parents stand behind her, doing that awkward waiting-to-be-acknowledged-by-the-rest-of-the-group waddle that happens when you follow someone larger than life into a room.

I pop up to give Sol a kiss and go make some more coffee.

"Don't you have a gig tonight?" I ask, after a brief kiss.

"Not til 10," she replies, her arms lingering on my waist as I walk past her towards the kitchen. She's been playing enough bass gigs lately to completely cover her tuition for law school. I can't decide if I'm more turned on by Sol the musician, or Sol the future civil rights attorney.

Both. Why not both?

Reluctantly pulling away from Sol, I pause to give my parents a group hug on my way into the kitchen. Mom follows me.

"You don't have to cancel a chimera attempt just because we're here," she announces casually.

"Ugh, Mom, I appreciate you trying to be cool and all, but I am not having sex with Az with you and Dad in the house. Az is… not quiet, and the energy spill-over gets everyone going—that's how the last experiment wound up using all of us. If you want to find out what it's like to be in a house with a succubus doing a power exchange, you can invite Az over to your place sometime, and please never tell me about it."

Mom frowns, but I can tell from the muscles around her eyes that she's mildly relieved.

"I appreciate the support of my lifestyle choices, though," I add, half jokingly. "Besides, Trev and Rhelia said they would be staying over tonight, so that really just could not get any more awkward."

Mom says nothing, while I get the coffee brewing again.

I had initially been pretty reluctant to rebuild the house in Flagstaff. I hadn't been sure I wanted most of the memories that went with it, and besides, it had been too large for just me to begin with, and the plans my parents had for the rebuild had been ridiculous. Or they'd seemed that way until I figured out that Sol and Seamus were both happy to move in with me, as long as we each got our own room, and that Mom and Dad—who were still splitting their time between Hel's realm and their own rebuild of our Colorado home—were going to be visiting almost as often as Trev and Rhelia.

Turns out a five-bedroom is barely enough space, half the time.

Besides, funding the renos had made Uncle Algy feel quite a bit better after the whole holding-me-hostage-to-save-his-granddaughters thing.

"How long are you in town for?" I ask Mom, once the coffee is going. I can hear everyone else chatting in the living room, but I'm in no hurry to rejoin the group. Everyone in there is used to each other by now, and it's nice to just listen to the peaceful conversation as background noise.

"Not sure. Albert has a new theory he wants to test out, but he says he can't leave because it's finals week, and he'd have to put Ms. Rebuke in charge, and no one wants that."

She looks bemused, like she isn't entirely sure what that means, but is going along with it anyway, and I have to laugh.

"Probably true," I say, not bothering to explain about Rebuke—who has been decidedly… different after flying off with a succubus during a certain demon battle.

"How's school?" she asks, quietly, as if the topic is a prey animal she's afraid of frightening away.

"It's good, Mom. And you don't have to sound so careful when you ask about it. I am not studying biology just to please you and Dad. Asking me how things are going isn't going to influence me unduly."

Can you tell we've had this conversation before?

"I just don't want you to think that you have to—"

"She's fine, Mom," Trev's voice calls from the front door. It accompanies the sounds of boots stomping and fabric rustling around. "I would know if she weren't."

I laugh, and take the distraction of Trev and Rhelia's arrival as a chance to escape to the living room with the pot of coffee and a tray of mugs.

A few minutes later we are all settled into the living room, which should be huge, but now feels delightfully cramped.

Everyone has coffee or tea, depending on their preferences, and there are multiple threads of conversation going on throughout the room.

I feel warm, and happy, and realize with a tinge of surprise that *this* has become my new normal, somewhere over the past few months. We're still working to undo all the harm that MOME has done. It's a task so huge that we will probably never accomplish it, but we are making progress—after the first few months of total chaos—and things are starting to finally feel manageable. I'm not in danger of being killed every day. No one is asking me to save the world multiple times a week and… I'm doing what normal

19-year-olds do; going to school, having roommates, having romantic escapades with said roommates and the occasional non-roommate. You know, college stuff. And my relationship with my parents is almost normal as well. I no longer feel rage at what they did, just a sort of deep sadness that hits me sometimes. It's a sadness I can talk to either of them about when it comes up, and we've done a lot of hugging and crying together since they've come back.

Things are, dare I say it, good.

Trev clears his throat.

"Rhelia and I have an announcement," he says.

The whole room quiets and we all look at each other, equal parts puzzled and excited.

Rhelia stands up and points to her sweater, which contains a slight bulge.

My Dad starts to cry, and Mom clings to his arm, but then the bulge twitches and Rhelia hisses while reaching a hand underneath her sweater.

"We have decided to adopt a kitten!"

And she holds up the tiny feline like it is the greatest treasure on Earth.

Then we're all on our feet, laughing and cooing at the tiny black cat with bright green eyes, as it stares bewilderedly at far too many big things crowding around it.

Almost at the same time, Sol and I shift to our cat forms and plop down on the ground in front of it. Rhelia sets it between us and it mews and squeaks, in the way that only kittens can. Sol gives it a lick, and I stick my nose out to give it a welcoming sniff.

Then it boops its tiny pink nose to mine, and everything is perfect.

OTHER WORKS BY VIRGINIA MCCLAIN

The Chronicles of Gensokai Series:
Blade's Edge
Traitor's Hope

Short Stories:
Rain on a Summer's Afternoon

Follow Virginia on Social Media:
www.virginiamcclain.com
twitter.com/gwendamned
facebook.com/virginiamcclainauthor

ACKNOWLEDGEMENTS

These books wouldn't have been possible without a fair bit of help from a number of people. My deepest gratitude goes out to the following people:

My editor, Aurora Wilson-McClain, for not only working with my sometimes ridiculous deadlines, but also for helping me sort out the best use of obscure spell references, the number of "s"s a certain dragon uses in her speech patterns, and where, exactly, everyone has left their clothes.

My husband, for putting up with me disappearing every evening for months on end in order to get these books written, for being my best cheerleader and for not giving me too much grief when I failed to get my half of the housework done.

Cedar, for letting me ignore her often enough to get formatting done, as well as promotion and marketing stuff, and for being so willing to hang out with her wonderful caregivers.

Anne, Lee, Jim, and Gabi, for keeping Cedar entertained, fed, and happy so that I could write.

To my Patreon supporters: Paul, Corey, Mishy, Marie, and Jessica.

To Paul (again) and Corey for reading ARCs and catching errata. (Now may be a good time to mention that my editor works her butt off to clean up my books, and my ARC readers volunteer their time to read and give me feedback. Any and all errata left in the books after these wonderful people are through with them are entirely my own doing.)

And finally, the folks at Stella's au CCFM for always putting up with me occupying a table for hours on end while only ordering a cup of tea.

Virginia McClain is an author who masqueraded as a language teacher for a decade or so. When she's not reading or writing she can generally be found playing outside with her four-legged adventure buddy and the tiny human she helped to build from scratch. She enjoys climbing to the tops of tall rocks, running through deserts, mountains, and woodlands, and carrying a foldable home on her back whenever she gets a chance. She's also fond of word games, and writing descriptions of herself that are needlessly vague.

For more information check out www.virginiamcclain.com.